To Seth

You will get a lot
out of this book!

Thank you for all your help

Best Wishes

THE EVOLUTION

First published in Great Britain in 2014 by
Gazelle Books
White Cross Mills, Hightown, Lancaster, LA1 4XS

1

A CIP catalogue record for this title is available from the British Library

ISBN: 1-85586-018-X
EAN: 978-1-85586-018-6

Cover illustration "The Pyramid of Illusions"
© Valerie Helmers

Printed by Book Printing UK
Remus House, Coltsfoot Drive, Peterborough, PE2 9BF

For my mother

Stephen’s Website: www.stephenmaybury.co.uk

*"The day science begins to study non-physical phenomena,
it will make more progress in one decade than
in all the previous centuries of its existence."*

Nikola Tesla

THE EVOLUTION

This is a fictionalised version of true events

PART I

THE PAST

1

A STRANGE MEETING

"I have to go, Karl, I can't stop." Grabbing my coat from the back of the chair and hurriedly heading for the side door, I left my coffee on the table with the steam still rising like a near-dormant volcano.

Gary was just about computer illiterate and had recently obtained an outdated laptop from his sister. The plan was to show him a few basics to get him started on the internet so finally he could join the rest of us in the modern world. Not only was it way past the designated time but the rendezvous was forgotten altogether, my mind preoccupied with matters of the heart as my recent separation from my partner was causing me a lot of anxiety and inner turmoil.

Being a regular at the local Cafe in the afternoons meant I had become friends with the staff, particularly Karl, who was in his late twenties. We shared many interests, talking for hours during the long, boring, cold winter months when the rain kept most people indoors and the café was for the most part devoid of life. Now it was May, spring was in full bloom, the temperature was increasing by the day and the anticipation of summer was slowly edging in as the days became longer.

"See you later, Karl," I called out, swinging my head around and pulling the door open. Then, to my horror, an old man walked through the door at the same time as my attempted exit. As I charged into him all his books and papers were sent flying across the floor. Thankfully the well-dressed gentleman stayed on his feet, but only just.

"Oh my God, I am so sorry," I apologised. "Let me get these things for you."

"It's okay, don't worry," he replied.

"No, please. It was my fault. I should have been watching where I was going." I put my coat and laptop on the nearest table and started to gather his books together. And then something grabbed my attention. It was a document, a paper of some kind which was clearly stamped with the words

'Secret – eyes only'. I tried not to look at it, but the words at the top of the page were clear – *'Viruses and the possible future desolation of Mankind'*.

There was also a book lying next to it – *'Maya Prophecies and beyond 2012'*. It wasn't a proper book with a normal cover one would find in a bookshop, it was more like a draft copy with a black and white, almost pencilled, image on the front. It was bound with string which was tied through punch holes and wrapped around the pages to keep it together.

I felt embarrassed but also a little concerned that I'd accidentally seen a secret paper of some kind. So many thoughts went through my mind in quick succession. Who was this man? What was he doing carrying such material openly in a public place? Why were the papers not kept in a briefcase, or something? Obviously he had connections in high places or he wouldn't be carrying secret papers. And now what could I do? Having seen these papers, was I now in trouble? Or was this some practical joke that Karl was playing? I was sometimes at the wrong end of the odd tease or two since life was often in the slow lane in the café.

I tried to pretend I hadn't noticed anything but the man's eyes were searching and it was undeniable he knew, so I tried to cover my new unwanted knowledge with a distraction.

"Let me buy you a coffee. It's the least I can do after causing you such trouble." I turned and headed back towards the counter.

"No," he said. His voice was stern and commanding. Immediately I stopped and turned around slowly, almost as if he had complete control over my every wish. "I will buy you a coffee. Now sit down, Mister Maybury, we need to talk."

What? How did this man know my name? Who was he? What was going on here? For a moment, the urge was to run out the door but this man already knew my name – what else did he know? And why did he want to talk with me?

I turned back to the man and his expressionless face gave away nothing, yet at the same time there was something sympathetic in his gaze. He gestured for me to sit in the corner of the back room, which was now empty as the afternoon was slowly turning to early evening.

"Two coffees, please," the man called out to Karl, who was now busily cleaning tables in the main area. It wasn't normal practice to be served at your table – the café requires you to go to the till and place your order – but even Karl immediately went to work making the coffee after the commanding voice bellowed through to the main area.

The man slowly, almost gracefully, joined me at the table. He was dressed in a black suit and his grey hair was flicked to one side. He was in his sixties and had a wrinkled face with bags under his eyes. His nose was slightly bent in the middle and it was clear it had been broken sometime in the past. He seemed tired and yet strangely energetic. A tough man but at the same time he appeared somewhat conscientious and emotional. In fact everything about this mysterious individual was contradictory.

"How do you know my name?" I asked, nervously.

"I know many things about you. You have recently separated from your partner. You are in between jobs. You have travelled extensively in South America and have studied the cultures there for many years. You have amateur knowledge of archaeology and astronomy. You studied psychology at university. You have spent the majority of your life studying and investigating the paranormal. You are an adventurous person with 'itchy feet'. You like travelling and putting yourself in danger. And in many ways the most important ability you have is a strange talent for memorising numbers. Do I have your attention now?"

To say I was stunned was an understatement. Petrified was more like it. It felt like some kind of personal invasion, as if I had returned home to find a burglar had ransacked the whole place, going through personal belongings as if they were of little importance.

"Yes, you do, but what do you want with me? And why have you bothered to find out so much about me?"

"Since you seem to have a little spare time on your hands I think this is the perfect time for you to go on another one of those dangerous travelling expeditions, don't you?"

He received a blank stare. What on earth was he talking about? Was this a dream? I decided to act cool and play along, but it was as if he had read my mind.

"This is not a joke, Mister Maybury. I have selected you to undertake a dangerous expedition. You will fly to China and cross the border into Tibet. You will be escorted throughout your journey, which is not without its dangers. You will be risking your life on occasions. And you will, at all times, be working for me and I have specific instructions for you to undertake. You have until this evening to make your decision."

He pulled out a small card from his pocket and handed it to me. "This is the hotel where I am staying. You can walk right in without announcing yourself. I am staying in room twenty. Be there at seven this evening. If you are not there at exactly that time I will be gone and this conversation will never have happened. And, by the way, you will be leaving on Saturday. Good day to you, Mister Maybury."

With that he stood up, nodded his head at me, placed a ten pound note on the table and before anything else could be said he walked out the door.

"Are you alright, mate?" asked Karl, as he brought the coffees on a tray. "Who was that guy?"

"I have no idea," I said.

"What did he want?"

"I have no idea," I repeated, not being able to conjure up any other words.

"He didn't want his coffee, then." Karl shrugged his shoulders, took the ten pounds off the table and he walked back to the counter.

I sat there with my mouth open like a naked mannequin waiting to be dressed. A dangerous trip? I would be risking my life? What on earth was he talking about? Why me? Who was this man? How did he know so much about me? And what the hell was he talking about when he said my ability to memorise numbers was perhaps my 'most important ability'? Why would that be so important? And how did he know that, anyway? That information was hardly on my résumé.

I checked the time – it was already five thirty. Exactly ninety minutes to get to the hotel and less time to make the decision. What the hell was I going to do now? Right now I wasn't even capable of getting out of the seat, let alone make such a life-altering decision.

But as the strange man was well aware, the decision was already made.

In three days I would be flying to China...

2

THE BRIEF BRIEFING

I drank both coffees and made my way back to my flat in a complete daze. I would be relieved to get inside the comfortable surroundings of my own private space. But first, I opened the door slowly and peered through the gap with one eye, looking around to see if anyone was there. Had anything been moved or altered? There was so much fear inside me after this strange man revealed so many personal details, almost as if he had been watching my entire life.

"Get a hold of yourself," I thought, "you won't be much use on a dangerous trip if you're scared of your own shadow."

My mind was racing with questions so I put on some soft music to clear the confusion and frustration and flopped on the sofa. The melodies slowly blocked out the thoughts and the memory of what was, without doubt, the most ridiculous five minutes I had ever encountered.

By the time it was six thirty I felt total internal ease – the calm before the storm, perhaps. The music had allowed my intuition to take over, my heart spoke and I realised that this was going to be a great and completely unknown adventure. There were many unanswered questions but they couldn't be allowed to cloud my judgment – I simply acknowledged them and then they drifted away. For sure there was nervousness but this seasoned traveller had been here before – dark shadows from the deep recesses of the subconscious creeping to the forefront of the mind and manifesting as a fear of the unknown – and the unknown is always a foreign country far, far from home.

I left the flat and caught the bus to the centre of town. The bus was half-full of returning shoppers, bags filled to the brim with items they probably never needed. No one knew where I was going or that there was about to be a secret meeting with a strange man in a hotel room. Perhaps I could ask someone if they thought it was a crazy idea to fly off to China without knowing why? Maybe the little old lady in the next seat would share her lifetime of wisdom which might help to change my mind. "Just stay at home and watch

TV," she would surely say – but that was the kind of life I would take any flight out of the country to avoid.

It was a few minutes' walk from the bus stop to the hotel and with each step my heart beat faster and faster. I arrived with five minutes to spare and walked down the corridor following the signs to the correct room. I found room twenty, took a deep breath and knocked.

The man opened the door and moved his head sideways in a little jolt that beckoned me inside. "Please, take a seat and make yourself comfortable. I have a few things to explain to you." He gestured towards the window, where I saw a chair in front of a desk.

"You knew I would come, didn't you?" I asked, as I sat down, facing him.

"Yes," he said, as if there was no doubt.

"And you purposely allowed me to see those papers, didn't you?"

"Yes. I timed my entrance well, don't you think?" he smiled.

I searched his face for a hint of what kind of a person he was, but he hid himself well. Was he a good person or a bad person? Who was he *really*? And what did he want me to do in Tibet?

"Let's get down to business," he said, as he sat on the edge of the bed.

"What do you want me to go to Tibet for?"

"I am sure you have a million questions to ask but first let me explain everything to you and then you can ask any questions at the end if anything is unclear."

"Okay."

"First, let me clarify perhaps some obvious things. You will never at any time reveal anything I say to you; not to anyone. As far as you are concerned, you have never met me. I do not exist. I am a figment of your imagination. Is that clear?"

"Yes."

"Good. When you leave you will take that bag over there. It contains some reading material, a fake passport and all the instructions you need for the journey. You will return to your flat after this meeting. You will pack only what is necessary – everything you would usually take if you were going travelling. You have spent the best part of a year in South America so you already know what is necessary to pack, but please pack lightly. You need to make sure you appear as any other backpacker. You must not raise any suspicions or do anything that will bring attention to you. Are we clear so far?"

"Absolutely clear," I said, wondering again if this was real.

"I do believe the only person who would be concerned about your absence is your mother. Is that correct?"

Trying to think of friends and family who would be worried about a sudden disappearance, I knew he was correct – only my mother would notice any absence if there was no contact for more than a couple of weeks.

"You will call her this evening and tell her you have been invited to a friend's house for a couple of weeks as there may be a job opportunity. You have friends all over the country so you can choose any you desire, providing she cannot contact them herself. Once you have packed, you will return to this hotel, this evening. I have booked a room for you and it is all paid for on account. You can request anything you desire from reception. You will spend the next three days studying the material I have given you. You may, of course, go into the town if you wish to enhance the idea that nothing is amiss. On Saturday you will be picked up outside at sixteen hundred hours. You will be driven to Heathrow airport and you will catch your flight to Chengdu at twenty one hundred hours. Any questions so far?"

"Yes. What is your name?"

He smiled wryly as if that was the most stupid of questions. "My name is not important. You can call me whatever you like but I am known as Charles."

"But who are you? And who do you work for?"

"I do not work for anyone – but I am part of a group of individuals who are aware of certain things in this world. You will come to understand these things yourself during your initiation."

"But you're obviously a wealthy man. What is your business?"

"Again, Mister Maybury, these things are of little importance to you and certainly of no relevance to this undertaking. You are asking the wrong questions. You should be asking more pertinent questions and, more importantly, asking those questions of yourself. You will be required to do more than a little, shall we say, *soul searching* during the next few weeks."

He obviously wasn't going to tell me anything about himself or what he did, or anything else for that matter. This was a one-sided situation completely controlled by him and whether I liked it or not this was how it was going to be, but what struck home was that he referred to the journey as an 'initiation'. What could that mean?

"Okay, so why do you want me to go to Tibet?"

"In China you will be met by a man called Chang. The information you need is in that bag. He will escort you across the border into Tibet, but listen carefully – the outside world does not know that the border into Tibet has been closed by the Chinese. It will be a very dangerous crossing. Once inside Tibet you will be met by others who will accompany you to another location. Once there, you are to report to me what you discover."

I sat in silence and waited for several moments, but nothing more came.

"That's it? That's all you are going to tell me?"

"Everything you need to know is in that bag. Naturally all your expenses will be paid. You have a bank card in that bag with the name that matches the passport. You have unlimited funds at your disposal. Enjoy yourself, if you get the chance, but it will be unlikely once you enter Tibet. And by the way – you will be paid handsomely for this endeavour."

"I'm not interested in any financial reward."

"I know that. This is half the reason you are going and not someone else. You see it as an adventure and even better if the journey is paid for by someone else. This is the person you are. I don't want someone who only sees financial gain as the incentive, for this journey has more important elements to it."

"How do you know so much about me?"

"Again you ask the wrong question. You will come to understand why you are being paid for your services. Okay, you can leave now." Charles stood up and held his arm out to shake my hand.

"That's it? That's all you're going to give me?"

"We will speak again. Have a safe journey."

Slowly raising my arm and taking his hand, I looked into his eyes and he stared back at me for what seemed an eternity. There was something strange in those eyes but it wasn't evil intent. This was a good man underneath the tough exterior and it was this, and only this, which convinced me to trust him.

"Good luck," he said.

I took the bag from the table, walked to the door and turned around. Charles was standing at the window with his back to me. I closed the door behind me and left the hotel. We would never meet again.

3

DECISIONS, CONFUSION AND BOREDOM

Confused but also excited, I returned to the flat still wondering whether this was all a figment of my imagination. I looked at the bag which almost seemed to be glowing as if a pot of gold had been placed in my hands. "All the answers are in that bag," I said to myself.

Did it contain the same documents from the café? Was that book there also? And then the title of the secret paper that slid across the floor in the café came into my mind – *'Viruses and the possible future desolation of Mankind'*.

"Viruses," I said out loud, speculating on the strange title. With growing impatience I slowly opened the bag to look at the contents and it suddenly struck me – this was real! I slammed the bag shut quickly before a more detailed search of its contents could be made; if I started now I wouldn't stop. I would have to wait until I returned to the hotel, for being side-tracked into some kind of pre-flight fear was not a good idea.

I phoned my mother and told her I would be visiting my friend Melanie in Lancaster for at least two weeks and that the stay could be longer if work was available. It wasn't a good idea to give her a return date because there was an inner feeling the voyage would be longer than was anticipated. She wouldn't worry about me. I had previously travelled alone in third-world countries, where at every turn tourists are mugged and robbed of their possessions, so there was little she would be concerned about in a provincial town like Lancaster.

Next, I telephoned Gary and apologised for not turning up. He was given the same story – there may be work in Lancaster so my absence would be for a while but I would contact him at some point. It was a good enough excuse for not going to his home that day. His initiation into the technological age would have to wait.

With the necessities out of the way it was time to focus on gathering what was required for a travelling expedition. Anyone who has ever been travelling, or real backpacking, realises how simple it is; just two sets of clothing, one to wash and one to wear. The same goes for all garments and it's easy to buy an extra t-shirt or socks if you need them. For me the most imperative item is army trousers. They are a necessity, the importance of which cannot be underestimated. First, they are light and comfortable with many pockets. Second, wearing them can give the bearer an aura of respect in a foreign country, and also a kind of psychological protection – if people think you have a military background then you can appear tougher than the average person, and this means any mugger will think twice before attacking you. They also provide the necessary camouflage if that need arises in the most dangerous environments. It may seem paranoid to some but often when travelling alone to foreign countries one is at the mercy of the natives. Many have been kidnapped in the jungle and it's not a fate anyone would recommend. Certainly in many third-world countries the white man is perceived as 'rich', a perception that is often misguided since real backpackers usually travel on a shoestring budget and save their pennies for a long period prior to leaving.

Among the other necessary items are a pair of light trainers for night comfort; a bathroom kit; Swiss army knife; water purification tablets; first aid kit and a headlamp.

I was hungry so I made a favourite meal of pasta and sauce – there was no telling when I would be eating my homemade version again. As I ate slowly, I pondered my fate – was Charles sending me to my death, using me as expendable fodder? Maybe he would get the information he wanted and then leave me to fend for myself. It was certainly a real possibility, for right now there was no reason to trust him. The meeting had been so sudden and only four hours had passed since then, but my intuition was my guide. Despite the fear and the uncertainty I was confident Charles was genuine. Most of the answers were probably in the bag so it seemed my concerns and fears were just pre-travel jitters. After all, I had already been through the experience of landing in an unknown country, not speaking the language and suffering from culture shock. I had also risked my life on many occasions in South America, so that wasn't something that would faze me in any way. The more I thought about it, the more obvious it was that I would be a natural choice for this undertaking, but the question still remains to this day – how did Charles know me in the first place? And why me – surely there were other people who had the necessary personality? That was one of many mysteries that would never be answered and later connections would only add to the mystery. And there would be a real shock later in the evening as the contents of the bag were to reveal almost nothing.

4

THE LEARNING PHASE: THE MARK OF DECEPTION

"You are booked into room five, Mister Maybury," the pretty receptionist announced on my arrival back at the hotel. "Just call reception if you require anything."

I hurried to my room and placed the bag on the desk and my backpack on the bed, then immediately headed back to room twenty. I wanted to ask Charles some more questions but on arrival I was met with a locked door and no one answered when I knocked. He was gone and for the first time there was a feeling of loneliness, my heart sinking into the depths of my body. There was no going back now.

I returned to my room and sat looking out of the window. As the birds fluttered around the trees and the sun sank behind the town centre horizon it brought a feeling of isolation as the long shadows cast doubts and fear in the back of my mind. On the desk the bag was beginning to look like an unexploded bomb that needed to be defused within three days.

I emptied the contents on to the desk. There was a folder of papers, a strange looking mobile phone, a lighter, the passport, a bank card, three pens and three small blank notebooks. There was also five thousand Chinese Yuan, although how much that was in sterling was a mystery, and the book that had skated across the floor back at the café wasn't there.

Looking at the passport I was shocked to discover it was my own. How on earth did Charles get my passport? So much for going undercover! My passport still had two years to run and was half full of stamps from country-hopping in South America. Sitting back in the chair, I wondered why Charles had told me the passport was a fake rather than my own. It didn't make sense and it certainly deepened my curiosity, but he had said it was important not to bring any attention to myself. It was nothing more than common sense to assume a well-used and well-travelled passport was more convincing than a new one. It also meant that at some point someone really had been in the flat going through my belongings. I laughed out loud at the irony.

The bank card was a credit card with my name on the front and the phone wasn't a typical mobile phone. The buttons contained only numbers and there were no letters for text messaging. It had no signature or make stamped on the front – it was just a blank, black phone – and it was a sinister looking device.

I picked up the folder of papers and opened it. The first sheet was a series of instructions with the headline:

Welcome, Mr Maybury. You are about to undertake a great adventure on my behalf!

That was the first insult. I was embarking on an adventure on his behalf, not my own. I was to take the risks while he sat back and gained the glory. There was more than a little annoyance on my part but that's the way the world works – those at the top reap the benefits while those at the bottom do all the grafting – but thinking of all my previous travel adventures I'd rather be doing the travelling than sitting back and waiting for news. All the dangers and life-threatening situations are worth it – any traveller knows these situations make you stronger and wiser. You see things that most people can only dream of, both good and bad. They are, in essence, the reason why people travel alone in the first place. For the most part it makes you a better person when you see things like poverty – you realise how lucky you are in this world. I continued reading...

This bag contains a lighter. When you have finished digesting this information you will take the folder to the hill behind the hotel and you will burn it until there is nothing left. Make sure it is totally destroyed. You must memorise all the information you need as your contacts and destinations are written here.

You are travelling to China for a short trip to enjoy the culture and experience Chinese cuisine. This is your cover story – you are simply a backpacker travelling the lands of the world. You have a three month visa and a return ticket but you will not be returning to China once you enter Tibet.

What did he mean? I wouldn't be returning to China and catching the flight home? Why was he leaving me stranded in Tibet? How on earth would I get out of Tibet once the task was completed, whatever the task was?

Strangely, not knowing only made it more exciting for me and I guessed that Charles must have known this.

The phone is a military phone that uses only military satellites for communication. It will have a perfect signal no matter where you are. Use it to contact me. The battery will last at least five years providing you only switch it on when you use it. Call me on this to report to me or to call me in an emergency. The calls are encrypted so that no one will be able to intercept them. Dial the number 5096 and this will give you a direct connection. Memorise the number. I don't expect you to call me until you reach your destination in Tibet.

This was my first clue as to who Charles might be – he had access to military technology which meant he was someone of high status and involved in the world of secrecy. He either had a military background or was high up in the 'establishment'. It only deepened my curiosity.

You must be wondering why it is you that has been chosen for this exercise. I have already made clear some of the things I know about you but most of your questions will remain unanswered. I will, however, add to what I have already told you. You have great knowledge in both archaeology and the paranormal. To be experienced in both is almost unheard of. You are a Gemini and born under the Chinese Year of the Rat. Both Gemini and Rat are intelligent, quick-minded and clever. These two traits are absolutely imperative for this mission. I imagine that you are surprised I would mention superstition. You will come to learn of the importance of these things. Don't be too surprised to find the ideas of superstition are very much embedded in every level of our society. Only the scientists tell you these things are nonsense but I can assure that those of us who are privy to certain pieces of information are well aware of how important these things are.

It was astounding that a man of his nature was referring to astrology. The 'science' of astrology was lost a long time ago but there are still some places that practice it, like India. At the time of Ancient Greece astronomy and astrology were the same science but they have long since diverged into what is now considered a science and a non-science, respectively. What Charles was intimating was that secret organisations like the Freemasons incorporate knowledge from places like Ancient Egypt. 'Superstition', as he put it, was an important element to understand when dealing with the scientific study of ancient cultures, for example, but it was still a bizarre thing for him to mention and I had a feeling there was something else he was trying to say – a hidden meaning for me to dwell on during the coming days.

The following pages contain information you need to learn before you leave. Memorise every part of these pages. The last two pages contain the contact details for your journey. The individual who will collect you from the hotel on Saturday at 16.00 hrs is in possession of your flight tickets. Good Luck!

That was it – nothing else. I let out a sigh and then turned to the last two pages to read the contact instructions.

The most important aspect of this journey is for you to write a diary of your daily experiences and you have already found the pens and notebooks for this purpose. Write as much detail as possible and you must write every evening if you can. Buy a new notebook, if you fill these. I do not want any information missing from this diary. You must write down everything. It is also imperative that you do not let this diary fall into the wrong hands. You will destroy it before this ever happens. Keep the lighter with the notebook at all times for this eventuality.

Why on earth did he want me to write a diary? Surely it would be easier to explain things when we spoke on the phone? It seemed odd because I'd also written a daily diary during my days in South America. Was he aware of that? Concluding that he must be, again my concern was how he had come to know so much about me. I even started to wonder if my trip to South America had been a grooming exercise for this expedition, but quickly dismissed this thought as paranoia – the decision had been mine and no one had suggested I write a diary, either.

When you reach Chengdu you will take a taxi to the hotel where a booking has been made for you. On Thursday morning, 13 May, at 08:00 hrs local time, you will be met at reception by a man called Chang. He will escort you across the border into Tibet.

And that was it. These were all the instructions he had given – precise, to the point and nothing more. I was annoyed, but then what else could he tell me? He could, perhaps, have told me *why* he was sending me to Tibet. That would have been helpful. Maybe the papers would reveal more.

I flicked through the rest of the pages and found that they were all blank. There was nothing except empty pages. "Son of a bitch," I shouted out loud, and slammed the folder shut.

Why did he fill the folder with blank pages? Why did he not just leave the few pages that did have information? What was the point? Maybe he just wanted me to think in isolation? Maybe he wanted me to fill in those pages myself? What was the point in me being in this room for three days? Having already memorised the instructions, what else was there to do? He must have known this, so why did he want me here for three days? The only conclusion was to prepare myself psychologically, but this environment didn't feel appropriate as it made me feel somewhat isolated, but maybe that was the whole idea. Maybe being isolated would teach me to be alone.

I decided to double check the entire folder by turning each page one by one, but there was still nothing. And then I had the brainstorming idea of holding each piece of paper up to the light. Eventually I came across a page right in the middle of the folder with hidden writing, like a watermark. Wondering what game Charles was playing, it began to feel like he was teaching me a lesson – to analyse everything in detail and make sure no vital clues were missed. Surely this was the message he was giving me.

The hidden message I found was only a few lines. In essence it was almost nothing, but it contained information that blew me away.

The fabled and lost city of Shambhala is thought to be situated in Tibet. It is said to have contained a vast library of knowledge and to be a place of total peace and tranquillity.

It wasn't the words that shocked me. Everyone has heard of the lost city of Shambhala. What disturbed and excited me was that this man was giving me an indication of why he was sending me to Tibet. Reading between the lines, was this a code of some kind? Or was Shambhala really there, hidden in the depths of the Tibetan wilderness? Maybe, just maybe, Shambhala had recently been discovered and he was sending me on a scouting mission...

5

UP THE CREEK WITHOUT A PADDLE

The next three days passed as quickly as an Arctic winter and I found myself walking around the room in such boredom that I might as well actually have been alone in the Arctic. The intense lingering left a feeling of near depression as the isolation started to take its toll. Going out for brief walks helped but for the most part there was no human interaction or conversation except for the receptionists and shop workers. What started during those three days was an in-depth analysis of the relationship that had broken down around me – bricks crumbling to dust as the deterioration became irreparable. It wasn't my decision to break it off, it was hers, but it should have been mine. The constant jealousy and insistence that I should have no female friends had made me somewhat fearful of her, to the point that I had become scared to even talk to women. I'd had many female friends prior to the relationship but they had been slowly eliminated, one by one. Arguments were many – a clash of personalities in many ways – but love is indeed blind. It's funny how, once on the other side of the fence, we easily see people as they really are.

The isolation of three days in the hotel suddenly made things very clear and those pre-programmed fears had manifested in a strange way – the dread of the loneliness of solo travel is, in many ways, almost identical to the fear of the loneliness caused by losing a partner, but at the same time there was a desperate need to get away from her and deal with those emotions, to be able let go and move on. While we were still living in the same small town, sooner or later we would bump into each other. Of course we had parted as friends – it wasn't in that sense a total breakdown – but seeing her would bring all the fears up to the surface and the emotional turmoil would be fresh and painful. That was neither needed nor wanted and this was the perfect opportunity to get away from it and move on. It would be difficult but necessary.

The isolation brought a change in my way of thinking and I found myself observing it with interest. It appeared that a slow internal psychological preparation was happening. What disturbed me was that Charles had known that this brief preparation was an absolute requirement. It made sense because it was a constant reminder of the trip to South America and I often wondered if this trip would be similar in its excitement. However, there was no doubt that I was about to enter a completely different culture, and the biggest difference was that prior to my South American trip there had been nine months of planning and preparation, but now I had just three days. The time to prepare just wasn't enough. Any solo traveller knows the real preparation is psychological.

The solitude of this hotel brought back memories of one particular expedition in southern Peru. I had particularly wanted to camp in the mountains far away from any living beings, especially human, and even before leaving England I had planned the time and the place where this could happen. Once settled in the city of Arequipa, my plans for a seven-day camping trip were explained to the hotel owner, since a taxi was required to take me as far as possible into the volcanic area north of the city.

"No, you must not do this," he replied. "It is a bad idea. It is very dangerous. You are crazy to do this."

His words would not sway me from my plans. I already knew how dangerous it would be and what possibilities may occur – snakes, spiders and even a puma attack could have left me dead or injured in the middle of nowhere with no help around. Then there was the danger of the human side of Peru – robbers and guerrillas had taken the lives of many lone tourists over the years. With Colombia winning the war against the drug barons Peru was, in 2005, the most dangerous country in South America, and this meant it was one of the most dangerous countries in the world. Certain areas to the east were, and may still be, off limits to travellers as this is where the coca leaf is grown in great quantities. Certainly at that time the land was owned and patrolled by the drug gangs and guerrillas who were armed with machine guns. Even the military rarely set foot in those areas. Thankfully by the time of my visit the political groups the 'Shining Path' and the MRTA had been somewhat subdued in their activities. Government troops under the controversial President Alberto Fujimori had been sent into the mountains to eliminate the drug gangs and had practically wiped them all out, families included, in a no-nonsense attempt to end the near civil war that had broken out between the drug lords and the government.

All this, however, was happening on the other side of the Andes, hundreds of miles to the north-east.

"Don't worry, I'll be fine," I told the hotel owner. Quite frankly I didn't know what he was so worried about. It was only a week's camping.

"No, you must not do this. It is too dangerous," he kept telling me, but nothing would sway me from this journey.

When the taxi driver arrived he was shown the map and the area I wished to get to – a hidden lake that was set between mountain peaks that are thousands of metres high.

"It is not possible to get there, not even on foot," he said. "I can take you to the road, but you will never make it to that lake."

"Well, I will try," I said. "It will be fine."

I then turned to the hotel owner. "I will be back in seven days," I said. "If you don't hear from me after nine days, then you can inform the authorities."

"Okay," he said, shaking his head.

From the city, my reluctant taxi driver headed north towards the mountains and the huge volcanoes of El Misti and Chachani. It wasn't the first or the last time that I would be journeying to some place with the knowledge I may not return, but that's all part of the traveller's life. It didn't scare me, it just made me more determined to do it.

The driver refused to take me any farther when we reached a bend in the road near a place called Aguas Calientes, which means *hot waters* and must be just about the most common place name in Peru. He told me it was impossible to reach the area by car and this was the closest he could take me. On the map, he showed me that there was no more road and the gravel track stretched around the mountain and headed back south on the other side. He continued trying to convince me to go with him back to the city, but I wouldn't be swayed.

I took all my things from the taxi and began struggling to carry everything towards a gap between two peaks. The taxi driver sat on his car bonnet for a while, watching me, before he finally decided my mind would not be changed.

"Thank God for that!" I said as he drove off. I wondered what all the fuss was about. After all, it was only a camping trip. Maybe South Americans don't understand the concept of camping, I thought.

My destination was at least a few miles farther north. Ahead was a huge hill and traversing it was all the more difficult because I had with me a week's supply of water – eight two litre bottles that weighed the proverbial ton – along with the backpack. It wasn't enough but purification tablets were in the pack in case of any trouble.

I wanted to reach the top of the hill, but very soon it became a near-vertical climb. At first I took the water up a few metres and left it on a ledge, then I returned to retrieve the backpack, but the climb eventually became impossible. With no ropes, at times I was hanging onto a ledge with a twenty or thirty metre drop below. The heat was relentless and in a very short time the sun would sink below the horizon. There could have been serious trouble without shelter in this unrelenting environment and high altitude and soon I had to accept defeat – I wasn't going to make it to the lake. Not today or even tomorrow. A quick decision was made to turn back and head towards the road once again.

Nearby, there was a fast-flowing river and a small area of sand where the river curved in a chicane and headed south down the mountainside towards the city. According to the map the area was two thousand metres above sea level and the river ran quickly as gravity and steep channels took it towards the ocean. It was only a few metres across, very narrow for a Peruvian river, but it was very deep.

The sun was dipping rapidly behind the mountains and it was becoming dark so I rushed to get my tent up by torchlight, finishing just as the sun disappeared.

The place was so beautifully serene and peaceful but always in Peru danger underlies the stunning beauty of this magical country. Wherever you go you must be on your guard, be aware, and always expect the unexpected. And on this first night, alone in the mountains with no one around, in just a couple of hours the serenity would be shattered and I would be fighting for my life.

Before that, however, there was total peace and freedom. It was just me and now I could truly enjoy the solitude and loneliness that only this kind of adventure can bring. It was the reason for being there – when you are alone and away from humanity, after a couple of days your thoughts change. You start to become one with your environment and thoughts seem to come from deep within your subconscious, rather than your consciousness. Memories from the far past come to the surface and events that you had forgotten suddenly become as fresh as if they occurred yesterday. This was a chance to make peace with the past – a chance to deal with bad episodes in my life, to allow them to surface, to deal with them and to put them behind me. However, I needed isolation for quite a time before this process could begin, and in reality it had only been about six hours since the hustle and bustle of the city of Arequipa had enveloped me.

As I was retiring for the night, a strange noise echoed through the darkness. It startled me, but only because I had never heard anything like it before. It sounded like a sonic boom from an aeroplane. On hearing the noise a second time I felt I should investigate, but there was nothing to be seen.

There were no aeroplanes in the sky, no movement, nothing. Then *boom!* There it was again. The sound echoed off the mountain peaks, which meant that its true direction could not be located. All I could tell was that it was becoming louder and more frequent.

"What the hell is that?" I asked out loud, becoming nervous.

Louder and closer the sound came until it was almost deafening. What on earth could be making such a noise? Had the volcano erupted? Was it the beginnings of an earthquake? Having only ever experienced a small earthquake with a magnitude of about 4.0, I knew a large earthquake or an exploding volcano would be thousands of times greater than this sound and the vibrations would be earth-shattering. No, this was something entirely different and more disturbing since it was totally alien to anything I'd heard before.

And then suddenly another noise could be heard. A loud hissing sound that became more audible very quickly. Another 'boom' – and then I realised the sound was coming from behind me.

I turned around just in time to see a wall of water hurtling down the mountain. The river in front of me changed in an instant from a calm but fast flow into an angry swirling monster that swelled up to the edge of the bank and swallowed the trees in front of me. For a moment I froze on the spot and then I realised there were probably just seconds before everything, including myself, would be swept away and lost forever. Taking a risky decision, I ran inside the tent and grabbed my boots and my hands were shaking as I put them on and tied the laces. "Do it calmly or you will make a mistake," I said to myself, knowing it required intense focus.

A split second can be the difference between life and death. My eyes darted up and down rapidly – up to the river just a couple of metres in front and down to the boot laces. There was no chance to salvage the tent, so I snatched the important things like my passport, bank card and money and then ran behind the tent and up the embankment. From that perspective I could see that I had pitched the tent on a sandy embankment that was, in reality, a river bed. I stood there waiting for my life to be washed away in front of me – all my possessions and everything I relied on for my survival.

Fortunately, and much to my surprise, the river never swelled above the edge of the first bank and the tent remained in place. I later discovered that the river reached a variety of levels during the year and, thankfully, it was currently at its lowest point.

The loud booming noises had been made by huge rocks, sometimes the size of houses and even bigger, pushed down the valley when rain water coming off the mountains collects and forces its way downstream. I have seen these rocks in Ecuador on the edge of mountain rivers – huge, round and smooth, they are pushed along by the water – the booming noise is the force of them crashing against each other, the floors and the walls of the river. They are beasts that weigh thousands of tonnes but water, one of the most powerful forces of nature, has no mercy on them.

I was very lucky that night. If there had been a larger rainfall farther east I would have been swept away in an instant and no one could survive such a powerful torrent.

The following day a lone man with a donkey walked past the road and he climbed the side of the hill behind me, a five hundred metre steep climb to the top. Checking the map there were several mines located nearby. In the afternoon another man appeared with a donkey and he stopped on the bridge that was behind me. He looked at me and pointed at the river, and I gave him the 'thumbs up' to indicate the dangers had already been made apparent. Again he pointed at the river, and again he received the 'thumbs up'. He probably thought I was a stupid gringo idiot and continued on his way up the mountainside.

On the third day things took another turn for the worse when I was attacked by sand flies. These little critters are worse than mosquitos and they relentlessly nibbled at my body. It was the only time during my whole year in South America that I had to use a head net, but that didn't save my arms. The sand flies had bitten into my left elbow and once blood appeared they repeatedly struck at that part of my body until the blood was literally running down my arm. It was too hot to take refuge in the tent and the decision was made to call it a day and return to the hotel. The danger of being swept away was one accepted problem but I wasn't going to be eaten alive by anything.

The quest to make it seven days alone had failed but I rationalised that I'd survived with a great tale to tell. I struggled up the mountainside and finally reached a tiny village several miles south, tired and hungry and in need of a real cooked meal instead of packets of rice. Luck was with me when the only bus that passed through the village each day arrived less than half an hour later.

The hotel owner was so relieved to see me alive he couldn't believe I had returned at all, and hearing my story he said I should never to do it again. Given the chance I would have done it again, but next time there would be more preparation. However, I never did have that chance and now, several years later, I probably wouldn't take it if it were offered – more because of my age rather than any common sense.

The current hotel room suddenly reappeared as my memories faded into the past and suddenly the realisation hit home that I was probably about to embark on an even more dangerous trip. Somehow these memories were an intuition of the future.

During the three days of solitude many things surfaced and in the end it was a battle with my own mind – the past and the present – wondering what I was letting myself in for and whether I still had the physical fitness to cope with it. Large amounts of time during the months prior to South America were spent preparing physically as well as mentally. Weight training for eight months, putting on a lot of weight and gaining all the stamina required for climbing mountains, at thirty-two I had been at peak physical fitness and ready to tackle anything, but this time I had been given no warning and had no time for any physical preparation. Whilst I was still fit and healthy, there was no way for me to replicate the kind of stamina I'd had six years ago, if it was required. This time I didn't fancy my chances in a fight against a puma. In 2004 I could have conquered the world. In 2010 I was wiser and more realistic about my own mortality – it was only after leaving South America that I had realised how lucky I had been to make it back home alive. Realisation was sinking in. What was I letting myself in for? At least in South America the decisions had been mine but this time I had no idea where I was going or why. I was a puppet on a string, a donkey chasing after a carrot. All I had were my intuitions and abilities to get me out of trouble and lead me forwards if need be, but even before reaching Tibet it would become clear that I would need them in greater quantities than ever before.

6

LETTING GO

Saturday arrived and I awoke with my heart beating fast because the next evening the plane would be landing on Chinese soil. I was both nervous and excited and I knew what these feelings meant and what emotions to expect when the plane landed in Chengdu. This time, however, I had no idea *why* I was going and this added a deeper air of uncertainty to the mix.

Charles had instructed me to write a diary, so the departing day seemed an appropriate place to start.

Saturday, May 8, 2010.

Bored after three days alone and scared. No, not scared, terrified. What does this idiot want with me? Strange man, but what can I do now? I am in this up to my neck – it's too late to turn back now. The only way is forward. Say goodbye to that psychotic woman. Glad to get away from her and that's a good reason as any to go. Despite my fear I can sense a new beginning, a new chapter in my life. I know this will lead onto something else and my intuition tells me this is something special. I am terrified but I've been here before so not too bothered. I'll be fine when I get going. Got to focus and take note of any strange happenings. Oh, the chance to travel at the expense of someone else is the greatest feeling of all...

Late in the afternoon I packed and went to stand outside the hotel and, as promised, at exactly four o'clock a car pulled up. The driver was dressed in a suit and he was tall and slender with a pronounced nose and a long face.

"Mister Maybury, I assume?"

"Yes," I said. "I wish everyone would stop calling me *'Mister Maybury'*. It's too formal."

There was no reaction. Instead he opened the back door and gestured for me to get inside. The car was impressive with its leather seats and drinks dispenser, rather like those limousines you can hire for parties, and I was about to strike up a conversation when suddenly the dividing black screen between us raised up, blocking any attempt to talk. Either he wasn't very friendly or he had been instructed not to talk with me.

On the seat next to me were the tickets to China and my heart leaped on viewing them. It once again added to the reality that all this was actually happening, my name stamped on the first class tickets, but at least I would be travelling in style rather than those cramped and uncomfortable aisle seats most travellers are so accustomed to when flying.

Two hours later we arrived at Heathrow airport. The driver opened the door for me and then shook my hand. "Good luck," he said.

"I'll need it!" I responded, sarcastically.

"I know you will," he replied.

Really, that certainly didn't help my nerves. I picked up my backpack as the driver disappeared from the set down. Loneliness suddenly took on a whole new meaning. Standing there for a moment and wondering what I was doing, there was the temptation to turn back. But I didn't.

There's not much worse than international travel – the waiting, the flying that causes jet lag between continents, the frustration and the sitting around in uncomfortable hard chairs. Thousands of people mill around in the terminal, screaming babies, bored children, tears of fear and despair as loved ones separate not knowing what the future will bring. If anything, that is what airport terminals contain: an air of uncertainty, a collective feeling of fear and anticipation, sometimes manifested as dread. Those who travel in family units or in pairs seem to be immune to these emotions but for the solo traveller it is always the same – fear on some level. For sure, most people have the thought at least once about the plane crashing to the ground. It's one of those things that we internally process. If a car breaks down we pull over, but if a plane breaks down there is only one outcome – death. No one wants to die alone. Only repeated trips diminish those feelings but nonetheless no matter how well you try and hide it, no matter how much you get used to it, it is always there hidden in the depths of your mind. Only the hardened traveller knows how to mask these emotions. And the bravest travellers of all must be astronauts. Can you even imagine the feeling of sitting in a rocket ready for take-off into space, tonnes of fuel lit up like a bomb underneath you as you leave the Earth's atmosphere in a matter of minutes? And people think *I'm* crazy? Huh! It's terra firma for me every time.

Two hours later we were taxiing down the runway and for a moment I looked out the window wondering if I would ever see my native England again, the patchwork of cultivated fields getting smaller by the second as we climbed into the sky. Cramming eight months of fear and preparation into three days I had barely had any time to think properly, but at every step I had been reminded of those emotions that had plagued me only six years previously. However, despite there only being three days preparation the emotions were not as bad as before. Was it the fact that there were only three days to prepare? Or was it the age-old saying that 'the first time is always the worst'?

Suddenly a strange kind of relief swept through my body, as if the clearer air of altitude brushed away my emotions and left them on the ground. It was an opportunity to clear my mind and allow some kind of coherence to form over recent events and also a chance to look out the circular window and stick my middle finger up at my ex-partner. That made me smile. I was jetting off to a foreign land on a great adventure while she was stuck with the turmoil and guilt of her actions. I hoped that she was suffering somehow. Not in a bad way, for there was a natural instinct not to wish her harm, rather I just hoped she was reminiscing on the mistakes she had made and realising she had thrown away a good person who would have stood by her through thick and thin.

Drifting in and out of sleep, each time my mind was snapped out of brief unconsciousness my heart leapt with a powerful adrenaline pulse of pure fear. Of course the questions kept coming. Of course I kept thinking that I had made a mistake. Why was I doing this? Was it a rash decision? Sure it was, but was it more an impulsive reaction to my relationship break-up, rather than jumping at the chance to go on a great adventure? Was I running away rather than thinking clearly about the implications of the dangers I was surely facing?

Thinking, analysing, reminiscing – there were moments during that journey when I wanted to open the door and fall into the sea from thirty-seven thousand feet, but all my thoughts went around in circles and I ended up right back where I started. In many ways this had nothing to do with my relationship. I kept using that as the reason to justify the decision, but in reality it was just the kind of thing I did on impulse. And why not? My life was going absolutely nowhere so what was wrong with jumping on a plane to a foreign, unknown land at the behest of an equally unknown person? Adventurers often make careers out of life-risking treks and readily find people to sponsor them – but I was no Ranulph Fiennes or George Mallory. Those who know me really well are well aware that this is the kind of thing I would do without question. To travel South America for a year, I had to work and save for two and sell half my belongings in the process. This time everything was being paid for by someone else. It was a no-brainer.

People may call me stupid, but the simple fact is they just don't understand the logic. What it's really all about is how we perceive life itself. Life threatening situations are not risks in my eyes, they are adventures and tests. So many people think this life is all there is – we are born and then we die, and that's it – so we should take all necessary steps to stay immortal. But for me this is wrong. The Western world has lost its connection to spirit; lost its connection with the wonders of the world. It was Teilhard de Chardin who said *"We are not human beings having a spiritual experience; we are spiritual beings having a human experience."*

Life is not about climbing ladders. It is not about acquiring material goods or getting a mortgage. Those are entrapments I have deliberately avoided at all costs. People want to feel a sense of security in their life and others who step outside that way of thinking make *those* people feel uncomfortable – it's *their* fear projected onto someone else, but the idea of security in this world is nothing more than illusion.

Although we are both, we are ultimately spiritual beings, not animal creatures. The more we experience the more we learn and thus the more we evolve as spiritual beings. So many people fear death, but when you know that death is not the end the world becomes an adventure playground. The people who would think it was a stupid decision to jump on that plane without question are the ones who fear the Grim Reaper. They are the ones who fear their own mortality.

Those climbing Mount Everest know there is a very high chance they will not even make it to the summit. The rates are one in ten deaths for the ascent, and one in twenty for the return. That's a ten per cent chance of not reaching the top. Those are high odds and yet people still climb the beast of the earth. So why do they do it? If you and nine friends went on a dangerous trek and were told one of you would not return, would you still go?

More psychological preparation happened during the flight than had been managed in the last few days. Somehow the situation seemed more real, but it wasn't a case of justifying the decision, it was more a case of settling in to the emotional turmoil that manifested and this was caused by being out of the comfortable surroundings of home – having the 'security' removed. This was also a reason why I never liked settling in one place for too long. There is always the illusion that everything is static and nothing changes but life has a way of biting us on the backside when we least expect it, and those who become too stable in their comfort zone are only inviting the shock of sudden change. Best to keep moving in life and go with the flow, for surely being stuck in one place makes life boring. So many people end up with regrets. They get a comfortable job and get a mortgage that takes twenty-five years to pay off, and before they know it they reach retirement age and wonder where the time went. What's the point in that? Sudden change can come in the form of the loss of that comfortable job, the consequent loss of the house and then they are left with nothing. So why bother in the first place? Why not experience life, go on adventures and experience the planet in all its beauty and wonder? Maybe there are two types of people in that sense. Would you prefer to be Ranulph Fiennes and trek to the pole, or Joe Bloggs who works at the office, spends his weekends down the pub and pays a mortgage?

The flight to Hong Kong was nearly twelve hours and there were a couple of hours to wander around the terminal before the connecting flight to Chengdu. After another three hour flight the plane would land in China and what a bizarre country that would turn out to be.

I fell asleep during the second flight. I dreamed of a strange place and when I woke up, I thought it must have been Shambhala. Perhaps the words in the folder had left me dreaming too much, literally.

Beautiful flowers adorned the edges of a low wall that surrounded perfectly cut grass-filled embankments. A small stream elegantly flowed through a man-made channel that surrounded a stunning temple, which looked like the Parthenon of Ancient Greece. Strange looking but attractive couples wandered around the grounds, talking of philosophy and the stars. As I walked towards the pillars of the temple a sweet sound entered my mind. "I'm over here," said a soft female voice.

I turned to see a remarkable and beautiful looking woman sitting on a bench surrounded by orange flowers. She was slender with slight shoulders and she had oriental eyes, rosy red cheeks with a cute button nose. "Where have you been?" she asked, "I've been waiting so long."

A sound of clinking glass in the cabin woke me, dispelling the serene world that had been created by the subconscious. It would have been nice to think I would soon be in that heaven of Shambhala, but that was not to be. Soon I would be in a hellish world of horrors that would make the trip to South America look like a summer's holiday on a golden beach.

7

CHINA, CHENGDU, CHANG AND CHA

"What is the purpose of your visit?" the thin security man asked me at the check-in desk.

"Pleasure," I replied. "Just visiting and travelling around a little."

"Where are you travelling?"

"I am not sure yet, I haven't made any specific plans. I hope that this book will provide me with the best places," I said, holding out the guide to China I had purchased in the local bookshop during my three days of boredom. "I was thinking of travelling to the East of China, it seems more traditional."

I didn't know if that statement was true but the hope was he would think I was just a stupid traveller with no clue about China. It seemed like the perfect cover but the main reason for saying this was to ensure he thought I would be travelling in the opposite direction to Tibet.

"Why didn't you fly to Shanghai?" he asked.

"Because I want to travel across the country and experience as much as possible," I replied, keeping a static smile on my face.

He looked at me suspiciously.

"How long are you staying?"

"Three months."

"When is your return flight?" he asked as he held my flight ticket in his hand. It's a mystery why airport security ask these stupid questions when the answer is right in front of them.

"The seventh of August," I replied.

He looked at my passport, comparing it to my face. Eight years had passed since the photo was taken, but there wasn't much difference apart from a little added weight. He stared at me for a moment trying to see if there was anything suspicious in my eyes.

"I hope you enjoy your stay," he said, stamping the visa that had magically appeared in my passport some time recently.

Thankfully, Chinese visas don't require a photo and if they did it would have been interesting to know how Charles would have arranged that. It would probably have the background of the café in the picture and a long lens would have created a fuzzy image.

As I walked towards the airport doors I was immediately met with the strange smell of China. My senses went into overload as my body tried and failed to decipher this new experience. My mouth became dry, accompanied by a weird taste in the back of my throat. Strange birds could be heard and the chatter of the Chinese language filled the air as the sensory shock had an instant effect. Here I was in the most populated country on earth – a country that grapples between its glorious past and its Communist present, even though the two are not so different in their political structure. A country that finds it hard to accept that its spiritual, Buddhist, martial arts history is now replaced with a technological society where the young are seemingly far wiser than the old. China is a once peaceful country of beautiful, open plains that have been replaced with flashing city lights and horrendous pollution. It is a country that, despite its economic growth and military power, somehow cries out for the long-lost ideals of fairness and spiritual equality. China is a contradiction, a society lost between two worlds that won't blend together.

Pounced upon by taxi drivers wanting my business I chose the most innocent looking man and gave him a piece of paper with the hotel details, and in no time at all we were whizzing around the streets of Chengdu, dodging rickshaws, bicycles and mopeds en route.

The effects of jetlag stayed with me for a few days and it seemed Charles was aware of this as my rendezvous with Chang was set for three days after arrival. I spent the intermediate days wandering the streets of Chengdu, trying out the cuisine and taking in the strange sights. It was a bizarre place of extremes. The streets were full of weird and wonderful shops and tens of thousands of people were milling around the city. Chinese food is a bit strange to say the least – they will eat anything from testicles to eyeballs, bugs and worms. Because of that, I was cautious and spent the time trying to find western-style restaurants that used a knife and fork, rather than chop sticks.

My sleep pattern was erratic and after the second day the tiredness eased but I never actually became accustomed to this huge city. Always preferring open spaces, smaller towns or villages and a quieter lifestyle, I was totally unsuited to the chaos that is Chengdu. Being summer it was also hot – very hot in a city full of so many people and so much pollution.

Chengdu is a fairly large city laid out over flat land with no great buildings to speak of and no dominating feature, although skyscrapers are plentiful. A wide river cuts a gouge through the city. It is a mishmash of the old and the new and many new construction sites were adding to the already overpopulated area. The city was filled with tens of thousands of cyclists, all trying to fight their way through the packed streets. Never wandering far enough from the hotel to get a real feel of the place, any tourist activities were completely forgotten as I spent the three days getting accustomed to the culture of China itself. On the night of the third day I wrote in the diary again.

Wednesday 12 May, 2010.

Chengdu, China. Stinks! Weird smells fill the air, a combination of food and pollution. There is no air to speak of. The people are a bit strange. They seem chatty but spend most of their time keeping to themselves. They seem oblivious to me. Just another tourist, I guess. Can't get used to it, it's too crowded, but at least some of the streets are wide and open, giving a feel of space occasionally. Food's a bit odd. I am amazed at how slim most of them are because the food seems greasy to me. Must be a genetic thing. I could never settle here but getting used to it. Looking forward to meeting Chang and getting out of this place. I just want to get on the move. Itchy feet.

On the morning of the fourth day Chang arrived in the foyer of the hotel. He was the complete opposite to what I had anticipated. I had expected another ageing man in a suit but instead Chang was in his mid-twenties, dressed in a blue shiny tracksuit, with short cropped black hair and a rounded face that made him look like a teenager. He also had a kind of impertinent look, the sort of innocent 'boy next door' image, but he obviously had a serious side to him. He greeted me with a beaming smile and I instantly felt comfortable in his company.

"Hello, Steve," he said, "I am Chang. Nice to meet you."

"It's nice to meet you too, Chang."

"I hope your journey was okay?"

"Yes, it was fine. I've just about recovered from the jetlag."

"That's good. Please, can we go to your room so we can talk in private?"

We reached my room, number fifty-two, on the fifth floor with a good view of the busy street below. It was funny – I hadn't taken any notice of the room prior to Chang's arrival but now that he was here I suddenly became conscious of my surroundings, as if there was a need for him to be satisfied in some way. The room had everything – TV, fridge, ironing board, two comfortable chairs with a small table sandwiched between them, telephone, and plentiful light switches. There were also a few peculiar 'modern art' paintings on the walls.

With their blue and yellow rectangles separated by a red line the paintings did little to inspire and for me they meant nothing whatsoever, but to be honest art is not in my repertoire of interests. I have always preferred a good book over a painting.

"Would you like a drink?" I asked, looking at the drinks tray on the table next to the wardrobe. There was nothing Chinese about this hotel. We may as well have been in London but at least it eased the shock of the culture change.

"Yes, that would be nice. Can I have cha?"

"Tea? Yes, of course."

The tray contained a menagerie of different teas.

"Which one would you like?" I asked, not knowing the difference between them. Neither were the labels readable.

Chang walked over and had a browse through the selection. "Ah, this one is the best. It's called *Longjing*, which means *'Dragon Well'*. Have you tried it yet?"

"No, I haven't actually. I am a coffee drinker normally."

"Oh, you must try *this* cha, it is wonderful," he said, smiling at me as if I was in for a great experience and pulling out a tea bag with a yellow wrapper.

"Okay, I will join you for Chinese cha," I said, looking forward to the new experience. It was at least six months since I'd indulged in a cup of tea. "When in Rome..." I thought to myself.

I wanted to ask Chang about how he became involved in this scenario. Who was he and what was his connection with Charles? However, knowing my questions would be futile I waited and hoped Chang would volunteer information, but he never revealed anything. His sole purpose was to get me across the border and into Tibet and then to meet with others who would take me farther into the interior.

"Once we meet at the village I will return to China," he said. "Tomorrow morning we will catch a bus to the nearest border town. Once there we will cross the border on foot, but I must warn you – the entire border of Eastern Tibet is patrolled day and night by the Chinese military. They won't ask questions if they catch us. Do you understand?"

Chang's eyes pierced my soul.

"Yes," I replied. There was nothing else to say about it. The message was clear – if we got caught we were in deep trouble.

"Tomorrow morning you will leave the hotel at seven. Walk across the road to the café with the red dragon above the door. You will see me further on but do not acknowledge me or speak to me. Stay a good ten metres behind and follow me. We must not be seen talking with one another. We will walk to the bus terminal and head west. Just follow me onto the bus, buy the ticket and sit in a different seat somewhere on the bus. At no time must we talk. At the other end we will do the same – you will follow me at a distance until we reach a safe house and then we can talk again. Are we clear with all of this?"

"Absolutely," I said.

His matter-of-fact way of discussing things was admirable and now it was clear that the way he was dressed was not normal for him – there was something in his seriousness that gave the impression of a businessman. But if Chang was wearing a disguise he was surely failing in every detail. The shiny blue tracksuit not only stood out but it was about twenty years behind the fashion. He looked ridiculous – and why he was wearing it was just one of many unexplained things that would plague my mind for a long time to come. Then again, nothing had been normal for seven days and nothing would be normal from here to eternity. It was clear though, that dressing in a way that brings attention to oneself is, in many ways, the best disguise of all.

"When we reach the safe house I will scratch the back of my head with my left hand. The house will be on the left. Enter this house through the front door. It will be open so just let yourself in. I will go around to the back of the house and join you inside. Before you go in, make sure no one is behind you. I am sure it will be fine, but if someone is behind you, no matter how innocent they may look, continue on down the street and then double back later. Make it look like you are simply lost in the backstreets. I am sure you are aware of what to do under these circumstances, I don't need to explain."

"I understand everything," I replied, "but wouldn't it be less suspicious if I went round the back and you went through the front door?"

"Ah, that is a question I hoped you would ask. It shows you know what you are doing. In normal circumstances it would be better if you did go around the back so you would not be seen, but trust me, Chinese people think differently. If the neighbours see you, which they probably will, they will be suspicious if they see a stranger wandering around the back of the houses, but if you walk straight in the front without hesitation they won't be concerned."

That made a lot of sense and it would work providing I didn't hesitate or do something worse, like wander into the wrong house.

"The border town... well, more a village really, is high in the mountains so make sure you wear appropriate clothing. It's very hot in the day but very cold at night. I won't tell you the name of the place – probably best you don't know. If you get caught you can play dumb and pretend you're lost. At least that'll give you some time."

"Some time for what?"

"What do you think of Chengdu?" he asked, ignoring my question.

"It takes a bit of getting used to, but it seems okay. Most people are friendly in an abstract way."

Chang laughed. "There is nothing friendly about the people here. It is just a front to be as polite as they can. Chinese people are very insular."

"What do you mean?"

"The friendliness is... What do you say in your country? Oh yes, 'two-faced'."

"But surely not everyone is like that? I mean, many people can be like that, but in this world people are generally either good or bad."

A smile ran across Chang's face as he peered towards the window.

"I find that theory a little too simplistic. There are many different types of people, I find. It all depends on their incentive in life and in China the state has created a mind-set that people must achieve and climb ladders. You must remember China is a communist state, despite its attempts to fool the world into believing it is democratic. The days of the Emperor are not over. Even though there is a government in place, behind the scenes it is not like that at all. Because of this, many people are selfish as the system puts the people into competition with one another. They become goal-oriented. With so many people in the country there is little room for error or failure. You only have to look at our Olympians for this evidence. Have you noticed how distraught they become if they win silver instead of gold? Pressure, pressure, pressure..."

It was difficult not to agree with Chang's view since he was himself Chinese, but I felt his opinion was coming from the stance of someone who was anti-government, someone who was angry with the state and against the way things were being run. For example, China is certainly more open and less communist than North Korea. The impression was that Chang was more an anarchist than a patriot – a young man with a little bit of anger at the way the system operated, and perhaps he had his own failures that gave him a world view that was slightly detrimental. However, if I thought Chang was just an angry man he offered something that made me a little more sympathetic to his views.

"You know, most Chinese people know nothing of Tibet. They think it is called 'Xizang' and don't even recognise the name of 'Tibet'. They don't understand that it has been a foreign country for so long. They have been brainwashed into believing that it is a part of China. They know nothing of the murder of the Tibetans by the Chinese military. They know nothing of the self-immolation of the monks there who protest against Chinese rule. They know nothing. Many parts of China are cut off from the outside world in that sense. The media is state-run and the news people hear is only that China is a great country with the best intentions. If that isn't communism then I don't know what is. And if you think we have moved on from Tiananmen Square then think again. The only difference is that you don't hear about these things in your media. Even your country has agreed with China to report very little about Tibet. The world's media are linked together hand in hand. They only report on what they want you to know. China is still ruled with an iron fist. For this reason you must understand the danger we will be in when we try to cross the border. These people kill first and ask questions later."

Chang once again stared into me making sure I understood what he was trying to tell me. Whether his view or his words were true or not, he was trying to ensure that I was prepared for what was to come.

Chang finished his tea and excused himself. Despite his anarchistic viewpoint he had a contradictory politeness that gave him a strange duality and this was something which made him good at the job he had to do – he could alter his thinking processes to suit the situation. In essence he had a great survival tool at his disposal. He left a lasting impression on me. There was something unique and curious about him that was unfathomable and I often wondered if his views were really his own.

Thursday 13 May, 2010.

Chang – funny kid! Or is he a kid? Can never tell the age of Chinese people, they all look the same. Only the elderly and the very young can be distinguished. Everyone else is either 20 or 40 years old. Starting to hate this place so glad I'll be leaving tomorrow. It's getting hot and humid and the sticky air in the city is stifling and uncomfortable. I've never seen so many bicycles. I still can't figure Chang. He's such a likeable character – relaxed, confident and yet I sense a small amount of fear somewhere. Is it the journey we are about to embark on? Or is it the fact he must be a marked man?

8

DROPPING PENNIES

I almost didn't recognise Chang. He was dressed in a suit and carried a briefcase. It was a stark contrast to his dress the day before and now the duality that I'd envisaged was clear to see. He now looked very much like Charles and the driver who took me to the airport. It was a reminder of the people I was dealing with. The sight did force a little giggle, though – Chang, the master of disguise!

It was a long bus ride to the far West of China, although where China officially ends and Tibet begins has often been debated, since China has claimed so much land from Tibet. Tibet covers two and a half million square kilometres. China, in an act which can be described as purely vindictive, has claimed 1.3 million square kilometres as its own, leaving Tibet with 1.2 million square kilometres. One doesn't need a degree in sociology to see that this is a humiliating slap in the face for Tibet.

The journey was around six hours across rugged mountain territory and by the time we reached our destination my backside was numb from the uncomfortable and cramped seating. Although it was an ambiguous border, we were close to it and now my nervousness started to show.

The small border town was set in a valley with large hills that dominated the area – the eastern end of the Himalayan mountain range. From a distance it would have looked like a child's toy town and certainly from above it would have appeared small and insignificant.

It was ironic that Chang looked more out of place than I did but it was a good ploy on his part since a man in a suit was a respected sight, especially in these parts, so no one took any notice of him. As for me, however, I was stared at by just about everyone and the place seemed devoid of foreign travellers which left a deeper feeling of unease.

Following Chang away from the small town centre and down narrow side streets there were tall, three storey houses that made the narrow lanes feel claustrophobic. Soon the pathway opened out, the streets widened, we were more out in the open and the houses became detached and separated. As we reached the outskirts, about a fifteen minute walk from the centre, we reached the safe house – a small bungalow with a typical traditional Chinese roof that sloped outwards as it angled downwards.

Chang scratched his head and I stopped a few metres behind him, bending down and undoing my shoelace before tying it back up again. There was no one in sight, so making sure Chang had disappeared I stood up and walked the last few metres and headed into the front door of the house he had indicated.

The main room was small and bare apart from a low table in the centre. It was devoid of any decoration apart from the painted walls and a musty smell hung in the air. This place was certainly not lived in.

Chang arrived a few moments later and called me into the room at the back. This room was altogether different, a complete contrast to the emptiness of the front room. It was decorated fully with chairs, a table, pictures on the walls of a Chinese family, a small fireplace and books. Lots and lots of books, old and dusty and looking like they had not been touched for a century or more.

"Please, sit down," Chang said, gesturing for me to relax and get comfortable.

"Thanks. What is this place?"

"It belongs to a friend of mine. This was his parent's house but they died many years ago and he inherited it. He has no intention of using it as he lives in Shanghai but he is planning on maybe retiring here, so he has left it as it is until he decides what to do with it. I can use it as often as I like so sometimes I come here to hide away. It is also the place I use as a base to cross into Tibet."

"Have you done that often?"

"A few times, mostly when I'm helping return Tibetan monks to their home land who have been arrested by the Chinese. I use a slightly different route each time before the river crossing, but always in the same area. From the river there is only one pathway into Tibet, so it becomes more risky each time I venture out. We are safe here but we must leave in an hour or so as we need to reach our destination by sunrise. We will eat and gain our strength before we leave."

This was not the best news under the circumstances. After that horrific bus journey all I wanted to do was sleep for a night but unfortunately that wasn't going to happen and it seemed that being static for too long was a bad idea.

"Wouldn't the neighbours notice different people coming in to this house?"

"Maybe they do, it is quite a close neighbourhood, but thankfully people here are sympathetic to the plight of Tibet. Being right on the imaginary border they are more aware of what is going on. It's a strange contrast, really, because in Chengdu no one would have a clue about it. Although I try to be cautious, I don't think people here are particularly pro-government and the *one child policy* has upset a lot of people, especially those in local communities like this who don't have the money to pay for a second child. Anyway, most people here are elderly and they tend to turn a blind eye to almost anything. A lifetime in China teaches you to mind your own business. Would you like cha?"

"Yes, please."

"I will make some noodles as well. We don't want a heavy meal but we need lots of energy so we will eat noodles and I have some sugar-filled cakes."

"Where do we go from here?"

"We climb up to the top of the hill behind the house, down the other side and onto a flat plain. You could call that *no man's land*, and this is quite dangerous as it marks the not-really-existing border point between China and Tibet. The real not-really-existing border, if that makes any sense, is actually the Yangtze River, which we have to cross at its narrowest point. Once on the other side we climb another hill and then down into Tibet. The top of the second hill is patrolled by the Chinese but on the few journeys I have made I have not seen a single soul on the route, so it seems like a gap in the defences as far as I am concerned. We should be quite safe but we cannot take any chances or be complacent about it."

Chang started to make noodles and I sat back in the chair. The thought of a long and dangerous trek, crossing from one country into another, forbidden land, left me feeling uncomfortable and nervous but surely once we hit Tibet things would be much easier. It was exciting to think that we would be crossing the mighty Yangtze River, though.

"I thought the Yangtze River was near to Shanghai and that it was very wide?" I asked.

"Both of those statements are correct, but it is the mouth of the river that exits into the sea at Shanghai. The Yangtze is about six thousand kilometres long, the fourth longest river in the world, and we will cross it right at the head, or close to it."

I wanted to check the guide book to pinpoint our location but I had left it at the reception desk in the hotel for another guest to use. Not only was it bulky to carry but Chang had insisted that it was better I didn't know where we were going so I could play the role of the idiotic tourist if we got caught. As Chang started to make dinner I took the opportunity to write a quick diary entry:

Friday 14 May, 2010.

We are about to cross the border and head into Tibet. I'm really excited about this daring trip but also scared, and underneath there's a feeling – a feeling that I can't explain. I don't know if it's just the danger of what we're about to do, or whether there's something else – an intuition that something's not quite right about this. It's not the illegality of it, or the fear that we might be killed. It's something else that I can't figure out. I guess we'll find out soon enough.

"How do you like your noodles?" asked Chang.

"I didn't know there was an option. I always thought noodles were noodles."

"Yes, they are. I was joking!"

He turned and smiled at me and for the first time I saw another side to him – a more relaxed Chang. It was almost as if he felt the hard part of his job had already been achieved and this in turn made me more relaxed.

"Why do Chinese people eat so many noodles?"

"It has been our staple diet for thousands of years – quick, simple, cheap and filling. Plus you can mix it with anything, like you can with rice or pasta. Talking of pasta, did you know it originated in China?"

"Really?"

"Yes. Archaeologists found some pasta in China that was thousands of years old and that meant it was long before the Italians 'discovered' it."

"Well, that's an interesting fact I never knew."

"It's true. In fact, many inventions or discoveries can be traced back to China. Our history is one of the oldest in the world."

"You seem proud to be Chinese," I said, waiting for a response that might contradict the views he gave me at the hotel.

"Well, I am I suppose, but only in a historical sense. I am not happy with the Chinese government and our secret society, not to mention our Human Rights record and of course the treatment of Tibet. I much prefer, and I am very proud of, our history."

"It certainly is an interesting history although I don't know too much about it. To be honest, this part of the world is rather obscure to me from a historical perspective but I do like Chinese films about the old days when people fought with the sword. That is where my history lessons come from."

"Yes, that is exactly what I am talking about. The days when people truly knew about Chi energy and things like that. The real days when people worked on and lived off the land, rode around the great plains on horseback and learned great wisdom from the old teachers. Give me those days any time."

"It certainly has an attraction to it, that's for sure, but life was not so easy in those days without medicine and things like that."

"Yes, but the old remedies were much better than modern medicine, and in those days we were at one with the land and I am sure we were more in tune with nature."

"I absolutely agree with that. We have lost so much in this modern world. People don't seem to realise our minds are filled with noise and nonsense day in, day out. Who actually bothers to sit in silence these days and allow their mind to drift away? And where is there any silence, anyway?"

"Exactly, yes, that is it." Chang turned and looked at me in a curious manner as if he had finally met someone of equal mind. "And how is your native country in this respect?"

"England is too overcrowded as far as I am concerned. There is no peace left and no big open spaces to enjoy. I never actually realised this until I went to South America. Peru is over five times bigger than the United Kingdom and yet its population is only around thirty million. About ten million live in the city of Lima so the whole country has vast open expanses of nothingness. You really feel at home with nature there, I can assure you."

"That sounds like large parts of China but nobody bothers with it anymore, except the farmers. People are too busy with their self-centred lives of selfishness and ignorance and they only seem to be interested in climbing the ladder or obtaining wealth."

"You hit the nail on the head there," I said.

Chang looked round at the noodles cooking on the stove.

"I did what?" he asked, wondering what he had done wrong.

I laughed at him. "It's just an expression – it means you explained the situation perfectly – hitting the nail accurately instead of missing it."

"Oh, I see. I hit the nail on the bed."

"No, on the *head* – you hit the nail on the head!"

"Oh, yes, I understand now. I hit the nail on the head." He mimicked striking a nail with a hammer. "Yes, it makes sense."

I smiled and turned my gaze towards the back window where the sun had already set. The air was warm and the world was quiet and still and a feeling of nervousness stirred within me. An intuition, perhaps, but it wasn't the normal kind of intuitive feeling – there was something else that bothered me. I could only assume it was because we were about to cross a border illegally and this was something completely new in my experience. Chang seemed more relaxed but he was becoming a little flustered at times.

"I notice there is no moon outside. I am guessing this will help our journey?"

"Since you mention it, we are here at this time because of this very reason. Dates are important. The moon is important and tonight is a new moon. The timing of this experience of yours is not by chance."

"Is that some of your old Chinese wisdom?" I asked the question seriously but it seemed to carry an unintended overtone of sarcasm.

Chang paused for a moment before answering. "Maybe, but this trip seems to be someone else's wisdom. It hasn't passed my notice, though. I can tell you that moonlight is a great hindrance because we could easily be seen. On the contrary, torchlight creates unnatural light and movement and is easily noticed by the patrolling soldiers. This night, we will need a torch during the first leg as the forest is very dense, but once we cross the river we will have no light to guide us."

I suddenly remembered what Charles had said about numbers and astrology. He had stated correctly that I was a Gemini and also born in the Chinese Year of the Rat but the connection between the Chinese birth year and the fact that I was now in China hadn't previously occurred to me. What was he trying to tell me? It was clear that what was written on those few pages of the folder wasn't meant as a joke but the irony seemed almost funny. Suddenly everything appeared to have a hidden meaning and these seemingly irrelevant things were critical, but the question was – what was the significance? What was worth remembering and what was not? Charles had said I must pay attention to detail but before now I hadn't even thought about it. Now it seemed as if the realisation of the connection between my Chinese birth year and the skills required to carry out this task had happened at the correct moment, like a trigger telling me to shake myself into *unreason*. It seemed that what might be termed 'scientific logic' was no longer a requirement and instead, intuition was paramount. Something had triggered in my mind. Something was telling me that things were not as they seemed. Those words in the folder were more important than I could have imagined. It was now obvious that Charles had chosen the exact day to enter the café, the exact day for me to leave and the precise time to meet Chang – all this so that we could cross the border under a new moon. Was it because of the darkness, or was there a mysterious astrological connection that was not apparent? Was Charles a believer in all things mysterious? It seemed it was necessary to read between the lines more frequently and I started to backtrack and try and recall little incidents that had raised my intuitive reactions...

"Noodles are ready," Chang said, breaking my thoughts.

We sat in the empty front room, kneeling down at the table. Chang passed me two chopsticks.

"Oh," I said.

"What's wrong?"

"I can't use these things."

"Really? I can teach you, if you like."

"Go for it."

"Okay, you hold one between finger and thumb and let the other one rest on the fold of skin between your thumb and first finger. Then you just pick up your food but you must control both of the sticks."

I tried many times but in the end gave up and ate with my fingers instead. We simply didn't have time for a chopstick lesson.

"Don't worry," he said, "it will come to you in time."

"Do you know Charles?" I asked.

"Who is Charles?" replied Chang, slurping as he ate.

There was no hesitation in the response and it was a stupid question.

"He is the man who sent me here."

"I don't know anyone called Charles."

"How did you know I was coming?"

"I was asked to escort you over the border. I don't ask questions, I just get paid for the job. Why?"

"I just wondered if you knew the person that gave you *this* job."

"No, I have no idea who it is. Why do you ask, does it matter at all?"

"No, I just wondered how it all worked."

Chang looked confused.

"I have no idea why you want to get into Tibet and to be honest I don't want to know. Everyone else that enters Tibet *this* way is going home. You have come from far away to do the opposite. Either you are crazy or stupid. And I don't know why you didn't fly into Tibet. The borders are closed, but the airports aren't."

Mortified, I dropped my noodles back into the bowl. It never crossed my mind once. He was right. Charles had never mentioned air space. He only stated the borders were closed. So, if the airports were open and I could easily enter Tibet as a traveller, why did he want me to cross a dangerous border on foot, risking the life of both Chang and myself?

9

D-DAY

I felt anger towards Charles but even more so at myself. How could I have not realised this before? How stupid of me not to have even considered it. It suddenly seemed as if Charles had hoodwinked me in some way and on my part there was an inward frustration that I hadn't done my own research, but to be fair he had left me no possible means of doing any homework in the few days at the hotel. Now, it was as if the situation had shocked me out of a trance, for it was unlike me to go anywhere without any background research. I was suddenly forced into a different reality about the situation – why was I blindly following his instructions? Only now, when we were moments away from heading into the danger zone, did I start asking more pertinent questions – what the hell was going on here? What on God's earth was I doing in the middle of nowhere going to some place that I had no knowledge of and with no idea why I was heading there? It was the kind of impulsive decision I *would* normally make and Charles had oozed an air of certainty about this trip as if it were my own grandfather urging me to do it, so in many ways my reaction to this news shouldn't have been a surprise, but there was something else going on that disturbed me, something that couldn't be explained. He did say I would be risking my life at times, but there was no indication of how deep that statement ran. The adventure side of the journey stopped me from thinking of any real danger.

Suddenly there was a sense of fear that I have never felt before – a fear so deep that my imagination had me flying out the door and all the way back to the city, running so fast I would even overtake the crowded buses. If I grabbed my rucksack and darted for the door once Chang went to the bathroom I could be gone before he realised, but what would I *really* do once I was out in the open? I could head back to Chengdu and try to get a flight home but that would entail withdrawing a large amount of money in case Charles suddenly cut off the finances – but it was obvious these ideas were fanciful and utterly futile. I had to calm down and stop my fear from overriding common sense. Perhaps Chang would offer some more information.

"So, why are the borders closed?"

"What? You mean, you don't even know?"

"No, I don't."

"You want to cross the border but you haven't stopped to think why it was closed in the first place? I am being paid to take you, but what about you? No perfectly sane person would try and get into Tibet this way unless they were totally desperate and had nothing to live for. I don't know why you are doing this and I don't want to know, but I can tell you that you're about to enter the cave where the dragon lives. If you enter Tibet like this, once you are there you are only a ghost. I can only think you have some *very* good friends in Tibet, or maybe the dragon himself is looking after you."

I found myself burying my head in my hands as reality was finally sinking in. How stupid could I have been? This was a far more dangerous trek than I had ever undertaken before. Not so different in the dangers, but more because I didn't know why I was going or why we were taking this route. Understanding the ultimate goal makes risks worth the effort and gives an incentive to attempt the dangerous trek, but this time not knowing the goal left me wondering if the perils were worth the effort. I tried to get this out of my mind and focus on getting the job done. No doubt there was a reason for all of this and it certainly wasn't the time to be having a panic attack. I needed to stay calm and focused. When I did clear my mind I realised it wasn't so much that it seemed I'd been tricked, it was more an intuition that something wasn't right. Something was lurking beneath the surface and it was slowly manifesting around me like a hidden disease suddenly showing symptoms.

"What happens when we get into Tibet?" I asked.

Chang looked at me and shook his head. "We must get to a village called Potala. There we will be met by someone. At that point we will part company and then you will be taken farther into the interior, but I don't know any more than this."

"Do you know the person we are to meet?"

"No, I have no idea who it is. This is not my normal job or route. I only get people through the border and once they get to the bottom of the hill I return. They are on their own after that. Once they are over the border they are literally in Tibet so it wouldn't be unusual for them to be seen on the other side of the hill. No Tibetan tries to come into China this way – it is a one-way route. In your case I have to escort you to the village since you won't have any idea where you are going, plus you have to meet with someone else and not to mention you are somewhat noticeable being a Westerner. My job is to make sure you are physically with the contact before I can leave."

"Yes, I think I might be a little out of place."

Chang laughed. "A little out of place! You people speak funny! In Tibet tourists stick to the tourist areas. They don't venture far off the beaten track. Finding a man like you near the imaginary border with China, where Tibetans are cut down like dogs just for being Tibetan, is a very suspicious thing indeed. China doesn't want the world to know what's going on here, believe me. Even your Western governments turn a blind eye. Why is that, do you think?"

"Trade, I guess."

"Yes, that is exactly true. It's all to do with money. A human life is nothing to these people."

It was shocking, to say the least. There were no words to say but there was a sense of logic behind this journey – if I'd have flown into an airport my presence in Tibet would be known. For some reason I wasn't supposed to exist here and it seemed Chang was reading my thoughts.

"It is obvious to me you don't even know what you are doing here, or why you are going to Tibet and the only logical explanation I can come up with is that timing is important for you."

"What do you mean?"

"From any airport it would take days or even weeks to get to Potala. For some reason you are being sent on the most direct route possible. Either your sponsor is a psychopath with no regard for your life or you need to get to your destination very quickly. Have you any idea which one of those possibilities would be the most accurate?"

"Probably both," I said.

Chang started to laugh again. "This is the funniest thing I have ever heard."

"Why did you take this job in the first place? Why not stick to your simple tasks?"

"So, you don't know *anything*, do you? I will be retiring after this mission. I am being paid enough to live a lifetime of luxury after this one. But I can tell you this – I don't like it at all. I don't know what is going on with you people but you are bringing a storm down on your heads. The Chinese soldiers don't mess around. If I was being paid any less, I would have refused this job. No one would be prepared to do this. I would normally only go as far as the hill and return. That's an easy job but actually going into Tibet is another thing altogether. The Chinese authorities are aware of me but they cannot catch me. I am the wind of the tiger."

I was stunned. What was so important about this that Chang was being paid a ridiculous amount of money just to get me into Tibet? None of this made sense but I had to stop asking questions, or thinking too much. Now was the time to be psychologically prepared. It was time to enter into 'survival mode' as we would soon be executing a military-style breakthrough – trying to sneak through the defences of one of the toughest, determined and most organised armies in the world. It seemed like an exaggeration, after all we weren't crossing through artillery batteries or entering a battlefield, but even though there would only be a few soldiers patrolling the area this was exactly the case. The Chinese have men dotted all along the border lines and Tibet is completely encased by the Chinese military. They don't want any foreigners getting in or out across the border and it seems they will stop at nothing to prevent this from happening. The Tibet that is being sold to foreigners is that of a peaceful nation of Buddhist monks and they prefer tourists to fly into the tourist areas and fly back out again without seeing the rest of it. The reality is a brutal regime of murder and silent occupation as China slowly stretches its arm out across the plains, dissolving a country into oblivion in the process. After all, the Dalai Lama is not in exile in India for nothing.

"I warn you, Steve, the Chinese do not stop to ask questions," Chang said, as we prepared to leave. "If we are caught, we are as good as dead."

"We'd better not get caught, then," I said as I locked eyes with him.

"I know. Don't worry. I am not complacent simply because I have made it through and back before. Each mission has exactly the same dangers but I will say one thing – if I get caught don't hang around, run like the wind. Do not stop for me or you will be caught as well. I won't be stopping for you, either. Once we reach the top of the hill, even though I am escorting you, you are on your own if something happens."

Chang's words were honest. It would be useless sticking together if anything bad was to happen. It would be better if one of us got out, rather than both of us getting caught. It would be a futile effort if we both failed. At least *someone* would know what happened to us, rather than unanswered questions and two rotting bodies in the mountains.

It was already dark when we left the safe house. We had to head south to the edge of town, climb up a hill, cross a river and then climb another hill before we could descend into Tibet. It seemed straightforward enough.

The streets were filled with a hazy orange glow but once we were near the edge of town there was only an ominous blackness beyond. Thankfully the street lights lit up the area just beyond the village, enough for us to see where we were walking for a short distance and this would allow our eyes to acclimatise to the darkness as we climbed higher into the rocky forest.

"How are we going to cross the river?" I whispered to Chang as we quietly walked down the deserted street. And deserted it was. There was a surreal feeling almost as if we were in a computer game and the area was so quiet it seemed there was a curfew in place.

"There is a tree that has fallen and lies on both banks of the river, making a bridge."

"That's a stroke of luck."

"Actually it was chopped down by others trying to cross the border about a year ago. It would be impossible to walk across – the river is a raging, fast flowing torrent, very deep and it is fifty metres wide at its narrowest point. Thankfully the Chinese haven't noticed the tree or they would have removed it."

"I thought it was forbidden for Buddhists to cut down trees?"

"It wasn't Buddhists who cut it down."

"Fifty metres – it must be a big tree."

"This area has some of the most wild, untouched forests on the planet but the Chinese are hacking it to pieces."

Wondering how we would have made this journey if the tree had not been felled, it seemed a lucky coincidence. Or was there another, more arduous journey before this route became accessible? I was about to ask Chang when he spoke.

"From here we must revert back to the rules of our previous outing – stay about twenty metres behind me and no more talking. We are together but from this point you are on your own. Understand?"

"Yes," I replied, wondering what we would do now if the worst was to happen. Getting caught on this side of the border was not an option – there would be nowhere to run or hide since we were still in China. Also it was pretty obvious what we intended doing. At least over the border we would know which direction to take.

Waiting for Chang to walk slightly ahead I then followed on behind, keeping the required distance. The night was chilly, about ten degrees, and the air was still which seemed odd since we were now in the mountains and on high ground.

At the edge of town Chang suddenly stopped at the end of a road. He peered around the corner and then turned back towards me, walking fast. He gestured for me to get tight against the wall of a house.

"It's the police," he said. "Hide behind this car until they pass."

We ducked down behind the car and waited, my heart thumping as our first encounter with danger had finally arrived. It made me excited, the 'buzz' of the threat creating an adrenaline rush that pumped blood faster through my veins.

The sound of footsteps became audible and voices of two policemen echoed down the street but thankfully they continued on the main road and ignored the side street where we were hiding. Breathing a sigh of relief, Chang gestured for me to get back up again.

"Wait here. I will go and check everything is clear. After I cross the road follow me between the two houses on the right, but make sure there is no one in sight before you cross the road."

"Okay," I whispered.

"Stay here until I have crossed the road." Chang wandered back to the junction. He looked around the corner again and waited a few moments before walking casually across the road. Taking the exact route, checking the street both ways before running across, I headed between the two houses and into a dimly lit lane.

After another fifty metres or so the lane ended and trees appeared. We had made it out of the town and into the forest.

We climbed the steep hill, away from the town and high into dense trees. It was tough going with no natural path and we struggled at a slow pace as the darkness hampered our progress. The roar of the river could be heard in the background, sounding like a train ploughing through the countryside. After around forty-five minutes we took a sharp turn to the right, continued on a straight path for another half an hour, clinging to the rocks and clambering through bushes, then headed back down again before reaching the river. We had travelled a long way and had taken an n-shaped route so that we were once again level with the town, which was now several miles distant. Chang was not wrong – the river was wild and unforgiving, deep and fast-flowing, with a deafening noise that meant we had to shout at each other to be heard. No one would hear us out here even if they were close by and this created a comforting sense of security.

"The fallen tree is around here somewhere," Chang shouted. "I think it is farther down."

We clung to the river bank and headed back towards the town, the distant orange glow giving a little illumination to guide us.

"There's the tree!" Chang shouted, jubilantly. It was a huge tree with a diameter of around nine feet and it was so long and the river so wide the bank on the other side couldn't be seen in the darkness. Only the black mass of trees opposite gave an idea of how wide this famous river actually is. It must have taken a long time to hack this beast of a tree down and it seemed sad that it was slain in its prime, but it was not in vain – the dead tree was now offering a new life to those who dared to walk along its back. It was the bridge between China and Tibet – a secret symbol of freedom that came with a price.

Walking along the trunk, the raging river below left me feeling slightly disorientated and I was splashed with water as the river churned and roared beneath me. Suddenly I slipped, but it was only a forward motion and I quickly regained balance. The trunk was a little slippery with all the water splashing on it and my misstep was enough to fill my body with adrenaline once again. True enough, one mistake would be enough to send me hurtling downriver towards the next town and no doubt by the time I got there I would no longer be breathing. It was ironic that I'd been thinking about the river incident in Peru only a week before. Not only did this give me the confidence to get across, but it made me wonder about the synchronicity. Had the memory been a premonition?

The crossing was a death-defying leap of faith into blackness and any kind of sideways slip would mean the end. It was as terrifying as a tightrope walk, not that I have or ever would try something as dangerous as that. Thankfully though, some ingenious person had carved away the bark from the top side of the tree and chopped grooves into the smooth wood leaving a steady path across the river and this gave my boots some grip along the route. It must have taken a long time to carve all that bark away from a tree this long but the incentive was a great one for the Tibetans – it meant saving lives. Certainly some people must have slipped and been lost forever but now was not the time to be thinking about that.

Continuing on, slow and steady, my heart beating fast and my concentration intense, just a few feet below the flowing water churned up waves of white bubbles and spots of water hit my face continuously as if it was raining. Juddering steps became a confident stride but it took a long time. Once on the other side I felt a sense of relief that I hadn't experienced for a long time – I ran the last few yards and jumped off the end of the tree, back onto firm ground.

"Are you okay?" Chang shouted in my ear as he grabbed my shoulder.

I nodded and let out a deep sigh of relief, allowing myself to drop on the ground, looking up into the sky and wondering how we ever managed to get across. The fallen tree stretched across the river, docile but meaningful, a silent witness to the hopes and dreams of all those who crossed it. How many of them made it across to return to their families back in Tibet?

So far all we had really achieved was to cross the official border which was controlled by the police, but the real defence was on top of the next hill where the military were strategically placed with a vantage point of both sides of the border. The police were there to simply check passports and allow people through but the military were there to stop people getting there illegally.

Onward we went, climbing another steep hill riddled with large rocks that gave shelter and camouflage before heading down the other side and reaching a flat plain that seemed bizarrely out of place. We stopped at the edge and waited for a short time.

The area seemed almost unreal, as if some worldly joker had put this place here as a test for anyone who dared to cross it. It was a flat, open expanse in the mountains, almost completely level and surrounded by impenetrable peaks that created a barrier around it. I might have said that the ground was an ancient lava bed – a volcano that had erupted and the solidified lava created a flat basin – but one didn't need to be a geologist or a volcanologist to see that this wasn't the case. The area was a bizarre freak of nature that gave us and anyone else a chance to cross into Tibet. Was it a gift from the gods? Or was it a temptation of the Devil? Whichever of the two, in reality it was a perilous path of open ground where we could easily be seen and without doubt danger would lurk with every step.

"We have to be careful here," whispered Chang, "we could be seen as we cross this field."

"Shouldn't we stick to the edges?"

"It won't make any difference. You can see the edges are rocky and they shine a little. We could be seen by our silhouette against the rocks but if we go across the field the grass will shield us slightly since it is darker. It's the lesser of two dangers I'm sorry to say, and neither of them are good. Once we cross this field we have to climb that hill. That is where the Chinese are located and they have a panoramic view over this field. Only the darkness will shield us. From this point on we don't speak to each other so if you want to say anything, say it now."

In that moment it felt like we were lambs being led to the slaughter. It was like the Somme battlefield and there was one simple equation – if we were seen we were as good as dead. We had to hope that no Chinese soldier was patrolling on the opposite hill and if they were we had to pray they were not looking in our direction. I shook my head and focused on the task of crossing the field.

"This is it, Steve. This is probably the most dangerous kilometre you will ever walk in your life. Are you ready for it?"

"Let's do it," I said, wanting to get on with it as soon as possible.

My nerves were already starting to shred. This wasn't to be an ordinary walk. At any moment we could be killed without question – it was the ultimate, terrifyingly exhilarating journey – a walk through the valley of the shadow of death with a fifty per cent chance of making it through. Our lives depended on whether a person's eyes were looking in our direction.

As we walked the half mile or so across the field it was clear how out of place it was – after all this was a mountainous area with forests. I tried to think of something to reduce the tension but it was important to concentrate fully on the walk and with each step the hill in front became closer and bigger, the black mass of trees casting doubts and fear in my mind.

Despite the darkness, the clear sky which had been our saviour by giving us a glimmer of light and showing us the way through the mountains, was now our enemy giving our location away to anyone in sight, but just as I was about to lay a curse on our starry companion, luck rolled in unnoticed like a snake sneaking through the grass.

Suddenly the stars disappeared as black clouds moved in swiftly from the west and within seconds the field darkened completely making it difficult to see. It was a total blessing as it gave us more camouflage across no man's land. We weren't completely out of sight but it was enough to give me the confidence we would make it.

Three quarters across the field we stepped up the pace as the base of the hill was within reach. All was deathly silent except for the sound of our walking – I was scared that the sound of the long grass slashing at our legs could be heard atop the hill.

The closer the trees became the more the adrenaline flowed. Faster and faster we walked until we were about a hundred metres away. And then we ran. We ran as fast as we could until we reached the bottom of the hill. It was one of the fastest one hundred metres I had ever run and once we made it we hid behind some trees, panting and sweating as the panic slowly subsided.

I crouched at the base of a tree and Chang and I stayed in our positions without moving until we got our breath back. Without doubt it was one of the scariest journeys I had ever undertaken. Somewhere, lurking around at any corner and at any place, was a silent enemy – sly, cunning and clever – waiting for us to make a mistake. They were there somewhere. I could feel them.

Chang waved his hand to call me closer and he whispered in my ear. "The soldiers patrol along the top of this hill. There is a path that will take us to the top but walk very slow and be careful of branches on the ground because the sound may alert them to our presence. One crack of a branch or a twig can be heard a long way off. Stay close and try to follow my exact footsteps."

He smiled and tapped me on the back, the camaraderie between us growing with every step as the danger intensified, but although we were in this together, at the same time our fates were our own.

Each step was slow and careful as we started the steep climb to the top and the wind suddenly picked up and started to whistle through the trees. The sky became darker by the second and it was even more difficult to see where we were going since we were now in dense forest. I wasn't familiar with this land or its weather patterns but it was obvious a storm was moving in very quickly. So quickly, in fact, it took me completely off guard. Slowly but surely we stumbled step by step until we reached a ledge a few metres from the top. Chang stopped and crouched down and I joined him at his side as we sat and listened. Then the rain started. A light drizzle at first but then a huge flash of lightning struck the other side of the hill, followed a few moments later by a crack of thunder. This seemed a blessing as the sound of the storm would cover our tracks but Chang had a different view.

"We need to move fast," he whispered. "If we don't get down the other side quickly it will be a treacherous walk. It is very steep and the rains make it impossible."

Chang quickly pulled himself over the ledge and on to the top. He looked around and then waved his hand for me to follow. The ground was already becoming wet as the rainfall intensified and I slipped a little trying to get over the ledge. I realised in that moment how lucky we were – if we had been just five minutes later we would have never made it up the hill for it would have been saturated and slippery and beyond climbing. Maybe the dragon was on our side after all.

I joined Chang on the path and we crouched down, listening out for any signs of life, but it was impossible to hear as the wind whistled in our ears and the rain came down heavily.

"Let's go," Chang said, quietly. "We need to get across to the other side before we can get down the hill."

Chang stood up and started to run across the level ground and I followed behind, making sure we stayed close together. It was a fifty metre dash, another adrenaline-crazed, life or death run through the darkness and when we reached the other side once again we hit the deck. We waited and we listened but there was no sign of anyone. The rain became heavier and the lightning flashes closer and more frequent, but it seemed we had made it. All we had to do now was get to the bottom of the hill and we would be in Tibet.

Feeling a sense of elation and achievement I was full of admiration for Chang's commitment to a cause that both of us were completely unaware of, but just as I thought we had made it and reached the safe zone, the angry dragon was about to come out of its cave.

10

INTO TIBET

As we cowered down behind a bush the rain slashed against our faces. Heavy, hard drops that began to hurt as the storm reached a crescendo. The lightning had crossed over the hill and was now behind us and with the rain following behind it was only a matter of time before the brief storm would pass. But it was already too late – the path ahead would be sodden, slippery and treacherous. In the distance the sky was once again cloudless and a lonely light stood out in between two peaks.

"That's where we have to go," Chang whispered, and he nodded towards the light.

"Jesus! That's got to be at least twenty miles from here. We've already walked about five miles and my legs are giving up on me."

Chang glanced towards me and turned to look around. He scratched his head and turned back slowly to face me.

"It's thirty miles," he whispered.

"Oh, you've got to be joking? My legs are dead already and you have to tell me that. I'll never make it. You should have lied."

"I *was* lying," he said. "It's actually forty miles!"

My mouth dropped and I turned to see a twinkle in Chang's eyes and a smile over his face. We both laughed quietly and I patted him on the back a couple of times.

"Actually I don't have any idea about miles, but it is forty kilometres."

"That's about twenty-five miles," I whispered.

"We have to get down to the bottom of this hill. There is a path down there that will lead us to the road to Potala. We have to cross to the other side of the road before sunrise as it is safer there. Once we get there we can rest. We must go now. We do not have much time. Be careful down this hill, it will be very slippery."

Chang stood up, grabbed my arm and pulled me alongside him. Taking one step forward, suddenly I heard shouting behind me to my left. It sounded so close. Chang pulled me forward and I nearly fell as his grasp sent me off balance. "Run!" he shouted.

The adrenaline kicked in once again but this time the danger was real and terrifying. In this area the shouting could only be coming from Chinese soldiers and that meant one thing – we had to stay ahead of them or we were dead.

Running behind Chang, thankfully the embankment soon dipped sharply away from the flat plateau and we were abruptly heading down the other side, but it was almost impossible to see in the dense trees. I kept up by watching a slight glimmer reflecting off the back of Chang's coat and followed his every step, whilst the shouting became louder and more voices joined the chorus. Sensing people behind me, the 'flight' reactions kicked in, time appeared to slow down and we almost seemed to be floating down the hill.

Branches slashed my face and bushes tugged my legs and arms but my panic was such that I didn't feel a thing. Then I started to slip and slide and it became more difficult to stay upright and the mud became more like ice as the rain made water channels down the slopes.

All of a sudden there was a loud 'crack' to my right and bark exploded from a tree next to me and hit me in the head as we ran past. It was a bizarre thing that startled me but then a 'whoosh' went right past my ear and I realised – they were shooting at us!

I ran faster, catching up with Chang and hoping he would move a bit quicker, but I didn't slow up and just moved around him, fear overtaking any sense of loyalty. A few more metres and then there was a 'ping' over to my left – another bullet, this time slightly off course.

The voices seemed to get quieter and it seemed we were outrunning the soldiers but that certainly wasn't going to slow us up as yet another 'whoosh' followed by the gunfire went past. It is such a surreal thing – a bullet travels faster than sound so it will hit you before you hear it – the bullets were flying past us before the gunfire echoed through the trees.

We kept running, not daring to turn around, and I was just about to shout to Chang when he called out, "Keep going, we are nearly there!"

Thankfully, he was right behind me. Hearing another gunshot, I slipped in the mud, falling over and sliding down the embankment. My legs crashed against a tree and spun me round. Chang also fell as my body rotated in a circle, the vision of him passing me as if I was on a roundabout, until once again I faced the bottom of the hill. I stopped only when I hit another tree and Chang rolled past me. Quickly picking myself up out of the torrent, covered in soaking mud, I stumbled down the few feet towards him and grabbed him by the scruff of his coat, trying to drag him to his feet so that we could continue running. He felt heavy and I fell again as his weight pulled me earthward. It must have been all that mud weighing him down.

Jumping up fast and sliding in the mud as I could hardly keep a grip on the sodden ground, once again I grabbed Chang by the arm and tried to pull him away from the gunfire. Falling down again, this time I hit my head on the floor which left me stunned and dazed.

Now facing up the hill and looking straight into Chang's eyes, they stared back at me, motionless and rolled upwards as if trying to give me one last telepathic message. Time seemed to stand still as I lay there staring into his face. Blood ran down the mud and over my hands as I still had a grip on his arm that was stretched out towards me. In the dim light I could see his chest was ripped open. He had been hit in the back, straight through the heart and the bullet had exited out the front. For a moment all was deathly silence and everything around me seemed to move into a different time frame. I had no idea how long it was – it must have been a couple of seconds – but it seemed like years as I stared into Chang's eyes. They stared back and pierced my soul but there was nothing there. No messages, no words, just a look of fear that was frozen into history like an oil painting hanging on the wall of a stately home. A person that time had forgotten but a face that would forever call out for help into eternity.

Suddenly voices could be heard coming down the hill. The Chinese soldiers were not giving up the chase and I jumped up and continued running. As much as it hurt to leave Chang there was no choice and I remembered his words – if we got into trouble we were on our own and not to wait for the other. As he said, it was better for one of us to make it than neither of us, and now there was an even more imperative duty.

So, I ran. I ran faster than ever before.

After just a few metres the ground finally levelled out. The trees became sparse and there was a pathway extending into some fields and along the tree line. Stopping at the bottom and hiding behind a tree to make sure there was no one around, I knew I had only seconds to make a decision but in reality there was no choice – if I stayed here my fate would be the same as Chang's. If I bolted for the pathway the better grip of the track would give me an advantage in the rain and the soldiers behind could be outpaced. But I couldn't outpace a bullet and all that could be done was to leave my fate in the hands of the gods, for the dragon had turned against me.

Running so fast and nearly falling several times, my legs seemingly moved faster than my body could keep up. I was petrified. I was alone. I had no idea where I was or where I was going.

There were no more choices except to run into the abyss, the dim light of my destination now seeming like a star, light years away. I ran for several miles on pure adrenaline, staying as close to the trees as possible until my legs buckled underneath me and once again I fell face down in the mud.

Laying there, my heart wanting to burst through my chest, I felt panic take hold when those lifeless eyes appeared in my mind once again. Scrambling toward the trees, unable to stand, my legs shaking in shock I managed to hide behind a bush. Trying to control my breathing as anyone in the near vicinity would easily hear me, I sat and listened. There was no sound except marmots and crickets. Looking back towards the steep hill it now seemed like a mound, I had run so far.

"Oh Shit. Oh Chang. Oh my God!" I whispered to myself as I tried to control my emotions, but I could not. With tears streaming down my face and nearly hyperventilating I looked up at the stars. All I could hear were his last words – *keep going, we are nearly there* – and all I could see were his lifeless eyes looking at me. It felt terrible. I felt something I had never felt before. It was without doubt the most horrendous moment of my life.

It seemed like my fear and instinct for self-preservation had caused his death, but if I had stayed behind him it would have been me lying in the mud and not him. Now that Chang was gone it made me even more determined to get to the destination and not to do a disservice to his good name, but the road still had to be crossed before I could rest. Certainly self-pity, sadness and crying were going to get me nowhere. With adrenaline still pumping through my veins, I picked myself up and slowly edged towards the pathway.

I decided that the best option was to ditch my backpack. It was becoming a hindrance and slowing me up and this was a desperate survival situation. There weren't too many things in there and nothing that weighed too much, except for water. And besides, the combat trousers had ample pockets to carry everything. I quickly took out all the necessary items – the diary, passport, money and bank card, and definitely my survival knife. I wouldn't hesitate to use the knife for the wrong purposes if that eventuality manifested, and ending up like Chang was not an option. Despite my spiritual beliefs and opinions it appeared I would have to kill if that situation arose, but even with my fitness and strength I didn't fancy my chances in hand-to-hand combat with a fully trained soldier, even though I was a foot taller and twenty kilograms heavier than most of them. My best chance of survival was to stay as far away from them as possible. All kinds of scenarios were swiftly going through my mind. It is amazing what the mind can do when faced with a survival situation. I thought about hiding when the soldiers were close and then jumping out behind one of them, plunging my small but deadly knife into his neck, placing my hand over his mouth to silence him once and for all, but was I even capable of such an atrocity? My belief system didn't allow me even to kill a fly, so what would happen if I was faced with my own death? Could I kill another human being to save my own life?

It's funny how, no matter what beliefs you think you hold dear, no matter what kind of a person you think you are, when you are facing certain death all that becomes irrelevant and your animal survival instinct becomes so strong you never even realised you had it. You suddenly see yourself in a different light, the layers of civilised behaviour are stripped away and you are left with the bare animal – the spiritual elements of our being become lost somewhere as if they never existed.

Filling my pockets with all the necessities, within a few paces it was clear this was not such a good idea – walking along with my pockets full was even more of a hindrance. I turned back and retrieved the backpack.

By now running was nearly impossible. There was no strength left in me so I hoped the road wasn't too far away, but twenty-five miles is a long way by anyone's standards. And where was the road in relation to the hill and Potala village? Was it the halfway point, or was it closer to the hill or the village?

Every animal that moved in the woods left me panic stricken, cracks of dead branches echoing through the night, my ears honed to the clear night air. The rain had stopped and the storm had passed long before but my soggy, muddy clothes were impeding my movements. Stumbling clumsily, my legs were so jelly-like they kept hitting each other, nearly sending me into the mud on several occasions. I felt like I was the only person on a foreign, desolate planet, and I was terrified. I tried to fill my mind with past memories...

11

A STROKE OF LUCK

"Hey, the gate opens!" I called to Jason and Neil. The gate opened fully and was stopped at a ninety degree angle only by a wooden block in front of six feet high stinging nettles. It was normally locked shut with a strong padlock.

"Let's take it in turns to stand on the gate, starting at the bottom, and then we'll stand one bar higher each time, and the other two push the gate against the post." There was no argument. Anything that had an inkling of danger and adventure was gratefully received without question. We were adventurous thirteen-year-old boys and anything to stop the boredom of teenage life was a brief high we all accepted.

Neil went first. Neil was short and stocky with thick, powerful legs, blonde hair, blue eyes and a bad case of eczema. On this particular hot summer's day he was the only one wearing shorts...

Jason and I pushed the gate hard with Neil holding on to the top of the six bars with his hands, his feet on the bottom bar and his body leaning into the gate to keep his balance. The gate thudded against the post and Neil held firm. He jumped off and the gate was returned to its starting position.

My turn. I found it easy to hold on to the gate as it once again crashed against the wooden block.

Last, but not least, Jason. Jason was the same height as me, a bit gangly in his early days, dark-haired, green-eyed, a wicked sense of humour and one of those infectious laughs that I can still hear echoing through my memories even today.

Jason had no problem keeping hold of the gate as the block did the job it was intended to do. The stakes were raised as it was the turn of the second bar, the excitement and laughing increased as the time drew closer when someone would fall.

Another round completed and up to the third bar. The third bar was slightly lower than half way and we all started to struggle, but we held firm.

Now, boys tend to have a natural instinct about angles and weights, along with mind-maps, and these are some of the traits have enabled our species to be so successful. It was obvious now that the fourth bar was above half way that the gate would be top-heavy and any chance of staying on it would be determined by the amount of force exerted on the gate when it hit an obstacle.

As Neil found his most comfortable position all it took was a look from Jason and we simply nodded at each other. We grabbed hold of the gate either side of Neil and ran as fast as we could, putting in all the effort we could muster. Just a couple of feet from the wooden block Jason and I let go and now the fruits of our brief labour could be enjoyed. The gate crashed against the wooden block and for Neil, well, there was no hope whatsoever. He somersaulted through the air, his body twisting and his arms and legs sprawled outwards like a new born deer. I am sure I counted three somersaults but my mind may have enjoyed the incident far too much and over the years may have added a few pirouettes to an already hilarious and magnificent display of gymnastics.

He landed facing us in a sitting position, the giant stinging nettles now bending down over his tiny, helpless body. As he sat there in shock Jason and I were laughing so much we had to hold on to each other just to stay standing. Tears streamed down our faces and Neil didn't dare move, the nettles were angry at being disturbed, plunging their stingers into him with each breath. Poor Neil was a piteous sight – a short thirteen-year-old sat in the middle of giant stinging nettles that completely encased him.

Eventually he stretched out his arm towards us and said in a pathetic and pleading voice, "Give me a hand, Jay."

That only brought even more laughter and Jason and I crashed to the floor in hysterics. When we finally dragged Neil out, he was in so much pain. He had a red blotch that almost covered his entire upper left leg and the right fared not much better. The combination of severe eczema and wearing shorts left him in a sorry state. Once we had checked he was genuinely okay and didn't require an ambulance, despite the horrendous pain he was now suffering, we laughed even more. As cruel as it seems, it was one of those hilarious moments that I can never forget. It's funny how the distress of your friends can bring so much amusement.

A smile ran across my face and for a moment I was in a warm and safe place. It was a welcome, albeit brief moment of peace in a world of hell but the images melted away as the first early light appeared on the horizon.

Concerned that my thoughts had created a lack of focus and concentration I stopped for a second or two and scanned the surroundings for any danger, and panic once again set in as the realisation hit home that I had to be across the main road and into the safe zone before daylight.

I clung to the tree line as slowly the mountain hills turned to flatter, arable land and my camouflage and cover was eroded as open spaces replaced potential hideouts. The tall trees changed colour as daylight slowly edged its way into the valley and unfamiliar birds started a dawn chorus. A distinct change in temperature was noticeable, as first it became very cold and then suddenly it started to warm rapidly. Mist slowly rose from the ground as the early morning sun started to burn the dew. The air was fresh and cold and I was breathing like a dragon.

I was close to the point of complete exhaustion and beginning to think that it may be safer to hide in the trees until the following evening when perhaps I could get some energy back and start again. But just as plans of defeat were manifesting in my mind there was a sudden noise to my left. It was a distinct mechanical sound that pierced the peaceful tranquillity of the valley. It sounded like a truck of some kind, rather than a car or something smaller, the unmistakable diesel engine chugging through the landscape.

"The road," I said to myself in relief and then it dawned on me that no chances were to be taken.

I had almost made it just in time but now there was a new danger to deal with. What was this truck? Was it a local farmer? Was it full of Chinese soldiers? Contemplating my options I realised that it was unlikely that any farmers around here would have mechanical devices. This was Tibet – a land of nomads who still lived a way of life thousands of years old. No wonder it was so peaceful and quiet. And no wonder, also, that the sound of the truck could be heard from a long way.

Noticing a small area of bushes about fifty yards to the right and running towards them, I realised I still had plenty of adrenaline when I needed it. I clambered through the bushes into the middle of a small mound, which seemed out of place in the field, but was safe enough while the vehicle passed.

Lying down, time seemed to slow and the wait was excruciating. Suddenly the vehicle stopped about a hundred yards away and shouting could be heard echoing through the landscape.

Nothing could be seen through the thick tree line but there was no doubt that these were Chinese soldiers, barking orders like a pack of wild wolves, and it was clear what they were looking for. Lying down and hiding myself well, for the second time in one night I prayed for a miracle. Through a gap in the bushes three soldiers were standing on the grassy path where I had just been, not fifty yards away from me. My heart started beating fast and lying back down again I hoped there were no footprints in the morning dew which would lead to my location and probably my demise, but by some miracle of nature the mist that was rising from the ground was creating a blanket, covering my tracks. Seeing the soldiers from the hips up they looked like long-lost ghosts on a forgotten battlefield.

They spoke for a moment and then all went silent. In those moments the stress was unbearable as there was no indication of where they were. They could have been right next to me and I shut my eyes and waited for one of them to drag me out, but there was nothing but an eerie silence. Peering through a gap in the bushes they were still there standing and looking around, listening for anything that might tell them where I was. After a few more seconds they said a few words to each other and walked back through the trees towards the road. The truck fired up again and slowly but surely the noise disappeared up the road. Lying back down and letting out the biggest sigh of relief I realised that I had once again outwitted them, but surely it would only be a matter of time before they found me and my luck wouldn't hold for ever. I had to reach safety or sooner or later my location would be pinpointed.

Sprawled out and feeling myself drifting, there would be no safety until I reached the other side of the road, but at least now with the sun rising fast nirvana was seconds away. The path was almost like the crossing point between heaven and hell and right now I was in the grip of the devil's jaw. Forcing my rigid body out of the bushes and back onto the path I clambered through the trees and the road came into view – a dusty single track with a few rocks randomly strewn here and there.

Hiding behind a tree, I checked both directions and then darted for the other side and dived into a ditch, receiving a mouthful of dust as a Tibetan gift. By now I must have looked a sorry state but there was no time to be concerned with my appearance as the next group of trees lay beyond another field. It was crucial to get there while the mist was still around to cover my location because as soon as it lifted the sun would be high and I would be at the mercy of the open ground.

A safe distance from the road and towards the trees there were some bushes behind a mound. With its protected view of the road, when I reached them I simply collapsed in a heap. In that moment, and just in the nick of time, there was no energy left in me. It seemed a slightly better option because the trees were not as dense as they first appeared and there were gaps amongst them. Instead I crawled into the middle of the bushes and fell asleep within moments.

12

HISTORY REPEATING

As the train stopped I jumped onto the tracks and I knew this was my only chance of escape. Through the undercarriage I saw the legs of a German soldier who was walking towards the field behind. All was deathly silence. Where was everybody – my parents, my brother? I looked up and saw a sign at the end of the line – 'Auschwitz.'

Running towards the back of the train and clambering between the couplings of two carriages, on the other side there was a terrifying sight. I froze as the smell of burning flesh hit me and the remains of dozens of mangled bodies came into view. There was not much to see except a ribcage sticking in the air and a skull, half melted with an eyeball looking straight at me. The rest was a black, charred mess with smoke slowly rising into the air and the stench was horrendous. The humidity made my mouth dry up and I felt sick. Jumping over the coupling there appeared a Chinese boy of about the same age as me.

"What are you doing here?" I asked.

"You are the one who is not supposed to be here," he replied.

For a moment we stared at each other and then he ran towards me and pushed me over. As I fell, something shiny caught my eye. It was a gun lying on the ground. I picked it up and without hesitation I pointed it at his forehead and fired, and as the gunshot rang out…

I jumped up and, breathing heavily with sweat pouring down my face, for a moment in the confusion I wasn't sure which was worse, the dream or my present situation. It's strange how in those few seconds between the dream world and the waking world sometimes we aren't sure which one is real. Only a moment passed and as consciousness returned it became obvious my current predicament was far more preferable.

For a brief time I thought about the horrors of Nazi rule and how millions of people suffered horrifically during those six years. How did history allow such things to occur? It never really made sense to me. Then I saw my grandfather's face. Wilhelm Jozef Cichorowski was a sixteen-year-old Polish boy when war broke out. An orphan living with a group of nuns, one day he was taken in a truck by German soldiers and driven to one of the castles that German officers had seized to use as their headquarters. Only his skill as a gardener kept my grandfather alive. He was forced to work and for nearly six years he suffered near-starvation but one German officer, impressed with his gardening abilities, looked on him favourably and sneaked him extra portions. My grandfather hid the food under hay in the barn and shared it with his comrades. Eventually, like most working prisoners, he was forced to fight for the Germans as the 'one thousand year Reich' came tumbling down and their resources and men dwindled. Old men and boys were the last line of defence for the despicable Nazi regime.

On the battlefield my grandfather and his friends were fighting and killing their own people as well as allied soldiers. During one of these battles, my grandfather turned to say something to his best friend and in that moment his friend's head exploded. It was a trauma my grandfather carried with him for the rest of his life and from which he never recovered.

My grandfather and two of his colleagues could bear no more and took the risky decision to make a run for it. They hid in the cellar of a house as the Allied soldiers swept across Western Germany. One day they heard tanks and soldiers outside and, emaciated and weakened to the brink of death, they decided to surrender, not knowing if the soldiers outside were German or allies. Thankfully it was an American battalion.

Eventually my grandfather was sent to England to be 'repatriated'. He met my grandmother, who had been in the Land Army, at a dance one evening and the rest, as they say, is history. However, he never recovered from the horrors of the war. My childhood memories of my grandfather are of a man who rarely spoke, either sitting in front of the TV smoking rolling tobacco, or in the garden tending his vegetable patch. I don't recall ever having a real conversation with him. He was aloof, distant and traumatised, but he was kind and gentle.

It's funny how history plays out sometimes. If the Second World War had never happened then my grandfather would never have arrived in England and I would never have been born. Most people alive in Europe and other places are probably alive because of the effects and displacement of people caused by the war. It's a very strange paradox, isn't it? Most people alive today, at least in Europe, exist *because* of the war.

What I had been through in the last twelve hours was a drop in the ocean compared to my grandfather's experiences. As this thought crossed my mind Chang's lifeless face once again reappeared in my head. It was clear what the dream was about – I was feeling terribly guilty about his death. Of course, those images will stay with me forever but I had to let go of any sense of wrongdoing. After all, it wasn't me who fired the fateful shot. And what a strange situation I now found myself in. The dream was all about Chang and yet it made me think of my grandfather, and here I was in many ways reliving the nightmare he suffered – my 'friend' killed in front of my eyes and on the run from the enemy in a foreign land. Can experience sometimes be a genetic programme that gets handed down through generations, like physical illnesses often do? Or was it just a coincidence? What was happening to me could never be compared to the experiences of those who lived through the war years but the similarity of my current predicament didn't go unnoticed.

Once on my feet and vaguely mobile I headed in the direction of the previous night's distant light, making sure the road was roughly parallel, as surely this led to Potala. The terrain was strange – rice fields, then grass, then areas of trees surrounded by distant shielding mountains and yet all the time at a high altitude. It was far from the familiar English summer countryside with its continuous fields of wheat and the odd pasture of bright yellow rape. There were tracks through the fields heading in different directions but it was hours before anyone appeared and I stuck to the edges of the fields so as not to trample on any crops, bring attention to myself or annoy any of the locals.

When any people did appear I panicked and felt like diving for cover but it was just paranoia – most people just passed me with confused looks on their faces as if I'd been dropped off in the wrong place, which was basically true. The locals were somewhat bemused by my presence, looking at me as if they knew that I'd crossed the border illegally and made it through. It seemed they didn't wish to help, talk, or get involved in any way and my conclusion was that if they were seen talking with me it would put them in danger. Because of this, I made a point of avoiding them as much as they did me.

My hunger had returned but I had no food left. With Chang by my side we would have arrived at our destination by now but I only had a rough idea of the direction of the village and asking any locals for guidance clearly wasn't advisable. If Chinese soldiers had stopped and questioned them, they may have told them I had asked for directions to Potala.

The sun started to drop in the sky, the colours changed as evening approached and my legs once again started to buckle. I was tired and hungry and now there was no water left either and I had seen no natural springs to drink from, although there was water in the rice-fields. Struggling on with a dry mouth and an empty stomach, I realised how stupid it was not to have bought a new bottle of purification tablets. Charles had given me limitless funds and the sense of security that this produced meant this kind of desperate situation had never crossed my mind once. How bloody stupid of me! How is it that money blinds us to the reality around us? With all my previous travelling wisdom, how was it possible for me to think so naively? But was I to blame? After all, I was under several illusions about what was going to happen because of the lack of information given prior to my arrival. I had certainly fallen for the illusion that I was being looked after all the way and there was no hint that I would end up in this mess.

As the sun disappeared, the sound of night creatures filled the air. A new fear filled my soul and this time it was total loneliness and alienation. Many times a similar situation had happened during my life but this time was like being on the surface of Mars with no human contact whatsoever. There were humans, of course, but now they looked like Martians – strange looking aliens with slanted eyes who said nothing and walked on without paying any attention to me. The more I thought about this, the more I believed it; at one point I really did think I was walking on the surface of Mars. I couldn't understand why it was so green, for surely Mars is a red colour. Between the delusions it was apparent to me that my mind was breaking down in preparation for death – it was nesting for a comfortable end. I collapsed in a ditch and blacked out.

13

BREAKDOWN

Finding myself digging human remains out of the ground, I pulled at the mud furiously and found the bones, one by one. Some were broken and all of them were separated from each other. First an arm bone, followed by a finger bone, and then a piece of jaw bone with a few teeth.

Concerned that someone would find them after I'd buried them here previously, it seemed the chosen location was not a good one, so I had to rebury them somewhere else. I felt people were close but I did not know who they were.

Songs from my childhood were ringing around my head, tunes that hadn't been heard for more than two decades and which I hated so much. Where were they coming from?

A creature of some kind crawled across my cheek, over my temple and into my hair, but I cared little. The delusions of being on Mars had diminished and I was back in Tibet. My conscious mind had rallied, forcing the subconscious back into its rightful place, the instinct to survive breaking through once again. I wasn't worrying about anything, I felt so peaceful that I could have died in that ditch and been quite happy about it. Lying face down with my head turned to one side, staring up into a blue sky with the clouds passing in groups of two or three, I thought they seemed like giant sheep dancing across the heavens.

How long had it been since Chang's death – a day, two, or three? The days seemed to blend into one large blur of faded reality, but this wasn't reality at all. My mind was definitely living in a dream world where fantasy and reality mixed together and created fleeting glimpses of a wonderful existence. Was it heaven, perhaps? Believing that would have been much easier if it wasn't for the pain that filled my body. Staying in the ditch was far more comfortable, but every time I moved I was reminded of reality as if someone was pricking me with a needle, making me aware of my surroundings and in the process keeping me fully conscious. Not being able to hold the comfort long enough to want to stay any longer, I made the decision to move on.

The first attempt was pathetic, even by my standards. Pushing my hands against the ground and lifting my upper body into the press-up position I fell straight back down again nose first. A mixture of mud and water covered my lips and an earthy taste hit the back of my mouth. Breathing out a despondent sigh, bubbles of brown rippled towards my cheeks and I turned my head to one side. Looking outwards I could see nothing but blades of grass and from my vantage point they seemed as tall as skyscrapers, reaching up into the sky.

"Get a hold of yourself," I thought and with a bit more effort I was up and in the sitting position. I scanned the horizon for any signs of life, but there was no one in the local vicinity and certainly the road was far enough away for there to be no real danger. Then the headache came; a little pulse at first but quickly followed by a regular pounding above the right eye socket, making me feel sick. It was that which made me realise this was a desperate situation. Five minutes before, I had been happy to die in the mud but now an urgency to get to my destination took hold of me and the seriousness of it all swung my mind in that direction. It was time to take stock of the situation.

Saturday 15 or Sunday 16 May, 2010

One dead, one half dead, no food, no water, a military force on the hunt for the remaining escapee, lost in a foreign land, no knowledge of the local language.

That covered just about everything. It's a good job it did because I was incapable of writing. I managed to focus on the page with one eye closed and my writing looked like that of a three-year-old child.

"Well, you've been in worse situations than this," I said out loud.

"Really, when?" a voice came back. Where did that come from? I looked around but there was no one there. Is that what happens when the mind starts to prepare for death; some other aspect of yourself comes forth and starts a conversation with you, keeping you in some kind of comfort during your final hours?

"What about that time I went wandering in the desert alone in Peru and I accidentally stood on that rock and tore my ligaments and couldn't walk at all? I had my backpack on with an extra eighteen kilograms bearing down on my ankle, it swelled up to twice the size during the evening and after pitching the tent I couldn't put any weight on it. I was miles from anyone. You see, that was worse than this." I held my hand out and waited for an answer.

"Then what happened when you woke up the next morning?" the voice asked.

For a moment I couldn't remember but then the memories came flooding back. The following morning the swelling had gone completely, there was no pain whatsoever and I could walk as normal. It was a miracle if ever there was one – the last time I had a similar injury it was six weeks before I was back to normal and a week before any weight could be put on the ankle.

"How did that happen?" I asked.

"I healed you so you could live and the vultures wouldn't peck your eyes out."

"How did you do that?"

"I can do anything."

"Yeah, sure you can! Bring me a plate of pasta right now," I demanded.

There was no response.

"I knew it," I said.

Standing up and reaching down to pick up my backpack a smile crossed my face, for this was the very same backpack that had travelled around South America with me, the very same backpack that had witnessed so many events and the same backpack that had been my saviour on many occasions. I realised how important this red and black thing was; it had become a part of me and I wouldn't go travelling without it. The day it broke and became useless I would stop travelling. I don't think I could buy another one, it wouldn't be the same. It was *this* backpack that had been with me through thick and thin, and it wasn't just South America – Denmark, Russia, India – no matter where I travelled, even if it was in the UK, this backpack accompanied me. It was *this* backpack that was my companion, not the voice in my head. I didn't need the voice in my head giving me stories about the past for it couldn't be trusted enough. But I could trust my backpack. I was sure it was the North American Indians who believed that you owned only what you could carry.

"Come on baby, let's go," I said, and with a swing of the arm I pulled my backpack over my shoulder.

The first necessary thing was to find a fruit tree or some other form of food. Water was also a priority. I felt dreadful but something had happened in the last few minutes that I couldn't explain. Something had given me a new lease of life. However, it didn't last long. I walked about half a mile, which was quite a feat under the circumstances, because I hadn't drunk anything for at least a day and I had used up all my natural energy supplies – but the worst thing was the headache. It's amazing how crippling a simple thing like that can be. It can stop you from even moving and unfortunately that's where I found myself in those moments – crippled. The headache became so bad that waves of sickness brought me to a halt and I couldn't go on any more. Even if an apple tree had been within reach, I wouldn't have made it. Noticing an innocent looking bush in front of a group of trees near the edge of the field, I found the most comfortable position to lie down, used my spare jumper as a pillow, and hugged the best friend I'd ever had.

This was it, I guessed – the end – but it wasn't so bad. I'd lived an interesting life and I wouldn't have changed a thing. I'd travelled to many places and seen wonders many can only dream of. I was happy with what I'd achieved and learned. And surely that was the whole point of it all.

Now it appeared it had come to an end. I wasn't bothered about it. I would know the whos and whys after my passing so no questions needed answering. It was a shame I hadn't completed the task, whatever it was, but life is such that the chance of making it through any situation is exactly that – chance. Having lived through so many life-threatening situations in the past, so many times my *luck* held firm and I made it out alive. It was just unfortunate that this time my luck had run out. Or was it destiny? Not even the promise of a fortune could get me out from behind that bush. I cared little for monetary reward; it had no meaning to me like it would to someone like Chang. Life isn't about money, it is about experience; it is about the inspiration we can instil in others; it is about helping people around us no matter how insignificant our actions may seem.

Now it was time to rest. It was time to let go of everything. It was time to sleep. So I did exactly that. Closing my eyes and watching as my life flashed before me, from my childhood right up until now, I saw everything.

"What a wonderful life," I mumbled, and then slipped into a comfortable coma.

14

LASYA AND YESHE

Waking on a hard bed with a blanket over me, my head was pounding with intense pain. Candle flames glimmered against the wooden walls and the sweet smell of incense hung in the air. For a brief moment I was certain I'd been captured by the Chinese, but the aura of the room felt too calm and relaxing. Certainly this wasn't death – the pain gave that away. Noticing movement to my right, I realised that someone was walking towards me. Their gait was elegant and light.

A woman sat beside me and wiped my forehead with a wet cloth. There was a large lump but I didn't recall hitting my head. I turned towards the woman and looked into her deep brown eyes – she seemed like an angel caring for my battered soul. She had long, black straight hair that fell down over her shoulders in two braids, and beautiful, soft, light brown skin. Her nose was thin and straight and she had high, defined cheekbones, a rounded face and soft, thin but pouting lips. She seemed to be around twenty-five years old. She was so beautiful – perhaps I *was* actually dead – maybe this was the place people talk about where the soul recuperates. She lifted my head slowly and offered a cup of water to my mouth. Her touch was so gentle and warm that it made me shiver. I drank, then she rested my head gently back on the pillow. Her beauty was so striking all I could do was lie still and gaze at her. She did not meet my eyes but she smiled as if a little uncomfortable with my stare.

Realising I was in safe hands the tears flowed as relief struck me in an immense wave of emotion. It was an outburst of feelings that had been held inside since Chang's death and the presence of a gentle, caring woman was the catalyst it needed. It was totally embarrassing – never before had I lost control of my emotions in such a way, but somehow this woman made it happen. It was purely a realisation that I was still alive.

This was also the first time there had been any intimate contact with a woman since my separation. In a strange way it felt that this outpouring of emotions was a kind of apology. Not an apology for any wrongdoing, but an apology for the relationship not working. It was like being in her arms again with a chance to say goodbye and move on, something that had not actually happened. It had been left so open, like a deep cut that hadn't been stitched up. The last thing I wanted was an infection in that wound but it hurt nonetheless.

Even if we feel no wrongdoing in a broken relationship there are always two factors that must happen before we move on. One is to say goodbye to that person and the other is to apologise. It takes two to make a relationship so it must take two to mess one up. When there is neither an apology nor a letting go, then bitterness fills the soul and can eat at us for the rest of our lives. We must make peace with ourselves so our soul can be free and so we can move on in our lives. So many people end up bitter and full of hatred after a relationship break-up but it is of their own doing.

This, however, was all ambiguous. All the anger and hatred that had manifested seemed to be washing down my face in these moments and was replaced with a sense of sorrow, but the sorrow seemed to be for me, not her. Being next to this beautiful woman made me realise how repressed I had been during my relationship and how trapped I was, for there had been no female contact for many a moon. There was some anger inside but somehow I was forgiving myself. It was a bizarre situation. What was I really crying for and what was my anger really about? Was I angry with her for her behaviour or was I angry with myself for my inability to see clearly and act accordingly?

The angelic face beside me looked confused and then an expression of deep empathy looked back at me. A tear appeared at the corner of her eye and she didn't move or react or say anything. She just sat there with total patience – my guardian angel. Exhausted, I slept.

I awoke to beams of sunlight shining through gaps in the wooden slats of the walls and dust particles moved whimsically through the incense filled air. Despite feeling better, when I tried to sit up pain wracked my body and my injuries had manifested in large bruises and scratches from the treacherous journey from China.

My guardian angel once again came and sat next to me. She gave me more water and then left the room, daylight bursting in as she opened the door, as if the gates of heaven had opened. Fear still filled my soul but oddly I felt safe – I supposed I was in shock after the events of the last few days. With everything starting to sink in, I was finding it difficult to keep my emotions inside.

My angel soon returned, followed by a short, stocky Tibetan monk. He sat down next to me and the woman stood behind him. "How are you feeling, my friend?" he asked.

"Terrible!" I replied in a croaky voice, my head pounding as I turned.

"Don't worry, you are safe now. We have been expecting you, Stephen. We are glad you are here. Where is Chang? Did you get separated?"

I looked at him and into his eyes and there was no need to say anything. He leaned back slightly and sighed.

"It is written," he said, looking upwards towards the ceiling as if expecting the gods to give him a sign. He said something to my guardian angel and she left the room again.

"My name is Yeshe. The one who has been tending to you is called Lasya. You have been through a bad time so you must rest for now. You will need your strength back."

"How did I get here?"

"Our friends found you two nights ago. You were in a bad way. We knew something was wrong when you did not arrive at the village on time. Chang is never late. They thought you were dead but luckily you were just unconscious. They brought you here as a safeguard because Chinese soldiers have been scouring the village and the surrounding area, asking questions."

Chang is never late. What did he mean by that? Chang said he had never done this before. He said he only got people to the border and then turned around and went back. Chang lied to me, but why?

"How far from the village did they find me?"

"About three kilometres, I would say."

Just three kilometres! I was so close to reaching the village. It must have been fate that I hadn't actually made it there. If I'd entered the village and there were Chinese soldiers around I would have easily been caught, for I would never have had the strength to fight or run. How strange fate can be at times.

"I was found two nights ago?"

"Yes. You have been sleeping for a day and a half but Lasya has nursed you well. You have many injuries but you will be fine in a day or two. You must have been through a bad time but do not worry to explain, I do not want you to fill your conscious mind with memories of this. Try to look forward now. What is done is done. Lasya will take good care of you."

"She already has. She is an angel. Is she married?" I asked, cheekily.

Yeshe smiled back at me. "Ah, I have heard of your famous Albion humour! No, she is not married. Maybe I can arrange a wedding for the morning, yes?"

I tried to laugh but pain hit my chest and I coughed instead.

"Go easy, my friend. You must rest. You are very important for us. We have been waiting many years for this time but do not bother yourself with this now for all will be explained to you soon. I will return your angel to you now. We will meet again when you are well enough to walk."

Yeshe held my hand for a moment and stared into my eyes. He smiled at me and then left the room.

You are very important for us. What did that mean? It sounded so surreal, but then this situation was equally surreal. Lasya came back and sat next to me and I gazed at her. I had never considered Tibetan women to be attractive but Lasya was extraordinary – an absolute beauty with an aura to match and her dark oriental eyes disguised her thoughts well, creating a deeper mystique. There was something very unusual about her, almost as if she wasn't Tibetan at all. She easily equalled my ex-partner in outward beauty but inside there was no comparison. While I didn't know her at all the aura she gave off was one I had never encountered before. There was no jealousy or possessiveness in Lasya. She was perfect in so many ways – a spiritually balanced soul.

It was a little bizarre, with zero conversation between us and the strange atmosphere that this created, but at the same time there was a calming and peaceful aura that was inexplicable, something in the air that stopped the awkwardness and ensured that stupid one-line comments didn't manifest. I could be an expert at those in uncomfortable situations, even if they were in a foreign language for the receiver.

I managed to eat in the evening – momos – balls of dough filled with meat, with two bowls of rice and an apple. I had not eaten for nearly two days but even so, by the time I was ready for sleep I felt that my strength had returned. Despite the pain from my injuries, I was practically back to full health and considering I'd been close to death this recovery was another miracle.

"I suppose you are responsible for this?" I asked the inner voice. There was no response. In fact I've never heard the voice again.

Lasya sat with me and ate a single momo during dinner but after this she left the room. She always seemed to know when to leave and was extremely courteous and polite at all times, allowing me the space and privacy one would require in an alien land with strange people everywhere. Despite

Lasya's amazing beauty and kindness I was still a little self-conscious at times and it was during these moments that she courteously left the room.

After sleeping comfortably and peacefully, the following day I managed to get up and walk around the room. It was amazing how undisturbed my sleep was, for even at home my nights were never so serene and calm. Was it the aura of the room and the scent of incense? Was it the area in which we were located? Was it Lasya who created such an ambience? I couldn't understand it, for recent events had been traumatic and at the very least I should be suffering sleepless nights accompanied by nightmares.

My body still ached badly but it was better to get my body moving than let it rest. As I stepped outside the sun shone too brightly, but in a shaded area by the door the overhanging roof gave my eyes time to recover.

The strange scene that greeted me was reminiscent of a medieval European village. Five small huts were set in a circular pattern surrounding what appeared to be a well in the middle, doubling as a religious shrine. A stone Buddha sat near the edge of the well and a picture of the Dalai Lama rested against the wall, with a garland of flowers hanging around both. Incense sticks were everywhere, some alight and some not. The huts were small and circular except for the one I'd been sleeping in, which was square. Made from slats of wood, the huts were raised about a foot from the floor and the roofs were thatched with long, dried grass. Only the square hut had a roof made from the same slats as the walls, which hung outwards and created a shelter, allowing a little respite from the blazing sun. The grass was worn down to bare earth in places and it created a circular pattern around the shrine with little paths that led to the huts and two main exits to the north and south. From above it would have made an interesting sight.

The area was a little strange. We were at quite an altitude and running south was a pathway that headed down the hill into the distant plains, and another path led northwards up towards the mountains. Around the entire site the grass was worn away revealing the brown earth below, so it was apparent that this place was frequented daily by a lot of people, or perhaps there had been hundreds here at a gathering very recently.

I sat down on the step by the door as Yeshe came walking towards me.

"Good morning, Steve. How are you today?"

"I am feeling much better, thank you. What is this place?"

"This is a stop off point for people going up or down the hill. The nearest village is a few hours down the valley and the next stop is equally far upwards. People can rest here, pray and relax, and anyone can stay as long as they want. You see that monk over there?" Yeshe pointed to an elderly man standing by the edge of the hill looking far into the distance. "He stopped here about five months ago and he hasn't left yet. Maybe he has found his nirvana."

Yeshe cast a curious glance towards me. I felt that life would be very boring here if one stayed more than a few days, but then the peace was something unusual and if anyone wanted to escape the modern world then this would be a great place to find inner tranquillity. The old man was motionless and staring out into space. Maybe he was contemplating his life's deeds in his final days. Was he regretting lost opportunities in his early youth? Had he let love slip through his grasp fifty years ago, the pain of which made him turn to a monastic life? Or was he just happy that he had fulfilled his life's ambitions and was now waiting for the soul of the Buddha himself to take him to the other side? It was probably none of those, but the image of that old man looking out into the distance is one that has stayed with me. If I were an artist I could paint a thousand renditions of that one image.

It was a serene location but perhaps not a good place to spend the end of one's life, for it would be freezing in winter up here on this windswept hill. A question has been in my mind ever since that day – before he stopped, was the old man going up or down the hill? Was he climbing high into the mountains to reach his heaven, or was he going back down to the village to continue his everyday duties? It seemed to me that he was stuck in no man's land and surely he needed to make a decision, one way or the other.

Yeshe was using a small wooden stick to clean his teeth. There was something about his calm nature that produced a powerful energy around him and yet he was so serene that if you weren't looking at him, you wouldn't even know he was there.

"So, this place is like a motorway service station?" I asked.

"Dear me, you people have a way with words in your modern world, don't you! Talk about ruining the vibration! But yes, I suppose it could be considered such a place. There is everything here. We are always stocked with food, water, fresh clothing and beds to sleep in. We don't have money here, so it's all with the added bonus that you don't have to pay. People bring things with them and leave them here for others to use. For example, you could bring a bag full of apples with you and in exchange you get a hot meal and a bed for the night. We are completely self-sufficient so you don't have to bring anything and are not expected to. That old monk is too frail to carry anything so he brought nothing with him and he's been here a long time, but that's fine – there are no rules."

It was an amazing way of life. So relaxed and peaceful it was hard to describe. There was no aggression or arguing and no one told anyone else what to do. There were no rules and no expectations and yet you could take what you wanted and were expected to give nothing. Equally you could bring items with you, drop them off and move on without staying or asking for anything in return. It was a system that functioned perfectly.

"I assume that's a well in the middle?"

"Indeed it is, and it is the best water you will ever drink. It runs straight off the northern mountains and is filtered through these hills. It's the perfect place. Have you noticed the land here is completely flat whereas everything else is hilly? Only this small piece of land is flat and then there is a well right in the middle. It's a bit of a coincidence. No one knows who discovered it, but there are those that say the Buddha himself created this place."

"What do you think?"

"I think monks built this place when they discovered the water but then I am a very conventional person!" Yeshe laughed. "Anyway, the Buddha never came to Tibet. He lived his life in India. Buddhism is an Indian export, but not the Buddha himself."

If there was any mystery about this place, Yeshe dispelled it instantly. In some ways, one expects a Buddhist monk to encourage dreams and fantasy but the more I learned about these people, the more pragmatic and normal they appeared. I understood then that Buddhism is a way of life, not a religion. It is the way they think which sets them apart, not any particular rituals, superstitions or beliefs. It seems they just live a more spiritual way of life and in my opinion this means that Buddhism, closely followed by Hinduism, is the highest religion on the planet, spiritually speaking. Have you ever heard of Buddhists fighting a war like the Christians and Muslims have been doing for what seems like eternity?

"When do you think that old man will leave?"

"I think he's already gone," Yeshe replied.

"What do you mean?"

"Can't you see? He's motionless. I think he's dead already!" Once again Yeshe burst into laughter. I really was starting to love Yeshe's humour but all it really did was show how stupid and meaningless my questions were. What did it matter when the old man would leave? Why would anyone care to worry about it? These are the cultural differences of thought processes.

Nobody cared about anything here. It was a life of peace, nothing more and nothing less. In the Western world everything is black and white – that old monk should be coming or going – but here everything was grey and, like Indian culture, there is always a middle road.

Talking of cultural differences…

"Where will he be buried if he dies up here?" I asked.

"Buried? We don't bury our dead. We take the body to the top of a hill, or up a mountain and while the ceremonies are occurring the body is chopped up using an axe. We leave the pieces out for the vultures and wolves to feed on. This returns the body to nature and is a wholly organic process. We return later to gather the bones and sometimes these are used in ceremonies. It all depends on the area of Tibet in which you live. There are many different customs in Buddhism and Tibet, there are no strict rules."

I wasn't sure if Yeshe was telling me the truth or making another stab at humour, but he informed me he wasn't lying about this. When I thought more about it, it made so much sense according to Buddhist belief. There is no fire to pollute the atmosphere. There is no burial to disturb the earth – in Tibet even cutting a flower is a kind of sin, for you are interfering with nature. All that happens is that everything is returned to nature and the animals get a meal too. And that is how it should be – the cycle of life. It has always been like this in nature. Our Western way of caring for our dead seems like a selfish ritual for the living, not a natural end for the dead. Not chopping a body into pieces and feeding it to birds is a reflection of our own emotional sorrow and not any consideration for the dead person.

"I wouldn't like to be the person swinging the axe," I said, as I thought about being consumed by feathery creatures.

"Well, family members don't actually carry this out, so it's not too bad, and when it's a part of your culture it is normal. In some communities if a woman dies it is the responsibility of the son-in-law to do the chopping."

"I couldn't imagine doing that."

"It's okay, some people don't like their mother-in-laws – they probably enjoy it!" Yeshe started laughing again, tapping me on the back. I would have laughed myself if Chang had not been slain so cruelly a few days earlier.

"How are your injuries, my friend?" Yeshe asked.

"I feel much better, thank you. A bit stiff and achy but I can't complain. After all, I am still alive."

Yeshe understood my implication. "Yes, you have suffered a terrible loss but one must not focus on the past. One must focus on the now. That was another time. This is a new time, a new future. And trust me – you have more important things to be looking forward to."

"Like what?" I asked, unconvinced.

"Like the future." Yeshe opened his arms and raised them up slowly like a false American preacher. "Just look at this glorious planet," he said in a stupid voice, "isn't it wonderful?" Once again he started chuckling.

I laughed along with him. Yeshe was such a loveable person, the grandfather everyone wished to have. He was intelligent and had a way of making me see things clearly but most of all he was warm and hearty and never took life too seriously.

"You can stay here and rest until you are ready and then we will move on."

"Move on where?"

"Why, onwards and upwards of course!" he said, pointing to the hill behind us, the path snaking away into the distance and disappearing into a blue sky.

"That is your stairway to heaven, my friend," he said, looking towards the Himalayas in the south. The huge mountains stretched up into the sky and disappeared into the clouds.

"I hope it's not as cold as up *there*," I said, nodding towards the beasts of the world.

"Nowhere is as cold as there," he replied with a serious tone. It was clear he had first-hand experience of those snowy peaks. "Make sure you rest. I will come and see you soon."

Yeshe walked off towards one of the huts. The old man continued staring out into the past. Looking at the same space I tried to find the answers he was looking for but there was nothing except the plateau below and the sky above. Shaking my head, I joined the Buddha and the Dalai Lama for a fresh cup of pure mountain water.

Despite the tranquil surroundings, it occurred to me again how isolated I was and a sense of desperation started to well up inside me. Every time I was alone, within a few minutes this emotion overwhelmed me. I didn't understand why. Was it the loss of Chang? Was it being alone in a foreign land? Was it an intuition of danger? Or was there something else – a feeling, perhaps, that was created by the energy of this place? Before I could try and figure out what was going on, Lasya crept up on me and was suddenly standing to my right, looking at me with her mysterious brown eyes. Noticing her intense gaze, I had a peculiar feeling that her arrival at the exact moment I started feeling strange was no coincidence. There was no question of her being responsible for it, but rather she was always around to counteract any negative emotions, as if these feelings created danger around me. At least that is what my intuition was saying and that intuition, I noticed, was increasing each day. What was creating these emotions I wasn't sure but the more this adventure continued, the more the words in that folder conveyed a deeper meaning. They spoke of Shambhala – a place of total peace – but this windswept hill and these wooden shacks were far removed from the idea of a lost paradise.

There was something going on here that was mystifying, to the point that there was a sense that this journey was not a physical one, but spiritual. The problem with this interpretation was twofold – firstly, Chang had died just a few days earlier and my emotions were raw and secondly, I was in the mountains of Tibet surrounded by spiritual monks. So, were these emotions an interpretation of what was happening or were they simply an internal perception that was false based on my surroundings and recent events?

As I stared at Lasya for a moment a voice called out from behind. It was Yeshe. "It's time to eat lunch, Steve, go back inside."

"Yeshe, what's the date today?"

"We don't care for dates, but in your calendar I'll have to check."

It was time to catch up with the diary, although I was sure I didn't need to write a detailed analysis. The last four or five days would never be forgotten. Even the delirium seemed clearer than things that had actually occurred and it was becoming clear that writing about these events was really quite unnecessary, for details would be remembered later. What was apparent, taking the folder's instructions into consideration, was that more attention must be paid to the *weird* things that happened.

Wednesday 19 May, 2010

Nearly died. Had no food or water and couldn't walk. I had the headache from hell and a very interesting conversation with myself. Or was it God? Some monks saved my life and took me to a village in the middle of nowhere, where I have been introduced to Lasya and Yeshe. Yeshe is a very funny man, always smiling and joking, free-minded, easy going and a pleasure to be with, but I know he's hiding something and he knows why I am here. Despite my frustration I must be patient, and pushing Yeshe for answers would almost seem like a crime of some kind. Lasya – wow! She is so beautiful it is hard to describe. She has an aura like an angelic creature sent from heaven, but there's something strange about her – she seems to feel my emotions, or something. Maybe it's just a coincidence. Time will tell. Not sure how long we have to stay here. It's boring, but at least I am safe... and alive.

Staring at the page, I felt there was nothing else to write about the last few days. I could, and should, have written pages and pages but the memories were etched indelibly into my mind. Although through trauma the present wasn't allowing any reminiscing over recent events, later the memories would be as clear as day, but it wasn't what had happened recently that was at the forefront of my mind. Instead there was something else. There was something happening that was making me think differently, making me see things that I wouldn't normally perceive. It was clear both Lasya and Yeshe were trying hard to stop me from tuning in to whatever it was; whenever I gained a glimpse of something unusual, one or the other of them would appear and redirect my thoughts – Yeshe with his humour and Lasya with her penetrating eyes and unusual beauty.

We ate a light lunch, just a small amount of rice and bread with an apple to follow, but it was enough to dispel the hunger. Lasya sat on a little stool and was smiling for some reason. I was unsure of what was amusing her but she seemed so content I did nothing to spoil her enjoyment, sitting quietly on the bed opposite her and eating slowly without making any hand gestures. Lasya really was in a world of her own. The lack of conversation was frustrating and it certainly added to Lasya's mystery but I really did want to converse with her. I wanted to know about her childhood, the things she liked and the things she didn't. I wanted to know what her parents were like. I certainly wasn't going to ask Yeshe for fear of him making fun or embarrassing me beyond manageable levels, but my curiosity created fantastic ideas in my mind about her.

Lasya continued smiling and after lunch she almost skipped out the door, like a child going out for a game of hopscotch. Despite my thoughts about her she was a rather peculiar person, childlike and immature on one level and then appearing as if the weight of the whole world was on her shoulders. She was unpredictable and confusing but all the time a joy to be with.

After lying down on the bed for a while, as the heat of the day increased and made the cabin very hot it wasn't long before I was back out on the porch again, cooling off in the shade by the door. I was feeling much better and almost ready to move on, but before a decision could be made about when exactly I should leave, events took another turn and control was once again taken out of my hands.

I watched a young man come running into the village – he was clearly in a bit of a panic as he spoke to an old monk who was standing by one of the huts. The monk directed the young man towards the cabin in which Yeshe was sitting. Within seconds Yeshe came walking purposefully but calmly towards me. He didn't speak until he was right next to me.

"Steve, gather what little you have here, we need to move on. Chinese soldiers have been in the village asking questions. We need to leave in five minutes."

I was speechless and panic-stricken, far more than the young man who had come running in to the peaceful village. Suddenly everyone seemed to be walking around with a purpose. Lasya came strolling past me and went straight into the hut. Everyone was wandering here and there, into one hut, out of another. If I wasn't so scared I would have been laughing at this funny show but everyone clearly had some kind of task to do. This was undoubtedly a finely tuned and rehearsed scenario. Only Yeshe remained totally calm and I watched him walk slowly back to the hut he had been in. In those moments I never reacted. Despite what I was feeling inside there was an inability to move – and then I felt a kind of pull to my left. I glanced across to see the old man standing by the edge of the hill where he had always been, but he wasn't looking out into the distance – he was staring at me. For a moment I locked eyes with him and then he raised his stick upwards into the sky. I looked up to see what he was pointing at – the sun.

There was no time to think or wonder what he was trying to say, but there was a strong sense that my inability to move for those few moments was because of him. The old man turned back around and stared outwards again as if he had never moved. Slightly unnerved by what just happened, I felt unable to do anything useful. Lasya was making everything tidy and ensuring that when we left the hut would look like no one had been staying there, and I grabbed my now filthy pack and stood waiting by the door. Perhaps I should have helped Lasya but it was better not to interfere since she knew better what to do. Lasya double checked to make sure everything was in order and then she turned towards me. As we locked eyes for a moment and stared at each other, I focused intently and tried to look inside her. Despite the darkness of her eyes I could somehow see her pupils widening. For a moment the door to her soul opened but then it quickly closed again as she moved her head slightly sideways like an Indian, then she nodded her head up and down a couple of times and made a light squeaking sound, while her brown eyes seemed to grow beyond normal.

I had no idea what to make of it but Lasya seemed to know *something.* Whatever it was there was no time to think or worry about it. We had to leave. The Chinese soldiers, like a pack of blood hounds, were not giving up the hunt.

15

BIRD TALK

We met outside the hut and were joined by two other monks, Pemba and Nawang, both who appeared to be too young to be away from their mother's breast. What alarmed me was that Pemba was carrying a rifle over his shoulder. Why on earth would a pacifist Buddhist monk be carrying a rifle?

I was unnerved by this for it meant only one thing – a possible gunfight with the Chinese. How would it be possible for a small Tibetan monk to take on the Chinese military? Surely this was just asking for trouble? Perhaps the rifle was solely for repelling wolves – but I knew this wasn't true. The only conclusion was that Pemba, at least, was not a monk at all, but disguised as one.

"It should take a few hours to get to our next stop," Yeshe said. "We can make it a relaxed walk and take it easy."

As we headed north up the path, the trek was steep for the first hundred metres or so and then the ground levelled out slightly, but we were always climbing in altitude. After the initial hike I lagged back and then stopped. I wanted a moment to myself. Looking back at the tiny village I saw that the old man was still standing at the ledge, staring out across the landscape and from our new vantage point he looked tiny against the backdrop beyond.

We continued the sloping climb to higher altitude. Breathing became a little difficult and it became much hotter. I stayed at the back of the group, taking in the views and enjoying the sense of freedom that this environment produced; away from civilisation and pollution, the fresh air was a delight to breathe.

After a couple of hours we stopped for a break at a flat ledge. We ate some rice and bread and I drank at least a litre of water as the early afternoon sun was relentless and harsh. Yeshe spoke to Lasya in Tibetan and for the first time I heard her string an entire sentence together. Her voice was as sweet as her face. Yeshe laughed out loud and then turned to me.

"Steve, Lasya says she is not worthy of your marriage offer!" He had a big grin on his face.

Totally embarrassed, I wanted the ground to open up and swallow me – I certainly wished my earlier joke had never been mentioned in the first place! Sure my face was beetroot-coloured but I hoped it was already this shade from the high altitude sun.

Lasya stared out across the immense plains below, her innocent and pretty face complementing the beauty of the nature that surrounded us. Could I really marry this woman? What was it about her? She had quite an effect on me and there seemed to be no flaws in her. Or maybe it was just the mystery of her dark eyes, her quietness and the gentle care she had given to me back at the village? My God! I had to snap myself out of this delusion! It must have been some kind of strange, *reverse* 'Florence Nightingale effect' that had come over me. Back at the village I had awoken expecting a Chinese rifle in my face and instead this beautiful creature had been looking at me. It must have been this experience that was creating my ridiculous ideas about her, for in reality I had only known her for a day and a night.

Shaking my head rapidly and closing my eyes, trying to shake off these strange delusions, I knew it was totally unlike me to be thinking like this. Once again I had the conviction these thoughts weren't my own at all.

It was imperative to get Lasya out of my mind and focus on the reality of my situation. And back to reality I came as I remembered Chang and thought of the very real danger that I was in. And then, suddenly, as if the voice came from a discarnate spirit, I said something so ridiculous I could have died. "It is I who is not worthy of a woman so gentle and kind."

Yeshe burst out laughing and wobbled sideways, leaning over to stop his fall, holding his stomach and coughing at the same time. Embarrassed and looking out across to the mountains, I couldn't believe the words that sprung forth from my mouth. I don't even speak like that. What the hell was I doing? The words just seemed to flow without any thought as if I had no control whatsoever. Lasya looked down as Yeshe translated my words. I sneaked a glance at her but she didn't move and neither did she turn her gaze from the ground. She was certainly an expert at hiding her expressions and emotions. Yeshe continued to laugh.

"Oh dear!" he said, "I see love blossoming here!"

He was enjoying every moment of this but I was more shocked and embarrassed than anything else. He calmed down and, thankfully, changed the subject. "Aren't the views stunning, Steve?"

I looked out across the plains and to the distant peaks. "Yes, it is so beautiful it is hard to describe."

"No, Steve, I was talking about the scenery!" Yeshe fell sideways once again and this time he rolled around on the floor as his hysterical fit took hold. And this time I joined him. I couldn't stop laughing, but more at his childlike behaviour and English-style humour. Lasya sat motionless and watched Yeshe with interest, like a schoolchild shocked at her teacher's sudden turn in behaviour.

"Okay, okay!" he said, as he finally returned to his sitting position. "I will stop teasing you now."

Without doubt it was one of the most embarrassing moments of my life, but Yeshe's taunting and humour had made me laugh properly for the first time in a long while and that was something that was greatly needed.

The journey continued upwards as the track started to wind and the tree line thickened, creating a protective shield from the wind, which was gaining in strength the higher we climbed. The trees were tall and luscious with fresh, new leaves and the branches swayed gently like the arms of puppets dancing gracefully to nature's symphony.

Suddenly something caught my attention. A little bird was sitting on a branch in a small tree next to the path. We locked eyes and for some reason my mind filled with strange images, almost like a collective film of my entire journey since my arrival in Chengdu. It was bizarre, like a DVD on fast forward, and I suddenly realised what was wrong.

"Stop!" I shouted.

Everyone stopped at the same time and collectively looked over their right shoulder. It was another one of those moments that would have been amusing under different circumstances, but this wasn't one of those moments.

Yeshe calmly walked back towards me. Lasya stopped a short distance behind, while Pemba and Nawang stayed put.

"What is it, Steve?" Yeshe asked with a curious but concerned attitude.

"Are you trying to tell me you haven't noticed anything unusual?" I asked.

Yeshe looked around as if I was talking about some peculiar physical manifestation in the local vicinity. "What is unusual?"

"Well, I haven't had the time to think before but now things are becoming clear."

"What do you mean?"

"I don't know how many people cross into Tibet in an illegal manner – it must be hundreds, if not thousands – but it seems obvious to me that the Chinese don't spend too much time sending soldiers half way across the country to look for any particular individuals. So, why are they so interested in catching up with us?"

"You mean, why are they so interested in catching up with *you?*"

"Thank you for that, Yeshe. Just add a little more pressure on my shoulders."

I really didn't need to hear that, but it was obvious and Yeshe wasn't trying to hide the fact.

Lasya had tilted her head sideways behind Yeshe. Then her eyes widened as she noticed the very same bird on the tree next to us. She lifted her head back upright, stared at the bird and then she pointed her finger at it and said something in Tibetan.

"Great," I thought, "now she's talking with the wildlife."

Yeshe glanced at the ground on his right side, and without actually looking at her he said something to Lasya which made her retreat a little further behind, halfway between us and the other two.

I looked hard at Yeshe and waited for an answer.

"Steve, it is not unusual for Chinese soldiers to enter villages looking for certain people. They do it quite often. There's no need to be concerned."

That was not the answer I was looking for and neither was it the correct answer. While the chances could be one way or the other, it was obvious to me what they were doing in the village.

"You and I both know they are looking for us, Yeshe, but why are they putting so much effort into it? I could be anywhere by now. Why do they appear to be on our trail?"

Yeshe let out a sigh and decided to come clean. "I think maybe they know something."

"You think they may know something about what?"

"I think they may know why you are here."

"Well, since I don't know why I am here that seems a little difficult for me to believe."

At that moment an image of Charles came into my mind and suddenly I realised this was no backpacking adventure – this was something far more serious.

"Steve, in the next twenty-four hours you will understand why you are here and why the Chinese want to stop you from being here in the first place. Or at least why they *think* they want to stop you from being here, at a place that may not exist."

That was a riddle too far. While it was a relief to learn that I would soon discover why I was sent here in the first place, being left in the dark about the dangers right now was not a comfortable situation.

"Okay, but *how* do they know I am here in the first place?"

"Well, some things are meant to happen and some people have the ability to see that those things are going to happen – and sometimes those people may want to try to stop those things from happening. That is all I can and will tell you."

What the hell was he talking about? Yeshe was making about as much sense as a Chinese washing machine instruction manual. I looked beyond Yeshe's shoulder at Lasya's innocent face and decided my best option was to leave this conversation until another time. Here I was, climbing up a mountain in Tibet with half the Chinese military after my blood, accompanied by a man who talked in riddles and a woman who talked with birds. My life was in the hands of two very odd, but wonderful people. If anyone can inform me of a more surreal situation, I would love to hear it. I let out a deep sigh and nodded at Yeshe. He turned around and we continued on.

Unfortunately the humorous and jovial atmosphere which Yeshe had worked hard to maintain was now destroyed by my brief outburst. Feeling a little culpable I tried to forget what had just happened but there was no doubt that something strange was occurring around me. As I reviewed the events that had happened since my arrival, a strange pattern to things was noticeable. It wasn't even something that could be put into words, for words were inadequate. It was a feeling, coupled with something that I could see – strange images in my mind that formed a coherent pattern without there being any language capable of explaining them. It seemed a good example, in a strange way, that spirit truly is separate from mind – that communication in spirit form is far more complicated than that of language. Of course, there is the argument about whether this is *spirit* or the *subconscious,* but the feelings that accompanied the images gave me a strong sense that these things were external, not internal.

It wasn't as if these things were new to me. I had experienced this kind of thing all my life. It's just that now, for some reason, these feelings and intuitions were magnified beyond anything I'd experienced before, and this made the reality and the clarity far more reachable than any time in the past.

Was it Yeshe and Lasya causing this to happen? Was it the environment we were in? Perhaps the village well had magical properties? Maybe as we climbed higher the magnetic stress on the fault line was perceptible enough to create strange emotions? Was this something to do with why I was here in the first place? Was it a test from Charles that I was supposed to discover a secret energy?

None of these explanations seemed adequate. Attempting to rebalance myself, I lagged slightly behind the group but the happy atmosphere was gone as we all concentrated on the climb. I felt guilty, as if I had destroyed the buoyant atmosphere all on my own but, on the contrary, it was clear Yeshe's comedy was just a way of masking what was really going on. I wasn't sure if he was trying to help me forget what happened to Chang, or whether there was something more sinister that he was trying to cover up. To be honest, he seemed to have little or no concern regarding Chang and why would he? It seems Tibetans mourn their immediate family and then only briefly, but for others there is no such attachment. In essence Buddhism is about having no attachments to anything, be it material goods or people.

Despite my attempts to lag behind the group and gather my thoughts, Lasya stayed alongside me the whole journey. This became a somewhat comical situation when I stopped to re-tie my boot lace and Lasya stopped with me. I tried other variations on the theme to amuse myself – when I slowed down so did Lasya, when I stepped up the pace she followed as well – she seemed to understand these games, throwing a glance or two in my direction when I changed tack, letting me know she was aware of my childish behaviour. But then, hers was hardly of the highest maturity, was it?

16

INTENSIFICATION

The last stretch of the journey was tough going as the inclination increased sharply but after another hour of hard, slow uphill walking the pathway levelled out and we reached a plateau.

I was astounded as before us stood a magnificent temple adorned with a beautiful, brightly coloured façade of red and yellow and a sloping roof of brown tiles. Just two floors high, the temple seemed as if it was carved out of the steep hill from which it protruded, or equally as if the earth itself was giving birth to it. At the front, on the ground floor, was a large covered courtyard lined with long, low benches and square columns that held the roof above it. The front of the temple was open to the elements and at the back an entrance led into the temple itself which, from my initial view, was obscured by the bright sunlight reflecting off the roof. Monks walked slowly through the grounds and an air of peace and tranquillity struck me as we passed through the gateway. Yeshe was right – the pathway *was* a stairway to heaven, for this building was astonishing.

The aura of this splendid place was so serene it was like walking into a dream-like state of transcendence, the total peace disturbed only by the quiet conversations of the mingling monks. Was it the aura of the peace-loving Buddhists which created the atmosphere, or was it the temple itself? Maybe it was both.

"We have arrived safely," Yeshe said, smiling.

"No kidding!" I thought, breathing a sigh of relief.

"We can all rest now," he continued. "I will arrange for some refreshments for us all. Steve, please relax and feel free to wander the grounds. No one will disturb or question you. I will send for you when dinner is ready."

I wandered away from the temple but stayed within the perimeter wall, which was a simple mound of earth about three feet high that surrounded the entire area, rather like the boundary of a well-worn British hill fort. But this certainly wasn't any kind of strategic military defence – it was more a garden fence.

A small wooden bench looked out towards the distant mountains and I marvelled at the astonishing view across the valley below. I was breathless from the walk and the high altitude, but more so because of the view in front of me. No words could describe the quiescence of this place. I looked downwards several thousand metres and outwards to what seemed like infinity; it appeared that this was the place where the worthy conversed with the gods. Ironically, despite this place being as close to heaven as it could be, Buddhists have no belief in any god.

Naturally, Lasya settled right next to me in total silence. Under normal circumstances it would have been quite annoying having someone stuck to me like a conjoined twin, but Lasya gave such an air of peace it often seemed as if she wasn't there at all.

To the left, a distant hill covered in trees brought Chang back into my mind again and every time I paused briefly, he was there. Now though, the image of his lifeless eyes was replaced by his cheeky, smiling face. Was it the surroundings that was causing this sudden change, or was it Lasya? It felt like a strange, magical energy was running through me as if all my negative thoughts were being replaced by a positive, spiritual force of some kind.

Now there was no doubt that somehow Lasya was able to tune in to my emotions without looking at me and with this came a great sense of security and safety. She was the reason, I concluded, and it required her to be in close proximity to me. Perhaps it truly was fate that Chang was not here with us, as if his death was predetermined. As this thought crossed my mind I noticed Lasya's face was directed at the ground in front of me, but she was looking at me from the corner of her eye, that typical way that young women always look at men, but this wasn't a kind of *I wonder if he likes me* gaze; rather, it was as if she was reading my thoughts.

Was this really happening or was I thinking too much and joining all the dots together, making a pattern that wasn't really there? It did feel like Lasya could somehow tune in to my emotions, but could she read my thoughts as well? Maybe that was one step too far. The resulting chaos of these powerful emotions and feelings was confusing and blocking my own intuitions. The higher nature of this place was certainly above the normal background level that existed back home, and most other places for that matter, but if my intuition was correct, had Chang known he wouldn't make it? He did say he was going to retire after our venture. Was this some kind of subconscious knowledge he held without really understanding what it meant? Was his subconscious telling him this would be his last journey, but he interpreted it in a material sense?

Is that one of the lessons we must learn on our journey through life; to understand that intuition and spirit have no time for the material world and that we often confuse spiritual messages for egoistic and materialistic empowerment? As I suddenly felt warmth that seemed to come from Lasya, a comforting that was like no other, my thoughts went deeper into this idea, as if they weren't my own, almost as if I was picking up these things from Lasya herself. Maybe Lasya was there purely to comfort me in my grief. If that was true then this would mean that Chang's death really was all part of the design, his dead body a decoy for my escape. This theory disturbed me more than any other because it meant pre-determinism was involved. While I could agree with this to a point, is it possible that someone's death could be predetermined? Was it plausible, when an important spiritual venture was undertaken, that a human life was of little importance to the greater goal? And then I suddenly remembered what happened when I first met Yeshe. When he understood that Chang hadn't made it he looked up to the ceiling and said the words; "It is written." What did he mean? Did he understand that by the occurrence of Chang's death some kind of unchangeable process was underway? I sensed, however, that Yeshe seemed to be shocked that Chang hadn't made it. Only when he understood he wasn't with me did he then consider some kind of pre-written plan. Was there a prophecy of some kind that would only start to function when a messenger or traveller was killed on the route?

All of this was well and good but then it would imply that whatever we were doing was of great importance and that was something I was not at liberty to accept. I was an ordinary person with an ordinary life, so why would I be involved in some kind of prophetic adventure in which the gods themselves had already written the story? Why not someone else, someone more deserving? On the other hand what did the words 'someone more deserving' mean? Who *deserved* to go through what I had been through? Who *deserved* to witness someone slain in such an awful way?

Whatever questions were raised, there was a paradox available, something that counteracted any of the arguments so that nothing made any sense. It was all too confusing, so to save my mind from going around in circles I concluded that the energy of this place, whatever power it had, was the cause of these unusual thoughts.

Thankfully I had gained control of myself by the time Yeshe approached. He stood admiring the immense valley stretched out beneath us.

"I cannot believe how peaceful it is here," I commented. "Surprising, considering China is so overpopulated."

"That is true, Steve, but remember this is not China and it never will be, even if they continue to populate our land."

And then I was given the first glimpse of something that was a clue to my being here. A statement so astonishing that no one would believe it.

"Tibet has a uniqueness that China will never understand, and the Chinese people will never be connected with the higher vibrational frequency that exists here."

"What do you mean by that?"

"Tibet has a slightly higher vibration than most places on the planet, probably all of them. This is where some of the original Atlanteans settled after the fall."

I had to pause to make sure I had heard him correctly. Did he say 'Atlanteans', meaning people from 'Atlantis'? Was the story about Atlantis true? I had no reason to think Yeshe would fabricate anything. It was not in his nature to do so and something about the factual way he spoke made some of my experiences make sense.

"Is this why I have been feeling emotional and why it appears I am tuning in to strange patterns that have been occurring around me?"

Yeshe looked around the horizon. "No," he said with his back almost turned towards me, "that's because of something else, but we cannot go into this right now as dinner has been prepared for us. Tomorrow will be the day that all will be revealed to you as we will start our discussions. Now, come and eat and regain your energy."

Yeshe walked gently back towards the temple and as I stood up Lasya stood up at exactly the same moment, mirroring my movements to perfection. As I looked into her eyes, they sparkled back at me before she looked down at the ground. I was, however, more concerned with what Yeshe had said. Standing still for a moment and trying to understand his words, Lasya must have sensed my distraction because she walked away from me and stood waiting about ten feet from the bench. What did he mean there was 'another reason' for what I was experiencing? Why would there be a reason for my emotional state, beyond the obvious grief? Why was I tuning into unusual patterns and coincidences?

Lasya was staring at me and I honestly felt a kind of telepathic thought from her as our eyes locked together. "Don't worry," it said.

We both walked slowly back to the monastery and as we entered the building the temperature dropped instantly to a perfect level, as if some kind of air conditioning existed inside, but since the front of the building was open to the elements this was more than a little difficult to explain.

The walls were brightly coloured with the same burgundy and yellow that adorned the outside and the columns were painted gold with green, white, yellow and red patterns at their tops. Above us the wooden ceiling beams were painted a bright red and in the middle of them were brightly coloured and detailed designs of circles and swirls and strange paisley-like symbols. It was magnificently decorated and the colours were almost ambiguous – bright and yet dull – creating a perfect ambience for the eyes. Although the temple was in essence a religious centre it was, in my eyes, a palace fit for a king.

We were all seated at a long, low table on large cushions with our legs folded, although this was not too comfortable for me – my legs were still stiff and the strenuous uphill climb to the monastery hadn't helped matters. The hall was filled with the endless chatter of monks and the echo effect around the hall was incredible, the natural acoustics creating a beautiful sound. The meal consisted of momos, bread, soup and rice, accompanied by water.

"Is this water okay to drink?" I asked Yeshe.

"Oh yes, even better than from the well at the village," he replied.

He was right. In fact it was the best water I had ever drunk in my life, crisp and clean and fresh.

"I hope you are recovering well, Steve? The walk to the monastery should have given you a chance to loosen the muscles a bit."

"I feel much better, but my legs feel like dead weights right now."

"I am sure by tomorrow you will be walking as normal and the pain will be gone," he smiled back reassuringly.

"I hope so," I said, searching his gaze to try and discover his wisdom.

"Lasya will show you around the temple after dinner and she will also take you to the room which has been prepared for you. Lasya will be in the same room as you."

I was bemused by this. Yeshe had that familiar playful grin on his face. Lasya, who was sitting next to me, obliviously raised an eyebrow while sipping her soup. Once again she appeared to be on *Planet Lasya*, but she was always endearing when in her own world.

"Don't worry," he said, "the room is divided into two with a temporary partition for your privacy. Please remember that Lasya is your protector and will remain close to you at all times for your comfort."

Lasya was small and slim, five feet tall and must have weighed all of forty-five kilos. I didn't feel that I needed a protector and I certainly didn't consider her in that regard. How could this woman protect me? Suddenly imagining her breaking into martial arts combat at the first sign of trouble, defending me from a handful of strong, burly men, just like those silly films, I let out a laugh.

Yeshe looked at me smiling and then, as if he had read my thoughts, he said, "Only in a spiritual and emotional sense!" Then he leaned forward and whispered, "By the way, Steve, try and stay within your half of the room tonight, okay? You know, certain activities are forbidden here."

The soup bowl almost slipped from my hand and Yeshe laughed out loud, causing me even more embarrassment. So much for him not teasing me any longer, but by now I was getting used to Tibetan humour. Thankfully, he quickly changed the subject.

"I know there are many things that seem strange to you but from tomorrow you will come to understand what this all means. We will start to explain everything to you."

"What I don't understand is *why* I am here," I stated, hoping for at least a small insight to take to bed with me.

Yeshe paused for a moment, seemingly trying to find an answer that was as tactful as he could manage. Leaning in close he whispered into my ear. "Well, for a start this is not something we can discuss here. There are too many people around. What you may not realise is that besides us there is only one other person in this room who knows anything about this. We must be careful at all times. I can tell you that what we are dealing with is something far beyond some of the greatest secrets that have ever existed. You have been entrusted with something of the utmost importance and it is imperative you keep that in mind."

It was very hard to comprehend what he was saying. Just under two weeks ago I was back at home – and as this occurred to me, a part of me wanted to be sitting back in the café with my boring life, chatting with friends and pondering on a meaningless future. Instead, in the last week I had illegally crossed a border, witnessed a man shot dead in front of me, I was being tracked and hounded by the Chinese military which wanted so desperately to dispose of me by whatever means necessary, and I was spending most of my time with a five feet tall, forty-five kilogram bird whisperer who, apparently, was here to protect me. Now, was it me or had my life taken a turn for the totally surreal? I had to pinch myself even to believe this was all happening in the first place, so to accept Yeshe's words wasn't something I could easily stomach right now. The only hope was this would all be worth it in the end, that this was something far more important than Chang's life, or the life of any person. But what could be more important than a person's life, no matter how unimportant and insignificant they may seem in the grand scheme of things? After all, everyone is *someone's* son or daughter, but in many ways what disturbed me most was that someone was entrusting this situation to me. Someone was gambling on me getting the job done, getting in and back out of Tibet without being caught, and at all times keeping my mouth shut. That is a huge risk on anyone's part.

Sitting mostly in silence for the rest of dinner, pondering on the various situations and outcomes, for some reason all my fear had disappeared. A few hours earlier the thought of being caught by Chinese soldiers was something that filled my soul with dread. Now I felt calm and completely unfazed by the idea. It is said that soldiers can only function properly in battle when they comprehend they are already dead. Only when they have no fear of death can they get the job done, function as a soldier and kill other human beings. I would never compare myself to a soldier – I could never, and will never, have that kind of bravery – but was this the key to surviving this situation and getting out alive? Was this my own personal test to overcome my fear?

After dinner Lasya escorted me to our room which was down a corridor and towards the back of the monastery. It was almost silent except for the sound of a bird singing outside, the beautiful song carrying through the open window and filling the room with a calm that was reminiscent of an empty English village church on an early summer's evening. Thankfully the room was divided by a wall and not a temporary partition. It was basically two rooms with a doorway connecting them, but no door. As I expected, it was sparsely decorated with a low, wooden bed, a desk with a chair and a bowl which contained water and liquid incense. And, unsurprisingly, the wall was adorned with a picture of the Dalai Lama, with his unmistakeable glasses and his intellectual smile. The picture blended in with the walls nicely, the burgundy colour mixing well with the Dalai Lama's robes. The window was slightly higher than normal and for some reason it gave the impression this place had been here a long time. It was an unusual feature but I never bothered to find out why it was designed in such a way. I don't know why but Tibetan temple window positions weren't high on my priority of things to ask.

After a few minutes Lasya popped her head round the corner and gestured that we should take a walk around the monastery. By now it was early evening but the sun was still well above the horizon and the high-altitude heat was intense. We walked around to the side of the monastery and towards the back where the ground sloped upwards.

Lasya walked close to me, her gaze towards the ground, and now I realised that she always stayed on my left side, for some reason. Behind the monastery the slope steepened into a hill and we slowly traversed the incline until we reached the top. The view was worth the effort. Breathless from the climb but now almost suffocating with incredible views, I felt as if we could see the whole world from our vantage point. We sat and watched as below us the monks wandered around the grounds, the trees swayed in the wind and the birds fluttered amongst the branches. It was so peaceful and serene I felt we could sit there for the rest of our lives, knowing that we would never have to worry about anything ever again. This was the nirvana Yeshe spoke of.

Conversation seemed a futile activity but nonetheless I tried to speak as normally as possible. To be honest there wasn't much to talk about and when I did make a comment it was met with a slight nod of the head and a downward glance at the floor. It occurred to me that despite her beautiful and elegant demeanour, a romantic date with Lasya would be a difficult and perhaps uncomfortable evening. Going out to dinner at a restaurant she would probably spend the entire night staring at her plate. As I dreamed the scenario Lasya smiled. I was beginning to truly wonder about the possibility of her ability to read my thoughts, or was she simply reacting to my body language, smiling whenever I smiled? I assumed, in this world without modern technology, people were more in tune not only with their surroundings but with each other. It made me sad to think how much we have lost in our Western world in pursuit of comfort and technological advancement. What have we really gained at the expense of our senses?

Lasya put her hand on my arm and looked at up at me with sadness, her glowing brown eyes reflecting the sunlight and sparkling like distant stars on a clear night. It was in this moment that I saw deeper into her soul and felt a much stronger connection than before. There truly was something remarkable about this seemingly innocent woman but I couldn't quite understand what it was.

I was still unsure where these thoughts were coming from, but the experience was not entirely new. I had experienced this before during my travels – being away from civilisation for a considerable time and starting to feel something beyond, something tangible that is within reach but invisible, a feeling that there is an energy in the universe that is hidden from us and yet responsible for our very being.

Wanting and needing to entertain Lasya in some way I looked for a large blade of grass and picked it. Lasya let out a disapproving sound and I suddenly remembered that even picking a blade of grass was not something Buddhists do. They believe strongly in the non-interference of nature in any way, but it was too late for me to go back and it was hardly the crime of the century. Putting the blade of grass on the tip of one thumb and holding it in place with my forefinger, I stretched it downwards with my other hand without breaking it and then sandwiched the grass between both thumbs at the top and bottom. Then I blew through the gap. The blade of grass vibrated and made a loud, screeching sound that seemed to echo through the valley and many of the monks looked around as if a strange, new species of bird had arrived in Tibet. This was something we frequently did as children back home and it was nothing new but it amused Lasya so much that she giggled and wanted to try for herself.

It took many attempts and several pieces of grass until she finally managed to make a noise and each time a new blade was required Lasya suspiciously looked around to make sure no one was watching, like a Russian spy sitting on a park bench concerned about enemy agents. This was amusing, for pulling a blade of grass out of the ground seemed to be the limit of Lasya's naughtiness. It was a powerful statement and an indicator that I was in a completely different world, but I also saw that innocence and gentle tenderness was in some ways the only real beauty left in a country that was being swallowed up by the industrial might of China. This defenceless country, Tibet, was at the heart of a battle of old versus new – the old spiritual ways of peace and tranquillity against the might of industrialism, capitalism, war and destruction.

As I looked outwards across the beauty a tear appeared in the corner of my eye. "What have we done?" I thought – poisoning the seas with our waste chemicals and oil, disposed of so crudely, cutting down trees at such a rate there would soon be no forests left, fishing the oceans to the point where fish stocks are so low we are in danger of making them extinct. And then there is our warring nature – the planet has an obvious problem in that there are too many of us, but is a cull of our species humanely and spiritually acceptable?

My thoughts shocked me. From the innocent pastime of making noises with blades of grass I suddenly found myself thinking again of the dark side of human nature. Where was it coming from?

Quickly snapping out of my trance and looking at Lasya, I saw that she was staring at me in a strange way with her mouth half open. Returning a slightly false smile and standing up, allowing the breeze to flow across my face, I closed my eyes and raised my head to the heavens. I wasn't sure where all these thoughts originated but they certainly weren't something new; not inspired by Tibet itself. The anger of world injustice had been growing inside of me since I was a child. In a place like Tibet, however, a new clarity of that injustice had become apparent. Whatever was going on around me, things were certainly changing within – while an obvious revolution was going on outside, an equally powerful evolution was happening in my own soul and with all my questions, weird intuitions and observations, there was now no doubt that something truly bizarre was going on here in the mountains of Tibet.

As we came back to the monastery, the sun was setting fast and it was surprising how rapidly it descended towards the mountains, with the temperature dropping equally quickly. Yeshe was nowhere to be seen and Lasya and I retired to our room. I lay on the not-so-comfortable, but much needed bed and fell quickly into a relaxed state, my body fatigued and my mind floating in the Tibetan altitude. Despite the confused thoughts my mind seemed free of worry.

Unsure what was happening inside of me, suddenly I started thinking about things that I already knew, and yet now there was a new clarity to these thoughts as if Tibet was clearing the clutter of everyday life and helping me to see things more clearly – in our towns and cities the noise of cars, the unseen bombardment on our brains of electricity and mobile devices, the lights of civilisation, only succeed in blocking our true intuition. So I started to wonder – what have we really achieved whilst destroying the beautiful nature around us? Was having a mobile phone, for example, a worthwhile sacrifice at the expense of truly understanding the world around us? Was it true that only when we come alone to a place like Tibet can we really start to *feel* the world? Was it possible that only when our brain is free of the continuous, monotonous drone that dumbs us down to mere robots can we start to understand our true nature?

It saddened me to realise that so many in our Western world have lost their souls – lost the belief in spirituality – because they are not in tune with the world. It suddenly seemed clear to me that living in a world of technology – lights, TV, computers, mobile phones, cars, and materialism – only enforces the idea that there is no spirituality. The idea of reincarnation, or that the soul lives on after death, was a well-known and understood aspect of life only a few hundred years ago. Throughout history, spiritual leaders and ancient priests spent their lifetimes studying what happens when we die. There was no doubt in their minds that these things were a part of the greater cosmos – the cycle of eternal life. The accepted wisdom, after thousands of years of study by the best human minds, was that this life was but a brief interlude in a much greater cycle. Then, suddenly, technology appeared and for some reason all that knowledge was written off as superstition – the unreasonable reasoning of primitive minds.

Now it was clear how arrogant we had become to be so sure of this, whilst living in a world where our minds are bombarded with a continuous flow of energy that only succeeds in blocking our senses. We assume, only because these things cannot be measured scientifically, or because we don't *feel* them anymore, that they are nonsensical ideas. We have removed the idea of spirit in the modern world. It has been replaced with greed and selfishness and the idea that a growing nation can only be measured by the amount of things it can consume. In the process we destroy the earth, invade other nations to steal their resources, killing hundreds of thousands of innocent civilians in the process, and become nations of obese people while thousands around the world die each day of starvation. And what do we call it? *Progress* – this is the so-called progress of a developed world. I realised it is Western civilisation – *it is I* – that is sick with disease and illusions about the world.

I must have been thinking these things for hours, for it was late when I snapped out of this trance. I could no longer hear anyone talking and certainly everyone was asleep in the monastery. Glancing up at the Dalai Lama on the wall I felt a sadness that was deeply upsetting – I sensed how empty he must feel to see his spiritual home swallowed up by the same evil that devours our planet.

Wednesday 19 May, 2010, continued...

There is something extremely weird going on here. Everything has shifted in ways that I cannot explain. I feel like my mind is no longer my own, as if replaced by a new consciousness. Something is being hidden from me and at times I feel very uncomfortable around Yeshe and Lasya, like they're both penetrating my mind and reading everything that's inside. On the other hand, there's something magical and mysterious about this place and it has definitely altered my thinking. I'm suddenly seeing the world more clearly.

I awoke some time during the night. Having no idea what the time was I was surprised to find Lasya sitting on the chair by the desk. The strange dream that had broken my peace was still in my mind.

Yeshe, Lasya and I were jumping around on a child's bouncy castle but we hung in the air longer as if the gravity was like the Moon. We were giggling like children and the atmosphere was tranquil and serene, as if we had no care or responsibility in the world.

Lasya stared at me across the moonlit room and then, after a few moments, she left and returned to her bed. Why was she there? It was almost as if she was waiting for me to have the dream and wake up, as only then could she retire and get her own sleep. Or did she have a part in my having the dream in the first place? I was starting to ask some very strange questions and it seemed that subtle and minor coincidences were increasing in frequency. It wasn't just my brain working overtime. There really was something magical about this place, something tangible that could be grasped out of the air only for it to disappear when an answer seemed within reach. What was this magical energy that was flowing all around us?

17

PANIC STATIONS

The following morning I awoke to birdsong and the room was filled with sunlight which created an ambient burgundy colour. It suffused the room as if the walls were emanating a glorious heaven-like energy and the smell of incense once again tempted my senses into sharp focus. My aches and pains had miraculously disappeared, just as Yeshe had said they would, and I felt invigorated and fresh. Even the bruises had faded and were almost imperceptible and the mysterious lump on my head had also gone.

Lasya was already up and moving around in her part of the room. On hearing that I was awake, she peered round the doorway and gestured for me to follow her. Out in the main hall she pointed to a door where a small shower room was located, which seemed rather out of place in a temple of this magnitude. In my ignorant naivety I had assumed everyone simply washed from a bowl or a stream, or maybe even buckets of water were filled from an outdoor tap. This may have been true for most people – maybe the showers were for guests – but in reality I had no idea how things worked in this place.

The shower was freezing and if you ever need to wake yourself completely I recommend the same torturous activity. Torturous because you find yourself gasping for air as your body recoils in shock. Cold showers are the norm in hot countries but high altitude Tibet was hardly Mumbai first thing in the morning.

Feeling very fresh and clean, I returned to the room to hear Yeshe talking to Lasya. The conversation seemed tense but Yeshe's manner changed when he saw me. "Ah, good morning Steve, how are you feeling today?"

"Fine," I replied. "All the better for the shower, thank you. And strangely, all my injuries appear to be healed."

"Good. I am glad to hear it," was all Yeshe could say, ignoring my recognition of his prediction.

Glancing at both of them, a sudden feeling of worry swept over me. "Is everything okay?" I asked.

"Steve, Chinese soldiers have been seen back at the village. They were spotted in the early hours of this morning. They will probably head this way."

My heart started racing and for a moment I was back at the hill running with Chang. Yeshe quickly put his hand on my shoulder and calmed me down.

"Don't worry too much, Steve. We have runners placed at strategic intervals along the route. If the soldiers are heading this way, we will have a head start."

"That's if they don't use a helicopter or something. And where do we hide? There is nowhere to run from here."

Yeshe looked at me blankly for a moment, as if the concept of flight hadn't reached Tibet.

"I would be surprised if they put that much effort into it. The Chinese use a lot of manpower since they have so much at their disposal, but they are often reluctant to use machines unless it is completely necessary. Since Tibet has no military of any kind they have no reason to deploy such hardware here."

"But if they wanted to find us so badly then surely a helicopter would locate us very quickly?"

"Then maybe they don't want to find us as much as you think they do."

My mouth opened halfway and then closed again, but my real worry wasn't whether or not they would use a helicopter – my real worry was *why* they were so concerned with finding us.

"Yeshe, what's going on here?"

"Steve, you will know everything soon. Please be patient. Today you will understand everything."

I was far from happy with this prolonged waiting game but I did have absolute trust and faith in Yeshe. And if Lasya was unconcerned about what was going on around her, then this alone helped me to relax. I had begun to look to her when I needed to know how to react to situations, and despite her small and elegant stature she was the rock on which I came to lean.

"We will know in good time if the Chinese are coming this way, so don't worry."

"Then why are you so concerned? And why do you need runners along the route?"

"The Chinese haven't been up here for years, that's why I am concerned. And the rest of it you'll find out if they do head this way. Since they have already reached the village I am sure this will be their next stop, so we need to execute the next phase of the procedure."

"What on earth are you talking about? And if the Chinese haven't been up here for years, then they obviously *do* want to find us as much as I think."

Yeshe looked at me with a concerned but stern look. "The scrolls speak of a chain of events occurring in sequence and since that chain of events is occurring exactly in that sequence, I can confidently say you are right in the middle of this mess. You appear to be the catalyst for these events."

"Thanks very much. That's just what I wanted to hear! Why don't you blame me for the ills of the world as well?"

Yeshe knew my sarcasm only meant that the content of his statements hadn't yet hit home. He sat on the edge of the bed and let out a deep sigh.

"Steve, it seems obvious that knowledge about your visit has been intercepted at some point. The Chinese have been looking for a place that exists here – and they know it exists – which is one of the reasons they have taken so much land from Tibet and claimed it as their own. There is a battle going on with some very powerful people in this world – a battle to acquire a certain kind of power and information. You could say we are involved in this battle, so I am thinking that your visit is known to them. From their perspective, all they have to do is follow us and they would find their Shambhala."

I stared at Yeshe in amazement, stunned by his words. A part of me wanted to scream out loud and that same part of me wanted to run outside and not stop until I reached another country. And yet something struck a chord with me. During those three days in the hotel I had read that strange passage in the folder that mentioned Shambhala. I learned about this magical place as a child – a fabled location of peace and beauty – but surely it was a myth, just a place that existed in the minds of ancient storytellers as an allegory or perhaps, at a stretch, a real place that existed long ago but was forgotten to history, handed down through countless generations as a yarn and embellished through the ages.

For some reason I sidestepped the obvious questions and asked a more stupid, but practical one.

"I thought the Chinese were taking land because they didn't like the Dalai Lama and the peaceful power the Buddhists hold?" I felt ignorant – my words seemed hollow and idiotic – but Yeshe answered me patiently.

"No, Steve. The real reason is that they want a buffer zone between themselves and India, Afghanistan and Pakistan. Both China and India are rising as the world's two great super-powers, and both are expanding exponentially in growth *and* population. Since Tibet has no military they are concerned that any conflicts could spill over into Tibet at some point, or that other countries could try to gain more land. Once over the Himalayas, access to China would be simple. India's military is far stronger than the world gives it credit for and like China they have large numbers of personnel at their disposal. India is not helping Tibet because of humanitarian reasons. Their reasoning is, like most things, political. However, Buddhism is widespread in India as well as in China, and housing the Dalai Lama in Northern India is an embarrassment to the Chinese. It certainly doesn't help their humanitarian reputation."

Yeshe's words were revealing, but his reasons were simple and obvious. He showed me how ignorant we are in the West about this situation and how our media continually shelters us from the truth but I was still a little confused. "But surely India and China would not dare to face each other in combat? It would be a never ending war?"

"That is definitely true. Both India and China contain more than a third of the world's population between them but political reasoning does not make sense to people like us. The Chinese government is so secretive that even their own people have no idea what is going on most of the time. A lot of their power is based on generating fear but also we must understand that we humans, as a species, are very territorial. In essence, we are like dogs when it comes to territory but this situation is exacerbated by the massive population increase in both China and India. China is not only creating a defence against India but it has also targeted the weakest country on earth, militarily speaking. Also, they claim to have documentary evidence that Tibet was originally a part of China and thus they can say that they are simply reclaiming their own land. Of course, this is not true. Tibet was never a part of China. Tibetans, although oriental in nature, are a different people and speak a different language."

Everything was starting to make sense – at least in the political sense – but it didn't help to explain our current situation and I certainly wasn't going to let Yeshe avoid the obvious.

"So what does this Shambhala place have to do with all of this?"

"To gain the knowledge and power of Shambhala would give the users of that power an advantage over their enemies."

"Are you trying to tell me that Shambhala *does* exist?"

"Well, not any more, no."

"Then what is all this about? Why do these people still believe it exists if it doesn't?"

A silence fell. Raising my arms in frustration and dropping them hard against my hips I headed for the door but before I could leave, Yeshe spoke again.

"Unfortunately, patience isn't one of your virtues, is it?"

"Are you kidding me?" I protested. "I mastered the art of patience travelling around third world countries. The problem here is that I am being hounded by a military force that will have no problems in killing me if they have the chance and yet I still don't know what they would kill me for. It's frustration, Yeshe, not a lack of patience. I don't mind dying but I want to know why first."

"Then trust me when I say that if you die you will know beforehand why you are dying. There seems to be a strange paradox occurring with your visit."

I turned to leave a second time, but Lasya was so close behind me I almost knocked her over. Clearly this conversation wasn't yet finished. Yeshe was staring up at the image of the Dalai Lama.

"What paradox is that, Yeshe?" I asked, although I was growing impatient with his riddles.

"No one, under *any* circumstances, is allowed to go to the place where you will be taken. In fact, the only circumstances in which you could see this place would be if the Chinese were trying to find us and your life was in danger. You have been sent here to see that place. This is why you are here. So don't you think it is ironic that the Chinese are trying to find us, because I would never show you this place if they weren't? Somehow the Chinese chasing after us and the fact that we are continually one step ahead is all a little strange. This is why I think a sequence of unavoidable events has been started."

I looked at Lasya. Her eyes were sympathetic and her gaze told me to hang on to my sanity for just a little longer. I scratched my head and then rubbed my eyes. "So, what you are saying is that the only reason you would show me Shambhala is if the Chinese were coming after us."

"No. The place you will be shown is not Shambhala. It is just a place."

"Okay, what you are saying is the only reason you would show me this place is if the Chinese were coming after us. As I was sent here to see this place, then somehow the Chinese being on our tail is all a part of the scenario. It is fate that they are coming after us, like some predetermined process has manifested, because if the Chinese were not after us I would have wasted my time coming here in the first place?"

Yeshe looked at me. "I don't think I could have put that better myself. I am happy you understand now."

"You think I understand? Ha!"

I looked at Lasya again. She was staring at me with puppy eyes.

"And what is this sequence of events?" I carried on, all the time looking at Lasya.

"Unfortunately that is something I will not be able to talk about."

"Then why mention it?"

"Knowing this is already written will help you to understand. Knowing the actual contents of the writing is an irrelevance and could put your life in danger."

At last, I saw a little bit of coherency in the story. Yeshe was only filling in gaps but it was enough for me to build a picture of what was going on here in Tibet, even if there was no sensible logic to it. I could see the connections in my mind but there was no way to understand them. This is what Yeshe meant about something 'written'. It wasn't that he was forbidden to tell me about the writing – he just couldn't find the words to explain it to me.

"Anyway, let's go and have breakfast and stop worrying about it for now. We will know far in advance if we need to be concerned."

He gave me that broad grin and it calmed me enough to put my faith in him again, and in Lasya.

Lasya went to the shower room and I followed Yeshe to the hall for breakfast, which was once again filled with the incessant chatter of monks, all dressed in the same robes. The laughter created a relaxed atmosphere, dispelling any concerns over the news that the Chinese were making great efforts to find us. I had naively thought they had given up and all was safe, but it seemed that underestimating the will of the Chinese was a mistake.

Lasya soon joined us, her wet hair shining and her smile tinged with concern as she looked at me. As usual the space next to me was empty and she sat down, grabbing her long locks of hair and dropping them over her left shoulder.

Yeshe and Lasya had a long whispered conversation during breakfast and it was frustrating not to know what they were saying to each other, especially since I was sandwiched between them, but I was sure they were discussing what to do next and they were obviously more concerned than they were letting on.

As I quietly ate, I became detached from my surroundings as an intuitive fear slowly swept over me. Something was amiss and a growing feeling of discontent and nervousness was starting to creep through my bones.

Whatever this written 'prophecy' was, and from what Yeshe had said it was indeed prophetic, the Chinese would soon be here in numbers.

After breakfast, Yeshe suggested I took a short walk in the grounds to get some air while he went to get some information. He advised me to relax a little so I returned to the bench to admire the views once again. For the first time since meeting Lasya I was on my own and it was quite a relief to be able to gather my thoughts without her sitting next to me. She must have been aware that I needed some time to myself or for sure she would have been stuck to my side as usual.

After sitting in total peace for about fifteen minutes, a blissful feeling of tranquillity gave me the illusion that I was completely alone up here. The air was fresh, the heat increased with every passing minute and the distant clouds casually and lazily passed between the mountain tops. The peaks lay mysteriously hidden as if the gods themselves were playing hide and seek. Were they hiding from each other, or were they hiding from me and laughing as they peeked occasionally through the gaps in the clouds? Did I just see one of these gods? Did I catch the giggle of the eternal cosmic joker, or was it just a part of the mountain that looked like a face, my mind playing tricks and trying to capitalise on the insanity that was surely lurking just below the surface of my own consciousness? Certainly if I thought about this situation too much then insanity wouldn't be too far behind. This was all too much for any human mind to grasp – prophecies, predetermined situations that I had no control over and whispers in the air that could be seen but not heard were all knocking on the door of my mind, but somehow I had to keep them locked out and concentrate on the here and now. Somehow, despite the confusion and ludicrousness of everything, I had to let this 'prophecy' play out and follow the path laid before me like an actor in a film.

Even with all these bizarre things going on around me, I was at ease and a feeling of peace was within my soul. This was contradictory since my normal senses were leaving me panic stricken. Somehow my soul was controlling my senses for a change. However, the serenity was suddenly shattered when voices behind me became animated and loud. Turning around, I saw several monks running in different directions and Lasya running towards me. She grabbed me by the arm. "Come," she said, as she tried to pull me up.

Struck by fear, my heart started racing as it was apparent something was wrong. We ran up to the temple entrance where Yeshe was standing with a concerned look on his face.

"They are coming up the path," he said. "They will be here soon. We must leave immediately. Lasya, make preparations for the tunnel entrance."

Lasya disappeared into the monastery and I turned back to Yeshe, surprised that Lasya understood his English commands. "Don't ask," he said, reading my face like an open book. He put his hand on my shoulder once again, making me calm down immediately, and then he spoke gently.

"The monks will tell the soldiers we left for the higher peaks in the early hours of this morning but we have a secret tunnel that will take us to safety, so please don't worry."

"Why don't they just tell them they haven't seen us?"

"If they say that, the Chinese will turn the temple inside out. If the Chinese think we *were* here, they will be satisfied no one is lying. If they are told we have not been seen, when they know roughly where we are, they will know for certain that we at least passed through here. Lying to them directly is never a good move. They'll probably leave a few soldiers to search the temple but the main group will keep moving."

Yeshe called over one of the elders and seemed to be giving him instructions. The elderly and frail man started shouting at the panic-stricken monks, who immediately stopped running about and went back to their normal mode of tranquil wandering. He turned back to Yeshe and they smiled at each other, as if amused by the unnecessary panic of their younger brethren. It was vitally important that everyone behaved normally when the soldiers arrived so as not to raise any suspicions, but for me it only showed the fear that the Chinese military instilled in these people.

"Steve, go and gather your things and make sure nothing is left behind. There should be no trace of our stay. Meet me back in the dinner hall in two minutes."

My backpack was already prepared so I threw it over my shoulder and began to check that the room was as I found it, but Lasya had already cleaned the place to perfection. Lasya was already in the dinner hall when I returned and Yeshe soon joined us with Pemba and Nawang.

"Okay, Steve, are you ready?" Yeshe asked.

"Yes," I said, although my heart was still pounding.

"Let's go," he said, and we headed into the darkness of the monastery.

Any fear I felt was not about my future – my fear was more the recurring emotion of my trek with Chang which was still fresh and bringing an automatic panic response at every thought of the Chinese. I, for one, had witnessed their callous and cruel treatment of anyone who dared challenge their authority. Soon, however, that fear would no longer be an issue because we were about slip down the rabbit hole and disappear into Alice's Wonderland.

18

THE TEMPLE WITHIN

In the far corner of the dinner hall the five of us went through a door that led into a much smaller hall, rectangular with a high ceiling and columns reminiscent of ancient Egyptian architecture.

There was something strange about this room and the symbols that adorned the walls appeared out of place. Carved into wooden panels, they seemed like a mix of Egyptian and Mayan hieroglyphs. On the ceiling was a strange, long, snake-like creature that stretched from one side of the ceiling to the other and pointed at the opposite wall, its tongue striking menacingly outwards. The room was dimly lit with just a few candles flickering in the darkness and it was devoid of the bright colours that appeared everywhere else in the temple.

At the other end were two small statues of the Buddha set about halfway up the wall in a small alcove, each about four feet apart. An elderly monk walked in through another door, carrying a small wooden box. He was so old and frail he looked like the living dead; he was very small and his body was just skin and bone and I wondered how he could even stand, let alone carry anything. As he limped slowly across the room I could see that the box he carried was very old and obviously well used. It was the size of a large musical box and I almost expected a dancing ballerina to pop up when the lid was opened, but instead Yeshe took out an unusual looking key. The key was obviously very old but it seemed in remarkable condition. Made of metal, it was shiny but there was something strange about it that produced an intuitive feeling that the key was most extraordinary. Leaning in for a closer look, I could see that the shaft was about five inches long and there was a crystal embedded in a circular handle. Looking at it horizontally from the end it looked like a cross.

Yeshe also reached for another, smaller key which hung on a chain around the old monk's neck. Astonishingly, he slid this into the wall between two blocks of stone. There was no key hole there, just the two blocks, but miraculously when he put this thin key between the blocks of stone, one of the statues moved outwards and to the side like a small opening door.

"Oh my God!" was all I could say.

My words echoed around the small hall and looking around again at the ceiling and the walls I had another insight into its antiquity – this place was much older than I'd imagined, and probably older than the temple itself. This must have been a part of the original structure and the temple presumably built around it.

Yeshe then put the larger key into a hole that was hidden behind the statue and turned it anticlockwise three times. A loud clunk could be heard behind the wall and then Yeshe pushed the wall between the two statues and it moved inwards, the sound of scraping stone echoing as the slow, lumbering, heavy door opened with a minimum of effort. There must have been a mechanism inside it, because it was enormously solid and heavy and opening it by hand like this seemed impossible, but just a push from Yeshe and it opened.

Beyond the door was a stone staircase that stretched so far downwards it reminded me of an escalator heading into a disused underground rail system. I fully expected our way to be lit by flaming torches, so it was a disappointment when the elderly monk reappeared from the blackness and gave Yeshe and Lasya battery powered, modern torches. They definitely ruined the atmosphere of the moment! Yeshe put the smaller key back around the monk's neck and shone his torch down the stairs, leaving the elderly gentleman to put things back exactly as they were. It was a surprise to see very little dust flying around and the air was fresh and cool. At the bottom of the stairs, a passageway could be seen stretching away at a slight angle. It seemed odd that the passage wasn't straight, but even stranger was the appearance of the walls, which were clean and dry, and the floor, which was impressively smooth and shiny. Yeshe thanked his elderly mentor and they embraced each other gracefully. When we were all inside Yeshe pushed the door behind him and we waited as the loud 'clunk' was heard once again. Now we were locked inside, the sudden feeling of safety was so powerful it was as if we'd outwitted a serial killer who'd escaped from the local mental asylum and was on the loose around the monastery.

"Okay. Let's go," Yeshe said.

Carefully navigating the steep steps, I stopped at the bottom. Everyone turned around.

"What's wrong, Steve?" Yeshe asked, impatiently.

"What about everyone outside? The Chinese soldiers are coming. I know about some of the things they do."

"Steve, I am sorry. Perhaps I should have explained more. Everyone will be quite safe. The Chinese soldiers, although they are looking for us, behave quite well towards monks in this part of Tibet. It is in the border areas where most of the problems occur. They will simply move on once they are satisfied we are not here and they won't find this secret passageway, either. They will search the monastery but they will find nothing. So, please do not worry. Your journey is at an end when we reach the other end of this corridor."

Was I now about to see the mysterious and fabled Shambhala? Was it really here, hidden behind these walls? Was it buried underground and that was why it had never been found? Or was it just an escape route, as Yeshe had said? As we slowly walked down the corridor the temptation to ask the question was too much, even for me.

"Is this Shambhala?"

"No Steve, this is the Great Hall of Knowledge. I told you Shambhala does not exist here," Yeshe replied.

"It's certainly a hall," I smiled, "but I don't see any knowledge in it!"

"Steve – you do not understand yet. At the end of this tunnel are all the answers. What I will tell you is that the place you are about to enter is the only Atlantean structure still in use on this planet. Shambhala is also Atlantean but it is not accessible to anyone – not yet."

I was stunned by his words and my attempt at humour was ignored. It appeared the time for joking was over but that wasn't an issue anymore because I was sure Yeshe had said this was an *Atlantean* structure. Did he really mean a genuine, still in use, Atlantean structure? I leaned on the wall with my arms folded.

"Right," I said, "so, why are we standing here?"

There was a long pause. Everyone looked at me blankly for a moment and then at each other. Lasya frowned in confusion and then turned back to Yeshe who was standing with a bemused grin. Yeshe turned around and walked down the passage, followed by Pemba and Nawang. Lasya stood in one spot staring at me in bewilderment and I had the impression she was trying to figure out how my mind was working since it must have appeared to her that I was never completely in control of my emotions. She seemed to be musing over my erratic questions and statements and then she smiled as if she had found what she was looking for deep in my eyes. She stepped towards me, grabbed my arm and pulled me forwards. We walked together hand-in-hand down the passageway like two scared schoolchildren on an adventure trip in a haunted castle.

After about a hundred and fifty feet we reached a turn in the passageway and this time it curved away so that we were now walking slightly east of our original direction, and after another hundred or so feet we reached another door.

There was a strange symbol on the door, set in relief, about three-quarters of the way up. It had a circle in the middle and around it were three concentric rings, rather like a target with a bullseye in the middle.

"What is that?" I asked.

"This is the symbol for Atlantis," Yeshe said. "In the centre of the great civilisation was this structure. It was a huge city. Each raised circle represents the land formation and the indented parts represent the sea. In a way, they represent earth and water and the circles themselves represent the akasha. The stone circles of Europe represent the akasha as well – it is the same symbolism. Everything in Atlantis was circular – all the buildings were circular – and the shape itself represents the continuous energy of the fifth element. The other four elements are different in that they can exist or they may not exist – earth, fire, water and air do not necessarily exist everywhere in the universe and their energy can come and go – but the fifth element exists in everything, and is everywhere."

Quite frankly, I didn't have the faintest idea what he was talking about. What did he mean by the 'akasha'?

Yeshe took off his necklace and removed a crystal that was inside a pendant. The octagonal crystal was cut and polished, with a strange blue tint inside a colourless outer shell. Yeshe then did something that left me gasping in amazement – he placed the crystal into the centre of the symbol on the door and the crystal disappeared inside. It was literally swallowed by the door itself and left no trace whatsoever. Taking a closer look, there were no marks or holes to put the crystal inside and my shock was such that I started blabbering.

"What the hell was that? Where did it go? How did that happen?"

I couldn't believe what I'd just witnessed. A part of me was fearful of the unknown but another part of me realised that everything that had happened in the last few days was worth it – I really was about to be shown something incredible.

Before anyone answered my worthless questions, the door made a 'whooshing' sound – a strange tone that was a cross between a blast of wind through a gap in a door and a fast car passing on the motorway. Then, to my total astonishment, the door opened inwards, on its own, in total silence. Yeshe looked at me very seriously.

"Prepare yourself," he said.

Beyond the door was another corridor, this time only about ten feet long and the ceiling, floor and walls were all made of the same material – a plastic-looking substance, lavender in colour with a shiny surface like glass. It had a strange depth to it as if the colour was behind the plastic front, giving the feeling of an extra dimension.

Once we had all entered, the door closed behind us again in silence as if it somehow knew we were all inside. I was utterly stunned when Yeshe's crystal came out of the centre circle on the inside of the door! Half sticking out of the hole, it sat there waiting to be pulled out. Somehow it had moved through the solid door and out the other side!

"Why don't you take it out, Steve?" Yeshe said.

"Are you sure?"

It was yet another stupid question on my part but by now there was little in the way of coherency going on in my brain. I pulled out the crystal effortlessly and watched as the door moulded back into a seemingly solid object. Blinking a couple of times and shaking my head, I gently held my hand out to Yeshe. The crystal seemed weightless, almost like a cheap, plastic fake you might buy from a market stall, but this was probably the most expensive crystal in the world.

Yeshe took the crystal from my hand, placed it back inside the pendant and hung it around his neck. He looked at me and smiled and I stood there open-mouthed, waiting for him to explain the miracle I had just witnessed. But he said nothing. Turning back to the door, I looked closely at the centre circle – there was no hole, nothing. There was only a solid circle on an equally solid door. How on earth did that work?

I realised that I was now in possession of knowledge that was forbidden to the world. I had become part of an elite group that was sworn to secrecy and was now entrusted completely with that knowledge. How did I end up in this mess? Five minutes ago I was an ordinary man on a strange adventure. Now I had entered into a different world, a world of which Charles was a part. I was no longer comfortable with this situation and well out of my depth. Standing at this alien door was more terrifying than when bullets were whistling past my ears a few days earlier. Both Charles and the seriousness of this undertaking suddenly popped into my mind and for the first time I realised I was in this way too deep, but there was no going back now, and it was like walking through a maze where, after every corner, the doors locked shut behind leaving only one way to go – forward.

There were no choices. It was unfathomable to back out of this now and it wasn't possible to turn around and opt out even if I wanted to. If I ran away, I could be perceived as a threat to Charles, or anyone else involved, so I had to follow it through no matter how scared I was, and standing inside a weird structure that was behaving in ways that were totally alien to me left me with a new fear. And yet, somehow, there was also an inner peace. Even though my animal responses were that of fear, deep inside my soul there was a new kind of tranquillity that was incredibly soothing and calm. And so I enforced the main rule that exists in my life – never allow animal senses to dominate the intuition of the soul – 'flight' reactions are born out of fear, but 'intuition' speaks the truth.

We walked the few steps to the end of this tiny corridor and it opened out into a small, circular chamber that was about eight feet across and was very dimly lit. The light didn't seem to be emanating from any particular spot but just filled the room with a dim haze. It appeared there was a reference point on the edge of my vision but whenever I looked in the direction of the apparent point of light it seemed to move to another location. It was so bizarre my brain could hardly comprehend it.

"What's that strange light?" I asked.

"Besides the door, this is the only Atlantean device in existence that still functions to its original design. It checks your soul's rate of vibration," Yeshe said.

Did Yeshe just say what I thought he said? This is a still-working Atlantean device – a genuine piece of technology from Atlantis? But instead of asking about Atlantis my brain sidestepped the obvious and concentrated on the perceived threat. "Why does it check my soul's vibration?" I asked.

"I'll explain when we are inside, but basically the device scans you to see if your soul's frequency is high enough."

I couldn't understand what Yeshe was saying and my focus was still on the idea that this place employed Atlantean technology. I had always imagined, probably like everyone else, that Shambhala was a real place hidden somewhere in the mountains of Tibet. Finding a beautiful, garden-filled paradise in the mountains was one thing, but walking into a building that employed a superlative technology to our own that was also thousands of years older and from a civilisation that apparently did not exist, was something else entirely. This was about as serious as things could get. Yeshe had said this was not Shambhala, but I couldn't accept this was Atlantis, either. And was this an Atlantean place, or was the door just technology that had been rediscovered? Or was it original technology that had been hidden away in the bowels of the earth for ten thousand years?

"The inner door won't open until we have all been checked by the scanning system," Yeshe said. "It senses the presence of people, but not in the way a camera would in our world. This structure is sensitive, rather like a plant. This is Lasya's first time here as well so don't be too worried. You are not alone."

A few more seconds passed and then a tiny hole appeared in the centre of the wall in front of us, spreading outwards like an opening flower, revealing beyond it a magnificent domed hall.

The room was huge, slightly bigger than the Royal Albert Hall in London in diameter. But it wasn't the size of the dome that initially struck me – it was the fact that the walls appeared to be moving. As I stepped forward, my legs crumpled beneath me and I found myself on the floor, the walls knocking my sense of balance into malfunction. It was like the nausea of a fairground ride. The wall of the dome appeared to be almost liquid and swirled around as if it were a living entity. It looked like a solid structure but at the same time it was constantly moving. Lasya was suffering the same fate and looked as bewildered as myself.

The impressive dome was a monumental structure and I had never seen anything like it before. From about ten feet inside the entrance the walls on either side were full of rows of pigeonholes that seemed empty. They stretched all around the dome with periodic gaps between them. In the centre there were circular seats and circular tables. It felt and looked like an ancient and alien library.

"Don't pay any attention to your nausea, Steve," Yeshe commented as he came through the door behind me, "this happens to everyone on their first visit. It passes in a few seconds."

"Why are you three okay?"

"This experience is so powerful and unfamiliar that the soul instantly adjusts to the effects, restoring an internal balance. The brain senses that this environment is life-threatening and adjusts rapidly. Soul and brain are then attuned and will adjust more quickly next time. However, if anyone truly unworthy did manage to reach this place, the effect on them would be more intense and they would be violently sick. They would not be able to stand it for more than a few moments. And in a very short time the energy field that exists here would cause their death since the vibration of the atoms would not be compatible with their own."

Yeshe helped me to my feet and as quickly as the effect had hit me, it disappeared and I was back to normal again.

"That's a bit harsh, don't you think?" I asked.

"No, this place must be protected against those with... ill intent, shall we say. The mechanism targets those people. It is a self-generating preservation mechanism. Don't forget, this place is partially alive. It will protect itself from harm. There's no need for a burglar alarm in here!"

"What if someone came in protected in a lead-lined suit?"

"The atoms would penetrate the suit. No earth-made material can protect anyone from this place. Anyway, they wouldn't get through the first door without the key, remember?"

"What if someone tried to blow the door open with explosives?"

"Explosives would be ineffective against the door because half of the atoms don't exist in this reality. They would destroy bits of it but the door would self-replenish and return to normal, only this time the door would contain more atoms from the higher frequency and this would make the door even more impenetrable."

Playing Devil's advocate, I didn't want to give up, but each time Yeshe had a fool-proof response. "What about a nuclear explosion?"

"A nuclear device would break through the door since it would alter the atoms inside it but there are two outcomes to this. Firstly, no one would be stupid enough to use a nuclear device in that small corridor – they would blow everything to smithereens within a square kilometre or more, assuming it was a very small bomb, of course. And secondly, if someone did manage to break the door open using that method then the dome itself would change its structure – its frequency – and 'rise up' so it would disappear completely and would not exist at all in this reality!"

I gave up. But more importantly I wanted to know what Yeshe was talking about when he kept referring to frequencies and realities because his answers only helped to confuse matters.

"This is why the walls move. This dome is partly fourth dimensional. From our vantage point, all Atlantean structures are in a liquid-like state, kind of half liquid, half solid. This dome exists partly in the new frequency and therefore it is prepared already for the shift. This dome is surrounded by a very powerful etheric field. We are accustomed to a magnetic field, or a gravity field, but here we have an etheric field and since the aether is made of dark matter it cannot be affected by normal matter. That is why it maintains its shape and density."

Yeshe was talking in riddles again but I didn't bother to question him. My brain, soul and body were in total sensory overload and I needed time to adjust.

"You can touch the walls if you like, it is quite an experience," he said.

He wasn't wrong. When I plucked up the courage to do it, the experience was like none I have had before or since. It was exactly as he said – like putting my hands into something half liquid, half solid. My hands were able to go right into it and it was as if the wall was reacting to me, as if my hands were being caressed by a structure that could sense my actions. It appeared exactly as Yeshe said – a kind of plant reaction. But this place was not organic – this was a construction, a building that was malleable but alive – and this made it a very unnerving experience.

I removed my hand and the wall returned to its original state. I expected to see fragments of the wall left on my hand but there were no traces whatsoever.

"Good, yes?" Yeshe asked, smiling.

"Amazing," was all I could say.

"Let's go and sit down. You have as long as you like here. This structure is self-sustaining and you could sit in this place until death, if you so desired. However, you might get bored because the energy here would prolong your life by a factor of fifty per cent. The energy field slows the ageing process and reduces the body's deterioration rate significantly."

Staying in this place until death wasn't such a bad idea. The huge dome had an energy that was far beyond anything I'd experienced before. As we walked towards the centre I could feel coolness against my skin, which was pleasant rather than uncomfortable. It felt as if something was pulling at me from all directions, rather like a magnetic field of some kind. It was such a pleasurable experience that it made me feel 'high', but only in the sense that I was connecting with something of a higher intelligence. Somehow, the whole place was interacting with my inner being. You could say it was touching my soul, communicating with my very essence and making me feel more alive. It was as if the dome and my soul were interacting and becoming one entity, feeding each other with energy. I could understand why life would be extended in this place – the energy field feeding my own body, interacting with it, creating a more balanced internal state.

The walk towards the centre of the room seemed to take an age and with each step the huge dome appeared to expand still further. It reminded me of Stonehenge, which had the same effect on me – once I had crossed the perimeter fence that keeps tourists away from the circle and headed towards the stones, they seemed to double in size with each step, and by the time I reached the monster sarsen stones and looked upwards they seemed to reach the sky. I had never noticed this before with any other structure – until now. Right here, right now, I was standing inside the strangest building that had ever been constructed on the planet - far stranger than Stonehenge. A building, it turned out, that didn't even belong here.

19

KINDERGARTEN

The large, sofa-like chairs in the centre of the room appeared to be covered in leather but in fact it was more like a fluid plastic substance – when we sat down on them, the chairs seemed to mould themselves around our bodies. It was a lesser variation on the wall effect and it created the most comfortable seating position – the chair could hardly be felt around me. It was like being suspended in mid-air, a feeling of weightlessness caused by levitation.

"Okay, Steve," Yeshe said, "it's time I expanded on some of the things I have already mentioned to you – I'm sure you are confused – but let me first explain what this place really is. This structure was built around twenty-five thousand years ago by the Atlanteans."

"This place is Atlantis?"

"No, this is not Atlantis. It is *Atlantean* in the sense that it was built by them. It is a later structure that was built during the fall."

As far as I was concerned, this *was* Atlantis. Even though Yeshe said this place was never a part of Atlantis, he'd admitted that it was *Atlantean* and for me this was the same thing. I was finding it hard to contain my excitement, for right now I was actually sitting in a remnant of the once fabled – but now real – city of Atlantis. It really existed.

Beside me, Yeshe was still talking. "This building is circular, like all Atlantean buildings," he was explaining. "You already know the design of the centre of Atlantis from the entrance door. All the structures were circular, dome-like, or even spiral in design. Humans are best adapted to circular buildings – it helps energy flow through us better. Modern, square buildings are a hindrance to human thought and actually block the universal energy. People in the modern world are often blocked from this energy by the buildings they live in. The Chinese practice of Feng Shui is actually a legacy of this knowledge and oriental martial arts use this same energy; *akasha*. The flow of this energy is spiral in nature. The blocking of it can cause ill health, spiritually speaking. Circular buildings amplify this energy by allowing its natural spiralling to flow through the building, thus allowing people to be more connected with it – and healthier."

"Akasha," I repeated, thoughtfully.

"Akasha is also known as the aether." Yeshe nodded, pleased that I was absorbing what he was telling me. "But we will come to that later. The scrolls that are usually contained within this room are copies of the original Atlantean scrolls, and were written around ten thousand years ago."

"Ten thousand year-old scrolls?"

"And they are merely *copies* of the original scrolls, which date back to the time of this building's construction – a date we don't know. For some reason it was not written anywhere here. No one has actually seen the original scrolls – they are long gone – but we had faithful copies. However, as you can see, they have also disappeared."

I looked around once again at all the empty pigeon holes. "Where are they now?"

"We don't know. They were here until about a year ago. Then one day I came in here with a colleague and nearly every scroll was gone. There were tens of thousands of them."

"What do you mean, they were gone? Who took them?"

"Steve, I am sure the scrolls are quite safe."

I found this mystifying. "If you don't know who took them, how can you be sure they're safe?"

"Steve, when you are dealing with a structure that dates back twenty-five thousand years and partly exists in another dimension, you don't worry too much when strange things occur. Anyway, I am sure no one physically took them. I expect they are still here but we just cannot see them."

"What do you mean by that? They are either here or they aren't."

"Have you never wondered why one person can see something but the person standing next to them cannot?"

It was a rhetorical question. Yeshe was trying to say that whilst neither he nor anyone else in the room could actually see the scrolls, this might be only because they partly existed in a higher dimension.

I didn't really understand this but it was comprehensible if I made a comparison with the electromagnetic spectrum. The electromagnetic spectrum contains all the wavelengths that exist in nature, from weak radio waves all the way up to powerful and dangerous gamma rays. In between are microwaves, x-rays, etc. We only see the visual range of this spectrum, which is but a tiny part. If we were to stretch the electromagnetic spectrum in a line that started in London and reached Rome, our visual range would be around an inch long. That is the only part that we can see with our eyes but birds, for example, can see the ultraviolet spectrum which is just above the visual range in wavelength. Now, just because we cannot see ultraviolet waves doesn't mean they are not there. The same principle applied to the 'missing' scrolls, except that we were dealing with different dimensions rather than wavelengths. Wavelengths can be perceived along a horizontal line that pertains to our third dimensional reality, while the actual dimensions of reality can be seen as vertical sections that can only be perceived individually, and not at the same time. But while it is possible to perceive other wavelengths in the electromagnetic spectrum by using certain technologies, it is not possible to view other dimensions by using the same technologies. In other words, while the third dimension remains within the boundaries of the scientific method, in the case of dimensions we are dealing with a more spiritual element to nature and thus access to them requires a different form of science.

In that moment I realised that if one's soul could vibrate at different frequencies, these changes might allow a person to view other dimensions.

"Can you explain to me about the soul's rate of vibration that you mentioned?" I asked.

"Each and every soul on this planet has a unique code within their DNA and each of their auras has a specific design. The aura design is dependent on when you incarnated on this planet. Since this structure is Atlantean, under normal circumstances only Atlantean souls can enter this place. In short, the door's scanner checks your soul. It is a very sophisticated device and if you are not an Atlantean soul the door will not open. Now, being an Atlantean soul – sometimes called 'Adamic' – refers to the time in history in which a person incarnated on this planet. However, your behaviour and your thoughts determine the person you are, regardless of your origins. This is still fundamental to Buddhist philosophy; the Buddha himself was in fact an Atlantean soul who was trying to reinstate the old philosophies. But that's another story."

"The Buddha was an Atlantean soul?"

"Yes. And also Mother Teresa, and many others. To answer your question, Steve, this is just a simplified explanation for the rate of vibration of your soul and thus the type of aura you have. But it is also related to the code in the DNA which determines what you are – and as we said this has more to do with at what time in history you incarnated on this planet. So, in essence your soul's vibration is your DNA code, or base rate of vibration. The Atlanteans were the first humans on this planet but in those days the frequency was higher than it is today. The system in place here stops anyone who is not an Atlantean soul from entering. However, there is a way of getting around this – you can work to increase your vibration, enough to bypass the system, but it takes quite a lot of work to do it. It all depends on how you think. Every person vibrates at a certain rate. You need to be vibrating well above ten thousand pulses per nanosecond to bypass this system. Most individuals on this planet vibrate at that rate. It could be termed the average rate, rather like the average rate of IQ being one hundred. Every thought you have creates energy waves that flow out away from your body and eventually they return. You know the old saying *what you think you become*?"

"Yes," I replied.

"It is based on this principle. It is all about negative or positive thoughts. Your thoughts determine your rate of vibration. The Atlanteans were of a higher nature. They were naturally of a very high nature because of the environment they existed in – like this dome – a slightly higher frequency. Since most individuals on this planet now live in a lower frequency because of the thought patterns that exist, it is almost impossible for them to enter this place."

I stopped for a moment before responding, digesting the information as best I could. "So, thought patterns determine the rate of vibration of the individual. How does that work? I think I understand, but how do you explain these differences in people and why is there a difference between people depending on when they incarnated?"

I asked the question but I had to work hard to suspend my disbelief. I had long known that soul existed separately from body because I had once gone through an out of body experience, but to say we *incarnated* on this planet implied we came from somewhere else. Many people assume the soul is created at birth along with the body. Even Buddhists believe this. However, in principle this is a Christian viewpoint – the idea that we are born and then we die and go to heaven or hell. It is the old Eastern philosophies that contain the idea of being incarnated on earth, rather than created, and then continually reincarnated. Were these ideas a truth, an ideology that was passed down by the Atlanteans?

Yeshe made no attempt to answer my question but left me alone while I was deep in thought. Then something even more intriguing occurred to me.

"If all you say is true," I challenged him, "then how did I get through the door?"

"Your life times have gradually lowered your frequency, as they have for many souls. This world has become a disease to us. So, this is what your 'dear angel' Lasya was doing this whole time – raising your frequency. She has been tuning in to your thoughts and counteracting your negativity, raising your frequency high enough so you could enter this place. She did a great job but it takes a massive amount of concentration and energy to achieve."

I now understood everything that had been going on – the strange energies, the bizarre thoughts – these ambiguous emotions were caused by my lower vibrational anxiety and Lasya's attempts to counteract it. I wasn't going crazy after all. She had been, quite literally, planting thoughts in my mind.

"Today," Yeshe continued, "there is no difference between an Adamic soul and any other, at least not in physical appearance. Everyone has become corrupted by the lower frequency which has existed for the last ten thousand years."

"What do you mean, there is no difference?"

"Everyone is living in *this* world. At the beginning the Atlantean souls were highly spiritual, having the legacy of Atlantis built into them, but thousands of years at this level of vibration has corrupted so many of them. At this level, people think in a material sense – they want more and more, they want a better life, but this is usually in the form of money or some other material aspect of reality. They want a bigger house, a better job, more money, and *nearly everything* they want is material. Even eating too much food is a spiritual sin. Occasionally there comes along a soul who will try to preach the real value of life – spiritual value. The Buddha himself, for example – he left his material life behind and went in search of enlightenment. He preached to everyone that the real reason of life is to attain 'moksha'. He wandered the land of India in rags and ate very little food. He was as thin as Gandhi – another Atlantean soul. All the great spiritual teachers are Atlantean souls."

I remembered the age-old teaching that everything must be in balance – waking, sleeping, working and playing – in order to create equilibrium and health within the soul and body. Too much of any can be unhealthy and so can too little – imbalance in the soul creates imbalance in the body and vice versa. In other words, ill health comes from stress – in old Eastern philosophies physical illness is a manifestation of an imbalanced soul. It was clear, metaphorically speaking at least, that the human form was a disease in itself – a disease of ill mind manifested by greed and the corruption of the spirit.

"You must understand," Yeshe continued, "that Tibet is only one of the places where the Atlanteans came after the fall. Some of us are descendants of those people, or rather we are reincarnations of those souls, and some of us have been quietly trained, from a very young age, to maintain the highest rate of vibration we can manage. We also have the advantage of being far from the developed world, away from all the corruption that exists; advertising, money, work in the recognised form, materialism, and so on."

I must have been looking incredulous, because Yeshe broke his train of thought to answer my unspoken question. "Yes, Steve, some souls here are indeed original Atlanteans. It's not so unusual, in fact. If all Adamic souls incarnated at the same time, they would make up about two per cent of the world's population."

I stopped him for a moment and tried to calculate the numbers.

"So, that's about a hundred and forty million people. That's quite a lot."

"But remember, not all these souls will incarnate together. The population of Atlantis was always around sixty million at any one time and the area of the land itself was the size of most of the Atlantic Ocean, so there were vast uninhabited spaces and really no large urban areas except the classic circular city. I'll explain more about that later. What you do need to realise, however, is *all* of the Adamic souls are incarnated at this time."

"Every Atlantean soul is currently incarnated on the planet?"

"That is correct, yes, and I'm sure you want a reason, but that will come later." Yeshe gave me that look again and I resigned myself. I saw that there was a good reason why he was giving me only pieces of information. I was gradually absorbing everything and he was telling me these things in a kind of sequence. I could also sense other things - information which I knew instinctively but which was just out of reach of my consciousness right now. I wasn't ready to know certain things at this time and there was a learning process involved that required subconscious processes and time for them to operate. There were also many things Yeshe would be keeping entirely secret from me – after all I was a fresh initiate and my new friends had been the keepers of this knowledge almost since birth. However, I realised that Yeshe was telling me only the things that I *needed* to know, so it followed that he had been *instructed* in what to tell me. That disturbed me.

Yeshe interrupted my thoughts again. "To return to our explanation… some of the Chinese elite are aware that some of those living in our monastery are Atlantean souls. They also know that this place exists, although they don't know where – they have been trying to find it for a long time. Their frustration and antipathy towards Tibetans is based around this fact, although this information is not in the public domain. The Chinese are angry that a peace-loving society like ours is the keeper of such power, but this is exactly their mistake – they think that they themselves should have the right to such knowledge because of their dominance as a powerful nation. Many nations, even civilisations, have been destroyed in the past because of their hunger for power. Imagine Adolf Hitler trying to gain the knowledge of the technology of this place – it would be misused."

Yeshe stopped talking. He could see that I was struggling to assimilate everything he was telling me and he waited for a moment before continuing. "Steve, do you feel Atlantis was a real place?"

"Yes," I replied at once, "there is not a doubt in my mind about that. There are so many pieces of evidence that fit together and I don't understand why the evidence has been so badly ridiculed by science."

"No, Steve. Do you *feel* Atlantis was a real place?"

I stopped for a moment and allowed my mind to 'ask' my inner self. "Yes, I do feel it was a real place."

"Exactly. Anyone who can effectively tune in to their intuitive sense will categorically answer that Atlantis was real. As for the scientists, they simply want solid evidence and that is hard to find since Atlantis itself existed in a higher frequency."

"So, the city does still actually exist somewhere."

"Yes – you've got it – somewhere. This is why it has never been found and also why Shambhala has never been found. They still exist, but on a higher frequency."

"So, what happened to the people – what was the fall?"

"The fall was not physical. To put it simply, all the negative, material thoughts worked to lower the vibration of the people. Atlantis slowly disappeared in front of their eyes; they found themselves on this level and became trapped here."

"How does a person know if they are an Atlantean soul?"

"It all depends on how you think. You will know if you are an Atlantean because Atlanteans can only learn through *feeling*. An Atlantean must feel a subject to learn it, but a Yhevic – the dominating soul that currently makes up around ninety-five per cent of the population – can learn through thought alone. This is why we have schools and learning in this way. Yhevics are clever at learning scientific subjects, whereas an Atlantean soul will struggle at school. However, this is not always the case. The Industrial Revolution was also created by the Yhevic. From around ten thousand years ago up until now, the Yhevic has dominated this planet and caused its destruction. This is also why there is disagreement between certain types of people – spiritual principles against corporate and financial greed, freedom of souls against control by royal lineages or central governments. In other words, Atlanteans disagreeing with Yhevics about how to live. Money is another invention of the Yhevic. They have no concern for the destruction of the planet. They swallow up everything for personal gain at the expense of the planet's resources and very few people actually care about it."

"So, we have gone from a spiritual existence to a material one."

"Yes, and in the space of just ten thousand years."

I suddenly understood everything – how and why our planet was being destroyed and why so many individual people care little about the devastation. So many people are only concerned with their own personal existence.

"And war is a construct of the Yhevic as well?"

"Of course it is. Now, I think we should leave this for a while so you can take a breather again."

Yeshe was correct. My head was going around in circles while I tried to comprehend all this information. It was too much for my brain right now – two different types of soul existing in the same kind of physical body but with conflicting ideas about how to live in the world, one a destructive entity and the other a spiritual being. The depressing part was that the destructive entities dominated by nearly fifty to one. This was the soul group that had basically taken over the planet and led us to the verge of ecological collapse, all in the space of just a couple of hundred years from the beginning of the Industrial Revolution – for surely mechanisation had brought about the total destruction we now see around us. It was astonishing and very sad in equal measure.

"In a moment we will have a look at the scrolls," Yeshe said, breaking the slight tension that had been created by my thoughts.

"I thought you said the scrolls had vanished?" I asked, confused at the sudden change of information.

"For some reason, a few have been left behind. I am not sure why, but we have three we can look at."

"Do you think they were left behind on purpose?"

"I am sure they were, yes. There are never any mistakes but I have no idea why these particular three were left behind."

"Do you have any *feeling* as to why?"

"Not really. Maybe they are just examples, clues."

It was an exciting possibility that the three scrolls might contain important information; perhaps they were a pointer to something significant and were left behind specifically to lead me on to some kind of greater discovery. Yeshe could see I was slowly beginning to understand the magnitude of the information they might hold and he encouraged my sudden enthusiasm to find out what the scrolls said. For sure, he had already read the three scrolls prior to my arrival and if they were meaningless he wasn't going to say so, but were these three scrolls the reason I was sent to Tibet?

"You will find the scrolls appear quite new, so you can handle them as much as you wish," Yeshe said, as we stood up and walked slowly to the far wall. "The way this dome has been designed enables the temperature to be maintained at a constant level and all microbes were removed from the atmosphere on completion of the construction. In fact, if you did decide to stay here until your death, your life would be prolonged for at least a further ten years since there is nothing in here that could attack your immune system. Over time, you would also be healed of any infections and severe illnesses as the energy contained within this building would increase your vibrational frequency to a much higher level. For that reason the Atlanteans lived much longer than we do."

"What you are saying is that because this dome exists partly in the fourth dimension, third dimensional microbes cannot exist here?"

"That is exactly correct, yes, you are learning well! Once the structure was completed, the energy level – the vibrational frequency – was increased to a point where nothing within this place that existed before could survive. And this is also why 'lower frequency' people would not survive – the energy does not match their own."

"So, it is comparable to an astronaut going to another planet and not being able to breathe the atmosphere."

Yeshe stopped and turned to look at me. "Perfect analogy, yes," he said. "Now, the *original* scrolls are hidden in Shambhala. Shambhala does exist, Steve, but you would be unable to see it. It exists completely in the fourth dimension and is of a frequency that we are unable to attain at this time. The physical location of Shambhala is in the Gobi Desert and it is contained within the etheric band."

For a brief moment I was disappointed but looking around the dome I realised I had already found my Shambhala. So what was the meaning of the text that was in the folder Charles gave me? Why did it mention Shambhala when it is not even visible to us?

"So, Shambhala is of a much higher frequency than this place?"

"Yes, it is. Shambhala is a magical place, and it is also why no one has ever been able to find it. For example, the Nazis tried to locate it in the nineteen thirties. They sent many archaeologists and scientists here and their program of measuring skulls to provide evidence for the existence of the Aryan race was a sideshow – in reality they were trying to find the lost scrolls. However, their basic idea of an Aryan race was correct – they were referring to the original Atlanteans. Since this was one of the original settling places of the Atlanteans you must question how the Nazis discovered such knowledge, especially since they were somewhat delusional in other areas of their thinking. Such people would never be able to access Shambhala."

It was amusing that Yeshe had referred to the Nazis as being 'somewhat delusional' – it was an understatement of great proportions. I was also stunned, but not because the Nazis came here to Tibet.

"What do you mean that their idea of an Aryan race was correct?"

"In essence the phrase 'the Aryan race' is referring to two things that are the same. The Atlanteans were the Aryan race, but an Atlantean would be someone who vibrates at a higher frequency. There is a certain irony in that – the Nazis were convinced that they were full-blooded descendants of the Aryan race and yet they themselves were most likely vibrating on an extremely low frequency. It is not known how they accessed this knowledge but there has been suspicion that somehow they used certain technologies to gain information. As you will know, they were dabbling with some very bizarre experiments at that time and had some of the best scientists in the world at their disposal. It is a shame, really. Imagine how different our world would be if the Nazi regime was of good intent – how far forward, technologically, could our world be right now?"

"I understand, but knowledge about Atlantis has been around since Plato's account, so why is it such a mystery that the Nazis knew about it?"

"It is not actually their knowledge of Atlantis that is in question but the idea of a 'superior race'. You see, they somehow knew the Atlanteans were of a higher vibration, although their interpretation of what that meant was completely distorted. It is how they knew about the higher vibrational frequency that is baffling, to the few of us who are privy to this information –

information that has been kept within a few closed circles for the last ten thousand years and more. When the Nazis came to power, one of the keepers of this knowledge must have given them the information, or perhaps it was forced out of them. However, there were no keepers in Germany during that time period. Somewhere there was a leak of information but no one has ever discovered where it may have come from."

"So, their entire ideology of an Aryan, superior race, was simply a misinterpretation of people having different vibrational frequencies."

"Yes." Yeshe looked at me with sadness.

"I think I might laugh, because if I don't I might cry, instead."

"I know, Steve, it is terrible."

"So, they started the mass-murder of millions because they thought *they* were the superior race and yet it was they themselves who were vibrating at a lower vibration?"

"Yes, and in the case of the Nazis, the lowest vibration possible."

"Oh, for Christ's sake, surely that has got to be one of the biggest blunders in human history."

"There are many similar, unfortunately. However, we must put things into perspective."

"What do you mean? Is there another perspective?"

"Well, we have to look at history and how this terrible blunder, as you call it, came about. The rest of the world does not take responsibility for what it did to Germany after World War One. In the nineteen twenties Germany was suffering because of sanctions to such a point that many people starved to death. It was this national anger that created the Nazi regime and World War Two. I am not condoning what happened or what the Nazis did but I sincerely hope that the rest of the world has learned that such punishment to a country can result in tragedy. We are all responsible for the monsters we create."

Yeshe's words humbled me. And of course, he was absolutely correct – how can we make such bad accusations against the German people when we were the ones who made them suffer after World War One? Is it surprising that the German people wanted revenge after they were so blatantly humiliated after 1918 and made to sign documents pertaining to defeat when no one won the war in the first place?

"Talking of the Nazis," Yeshe said, "the difficult thing to comprehend is that Adolf Hitler was an Atlantean soul, believe it or not."

"Really, that doesn't make sense."

"Steve, you must understand that by being an Adamic soul does not mean you are a good person. The vibration at this level has corrupted so many souls it is ridiculous. Adolf Hitler's Atlantean soul could also explain their ideologies about the Aryan Race. He could well have known this information internally – he could have had an inner knowing – about Atlantis. Hitler could have had memories of this and his soul may have wanted to return things to the way they were in the past, but his lifetimes of bad karma had created a very negative aspect to his soul. The Nazis were so corrupt their minds believed all others to be beneath them, so in their ideology the Nazi race – the Germanic people – were superior. But there is no superior race, just the Atlanteans. Although they were correct in stating that the Aryans were the Atlanteans, the centre of their lineage was not in the Germanic region. It's the correct theory, but with the wrong set of people!"

"I understand, but what you are really saying is that the Aryan race is not a race at all, but a soul group and it doesn't matter which race you belong to today – you can be black, white, or even green for that matter – it's the soul group that determines whether you are Atlantean or not."

Yeshe had a broad grin on his face but I wasn't happy with the explanation.

"The problem I see is that you've already told me the Atlantean soul is a superior race because the Yhevic soul is the one which has caused all the destruction."

"What about Adolf Hitler?" he replied. "Look at the destruction he created. You need to think about it, Steve, it's not so simple."

This information was so amazing and fascinating but as Yeshe said, the question that stood out was how the Nazis came upon this knowledge. How did they know that, in essence, the Adamic soul was the original Atlantean? It seemed there was no answer, or if there was Yeshe never mentioned it. Instead, he changed the subject.

"In the case of the door," he said, "it checks the soul itself to see what level of vibration it has. So, although Adolf Hitler was an Atlantean soul he would never have got in here due to his lower vibration. And don't get confused between 'soul' and 'aura'. The aura is generated by the body – it is the electrical field around the body. The aura cannot deduce your level of vibration, but the soul does."

20

THE SCROLLS

"Let's take a look at this scroll," Yeshe said, as we finally reached the pigeon holes, our conversation making the short journey last an age. "You won't be able to understand the script but I can translate for you."

Each pigeon hole had a symbol to the right of it that consisted of dots in various configurations. It reminded me a little of Braille. Yeshe explained that the symbols were part of the original cataloguing system.

Yeshe pulled out the first scroll, turned around and placed it on a lectern. Each set of approximately twenty pigeon holes had a lectern positioned before it, giving the impression that the dome was a busy place in its heyday. The pigeon holes themselves were approximately two feet square and would probably contain around twenty scrolls, all neatly placed on shelves within. Taking out a scroll and placing it on the lectern in front, the system ensured the scrolls were returned to their exact place afterwards.

"Open it," Yeshe said.

The scroll was rolled very loosely and there was nothing to tie it together, which seemed very odd until I actually handled it. It was made of a strange material that was as strong and smooth as metal, but as thin and malleable as paper.

"Strange, isn't it?" Yeshe said, smiling.

"Yes, it's weird. It feels as if it should break apart – it feels flimsy and delicate."

"It is hard to believe but the scrolls are made from metal. It is an alloy of two metals – one of them is zinc and the other is one you will not find existing normally. The periodic table of elements is incomplete – there are actually metals within metals – and it all depends on the frequency of the planet as to whether these metals exist or not. From a monetary point of view, each individual scroll is priceless on this planet but if you took one of them outside of the dome it would no longer function as a scroll. Its molecular structure would change instantly and the atoms would collapse into the two base metals that it's made from."

"What is the second metal? Where would it be in the periodic table?"

"Well, it might sound odd but it is similar to a combination of copper and lead."

"But they're not next to each other in the periodic table."

"No, they are not and I said only 'similar to', but that is what it is and it is this metal that enables the scrolls to be easily folded and strong at the same time."

Yeshe wasn't wrong. As I rolled out the scroll and laid it flat against the lectern it was amazing to see and feel. We are accustomed to a rolled out piece of paper returning quickly to its curved state when we try to flatten it out and we are used to metals not bending easily, but this strange metal behaved exactly as I wanted it to. The scrolls had a golden colour to them, like a very light copper, and the writing consisted of a series of symbols that were unlike anything I had seen before. They were not hieroglyphs or cuneiform, they were something quite unrecognisable. Rather than lines or dots, all the 'letters' were curves, each one a different size or length – circles, semi-circles, part circles, two quarter circles facing each other, and so on. It was a very simplistic system and I felt that learning it should be easy, provided that each symbol corresponded to a letter, rather than a word. Symbols were carved into the metal plate, rather than written, and their perfect symmetry was reminiscent of stencilling as opposed to hand-written, or hand-carved.

"What does it say?" I asked.

"It says – *From the source the human form was moulded from the divine elements*. Now, we don't know how this occurred, or what the 'source' actually is – there are many things we cannot understand – so all we can do is accept the words on these scrolls as truth."

Yeshe rolled the scroll up again, put it back in its pigeon hole and replaced it with the next one.

"Is that all it says?" I asked.

"Yes. Each scroll has only one or two lines, some have more, but each one is a story in itself. A whole book could be written from each one."

"So, human beings were made from some divine source, just like the religious texts say."

"Yes, basically, but I don't think we were made 'in the image of God' as some texts say, just that we were created *by* the source itself. As to what the source really is, well, that is totally open to debate. Another point is this – does it mean the source created us, as in we were 'made by a God', if you like, or is it telling us that it is a natural process – that we are a natural evolutionary aspect of creation?"

Yeshe was correct – it wasn't a simple question of accepting the words – the interpretation of those words was important. From Yeshe's smile it was clear he knew but he wasn't going to give me answers – I had to work it out for myself.

Yeshe passed me the second scroll. "This one says – *time is the illusion of the third dimension."*

"What does that mean?"

"It means exactly what it says. On this lower level of vibration time is illusory. We perceive time as linear but it is not. Time is linear in our minds but at the subatomic level there is no such thing as time. We perceive time as being linear for two reasons. First, we see things as being born and then after a certain time they die, so we see time as moving forwards. That forward motion, however, is a bit of a trick. The other reason is the way the universe functions. We think there was a 'Big Bang' that started everything and since then the universe has been evolving in one direction, but this is not strictly true."

"Are you saying that the universe is not moving forward in time?"

"I am only telling you the facts. You have to figure it all out for yourself but what you must realise is that the third dimensional level is the lowest form of existence. There is a lower dimension – that of a two dimensional world – but life as we understand it does not exist there. The two dimensional state is like a drawing of a house on a piece of paper. A real house is three dimensional, but a drawing is two dimensional."

I wondered - if the two dimensional world is like a flat piece of paper then what was the fourth dimension like compared to the third?

Nawang and Pemba were playing some kind of chess game over by the wall to my left. Lasya was across the room, putting her hands in the walls and moving slowly in our direction in the process. She looked tiny against the huge dome and I sensed she was relieved that all her hard work had come to fruition. On turning back to Yeshe, I saw that he was also looking at Lasya, shaking his head slowly, smiling as if watching his granddaughter at the fairground. "Lasya," he called out, "don't put your whole arm in or you might disappear!"

Laughter echoed around the dome and it amazed me how good the acoustics were in this place – it would be a perfect arena for a music concert.

"Okay, where were we?" Yeshe mumbled. "The third scroll says – *Think and you become, for thoughts create the universe around you.* Well, we were discussing that earlier."

I stared upwards for a moment, trying to understand the implications of these words. I couldn't imagine how much information had once been contained in this great dome. Each scroll, as Yeshe said, was like a book in itself and once there were tens of thousands of them. It reminded me of the sad loss of the Great Library of Alexandria, which must have been a similar place and may well have also held the secrets of our origins and our history. It is this kind of loss which has left modern man rummaging around in the sand looking for pieces of a puzzle that will never be found, with only scraps of archaeological evidence giving us a one-dimensional, lopsided view of our past.

Yeshe had more to say about the third scroll. "This scroll tells us that humans have always existed – and normally exist – in a fourth or fifth dimensional state and that in these states all things are created by thought alone. For example, if you were to imagine yourself on a desert island, you would suddenly find yourself there. You could think of any location and you would instantly be there – but you must understand that those places are illusory – they are creations of consciousness."

That explanation struck a chord with me. It made absolute sense.

"So, is that why some people say we should be careful with our thoughts?"

"Yes, because you can attract what you think. If you think your life is hell, it will most likely be that way. Even quantum physicists have noticed this effect – our reality conforms to our expectations."

"But how does that apply in reference to the dimensions?"

"You can create anything by your thoughts. In the fourth or fifth dimension these thoughts attract instantaneously, but in our third dimensional reality the response is not immediate. Also, the universe does not distinguish between *want* and *don't want* – you will simply create what you think."

I was silent. Not because I didn't understand, but because I had no words. Interpreting my silence as mystification, Yeshe tried to explain it further.

"A good example would be the journey we made to the temple. I know you have been very worried about the Chinese catching up with us. In that situation, you might think in this way: *'I don't want the Chinese soldiers to catch me'*. But the universe does not differentiate between *'want'* and *'don't want'*. So, because in your mind you are seeing images of the Chinese soldiers capturing you, you create that exact situation in reality, simply by summoning those images to your mind. It doesn't matter if you want it or don't want it – if you think something you can create it. That is why some people seem to have bad luck all the time and others have good luck. The way we think creates the reality around us."

I felt guilty for thinking bad things on the journey. "Do you think the Chinese will come now because of my thoughts?"

"You don't have to worry. I was picking up your thoughts and all of us are well versed in this knowledge, so any thought waves you sent out we counteracted with positive thoughts. We simply imagined we were in another place and Lasya focused on dissolving your thoughts into the aether. Like the etheric energy, our thoughts are waves that go outwards. You can imagine them like radio waves. They start in our mind, the thoughts expand and move away from our bodies and they can be felt by others. They can be sensed and interpreted, just as a radio set interprets radio waves. This is why people sometimes don't feel comfortable when they meet a new person, because they are picking up their thought patterns and instantly know that they do not think alike or share opinions. This same principle applies when you meet a potential partner. You say that there is chemistry between you. The term 'chemistry' is a good one to use and in effect it means that you have simply met someone who thinks the same way as you – you tune in to one another. It can be a very powerful experience."

A shiver went through me as if I had just discovered a lost Da Vinci painting. I really identified with what Yeshe had described. I had often wondered about the many times when I had not felt comfortable around someone and taken an instant dislike to them. On the flipside, I had met people where there was an instant attraction and these people had often become a great friend, or even a partner. There was, however, a contradiction. Sometimes the person I disliked later proved to be a good friend and more than once a person I felt drawn to was quickly dismissed soon afterwards and all contact lost. I mentioned this to Yeshe.

"That is because the initial experience is powerful and the connection confused," he explained. "When you are in a group, the collective thoughts are picked up by each person and the powerful connection between you and the correct person is often lost in that confusion. You could say the energy lines between you and that person are contaminated by the others in the group."

This is a common occurrence, I realised. Often, married couples would say it was 'love at first sight' when they met their partner, but just as often they may say they didn't like each other at all. Thinking about the couples I had seen come together, I realised that those who didn't like each other had first met at a gathering where there were large amounts of people, whereas those who claimed 'love at first sight' had met in more intimate places; walking their dogs, for example, or at dinner parties. A further contradiction, however, was clear in that often a person's intuition was correct – sometimes an initial dislike towards another person was proved later because their relationship broke down. There were many variations, none of this was simple and it required deeper thinking, but however interesting this train of thought was, right now my concern was about my own negative thoughts on the journey to the temple.

"Stop worrying," Yeshe said, before I could react to his gaze, "your fears are ungrounded. Think of the place you are in and ask yourself – do I need to fear what is happening around me? You are a part of a great adventure and a future that is already happening. Don't be concerned with the fear that you absorb when you are living out there in the world. This will pass during your time here. This great dome will erase your worries."

"You can read my mind," I said, as the realisation hit me.

"I can, yes, but not the words that you construct. Like Lasya I can feel your emotions and this in turn allows me to understand what you are thinking. It is a natural ability, one that we all have, but mostly it is blocked by the world in which we live. Here we are fortunate to live in an environment that is isolated from the outside world and our learning enables us to be free of fear. It is fear that blocks all our natural abilities and keeps most people locked in a cycle of life that is rather like a prison. Basically, it keeps the mass population in a control system, like religion. Religion uses fear to control people," Yeshe looked around, his eyes reaching high as he scanned the entire dome, "but this incredible structure gives off an energy that is unparalleled in our world. It allows you to access those special abilities that are blocked. It creates an energy field that is so powerful that it alters your very being to a higher frequency. However, it is currently only activated to a percentage of its capability. We would not be able to exist inside here if the energy field was at its full capability, because we are dealing with two different dimensions. The dome and our low vibrational bodies are not yet compatible."

It was a struggle to cope with the concepts Yeshe was teaching in the great dome. While it all sounded simple in theory, in practice it was difficult to digest all the information. What was required was a more detailed explanation on some of the aspects of the scrolls.

"Going back to what we were saying before – are you suggesting that humans are not part of the natural evolution of the planet?" I asked.

"That is correct. Darwin's theory of evolution is wrong but only in the sense of origins. Evolution does happen, but not the way the *Theory of Evolution* describes. Changes to a species are not gradual. Instead, there are leaps in evolution. Any creature on this planet can evolve new adaptations overnight and these adaptations normally occur in the entire species, even if they are on separate sides of the planet. Signals are sent out – rather like the thought patterns we talked about – and then an entire species can develop overnight. I think it has been called the *Hundredth Monkey Effect*. For example, if there is a catastrophic global event that threatens an entire species they can all evolve in one day to adapt to the threat and survive. Normally this does not occur quickly in larger mammals – the smaller and simpler the creature, the quicker the change. If we look at the dinosaurs, the events that caused their extinction could not be adapted to – the atmosphere became stagnant and dangerous to breathe."

"That actually makes sense because even though Darwin was convinced of his theory, he was adamant there was divine intervention."

"That is exactly true, yes. Evolution is in fact a genetic code or program that instigates instant changes, not the gradual changes of selective breeding, although they do occur as well. And yes, Darwin was a very religious person. He knew, or at least he thought, that gradual evolution was the way that species evolved, but just like the 'Big Bang' theory he could not explain the original spark of life and he correctly stated that the only explanation for this mystery was divine intervention and that everything was originally created by a higher intelligence. How he must have struggled between his faith and science."

For a moment I contemplated how Darwin must have contested his scientific mind and his religious beliefs and how worried he would have been in those days not to upset the Church in which he believed so greatly.

"Did you say that this swift evolution in entire species does not occur in larger mammals?" I asked.

"Yes, that is correct, and right now we are seeing this happening in our own species. What is required in larger mammals is to achieve a state that is known as a 'critical mass', which has been shown scientifically in the *Hundredth Monkey Effect* experiment. Right now, our consciousness is expanding rapidly over a short space of time. We are witnessing a global evolution in the human race and it has been happening for the last fifty years. It will continue into the future and we are observing a very rapid growth in both available energy and population. You must understand that the spark of any evolution comes from the divine source – the etheric – and changes are occurring from there, not from here. This is consciousness evolution, not biological evolution, and you must understand the two are very different – it is consciousness evolution that causes subsequent biological evolution. However, this will peak and then decline as we enter a new age of consciousness and resources become depleted."

"What do you mean by 'peak and then decline'?"

"The Earth has limited resources and we are swallowing everything up at increasing rates, destroying habitats like the rainforests. This consumption is increasing day by day as the world's population multiplies at an alarming rate. It is an unsustainable situation and something will happen to make reverses to this process. Our species could be looked upon in different ways, but you could say we are a planetary disease that is eating everything up as we spread throughout the planet, rather like a cancer. We are very much like ants, did you know?"

"Are we? In what way?"

"Ants are very human-like in their behaviour. They travel across the land, consume everything in their path and then move on to the next place. And a very interesting fact – ants are the only creatures other than human beings that wage war on their own species."

"I have never thought about that," I smiled.

"Despite their size, their behaviour is very similar to ours in many ways. They have organised societies with workers, guards and queens, just like we do. Even most of our so-called cousins, the apes, don't have these behaviours. In so many ways we are more like ants than any other creature, which makes you wonder about the order of things in nature."

"It certainly does." It seemed ridiculous that we could be compared with ants but it was an obvious recognition once an analogy was made using behavioural patterns. So here we are, nests of ants, running around the planet eating everything in our path and fighting with other ants for resources...

As the hours passed Yeshe told me countless stories and gave me information that was at best difficult to digest and at worst downright ridiculous and hard to believe. Many of the stories, it turned out, were irrelevant to the quest I was undertaking, but some would reveal themselves later as being an integral part of the path I was travelling – the information was absolutely vital to what would happen much later. Without it, a complete understanding of what I was dealing with would not have been possible. He even told me the secrets of the pyramid builders – how they built them and what tools they used – and he told me this information would be required later. When it was required, he said, it would become apparent at that time. Until that time, he said, I must keep it quiet.

In between stories, we took short breaks which gave time for me to absorb all the information, for Yeshe to take a breather, and for Lasya not to disappear into another dimension. Eventually Lasya became tired of playing with the walls and calmed down a little. She relaxed in one of the chairs and listened intently to Yeshe's great story telling abilities, whilst Pemba and Nawang continued playing chess and were on to their umpteenth game.

By the end of the evening I had an overload of data and felt like a computer that was about to crash. Yeshe told me that most of the facts he had given me must remain secret and that my concentration must be focused mainly on the information contained in the three scrolls that had miraculously been left behind. Everything else would either reveal itself at the right time or I must keep it within me for eternity – what details I had been given were necessary for me simply to grasp the greater picture. It was clear to me that much of this information could be dangerous if it was in the wrong hands and to this day it remains a secret.

Finally, Yeshe said, "There is not much more information I need to give you, Steve, so we can leave this place now. Our time here is finished."

And that was it. It ended as abruptly as it had started.

Lasya let out a childlike whimper showing her disappointment. I smiled. The strong, aloof woman that she had appeared to be when I had first met her had slowly been replaced with the feminine, soft-natured person I always sensed she was.

"Will it be safe outside?" I asked, concerned the Chinese might be waiting for us.

"Oh yes," Yeshe said. "We have been here much longer than you think. How long do you think we have been in here?"

I thought about it for a moment but my brain seemed to have a malfunction of some kind. It was like the answer was right in front of me but it couldn't be reached. "I have no idea. On the one hand it seems like an hour and on the other, an entire day. And I haven't felt hungry at all."

"The lack of hunger is caused by the suspension, or alteration, of time as we perceive it. Time exists here in a different way to the outside. An hour in here could be several beyond the dome and vice versa. At least, that is the perception. It can be a strange feeling when you walk outside and find it is the middle of the night, when in fact you expect it to be the afternoon. It's a little like international flight."

"How do you know which way around it is? How do you know if time has not reversed for us and we end up outside at the exact time the Chinese arrive?"

"Because Pemba has a watch on his wrist and I can see what the time is!"

Laughter echoed around the hall as all five of us started to chuckle, and then the strangest thing happened – the walls seemed to churn a little quicker as if there was an understanding of the humour between us. But how could a structure understand our language? I asked Yeshe.

"It doesn't," he answered. "As we discussed before, this structure is rather like a plant and since it is in a higher dimension it is responding to the changes in our souls, our auras, but this is nothing new – plants have this reaction in our dimension too. The electrical signals they give off have been measured through countless experiments and the results have proven that plants react to people's thoughts."

"How does that work?"

"You must understand that we exist in all realities at the same time. Our souls are within us but they also extend outwards into a slightly higher frequency and this is why we cannot see them. The dome can 'feel' our aura but not our physical body. When we have emotions, be it laughter, sadness, anger or happiness, the world around us changes accordingly. The aura changes vibration slightly and, for example, laughter makes it rise up a notch or two."

With that sentence I had another one of those 'Eureka' moments.

"So *that* is how our thoughts create our reality! The changes are in our spiritual bodies and not from our actual thoughts?"

"That is correct. Your thoughts change the electrical, and thus the auric, pulses that exist in and around the body. In the physical body there are the electrical pulses and in the aura there is an increase or decrease in vibration. The two function together. It is these changes that go outwards into the universe and affect everything around us and it is those same electrical pulses or vibrations that come back to us as Karma."

"And this is why we can feel someone's mood from a distance."

"Yes, because the energy field around a person changes depending on their thoughts. It is what we might term a 'bad mood', or a 'good mood', but it is not an actual *mood* – that is basically a physical term used to explain the energy that a person has created around themselves."

"But another person can actually give someone a bad mood, right? I mean, if someone wakes up happy in the morning, for example, and then on their way to work they have an argument with someone, then that person can create bad energy within the other person."

"No, that is wrong. We can only do this to ourselves. What you must realise is that all of this understanding has been lost. People are much weaker nowadays. We have lost the ability to create a boundary around us which can't be penetrated by others. Have you ever wondered why some people are unaffected by someone else's criticism, while others go into a mini-depression? It is because the person who is little affected has a closed aura around them and criticism becomes – what do you say – water off a duck's back. However, don't make the mistake of thinking that the person with the closed aura is a stronger person, thinks more positively or may even be an Atlantean soul, because that is not the case. There are many factors that can affect the auric body. Childhood experiences are one obvious factor, especially abuse. But an equal factor is an accumulation of previous lives, because they create the soul that you are today. Your personality is not just derived from your current life. These various factors make it a far more complicated thing than you might imagine, so it is just something you'll have to think about later."

Pemba and Nawang had packed away the chess game and it seemed to disappear inside the table, the semi-liquid structure moulding itself around the board and swallowing it like a magician's rousing finale.

"How do you know which way time will go? I mean, how do you know if it will go forwards or backwards?"

"We don't. It can go either way, but reverse time is a very unusual phenomenon, although it does happen. However, when time goes forwards the rate of speed can vary. In the third dimension there is the constant illusion of forwards time. I say 'illusion' because time itself is an illusion in our reality. In this dome, which exists partly in the fourth dimension, forwards time can be slowed down or speeded up. In the fifth dimension, time can go forwards or backwards although it doesn't actually *run backwards* – it can simply be returned to an earlier point in time. However, we don't really have the brain capacity to understand the concept of backwards time and our reality is such that we see time as an arrow, but our science is limited to *measurement* and this is not something that can be applied in higher dimensions."

"So, the science of matter – our science – does not function in higher dimensions because the universe operates as consciousness, and not physical cause and effect."

Yeshe's broad grin confirmed that I understood. It was bizarre to think that the higher the dimension we exist in, the more consciousness has an effect. In our reality it seemed that our thoughts didn't necessarily have an immediate effect on our surroundings, but the higher the dimension, the quicker the response. In other words, the higher the dimension, the closer we are to the source of the universe itself, and this means the closer we are to what the universe itself actually is – consciousness. In this reality, although our thoughts have more of an impact than we imagine, we still pretty much live in a 'cause and effect' world, but the important thing to note is that cause and effect is more an act of our thoughts, not our actions. Actions are created by the thoughts that precede them – an action requires mental planning before it is carried out, therefore it is thought that causes the effect, not the action itself.

There was little more to say on the subject. While it was hard to imagine in practise, it was fairly simple to understand and I was able to apply this new knowledge to the world outside. And then another thought struck me like a sledgehammer. "Does this mean that our entire world is a construct of the collective thoughts of every individual on the planet? Is this how people can communicate?"

Yeshe smiled yet again and nodded his head in a way that illustrated his pleasure at the rapidity of my understanding. "That is *exactly* how the world works. Wasn't it Carl Jung who called it *The Collective Consciousness?* Even though he was mostly referring to how information can be passed from one individual to another across space, the concept applies to the entire world. Since the universe is consciousness, then everything that exists in it is also consciousness and that includes our world."

"What about animals? Do they have the same consciousness as us?"

"Yes of course they do, but you must understand that animals don't think in the way we do. Don't confuse thinking patterns with consciousness in that sense. Only animals have a thinking brain or react to stimuli, but everything is alive. If you imagine the entire universe as a brain, and the contents of that brain are the contents of the universe, then you realise that everything in that brain is alive. Just as the whole functions as a collective consciousness, the individual atoms are alive within it. Since the brain is made up of atoms and the brain is conscious, then those atoms must also be conscious. The atoms don't suddenly become alive when they collect together to form a whole, they are already alive as individual atoms. In other words, consciousness exists already, prior to the brain's existence, so therefore consciousness is nonlocal – it is not constructed by the brain."

"It is so simplistic that it's amazing no one has noticed this before."

"It is simplistic, yes, but it does require us to review our understanding of what consciousness is. We are taught in our schools that consciousness is the construct of a living brain but once you remove that idea and start again then you can rebuild a new view of the universe."

What Yeshe meant was that consciousness was not generated by the body. It is the mind that is generated by consciousness. That consciousness exists in the form of our soul. The physical body requires a soul to be able to function. Without one, it is dead. It is the soul that is the life force of the body, not the electrical firing of the brain.

There were many other things that Yeshe told me but much of it was only part of a larger story. He said that later everything would be understood and I assumed he meant I would be going home now, that this adventure was over, and things would slowly make sense over time. But if I thought I would be returning to a boring life in England, a messy relationship break-up and visits to the local café, I was in for a major shock.

21

A SLIGHT DETOUR

The new experience in the dome had filled my soul with an unrivalled sense of freedom and peace. Sure, I had felt great inner calmness on many occasions but this was something entirely different. The energy field produced by this awesome structure had lifted me to a higher state of being where absorbing all Yeshe's information seemed easier than normal, as if I'd managed to remember every word. Even today, when I recall the things Yeshe told me, in my mind I am suddenly standing in front of him and I can see and hear our conversation as if I'm watching a recording. I didn't know it then, but this would be a vital ability during everything else that was to happen in the coming weeks.

As we reached the door, we all stopped and turned around in unison, as if paying respects to a great Tibetan guru who had given us insights into life that before had seemed impossible to attain. One last time, I scanned the entire structure, taking in the beauty and the unique way in which it had affected my senses. The dome was undoubtedly *The* Greatest Wonder of the World, and what a shame it had remained a secret for so long; what a shame the human race was such that a place like this would only be abused.

As we faced the door, it suddenly opened automatically as if the dome knew we were leaving, allowing us safe passage back to the outside world. It was strange how, once outside of the dome, my normal fears returned quickly but inside the dome I had no concerns whatsoever – the energy had raised my soul to new levels of awareness. We reached the outer door and Yeshe produced the crystal and pushed it into the middle of the three concentric circles. The door casually opened and the 'whooshing' sound once again echoed in the hall beyond.

Outside, an immediate sadness swept over me, coupled with a sense of relief, as if somehow my body was reacting, readjusting on returning to its normal state of being. This was surprising but it wasn't without explanation – even though the dome existed in a higher frequency it was difficult for the body to adjust to it. As Yeshe stated, we humans are no longer compatible with the fourth dimension.

No one had said a word up to this point and we traversed the long, dark corridor in silence, back to the huge door that opened out into the monastery, each one of us dealing with an experience that was both collective and personal. Despite Yeshe having been there many times, his demeanour told me that the experience was equally as powerful on every visit. Now the experience was over, readjusting to a normal state of being resulted in an overload of the senses.

I worked on memorising the few sentences contained in the three scrolls, for surely these were of great importance for whatever it was I was supposed to be doing here in the first place. *From the source the human form was moulded from the divine elements; Time is the illusion of the third dimension; Think and you become, for thoughts create the universe around you.*

Those three sentences were powerful, for they explained that our world was not the way I had perceived it to be. Firstly, we were created by a divine force of some kind. Secondly, time is an illusion and thirdly, what we think, we create. But what was I supposed to do with this information?

"How do we get out?" I asked. "Isn't the key on the other side?"

"No, it is a much simpler process," Yeshe replied.

It was apparent that gaining entry to the dome was far more difficult than getting back out. The security devices which had to be navigated to enter the dome were as tight as a bank vault but once inside it was as if we were accepted as a part of the structure, almost like a family member, so releasing us was unsophisticated. Therefore, I almost laughed when Yeshe stepped forward and pulled open one of the wall stones like a small door – inside was a small handle poking out of the middle, which Yeshe pulled towards him until a loud 'clunk' could be heard. The heavy door opened slowly but just a little and Yeshe then pulled it effortlessly towards us by grabbing the exposed inner side.

A blast of warmer air quickly flowed through the door as if we had just stepped outside into a summer's night. It was fresh and clear and although the air inside the corridor was clean enough, it had a different feel to it, like a house that had been cooled with air conditioning.

I suddenly felt as if I were ten years younger – all the natural aches and pains of a 38-year-old had simply vanished and I felt I could climb Mount Everest. I mentioned this to Yeshe.

"Unfortunately this does not last," he said, "and by the time you get outside you will be feeling back to normal. Even though your vibrations have been increased inside the dome they quickly lower to the current frequency when you get outside. And before we say anything else, I need to tell you that once we go through this door and back into the monastery we do not talk of this place. It does not exist. Understood?" He gave me a long stare.

"Loose lips sink ships," I said, referring to the wartime call of silence and the need for secrecy.

Yeshe smiled and nodded his head slowly. I don't think he had heard that expression before but he understood the implication. "If you have any questions please ask them now, because if you have any after this I forbid you to speak of them, even if it seems we are alone."

My mind was blank and I shook my head. For sure, there would be dozens of questions later but I was still in awe of what had happened. Oddly, it was easy to accept that any later questions would be unanswered and maybe there would never be a response, because somehow I also knew that the answers to those questions lay within me, as if the dome had planted everything inside my soul like a seed from a tree.

Yeshe turned towards Lasya, making sure she was ready, and then we headed out to the main hall. It was dark outside and just as predicted it seemed time had differed from inside the dome. A brisk breeze swept across the hill and filled the air with a slight chill that was pleasant and not cold, but it cleared my mind quickly. I felt dizzy, as if I'd suddenly leaped out of bed after lying down for hours, and my head was spinning as it tried desperately hard to return to normality. Thankfully it didn't last long – it was just a reaction to the outside air.

The dinner hall was devoid of monks who, for the most part, had already retired for the evening and a sudden confusion swept over me regarding the time of day. We had gone into the dome in the early afternoon and now it was late at night. Although we had been talking for many hours it seemed that time had not altered on the outside in any way at all. Maybe time only altered if one was in the dome for longer periods of time. Either way, there was not a Chinese soldier to be seen.

"What are you going to do now?" I asked Yeshe.

"I shall continue my work here. I am waiting for the time when change comes. I am hoping for a better future for Tibet and hopefully this will occur soon. We are not asking China for an independent state because we know they won't give it to us, but we do want autonomy."

Tibetans have no means and certainly no desire to fight the Chinese, either militarily or otherwise. Only peaceful protest can be their weapon but for the most part their plight is being ignored by the rest of the world.

I turned to Lasya. "And what about you, Lasya? What will you do now?"

"I will do the same as Yeshe," she said, smiling as if the question was irrelevant. I wasn't even sure if she'd heard the question at all. She was on autopilot. Lasya had been changed by her day in the dome. She seemed distracted, aloof and in a different world, but all the time a smile was on her face.

"So, how are you finding Tibet? Do you like it?" Yeshe asked.

"It is an amazing place, a beautiful country, but I haven't really had a chance to take a step back and absorb it all. So much has happened since I arrived. But I can say the vast expanses have opened my soul to a whole new experience."

He looked at me with an expression of curiosity and even I realised my words were different, but my statement wasn't a fabrication – my soul had awakened to a great extent and that was not entirely due to being inside the dome.

We finished dinner and Yeshe suggested we all rest. "It is time to retire for the evening," he said. "It is also time for us to move forward."

Yeshe's statement was blunt – it was time for me to leave – but in any case it felt like the journey had come to an end. There was nothing else for me to do here. It was time to call Charles, get out of Tibet and go back home to England. Despite the desperation and emptiness that could be felt when I thought of leaving my new friends I was never truly comfortable in this country. It is a magical, peaceful place but the constant worry of Chinese military rule and hard line abuse they meted out to the people here left a constant air of trepidation and fear, like a persistent skin rash. Not to mention the fact that if they caught hold of me I may never return home at all. This was a contradiction to what Yeshe had said but there were two experiences – one on a much deeper level to the other – one surreal and spiritual and one based on what was happening in the real world. It was practically a metaphor for the dome itself.

Returning my backpack to my room and taking a walk back to the bench that overlooked the vast plains below, I made sure I was alone and that no one could overhear the conversation that was about to take place. Everyone appeared to have gone to sleep long ago, and taking a deep breath I dialled the number – 5096.

"Mister Maybury! I expected you to be calling me today. Everything is going to plan. Good. How are you finding Tibet?" Charles' voice was expectant and calm, but the same commanding and dominating tone was still apparent.

"Tibet is interesting," I said, not wanting to give any information. I felt a need to hear what he was going to ask before volunteering anything that I'd supposedly 'discovered'. Neither did I want to say anything that could be intercepted by someone else. Even though he had told me that this was a secure line, I realised that anyone else with the same technology, or those with an equal standing to Charles, would understand how to use it as well. There was no telling how many people at his level were involved.

"Yes, it is an amazing place," Charles said, "full of interesting people. The architecture is stunning too, don't you think?"

"There are some interesting buildings here, yes. I like the monasteries especially, they have an unusual design. Have you been to any of the monasteries?" I asked.

"No, I have never been to Tibet."

That was not the answer I expected. He had never been here? I was intrigued and confused in equal measure.

"So, how do you know about the monasteries?" I asked.

"I have seen pictures of them. Anyone can see pictures of the monasteries on the internet. I am also aware of the daily events that go on there. Tibet is a peaceful place, I am sure."

"It is not so peaceful at the border," I said, breaking the tactical conversation and getting to the point of Chang's death.

"I did hear of this unfortunate event."

"You don't seem too bothered about it."

"In a game of chess, pawns are always sacrificed to protect the King."

"Are you telling me you knew this would happen?"

"Destiny is often written prior to the events that happen."

What the hell did that mean? "So, you employed someone's services by offering them wealth, knowing they wouldn't make it and you would never have to pay them anyway? That is quite sick if you ask me."

"Don't be silly. If you could guarantee the life of your family would you sacrifice an unknown person?"

"Oh, so I am your family now?"

"Don't get smart with me. You must understand how these things work."

"I understand how this works. Just to get me to see a few sights in Tibet you knowingly have someone murdered. You could have told me about this place back in England and saved all the trouble." I was irritated by the man's coldness.

"You really don't understand," he said. "Sometimes we can see things before they happen but that doesn't mean we can stop them. Secondly, you need to be there for particular things to happen and experience those things which you could not experience back home – certain events must happen before other events can manifest. You cannot boil water in a kettle without first turning on the switch."

I tried very hard to comprehend what he was saying. How was it possible that Chang's death could have been known before it occurred? Suddenly I remembered Yeshe's narrative about time not being linear and now I understood how it can work outside of our reality, provided that certain techniques could be used – like remote viewing – but still it made no sense. My mind could not grasp this possibility, maybe because I was so personally involved in Chang's death. It would be impossible to take myself out of that situation and look at it from an objective viewpoint. But right now, I had to stay focused. Everything Charles said always had a million implications and the meanings were at times obscure and hard to understand.

"So," I asked him, "how do I get home now? I assume that whatever I was here for has been completed, although I don't exactly understand the point of all this. If you already know about the monasteries then why did you send me here in the first place?"

"You don't quite understand because you are misunderstood."

"What the hell does that mean?"

"This was just an introduction. You only understand about a third of what you need to know. And if you think crossing the border was a scary experience, wait until the next part."

Part of me wanted to scream at him, but instead I was stunned into silence. What experience could be scarier than being shot at? What could be more terrifying than seeing a man dead in front of you with his chest blown open; a man who, only a few seconds previously, was a talking, walking, living person?

"I believe you have good knowledge of the Maya Calendar," Charles said. "Is this correct?"

"Yes. Well, I haven't looked at it for a couple of years. Why? What does that have to do with anything?" I asked, disturbed by the sudden change of direction.

There was a very long pause. I waited.

"The second stage of your task is to go to Mexico."

"What?" I shouted.

"Careful, Mister Maybury, someone might hear you."

I looked around, checking no one was in sight but also instinctively looking for Charles, because it was once again beginning to feel like he was watching me from somewhere, as if he knew exactly where I was.

"Why on earth do I have to go to Mexico?" I had dropped my voice, but my anger was still apparent.

"It's all part of the plan. Did you think this would be the end of your journey? What have you actually achieved so far?"

"How the hell should I know? You sent me here, remember? I didn't realise I was going to be country-hopping round the planet for you."

"Calm down, please. Emotions are not necessary and neither do they suit you. Try to stay focused and listen carefully."

I said nothing and waited in silence but I was seething.

"A new site has been discovered in the jungle. You need to go there and find out what is going on. Your knowledge of the Maya Calendar is important for the next stage."

"The next stage," I interrupted. "How many more stages will there be after this one?"

"Did I not just say listen carefully? Tomorrow you will leave. You will be given instructions how to proceed. Your journey will enable you to leave the country easily. You will fly to Delhi and from there you will continue on to Mexico."

I laughed.

"What is so funny this time?" he asked.

"Nothing," I said, but I was laughing at the ludicrous way in which he could pull strings in every corner of the world.

"This is not a joke. Have I joked at any point up until now? No one will ask you questions. Your exit from Tibet will be trouble free."

"Then why didn't you get me into Tibet the same way? At least Chang would still be alive."

"I wish you would stop asking irrelevant questions. Getting into Tibet is not so easy. The Chinese do not like visitors. They are happy when you leave

Tibet. They are not so pleased when you arrive. Please trust me that everything is happening as planned and there were, or are, no other ways of carrying out this process."

"Okay. So, tomorrow I am leaving for Mexico, great. Why do I get the feeling I am jumping out of the frying pan and into the fire?"

"It is not without its dangers but that is to be expected considering what you are doing."

"And what am I doing exactly, besides risking my life for reasons which escape me? Why can't you just tell me what this is all about?"

"You will know this in time, but let me tell you this – you are about to have the most amazing experience of your life. In a very short time your life will have changed beyond recognition. Sometimes you go through so much fear that you come out the other side with no fear at all."

Before I could speak the phone went dead. I almost threw it away, but I recognised that my frustration and annoyance would get me nowhere. I had to deal with this situation and go with it and hope that sooner, rather than later, there would be some answers. For now, though, I was as confused as ever. What drivel was he talking about this time? I ignored the part about the fear. My brain didn't want to know anything about that. Instead, I concentrated on the fact I was now heading to Mexico.

He said a new site had been discovered and I would require my knowledge on the Maya calendar. Did this mean a new *Maya* site had been discovered? What was so special about this site and what did it have to do with Tibet? What could possibly be the connection between the two and how was it possible that ancient Tibet could be related with ancient Mexico?

I had actually been looking forward to going home to face my boring life once again and the idea of going to Mexico had filled me with fear. But it didn't take me long to rethink and before many minutes had passed, the idea of going home horrified me and the idea of a new adventure, no matter how perilous, filled me with a new invigoration. No matter what the dangers and no matter how strange it may seem to some, I'd rather be running from a gun than sitting in that café pondering on a lost relationship.

A smile ran across my face.

"I'm going to Mexico," I said.

22

PENGUINS AND PANDAS

Sitting on the bench and staring out across the blackness, my mind was awash with confusion. I was excited, but also frustrated at having no control over what was happening. I wasn't going where I wanted to go – I was going where someone else wanted me to go. I was on a weird guided tour, rather than planning my own route through unfamiliar terrain. Charles must have known that underneath I would be jumping with joy at the thought of going to Mexico but I also knew there would be no time to lie on the beaches of Cancún, or some other desirable place. Charles had stated clearly that this trip would be like no other, so my excitement was coupled with a new kind of fear. A fear that, over the coming forty-eight hours, would grow and grow the closer the shores of Mexico became. Looking upwards, the sky was clear and the stars twinkled as if they were communicating with me, flickering in sequence like a coded message.

Lasya was sitting on the end of my bed with her arms folded like a wife waiting for her wayward husband to come home late at night, but a smile swept across her face when she saw me enter. Then she saw that I wasn't smiling back. "What is wrong?" she asked.

"It's just that I will be leaving tomorrow."

"I know. Sad I am for this too, but do not worry." Lasya's dark, oriental eyes spoke a thousand words and yet there was no understanding of their meaning. Even when sitting next to me she was always a million miles away. She touched my hand and looked out of the window.

"I know it is difficult for you to understand but important is this journey of yours. You will come to know everything in the soon time."

"What will I know, Lasya? And why didn't you tell me you spoke English in the beginning?"

She turned back to me and once again looked into my eyes, her sympathetic gaze having a calming effect. I'm not sure why but whatever words she said to me were far more powerful than anything Charles said. There was a gentleness that made me listen to her intently.

"There are things you cannot know, things you will never understand, but important this is not. You are a penguin in the Antarctic and you must reach the safe ground before the mid-winter freezes until death your body. Time is running out."

I laughed at her analogy, for surely no one has ever heard one like that before. It was very silly but there was clearly a meaning in there, even if I couldn't see it at the moment. I tried to get her to give me more information, playing with her words.

"And what if the penguin does not reach the safe ground?"

"Clever is the penguin. He has the ability to achieve the goal. This is why he was chosen to get there. The penguin can be resilient and stubborn. There will be mountains to climb, but they are not as high as he thinks."

"But what if the penguin does not climb these mountains and starts to freeze in one spot and doesn't reach the safe ground?"

"The penguin does not do this. Fear will push him forward. When faced with danger, the penguin is not stable. Many penguins will perish on this journey but the strong ones will survive."

Lasya had a way of speaking that made me believe everything she was telling, no matter how obscure it was. Her analogy was understandable enough – I should have faith in my abilities to overcome any fears about future situations. Her method of storytelling was normal for her but why she talked about penguins, which live on another continent, was baffling. Why didn't she talk about yaks or something closer to home? Her words were odd but it was this quirkiness that made her unique, along with her innocent personality.

"You must rest now. Important is sleep, for restless in the coming weeks will be your nights. Goodnight." Lasya gently patted my arm and then stood up, leaving the room in her usual elegant manner.

"Goodnight, Lasya, and thank you."

She stopped in the doorway, turned around and smiled at me, and tilted her head to one side. Then she left, gently and lightly as only she could. She was only in the next room and yet when she wasn't in sight it felt like she was a million miles away. Lasya really was a strange creature but somehow she was set very deep in my heart.

Moving my pillow to the opposite end of the bed gave me a clear view of the sky and I lay there thinking about what Lasya had said, but one thing more than any other struck me; *fear will push him forward*. Again I was left wondering what terrifying situations lay ahead – situations where fear might once again override loyalty to another person, that selfish human ability to allow someone else to die in your place at any cost. Was I really that kind of person? I had always thought my spiritual side gave me a more empathic attitude towards others, but already I was guilty of running ahead of Chang and allowed him to succumb to a bullet or two. I felt I had betrayed him. The more I thought about it, the more I was learning things about myself. Were the spiritual principles I adhered to at great cost just the lies of a mind that wished to be something it was not? Was it a mind that not only lied to others for self-preservation, but a mind that lied to itself without realising it? Or was it just that, no matter how spiritual we may be, our animal fears and reactions always come to the fore when faced with danger, pushing our spiritual being into the background? And if that is the case, then how spiritual are we in the first place? It seems that it takes a lot of bravery for one to counteract one's fears and allow one's spiritual side to override them. We are, in essence, two beings in one body because the soul is a separate entity from the mind. It seems that, for the most part, our soul is in control but when faced with danger our animal instincts override our soul, since we live in a world dominated by animal senses – the physical third dimension.

Feeling rather doleful, I reluctantly pulled out the notebook and the pen and lay there for quite some time wondering how on earth I was going to record this last day on paper, but I soon realised that I couldn't write a single word about the dome. What if the notebook became lost? I should have thought of writing in some kind of code, but the strange events inside that bizarre place had left an indelible memory so that writing about it was really unnecessary.

Thursday 20 May, 2010

I have memorised the three important sentences. I am not sure what they mean right now but in time I will discover the truth. Don't know if it's possible to say goodbye to Lasya. My heart feels empty when I think about it but it's time to move on. Surely staying in one place is far too dangerous. Such bizarre things have been happening since I met her but now I know why. Still not making any sense of the 'accident' that happened en route, though. Not sure why someone has to move aside to pave the way for future events. It doesn't make sense to me. Trying to go with the flow of it all but there's a feeling inside of me, something growing from within. There's something bigger than I can imagine right now. I can feel it, but not see it. Soon I'll be on the other side of the planet. In many ways I'll be glad to get away from here and the horrible memories of that event, but will things be any better over there?

A new morning; birdsong and a stream of sunlight penetrated the room. I felt a new peace within myself, as if my body had been regenerated and there was freshness in the air that cleared my mind and made me more alive than normal. Was it the experience in the dome, or was it being so close to that bizarre place that it had an effect on everything around it, creating a new energy that was hidden and yet noticeable? Or maybe it was Lasya's presence that made me feel this way – perhaps her powerful aura and thought distraction created the peace that lay within me. Either way, it was time to move forward. As sad as it was, I had to say goodbye to my new friends and fly all the way to Mexico, which was surely as far removed from this peaceful place as it was possible to be.

Lasya popped her head round the door. "Good morning, Steve," she said, in her sing-song voice. I raised my head and watched her as she brushed her long black hair in the doorway.

"Good morning, Lasya," I replied, returning the tuneful tone playfully. She smiled, tilted her head and disappeared again.

It was quite an effort to crawl out of bed and have a shower, but eventually Lasya and I walked slowly to the dinner hall where Yeshe was already waiting, sitting in his usual meditative position. The atmosphere was calm and happy, a new vibrancy filled the hall and suddenly I felt a revitalised enthusiasm for the coming journey.

"Steve, are you ready to leave?" asked Yeshe.

"As ready as I will ever be, I guess."

With that I was introduced to a man who was sitting next to Yeshe, but until now his head had been turned the other way. Dzengin, much to my surprise, was Chinese, or so I was told. He was fairly tall and thin, with a long face and a protruding chin, a Roman nose to match and deep set eyes that spoke of a thousand secrets. His face was far from the typical rounded face one might expect from a Chinese person. His eyes were brown but sparkled green glints around the edges and his cheek-bones were high. He had one of the most interesting faces I had ever seen, but he was also an anomaly. Maybe he was Chinese by birth, but there was no telling where his ancestral line lay and Dzengin was obviously not a man to be getting personal with. In fact, I wasn't sure I liked him.

"Dzengin will take you from here back down the mountain and safely out of Tibet," Yeshe continued, "and so it is time for us to say goodbye. I hope you have enjoyed your stay?"

"I cannot thank you enough," I said. "It has really felt like I am with family here and it has been a wonderful experience staying with you."

"You are most welcome."

Yeshe walked around to the side of the table where Lasya and I were sitting. I stood up and we hugged, his large frame squeezing the air out of my lungs.

"Take care, my friend, and good luck."

"Thank you," I replied.

With that he walked away and wandered towards the gardens outside the monastery.

It was a swift and unemotional farewell but there was turmoil in my heart. After all, I had just shared the most amazing experience of my life with Yeshe, not to mention all the things he had taught me. Now he was gone and I would never see him again. However, the worst was yet to come – saying goodbye to Lasya would be a different thing entirely. Her gentle awareness had been the solace I leaned on after Chang's death and the pillar which kept me upright. I suddenly realised just how gifted she was and that she hadn't been around me simply to raise my vibrations – and as I realised that, Charles' words that Chang's death was predetermined hit me again. That had disturbed me more than anything, even more than the experience in the dome. How was it possible that these events could have been known before they happened? How was it that Chang's death was already written before we even met?

None of these things made sense to me and it was a whole new concept that meant my entire version of reality was completely wrong. Pre-determinism, or in this case predestination, was not a concept that sat comfortably with me. The idea that everything was mapped out – had already happened before it actually occurred in our time – was an idea that left me feeling very uncomfortable. What was the point of life if all our choices were not actually our own?

I was sure, however, that we still have free will. Perhaps the major things in life may be part of some destiny but the smaller, everyday decisions must be our own. It is difficult to understand where free will ends and destiny begins.

Lasya broke my daydream by clicking her fingers in front of my face, giggling to herself, and as I turned she seemed to be moving in slow motion, her white teeth gleaming and her smile so sweet and innocent. She didn't seem sad about my coming departure; like most Tibetans she took things in her stride. Getting emotional wasn't something these people seemed comfortable with and their surroundings and life meant that things were hard enough without sentimental connections. For me it was different. I had made emotional connections with both Lasya and Yeshe and letting go would be much harder than the decision to leave my life back home.

I returned to the room to gather my things and Lasya followed me in her usual, quiet way. For a moment I sat on the bed and let out a deep sigh as I contemplated the long journey ahead. Lasya entered the room and one last time she sat next to me. "Are you ready to leave?" she asked.

"I am not sure I would ever be ready to leave this place. It is so peaceful."

"It is true, but elsewhere is your destiny. It is time to fly away," she said, flicking her hand open and mimicking a bird.

"I know."

"It is sad, but to make this journey somehow you must find it within yourself. Wondrous things await you, I am sure."

I turned to look at her. For sure her words meant something and I had a feeling she knew what awaited me in Mexico.

"It is a long way. I will be on the other side of the planet in a different environment. It will be strange."

"Yes, it will be strange, but accustomed to your surroundings you will become. Things will be okay. But settle you will not."

"What do you mean?" I asked.

"Not being completely comfortable where you are going will help you to stay alert."

"How are you so sure about these things? How do you know I will be okay?"

"I don't *know*, but in my spirit I feel it strong that you will succeed in your journey, for without an ending it is pointless."

"A good ending, you mean?"

"I don't know if it is good or bad, but the correct ending it will be."

"That is not very helpful, Lasya. What if I might die?"

"If you succeed and then die, then fulfilled will be your journey. You should not fear death – it is a part of life. Know that what you are doing is far more important than your own life."

"What do you mean by that?"

Lasya looked at the walls trying to find a way to explain what she was trying to tell me and then gave me another of her peculiar analogies.

"Imagine you know there are only two pandas left on the planet and you are searching for them. There is one male and one female and if you save them you will ensure the survival of their species. One day you find them. You put them on a truck to be taken to a haven so they can breed and continue their species but an unfortunate accident occurs – the truck accidentally runs you over and then you die. Do you think your journey was successful, despite your own death?"

"Can you not come up with a better story than that?" I laughed. "Yes, I would think I succeeded. So, you are saying that if I die I should be happy I fulfilled my destiny. Do you think I will die, Lasya?"

"No. I think you will be fine, but a good story it is, yes?"

Lasya nudged my arm playfully, giggling as usual, and in turn I pushed her harder so she fell sideways onto the bed – she had fooled me for a moment with her serious face. She rolled around on the blanket laughing and I shook my head at her as she enjoyed her latest, and last, game. When she finally calmed down she sat up and looked at me more seriously.

"Everything I say is true. Except for the panda story, of course! Please, about your adventure do not be worrying. It will be difficult but for the better you will be changed and you will experience great things."

"I hope so. I wasn't expecting to be going somewhere else after this, I must admit."

"Your journey, when it ends, only the beginning it will be."

"What does that mean?"

"It means when this journey has been completed it will be the beginning of your whole life. The start of a whole new adventure it will be."

"I hope this will end at some point."

"End this particular journey will, but also it will begin your life adventure."

I understood. It was pointless continuing with this narrative even though I could have listened to Lasya's sweet voice for a long time. It seemed we were going round in circles and Lasya was only repeating what she had said at the beginning, but in a different form. Despite Lasya's statement that her panda story was just a joke, I knew exactly what it meant. She was referring to Chang, but the story was also about myself – what I was doing was far more important than my own life. No matter what was going to happen, I had to ensure the safety of her proverbial pandas.

It was time to leave. I wanted to get it over and done with. It wouldn't be good to hang on to any emotions so it was best just to say goodbye and get on the move.

I stood up and looked at Lasya as she sat on the edge of the bed, smiling at me as if I had just arrived. For the first time, she seemed oblivious to my emotions and I tried hard not to show how upset I was to be leaving her and this place.

"Steve," she called out as I reached the door.

I turned around and Lasya walked towards me. She stopped right in front of me and to my surprise she said, "I will miss you."

She threw her arms around me and for a moment my heart burned. Then she let go and took a step backwards, looking deep into my eyes.

"I will miss you too, Lasya. I will never forget you."

She smiled, then without another word she turned around and went back into her room. I didn't follow her. It was best left as it was. I turned around and walked back down the corridor, feeling a wrench as I tried to leave Lasya to my memory.

"Pandas and penguins," I said out loud as the sunlight stretched down the hall, filling me with warmth. Lasya's analogies were so innocent and cute but I imagined that after a year of living with her one would find them really irritating.

"I'm going to the market to buy some carrots," I would say.

"Be careful," she would respond, "when the penguin crosses the road..."

"Shut up, Lasya!"

Outside, to my surprise Dzengin was still sitting at the table, waiting patiently and sipping water from a bowl. When he saw me he stood up and nodded, gesturing me to follow him.

He walked away towards the outer entrance of the monastery grounds and when I reached the gardens I turned around for one last look at this fabulous building. It was hard to believe what lay hidden deep inside this innocuous-looking place. It was the secret of all secrets.

23

HORSES AND CARS

On reaching the gate a horrific scene struck me and sent shockwaves through my body. Two horses were tied to a small post and Dzengin was adjusting the saddles. A total fear of these creatures was firmly implanted inside me after an incident many years before and I certainly wasn't keen on getting on one now. "Don't you have another form of transport?" I asked. "A couple of giraffes would be better than this!"

Dzengin shook his head without turning around, like a disapproving father who had spawned a total idiot for his only son. Probably he would blame his wife for the rest of her life for the bad genetic material that created this unfortunate mutation; a son he expected to be tough like himself but instead spent his life clinging to his mother's leg and feared the cold outside.

"I guess you have a problem with horses. Don't worry; these horses are not wild so please, we don't have time to play games."

Dzengin was living up to my original reading of him – a no nonsense man with little time for humour. But despite my nerves, Dzengin's strong character removed any fears. He was the kind of man you listened to and believed wholeheartedly, although you wouldn't want to mess with him. Although he was thin, he had a powerful energy that made me think he had a military background and may even be trained in some useful martial art.

Dzengin helped me get on the horse, which seemed a fairly placid individual, and once in the saddle I was reasonably comfortable. There was a little nervousness after what happened in the last week and if riding a horse had been necessary at the beginning of my journey I would have been more than reluctant to get on, but recently I had seen a man murdered and I had been to Atlantis, so it wasn't going to bother me at this juncture.

"From here," Dzengin informed me, "we will take an alternative route down the hill. We cannot go back to the village so we will head through the valley and into the next town. It should take no more than a few hours. Your horse will follow mine so just sit back and let me take the lead. We will gallop for a part of the way once we reach level ground, so be prepared for that."

"Okay," I responded, holding on to the reins.

Without a word from Dzengin the horses started walking slowly away from the monastery. As I turned around to take one last look at this magnificent place, to my surprise I saw Yeshe and Lasya standing near the edge of the gardens and they both waved at me. Returning the gesture, I then kissed my hand, raising it and sending it to Lasya. It was a wonderful sight and one that will stay in my heart for eternity – I hadn't wanted the last memory of Yeshe and Lasya to be the image of them turning their backs and walking away from me. It was a wonderful end to the most amazing adventure.

As we headed down the hill the monastery disappeared behind, leaving us alone in the stunning Tibetan wilderness. The wild shrubs and bushes intertwined with dense trees and the going was slow and arduous as there was no natural path on this route, but after just half an hour the trees were fewer and before long we were in open country, the short grass allowing free passage down the steep hill. Another half an hour passed and we were on level ground. Dzengin stopped and turned his head, waiting for me to come alongside him.

"We will take a gallop now."

"Okay," I replied, gripping the reins tighter, more in expectation than anticipation. Within moments we were galloping along the open valley with the wind whistling past my ears. I had never imagined what a beautiful experience this could be. It was a sense of freedom that before I had only experienced when riding a motorcycle. But this was different. This was a living creature, allowing me to ride on its back.

We had galloped several miles before we slowed once again to a walk and after a few hundred feet we stopped near a small stream. The area was lined with trees that ran alongside the stream all the way back to the hill behind us and the sound of trickling water delivered a soothing effect on the ears. It was a very peaceful place, like most of Tibet, and all that could be heard was the running water and the singing of birds which fluttered around and chased each other in the branches.

"We'll give the horses a rest and then we will move on," Dzengin said.

After we climbed off, the horses immediately wandered to the water and started to drink the fresh mountain nectar. Dzengin also walked to the edge of the stream. He leaned forwards and cupped his hands, gathering water and drinking it.

"Drink," he said.

"Is it safe?"

He shook his head at me. "It is much safer and cleaner than your tap water. This is the purest water you will ever drink. It is even cleaner than your bottled water. You Westerners make me laugh," he said with disdain.

I felt stupid at my ignorance. Dzengin's scorn had an element of negativity attached to it, almost as if he hated Westerners, but he was absolutely correct – how could water get any better than this? Flowing down the mountainside picking up minerals as it travelled, this was some of the freshest water to be found on the planet. It tasted incredible, even more so than the water from the monastery well. It was extremely cold and fresh.

"It is good, yes?" asked Dzengin.

"It's incredible. So fresh and it even has a taste to it – a natural taste, not like the chlorine in tap water."

Dzengin frowned at the stupidity of my words. I plunged my hands in for another cupful and drank it quickly and the hot sun, which was beating down on my back, was a complete contrast to the cold water filling my body.

We didn't stop long and as soon as the horses finished drinking and their breathing was back to normal we moved on across the valley, following the path of the stream.

It was another hour before we saw the first signs of human life. A lone man was tending his sheep in an open field close to the stream. The man was small and frail and he seemed no taller than the Tibetan mastiff that was near him. He walked slowly and was slightly stooped, an age of mountain life taking its toll on his rickety bones. He didn't even turn to look as we passed him and turned onto a bridge that crossed the stream and on to a dirt track.

Within ten minutes we reached the outer edge of a small town. I had no idea where we were but it was the first time I had seen any signs of modern living since the border town in China.

People wandered slowly and purposefully around the dust-filled streets but the market stalls were devoid of shoppers apart from an old woman buying fruit. As the main street headed into what appeared to be the centre of this quiet town, we took a left turn and headed downward towards a lone house that was set back against some trees. Behind the house was another hill that stretched away at a low angle, and yaks could be seen grazing on the upper levels.

We stopped at the back of the house where there was a large, open area that was fenced off, rather like an animal enclosure, although there was not a creature in sight. The place seemed eerily quiet and a strange emptiness filled the air as we climbed off the horses.

A large shed was set to the far corner of the house, rather like a barn, but again there were no signs of any activity. The large doors were locked shut and the wind created miniature dust devils in the open yard in front of them.

"Are we staying here?" I asked, concerned about the strange and bizarre energy swirling in the wind.

"No. From here we move on. You can freshen up if you need to but we will leave here straight away."

"Then what was the point in stopping here?" I thought to myself.

With that an elderly man appeared from inside the house. Standing at the doorway he nodded to Dzengin and then turned to look at me. He seemed a wise man and his piercing stare made it clear he had a secret or two hidden in his soul. I don't know why but I instinctively knew this old man was connected with Charles. As he stared without saying a word, I could feel my soul stirring within as he fixed me with his gaze. After a few moments he turned around and went back inside and the whole incident seemed like a figment of my imagination.

Dzengin, who was standing by his horse, gave no hint as to what I should do next. Instead he looked at me and shook his head as if I was staring at something that didn't exist. With no clue about what to do, I waited for him to prompt me, the uncomfortable feeling leaving me a little nervous once again.

"There is what you might consider a bathroom at the side of the barn," he said, putting me out of my misery and lifting the gloom.

"Thanks," I replied, heading for the gap between the house and the garage.

"There is what you might consider a bathroom at the side of the barn," I repeated in a stupid girly voice, not knowing what to expect.

I have been in some dreadful places during my travels but this one came top of the 'worst bathroom' list. Accompanying a small covered pit, which had a whole in it for a toilet, was a large tub full of green water. Dead flies and a layer of scum floated on the top and the stench was simply morbid. I did what I had to do and left the putrid place as soon as possible.

As I emerged from the side of the house, Dzengin looked up at me and smiled. It seemed like he had been testing me or simply trying to unsettle me.

"I hope you managed to get a drink? It could be a long time before the next one," he said, pointing up at the sun.

"I am fine, thanks. I had enough at the stream." I smiled back at him. I didn't want him to win the battle of wits that he had suddenly judged necessary to play.

"So, what now?" I asked, trying to change the subject.

"We will leave at the exact time we are supposed to," he replied, and then he walked into the house. He did not invite me to join him. I scanned the area to find signs of anything unusual, but despite the lack of animals on the farm everything seemed as it should be. There was a large tree set back from the house that offered shade, so I headed for that and sat underneath as the heat of the early afternoon became intense and stifling.

Thankful for the relief from the baking sun I rested and waited as the dust swarmed past my eyes forcing me to squint. Picking up small stones and throwing them far towards the edge of the house, I tried to hit a small bucket that was placed near the edge of a set of steps. The steps were out of place. There were three of them, and they rose upwards but led to nothing, just the wooden wall that was part of the side of the house. Were the steps made first and then the door that was supposed to be there never built, or was a door there previously and it was removed later? I could see no evidence that a door had been there before, so I concluded this was one of Dzengin's stupid ideas that never came to fruition.

I never managed to hit the bucket either, despite imagining it was Dzengin's head – I was certain he hated me. The stones were far too small to allow any real direction on the throw, and each time they either fell short or drifted off towards the horses or the farm entrance.

I was trying not to think but the boredom forced me to start dwelling on the past few days. All I wanted was to move onwards but being alone for the first time in a while allowed too many thoughts – Chang's awful death and the dangerous crossing into Tibet; the constant danger of Chinese soldiers; the dome and its bizarre walls; Yeshe's amazing stories and, of course, sweet Lasya and her smile which I already missed so much.

"It certainly has been quite an adventure already, but I still don't know what the hell I am doing here," I said out loud, frustratingly throwing another stone aimlessly as my discouragement gained in abundance. I heard a 'ping' as the stone hit the bucket. I laughed out loud. "Typical!" I shouted, my voice echoing against the walls of the wooden house. For the life of me I couldn't hit that bucket while taking aim, and then without any real direction on my throw the stone struck it cleanly.

I suddenly remembered an incident that occurred while living at home with my mother as a teenager. I was playing a game of darts in my mother's garage, trying to hit the bullseye in the centre of the board. Despite taking at least ten minutes and dozens of attempts to strike the centre of the board I could not do it and my frustration slowly turned into teenage angst. With total infuriation I turned to my side and threw a dart as hard as I could towards the board without looking, and when I turned around the dart had landed smack bang in the middle of the bullseye! How funny life can be at times.

Strangely, it was that memory which suddenly put things into some kind of perspective. I couldn't quite figure it out because the meaning was far too complicated and mysterious, but somehow my mind could 'see' the pattern of events that had occurred – but it wasn't my mind. No, my mind was full of confusion. It was my soul that was seeing things in some kind of spiritual coherence, an order to things that was far too complicated for my animal brain to comprehend. The answer was within reach but at the same time it was too far away for me to attain. It was this time of being alone that allowed my soul – my *subconscious* – to start working things out for itself. After all, this entire journey was of the soul and not of the body. The memory of the dart game came from my soul. I could see it so clearly and yet couldn't find the words to explain it. It seemed my soul had figured something out, found the memory of the dart game in my subconscious, and then sent it to my consciousness like a coded message for me to understand. I thought about it for a moment, trying to see the light in the story.

"I couldn't hit the bullseye when I was looking at it, but I could when I turned my back on it," I said to myself, throwing another stone that landed on the ground.

I couldn't figure it out, my mind was far too confused and the heat didn't help matters, but somehow there was an understanding of sorts on the edge of reason – only when I was away from this place would I understand what had happened, only away from Tibet would the connections and synchronicities be visible.

The horses were standing silently in the heat, not making a sound or any movement. They almost seemed like statues as they stood parallel to one another, their heads in the same position and their eyes watching me with what seemed like a bored curiosity. I wondered what kind of things they were thinking. Surely they can think things the same as we do? They weren't calculating *pi* of course, or any other mathematical or logical problem, but certainly they were thinking something. Maybe they were wondering why I was talking with myself? Or maybe their thoughts were more basic and only concerned with food and water?

I've always thought horses are quite strange creatures in their placid ways. They appear calm and accepting but like most animals they probably have higher thought processes than we give them credit for. Surely animals, like us, are spiritual creatures that are a part of the same grand design of the universe. We, for some reason, measure intelligence by the ability to solve problems, build, and how to be logical and mathematical, but that seems an odd way to me. After all, in many ways we are the most stupid of all creatures with our incessant and self-imploding destruction of the world.

One of the horses started nodding its head up and down almost as if it was agreeing with my thoughts and with that Dzengin reappeared from inside the wooden house which, incidentally, reminded me of an English barn, its lack of windows seemingly an oddity in the heat of Tibet. The horse must have known Dzengin was coming out. Could the horse hear something that I could not, or could it sense things beyond human capabilities?

Dzengin looked at me sitting on the floor under the tree and shook his head again. "It is time to leave," he said. As I got to my feet and walked towards him, he stroked one of the horses gently and spoke to it in Tibetan. The horse closed its eyes for a moment as if it enjoyed being touched and then Dzengin headed towards the garage.

When he opened the doors I couldn't believe my eyes.

"You've got to be kidding me!" I said, laughing.

As sunlight struck the interior the shape of a car appeared under cover of a large white cloth, and with one pull on the corner a perfectly clean and dust-free black beast was unveiled. It looked brand new and its gleaming surface appeared as if it had just been delivered to a show room.

"Get in," he said as he opened the back door, "you'll find everything you need in here. I'll be back in a minute."

With that he shut the door and went back into the house. This new turn of events left me stunned – I had honestly thought we would be horse-riding all the way to India, even over the Himalayas. Now the journey would be comfortable and stylish. What a relief!

The back of the car was very roomy – I could stretch my legs out straight and there was still some distance to the front seats. There were also little doors and handles in various places, and when I pulled one of them open I was astonished to find a small fridge, complete with cold drinks inside. Grabbing a small bottle of orange juice and drinking it in one go, it felt as if I'd suddenly landed on a fruit-filled desert island after days drifting on the open sea.

After a few minutes Dzengin reappeared and I laughed out loud when I saw him – he was wearing an official driver's uniform!

"Don't say a word," he muttered, watching the smirk across my face as he got inside, but I couldn't resist a quick quip.

"You look lovely," I said in a sarcastic tone.

"Shut up," he replied, angrily.

I laughed again. The tables had turned but in all honesty it was an extremely uncomfortable situation, for I was not born to be driven around in luxury as if I was some kind of important person. It was clear, however, this was our escape route from Tibet and by design the windows in the back were blacked out so that no one from the outside could see who was inside.

The frail old man once again reappeared and he took both the horses by the reins and moved them to one side to allow the car to pass, and as we drove out he led the horses towards the empty garage, which I now saw was obviously a stable enclosure. Out of the farm and on to the dirt track, a trail of dust levied in our wake as we drove slowly back up the road towards the centre of the town.

People stared as we passed the main centre and must have wondered what on earth this bright gleaming car was doing in the middle of Tibet. It was so out of place it was ridiculous, like an alien spaceship in the middle of London.

"So, what now?" I asked Dzengin, who had so far been silent about this latest turn of events.

"We will head for a private airport which is situated near the edge of the Himalayas, and then you will fly to Delhi."

"I understand, but what about this car? What's this all about?"

"If we come across any Chinese military they will assume this is a government car and will let us pass any roadblocks or checkpoints without even asking us to stop or requesting to look inside."

"Great plan!" I said, exuberantly, "but surely anyone trying to escape Tibet can use this method?"

"Only those with large amounts of money could do this, but anyone with large amounts of money wouldn't be trying to escape Tibet in the first place. You could say this is a first."

"How long will it be until we reach the airport?"

"It will take many hours. It will probably be late evening when we arrive. I was told to leave at an exact time but I wasn't told what time to arrive. I am guessing our arrival will be expected at the time we get there. I don't question things, I just do them. Maybe you should take this advice too?"

"Maybe," I responded, sensing Dzengin's annoyance at my questions, "but then again, I'm not a eunuch," I added, enjoying the turned tables.

Dzengin stared in the mirror at me with such a strong choleric look I was certain he would have punched me in the face if we were standing outside.

"Are you sure about that?" he quipped, making sure he had the upper hand again.

He was right – I was Charles' eunuch.

Leaving the small town we headed south west through the Tibetan wilderness, up steep hills and down the other side once again to the flat plains. The scenery changed frequently from grassy hills to fields full of crops – wheat, rapeseed, and rye. Each time we reached the peak of another hill I waited excitedly to see what would appear over the other side, but it was always the same contrast of grassy hills and crop-filled plains. The mountains are the perpetual backdrop in Tibet and no matter how far you travel they always seem to be so far away as to be unattainable – a distant, lonely place forbidden to all who attempt to conquer them – the boundary of the whole world. Every time I thought we were getting closer to them they gave the illusion that they were getting farther away. The Himalayas are the mysterious monsters that govern everything in Tibet. Mountains are the gods themselves and it is no wonder that ancient peoples all over the world saw them as such – their dominating and massive presence gives the impression of impenetrable barriers that are untouchable by humans.

Up and over the hills we travelled, along dry dirt tracks that left clouds of dust behind. There are few tarmacked roads in Tibet and no transport infrastructure to speak of, certainly not in the places I saw. Tibet is a country still clinging to its past way of life with a reluctance to move into the future, but China is slowly edging its way west across the country, and in the process diluting and eliminating all traces of a beautiful and peaceful way of life – its hunger for economic growth and vast natural resources has no sympathy for the serenity and tranquillity of a virgin environment like Tibet.

I felt myself slowly drifting to sleep as the smooth running of the car put me into a trance state – even the rough roads didn't stop the black beast from maintaining a comfortable ride. When I awoke the sun had already dipped behind the western hills but the wilderness was filled with a strange purple glow. The Himalayas seemed as far away as ever, the massive peaks disappearing into the clouds. Noticing me stirring in the back, Dzengin peered into the mirror.

"We are not too far now, maybe an hour more."

"We seem to be a long way from the mountains," I responded.

"They are not too far but the airport is quite a distance from them."

"I wasn't aware they had airports around here."

I wasn't sure why I said that since I know very little about this great country.

"It's not an international airport. I already told you it is a private airport."

Surely Dzengin was as confused as I was when it came to Charles' choice of individual for this adventure, but equally I had no idea how much he knew about all of this. He must have thought that a military man would be more suited to this task, whatever it was. To be honest, I often thought this myself but it seemed it was not necessary to employ a person with survival skills of a murderous nature. Dzengin certainly had a lack of respect for me, or maybe he was like this with everyone.

Slowly we descended the hills and reached the last flat plains before the edge of the Himalayas rose up into the sky. Only now did it appear that we were close to them. The altitude of the journey had given the illusion the mountains were unreachable but as we traversed onto low ground the monsters of the Asian world dominated everything around. Finally they showed their true nature – the largest and highest peaks in the world. I was in total awe of them. I had travelled over the huge peaks of the Andes in South America and had been blown away by the stunning vistas offered – the most beautiful I have ever witnessed – but the Himalayas are the real monoliths of our planet.

We arrived at the airport as the long, dark night reached out and left Tibet in a silent blackness. It didn't look like an airport. In fact, it seemed like just another large farm with a strip of concrete running alongside and only a few dim lights emanating from the homestead gave the impression there were any people around. Moonlight reflected on the runway which stretched south into the darkness like a guiding arm pointing to the mountains but for some reason the runway had a sinister aura around it.

"Where are we exactly?" I asked Dzengin.

"We are near the border of Bhutan."

Surprised by this answer I suddenly realised Tibet was a far bigger country than I'd imagined.

"I thought we were farther west than that, nearer Nepal."

"It would take several more hours to get to the Nepalese Himalayas. You entered Tibet from the east, headed north-west to the monastery, and now we have travelled south-west to get here."

"So, how long will the flight be to Delhi?"

"About two hours."

As we drove into the farmstead a strange feeling welled up within and I felt shivers down my spine as if we were in a haunted house. The menacing aura of this place left me wondering about its history. There was only one reason why this place could be here and why the Chinese would allow it to exist at all – it must be owned by the Chinese government, or by some rich Chinese businessman who had connections all the way to Beijing. No Tibetan would be allowed an airport with free access to the outside world, and no Tibetan would be rich enough to own it. How ironic, I thought, that my escape would be provided by the Chinese – right under their noses.

24

A SYNCHRONICITY TOO FAR

We pulled up alongside the farmstead and were greeted by a middle-aged man who, much to my surprise, was of European origin. It was the first 'familiar' face I had seen since the European tourists in China and I felt a sense of homeliness at being introduced to François.

François was from Paris and spoke fluent English. He had a wrinkled face which gave the impression he was much older than his personality, a large, thin straight nose and a powerful stare with tired eyes. He had thin lips and a short beard that had been carefully and professionally trimmed close to his face. He escorted me inside while Dzengin parked the car.

"Have a seat," he said, "there's plenty of space. We will eat soon."

The big open room had four large leather sofas that surrounded an expensive wooden table and pictures of small jet planes hung on the walls. There were several photos of people in suits which led me to the conclusion that this was a place used for important meetings; perhaps this airport was used by the Chinese elite for engagements on the Indian sub-continent, but why they would fly from the middle of nowhere was a mystery. François disappeared into another room and Dzengin followed.

Left alone, something caught my eye and I was left stunned, for on the wall was a picture of two men shaking hands, but these were not just any two men – it was Charles himself, and I was shocked to find that I recognised the other man as someone I had known back home. To say I was fearful was an understatement. In fact it left me so scared I wanted to run out the door.

Peter Froude had lived in squalor and spent his life as a loner. His house was a total mess – his bathroom ceiling had collapsed into his bath and was never repaired, which led to some obvious conclusions. The kitchen was rarely cleaned and the whole place was full of dust. Everyone who knew Peter had the impression he was a man living in poverty in retirement who couldn't look after himself properly. However, when he passed away it was discovered he had a large amount of money in his bank account, his house was fully paid for and there was no family. He left all his property and money to a cat's charity and then the questions arose about how he came into possession of such wealth. Peter had been a very gentle man and never had a bad word to say about anyone, but how was it possible that a man who seemed to be living in such squalor was connected with Charles?

My personal connection with Peter came about because he was a spiritual medium. I had been introduced to him by a friend and had attended weekly meetings, infrequently, over a three-year period before his death. Peter would help anyone in need of spiritual guidance but he never let on about his wealth. His whole philosophy was that spiritual practices are everything and material things are nothing – offering your heart and soul is far more important that helping someone materially. Give someone money and they will thank you but give someone your heart and that kindness will be remembered. Peter never charged for his services – not that he needed to, as it turned out – and he was available twenty-four hours a day for those requiring spiritual guidance, even though at times it was obvious he was uncomfortable with certain visitors. He was a true Christ-like character, always offering his help to anyone who needed it.

Peter had obviously kept certain things a complete secret but now they were becoming apparent. For a start he had obviously known Charles, but to what extent had he been involved in this game? What could Charles possibly gain from someone who channelled spiritual information when he was already in possession of such knowledge on paper? Channelled messages were considered, by the scientific community at least, a load of nonsense, so what use was Peter to a man who already appeared to know everything?

However, Peter had been in possession of a great amount of knowledge regarding many secrets of the past and during sessions that I attended he had also accurately predicted things that came true. He had been a man of total mystery during his life but after he had passed away he became an enigma of much greater proportions. Was it possible that Peter's wealth had come from spiritual guidance given to Charles? Was it possible that these messages were the reason for the knowledge Charles held? Both these scenarios seemed unlikely, but nonetheless there was a connection that was making me disorientated.

Just as I was standing up to take a closer look at the picture, Dzengin and François reappeared. Pretending I was adjusting my position and taking off my jumper in an effort to look as innocent as possible, a part of me wanted to ask who these two men were but I held back and played safe. A million questions went through my mind and with great difficulty I managed to stay calm. Thankfully François and Dzengin didn't notice my sudden mood change.

"Did you pass any roadblocks en-route?" François asked Dzengin.

"No. I didn't see any military or any road block at all. We had a free pass all the way."

"That is surprising."

"Yes. It was. Maybe they are concentrating in other areas since it is difficult to cross the border this far south."

"That is true, but they know that many people do take this route along the southern edge, especially west towards India."

I was becoming visibly shaken and had to excuse myself and get to a bathroom, needing a moment alone and time to think. Locking the door, I leaned heavily on the sink. What the hell was going on? How did Peter know Charles and what relationship did they have? What was so important about Peter that there was a picture of him and Charles together hanging on the wall? What was significant about the meeting in which the picture was taken? Was it possible that during my meetings with Peter I had been groomed by him for this journey? Peter was such an ordinary man with a basic lifestyle and he spent all his time indoors. How was all this even possible? Deciding to get a closer look at the picture to discover how long ago it was taken, I then realised something – If I had my picture taken with Charles during this expedition and then one of my friends came across it later in the same circumstances, they would be thinking the same as me – that I was just an ordinary person and what was I doing in a picture with Charles? Maybe Peter had been chosen before me to undertake another task given by Charles. Maybe this explained his confusing wealth. But if Peter had undertaken a task similar to mine then why was I chosen for this one? If I was chosen because of specific skills, then it was too much of a coincidence that Peter would have been chosen for another task since we knew each other. If Charles was choosing people because of certain skills the chances of finding two random people who actually knew each other would be almost impossible.

My only conclusion was that Peter and Charles did have some connection that meant they both knew about my journey. It was something that left a very uncomfortable feeling but somehow I had to find the link. I could accept many confusing things about this journey, forget the coincidences, not ask questions and move on but this situation required answers and I was going to find out one way or another. Since Peter also lived in Bournemouth there was no doubt that my involvement in this 'game' had to have originated with him, either directly or indirectly. Another 'coincidence' was that the café where I first met Charles was only a few hundred yards from Peter's house.

Knowing Charles, nothing was left to chance. He must have known that I would see that picture. That is why it was placed on the wall in the first place. Of this there was no doubt. These people were thorough and took no chances; this was not a silly mistake. This strange game I was playing was more than bizarre – nothing was as it seemed.

As I returned to the main room, François and Dzengin were engaged in a conversation about jet engines, a boring dialogue that I certainly wasn't going to enter into. I took the opportunity to wander around the room and look at the pictures in sequence, naturally starting at a different picture than the one I really wanted to look at, casually meandering around the walls in the process.

The picture of Peter and Charles had been taken quite a few years ago. Peter looked to be in his early fifties and he had died quite recently at the age of sixty-six. It must have been taken at least ten years before I even met him, which created yet another mystery that couldn't be understood – if Peter really had been involved, it was for a long time. My being here could not be a coincidence.

Synchronicity – the phenomenon of events having a connection outside the normal laws of physics – is very real. Scientists would call it 'coincidence' but synchronicity is growing in recognition as a part of our reality and such events appear to happen more while travelling. When we are in a mundane, repeatable, everyday existence we do not recognise them, or they do not happen as often, but when travelling they seem frequent and this makes people wonder if there is a bigger picture to reality than we realise.

One synchronicity that occurred to me actually involved Peter Froude. I had travelled to Russia for five weeks in November 2009, just six months before this adventure started and less than two months before Peter's death. My electric toothbrush had a European two-pronged plug so I assumed it would fit into a Russian socket since they have the same system. But it turned out that Russian sockets are slightly wider than in Europe and my toothbrush plug didn't fit. After about a week the toothbrush battery was almost depleted and it was soon to be used in the old way of brushing one's teeth – manually.

Each day I visited the same café that was situated below the hotel in Saint Petersburg, and I always sat at the same table. Peter, who was always sending emails about strange phenomena and unusual events, sent an email that was talking about synchronicity. He wrote:

The famous British actor, Anthony Hopkins, was starring in a 1974 film called 'The Girl from Petrovka', written by George Feifer. Wishing to read the novel, Hopkins tried a number of bookshops in London but he found no copy. While waiting in a London station to catch a train home, he happened to notice a discarded book on a bench. Looking closer he discovered the very book that he was looking for.

Two years later Hopkins and Feifer met. The author mentioned to Hopkins that he didn't have a copy of his own book because he had loaned the very last copy to a friend who had lost it. Hopkins then discovered that he had found that lost book – the copy he discovered on the bench had Feifer's own notes written in the cover!

Is this a coincidence or synchronicity?

I responded to Peter's email, stressing that synchronicity was something I had become very familiar with during my travels, and I gave an example.

The following day, sitting in my normal seat in the café I opened my laptop to find another email from Peter regarding synchronicity:

You have probably have come across this synchronicity before regarding the assassinations of two Presidents – Lincoln and Kennedy. People look at it and can find no explanation. Two events coming together can make a person feel that life could be ordained by an invisible storyteller:

Lincoln became President in 1860 and to congress in 1846; Kennedy became President in 1960 and to congress in 1946.

Both Lincoln and Kennedy were shot on a Friday; both had their wives with them; both were shot in the back; both were succeeded by 'Johnson'.

Andrew Johnson had been a senator and Lyndon Johnson had been a senator.

Andrew Johnson was born in 1808 and Lyndon Johnson was born in 1908.

Lincoln died in the Ford Theatre and Kennedy died in a Ford Lincoln Continental.

Lincoln's secretary was called 'Johnson' and Kennedy's secretary was called 'Lincoln'.

Lincoln's killer, John Wilkes Booth was born in 1839. Lee Harvey Oswald, Kennedy's killer, was born in 1939.

Both Mrs Lincoln and Mrs Kennedy lost a child while in the White House.

Both the killers had 15 letters in their names.

Both killers predicted their deaths before coming to trial and both were killed before coming to trial.

Again responding to Peter, on the third day I returned to the café, but to my annoyance the table was taken by someone else so I had to find another place. I scanned around the room until I found the only table I was prepared to sit – against the wall where prying eyes could not see my writing or my private emails. I could sit comfortably by the window knowing no one could look over my shoulder.

Opening my email there was a third, and last, email from Peter regarding the subject of synchronicity. It read:

You should have come across this synchronicity before, but the question has never been answered – why did a work of fiction so accurately correspond with an event twelve years later? In 1898 J Morgan Robertson wrote a book called 'Futility', which was about a great ship called the 'Titan'. After that literary effort there was built in Belfast the White Star 'Titanic', which was owned by the super-rich J P Morgan.

Both ships were uncannily the same:

The Titan had 40,000hp and the Titanic 50,000hp. The Titan could carry 3,000 people and was 800 feet long; The Titanic had a compliment of 3,360 people and was 882 feet long. The Titan had 24 lifeboats and weighed 45,000 tonnes; the Titanic had 20 lifeboats and weighed 66,000 tonnes.

Both ships had double hulls, three props and two masts. Both ships were on their Maiden Voyage and had a top speed of 25 knots; both hit icebergs; both sunk in the month of April. Both ships were the largest afloat, the most luxurious, both were unsinkable and both had a rich US owner.

Two Important Questions:

Did the author of 'Futility' actually see psychically fourteen years into the future to 1912? If not, did J Morgan Robertson unwittingly create this future by writing the book?

Anyway the story does not end there because William Stead was a well-known Victorian spiritualist who wrote a story in 'Review of Reviews', a UK magazine that he had founded. The story was called 'From the Old World to the New' and was printed in 1891. It was about the iceberg danger to North Atlantic shipping and a British family travelling from England to Chicago to start a new life. At the time they were unfortunately travelling in a massive liner called 'The Majestic'.

Twenty one years later the Titanic sunk in April 1912, and both the Titanic and the Majestic were commanded by a Captain Smith. The trouble was that William Stead was actually a passenger on the Titanic and he died a horrible death in those ice cold waters.

What were his last thoughts as the unsinkable sunk?

As the irony of the last of Peter's synchronicity emails struck home I was about to press the 'reply' button when my laptop sent a warning – *'battery 10%, plug in or find another power source'*.

Reaching into the laptop bag and pulling out the charger I turned around to the socket behind me and as I stretched down something caught my eye. I knew exactly what it was as soon as I saw it – the extension socket required for my toothbrush!

Someone had obviously left it there by accident but the irony was comical and the synchronicity astonishing. Not just the timing of the event since Peter had started a discussion about synchronicity and I was about to press 'reply' on the email with a response on the very subject, but also my change of table seemed an event that was predetermined. On top of this the actual synchronicity itself – the plug required to charge my toothbrush sitting in the wall waiting for me.

The synchronicity of the extension plug was one miracle but then we have to look at the other aspects. Was Peter's sudden discussion about synchronicity actually creating the future regarding the extension socket? Were the thoughts created around the synchronicity stories that Peter was sending actually going out into the universe, just as Yeshe had described, and returning as another synchronicity? The mind boggles at the complications and possibilities.

Continuing to look at all the pictures around the room, most of which were uninteresting, I returned to the seat as François was asking Dzengin questions about our journey from the monastery. Then he set about explaining what was going to happen next.

"We're going to fly to Delhi within the next half hour," he said, "and it will take about two hours to get there. Once we arrive you will transfer to a commercial airliner and head off to Mexico but be warned, it is a twenty-two hour flight."

"Ouch!" I said, not at all looking forward to it.

"You will fly into Chicago and change planes before you move on to Cancún, in the Yucatan peninsula. You will be flying first class so it will be comfortable and I suggest you get as much sleep as you can – you'll need it. When you board the plane waiting outside you will find a folder on the seat. You are instructed to read the information inside it."

"Great!" I whispered to myself, remembering the ludicrous contents of the folder in the hotel back in Bournemouth.

"Pardon?" François asked.

"Oh, nothing, don't worry, continue."

Dzengin looked at me and shook his head with his usual displeasure.

"There is nothing to continue with, that's it. Say *'au revoir'* to your new friend, we need to board the plane now."

François stood up and disappeared through the door at the back of the room.

"Well, it's been a pleasure, kind of," I said to Dzengin.

It was the only way I could really talk with him. He seemed a fairly cold-hearted man and emotional communication was not the way to get his attention. Only sarcastic or even abusive talk would get a reaction. If I told him I hated him and wished him dead he would respond but if my words contained a hint of empathy he seemed to consider me a weak individual and would ignore me. Now I understood his behaviour back at the farm where we left the horses behind but just as I was getting to understand him, it was time to say goodbye.

"Likewise," he said. "By the way – you are in for a rough ride when you get to Mexico. I suggest you prepare yourself."

"What do you mean by 'a rough ride'?"

He smiled and snorted a little. "Well, it all depends on you. It could be the adventure of your life or it could be your worst nightmare. It all depends on how you'll react to it. Either way it'll make a man out of you."

And that was exactly Dzengin's opinion of me – that I was much less a man than he was. Aware of his attempts to unnerve me at every opportunity, I took his words with a pinch of salt, but at the same time what he was telling me was the truth – this was going to be something on a level much worse than the incident with Chang. I could feel it inside, growing and eating me from within and I could only wonder what perils lay ahead in the stifling heat of the dangerous jungles of Mexico.

25

AIR PRESSURE, HEAT AND DELHI

Dzengin escorted me to the back of the farmhouse and out into the open. The small jet was sitting on the runway, its engines running with a high pitched squealing that pierced my ears like a screaming cat. A small set of steps led to the open door and for a moment I stopped, wondering if I should climb them and accept the next part of the journey. There were many moments like this, questioning what I was doing with my life and where it was going – but what real choice did I have?

Dzengin nodded towards the plane, gesturing for me to climb the stairs and once again into the unknown.

"Take care," I said, "and thanks for everything."

I held out my hand. Dzengin nodded and without words he shook my hand and then took a step back as he waited for me to climb aboard.

Entering the small jet I was greeted by another Frenchman. "Hello Stephen. My name is Louis. Your seat is over there, please make yourself comfortable."

The place looked more like a hotel than a plane, its leather reclining seats, wallpapered walls and rectangular meeting table making it appear more like the Marriot than a machine that flew through the air.

"I am here to service your needs," he continued. "If you require anything just press the red button on the seat and I will come quickly. I will be in the cockpit with François and if you wish to speak with him directly pick up the phone and this will connect you. Have a nice journey."

With that he disappeared. He must have been instructed to leave me alone, the folder lying next to me was to be read in peace, but first I picked up the phone to speak to François.

"What is it, Steve?"

"Why are we taking a private jet for a two hour journey and then a normal commercial airliner for the rest of it? It doesn't make sense."

"I am sorry, I cannot answer your question because I do not know the answer, but I do know it is not so easy to fly into Mexico in a private jet. Any private jet will be searched on arrival, regardless of who is inside, because it may be loaded with drugs. Only the President could get in without a search."

"But I thought strings were being pulled?"

"Strings are being stretched and broken as far as I know but Mexico is a different prospect. It is best to go there unnoticed. You don't want to raise suspicions over there. I am under the impression that you are going there for something very serious. Sit tight, we are leaving now."

The phone went dead and the engines increased their screeching to maximum. As I took the folder from the seat next to me, François' French accent rang through my head like an alarm bell.

As the plane pitched at an angle gaining altitude my ears popped and the pressure increased, but it was a comfortable flight and much better than a commercial airliner. Not knowing what to expect, I took a deep breath and opened the green folder.

Congratulations on completing the first stage of your adventure.

There was a clear sense of sarcasm in this phrase, like Charles was goading me into the next step, as if there was something good done by my adventure in Tibet. This wasn't the time to take stock of what had happened but, now I was leaving I couldn't help but analyse what had happened in the last week – Chang's horrible death, Yeshe and his humour, and the lovely Lasya all filled my heart with equal amounts of sadness and joy, but it was the bizarre and wonderful dome that was most prominent in my mind. It was starting to have an effect on me, like it had gone right into my soul and touched me, and it was a welcome relief from the thought which had previously been at the forefront of my memories – Chang. Was I finally recovering from that awful incident?

It is now necessary for you to renew your knowledge of the Maya Calendar. You will need to have it fresh in your mind when you reach your destination.

Charles had asked about my knowledge of the Maya Calendar and whilst I had studied it and was familiar with it, he was right in saying that if it was required in Mexico I would need a refresher course. It had been a couple of years since I had even looked at it.

Hold on to your hat, the rug is about to be pulled from underneath you.

There were no more words.

"Great," I said out loud, "thanks for that."

It wasn't the kind of news I wanted to be hearing right now. I just wanted to forget everything and had thought that the next twenty-four hours would be an opportunity to relax and clear my cluttered and confused mind, but once again a fear was instilled into my being. What was going to happen in Mexico? Why would the proverbial rug be pulled from underneath me? Turning the page, I saw texts regarding the Maya Calendar but I decided that this two hour flight to Delhi could be used for better purposes, like relaxing and closing my eyes. The Maya Calendar could wait until the long haul to Mexico. I didn't want to think about this anymore. I wanted to forget everything. Despite the long flight that awaited me there was little time to prepare myself for what was to come and like the air around the plane, the pressure was building inside my mind like a balloon that was about to burst. And now, suddenly, I felt something stir within – a certainty that what was going to happen in Mexico was something truly extraordinary.

I closed my eyes and thought about Delhi – the capital of the great country that is India. Or should I say New Delhi. Nothing new about it, though. It is a stiflingly hot city even at night, with its massive population of dark-skinned people. The Taj Mahal is just a short distance south. Well, a short distance in Indian terms. In English terms it is half way across the country, but the 128 miles from Delhi to the Taj Mahal means it is a local tourist attraction for Delhiwalas.

Delhi is a place to visit for travellers – after all it is the Capital – but it's so hot most people only stay for a day or two. And then there is the smell, which is much worse than Mumbai. At least Mumbai has a mixed smell of incense and spices on top of the pollution, and the surrounding sea dispels the choking air, but in Delhi many places just smell of stale urine, the heat making the stench unbearable in the poorest areas. But all of this is doing Delhi a disservice. It is an amazing city with an incredible history.

India is the most diverse country on the planet, with twenty-four languages exclusive to the country, from Hindi and Urdu to Tamil and Malayalam. Although mother languages run into the hundreds, the two main official languages are Hindi and English. Indians who speak different native languages often find it easier to communicate with each other in English. This is one example of the diversity of this huge country of over a billion people, and other examples are the food and historical origins, whose wide ranges stretch to all four corners, from the cold Himalayas in the north, to the hot Southern peninsula.

I love everything about India – although it's not for the faint-hearted – the food, the people, the music, the films, the Hindu religion and the different languages that make up this beautiful country. The Hindi language is the most beautiful – it has a sound that is like music to the ears.

Long ago giving up on the films of Hollywood and Europe, sick of the violence and repeated storylines that bored me, I turned to Indian cinema some years previously. Hindi films have a sense of innocence and purity – the way films should be made. Not all of them, of course, but mostly. Nowadays our Western films tend to be too serious and they glorify violence and horror far too much, the filmmakers producing them as realistically as possible. What are they doing to people's minds? Before, I thought I was immune to them, watching films frequently and never feeling that they affected me, but after turning to Indian cinema my mind changed and my very thoughts purified a little. Once, after a year or so, I again watched a Hollywood film and the violence left me rattled, wired and nervous – it was only after a long break from these films did the impact become apparent.

There is an issue with those who see truth in something because 'it was on the TV'. Television is pure propaganda, like the daily news, and it is clear to me that people's minds are being led in a direction that is not a positive one for the soul. After all, it's not called *programming* for nothing. Advertising on television also makes me wired and angry. And it's true what they say – ask a child to name ten birds or trees from the garden and they won't have a clue, but ask them to identify symbols from giant corporations who advertise often on television and they will score ten out of ten. Now, is it me, or is that fundamentally wrong? What kind of society are we really creating for our children? Why are our children being programmed into a corporate, materialistic environment?

I cleared my mind of thoughts of India and television as we touched down at the airport and taxied to a hangar set at the end of one of the runways. Louis appeared.

"I hope you had a comfortable flight?" he asked.

"Yes, fine, thank you."

"Can I have your passport for a moment, please?"

Much to my amusement, Louis placed my passport on the table and stuck an Indian tourist visa into an open page and then stamped it. Then he turned to the Chinese visa page and stamped that too with a different stamp.

"Just wait a moment for that to dry," he said, passing the open passport back to me.

Looking at both pages there was an exit stamp on the Chinese visa dated three days before and the Indian visa, complete with my photo, had an entry stamp for the same day.

"Pretty cool, huh?" he said.

"Just three days visiting as a tourist? And the visa photo is the same as in my passport, which is about eight years old!"

"They don't care. This is India! You could walk in without a visa and if you pass the correct amount of money over the counter they'll most likely let you through, but we don't want to try that, just in case."

After the engines had stopped François appeared.

"A car is waiting outside. It will take you and your backpack to the main terminal. From there you will go into the main airport lounge as if you are a normal tourist. Your tickets are in the car and they will tell you which gate you need. Your flight is leaving soon so there will be no waiting around. Unfortunately, you cannot bypass security – from here everything is normal so take your mind out of the luxury transport you have enjoyed recently and return to the state of mind that you are a lone traveller, at least for half an hour. Once inside the aircraft, however, you will feel luxury again. Your friend has bought the entire first class area just for you, so you will be alone and with plenty of time to prepare yourself. Good luck."

François held out his arm and as we shook hands Louis opened the door, the heat of New Delhi bursting in like an open oven. Even though it was the middle of the night it must have been about thirty degrees with the humidity of a jungle.

"Holy crap!" I said, as the heat hit me.

"Yeah, it's a bit hot here," said Louis.

I picked up the folder and headed for the door. The car was waiting below, this time a standard yellow Indian taxi. Inside, the smell was like a musty room and in the front a picture of Lord Krishna hung from the rear view mirror. A garland of flowers stretched across the dashboard but they did little to extinguish the smell of Delhi which had penetrated every hinge and bolt. We sped off towards a side entrance that was manned by security, back onto the main road and through dense traffic towards the main terminal.

There was no conversation en route – not all Indians speak English – and on reaching the terminal the driver took my backpack from the boot and set it on the ground. Then he returned to his car and drove off. I took a deep breath. I hate airports and the long, boring queues, bag scanners and passport checks.

After the last week of almost serene tranquillity India was not the place to become accustomed to large numbers of people. Tibet and India couldn't be further apart when it comes to cultural differences, despite the historical connection between them and their shared border.

After chaotic formalities, by the time I reached the gate it was less than five minutes before all first class passengers were called up. I was slightly embarrassed as everyone gathered around the desk but only I was allowed through. In fact, it turned out that my accommodation wasn't first class at all. I was escorted to the plane by a stunning Hindi woman, wandering along the temporary walkway that shook underneath my feet, and I was amazed to be shown into an area that was set below the main cabin in an isolated part of the plane. It appeared to be a private area which contained only four reclining leather chairs, with luxurious surroundings and everything I could wish for. It seemed a secret little place, with just two small windows on the left from my forward seating position, and on the right were cupboards. Behind was an area large enough to walk around and stretch the legs. I had all this privacy to myself. Wonderful! Maybe this wasn't going to be such a bad flight after all.

26

OUT OF THE OVEN AND INTO THE CASSEROLE

Anjali introduced herself and told me how the room functioned and where to find things. The best part was a seat at the back of the room that could be used as a bed once it was unfastened from the wall. There was even a small shower room in the corner. Anjali told me to press the button on the edge of my seat if anything was required and it seemed she was instructed to otherwise leave me alone, for as soon as she had given me the lowdown she disappeared again through a small door in the corner of the room.

It was an hour into the flight before I pressed the button. Anjali appeared and asked what I required with a smile that would melt even the most hardened of men, but it wasn't food or drink I wanted – I needed female company. To deflect my intentions I ordered a coffee and only on her return did I politely request she sit in the seat facing me. I was feeling very alone, the last few days had left my mind in search of answers that were unattainable and I felt isolated and somewhat deserted in this small secret compartment. There was more than a reluctance to be on my own – something was stirring within me that commanded attention, but not knowing what this bizarre feeling was, I chose avoidance. I missed Lasya, I concluded. At least, that was the fabricated reason I gave myself to escape it.

Anjali seemed a little bemused but happy enough to sit down and relax.

"Do you like Hindi films?" I asked her. It may have seemed a silly question, but one is always surprised at the amount of Indians who don't like their films – it's very much a 'deep love' or 'absolute hate' relationship.

Anjali looked at me first with a confused look and then that big smile crossed her face. "Yes, I love films, when I get the chance to watch them. I am always working long hours. Do you like Hindi films?" she asked with an expectant stare.

"Yes, I love them. I only watch Hindi films these days." She seemed quite surprised by that answer.

She was so beautiful, her long black hair tied up at the back, and her full lips seemed to stretch from ear to ear when she smiled, showing her perfect white teeth. She had a small nose, high cheek bones, mid-brown skin and deep but sad-looking dark brown eyes. Her smart red uniform, which clung to her body showing her curvy figure, made her all the more attractive. The icing on the cake was the small red bindi between her eyes, perfectly symmetrical between her eyebrows.

It was quite a ridiculous conversation but I wanted to break the ice and make some kind of connection with her. We had a long conversation about Hindi films and music and all the while I was watching her closely, as her eyes darted up and down occasionally. It wasn't really necessary to try and make a connection with Anjali – the chemistry was there from the start, an instant attraction that was apparently mutual.

Brown eyes can often hide someone's emotions more than blue or green, but I could clearly see that Anjali was hiding a lot of emotional pain which was so vivid that it was practically advertised on her forehead. It didn't seem like she'd had an unhappy childhood – she was far too cheerful and bubbly for that. For sure, her childhood was a wonderful time with a lot of love from her parents. But there was something else, something that she was trying hard to forget, and it seemed the pain in her soul could not be hidden by her eyes or her smiling face. Something had hurt this beautiful woman and I sensed her inner sadness – a sadness which had caused her a lot of trauma in the not-too-distant past.

My perception of Anjali's inner turmoil was heightened for some reason. Perhaps the experience in Tibet had left my soul more able to reach out to other people when we came into close contact, or maybe it was some kind of emotional connection that before was only glimpsed in others by fleeting intuitions. Or maybe there was just a connection with Anjali. Whatever the reason, the openness that existed between us was apparent from the first moment and, like Yeshe had said, sometimes you meet people and you instantly make a connection with that person...

"You pronounce Hindi so well," she said. "Do you speak the language?"

"No, I don't speak it, but I do know a little. It's amazing what you can pick up from watching the films. I know a few phrases, enough to get by in India, I think."

I had dropped myself in a hole with that phrase, because it led to the obvious next line of enquiry which I was totally unprepared for.

"So, what were you doing in Delhi?"

I couldn't lie to this beauty and then dig a deeper hole by saying how much I liked Delhi and which places I'd visited, after all we would be spending an entire rotation of the earth's sphere in close proximity, so the question required a diversion and a subject change.

"Oh, I was just there on a connecting flight, I didn't stop over."

Anjali looked at me with a confused face, as if she tried to work out which connecting flight had brought me here and found none. Or maybe she was thinking it was strange that I had such an interest in India but wasn't stopping even for a day. She just smiled and waited for my next move.

"I have just been to China but I needed to get to the United States quickly so I didn't have time to stop, unfortunately."

She seemed adequately satisfied with my answer, not that I needed to be concerned with what she thought about me. It seemed a little odd that I should be concerned, but I have always disliked lying, even to a complete stranger and for my own benefit. It also occurred to me that Charles would have also checked or even chosen the person to be the flight attendant during this trip, so she probably knew more than I thought she did. After all, everyone else so far appeared to have been strategically placed along the route, all having a slice of knowledge about something small which at the same time didn't allow me, or even them, to see the whole.

"Cogs in a wheel," I thought, as the design of the Maya calendar flashed before my eyes.

"Where do you live?" I asked, changing the subject and trying to get the clicking mechanism out of my mind.

"Oh, I live in Bengaluru," she said, her face lighting up as if comfortably startled by my interest.

"Ah. Bangalore," I said, throwing up my peacock feathers.

"You really do know Hindi!" she smiled.

I passed the test. Good.

"I live with my parents," she continued. "As I am travelling all the time I don't need so much of my own space when I go home and my mother is ill so the extra help is always welcome. We have a big house and my brother is already a successful businessman with his own large apartment in Mumbai, so I will inherit the family home. For that reason there is no need for me to buy another property."

"Oh, that's nice. It's good to know your future security is already assured."

"Yes, it is, but sometimes I feel there are not many challenges to be had in life if everything is so simple. I consider myself fortunate but sometimes I want things to be a little more difficult."

"I understand exactly what you mean. When life is not a struggle you don't feel *alive*."

With that comment we seemed to strike a deeper connection. There was something interesting about Anjali but I couldn't put my finger on what it was. Ignoring her obvious beauty, I tried to look within her to see what else was going on inside her soul besides the pain of a possible lost relative. Anjali's openness and comments about her private life were not intended as a statement of wealth. She just wanted to offer a reason why a Hindi woman in such a well-paid job still lived at home, but the closeness of Indian families is well known, and it was also clear the main reason for her still being there was that she was unmarried. At around thirty years old it was unusual for a Hindi woman to be unmarried, and I wondered if she had even considered it at all since she appeared to be jetting all over the world. Would she hang up her uniform at any time and get married, or was her statement about inheriting the family home an unconscious way of telling me she had no intention of doing so? We locked eyes and stared for a moment. I suddenly felt Charles *had* placed this woman near me for some reason, rather like Lasya, but I was also aware that I needed to end our conversation and get on with reading the folder. There were many more hours to go and it seemed the correct juncture to allow our personal conversation to be left until later.

"So, what's on the menu?" I asked.

Anjali jumped slightly as if she had been in a trance, her gaze firmly fixed on the carpet.

"Oh, here is the menu," she said, passing me a laminated card. "Just press the button when you have chosen something and I will come back straight away."

With that, she began to walk towards the door.

"Uh, Anjali," I said, "this might seem a strange question, but what is the date today?"

Anjali was startled and she stuttered slightly. "It's... um... the night of Friday the twenty-first of May, almost Saturday the twenty-second."

"Thank you."

She stood still for a moment and I could almost see her thoughts – 'Is this guy crazy, or what? How can someone who's just got on a flight not know what the date is?' Then she turned and walked away, closing the door behind her. I looked at the menu. I wasn't hungry. I looked out of the window and there was nothing to be seen except blackness.

Friday the twenty-first of May. I had left England on the eighth, almost two weeks previously. Chang and I had entered Tibet under a new moon and today, exactly a week later, it was now a half moon, or 'first quarter' to give its scientific name. Right now there was no telling if there was any significance to that. Certainly Chang and I had crossed the border at a specific lunar time that had been previously planned, so making sure I kept an account of the moon cycles seemed important.

I thought of Lasya once again and then of Anjali. They couldn't be more different if they had tried – one a nomadic Buddhist with spiritual knowledge, and the other a city girl living the commercial dream – but the more their differences were compared, the more similar they seemed. Amusing myself by swapping their roles – Anjali out in the mountains of Tibet and Lasya dressed in a red airline uniform – I couldn't come to any conclusions about how either of them would cope. That one could stew inside me until later.

And now Anjali was stuck in my head like a repetitive song. There was something going on inside her that I couldn't quite understand – a secret of some kind that she was fighting to keep down but which was bursting at the seams trying to get out.

Letting out a deep sigh and reaching for the green folder, It was time to re-familiarise myself with the Maya calendar.

I pressed the button and Anjali immediately came into the room, almost as if she was standing behind the door.

"Can I just have a black coffee, please?" The caffeine boost was needed to keep me alert for the next few hours.

"Yes sir, I will get it right away. Do you want sugar?"

"Yes, please. Anjali, please call me Steve. I am very uncomfortable with formalities. I am no one important."

"Yes, of course, Steve." She smiled and turned away.

Contained in the folder was not a book on the Maya Calendar but a hundred or so pages of typed manuscript. There was no evidence of any reference to where this manuscript came from, or from which source it was copied, but there was something very odd about this version. My knowledge of the calendar quickly returned once I started reading the text but there were discrepancies that I couldn't explain.

Maya Calendars are basic as individual units. However, combined together they create a complex series of interlocking calendars spanning great periods of time.

The first thing to comprehend in order to understand these calendars is all to do with Maya consciousness, or the way they calculated time. The Maya did not count using a base ten system as we do. Instead, they used a base twenty system.

One of the simplest means of understanding the Maya system is achieved by calculating time. For example, we have an almost crude modern way of calculating the year – the Gregorian calendar. We simply divide the 365.24-day solar year into twelve months, adding a day every four years to compensate for the extra quarter day in each single year. Our calendar is accurate, but it is a little awkward in the way it divides the year into months – the months are of unequal length.

The Maya, however, stuck to their base twenty numbering system and had eighteen months of twenty days, making 360 days. The extra five days were considered 'unlucky' and were unnamed. As we add on a day every four years, the Maya added five days at the end of each year. The Maya, however, did not compensate for the extra quarter day in each year (even though they calculated the year extremely accurately – see below) and because of this their calendar tended to 'wander' through the years. This is not a major issue within the Tropics, since there are no seasons and the amount of daylight changes little through any year. The total change in the length of the day in Mexico fluctuates within a range of approximately 2.5 hours each year, whereas in the UK the day length changes greatly over a six-month period, around six hours.

It might seem strange that the Maya calendar drifted through the years, and it added fuel to the notion that the Maya were 'stupid farmers who could not calculate the year correctly', but the reality is that the Maya had little or no interest in the solar year. They understood the length of the solar year, but it was of little importance. They were looking at something far more interesting.

To provide evidence of their use, or knowing, of the solar year the picture on Page 23 of this document shows the Pyramid of Kukulkan. This pyramid has stairs on each of the four sides, each containing 91 steps, and the platform on the top makes the total 365.

I was confused by this information as there were two versions of the Maya 'Haab' calendar – one earlier than the other. In fact they were almost two different calendars. If my memory served me correctly, the earlier version of the Maya solar year was 360 days long. This was the reason the calendar 'wandered through the years' because there are 365 days in a year. It was only later that the Maya made an adjustment to this calendar and added the five 'unnamed' days. The other confusing factor was stated clearly in the text – the great Pyramid of Kukulkan. This pyramid was undoubtedly created to mark the solar year, so if they had 'little or no interest in the solar year', why did they build such a huge monument blatantly stating the number of days in the year? To say it was *written in stone* would be an understatement.

What was the purpose of this deception? Was Charles trying to point me in a direction that made me think of the Maya solar year? I had to try and figure out what it was.

The Maya had three main calendars in use. The solar year – called the 'Haab'; the 'Long Count'; and the 260-day 'Tzolkin'. Only the Haab has a relation to the solar year.

The Tzolkin.

The Tzolkin is basically a 260-day calendar of two week lengths. While we use a week of seven days, the Maya used a week of thirteen days, and a month of twenty days, which combine to make a calendar of 260 days. The thirteen-day week was numbered from 1-13 and the twenty days of the month were named, rather like the names in our week (and numbered 0-19). If you start the 260-day calendar with the first number – 1 – and then combine that with the first named day – Ahau – it is 260 days before the calendar resets at 1 Ahau (13 x 20 = 260). The day you were born was significant, as each of the 260 days had a different meaning. For example, the day '6 Ahau' only occurs once in 260 days and, rather like our astrological calendar, this day determined your personality and what kind of life you were to lead.

The Haab

The Maya somehow managed to calculate the solar year more accurately than we do today. Their calculation of the solar year is 365.242036 days, and this is more accurate than our Gregorian calendar, which calculates the year as 365.2425 days. How they achieved this calculation is straightforward, but how they measured it is a mystery since they did not have the technology we use today. This shows the Maya were aware of the complete length of the solar year but, as stated before, they did not regard the solar year as having much importance.

The eighteen Maya months of twenty days were named and the days were numbered 0-19. It is thought that the Maya were the first culture to make use of the number zero, long before Europe and Asia. The years of the Haab were part of a larger counting system of fifty-two years, the Calendar Round. This 52-year cycle occurs when you combine the 365-day Haab with the 260-day Tzolkin. The smallest even division of these two calendars is 18,980 days, or 365 x 52 and 260 x 73. When these two calendars are combined it is only every fifty-two years that the calendars reset at a single date. To simplify this – if the Tzolkin started at 1, and the Haab started at 1, the following day would be 2 and 2. After 260 days, the following day would be 1 in the Tzolkin (since it has reset to the beginning), and the Haab would be 261. It takes fifty-two years for both calendars to reset at 1 and 1. In essence, you could say the Maya year is fifty-two solar years. However, the Tzolkin is considered to be a year, the Haab is also considered to be a year – they are simply using various calendars at the same time.

The 52-year Calendar Round is a larger version of the 260-day Tzolkin – they both continue clocking forwards and are recognised as beginning again only when they reset to the combined first date. It is a more complex version of our calendar resetting each year on January 1.

The Long Count

The Long Count calendar was altogether different and much larger. Again, it is based on the notion of calculating the base twenty and base eighteen systems. The following is a list of the calculations of time in the Long Count calendar.

Uinal	*1 Uinal = 20 Kin = 20 days*
Tun	*1 Tun = 18 Uinal = 360 days*
	approx. 1 solar year = 1 Maya year
Katun	*1 Katun = 20 Tun = 7,200 days*
	approx. 19.72 solar years = 20 Maya years
Baktun	*1 Baktun = 20 Katun = 144,000 days*
	approx. 394.52 solar years = 400 Maya years

It is the Long Count calendar which is used in reference to the year 2012. This is because their Long Count calendar started at 13.0.0.0.0. This date has been calculated to be 13 August 3114 BC. When this calendar resets at 13.0.0.0.0 the date in our calendar is December 21, 2012. This cycle of the Long Count calendar is 5,126 years long. It cannot be a coincidence that the calendar ends on the winter solstice of 2012.

It is interesting to note that the Maya believed everything could be multiplied and divided infinitely. It is an extension of the old Greek knowledge that philosophised about atoms being the smallest components of the universe, but the Maya knew that numbers (time and matter) could be broken down into smaller components infinitely. Likewise, these calculations could be multiplied infinitely. Only modern science has understood how small or large things can actually be and the atom is a monumental structure in comparison to what has been discovered in the modern age of quantum physics. It is an important thing to understand about Maya consciousness.

There were pages and pages of other, more meaningless information – artefacts that had been dug up recently, references to the calendar carved into stones, stories about Maya history. Most of this information I had researched before, except for the latest interesting items that had resurfaced after a thousand years, more or less, of hiding in the mud or trees. Maya artefacts are being found on a daily basis since many sites are still covered in jungle, so it is impossible to keep up with it all. I hadn't done any research in that field for a year or more as my interests were diverted into new areas. Only the more interesting finds were given public attention. But I was left scratching my head at the obvious mistake that was put into the text. I read through again and again to make sure it wasn't my misunderstanding but the statement was clear and concise. I couldn't understand why it said the solar year was of no interest to the Maya, when clearly it had a major significance.

Friday 21 May, 2010.

Strangely, Tibet seems like a long time ago. I'm not sure I'll ever recover from it and I certainly won't forget it. It all seems like a bizarre dream, almost as if I'm back on the plane flying to China all over again. I'm glad to get away from there, to be honest. The monastery was only masking the real emotions I was feeling, and there's a perceptible air of fear all over Tibet. I miss Lasya but I have a replacement in Anjali! I can't stop myself from comparing them but they couldn't be more different. Lasya was more like a sister or a nurse in many ways, but Anjali… she's just stunning! There's definitely a connection between us. I don't know how I'm going to say goodbye to this one, it will be very hard, but I seem to have more important things to be doing. And on that note I'm feeling like the devil is creeping up on me from somewhere. I don't want to think about it and I don't know what it is but it's coming. And it's filling me with fear.

27

THE PASSENGER, THE BEAUTY AND THE MAGIC DOOR

Beams of strong sunlight penetrated the cabin through the small oval windows, waking me from a long sleep, a red glow on the inside surface of my eyelids as if someone was shining a torch in my eyes. The folder had fallen onto the floor and for a moment I wondered where I was, unsettled by the strange feeling of sleeping in different places each day. There was nothing to be heard except the high powered engines and my ears popped again as I yawned and stretched my legs outwards under the table in front of me.

"Damn," I thought, "I never used the bed."

There was no telling what the time was but I must have slept for a long time because I had a raging hunger and the sun seemed high in the sky. After regaining my senses, I went to the bathroom to freshen up and then came back to my seat and pressed the button. Anjali appeared within moments.

"What time is it?" I asked.

"It is eleven forty... and it's Saturday the twenty second of May, in case you were wondering! Would you like something to eat or drink?"

Eleven forty? I must have been asleep for a long time, maybe eight hours.

"Yes please. Water, black coffee and whatever you recommend from the menu?"

"In that case I recommend salmon and vegetables. None of it is frozen. It is all fresh. Well, in this compartment anyway."

"That sounds great."

It may have seemed a strange thing to eat for breakfast but it had been a long time since the last meal and I was so hungry Anjali could have recommended spider soup and it would have been eaten without question. To be honest, I hadn't even been listening to her when she suggested it – I just agreed to whatever she recommended because I was too tired and lethargic to even think straight. Anjali obviously hadn't been in the room or known I was asleep for so long or she would have suggested breakfast instead. It was the first time I had properly rested since leaving England and certainly the first time I felt *safe*. Physically and mentally, things had caught up with me but it was also apparent that round two of this adventure was probably going to be more stressful than the first, if the information gleaned so far was anything to go by.

While Anjali was preparing the meal I spent a good five minutes walking up and down the cabin to get the blood flowing through my body again and then I peered out the window. All that could be seen was the vast expanse of the Atlantic Ocean, and since there were no clouds the curve of the earth could just be made out in the distance. It was a humbling experience and where sea met sky there was a whitish-blue haze, a ring that circled the planet as far as they eye could see.

Anjali returned with lunch and we engaged in a brief conversation before she disappeared again through her magic door; she vanished through it and there was no telling where it was taking her. I had entered through another entrance near the back of the room and I imagined Anjali's door was mysterious, like the portal in the story '*The Lion, The Witch, and The Wardrobe*', and when Anjali was on the other side of it she was actually sunning herself on a beautiful hot beach somewhere, complete with strawberries, grapes and the best iced fruit juice imaginable.

We were now around twelve hours into the flight, which left me just a few hours to re-read Charles' version of the Maya calendar. I say 'Charles' version' because it wasn't one familiar to me. The idea that the Maya had no interest in the solar year left me in a distinct state of confusion. Surely there was a reason this was stated in the text, but why the discrepancy? Was the accepted version of the Maya calendar wrong? Was Charles' version the definitive account of this timepiece, or was a deliberate mistake designed to make me focus on a certain aspect of the calendar? Was this discrepancy a clue to something I had to figure out? One thing was certain – if they were clues there wasn't much time to decipher them. There were only a few more hours on this flight and then surely only a few more hours to Cancún from Chicago.

When I picked up the folder again, something dropped onto the floor.

"Strange," I thought, "I am sure that wasn't in there before."

Picking up the small white envelope, inside there was a note and a bus ticket. The destination was the town of Candelaria, a place I had never heard of before.

Dear Stephen, the note began, very formally.

When you arrive in Cancún, go to the main bus terminal. From there you will take the bus to Candelaria. Once you arrive, take a taxi to the Hotel Royal, situated on the main plaza. Take some rest. On the morning of Monday 24 May wait in the hotel reception area at 08:00 hrs where you will be met by Professor Santiago Sanchez. Good luck.

"Professor Santiago Sanchez... Santiago Sanchez," I repeated, "I know that name..." But I couldn't remember where I had last come across it. I tried to get back to reading the notes on the calendar, but that name played on my mind and I couldn't concentrate. The words were being read but they weren't forming correctly in my consciousness. For some reason the name Professor Santiago Sanchez was melted into my mind and I couldn't get rid of it. Something was rousing within me; an odd feeling that made me excited, but also left me feeling nervous. Never before had the sound of a name left me with such intense emotions, but the feelings were so ambiguous they became frustrating and I needed to do something else to take my mind off it.

I requested a coffee and asked Anjali to sit with me for a while. We talked, but no matter what we discussed, the name *Professor Santiago Sanchez* was ringing around my head like church bells on a Sunday morning during a hangover. And wherever I turned it seemed his name was everywhere – on the walls, the floor, and even on Anjali's clothing – almost as if his name was stamped onto the inside of a pair of glasses that were permanently glued to my face.

"When I was young my father taught me many things," Anjali said. "He said it was important not to have attachments to people."

Where the hell did that come from? What was she talking about? From our first meeting I had realised Anjali was an open person but this new direction in the conversation left me bemused. However, it did stop that name reverberating in my mind.

"What did he mean by that?" I asked. "Surely we cannot avoid attachments to others?"

"He said it was unhealthy to be attached to people because we all walk this earth alone and we are all on our own individual spiritual path, regardless of who we meet."

That was a strange statement coming from a woman who I perceived to be a materialist and certainly non-spiritual. Maybe she *would* cope as a nomad in Tibet.

"But surely a mother is attached to her child in a very strong way. What did your mother think of this?"

"My mother has the same view. They said it was important for our individual spiritual development to be detached from people and that a mother should not be too close to her child, but should allow the child to develop its own pathway without the influence of the parents."

Anjali's view was confusing. On the one hand what she was saying was clear, but on the other there were contradictions. In a child where does freedom end and discipline begin? How free can a child be before it develops bad behaviour?

"Surely parents must bring up a child to instil good behaviour and the importance of caring for others?"

"Yes, this is correct, but once the child develops its own personality he or she must be allowed freedom to conduct themselves in the way the soul wishes. Too much discipline and control over a child is very damaging."

"Okay, but what about when two people meet as adults? It is important for a couple to stay together when a child is born because healthy development requires both parents."

"This is true, but if the parents themselves are free spiritual beings then they will also not be attached to each other."

It was clear what Anjali was saying but there was no telling where on earth all this was coming from. She was up to something, maybe trying to find something specific about me, but if that was the case why wasn't she being more direct? I continued to play Devil's advocate.

"How is that possible if they live in the same house bringing up a child?"

"It is possible by the way they live. If they are of a free spiritual nature then they will naturally have space within the relationship, which maintains a healthy balance. It is important not to have any control over the other person. That way they can be free. Too many people control their partner in a relationship. As soon as this occurs resentment begins and the relationship starts to breakdown. Jealousy is often the main cause of this."

Anjali was starting to sound like a guru rather than a flight attendant, but her words still ring true today. And it didn't pass my attention that I had just escaped from such a relationship.

"Ah, jealousy, the little green monster, as my mother would say."

"Yes, it is a monster and life is far too short for this destructive emotion. It is the basis for control in a relationship and it comes out of fear. Fear that the other person will leave them, or be unfaithful, but this fear is usually put inside of them by the way their own parents bring them up, or from early experiences. This is why my parents taught me to be a free spirit."

I understood the circle. If parents are too close to their children, their fear of losing them teaches the child to understand fear, but if the child is left to develop naturally then they will not require the attachments that create the fear that causes bad relationships.

"I understand, Anjali. I have always been mystified when a person tries to control another in a relationship. My advice has always been; if a person wants to be unfaithful, they will be and there is nothing you can do about it, so why spend your time worrying about it? People do things because they want to and no other reason. It's best to live your life outside of this fear and worry."

Anjali smiled and leaned forward slightly.

"Exactly, Steve, and I am also sure you understand that what you put out will come back to you. This is the fundamental law of the universe. If you are always worrying that your partner will be unfaithful and you start to control them because of this fear, then the likely outcome is that you will create that situation. If you control the other person they will become unhappy and eventually the worst of your nightmares will come forth, but many people don't realise that these events are their own creation. What you give to the universe you will receive."

Now Anjali was starting to sound like Yeshe, the message of the scrolls clearly echoing.

"Yes, I understand this principle. I was taught this some time ago. The universe does not differentiate between 'want' and 'don't want', so if you create an image that you don't want your partner to be unfaithful then it is that image which the universe receives, not the 'want' or 'don't want'."

"Yes, you are absolutely right, but it is not as simple as this. It takes two to create this situation. A person can be strong and avoid these creations. A partner will not be unfaithful solely on the basis of the other person's thoughts. They have to want to do this in the first place, but it is those thoughts and conflict that create the unhappiness in the individual in the first place."

"Of course, there are those who are just naturally unfaithful," I said.

"That is true, but this could be considered an illness in some ways. That selfish behaviour is one learned in childhood; the inconsideration towards the feelings of others, putting the self before others."

"But there is also the argument that human beings are naturally polygamous animals."

"But we are not animals, Steve."

Anjali was proving to be an interesting woman. Her view on the world was really fascinating, but certainly not unique in the Indian spiritual or religious way of thinking. Her parents had taught her not to be reliant on others for emotional support, but this didn't mean she was a cold-hearted person. On the contrary, her parents' teachings had made her a very balanced individual and obviously extremely unselfish and empathic. It also allowed her to follow her own career path without the pressures of someone else's ideas. So many parents try to direct their children into a certain career path without allowing the child to discover their own. Once again, it's that control aspect of our behaviour. The interesting statement, however, was the last one. Anjali had stated that being unfaithful was an act of the animal brain, and not a part of a spiritually evolved individual and again it showed this contradiction of animal versus soul. It seemed that perhaps this behaviour depended solely on which aspect of our being we allowed to dominate over the other.

It was the end of another interesting conversation and Anjali disappeared into her magical world beyond the cabin door. Something was happening with our conversations that I couldn't figure out.

I once again picked up the folder. Then I put it straight back down again.

"What the hell was all that about?" I asked out loud.

Why was Anjali talking about these things – repeating the principles that Yeshe had taught me only a couple of days before? Was the conversation with Yeshe about creating our own world somehow being picked up by Anjali subconsciously? Was the similarity between our conversation and the scroll's teachings just a random coincidence that had no meaning? Was she just being friendly but, without realising, connecting to the universal consciousness? Or was there a deeper meaning to this bizarre conversation? Was she a part of the game or was she talking randomly without realising the importance of her words – another one of those synchronicities, perhaps?

28

THE CONNECTION

With only a couple of hours left of the flight to Chicago I asked for yet another coffee from Anjali. Already feeling sad that we would be saying goodbye, I was astonished when she informed me she would be accompanying me on the connecting flight to Cancún.

This was a strange turn of events, since the airline taking me to Mexico would obviously not be the same one that flew from New Delhi. After all, Indian airline companies fly from India and back, not from the United States to Mexico. Now there was no doubt in my mind that Anjali was employed by Charles – another one of the characters gently urging me forward on this unknown quest.

It was frustrating. While I understood the role of people like Yeshe and Chang, Anjali's purpose – on the surface – was solely to serve me coffee, demeaning as that may sound. That was until she started talking about strange things. Now it was necessary to go over the entire conversation once again to see if anything significant was lurking beneath her seemingly innocuous words.

Since Anjali had repeated things that Yeshe had already taught me, she was either reinforcing those ideas or she was telling me very clearly that I must make no emotional connections in Mexico. Perhaps it was both, or maybe it was something else.

To suggest all of her words were planned would be, at best, paranoia on my part but it did appear that Anjali's narrative was a subconscious and synchronistic aspect of the whole. Certainly she never calculated her sentences or her conversation – I was the only one seeing the connection – the synchronicities were happening to me, not to her, but there was no doubt Charles knew exactly the correct person to place in this role. This was more bizarre than anything else. Anjali, like me, was a seemingly ordinary person going about her daily business. Had Charles painstakingly chosen her from the hundreds doing her job, picking the correct candidate for the role as he had done with me? Or was she in fact employed by Charles – perhaps she was the person who travelled on his flights – and was briefed by him beforehand? Maybe she was even one of 'them'. Or was this *really* paranoia? Maybe I had been thinking too much about all of this, making connections that weren't there, the experience in Tibet a little too much for my mind to cope with.

Even if it was paranoia I took Anjali's words as a direct sign – be careful in Mexico and keep my emotions in check. There was no other choice. I could ignore her words and slip up, or I could take them as important and perhaps learn something from them later. Making the presumption that the universal consciousness was speaking to me was a far more favourable attitude to assume.

In Tibet I never had a chance to really think about the things that people were teaching me. I had probably missed many subtle clues because Chang's death had upset me more than I'd realised, and now Anjali's words about not being attached to people were echoing in my head.

Did this mean that more people were going to die in Mexico? Were things going to get worse? Was there going to be a lot more danger? The area I was going – the East – was a haven for tourists, with its Maya ruins and great beaches. It was clear, however, that any dream of sunning my body on golden sands was never going to happen. On the contrary, there was a very strong feeling that I was heading for dangers that had only previously existed in my nightmares and that feeling grew stronger the closer we got to Mexico. I recalled what Dzengin had hinted at – that Mexico was going to make a man out of me.

Anjali had brought coffee and she sat down briefly, staring at me across the table. I wondered if she could sense the fear growing inside me. Then she dropped a bombshell. Actually it was more like she triggered a nuclear explosion.

"There have been some very unusual finds in Mexico," she said – and then she got up and walked out.

"What the devil is she rambling on about now?" I thought. Sure, there have been many unusual finds in Mexico over the years. Was she also interested in archaeology?

And then it hit me.

Like a computer program that gave commands, her words suddenly activated something in my mind. I felt like a 'Manchurian Candidate', as if the sentence she just said had previously been programmed into my mind while under hypnosis and would bring out the memory when it was required.

Professor Santiago Sanchez was Mexico's leading authority on Maya ruins, the top archaeologist in Mexico. He was also responsible for the major archaeological discoveries in Mexico over the past thirty years. A powerful intellect, he was the most respected archaeologist in the Americas. How could I have forgotten him? Having come across much of his work during many years studying Central and South American archaeology, he was *the* most respected man in American archaeology. How blind could I have been? How did I not remember him before now? It was a strange feeling, but now all my fears turned to excitement – Professor Santiago Sanchez was coming to meet *me*!

I was going to work alongside the most respected and knowledgeable archaeologist in the Americas, one of the best in the world. This could only mean there was something of great importance going on in Mexico, but did it also mean that Professor Sanchez was part of the group of people that were aware of all these pieces of secret information? Was Professor Sanchez the Yeshe of the Americas? Had they discovered yet another Atlantean dome? Or was it something entirely different?

One thing was for sure – it was now time to put my archaeology hat on. It was time to use all the knowledge I'd gained in the world of archaeology, but with a man like Professor Sanchez at the helm what could I possibly bring to the table? I wasn't even a post graduate on the subject. In fact, I had never studied archaeology academically. Then I remembered Charles saying that my alternative view on these subjects was the requirement. From all this, it appeared that I was required to bring a non-scientific aspect to whatever was going on in the heat of Mexico. And Anjali's concepts about spirituality were reinforcing certain ideologies I held about life. But what could possibly be both non-scientific and spiritual at an archaeological site?

29

THE LAST LEG

Landing in Chicago sooner than expected, Anjali escorted me through the airport and straight onto the connecting flight. She took care of all the necessities and personally logged my passport into the system before we boarded the plane. It was another three hours until take-off but once again I was subjected to luxury treatment. Wandering around the airport terminal would have been preferable but for some reason solitude was being openly forced onto me. Once again the private lounge was reserved entirely for me and now I felt both excitement and nervousness. Excitement at meeting Professor Sanchez – but also nervousness because once we landed in Cancún I was on my own. It was as if the trip was starting all over again – landing in China, meeting Chang and then all the dangers and adventures that happened afterwards. Was this journey going to be a similar experience?

The flight was to take three-and-a-half hours and I made the most of the luxury that surrounded me, for I was going to be out of this comfort zone and into the Mexican heat before I knew it. Once we were in the air Anjali reappeared, smiling. "Would you like something to eat? I suggest you get a good meal inside you before we land."

"I would, yes. What do you recommend this time?"

"We have a leg of lamb. It is being taken off the menu and replaced with beef, so I recommend that since it is the last leg. It comes with vegetables and gravy."

"That sounds great."

My mouth watered at the prospect and it would surely be a long time until another familiar English-style meal would be eaten. I rarely eat red meat these days but the occasional gourmet feast is never rejected when it is offered.

My body clock and meal times were completely out of sync, but things would settle once we hit Mexican soil. I had always wanted to go to Mexico but never before had the chance. The excitement of meeting Professor Sanchez, however, was slowly being overcome by that same sense of fear and trepidation. Something was stirring within me yet again, an intuitive feeling that was brewing from the solar plexus. I tried to ignore it, but it became something that couldn't be disregarded and the closer we got to Mexico the stronger it became. My instinct told me this journey wasn't going to be a fun adventure – it was going to change everything inside me and everything around me – and there was very little time to prepare myself.

As we headed south across the Eastern Central United States it was two hours before we hit the Gulf of Mexico. Out of the window, the Atlantic Ocean stretched out below as if the entire universe was a sea surrounded by stars.

"We'll be landing in the next hour," Anjali told me as I was staring out of the window.

I had been standing for at least half an hour without realising it, the ocean mesmerising me into some kind of mild trance. My subconscious was trying to prepare me for what was to come, the black blanket below and the star-filled sky acting like a hypnotic dream world.

"Would you like anything before we land?" she asked.

"I would like one last coffee – and if I can take a bottle of orange juice or two with me, that would be great!"

"You can take whatever you like. The cupboards are full, help yourself," she responded with a large smile.

It was difficult not to let my thoughts deteriorate under the circumstances. Anjali was an incredibly beautiful woman and her soul and her view on life only added to it – the inner beauty matched the outward appearance, and was even more captivating.

I filled my backpack with as many items as I could until the side pockets bulged with curved bottles, which made it look like a small robot with arms. The heat would be a struggle inland and while drinks could be purchased in various places, my previous travel experiences had taught me that taking extra fluids was never a bad idea. I put chocolate well inside the pack, since it would melt quickly if exposed to sunlight and would probably be forgotten by the time the sun was high in the sky the following morning. There's nothing worse than opening a chocolate bar to find a thick brown liquid inside the wrapper, when there is no other food around and you need an energy boost in the jungle. Actually, there are far worse things in the jungle – giant hairy spiders bigger than your hand, snakes so deadly they can kill with one bite, insects so large and scary you think you are on another planet entirely. Even ants can kill you if you are not careful. They are huge, several inches long in some cases, and if you fall and break your leg near a nest of those critters and become unconscious, with an open wound you'll be eaten alive in no time. The jungle is an environment where human beings are neither welcome nor adapted to. We, the great hunter, become the hunted. And that reminded me, rewinding five years...

Riding a motorcycle through the Amazon one afternoon, off road and through dense trees, I had to swerve to miss a snake on the track and my excitement was such that I slammed on the brakes and ran back after the slithery serpent just to get a photo. The snake tried to escape but I caught up with it, readying the camera for a shot. It was a beautiful creature with red, yellow and black circles covering its body. I had seen this creature on TV many years before and couldn't recall its name, but I should have remembered that a snake with any form of bright colouring is dangerous. The friend who had accompanied me on the journey was a local girl who was so familiar with the jungle she practically knew where all the animals lived and their personal names. She was screaming and shouting at me but I paid no attention – nothing was going to stop me from getting this photo.

"Beevora! Beevora!" she shouted as I got closer, although at the time my Spanish wasn't very good so there was no telling what she was talking about. When the snake stopped and allowed me to get closer I crouched down, leaned forwards and clicked the shutter.

On returning to where the girl was standing I was given a deafening earful of local expletives which I failed to understand, along with, "You are stupid! You can die!" which I did understand. She was absolutely furious. I thought she was overreacting far too much.

"It's just a little snake," I said.

Later in the evening I remembered the sounding of the letters 'v' and 'b' are the other way around in South America, so I scanned my dictionary for the correct word – Víbora. *The sight of that name left me hyperventilating and I had to drink an entire litre of water to calm me down as I realised I had been less than twelve inches away from the jaws of an Amazonian pit viper.*

The memories of my days spent in the Amazon gave me a tiny amount of preparation for Mexico, but it was just a glimmer. Remembering how humid the jungle can be was more of a premonition than a recollection and the deadly creatures that inhabit these places are not for those with serpent, insect or arachnid phobias.

It wasn't long before Anjali and I would be saying goodbye and she sat with me for one last conversation before we landed in Cancún. I didn't have the same feeling I'd had when I parted company with Lasya. With Lasya it was a very strong emotional connection – with Anjali it was more a case of physical attraction, but we had also covered ground that was familiar to both of us and that left an understanding on a different level. There was a deep spiritual connection with Anjali that was quite powerful – a meeting of mutual minds – but this was different from Lasya. Lasya's effect had been one of a nurse healing a wound, but Anjali's view on the world had given our connection a more mental and spiritual overtone, rather than emotional. I also had the sense that any genuine closeness to a female was going to be non-existent in the near future and this left me feeling even closer to Anjali. Choosing between the two of them was an easy task and the physical beauty of Anjali only added to the attraction. My interest in Lasya had been brought on by her tuning into my thoughts so it wasn't *real*, but with Anjali the attraction was natural and mutual.

There was something else more pressing, though. I couldn't explain why, but whenever I closed my eyes I saw visions – flashes that crept into my consciousness from an unknown source – images of being isolated and in fear.

"My mother always taught me not to fear anything," Anjali said, as if she was viewing the images in my mind and tactfully diverting my attention. "It is important to understand that we are spirit and that spirit is greater than the body. We must not fear death. We must embrace it, for it is the next stepping stone on our journey through the universe. In fact, this short life we have *is* the real death, for we exist in a level of the universe that could be considered dead."

Anjali was starting to sound like Gandhi, or even the Buddha himself. Certainly, and for a second time, she appeared to be repeating the things Yeshe had taught me. Not sure what to make of it, I went along for the ride.

"What do you mean by that?"

"This life is to experience pain and suffering, love and compassion. These emotions can only be experienced in this reality and you need a physical body to have this experience. The physical body does not exist after death, for we move forward to experience a more spiritual environment."

"And you are convinced of that state of reality?"

I too shared the same belief system, but I wanted to hear her reasoning for this understanding. Then she gave the best answer possible.

"It's not about conviction; this is not a *belief* – it is a *knowing.* A belief system is not useful in this world. It can bring misleading hope and always there is a little bit of doubt in the back of your mind. Knowing is different. When you know something, it shapes the environment around you, whereas a belief allows the environment to shape you. I know things because I have experienced them. Things have happened in my life which show beyond doubt these things are real. So, I know things, rather than believe them."

Anjali's words were profound and yet so true. What is the point of belief? It can bring false hope and often our view of the world is shattered when these beliefs are proven to be incorrect. Belief can also breed arrogance in an individual and can even destroy a person's life to the point of insanity. It is best to wait until experience provides us with truth, but what sort of experience can give us the kind of truth that leaves us with a knowing so powerful that it shapes the world around us? What can make us *know* that the world is contradictory both to science and what our eyes can see?

Anjali anticipated my next question and spoke as I took a breath to speak.

"When I was a child, I had what is called a near-death experience. We have an old traditional style house, which has two levels and an open courtyard in the centre. When I was five years old, I climbed over the railing on the second level and fell into the courtyard below, hitting my head badly. I have a six-inch scar on my head."

"That sounds like a terrible injury," I said, scrunching my face up at the thought of how life-threatening that would be to the delicate skull of a tiny five year-old girl.

"I was almost dead when the ambulance arrived. They barely managed to keep me alive on the way to the hospital and then in the evening I flat-lined and they had to resuscitate me. It was then that I went out of my body and could see what was going on in the hospital room."

"So, you were floating above your body and you could see the doctors working on you?" I asked, leaning forward with excitement. I was familiar with NDEs but had never met anyone who'd experienced one.

"Yes. Do you know about these things?"

"Oh yes. I have studied NDEs and I've even had my own out-of-body experience."

"Really? That's a coincidence. So, you understand what I am saying?"

"I've understood everything you've said; I'm just interested in your point of view on these things. Your Indian philosophy is very interesting for me."

"I remember it so clearly, even though I was only five years old. As the doctors were trying to resuscitate me I felt a pull behind me and suddenly I was floating away from the room, through the ceiling and away from the hospital itself. I could see a tunnel with a light at the end and I felt myself being pulled through it. When I came out on the other side I was in a beautiful landscape with trees, fields of flowers, mountains, a lake, and even waterfalls in the background."

"That's amazing! Was it real, like a scene here on earth?"

"No. It was more real than here. The colours were intense and bright, nothing like we have here. It was more *surreal,* like everything was blended together by a fabric that connected everything."

"What do you mean by that?"

"I am not sure!" Anjali laughed.

I could see she was struggling to explain what it was like. She looked upwards trying to find the words to express the experience.

"It was like the whole scene was bound together by some kind of energy that ran through everything. It is impossible to explain. Only you feel it when you are there."

"Okay, so what happened next?" I asked, sitting on the edge of my seat.

"I heard a voice that told me I must go back and that my time was not now. It was a gentle voice, familiar, as if I knew who it was, but I never actually saw anyone the whole time I was there. It was strange, because as a five year-old I wouldn't have understood this on earth, but I knew in my soul and understood what this all meant. Then I was ejected from the field and I felt myself flying back down the tunnel and with a bump I was back in my body. The doctors had saved me and were so relieved and my parents were in tears near the bed."

"Did you report this to the doctors? Sometimes they are very interested in these stories because they do hear about them more frequently than people realise."

"No. Absolutely not! I was too young to understand what was going on. Even though when I was in that place I understood what was happening, when I returned here I was back in my five year-old mind. Plus I had the worst headache you can imagine! After leaving hospital I started drawing pictures of it and then my mother began asking me what I was drawing. I explained to her what had happened, at least from the mind of a five year-old. She wasn't shocked at all and encouraged me to remember what had happened without giving me any hints, so she certainly didn't plant any false memories in me. She was very calm about the whole thing. She seemed to know all about it."

I was not surprised by Anjali's story at all – this was a typical near-death experience and it is very common for children to start drawing their experiences after similar incidents.

"What happened after all of this?" I asked, wondering about any conclusions.

"My mother asked me when I was about twenty years old if I remembered anything from my time in hospital. I guess she thought I had forgotten it, but I told her that I remembered everything and told her the whole story again. She said that it was exactly the same story I had reported when I was five, although naturally my language of explanation had improved considerably."

Anjali smiled, and looking into her eyes I saw something different. An old soul looked back at me, and for a moment our eyes locked together. I saw the *real* Anjali – a beautiful, all knowing spirit of antiquity, yet tinged with a youthful innocence. If we could all be like this, I thought, the world would be a wonderful place to live.

"We will be landing very soon," Anjali said, breaking the connection.

It is difficult to hold a stare with someone when you see into each other's soul. It is never a negative feeling, but when you see someone's soul through their eyes it stirs something within you that cannot be held for more than a few moments before it becomes a little uncomfortable.

Anjali disappeared for a few minutes and left me contemplating our interactions. I wanted so much to spend more time with her because everything she said had underlying meanings and interpretations, but right now another destiny awaited me.

Anjali returned and asked me to fasten my seat belt and then she passed me her email address, written on headed notepaper from the airline.

"Contact me when you are settled," she smiled. "I'll be back when we have landed."

She walked gracefully back to the door. I folded the paper gently and placed it safely in my backpack in an inside hidden pocket.

There are times when we meet someone and the connection we make with them is so strong that we wish to keep in contact with them. It's a knowing, a meeting of similar souls who share similar ideas. For me, Anjali was one of these people. It was strange, really, because I had more of a connection with Lasya – or so I thought. While I considered that Anjali created more of a physical attraction, on my part at least, with Lasya it was a more an emotional connection but I never gave any thought of keeping in contact with Lasya, even though it would have been near impossible without modern technology. And then it occurred to me – maybe it was the other way around? Maybe in reality Lasya was Anjali, and Anjali was Lasya. In some ways what Anjali was saying to me resonated more powerfully in my soul than anything Lasya had said. Maybe sometimes, when we are clouded by physical attraction, we miss the spiritual connection. Right now I was certainly learning the difference between emotional and spiritual connections. One could easily think they were one and the same, but they are not and Lasya and Anjali had clearly, perhaps unwittingly, shown me the difference.

The plane dipped sharply to the right, levelled out, then took another right turn as we circled Cancún. We were dropping quickly but gently out of the sky.

It wasn't long before we hit the ground with a jolt and the braking of the plane forced me forwards in my seat. My heart jumped because I was getting closer to a new and dangerous adventure, but my nervousness had diminished because of Anjali's calmness. As the plane taxied to the end of the runway and headed for the main terminal she appeared once again, smiling like a child.

"Well, this is it," she said.

I unfastened my belt, stretched my legs and then passed her a piece of paper with my own email address.

"Contact me if you don't hear from me. I don't know what's going to happen or where I am going to end up in the next few weeks."

"Steve..." Anjali's voice made me stop everything and her voice was such that I sat back in the seat. She sat opposite and looked at me for a few moments.

"Is this about penguins?" I asked.

She was startled and gave me the same look she had given me when I had asked her what the date was.

"Never mind," I said, "carry on."

"You must pay attention to what is going on around you. Try to read between the lines and look for the signal that something other than what your eyes are telling you might be happening."

She said it in such a gentle way it made my spine tingle. I didn't respond. I couldn't tell whether this was some kind of intuition or whether she was just talking in general terms, a kind of overview based on her world view. Looking straight at her I repeated the words several times in my mind, trying to etch them into my memory so that I could remind myself in times of need.

"Okay," I said, standing up and turning to pick up my backpack. I felt like an idiot and my reaction was almost childlike, but how was I supposed to respond to a sentence like that?

"Are you ready?" she asked.

"I was born ready!"

"Then let's go."

Anjali escorted me through to the gate and out into the airport lounge.

"Just walk through that door and you will be at passport control. Good luck, Steve, I'll be thinking of you. Keep in touch." With that she smiled, turned back around and headed towards the gate. As I watched her she suddenly stopped, turned around and walked back towards me. When she was within five feet of me, she said, "It's almost midnight on Saturday the twenty second of May."

She turned away briefly and then stopped, turning her head to face me once again. "And there aren't any penguins here," she added.

She let out a feminine giggle and held her hand up to her mouth, her eyes twinkling like stars on a moonless night. A sudden fire lit inside me, burning intensely, and in that moment I could have grabbed her and kissed her. She turned around one last time and walked away.

Alone once again, suddenly the warm feeling that had filled my spirit disappeared rapidly. It was time to gather my thoughts and strength and prepare myself for whatever was to happen in the coming days. I exited the airport without any fuss and headed for the bus terminal which was situated close by.

This was it.

I was finally in Mexico.

But if I had known what horrors awaited me in the jungle I would have turned around, grabbed Anjali by the ankles and, as I was being dragged along the terminal floor in a childish tantrum, I would have pleaded with her to take me back to India.

PART II

THE PRESENT

1

THE ROYAL CAT OF CANDELARIA

It was hot! Very hot, but thankfully a sea breeze filled the air and lessened the humidity. It was only a half hour wait before the bus pulled in and I climbed aboard, sitting as close to the front as possible on the driver's side. I had noticed that his window was wide open and the breeze, once we were moving, would be a godsend. Before we set off, under the lights of the bus terminal I quickly wrote another diary entry.

Saturday 22 May, 2010
I am utterly terrified. I don't know what it is but it's worse than when I left the UK. Maybe it's the shock of Chang's death, or maybe it's the suddenness of being alone in a strange, foreign country. It's hard to gain any clarity and things are moving so fast I hardly have time to think. I already miss Anjali. A lot. I know there's a deep connection between us, but I'm not sure if these emotions are genuine or whether there was just a clinging on my part, a need for female company. Either way, women as beautiful as that don't come along very often and then there are the shared interests. Damn it! Oh well, such is life. Anyway, I need to start focusing on what's going on here in Mexico and put all of the last two weeks behind me. That was then, this is now. I wonder what on earth is going on over here...

Very soon we were away from Cancún airport, heading south along the Mexico 307 road and hugging the coastline. It was a tortuous eight-and-a-half hour journey on an uncomfortable bus which stopped at several places en route for refreshment breaks, but thankfully the night run meant the roads were clear. The coastal route offered not only a cool breeze but also magical views of the ocean, and the sea was a glorious dark mass of nothingness, apart from the lights of lonely boats which looked lost on the horizon.

Heading away from the next town – Bacalar – the road ran alongside the huge Laguna Bacalar for miles. Reminiscent of Loch Ness, it stretches for thirty miles along the highway, a narrow gouge in the landscape filled with fresh water millennia before, probably during the great ice age melt and today replenished by tropical rains. At the end of Lake Bacalar, after passing the small village of Xul-Ha, we turned onto Highway 186 and headed directly west, deeper into the Mexican landscape. It was a straight 120-mile dash westwards and the farther we headed inland the hotter and more humid it became, the fresh sea air becoming a distant memory.

The coach driver put his foot down on the 186, its long, straight roads allowing for good, safe driving at high speed. We reached the town of Escárcega in just two-and-a-half hours, after passing through the beautiful Reserva de la Biosfera Calakmul, a large protected forest where the trees seemed to reach the sky.

After leaving the town of Escárcega, the road stretched west and then south and another hour later we finally reached my destination of Candelaria. Apparently this place is officially a city, the municipal seat and the capital of the state of Campeche. With fifty thousand inhabitants, Candelaria is the biggest of the eleven municipalities of Campeche but, in the days that followed, never once did it give the impression of a bustling city. Instead, it always appeared to be gliding through a version of Yeshe's aether, in a state of drowsiness where everyone seemed to be under a collective spell of robotic conformity.

The perfect place, one would imagine, to hide a great secret.

To say I was shattered would be an understatement. After travelling half way across the world non-stop, I needed a long sleep. It was early morning when I arrived and the somnolent city was far from awake, with just a few people wandering lazily through the streets and across the plaza in dreamy states of indifference. It was a strange place. The plaza was far too large for such a small, sleepy city, as if the original Spanish designers had been expecting Candelaria to expand into a metropolis. Clearly it had never reached its anticipated size.

The taxi ground to a halt when we reached the Hotel Royal, on the corner of a side street, overlooking the plaza. It was a three storey colonial-style building and in its heyday must have been a grand place, offering luxurious rooms to the wealthy. Now it was a slightly run down but extremely clean hotel, giving visitors a feel of the past.

The reception area was bland and sparse, with a simple desk and a sofa for visitors. I was greeted by a middle-aged man who seemed surprisingly hyperactive and eager to process my booking, while maintaining an expressionless face throughout our encounter. He gave me a key, said my room was on the top floor and gave me directions on how to find it. It was obvious that climbing two flights of stairs was something he was not intending to do, although a little exercise would probably have reduced his sprightliness.

Beyond the reception area a great hall appeared that seemed to stretch forever in both directions and a grand staircase rose upwards to the upper floors.

The staircase appeared to be original, made of some native hardwood, with beautifully carved balustrades. The rail was smooth and cool to the touch. I wondered about the tens of thousands of hands that had glided up and down over the past hundred years and more. Imagine what stories these stairs could tell.

The staircase curled upwards and around, its solidity a memory of past grandeur. The smooth tiled floor was gleamingly clean and reflections from the hall-lights followed my steps as I walked along a brightly lit corridor with painted white walls and wooden supporting beams – a contrast of the modern and the old.

On reaching the top floor I was so exhausted I could easily have collapsed and slept right there in the hall, but there was just one more stretch to go to find a bed – surely mustering up one last ounce of energy would be worth it when a soft surface awaited me. This excursion had started in Tibet two days ago, I hadn't slept in a bed since the monastery and now there were just moments until its end.

As I dragged myself towards the end of the hall there was a single chair that seemed out of place, half way along. I stopped suddenly, for I had a dopey realisation that I'd seen something on the chair, but my exhausted brain didn't comprehend what it was. I turned around and saw a black cat curled up on the chair, its eyes glaring at me menacingly as if I were a new invader daring to interrupt his peaceful morning.

I crouched down and the cat stared back at me, annoyed. Looking into his eyes I told him he had nothing to worry about and he watched cautiously as my hand reached out to stroke his soft fur. At least I thought it would be soft fur. Too late I realised that a filthy layer of dust covered the black moggy from head to toe. It seemed pretty obvious this dirty animal had not moved from this chair for quite some time, only leaving this spot to eat and then returning to his sloth-like existence. As I would be here for the next twenty-four hours at least, that theory would be put to the test.

"Goodnight you filthy cat," I said, somehow managing to stand upright.

Filthy Cat had the same expression on his face throughout our brief encounter. He was not impressed by the disturbance but he seemed satisfied now his layer of dust had been transferred onto my hand. Certainly he appeared to be laughing behind his mafia don face.

On reaching the room at the end of the corridor I placed my backpack against the wall and without even the slightest concern for the décor, I closed all the shutters, fell onto one of the beds and into a coma that lasted for ten hours.

When I awoke it was late in the day and beams of sunlight were penetrating the wooden shutters. Dust motes were dancing in the air as if levitated by some magical force.

I took stock of my surroundings. The room was large, with three single beds each with a small desk alongside. The floor was covered with varnished wooden panels that were probably original – their unevenness gave a clue to their antiquity. The walls were painted with the same white paint as the halls, but the best features were the window shutters – old and wooden, double-folding and shielding all sunlight except where tiny gaps had appeared over the years.

Opening all the shutters filled the room with sunlight that left me squinting. My room was at the corner of the second floor so one window faced the street that ran from the centre, one faced the plaza and the central window, which was right on the corner, gave an angled view of a large church at the left of the main square.

The humidity was uncomfortably high and as I opened the window the noise of the busy centre of Candelaria burst into the room like the sound of trumpets. I was amazed how these old windows had kept out so much of the noise of the world outside but now, for the first time, it hit me – I was in Mexico, and bang in the centre of Maya territory.

Outside people wandered around in all directions. A group of schoolchildren stood outside the church awaiting instructions from their teachers. There was nothing fundamentally wrong with that scene except that today was a Sunday. No doubt these were extra brainwashing lessons for the young. Surprisingly, the side street beside the hotel seemed almost empty apart from a few taxis that slowly caressed the kerbside as they drifted through the town waiting for fares. On the main street and in the plaza it was apparent that everyone seemed to know everyone else. Not a good place to be inconspicuous but Professor Sanchez would be meeting me tomorrow morning, so my stay would be brief. Now, however, I had a chance to sample a taste of Mexico and also my first opportunity to use the credit card Charles had given me just two weeks ago. It was time to find the most expensive restaurant in town. After all the crap Charles had put me through I was tempted to go completely crazy with his money, but brothels and gambling casinos are not my style. In fact I've never been to either, but I guess Charles knew that. It was doubtful that there were such places in a city like this anyway, and if there were they were probably hidden down side streets and back alleys.

I headed for the shower room adjacent to my own. Filthy Cat was sleeping on his chair. He was in exactly the same position he had been in when I first met him.

"Good evening, Filthy Cat," I said, giving him another stroke.

A fresh layer of dust rose from his soft fur and he seemed to like the attention. Filthy Cat really was filthy, and his temporary name very apt. It was obvious he cared little for personal hygiene, but then neither would I want to tongue wash my body with all that dust. We had already struck up a good relationship – Filthy Cat would get his coating of dust removed and a quick massage and in return I would get nothing. To be honest, it was a typical human-cat relationship, but the interaction was enjoyable for all that.

After my shower and fresh clothing, it was time to taste the atmosphere of Mexico.

"See you later, Filthy Cat," I said, passing his chair. He looked at me with those annoyed eyes and his thoughts were almost written on his forehead – *where's my stroke?* – but my hands were too clean to pay him any attention this time. "When I come back, okay?" He rested his head back on his paw and closed his eyes.

Leaving Filthy Cat to dreams of mice and tuna fish, I was looking forward to getting outside and feeling a breeze but much to my horror there was no draught at all. Instead, a sticky humid wall of thick air greeted my every move as I walked aimlessly across the plaza. Still, it was nowhere near as bad as New Delhi. I stood in the centre of the plaza and took a moment to look around and see what delights awaited me, but there was simply nothing of interest. It was quite apparent this was not a tourist haunt. Candelaria really was an obscure city in the middle of nowhere.

I found a bench and sat down whilst I decided what my next move would be. My Western appearance was hardly inconspicuous and the curious eyes of passers-by stared unashamedly at me. "Yes, you're right – what the hell am I doing here?" I muttered, but not loudly enough for strange eyes to conclude that a crazy gringo had landed in town. But it was a valid question – what was I doing here? Why had a meeting with one of the most important archaeologists in history been set up in this godforsaken place? Certainly it had something to do with the Maya calendar – that much was obvious. I tried not to think too much but I was exceptionally excited that Professor Sanchez would be coming to meet me in the morning.

On the edge of the plaza there was a restaurant serving a mix of typical Mexican food and also more unfamiliar local dishes. Thankfully I have a good grasp of Spanish or the menu would have been indecipherable. From the lack of any English translation it was obvious that few foreigners ever passed through here.

I stayed in the restaurant by the window for nearly two hours, watching people wander through the plaza, their small shadows changing shape and direction as they passed under different street lamps. When a feeling of tiredness hit me I once again headed back to the hotel.

Filthy Cat was sleeping in his chair. I sat with him for a good five minutes, stroking him and giving him all the attention he desired, before taking my dusty hands to the bathroom for a wash.

Sunday 23 May, 2010

The first day I've had to myself since Chengdu and I really needed it. Nice just to sleep, wander around and not think about anything. This so-called city is a very strange place. I don't know why it's called a city, it almost seems as if it's existing in a slow-motion dream. Everyone seems so relaxed and they walk slowly. Maybe it's just because it's a Sunday. Tomorrow is the day I will meet Professor Sanchez. I'm really nervous and excited but I don't know what's going on around here, or why I am here. I guess I'll find out soon enough. That terrible feeling of fear is still there but I've managed to push it deep inside. When I think about it though, it rushes to the surface like a boiling saucepan about to overflow. Am I ready for what's coming?

It wasn't long before I fell into a deep sleep. The last couple of weeks had left me shell-shocked and more tired than I realised. I told myself that I just needed to lie down and allow my mind to rest. And rest I did, sleeping all night and waking at 7am, which was lucky since there was no alarm clock in sight. It's funny how our internal system seems to 'know' when we need to wake, like when we fall asleep in a moving car for a couple of hours and then wake up just two streets from home.

2

POWER AND PROWESS, CONFUSION AND SUSPICION

Sitting in the reception area I was both nervous and excited to meet Professor Santiago Sanchez. I was familiar with him after seeing him in several TV documentaries, but meeting someone in person is a different situation entirely and I wondered about the kind of energy that would emanate from a man of his reputation.

The morning was humid but fresh and the sun had just risen above the buildings, casting long shadows across the plaza. The small town was coming to life with people going to work and children heading off to school for their daily dose of indoctrination.

As the sun rose higher into the sky the reception area lit up as if someone was shining a huge search light across the plaza. A jeep pulled up outside and a silhouette came towards the doorway, eclipsing the sun. It was ironic – and iconic – since the sun worshippers of the Maya would have revered such an alignment with awe and superstition. So it wasn't a surprise when Professor Sanchez burst through the door like a tidal wave, his bulky frame quite intimidating. His presence was powerful, to the point where everyone around stopped and looked at him. He was a man to be respected even if you didn't know who he was.

His hair had greyed but thick black wiry strands stuck out in various places. His face was rounded, with a long flat nose reminiscent of native Indians. Surprisingly, he had fewer wrinkles than I would have expected for a man of around sixty years, particularly as he lived in a climate where the sun did no favours to the ageing process. But his most striking features were his eyes. They were typical Mexican brown, but what was apparent was that this was a man of awesome intellect. Looking into his eyes left me with a distinct inferiority complex that never diminished, but it wasn't a negative emotion for there was far too much empathy in this man. Professor Sanchez was simply an extremely intelligent being who naturally attracted respect and received it wherever he went.

"Good morning, Stephen," he said, holding out his hand as he reached me.

I stood up and we shook hands. I wondered how he had recognised me but being the only gringo in the entire town, and certainly the only one in the hotel reception area, had clearly given the game away. Sherlock Holmes was hardly needed to find the culprit on this occasion, but it was the professor's confidence that struck me – I would have been reasonably cautious approaching a stranger for fear of introducing myself to the wrong person.

"Good morning, Professor, I am so pleased to meet you."

For a moment we locked eyes. There was an indescribable and discreet sense of searching from the professor. After all, why was he instructed to go and pick up a man from England who was basically nobody? I wasn't even an archaeologist, at least by trade, so he must have been wondering what this strange man was doing here, but neither of us asked any questions.

"Are you ready?" he asked.

"Yes, I am."

"Good. Just take whatever you feel you need, we will be back in the next few days, a week at the most."

I had already packed all I needed and paid for my room in advance for a week, so we headed outside. In the waiting jeep was another man, introduced to me as Carlos, who was Professor's co-worker and a fellow archaeologist at the National Autonomous University of Mexico. Carlos was about five years younger than Professor but he had the same physical shape and size, the same grey hair and thick skin, although their faces were very different and Carlos had an unusual 'feel' compared to Professor Sanchez. While the professor's aura was powerful yet calm, Carlos seemed to exude a slight edginess. Despite this, he seemed like a decent man and another intellectual powerhouse, if not quite on the same level as the professor.

Professor and I sat in the back as we headed away from the plaza and through a side street, and within minutes we were out on the open road and heading south towards Guatemala. Professor waited until we were away from the town before he started to tell me anything. Finally, I thought, I was going to discover what we were doing in the land of the mysterious Maya.

"So, how much have you been told about what is going on here?" Professor asked.

"Absolutely nothing," I said, "I was told only that you would be meeting me at the hotel and that a site had been discovered somewhere."

Professor looked a little confused and Carlos was peering into the rear view mirror. "Well, maybe it is for security reasons, that's okay," Professor said, as he glanced at Carlos.

"Who told you to come and get me?" I asked, wanting some answers and to see if they might tell me something about Charles, or someone else involved.

"I had a phone call from someone at the university who told me you were going to help us on the dig."

"Who was it?"

"It was one of the Board of Directors – but I thought you knew that. Otherwise why would you be here?"

"I don't know anyone in Mexico. I've never been here before."

It was suddenly quiet enough to hear a pin dropping. The confusion on Carlos' face was matched by Professor Sanchez's bewildered expression. His mind must have been doing cartwheels.

"You do not know anyone in Mexico?"

"No."

"Then where did you come from?"

"I came on a flight from India."

"India," he said slowly, the confusion clearly etched on his face.

Professor stared at Carlos in the rear view mirror again. I will never forget the looks on their faces. They seemed so disturbed by the situation they probably wanted to turn around and drive straight back to the hotel. I glanced out of the window to divert my eyes for a moment. I hadn't wanted to make things more complicated, I just wanted to see if the professor and Carlos were connected with Charles, but it seemed they were unaware of him. Now I wished I'd never asked. Then Professor spoke and eased the sheepish look on my face.

"Look Stephen, I do not know who you are or why you are here. In fact I have no idea what is going on. No one, and I do mean no one, knows where we are or where we have been lately, so it comes as a surprise that someone at the university seems to know our location and what is happening. It is even more of a surprise that an Englishman has come from India to join us. However, I cannot argue with the person who told me to come and collect you, despite my authority. Mexican archaeology, and Maya archaeology especially, is riddled with secrecy and control. There can be a close relationship between one or two government officials and drug cartels, although that's rare, so archaeological finds are often prone to strict regulations." He paused for a moment. "On the contrary, I have experienced weirder things in my career."

Looking the professor straight in the eyes, I could see his suspicion. He was searching and trying to find some clues in the deep recesses of my mind, but he didn't realise I was equally in the dark. Something needed to be said.

"Then let's break the ice," I said. "I have no idea why I am here. I don't even know the person who is funding my trip, or why he has sent me here. He hasn't told me anything yet, only I have to be here to be a part of whatever is going on. He said my knowledge of the Maya calendar and my other experiences were important for this trip."

Professor relaxed a little on hearing my words but at the same time he seemed no less confused.

"So the person I know is familiar with the person that you do not know. That's fantastic!" he said sarcastically. "So how much do you know about the Maya calendar?"

"Probably nowhere near as much as you, Professor, but I have an alternative view of things. My approach is more, shall we say, spiritually based rather than scientific."

The professor eyed me cautiously. He was not impressed. I could see him wondering what a 'spiritually based approach' to the Maya calendar entailed. Certainly it implied a non-scientific approach, so that probably wasn't a good start.

"So, where did you study archaeology?"

The question caught me off guard.

"I haven't. Well, I've studied it in my spare time. At university I studied psychology."

"You studied psychology at university and you flew here from India."

"Yes. But there's not really a connection between those two things."

"No kidding," Carlos retorted.

"What were you doing in India?" Professor asked.

"I was catching a connecting flight from Tibet."

"And what were you doing in Tibet?"

"I haven't quite figured that out yet."

The jeep was a balloon filled with all the collective sarcasm that had ever been dished out in the world and I wanted the floor to open up and swallow me. This was not a good start. It was like being interviewed for the best job in the world and completely ruining any chance of getting it. Professor let out a deep sigh and raised his eyebrows as he looked down at his papers.

"What do you think, Carlos?" he asked.

"Psychology won't be very useful where we're going. I think there is something very strange going on here, but what can we do about it?"

There was no choice but to lay my cards on the table.

"I think there is something strange going on as well, but please trust me," I said. "It seems I am in the same position as you, so it would help if we just forget about all of these strange things and got on with whatever it is we have to get on with. I am a fish out of water in this bizarre place. I don't know where we are going or why we are going there, so it would help if we trusted each other and helped each other. I don't know who sent me here or why. All I have been told is that my skills will be required. There is a lot of secrecy around this – whatever it is."

Professor let out another long sigh and scratched his head. He was still stressed and confused and probably wanted to open the door and kick me out, but at the same time the fact that I knew nothing had calmed him. Whatever was happening here was being kept a closely guarded secret and the fact that I knew nothing was running parallel with his plans. But did the professor and Carlos really believe that I was as just as much in the dark as they were?

"Carlos?" Professor looked up at the mirror again.

"There appears to be a conspiracy and some very important people seem to know what's going on, but I think our new friend may really be in the same position we are. If *you-know-who* sent us to collect him, then we have no choice but to trust him."

It was a shock to learn that neither of them had any idea why they were told to come and collect me. If Professor Sanchez – one of the most respected archaeologists in the world – was an unwitting player in this game, then that alone gave a clue as to the kind of people we were dealing with. It was also clear that Professor and Carlos probably didn't want me here but it seemed their hands were tied. It seemed they either had to take me on board, or someone else would take control of the site in their place.

"Okay," Professor reluctantly gave in, "but let me tell you something, Stephen. What I am about to tell you is going to change everything you know, so prepare yourself. Are you aware of the history of Maya culture? I mean the historical time lines?"

"Yes, I am. The classic period around a thousand years ago, the Spanish invasion during the fifteen hundreds, and the Maya culture probably descended from the Olmecs around two thousand years ago and probably longer, as far back as three or even four thousand years, depending on which source you look at, but the best bet is 2,500 years ago."

"That's good enough," he replied. "Now take a deep breath and forget all of that, because after this conversation it will no longer apply."

We turned off the main highway and headed down a minor road. Trees were scattered infrequently and farther away a dense jungle could be seen.

"You appear to know a fair bit about the Maya," Carlos commented.

"As I say, I have studied archaeology in my spare time – and for a long time. Sure, I don't have a certificate from a university but as far as I am concerned that just makes you a 'member of the club'. I think it's a joke that anyone who isn't a 'member' is ignored and ridiculed. People with university degrees are programmed into thinking in a certain pattern and scientific funding is often dependant on the results that corporations wish to achieve. If the correct results don't surface, you lose your job. Anyway, that's veering away from archaeology. My point is that despite studying the subject for twenty years I would still be disregarded if I came up with any new ideas because I haven't 'joined the club'."

This babbling statement wasn't intended as a dig at these two men; it was a general assault on the scientific establishment, but at the same time it came more from the awkward situation in which I found myself – a defence mechanism. Professor seemed to be amused by my words, a slight smirk appearing on one side of his face.

"Is that what you call a 'spiritual view'?" Carlos asked, sarcastically.

Professor Sanchez let out a snigger, so out of pure embarrassment I continued explaining my standpoint.

"I spent a year in South America, mainly Peru, and travelled around the country visiting as many sites as I could. I volunteered on the dig at Cahuachi and worked in Nazca for a month. I have basic knowledge of ancient cultures in all areas of the world, mostly Central and South America as that's my main interest, but I lack the speciality focus of one subject. What's that quote? Oh yes, *'It's better to know something about everything, rather than knowing everything about something'*. I have adopted that philosophy throughout my life. It gives me a better viewing platform rather than tunnel vision, which is what most scientists have."

Thankfully neither Professor Sanchez nor Carlos took my words personally and they understood my viewpoint, or so it seemed. Now they could see where I was coming from, at least from my personal perspective.

"Okay, Steve. Let's not worry anymore about all of this. I can imagine how uncomfortable you are feeling after arriving here for the first time. So, are you ready?"

Taking the deep breath that had previously been requested I sat back in the chair, waiting for whatever Professor was going to tell me and anticipating nothing. Professor paused for a moment, as if he was having trouble articulating what he wanted to tell me.

"We have discovered a pyramid in the jungle, just north of the Guatemalan border. It seems no one else has ever uncovered it before. One of our guides found a strange artefact nearby and alerted me. His name is Felipe and when we are working in this area of Mexico he always accompanies us on the digs."

"What was the artefact?"

"It was a small bowl. Felipe noticed immediately it could not be placed in the area or connected to the known sites, so we immediately came over here. Once Carlos and I looked at it, we realised there was probably a site nearby, but the bowl was not familiar. It did not seem to be Maya. We realised it was old."

"How old, exactly?"

"Older than the culture of the Maya, which led us to the conclusion that it was probably not Maya – but no other culture ever existed in this area, as far as we know. The Aztecs were to the west, but of course they were even more recent than the Maya, in comparison with the bowl. Although the Olmecs were much older, they were farther to the north, so it could not have been theirs either."

It might have seemed strange that I had more interest in the bowl than the actual site but somehow the words that a new pyramid had been discovered went right through my head and out of the window. Charles had said that a new site had been discovered but I hadn't even thought about what it might be, beyond the idea of a few huts or another dome. The thought of a newly discovered Maya pyramid was the stuff of dreams.

"Is it possible the bowl is unconnected to the pyramid?"

"We have our suspicions, but not far away from the bowl we found the pyramid. There is a contradiction here. The bowl cannot be connected with any of the cultures that existed but then, neither can the pyramid. Except we have proof the pyramid is Maya."

"What proof do you have? And how can a pyramid be Maya but not connected with any known culture? That doesn't make sense. It's either Maya or it's not."

"Nothing here makes sense, Stephen, but we have these contradictions nonetheless. What I am trying to say is that, archaeologically speaking, there should not be a Maya pyramid that predates the Maya. We have proof that not only is the pyramid Maya, but it is *at least* two thousand years older than their culture!"

"You are joking, right?"

"No, I am not. This pyramid is five thousand years old."

"That's just not possible," I categorically stated. It was totally ridiculous.

"How do you think we feel?" Carlos said, from the driver's seat. "Our life's work is down the drain."

"Are you sure? Is it possible you have made a mistake?"

It was utter stupidity to ask that question – after all, these two men knew more about the Maya than anyone else on the planet.

"We are sure, Stephen, and we will explain it all to you in a moment," Professor replied.

Trying to imagine a five thousand year-old pyramid in the jungle was almost impossible. Not only did it outdate the Maya, but it pretty much outdated every culture known in Mexico. Even the Olmec, who were considered to be the first civilisation in Mexico, were not judged to be that old. The Olmec culture probably started around four thousand years ago, although some farming communities had been discovered which were estimated to be up to seven thousand years old. However, no structures were built prior to the start of *culture*, so this pyramid was at least a thousand years older than anything that had previously been found. In reality, however, there were few, if any, sites dating prior to 1000 BC, which made this pyramid two thousand years older than any known structure in Mexico.

I pressed my fingers into my forehead, struggling to absorb this new information, which disagreed with all my previous knowledge. I had no idea how Professor and Carlos felt but I guessed that it must be both devastating and exciting for them.

Professor was waiting patiently for me to process the information and, looking at him, it was apparent there was more to come.

"Go on," I said.

"At the base of the pyramid we have found a stone slab depicting the Maya calendar."

I started to laugh. "You are joking, right?"

"No, I am not," he said in a strict voice. "The slab appears to be a lid of some kind, but we do not know if underneath is a tomb, or another kind of chamber. There could even be a solid block underneath and the slab is just a piece of stone resting on top of it."

Professor smiled at me. My heart was thumping. I couldn't believe it. I was beginning to understand the full implications of what he was telling me and suddenly the world seemed to crumble into pieces around me. This incredible discovery was nothing less than shocking, and when you are faced with evidence that destroys previously known history it takes a while to come to terms with it. Professor and Carlos had had time to digest the information since they had made these discoveries one by one over a space of time. For me, it was being thrown in my face in one sitting.

"Yes, I know, Stephen. We are all stunned as well."

Professor Sanchez was fully aware of my difficulty in grasping what we were facing and he seemed surprisingly empathic.

"Let me get this straight," I said. "You have a five thousand year-old, previously undiscovered pyramid in the middle of the jungle which predates the Maya by at least a thousand years, and it contains a slab with a depiction of the Maya calendar?"

"That is most of it, yes, but don't forget the accepted date for the evolution of the Maya from the Olmec is about 2,500 years ago – about 500 BC. It is only an argument that they go back as far as four thousand years. So, in reality this pyramid gives us hard evidence that takes the Maya back *twice as far from today* than was previously thought."

For me, having a deep interest in Central American cultures, this was far more important and almost more unbelievable than a hidden dome in Tibet that exists in a higher dimension. Five thousand years ago, Central America was supposed to have been full of farming communities and hunter-gatherers. While the imagination could be stretched to accept that maybe, just maybe, some clever people had built a pyramid somewhere, it was near impossible to grasp the idea that a fully completed, in-use version of the Maya calendar was also found, dating to the same period. It not only suggested these people could build mathematically difficult structures a lot earlier than was previously believed, but also they must have had a complex knowledge of astronomy. It could only mean that the calendar itself was even older than the carving I was learning about, for the knowledge to construct such a complicated piece must have taken generations to evolve.

"Anyway," Professor continued, "the point of all this is we are going to lift the lid tomorrow. We have been ready for three days. We were just waiting for your arrival."

I barely heard his words through the churning chaos that was turning my mind inside out. If this was all true, this discovery was one of the most important in archaeological history.

3

THE FIRST WONDER OF THE WORLD

We turned off the road and headed down a dirt track into the forest, where the terrain soon became muddy and bumpy. The trees blocked out the sunlight but that only increased the humidity and the air conditioning was turned up a notch. After an hour or so, the jeep slowed to a crawl as we turned off the track and started to climb up a shallow hill. The forest became dense and driving more difficult as nature, rather than human tracks, dominated the terrain. A slow, lumbering and bumpy ride lasted another two hours before we ground to a halt at the edge of a steep hill. When the engine was switched off the sound of the jungle echoed through the trees and unrecognisable birds with strange, unfamiliar song alerted the forest to our arrival. Insects buzzed all around and larger mammals rustled in the bushes.

"We go on foot from here, but be warned – you will get a blast of heat when you open the door," Professor said.

He wasn't wrong. The air conditioning had given us a false sense of comfort and when the door was opened the humidity hit me as if we had stepped into an industrial oven. Within minutes sweat dripped from my nose. I had forgotten how uncomfortable the jungle can be. From a personal perspective the jungle is a wretched environment, but at the same time the aura it creates is incredible – *everything* is alive and the energy is powerful and intense. This is why the chopping down of the rainforests is such a crime against the planet. In the case of the world's great jungles it is not solely the cutting down of the trees which is the issue – it is the powerful energy of the earth that is being removed, the life blood of the planet, not to mention the irreplaceable habitats of millions of creatures.

"Bloody hell," I cried out.

"Yes, it is a bit of a shock," said Carlos, "you'll get accustomed within the hour, but we have a long walk yet."

Unfortunately, coming from a colder climate, that prediction didn't ring true for me. The jungle has never made me comfortable. Even after acclimatisation it's impossible to feel comfortable and there is always a longing to leave for a cooler area. I had once spent a month in the Amazon jungle; after about four days I did become accustomed to the environment but the stickiness caused by the intense humidity still left me feeling distressed and nights were often sleepless under the dreadful heat of a mosquito net.

After gathering all the necessary equipment, as well as our own packs, we set off in the stifling heat towards the pyramid. The huge trees gave cover from the intense rays of the sun but in contrast this only increased humidity under the canopy and the trek was slow and tortuous. There was no natural path along this route – we had to fight our way through the dense jungle. Occasionally there were chopped branches lying on the floor from the team's original expedition and somehow they had remembered the route, but for the most part it appeared like virgin forest, almost as if the trees had already reclaimed the path that had been cut. My back was soaked with sweat, my rucksack stuck to my back, and water dripped from the end of my nose at regular intervals like a broken tap. Flies and mosquitos were everywhere, despite the fact it was nowhere near dusk, and periodically a sharp prick to the neck was swiftly followed by a high pitched buzzing sound. Mosquitos have this incredible ability to creep up on you in silence and you only seem to hear them when they fly off, only after they have had their fill of your life force.

"So, how far away from the pyramid was the bowl found?" I asked, panting like a dog after a run in the park.

"Felipe found it about three hundred metres north, just off this route," Carlos answered. "We started scouring the area and fanned out in all directions. We had found nothing for over a week and thought that maybe it had simply been discarded by someone passing through millennia ago, or even recently. We were about to give up when, on the last day, we came across a clearing in the forest. That's where we found the site but at first glance we couldn't see anything. Ironically, we had searched everywhere else before we found the site. Sometimes you find what you are looking for on the first day, and other times you find something in the last location. There seems to be little in between."

"So, what makes you think the bowl is connected with the site?"

"We don't. Both are complete anomalies. We have a bowl that doesn't fit into the historical record and a pyramid that is equally out of place. In scientific terms that's the only thing that connects them, but it's not enough evidence to put them together in history."

Carlos was right. If the bowl had been found with the pyramid then they could have a good argument that they were linked, but the fact that the bowl was some distance away meant nothing.

By the time we reached the site, it felt as if the temperature had increased enormously. The humidity was almost unbearable. It had taken us about two hours to reach the site on foot. It had been a treacherous journey and I had ensured my trousers were tucked into my socks during the walk, for obvious reasons.

"Okay, we are nearly there," said Professor, "you see that tree over there with the large branch that looks like a raised arm?"

Looking in the direction he was pointing, about a hundred metres away, there was a clearing. Through the dense forest and down a slope was an odd looking, but very large tree.

"Oh yes," I said, "the one with the dense foliage on the right side."

"Yes. What do you see there?"

Browsing around the tree line there was nothing but more trees, yet glancing downwards slightly there was the unmistakable outline of a beautifully constructed pyramid. It was almost completely camouflaged and although the area had obviously been cleared by the team it was still cleverly concealed within the jungle.

"Wow!"

"That is exactly what I said."

"That's unbelievable. You can see almost nothing at all. It just looks like a natural hill."

"Yes, it is very much concealed, from this angle at least. Before we cleared it you could easily have walked past and not notice what it actually is. I am sure we could also have passed it in ignorance if Carlos had not walked across in front of it. Considering how experienced we are, that shows you how well it has been concealed. But, in reality, it is not concealed. The shape of the pyramid is obvious in relation to the surroundings but it has a strange kind of camouflage – an illusion – and it blends in almost unnoticed. It is either a fluke of nature, or there is an advanced and clever design to it. From the front, it is obvious what it is, but from any other angle it looks like a part of the landscape. It is a bit like one of those 3D images that show a jumbled mess, and only when you defocus your eyes do you get to see an image. However, for my own sanity, I have concluded that it is just a coincidence."

The pyramid was definitely out of place in its form but from a distance it certainly looked like a part of the landscape, especially from the back where the trees were many. I had expected to see a steep sided, typical Maya structure so that was another reason I hadn't seen it at first glance, for this pyramid was small in height with a shallow angle to the sides. There was something very peculiar about this place and I couldn't figure out what it was, but from the outset its design felt slightly otherworldly. If the professor had the same feeling then he must have been extremely confused. For me, the obvious comparison that came to mind was the dome back in Tibet, but this was hardly the same thing. The dome had looked new even today but this long-forgotten pyramid, although in good condition, was looking rather sad and it certainly fitted in with the other cultural buildings of Mexico, even if it was much older. While the dome was unlike anything that had been built by previous cultures on the planet, this pyramid was similar to any other pyramid. Only its supposed antiquity was in question.

Professor and Carlos were both staring at their discovery in a strange way and there appeared to be a marked reluctance to move on both their parts, almost as if they didn't want to go any farther. Carlos took a deep breath and headed towards the pyramid and I stood silently with Professor Sanchez, who appeared hesitant and dismayed.

"I need to ask you something," he said. "I do not know what is going on here and I am really not happy about it. No one knows about this site. I told no one. So the fact that I received a phone call from someone at the university telling me to drive to Candelaria and collect you was a considerable shock. It also meant that we had to halt the dig until your arrival. I do not know who you are, or why you are here, and I certainly do not know how anyone found out about this site. So, if you want me to trust you, is there any information you could give that might enlighten me? Because, to be honest, the only conclusion I can come to is that someone in my team is no longer trustworthy."

"How did you get a phone signal out here?"

It was a stupid question under the circumstances, but the image of Professor Sanchez receiving the phone call made me think of the phone that was in my backpack. He looked at me, startled.

"I was in Candelaria picking up supplies. Once we found the site we realised we would be here a while."

"When did you get the call?"

Professor looked back at me with a deep frown.

"About three weeks ago. Why?"

"Three weeks ago." I ran my hand slowly through my hair, pushing back a lake of water and trying to hold my brain in place – I was sure it was about to explode. Three weeks ago I had been back in England and my strange meeting with Charles hadn't even occurred.

"You've been waiting three weeks?" I asked, my surprise all too apparent.

"Yes and no. We continued working here. We had a lot of work to do, clearing the site and uncovering the slab from layers of mud. We finished about three days ago and since then we have been waiting for you."

So, it was almost certain that the discovery of the pyramid was the event that had prompted Charles to send me to China in the first place. Now I was torn between the idea that everything was predetermined and I was simply playing out an already written role and the other possibility – that these people, whoever they were, were connected all over the globe and had ways of communicating that I was unaware of.

"It might come as a surprise to you," I told Professor, "but I only discovered I was being sent to Mexico three days ago."

"You did not know about this at all before then? So what *were* you doing in Tibet?"

"Escaping death, most of the time."

Professor looked at me. He must surely have been wondering if I was making this all up. Something had to be said and I really needed to be honest with him.

"I understand your position, Professor. First of all, I am no one special and certainly not a threat to you or your dig. I will be working under your jurisdiction at all times. This is your dig and nothing will change. All decisions will be yours and I have not been sent here to oversee or take control. The word I was given is to 'assist' you, not 'control' you, so please don't think I am one of 'them'. As far as my time in Tibet goes, there are things I can't tell you, things I haven't even figured out for myself yet. I am still confused about it all but I get the feeling that if what is happening here is as weird as Tibet, I'll be telling you some very strange stories pretty soon. As for whether someone in your team is untrustworthy, I can't answer that question, but it's unlikely. I can tell you things may be far stranger than you can imagine. Between you and me, there's a possibility that a certain amount of weirdness may be involved here."

"What do you mean by that?" he asked.

"I mean that there may be greater forces at work."

"This still does not explain to me how someone at the university knew about this site when it has been kept a secret, so the only conclusion I can come to is that someone in my team has leaked the information."

Talk about being in a difficult position. It was necessary to remain secretive about what I knew and certainly it would be unwise to talk about Charles at all but, at the same time, I felt a real connection with Professor Sanchez and I was impelled to be as honest as I could, without jeopardising my position.

"I don't have the answers myself, Professor, but may I suggest that the most likely explanation is that the person who sent me here probably informed your superior. But how that person knew about this site is as much a mystery to me as it is to you."

Professor paused for a moment, staring blankly into the sunlit sky and then he let out a long, disbelieving sigh. I couldn't imagine how I was ever going to gain his trust.

"I am sorry Stephen, but that does not make sense to me. The most likely scenario is the one that is most obvious."

"Well, after what I have learned recently, I would be inclined to disagree with that."

"Would you care to elaborate?"

Certainly I didn't want to tell him anything, for I didn't think he was ready to know the things I had seen and heard in Tibet, at least not yet. What was required was an analogy.

"You know how the Aztecs were expecting a bearded white man to turn up in the year of *One Reed*? Cortés arrived in that year – the Aztecs probably thought he was the returning God *Quetzalcoatl* – that one incident bringing an end to an entire civilisation. We know that's historical fact but explaining it is almost impossible, if you exclude coincidence."

There wasn't a better explanation under the circumstances. At least the professor would be able to relate to the story. The confusion surrounding Cortés' arrival in exactly that year is a mystery that most scientists have ignored, or at least they say it's just coincidence, but surely it is more of a synchronicity. It is almost certain that Cortés manipulated this event to his advantage, a single synchronicity that brought an end to the native Mexican civilisations that existed during that time. It's quite possible that if Cortés had arrived in any other year, the Aztecs may have attacked and killed the Spanish invaders and Central and South America could have been dominated by the British, French, Dutch, or any of the other empire builders that went to the

New World. It's even possible that the country we now call the 'United States' could have taken control of the entire continent. It's incredible to imagine how one simple, seemingly unimportant, event can shape an entire continent, but can we call this synchronicity? Can the total desolation of an entire country – the murder of tens of thousands of people, the eradication of entire civilisations through alien diseases, the burning of nearly all historical and religious documents, and the extinction of many languages – be compared to finding an extension socket for a toothbrush? Where does coincidence end and synchronicity begin? Come to that, where does synchronicity end and destiny begin?

Thankfully, judging by Professor Sanchez's reaction, he was well aware of how inexplicable the event of Cortés' arrival was.

"Do you honestly think things could be *that* unusual?"

"You could well be the Cortés of the twenty-first century – without the bloodshed, of course. When the time is right, Professor, I will tell you things that will put hair on your chest."

He looked at me with a frown.

"It's an English expression," I said.

There was a very long silence. For at least two minutes we stood there looking across at the strange pyramid that was undoubtedly in the wrong place as well as the wrong time.

Then Professor turned to me. "Okay, let's go. Are you ready for this?"

"I guess."

Never in a million years would I have imagined that events in Tibet would be child's play compared to the terror that awaited us in the jungles of Mexico, but as soon as we stepped forwards and headed down the slope the Maya calendar – *our Maya calendar* – started ticking.

4

THE MOTHER OF ALL PYRAMIDS

A feeling of excitement and anticipation welled up inside me and for once the heat wasn't bothering me. We walked the last hundred metres down the shallow slope and when it levelled out the ground was slightly sodden due to a recent downpour of tropical rainfall. The front of the pyramid came into view and only then, once it was just a few metres in front of us, could it be seen it in all its beauty.

The pyramid was surprisingly small and only about twenty-five feet high, but its general design was unusual and not the typical style of the Maya. A surprisingly shallow angle led to a flat platform at the top and a narrow stairway was located in the middle, but it was the angle that was so bizarre. The forty-five degree sides made the pyramid look as if a fat God had been sitting on it for the past five thousand years, slowly squashing it. Imagining a giant Buddha sitting on the top, I laughed out loud to looks of bewilderment from Professor Sanchez and Carlos.

The weird thing, though, was that when we reached the cleared area a strange echo effect came into play. Wherever any of us stood, whether we were near the pyramid or near the trees, our voices seemed amplified and could be heard anywhere around the site. It turned out to be only one of many strange things that would occur during the coming days – things that were experienced by us all but which were so bizarre they would be left unmentioned.

We reached a low wall immediately in front of the pyramid and slightly to the left, which enclosed a square with a deep hole.

"We excavated this area first and now you can clearly see the size of the pit," Professor said.

"You excavated *this* first?"

For me this decision was more than surprising. I would have been draped over the steps of the pyramid like a bikini-clad model over a new sports car if I had discovered this place.

"We had a look over the pyramid and saw nothing obvious so we decided clearing it could wait until later. What we wanted was another piece of archaeology that could give us a time period and even a culture to attach to it. Unfortunately we never found anything here. It took us an entire week just to clear the branches and dig a half metre-square pit. We only managed to dig down about twenty centimetres."

"Surely if the pyramid is five thousand years old you'd need to dig down much farther than that?"

"Call it experience, Stephen. I can assure you that pit is empty. Anyway, at that time we had no idea the pyramid was very old. We had not really noticed the strange shape jutting out from the corner. Well, we had noticed it but it appeared to be a pile of mud so we had assumed it was a fallen stone, or something, that had come off the side, or maybe it was a natural boulder. Stupid really, considering the size of it, but we were focusing on finding a connection between the bowl and the pyramid and from my experience the most likely evidence would be pottery shards or something like that. These things usually turn up in the most boring places."

I stared down into the hole. The floor, full of mud, was about four feet down.

"Is this a sacrificial pit?" I asked, my voice bouncing off the low walls and out into the forest.

"No. There is no evidence any sacrifice took place here and it is also illogical to think they would have filled this pit with victims, since it is so impractical. We think this site was for something else but we do not know what. We are scratching our heads over this because of the age of the slab."

I had almost forgotten about the slab but now my attention was drawn to the bottom of the pyramid on the right corner, the left side as we faced it. The slab was big and looking at it from a distance I suddenly realised how strange this place really was and how surreal the situation. There I was, standing next to the world's best intellect on Maya history and he didn't have a clue about this place. In fact the only thing he was certain of was that the pyramid was, indeed, Maya.

As we passed the steps, the unusual angle of the pyramid compared to other Maya structures was even more apparent.

"That's really not as steep as a normal Maya pyramid," I remarked.

"Yes. As we said before the pyramid is at an angle of *exactly* forty-five degrees, which in itself proves that no sacrifice was ever carried out here. Normally, the Maya would sacrifice their victim at the top, on the platform, and then they would cut off the head and throw both the head and the body down the steps. The shallower angle of the slope means that bodies would not fall to the bottom – they would probably come to rest a few steps down. Sacrificial pyramids also tend to be very tall in comparison to other structures. They are a show of power and dominance and you would want everyone to see that power. This place is far too small. In essence the design is of a typical sacrificial temple but it is too small and the angle too shallow. What I think you must understand is that it is very unlikely sacrifice was a part of life in this area during that time period. Sacrifice came about thousands of years later, as far as we know, and anyway the Maya were not as barbaric as they have been made out to be. Sure, they did use sacrifice but not on the scale of the Aztecs. I think people often confuse the Maya and the Aztecs, especially since they were contemporaries. Anyway, that is not the significant thing here, either. This is actually the earliest known use of the forty-five degree angle in the Americas. That is one new discovery – it is perhaps the earliest known use of this kind of geometry."

"There will be plenty more new discoveries to come, I am sure," said Carlos, who was unpacking the supplies by the tents.

"Is it really the first known use of a forty-five degree angle?" I asked Professor.

"Yes. Although the pyramid itself contradicts later constructions in its slope angle, the use of the forty-five degree angle is an indication that the mathematics of the Maya was in place a lot earlier than we've previously assumed."

"What do you mean?"

"Well, you'll be familiar with the fact that the Maya year was 360 days long, using their calculations of a base twenty, plus the five unnamed days. This implies the use of sexagesimal numbers in their mathematics."

"Sorry?"

"Sexagesimal numbers – calculations using a base sixty. To be brief, it implies that the constructors had knowledge of circles and pi over five thousand years ago. The Sumerians have been credited with using sexagesimal mathematics in the third millennium BC, but we seem to have it in use here at this pyramid, and around the same time period. The fact the calendar is 360 days long suggests the use of a sexagesimal numbering system. A circle can be directly linked to the solar year, since certain calendars contained 360 days, and the sun travels through the ecliptic at a rate of slightly less than one degree per day, making 360 degrees over a 365-day year.

The fact that the Maya calendar was 360 days long may have more to do with circular mathematics and the path of the sun than a mistake in their logic and their calculation of the solar year, which some people might want you to believe." Professor turned and stared at me. "Not that they made any mistakes in their logic. They were well aware of how long the solar year was. In fact their calculations of the solar year were accurate to the point of stupidity."

I was managing to understand what Professor was telling me, but only just. It had never previously crossed my mind that the Maya Haab calendar – their solar year – may have been directly linked to the sun's voyage through the ecliptic and circular mathematics, rather than the number of days the earth takes to circumnavigate the sun. But it made sense. Their calendar was 360 days long, not 365 – the five extra days were 'unnamed' – and this could be more easily linked to circular mathematics and the degrees of a circle. It was clear that these were two completely different systems in place – the solar year and the 360-day calendar. But the implications were that the Maya were well aware of circular mathematics long before this knowledge supposedly came to the Americas, and all this because of one obscure pyramid seemingly half-buried in the middle of nowhere in the Mexican jungle.

"How do you even know that this site is Maya?" I asked.

"Well, that is the problem, is it not? We do not actually have a reference for the finds. We have a pyramid with a Maya calendar and Mayan hieroglyphs, but it is two-and-a-half millennia older than their culture. We're saying it is Maya because that is what it looks like, but does it mean the Maya adopted their calendar and language from whoever these people were, or does it mean the Maya culture is at least 2,500 years older than we thought? Either way, we have a fully completed calendar with all the necessary calculations of astronomy and circular mathematics built into it. If this calendar goes back even further, then it is quite possible it was these people who discovered the mathematics, not the Sumerians."

Whatever the explanation, it was shattering. I couldn't even grasp the concept – my mind was struggling more with this information than the Tibetan discoveries. What confused me more than anything, though, was the angle of the pyramid. Later pyramids, all over the world, were built with a steeper angle of around fifty-two degrees because otherwise the very weight of such a structure means that the pyramid will collapse in on itself. There was no logical explanation as to how this pyramid, with its forty-five degree sides, had managed to stay standing at all, let alone for five thousand years. There must have been an advanced technology involved in its construction to make the interior strong enough to withstand the weight bearing down on it, especially closer to the centre.

However, the pyramid wasn't particularly high in comparison to later Maya pyramids and the most amazing thing was that there was a pyramid here at all. The engineering and construction work required to build such a structure is so complicated it requires an advanced level of mathematics and architecture. The builders of the Egyptian pyramids at Giza, for example, had a technological knowhow that surpasses modern techniques. Modern engineers have admitted it would be impossible to replicate one of the Giza pyramids, even with our technology.

This simple fact cries out across history – a question that cannot be answered and which, for the most part, is brushed under the carpet by scientists who are convinced the Ancient Egyptians cut these stones with soft copper tools, dragged them across the land, and then stacked them on top of one another in such a way that their precise alignment has an accuracy which can only be achieved by using something similar to a laser beam. And that's the easy part. When you start taking into account the precise measurements of the internal chambers and tunnels which, by any normal engineering principles, should collapse under the weight of the pyramid, you begin to realise one simple thing – technologically our ancestors were so far ahead of us it is totally ludicrous.

Something is seriously *and* fundamentally wrong with our history and most people seem to ignore it. The level of technology required to build such structures can only mean that all the pyramids in the world have to be a *legacy* of an even earlier time period.

So, there we were, standing in front of a pyramid in Mexico that was at least 2,500 years older than it should be, which could only mean that the technology involved in building it was inherited from an earlier culture. Of course, this little pyramid was in no way comparable to the monsters of Egypt, but the principle still remains – architecturally, mathematically and scientifically, pyramids are very difficult to build. So, why didn't these ancient people just build a square house and be done with it? Pyramids must have had a function that is lost to us. Tombs for the dead, places to sacrifice or religious centres are not adequate explanations for these structures. These people knew something that has been lost through history and there is no doubt there must be some connection between the different cultures who built them - how do we explain that people in different parts of the world were building similar shaped structures at the same time?

I looked around the site. Our sleeping area was placed beyond the corner of the pyramid, about twenty feet away, and near the side of the pyramid was an area that was obviously used as the kitchen. That only left the most important thing – the slab – which was resting on a large block of stone on the right hand bottom corner of the pyramid. It seemed to be in a rather strange position, offset from the centre and protruding from one corner.

I walked over to it and then, looking at it properly for the first time, I almost fell to my knees, for it was undoubtedly the most incredible piece of archaeology I had ever seen. The slab was huge, about six feet square, roughly six inches thick and covering what at first glance appeared to be a sarcophagus.

The image in the middle of the slab was an exact copy of the later calendar stone but this calendar was set within a square border, carved into the solid block. The stone had been smoothed level very precisely and only after this was the calendar cut into the slab. It was an incredibly complex piece of artwork that employed highly skilled carving.

The earth above the slab had been cut away and the amount of work that had gone in to revealing the top of the slab could be clearly seen. The soil was cut at an angle and an A-frame had been attached with all four corners of the slab tied with rope. The slab was ready to be lifted and it was apparent how impatient everyone must be to get started.

"She is beautiful, is she not?" said Professor, who was proudly looking over my shoulder at this, his greatest of finds.

"She certainly is. It's incredible workmanship for such an old stone."

"That is what I thought."

Suddenly I was startled by an irregularity.

"I thought you said this was a copy of the *Maya* calendar? Surely this is the *Aztec* calendar."

"Well done for noticing that. First, let me clarify that the Aztecs called themselves 'Mexica', the word from which Mexico gets its name. The term 'Aztec' is modern. But don't be fooled into thinking that the Aztec calendar stone, or Mexica sun stone, is originally Mexica. If you look at the mathematics incorporated into the stone you will see the Maya calendars in there. Both the Aztec and the Maya used the same calendars and system of calculation, as did many Mesoamerican cultures, and since the Maya existed two thousand years prior to the arrival of the Aztecs, then the system must have been originally Maya."

"Yes, but surely the Aztec calendar is 'Aztec' because it depicts Aztec deities?"

Professor was smiling at me again. It was obvious when the next part of the story was coming because each time he had that same expression on his face.

"Do you notice anything strange about the calendar?" he asked.

"No, it's just an exact copy of the calendar stone."

Staring at it once again I could see nothing that implied any difference to the later version. I was simply in awe at this marvel of archaeology – the Eighth Wonder of The Ancient World. Or was it the First?

"Are you sure?"

"No, I can't see anything out of place."

"Keep looking," he said. He moved around to the side of the slab and watched me with a big grin on his face. He wasn't going to point out whatever it was he wanted me to know – I had to figure it out for myself. Just as embarrassment was about to take hold I suddenly realised what it was, and it was the most obvious thing imaginable.

"Oh my God, the centre circle is missing!"

"Exactly. And this leads us to the conclusion that this calendar was made towards the end of the fourth Sun, which ended around 3114 BC. This also coincides with the approximate age of the mud layers, so we have something to back it up with."

It was an astonishing discovery and it meant the later, well-known calendar stone was a work in progress.

The modern Aztec calendar stone, or Mexica sun stone, has one large circle in the centre. Four squares on the outside connect to it, rather like the geometric design of 'squaring the circle'. Two more circles are placed between the squares in the east and west position. There is an arrow design in the northern position and a series of dots set in two squares in the southern position. Surrounding these, concentric rings make up the outer circles, each representing separate time periods in the different calendars. Each of the five central shapes – the circle and the four squares – is called a 'Sun', representing a time cycle of 5,126 years. Five cycles, or Suns, amount to 25,630 years, which is thought to be the exact length of the precession of the equinoxes – the wobble in the Earth's rotation. How the ancient Maya predicted this cycle so exactly is a complete mystery.

The earth spins on its axis rather like a gyroscope, and it takes approximately twenty-six thousand years to make one complete circle. Since the current 'Sun' began in 3114 BC, and the circle representing that Sun was missing from the slab, it was an obvious deduction that this slab was made to represent the previous four cycles – and not the current one. This piece of evidence, coupled with the age of the mud layers, made it unquestionable that this calendar stone was indeed five thousand years old. It was an archaeological miracle.

"As you rightly said," Professor explained, "the centre circle is missing. The modern Aztec calendar stone depicts the Aztec God of the sun, Tonatiuh, in the centre circle. Now, since the Aztec calendar stone incorporates Maya time periods, or calendars, I believe strongly that the Aztecs were in fact influenced by and partly descended from the Maya. Most scholars seem to think they appeared independently, probably due to geographical location, but through my years of research I believe the Aztecs were influenced by a group who left the Maya heartland and started their own colony. What is termed the 'classic period' of the Maya came to an end long before the Spanish arrived, so I think that when this so-called collapse occurred, a small number may have moved west and eventually started their own culture with natives they found there."

"That doesn't make sense," I frowned. "I'm not an expert on this, but I thought the Classic Maya collapse was somewhere around 900 AD and the Aztec civilisation started in the early fourteenth century. That's a four hundred-year difference *and* a long way for a migration."

"That's correct, but let me give you the reasons for my logic. First, the collapse of the classic Maya may have been related to climate – possibly drought, although I am not fully in agreement with that theory – and this could have been the reason for the long distances travelled through Mexico. Secondly, I think the Aztec Empire was started by a mix of this small band of people and others already living in the west of Mexico. I believe this because of the strong influence of the Maya in Aztec culture. I think their calendar was exported from the Maya heartland. There are obvious differences between the two cultures, but too many similarities. Also, the primary bases of the Aztec culture can be traced to around 1100 AD, only two hundred years after the Classic Maya collapse. They spoke different languages, but that can be explained by the influence of the group majority in the west."

"So, even though this is the *Aztec* calendar stone, you believe it to be the *Maya* calendar?"

"Absolutely. Let's not forget we have *Mayan* hieroglyphs here, not Aztec. It is a bit of a problem because this version of the calendar only appears in the Aztec heartland – not the Maya – but this calendar stone here is *four thousand* years older than the Aztec! It is too confusing, but if you accept that the calendar stone is Aztec, then we have a mix of Maya and Aztec here at this site. However, I do not believe this to be the case, because of other factors. Therefore I am proposing that this site is purely Maya."

"Okay, I'm getting confused by this. Why do you think this site is purely Maya when you have a Mexica sun stone?"

Professor smiled again. He leaned in towards the beautiful stone and we both stared at the gorgeously carved inscriptions.

"You see the inner circle, depicting the twenty-day calendar. Do you notice anything about the twenty pictures carved there?"

"No, I don't know the different images for each day, to be honest."

"In the Mexica sun stone and the Maya calendar they are different pictograms and they have a different meaning. The ones you are looking at are not from the Mexica sun stone – they are from the Maya Tzolk'in calendar!"

It was clear what Professor was saying – since this calendar, although an exact copy of the later Mexica sun stone, incorporated Maya pictograms it must have been the original version. He must be correct in thinking that the Aztecs obtained or imported an earlier version and then made their own calendar based on a new, slightly different, belief system. His proposed theory that the Aztec evolved from the Maya was practically proven by the evidence in front of us.

Standing for so long in front of this huge square stone had created an intense sensation within me, as if the stone had a power all of its own. It was a statement, a message from the past that told of the future, but the future was, at this point in time, unwritten.

"It's a bit of a coincidence that you have found this stone when the later calendar is about to end. It's only two years until 2012."

"Yes, that was the first thing that caught my attention," said Professor, "which brings me on to the carvings we discovered at the other end of the pyramid." He led me past the steps and on the base of the pyramid I saw a series of Mayan hieroglyphs. Bizarrely, they seemed to me to be very similar to later writings, which meant that the Mayan language, at least in written form, had been in use in the same form for thousands of years. Mayan hieroglyphs are not easy to understand, but thankfully I was with an expert on the subject. There were five of them, but they would turn out to be the most important Mayan inscriptions ever found. Professor pointed to the first symbol.

"In principle, it says - *This site represents the end of time and a return to the original system*. We can deduce what it means by 'the end of time' because of the calendar, but we do not know what it means by 'returning to the original system'."

"Maybe it means the starting point of the next cycle of precession."

"I had thought that, but since the Earth is a sphere there cannot really be a starting point of precession because it simply rotates in a circular motion, like a gyroscope. What has never been fully understood is why the five cycles start at the time they do – 23,618 BC – and what that date actually signifies. It could just be a mythological date referencing something like the beginning of time as they knew it. Nobody really knows – and since American archaeology began in earnest only relatively recently, this site is the only link we have to this time period. It is quite frustrating because there is nothing of significance here other than what we have found. However, what we do know of course is that there are five Sun cycles in the Maya calendar and this current one, the one we're living through, is the last. So, we do have a beginning – and an ending – in that sense."

"But the calendar doesn't actually end in 2012, right?" I asked, as we walked back towards the slab.

"Well, yes and no. There is no doubt that at the end of this cycle there will be the beginning of a new one – another 5,126-year period. But there were five Sun cycles of the Maya – this is the last one – and according to the mythology, each of those worlds are destroyed by some catastrophe. Since there are five cycles and the total of those five cycles is exactly, or close to, the number of years in the precession of the equinoxes, then they must have known about precession. If that is the case then we have to ask why they broke that cycle down into five equal lengths of time."

"Is it possible that, since the precession of the equinoxes is a cycle, they knew something about it that we don't? Maybe at some point during precession there is some kind of mechanical event that can be measured at the end or the beginning of each cycle."

"But then you would be insinuating that these people were advanced enough to have measured that frequency, and that they were in existence early enough to experience that event. That is not something I am willing to accept. It is difficult enough to believe they even knew about the precession of the equinoxes."

"No disrespect, Professor, but maybe that has more to do with your preconceived ideas than any evidence?"

"But what you are proposing is, at the very best, circumstantial or even guesswork."

"That's true – but you've found a pyramid that's twice as old as it should be. Maybe you need to start stretching your imagination?"

"I can stretch my imagination back five thousand years, no problem, but not twenty-five thousand years. There is simply no reference point or evidence to take this knowledge back *that* far in history."

"Maybe if there is a tomb under the slab, the occupant will give you more clues."

"Yes, maybe, but it is an odd shape for a tomb, don't you think?"

"Maybe there are two people in there," I responded, running my hands over the smooth edges of the slab.

"Possibly. Or maybe it's just a solid stone block made specifically to hold this lid in place and keep it secure. As an archaeologist I have learned, over the years, to expect nothing but to plan for a miracle. Certainly, it is wise to think the worst rather than expect something wonderful, because ninety-nine times out of a hundred you will be very disappointed. Most digs turn up nothing, as you doubtless know."

"I see that, but in this case you've already found the Holy Grail."

"Yes, maybe, but really we have only uncovered more questions and absolutely no answers. It is very exciting but frustrating from that perspective. Anyway, if there is nothing under the lid I think we will just pack up and leave."

"Aren't you going to take the lid with you?"

"Eventually we will, yes. We will return with a bigger team and extra transport but it is a logistical nightmare considering the location. It must weigh several thousand kilos and you've seen the terrain around here. However, once the correct authorities are informed I expect it to be removed by helicopter when they realise the value of it. A land removal will risk breakage."

Standing in front of the pyramid and looking around it became apparent that even without the inexplicable archaeology this was not an ordinary place. The area in front of the pyramid was devoid of trees and although this may have been part of the original design, there was no reason why the jungle should not have reclaimed the land during the five thousand years since then. In front of the pyramid there was a clear area of around sixty feet extending outwards before the dense jungle swallowed everything. Around the sides of the pyramid there was also bare ground extending from the base for about fifteen feet, but the area to the back of the pyramid was covered in dense forest. The strange thing was that in front it looked like a perfect rectangular pattern of deliberately cleared ground. Professor had said they had come across a 'clearing', but I decided to check anyway.

"Did you clear this area?"

"No," was all he said.

"Then how come the area is clear and why has it not been filled in with trees and dense jungle?"

Professor's head turned slowly towards Carlos. Their eyes met but no words came from their mouths – a silent response. They had no answer to this question and thus the conclusion was that there was no logical explanation. I sensed the same feeling from them that I had when we first arrived. Something wasn't right here – beyond the obvious mysteries.

Carlos, perhaps in an attempt to break the silence – or to change the subject – suggested that we should think about eating after our strenuous walk here. I was just about to wholeheartedly agree when two men appeared from the trees, one carrying a rifle, which made me instantly nervous. But it turned out that these two were part of the team.

From a distance they looked almost identical. They were the same height, the same build, and had the same weathered look from spending most of their lives working outdoors. I was first introduced to Juan, who may have been around forty but looked ten years older. He had piercing brown eyes and I suspected that in his younger years he had been quite a lady killer. Felipe was a little younger but also slim and muscular – I was jealous of his ethnic build, with no body fat and a 'six-pack' to die for. Felipe, I remembered, was the one who had originally found the bowl. He also had piercing eyes but there was a green tint to their darkness. He didn't quite have Juan's looks, but certainly he had the same appearance as his ancestors – high cheek bones and a powerful, masculine face. Even though both of these men were much smaller than me, it certainly wouldn't be a good idea to engage in physical combat with either of them. It was easy to imagine them as Maya warriors. They were both native Mexicans of Maya descent and were expert trackers and hunters.

"Did you find anything?" asked Professor.

"Not a thing," replied Juan, "and I think we've now covered about a kilometre in all directions. There is nothing but trees and mosquitos."

Professor explained that Juan and Felipe had been scouring the area for some time trying to find any trace of other possible structures, but without success.

"We did discover something you may find interesting, though," Juan continued. "It was on the ground a few hundred metres away."

He passed the object to Professor. It was a spear head, rusted and dented and about three inches long.

"A tribal spear head," said Professor. "Any ideas?" He looked cautiously back at Juan.

"The nearest tribe is about twenty kilometres from here. I suspect it's one of theirs, although that's quite a distance for a hunting expedition. Anyway, it's been there quite a while. I don't think we will be interrupted in the near future."

Professor was obviously concerned that unwanted visitors might arrive and lay claim to the pyramid and its secrets, but thankfully Juan dispelled any misgivings on that front. Not only did he have excellent tracking skills but he knew the area well and was an expert on tribal behaviour. The term 'tribe' is misleading since there are few real native tribes left in Mexico and those that remain have modernised themselves with mobile phones, televisions and modern clothing, but there are still Maya villages that practice the old ways, including traditional hunting.

Professor was more than adequately satisfied that no one had been in this area for a considerable time and thus we could continue without any fear. It was obvious even to me that the spear head was rusted so much it must have been there for years, rather than months.

The most satisfying thing, however, was that my understanding of the *Castellano* Spanish language – although the Mexicans call it *Español* – had not diminished in the years since my travels. Up to now, the conversations with Carlos and Professor had been in English, but neither Juan nor Felipe spoke the language, so from now on our group conversations were in Spanish. Occasionally Felipe and Juan spoke to each other in Yucatec Mayan, a language that Carlos and I had no knowledge of, but the intellectual Professor was fluent in that too. I wouldn't have been too surprised if he knew Mandarin, Hebrew and Russian as well.

Juan and Felipe decided to take a break and headed for the area set aside for cooking. I turned back to look at the pyramid. I was beginning to realise that one of the weirdest things about it was its state of preservation. Many Maya pyramids have been completely destroyed just by being in an environment where trees and shrubs grow so rapidly that, over the last thousand years, they have turned once great structures into nothing but mounds of earth and rubble.

"How long did it take to clear the pyramid of all the undergrowth that must have overtaken it?" I asked Professor and Carlos.

"Not long," Carlos replied. "There were some tough-rooted creepers and a few trees had managed to grow on the slopes and break through the structure, mostly on the sides and on the back. But there was no real major damage – only surface damage on the outer shell."

"Okay, but how is it that the pyramid was not completely covered? I mean, I am no expert on growth rates, but I would have expected that five thousand years in an environment like this would have buried this place beyond recognition. Trees taking root on the pyramid should have broken the structure apart completely. It's almost like it's been cleared periodically, as if a gardener has occasionally appeared and tidied everything up."

Professor and Carlos once again looked at each other in silence and then Professor stared at me. "We do not know," was all he could say.

Maybe it was Professor's answer or maybe it was a subconscious understanding, but for some reason a strange feeling swept over me as if we were suddenly living in a dream-like reality. This was a disturbing situation. There was no doubt something was *wrong* with this place. There were only two possibilities – either somebody had indeed come along every now and again and cleared this site, or there was some kind of material or energy acting like a weed killer, keeping five thousand years of growth to an absolute minimum. Both of those explanations were unsettling. In the first instance, it would mean that people had been coming here for thousands of years keeping the place up to a standard of cleanliness – and obviously the last time was fairly recent, considering the cleared area in front of the pyramid. Or, five thousand years ago the people who built this pyramid were aware of, and used, some form of chemical or a natural plant extract that was still actively repellent today. Either one of those explanations gave me goose bumps. The real truth, however, was even more disturbing and it would slowly manifest over the coming days.

5

HISTORY LESSONS

"We will camp tonight and then lift the slab first thing tomorrow," Professor said. "Let us get comfortable and eat."

By now it was mid-afternoon and time had flown by with all the excitement.

"You will sleep in this tent over here," he told me, "but make sure you keep it sealed at all times so no tarantulas come visiting during the night."

Professor was smiling as he said this and I realised his joke was meant for somebody with arachnophobia. I wasn't actually bothered by the thought of spiders but I was always concerned about the multitude of nasty bugs in the jungle – there are plenty of creatures in that environment that can cause serious damage. In many ways, the smaller the creature is, the bigger the danger.

"Don't worry," Professor continued, "these tents are specially designed for the jungle. They have a double inner tent – once you open the front you climb inside and close it behind you, then open the inner tent and close that behind you. It keeps it sealed but it can be hot. Just make sure you have nothing crawling on you when you climb in and you should have a good night's sleep."

Testing the theory and putting my rucksack inside, I first made sure nothing was crawling on it or me. It was, as Professor had said, very hot inside. Hopefully it would cool down a bit before bed time, but often the humidity of the jungle can be worse at night. Crawling out of the tent and zipping it up tightly, I looked at the other two tents and counted four people.

"How do you four fit in those tents?" I asked Carlos, who was breaking twigs into smaller pieces near the stove. He turned to look at the tents.

"Juan and Felipe sleep in the hammocks over there," he nodded towards the jungle. Opposite the pyramid there were two hammocks already set up between trees.

"Why don't they sleep in tents as well?"

"They'll be keeping guard overnight. Anyway, hammocks are fine to sleep in as long as they don't touch the ground. Most of the nasty things crawl along the ground, so if you're in a hammock you're quite safe. Snakes are the only real problem because sometimes they slide down a tree and startle you."

"That's funny, I never noticed them earlier."

"Steve," he laughed, "when you have a five thousand year-old Maya calendar in front of you, it's hardly surprising you don't notice anything else!"

It was a good point.

Juan and Felipe were preparing a meal on a camping stove and I marvelled at the new design. This stove needed no chemically based fuel because it was made of a high quality, expensive metal which conducted heat unbelievably well. All that was required was to fill the base with twigs and light them. The heat was tremendous and worked as well, if not better, than the gas fuel versions. A prepared mixture of fish and salsa was heated in a large saucepan and tortillas were warmed to perfection. We ate mostly in silence as the heat of the day reached its tortuous height.

After we'd finished eating, I was given a complete tour of the site.

Since the pyramid was not as steep as the typical later Maya structures the steps were not sharp and were easy to traverse. They showed little wear which led me to believe the structure had not been in use for very long or, at least, not used by many people. Once we reached the top it was doubly obvious that this pyramid was ridiculously small compared to the dominant sizes of the later temples.

At about twenty-five feet from the ground the pyramid levelled onto a platform about ten feet square. The view gave us only glimpses of the surrounding area, the trees being at least as high as the pyramid in most cases. The base of the structure was extremely wide because of the forty-five degree angle and as I looked down, the pyramid almost seemed flat and two dimensional. Only seeing the ground below us gave me any sense that we were above it. It was a bizarre effect and I felt that if the pyramid had been built in any other way, it wouldn't have given this illusion.

"So far we have no idea what this platform was used for," Professor said, "because there is no evidence of any bloodletting and there is no damage to the structure that may have been caused by warring factions. My best guess is that this was a religious temple of some kind, but then the term 'religious temple' is used by archaeologists as a cop-out when we don't know what a structure was used for. It could be a burial tomb, though, and we might find evidence for that under the slab."

"It's a strange place to put a tomb," I commented, "on the outer edge and on a corner."

"It is, yes. Stranger still, the pyramid was not aligned with the poles and it seems to have been built without any astronomical considerations at all, which contradicts most of the later buildings."

"That *is* strange taking the calendar into consideration. So, basically, they built it for a purpose that isn't obvious and it doesn't really conform to the known Maya methods of construction."

"Precisely," Professor said, nodding his head. "We even have to question whether it is Maya at all. I mean, it is Maya, but since it predates the accepted Maya chronology by at least two thousand years, we have a big problem. The Calendar points to a Maya structure, the hieroglyphs on the bottom of the pyramid are Mayan and the structure in its design is Maya. It is such a mystery. Placing this in the historical record is going to be a very difficult task indeed. Of course, the builders may be ancestors of the Maya, as we mentioned before, but this makes little sense because of all the other cultures that predate them. Looking at the historical record, there is no place to fit another culture into it. I have been going crazy trying to figure it out."

"Well, you certainly have me confused. I can't suggest anything, that's for sure. Maybe the tomb will reveal everything?"

"That is what we are hoping. Supposing it is a tomb and the occupant is still inside, we may find some artefacts that could give us clues. One thing I have noticed, however, is the similarity between this pyramid and the ones at Lubaantun but, of course, even those pyramids have steeper sides. They are on the coast in Belize, supposedly where Mitchell-Hedges found his crystal skull. I stress the word 'supposedly' due to the controversy surrounding that story. Anyway, this pyramid is very similar in height to those at Lubaantun and it has been built using the same material – black slate, rather than limestone – and there are no structures on top, unlike most of the classic Maya pyramids which have a wider platform. The stone blocks have been laid with no mortar but this pyramid does have angled corners, whereas the pyramids at Lubaantun have mostly rounded corners. No one knows which civilisation built those structures, although it has been argued that they are Maya, and they are about thirteen hundred years old."

Professor paused for a moment. I knew what he was thinking; that there were other, stranger reasons why this pyramid was unlike any other. "What really strikes me as odd," he continued, "is the fact that this pyramid shows no signs of erosion compared to the Lubaantun pyramids – it is still completely intact – and what I mean by that is all the sides and stones are exactly in place, and nothing has sunk into the earth as you would expect from such an old site. It is unlikely the pyramid is resting on a hard base, that's for sure."

"I thought the age of Lubaantun was questioned? I mean, some people think it is much older than thirteen hundred years."

"Yes, and I have been one to dismiss that theory. Now, though, after finding this site, I've had to reconsider. Considering that we are very close to the Guatemalan and Belize borders, I have a suspicion that these two sites may be linked."

"I remember the Mitchell-Hedges crystal skull and I can vaguely remember the pyramids. I do recall they are quite small in height."

"And most have an even steeper angle than the later pyramids, which makes it slightly easier to make a connection with the classic Maya. One argument is that those structures were built by a seafaring people who arrived on the coast and if that is true it would mean that Maya culture did not even originate in Central America. That is the thing that most people cannot agree with."

"Well, it doesn't make sense because the Maya are in essence biologically Mexican."

"I know, but it is possible. One study has even shown that the basic Mayan dialect is twenty per cent Hebrew in origin – but that's an argument that will take us well away from where we are now, so let's leave it. Another, more important, fact is that this pyramid is very similar to the pyramids in Teotihuacan – and the builders of that city are also unknown."

What was confusing was that black slate was used to build this pyramid and this was also the construction material used at Lubaantun; the Lubaantun pyramids are supposedly dated to 730 AD but they consist of the kind of design used in later pyramids; Professor's pyramid was five thousand years old and was similar to the design of the pyramids north of Mexico City, but those were made using limestone. These were strange contradictions that added more mystery to the site. Professor's pyramid was like an amalgamation of different time periods, and yet it predated all of them. Helplessly, I looked around to see if the landscape could shed any light on why this strange construction was here – but given the surrounding jungle, there was no visible clue.

"Are there any natural structures at all within sight of this place that might be meaningful?" I asked. "Is there anything that might hint at a pattern?"

"No, there's nothing," Professor assured me. His quick response told me he had examined the contours of the landscape carefully, looking for the same clues. “There are no hills, no mountains and the maps don’t reveal anything. The area has been physically searched for up to a kilometre around and, so far, nothing. We have not found anything else around here either, just the pyramid and everything you have seen so far. Anyway, if we climb back down we can take a closer look at the calendar.”

As we walked down to the bottom of the pyramid I counted the steps – fifty-two in total. “I assume there is a mathematical meaning to the structure, like the amount of steps, for example?”

“Ah, this is Carlos’ territory,” Professor said, as we turned towards the slab. Carlos had overheard our conversation and was already walking towards us. Professor went to his tent to arrange his things and Carlos took over the conversation.

“I am glad you asked that question. We have taken all the measurements but I cannot see a system of unit yet. The builders must have used a mathematical system but I don’t know what it is. I have been trying to calculate a common measurement but I have not found one. Soon I’ll sit down and look at the numbers more systematically and see if I can figure something out.”

“What about the steps? There are fifty-two of them. Professor said they were all fifteen centimetres high and the pyramid 7.7 metres high. Maybe there is something there?”

“Not necessarily. Yes, there are fifty-two steps, but the pyramid is 7.766 metres high to be precise and that is from the base which we dug around the sides. If all the fifty-two steps were exactly fifteen centimetres high then the pyramid would be 7.8 metres, so they are each slightly below fifteen centimetres. None of the measurements make sense, except for the fact that both the Maya and the Aztec used the number fifty-two.”

“The Calendar Round,” I said, as I suddenly realised the obvious.

The Maya and the Aztecs – the Mexica – used the same measurement of time based on the calendar. Every fifty-two years, both the 365-day Haab and the 260-day Tzolk’in reset to ‘one’ and ‘one’ when the simplest even division of those calendars was reached – 18,980 days, or fifty-two years. It was a time of rebirth and renewal. This was a very significant number for both the Maya and the Aztecs and so it seemed unlikely that there were fifty-two steps for no good reason.

“The base of the pyramid,” Carlos continued, “has a length of 16.76 metres and the platform at the top is 3.05 metres square. And, of course, there is a precise forty-five degree angle to the sides. If none of the other measurements make sense, at least we know they did measure it out precisely because they were aware of the forty-five degree angle and made use of it."

I frowned. "Are you telling me that none of the pyramid measurements conform to any precise unit?"

"Well, naturally if you make a pyramid 7.766 metres high and use a forty-five degree angle on the slopes than there is an exact measurement for the base and the platform because they will conform to the height and angle. But we see no significance in the calculations or numbers, except for the number fifty-two."

Professor returned and we walked the few metres to the slab. It truly was a beast of a stone and had a menacing but beautiful aura. The slab jutted out from the edge of the pyramid about two feet above the base. Whether by chance or design the slab was the same height as the wall surrounding the pit. It was the perfect height for manoeuvring the huge slab from its position – if the slab had been much higher it would prove difficult to control, any lower and it would be difficult to lift. Strangely, it seemed that the positioning of the slab was deliberate, in order to enable easy removal. But why? Did the builders actually want the secrets inside to be uncovered? Or was it a solid block underneath as Professor said?

The calendar was remarkably well preserved considering it had been in a damp, albeit protected environment. Many stones that have been found with carvings on them, lying on or buried in mud, have not survived and have crumbled away, practically disintegrating on contact with the air in some cases because the damp has penetrated the stone. Since this slab was also found in a similar environment it was very hard to believe it hadn't suffered the same fate.

"We can't understand that either," Professor said, "we're just hoping it does not disintegrate when we try to lift it tomorrow. It seems very solid. I only hope it actually is."

"What stone is it made from?"

"I was wondering when you were going to ask that. Do you notice the colour of the slab compared to all the other stone?"

"Yes, it's lighter, probably because it's been buried for so long."

"Ah, but the block underneath it isn't lighter – it's the same colour as the other stones, can you see?"

It hadn't been immediately obvious but still I felt foolish. Professor was a patient man, though, and a good teacher; he could see I was grasping all the odd details of this site and informed me of other facts only to speed up my learning process. After all, he and the other three men had been investigating the site in depth, whilst I had just arrived. He needed to bring me up to speed.

"I have to tell you," Professor continued, "this pale stone is not from Mexico. I have never come across it before, in all my years in archaeology. It is very similar to the stone in Peru with its desert-like colour, but it's not the same. This stone appears to be far more compact, more like the stone in Arizona – but to be honest I have no idea where it comes from. It looks like a kind of sandstone."

It was yet another mystery to add to the list. The slab was made of a stone that did not appear native to Mexico. It weighed several tonnes at the very least, so how it got here was a mystery in itself, but Professor seemed unconcerned about this fact right now. At times it seemed as if some of these facts were too bizarre to warrant any consideration – as if there is only so much the mind can take.

"I thought sandstone was soft."

"The hardness of sandstone can vary depending on where it is found. It can be soft or as hard as any other strong stone. I have had a close look at this slab because we need to lift it and thankfully it is very hard."

"Have you contacted a geologist about it?"

"Not yet. As you know the site is still a secret and I do not know anyone I could tell about the stone without having to answer too many questions. I would rather wait until we know what we're dealing with here. Discovering what kind of stone we have here is not the main concern at the moment."

Looking at the dominant centrepiece of the calendar, it seemed very strange without the centre circle. The four squares that surround the centre circle are about half its size, so it just seemed bizarre that the centre of the calendar was literally left blank. In artistic terms it could be compared with painting the Mona Lisa without her face.

"About that missing centrepiece," I said to Professor, "your theory is that the centre circle is missing because that represents the fifth Sun, and you think this calendar was made to depict the end of the fourth Sun?"

"Precisely. Unfortunately we do not know what events occurred at the end of the fourth Sun. And since this discovery contradicts all the known archaeological history we will have to rewrite it in order to be able to understand what happened."

My mind did some rapid calculations. "Professor," I said, slowly, "if the later calendar represents the fifth Sun, and it was probably made at the start of that cycle, not the end, could that mean that this calendar was actually made at the *start* of the fourth Sun?"

"You know, I am starting to think I should not have brought you here!" Professor smiled. "That would make the stone over ten thousand years old and that's not a concept I am willing to even discuss, let alone consider. Since the evidence states this stone was laid here five thousand years ago, and the calendar itself is giving us that date, I'm not going to dispute it. Historically we have to look at what was going on around 3114 BC. In fact if the Maya calendar is as accurate as people think, and it ends on December 21, 2012, then we have an exact date of August 12 in that very year. However, checking the historical record is not going to help since our accepted ideas about that period are so muddled and inaccurate."

"You mean, like the date of the Sphinx?"

"Yes, the perfect example. That Sphinx is obviously much older than anyone will recognise. But, of course, Mesopotamia and Egypt are always stated to be our first civilisations. It simply isn't logical to think that there weren't highly developed civilisations before that time."

I nodded my head in complete agreement. "It's obvious there were others, long before those two. I have never accepted the supposition that the pyramids are the first really big human structures because even modern engineers with all their technology could not build one with any great accuracy. To reach that level of complexity requires many years of tried, tested, failed, and tried again techniques. You cannot just come out of the fields and build pyramids."

"Exactly, and many new places are being discovered that do take these dates back further. Göbekli Tepe, in Turkey, is believed to be twelve thousand years old."

"And in Peru there is Caral."

"Yes of course. Didn't you say earlier you had been there?"

"Yes, I went there in 2005. Most of it was still under the sand at that time but they think it's probably older than Mesopotamia, and at that time it would have been the oldest known civilisation in the world. I think many historians were uncomfortable with the idea that the earliest known civilisation was in Peru, of all places, but since the dating of the Turkish site they are happy that the balance has now swung back to the Middle East area. It seems, since they are convinced civilisation started in that area, they won't accept it if it is found elsewhere. You'll have been there yourself, of course, since it is near your territory?"

"Well, I have been so busy in Mexico for so long I have not been to Peru for a long time now. Anyway, let us go and have dinner."

As Professor cut the conversation short, I realised with a start that time had flown by once again and the sun was starting to sink low in the sky. We had spent at least an hour in front of the calendar, discussing various aspects of the Maya and the other cultures of Mexico, but even so, time seemed to be moving quicker than normal. It must have been all the excitement.

I was convinced that I had gained Professor's trust. My amateur knowledge of the Maya and archaeology in general was well beyond that of someone who had read a few books and I had field experience in the Americas as well. What I lacked was the detailed knowledge one would expect from an archaeological degree, or years of field work, but Professor seemed more than impressed with my enthusiasm for the subject. I was never going to win him over completely, but at least he could see the reason for my being there was to assist him. The problem was, while we'd both been told I was there to assist him, neither of us actually had any idea whatsoever what that meant.

"I think it's time to get dressed," said Juan.

"Definitely," said Felipe.

"Get dressed? Do we have to wear evening suits for dinner?" I joked.

"No, we cover ourselves as best as possible because when the sun goes down the mosquitos have a great time!" said Felipe, smiling.

After putting on long sleeved shirts and covering ourselves the best we could we were just about to sit down when Carlos reappeared from the other side of the pyramid.

"You have got to see this," he said. "I've found something."

6

THE MYSTERY DEEPENS

Carlos escorted us to the rear of the pyramid where he had been finishing the task of clearing earth from the base. Prior to my arrival the back of the pyramid was the only part that had been covered in dense trees, bushes and foliage and it had taken Carlos an entire week to clear it.

"Here, look at this," he said, pointing at the base of the wall.

We all gasped when we saw dots and lines in a sequence – the unmistakable numbering system of the Maya.

Maya numbers are simple but effective – a dot or circle represents the number one and a straight line represents the number five. Combinations of the two make up all the other numbers. Nine, for example, is shown as a line with four dots above it. The number zero is different – denoted by a 'conch shell' shape; an oval with three vertical lines running half way through it, meeting a horizontal line across the middle. It is thought that the Maya were the first culture to use the number zero, even before Europe and Asia.

The Maya written number system looks complicated but only because they use a system of multiplications of the number twenty. It's difficult to grasp at first but actually quite simple if we apply our own version in the same way. We use the following base ten: 1 by 10; 10 by 10; 10 by 100; 100 by 100, giving us 10, 100, 1000, and 10,000 respectively. The Maya, using their base twenty, give us 1 by 20; 20 by 20; 400 by 400, giving us 20, 400 and 8000, respectively.

Along the base of the pyramid, right at the bottom, was a line followed by a dot or a circle next to it, then a line with four circles above, and lastly a line with another circle above it.

"What does that say?" asked Juan.

"They are Maya numbers," said Carlos, "and these say five, one, nine and six. Beautiful, aren't they?"

"What's that all about?" asked Felipe.

"I have no idea," Professor responded.

"I have no idea, either," I said slowly, as my brain started doing overtime.

We all looked at Carlos, expecting him to tell us he had figured the meaning, but it seemed all he had done was find some numbers.

"I don't know," he said, "but this is a simpler way of using the numbering system. This is not the number 5,196 because that would have been shown as a complete number. These are individual numbers, separated."

"What do you mean?" asked Juan.

"It doesn't say 5,196. It says 'five, one, nine and six'."

What was the significance of the separated numbers as opposed to a complete number? We were all left a little confused as the sun dipped low behind us and only sprinkles of light were hitting the pyramid, the slow moving branches of the trees showering the pyramid with intermittent specks of light.

Carlos pointed to the other end of the pyramid on the same side where there were more numbers.

"Two, one, three, eight and four," said Carlos.

"What's that?" asked Juan.

"I don't know what it means."

I turned to Professor who was squinting at the carved numbers, running his hand over them as if that would help him decipher their meaning. Then once again his intellectual abilities came to the fore. "It is not five, *one,* nine and six," he said. "It is five, *zero,* nine and six."

"Don't be ridiculous!" snapped Carlos. "How can that be possible? You know the number 'zero' was not in use until the Maya applied it in 36 BC."

"And you should know that is not strictly true. The number 'zero' was found in the Olmec heartland before that time."

"Yes, but it was found *after* the Olmec disappeared, so it cannot be placed with either the Olmec or the Maya, since the Maya never existed in that area. You know that has always been a mystery."

"Yes, it has. Maybe we have just found the solution."

"Explain it, then."

"They are not individual numbers, either. They are complete numbers. It is not five, zero, nine and six. It is 5,096."

"How is that possible?"

"Look – if you change the 'one' in the other number to a 'zero', that number is four times the number 5,096. There is something strange about these numbers. They are not written as the Maya would normally write large numbers, they are written as individual numbers, but the number 5,096 multiplies into the larger number by a factor of four."

"Okay, you've lost me now," Juan said.

"It could, and I stress the word *could*, imply that this was an earlier numbering system. The later numbering system that used large numbers more concisely could have evolved from this system."

"I'm going to dish up," Felipe said, turning and walking away from the scene in confusion.

"How can you come to that conclusion?" asked Juan.

"Because this number here – 20,384, is four times 5,096. It means the number 'zero' was applied by using a single dot, or circle."

Poor Carlos was almost embarrassed by Professor, taking a step back and letting out a sigh of defeat.

"Then what about the number 'one'?" asked Carlos, waiting for the explanation.

"There is a subtle difference between them, but we don't have a number 'one' to show us. However, if you look closely there is a residue of blue paint on this circle. They identified the number 'zero' by painting it blue. It also has a slight indentation in the middle and since *this* number is four times *that* number I think we're correct. It also means that whoever built this pyramid were the first people in human history to make use of the number 'zero'. I expect the conch shell 'zero' was applied later to distinguish it more clearly from the number 'one'."

It was another amazing discovery. This version of Maya numbers had never been found before and, as Professor said, the most likely explanation was that this was a forerunner to the later numbering system. It may not have been anything significant in the eyes of Felipe, but for us it showed the evolution of the Maya literally written in stone. And here we had the best evidence yet – the calendar stone, the hieroglyphs and now the numbers, all pointing us in the same direction. Now there could be no doubt – if this structure was not Maya, it was definitely from their mother culture.

This realisation brought its own problems, though. If this pyramid really did originate with the mother culture of the Maya, then there were complications that needed seriously looking at. The Maya were thought to have evolved from the Olmec, a culture that existed in *south-central* Mexico, only two hundred miles or so from where we were in the *south-east*. However, since the land mass of Mexico is an odd shape, the Olmec culture existed literally two hundred miles in a *straight line west* from our current location. So, was this the mother culture of the Olmec? Was it in fact the Olmec who evolved from the people who built this pyramid, making history turn around? The problem with this theory was the hieroglyphs on the pyramid were Mayan – they never existed with the Olmec. It would mean that the hieroglyphs existed at the beginning, were then removed and not used by the Olmec, and then magically reappeared in their original form several thousand years later when the Maya appeared. This seemed far too ridiculous to be a real possibility, and that left only one solution, another nail in the coffin of the accepted chronology of Mexican civilisations – the Maya had not evolved from the Olmec at all.

Carlos looked at Professor and they stared at each other for a while, their minds seemingly recalculating history. Carlos examined the larger number and found the same blue paint, faint but visible as a dark residue, the thousands of years in the jungle almost eradicating the evidence. Plus, on close inspection, the indentation was clear to see.

"I think you are correct, my friend." Carlos stood up, smiling.

Now it was clear how their relationship had stood the test of time. These two academics were never in fear of admitting when they were wrong, even if it was nearly always Carlos who had to stand down. Their excitement at this new discovery was evident but at the same time they were struggling to understand what they had found – they had without doubt discovered the use of the number 'zero' in a five thousand year-old pyramid and this meant the entire history of the world needed to be re-written. But that wasn't all...

"Are you thinking what I'm thinking?" asked Carlos.

"Congratulations, my friend," said Professor, "you've just discovered the oldest numbering system ever found anywhere in the world."

"Really?" asked Juan, stepping forwards and taking a closer look.

"Yes. Although the number zero and a numbering system we would recognise appeared much later, the Sumerians produced the first real counting system somewhere between four and five thousand years ago. This isn't even comparable to a counting system – these are *real* numbers. *Real* numbers with a *place value* didn't appear until the Mesopotamians with their base sixty sometime after 3000 BC. The Egyptians came up with the base ten around the same time. This is a base twenty system, just like the Maya, but it is at least a hundred years older than the original Mesopotamian system, and most probably older."

We stood in silence as these facts sank in and I felt a tingling down my spine that made me shiver. This discovery, that should have made me feel elated, left me instead feeling fearful. It felt as if we weren't supposed to know about this; as if we had opened a box that was meant to be locked forever. Professor and Carlos looked deeply satisfied, but their happiness did nothing to allay my fears - my intuition was telling me there was something sinister in the meaning of those numbers.

The elation hadn't died down as we sat in a circle around a pot that was simmering gently with a concoction of vegetables and a decent helping of chillies. The temperature had dropped a little but it was still uncomfortable and the humidity had only decreased slightly, so it goes without saying that a meal with a large chilli content was not exactly an ideal solution. However, the dish was made perfectly with a tangy, tomato flavouring and an after-heat that was more pleasant than hot. Over thousands of years the Mexicans have worked out exactly how to make chillies work in the best possible way.

Once the sun dipped behind the trees the mosquitos were out in numbers and we were attacked relentlessly, but I wasn't unprepared. I unpacked the head net that had accompanied me in South America years before, which amused everyone because admittedly I did look ridiculous. Every time I took a forkful of food I had to lift the head net up, but it was worth it because in the end I was bite-free, apart from a couple on my hands.

After the meal a couple of bottles of red wine appeared and these were passed around as we took turns, swigging into the night. It was enough for a light drunkenness and would help us all have a good night's sleep.

"So, what does this number mean?" Felipe suddenly asked, taking the thoughts from my mind.

"Which number?" asked Carlos, as if it had all been a dream of some kind.

"5,096," he said with a slight slur.

"I have absolutely no idea."

But what did it mean? No one else seemed too concerned with the actual significance of the numbers. They were just happy they were there. They were here to lift the lid and that was enough to think about; the numbers could wait until later. I kept thinking that something under the slab might give us all the answers, so maybe Carlos was thinking the same.

As the conversation continued it became apparent that no one had any sensible suggestions. The only useful comment was that the number was very close to a Maya Sun cycle, which is 5,126 years – thirty years difference from the number given on the back of the pyramid – 5,096.

However, there was one obvious correlation that I had noticed, and for sure Professor and Carlos had recognised it as well. Neither of them had mentioned it so I kept my mouth shut too, although I wasn't sure why they were keeping quiet. Since the calendar stone at the base of the pyramid represented the end of the fourth Sun, then that implied four Sun cycles had been completed – four Sun cycles of 5,126 years, equalling a total of 20,504 years since the beginning of the first cycle. The numbers on the back of the pyramid could be applied in the same way, although there was a difference of 30 years per cycle – 5,096 multiplied by four gave us 20,384 – both of these numbers appearing on the back of the pyramid. It was an obvious conclusion since the calendar stone seemed to be indicating the end of the fourth cycle, but why was there a discrepancy of thirty years in each of the cycles? And if that wasn't the correct interpretation, then what else could it mean? And why were Professor and Carlos keeping quiet about this obvious conclusion? Was it simply because it caused too much of an issue? Or were they, like me, secretly hoping that a body under the lid would reveal secrets that would give us all the answers?

The looming pyramid above us had an eerie feeling at night, as if it was watching us and listening to our conversations – the dark silhouette making a claim on its territory, asserting that all below it were only subservient visitors. And seemingly unwelcome visitors at that. There was a strange energy that could be felt, an aura of power and dominance that filled the air and gave us a sense of inferiority. I felt the pyramid was laughing at us in some way, goading us and daring us to unravel its secrets.

"So, what about this calendar of yours?" asked Felipe.

"What about it?" asked Carlos.

Juan sniggered and nudged Felipe's arm.

"What does it mean – the one behind us?"

"It doesn't really mean anything. It is what it is – a calendar. You know the calendar anyway, so why are you asking silly questions?"

Juan laughed again.

"Yes, but this one has the centre circle missing, so what does it mean?"

"We had this conversation two days ago. Have you forgotten already?" Carlos shook his head.

It was apparent they were accustomed to Felipe's stupid questions, and it was also apparent this only occurred when he was under the influence of alcohol. It seemed he was a person who couldn't handle his drink very well.

The kitchen area had been named 'base camp', and this is where we ate and drank and socialised. It would become the centre of all our activities. It was the place from where we would set off each day to explore our surroundings – a miniature mountaineering expedition in the hot jungle. But this was no mountain. This tiny little pyramid was proving far more difficult to climb than a real mountain. And then I suddenly remembered what Lasya had said to me – "There will be mountains to climb, but they are not as high as he thinks."

Did she know about this pyramid, or was she talking in general terms about the patterns in a person's life? The latter would have been the obvious conclusion but the more this journey continued, the more my ideas about what was going on suggested that everything was connected and woven together in a way that was way beyond comprehension. It was something that was only glimpsed in my subconscious, but slowly I could see things were connected to a greater picture, like those 3D images that Professor had mentioned previously. I could only hope that by the end of this journey I would be able to see the real image, the real truth as a complete whole but, as I was to discover, this pyramid had no intention of giving up its secrets so easily.

Monday 24 May, 2010.

What a day! I have to say this has been to most exciting day of my life! A Maya pyramid 2,500 years older than it should be; Mayan hieroglyphs equally as old; Ditto Maya numbers; and a copy of the calendar which suggests an earlier time period, taking Mesoamerican cultures back twice as far as they should be. Never in my wildest dreams could I imagine this is what I was coming to Mexico for. It's so exciting it's unbelievable, but that's where it ends. I don't need to be reminded of the things I was told prior to coming here, and it hasn't passed my attention that this place is weirder than anything I've experienced before. There's something lurking underneath the surface, hiding somewhere, watching. We aren't supposed to be here and that's that. This place should never have been discovered. That pyramid holds secrets that are way beyond what we can handle. I don't know why I feel this way, but I do. That pyramid scares the hell out of me. Something is wrong here. How can the Maya be 2,500 years older than they are supposed to be when there is no evidence of ANY civilised culture anywhere in Mexico that far back? Who were these people? How did they create that calendar? How did they build this pyramid? Where did they go? But the things that keeps nagging at me – why is the pyramid completely intact and why is the area in front of it clear in a near-perfect rectangle? Why aren't trees growing in that area, and why has the pyramid kept its shape? I don't know how I'm going to sleep…

7

LIFTING THE LID

A drop of sweat ran down my cheek and I awoke as it tickled my face. It was already very hot and it was only 8am. I could hear that everyone else was already up and about so I crawled out of the tent quickly to ensure I didn't miss out on the adventure of a lifetime. Professor and Juan were making final preparations to remove the lid, ensuring the straps would not slip when the slab was moved for the first time in five thousand years. Ropes were attached to leather straps that gripped all four corners of the slab, tied together in the middle so that the weight was focused above the centre, bringing the weight inwards and giving a firm grip on the corners. This, in turn, was attached to an A-frame that had been cleverly assembled using the natural resources around the site.

"Good morning, Stephen," Professor said, as I yawned at the pyramid above.

"Morning," I replied, scratching my head as the heat affected my skin.

"There is plenty of coffee in the pot. Help yourself. There are some warm sandwiches in the yellow box if you want to eat something. We should be ready soon."

He looked at me and smiled like a child that was about to open his birthday present. It was quite a surreal look – the first time I'd witnessed an academic looking like a five year-old.

Rarely eating breakfast, I settled for a good dose of caffeine to wake me and then wandered back towards the slab.

"Anything I can do?" I asked Professor.

"No, it is okay, just get yourself together and we will get the thing removed."

He stared at the slab and stroked it like a teenager with his first car, and then turned to me. "This could contain one of the oldest bodies ever found in archaeology and certainly in the Americas. Or, it could be an empty box – or even a solid block of stone."

"Well, I have a distinct feeling that something is in there. The thought of an empty tomb or a solid block has never crossed my mind once."

"I have the same feeling, but let us keep our feet on the ground."

"I know. I better get washed up, then." I headed for the shower – the result of magical engineering on the part of Juan and Felipe. The base was a plastic tub about six inches high and two feet square, full of water. Using a crude water pump powered by a car battery, the water was pumped electrically up a hollow vertical pole and through a spout at the top, and then recycled as it passed back into the base. It became slightly murky once a few people had used it, but it was a million times better than no shower at all and the water could be changed easily. Even river water would do the trick, although it was important to keep one's mouth closed at all times. It was a perfect device for this type of expedition and it even had a shower curtain for privacy. However, it was imperative to shower fast and get back inside the tent swiftly as mosquitos would quickly go to work on bare skin.

When I returned to the slab, everyone took up their positions. Professor was monitoring the slab itself, Carlos was keeping a close watch on the A-frame and the four extending ropes, and the rest of us grabbed hold of the main pulling rope from the other side. It seemed only fair that Professor should be the first one to see under the lid. There was a lot of concern that the slab could be brittle and the corners would simply break off when we tried to lift it. There would be a lot of force on those corners and, although the weight was centralised by the four ropes meeting in the middle, only a very hard stone could withstand the weight of the entire block pulling on its corners. If that were to happen, the only way to look inside would be to smash the lid, and that was not an option. I closed my eyes for a moment and prayed.

"Right, listen, men," Professor said in his commanding voice, "I want you to pull hard but very slowly. Once the tension is reached, steady it down to a near stop. I want this lid lifted one millimetre at a time. We do not know what condition it is in so it may break apart. So, we lift slowly, and if it does come away from the surrounding stone then we can move it out of the way. Are we clear?"

"Yes," we chorused.

The anticipation was intense. Would we find anything underneath? Would the slab disintegrate when it was lifted? It was an agonising wait and each moment seemed like weeks.

"Okay, pull on my count, but very slowly. To begin with just take the tension and once the lid moves we will raise it a little at a time and I will keep it steady. Is everybody okay?"

"Yes," we all said in unison again.

Professor looked at each of us individually, smiling as if we were going into battle and might not return. And that is what it felt like – entering the unknown – for if we found something significant we would all be dramatically changed by the experience.

"Good luck, gentlemen," he said.

The four of us pulled the rope back and the A-frame tilted upward towards us until it reached its optimum position and the straps holding the slab were stretched and tense.

"Right, now pull a tiny bit," Professor said.

We all pulled a bit more and the straps stretched further.

"Okay, a bit more – three, two, one – now!"

Again the straps stretched even more but there was no movement.

"Okay, good, again – three, two, one, pull!"

Another pull on the ropes and the forest echoed with the sound of scraping stone. The bizarre acoustics around the site made it sound as if the slab had moved half way across Mexico. It slipped slowly to one side, turning anticlockwise a little and lifting slightly, creating a gap of a millimetre or two above the base. And then it dropped back down against the block.

"Hold it," Professor shouted, concerned that the drop could have caused cracks in the slab. He went around the stone checking it for any damage and then turned to us and smiled.

"Good. The hard part is done – the slab moves. Now we can remove it completely. Again – three, two, one – pull."

The slab moved again and a small gap appeared between it and the stone underneath. It swayed about half an inch and Professor put his hand on it to stop it from moving.

Strangely, for a moment I had a feeling that the slab should be left where it was, as if we were committing an ancient crime, but when further instructions were called out that thought was quickly lifted into the forest like an eagle stealing a mouse. Another millimetre appeared between the slab and the stone, quickly followed by another. There was now a one-inch gap and we could all see the strip of darkness that had appeared.

"Okay, hold it there," Professor said.

As we stood leaning back with the rope tight in our hands and sweat flowing down our faces, Professor went around the slab and placed several small wooden blocks between the slab and the stone, one in each corner and one on each side.

"Okay, now let it rest slowly."

We all let the tension slip, bit by bit, until the slab rested on the blocks and held its position.

"Okay, good work men, take five," Professor said.

The sweat was dripping off my face and I was panting like a dog that had run around a field all afternoon. It wasn't the heat or even the pulling of the rope, which was far easier than I imagined, it was the sheer stress of what we were doing – lifting a five thousand year-old slab away from its final resting place left me feeling like a grave robber. Professor grabbed his torch and peered into the darkness.

"Anything?" I asked.

"Hold on," he said.

There was a long pause and Professor seemed to go into a trance. For a moment only the insects could be heard. A toucan's call screeched through the trees and I jumped as if the creature was sending out a warning across the jungle – a warning through time, telling us not to continue with this barbaric act.

"Carlos, come here for a moment," he said.

Carlos walked across and knelt down next to Professor and peered inside. Again there was a long silence. Professor walked around each of the three sides and checked all angles of the interior.

"Come on, you two, the suspense is killing us!" I cried out.

"Sorry men, just give us a minute."

Yet another long silence. Professor and Carlos looked at each other for what seemed like minutes and they both smiled – the kind of smile you only give to a friend you have known since childhood. Without speaking, they indicated that we should attempt another lift and so Carlos returned to the A-frame and we raised it to the rigid position. Another pull and the slab was raised another half inch or so. Another pull, and then another until there was at least five inches between the slab and the block. Professor placed more wooden blocks in the corners and the slab was rested down a second time. Carlos once again joined Professor and they both peered inside with torches.

There was yet another long silence.

Suddenly the mood turned to elation as Professor and Carlos stood up, smiled at each other and shook hands. And then they laughed with joy and hugged each other like two lost friends who'd been reunited.

"It's a bloody staircase!" Carlos told us in stunned disbelief.

I couldn't believe what I was hearing. A staircase! For a moment my mind couldn't comprehend the words. Never was there a thought of anything beyond a burial tomb – the idea of a long-lost king lying in situ was the best my mind could come up with – but a staircase meant there was an even larger chamber down there, somewhere underneath or inside the pyramid.

"Come and see for yourselves," Professor replied, with great excitement.

We all hurriedly walked over and peered inside. A stone staircase led into the darkness and there was no suggestion of an ending – at the bottom of the stairs a stone floor led away into the abyss. I started to wonder what on earth could be down there. Was this the tomb of a king or a queen? Maybe a store of gold – could this be the hidden cache of the fabled El Dorado? Or was it a storehouse of knowledge – books like the great library of Alexandria, finally revealing the secrets of our past?

The excitement, however, was tinged with an unmistakable feeling of trepidation and the whole scene suddenly became as surreal as a painting. I couldn't help it – something didn't feel right. While my mind was ecstatic, my soul was reeling in a strange kind of terror I had never experienced before. I looked at the others and could see it on their faces also. What was this fear that had suddenly manifested in all of us? Was it simply a fear of the unknown, the realisation of what we had discovered? Or was it something more sinister?

Kneeling together around the block, we could only stare at each other in shock. Here we all were, in front of a five thousand year-old calendar, underneath which was a staircase that hadn't been walked on since the time when Egypt was in the height of the Old Kingdom and the rest of mankind was still in the Bronze Age.

It was a powerful and emotional experience which brought tears to the eyes of most of us; one of those moments in life where everything seemed to fall into place at the right time, a kind of personal 'eureka' moment. But although we all felt the hard work was over, the lid was still a long way from being removed. Now it seemed the discoveries at this site had not even begun. Whether or not the chamber inside was empty mattered little to us, for the pyramid suddenly took on a whole new level of technological understanding – building a pyramid on top of the ground was relatively straightforward, but incorporating a chamber inside required a level of ingenuity and mathematics that was still confusing modern scientists in Egypt – such a structure relies on complex weight distribution to maintain stability. In Mexico, chambers *inside* pyramids are quite common, but a subterranean room was unheard of. There was also the confusion of the base of the pyramid – the pyramid seemed to be resting on top of it. Was the base solid, dividing the pyramid above and the chambers below, or was the base just a wall that surrounded the edges? Only further inspection would give the answers.

It took the rest of the morning and part of the afternoon to raise the slab high enough into a safe position and remove it completely. A pallet had been made by Juan and Felipe for the slab to be rested on and it was a serious logistical effort to move the slab away from the block. It needed to be high enough away from the block to ensure it didn't hit anything and break apart as it swung around. Lifting it was the easy part; manoeuvring it was an altogether different undertaking. Eventually we gave up trying to swing it across since it became too unstable and eventually Felipe came up with the brainstorming idea that we should simply lift it by hand. The five of us together should be able to take the weight, he suggested. No chance. It was much heavier than we'd imagined when we tried to lift it. We were dealing with a stone block that even between five of us was around half a tonne per man. Eventually the pallet was raised higher and placed parallel to the block.

It wasn't until the sun was dipping into the trees that we managed to place the slab securely on the pallet. We had achieved this by resting it onto the edge of the block, stabilising it with wooden stilts, and then moving the A-frame slightly to give a different angle. We repeated this several times in a crane-like motion until the slab could be moved away from the block completely.

By the time we had finished, night was approaching. We covered the entrance with thick plastic sheeting and blocks to hold it down. The staircase beckoned, but no one was willing to go down there in the dark. It would have been foolish, at the very least. I for one was scared of walking down that corridor and the strange feeling of fear that had filled me to my boots had only increased, creeping over my skin like a swarm of ants in the night.

There was something. I couldn't explain it in words, but something was there in the forest.

8

TERROR IN THE TREES

Gulping wine from the bottle and staring up at the nearly full moon, I felt as if all the forest wildlife and even the trees were watching us, keeping an eye on each and every movement we made, waiting for us to take a deep breath and walk into the unknown.

Our general mood was cheerful and excited, but the looming presence of the jungle wouldn't let us alone for a moment, making sure we all knew we were out of our depth. We had uncovered a secret; a secret that had been hidden for five thousand years and kept under guard by the jungle itself. If I stopped to think about it too seriously, it seemed that some kind of retribution was inevitable.

Our dinner was somewhat celebratory, one that none of us would forget, because the following day our lives would never be the same again. We had entered into the realm of history-making and very soon we would be travelling back in time, and in the process discovering our future.

Once the ritualistic wine-drinking had made us a little tipsy, the conversation turned to the staircase. Not one of us had dared to mention it so far during the evening, so it could only be Professor who broke ranks on the unspoken agreement.

"Does anyone have any idea what is down there?" he asked casually.

A silence hit the camp. Professor looked at us all, one by one.

"Well, I think we should lighten the tension a bit. I suggest we should all have a bet on what awaits us."

It wasn't his proposition that was surprising. The astounding thing was that he sensed the fear. Ever since that lid had been removed, the whole area's atmosphere seemed to have changed, as if something had been unleashed from inside the pyramid. Professor's attempt to lighten the mood only confirmed to me that I wasn't alone with these feelings.

"The winner pays for a night of beer when we get back to Candelaria," he continued, "because I don't know about you, but I'm sick of this disgusting red wine!"

Laughter echoed around the camp. Professor was right, the tension did need to be broken and he had expertly chosen his lines and his moment – but before we could even begin to lay our bets on what was inside the pyramid, the tension returned like a horror film when the loud crack of breaking wood echoed through the trees.

We instantly fell silent and Felipe grabbed his rifle, loading the chamber as he turned towards the trees. The sound came from directly in front of the pyramid, not twenty yards away from us. An eerie calm filled the air and for a moment we all listened. We could hear nothing except a weirdly audible silence, brought on by the sudden stillness of the forest. Even the insects had become dormant and the air was filled with a thick layer of fear.

"Was that an animal?" I whispered.

"I don't think so," Juan hissed, "it sounded more human."

My heart started beating so hard I could physically hear it. Juan and Felipe stood up and headed for the tree line, Juan pointing a torch and Felipe aiming his rifle wherever the beam of light reached a target.

Juan and Felipe reached the trees and carefully studied the area. After a few moments they crossed over the threshold and into the forest canopy, disappearing from view until the only thing that could be seen was the torchlight shining through the branches like a ship lost at sea.

"What do you think?" I whispered to Professor.

"If they say it is a person then it is a person – you can bet your life on it."

"For some reason, I don't think they will find anyone," Carlos replied.

"Why?" I asked.

"I don't know what it is, but let's just say this place is scaring the hell out of me. I think we all know there's something strange going on here."

Professor gave Carlos an angry look, as if by saying the words he had risked making the situation worse. If we all kept quiet about the obvious then maybe it wouldn't stretch its arms out and touch us. Surely fear could only enter our souls if we let it in; speaking the unspeakable was like summoning the Devil himself.

We sat in silence and listened, waiting for the other two to come back and join us, but several minutes passed before Juan and Felipe returned to base camp.

"Did you find anything?" Carlos asked.

"There was nobody there, no tracks, nothing," Juan replied.

"Are you sure it wasn't an animal of some kind?"

"Definitely not – it was a person, but there is no one there."

"You mean they ran off?"

"No, I mean there is no one there and there never was anyone there."

"We all heard it, Juan. Are you saying it was a ghost?"

"I am only telling you the facts. No one is there. No one was ever there. There are no tracks at all, nothing but dense bushes. It's not even possible to get through that area because the bushes are so tightly packed together. Go and see for yourself if you don't believe me."

More silence. We all sat motionless and scared. Certainly no one was going to take up Juan's offer to go and have a look.

"Don't be too scared about it. It was nothing unusual. Strange things often happen in the forest," Juan said.

"I am not scared," I retorted, "I've experienced far worse things than that."

"Like what?" Felipe asked, inquisitively. Anyone could have guessed he would ask that question.

In a way, I was lying through my teeth, but at the same time it was true. It wasn't the sound of the cracking wood that concerned me – it was the atmosphere and the silence of the forest that gave the game away. This was a typical paranormal experience – often during these types of events all the creatures become silent as if they are all aware something unusual is happening, or there is some kind of altered reality.

I looked at Professor to see if there was going to be any objection over telling a scary story, under the circumstances. He motioned me to go ahead.

"When I was in the Peruvian Amazon back in 2004," I began, "I was staying with friends in the town of Moyobamba. It was just after Christmas – after that big tsunami in Asia – and the environment wasn't much different to this one, hot and humid all the time. Miguel and Maria are both chefs and the family home a restaurant, so I had free board and food whenever I needed it. I also had the use of the family motorcycle. One evening, I went out to the bike to ride into town – it was dark and just as I put my hands on the handlebars I heard a noise, to my right. The trees rustled and two large fruits hit the floor. When I turned, I saw a man standing in the trees, not ten feet away from me. His head was hidden behind a branch but very clearly I could see he was wearing what I can only describe as a thick fireman's coat, with what looked like silver buttons down the middle, and in the heat of the jungle I thought that was the strangest thing for someone to be wearing. My initial thought was that he was stealing fruit from the trees.

"I quickly ran inside to get Miguel so that we could confront him together, since my Spanish wasn't good enough at that time for such an encounter. By the time we returned, only a few seconds later, there was no one there. We looked out the front of the house, up and down the road, but he was gone. Since the road was straight, he would have easily been seen so we knew it wasn't possible for him to have escaped that way. That left the garden, which was surrounded by a high fence. He must have been in there, but after an intense search we found nothing.

"As we went back into the kitchen, I explained exactly what I'd seen to Miguel. 'It was a ghost,' he said and laughed at me. He wasn't laughing at me for seeing ghosts – he was laughing because I'd thought it was a real person! The paranormal was a part of everyday life for this family. Miguel also pointed out that there were no fruit trees in that part of the garden – but there had been once, nearly twenty years earlier. I never did understand what actually happened that night, but I experienced many more paranormal activities in that restaurant."

"So, do you think that what you saw really was a ghost?" asked Juan, inquisitively.

"Well, yes, I do. There is no other explanation – the person was wearing very strange clothes for such an environment and he couldn't have got away without us seeing him. And there's the fact that I distinctly heard fruit falling from a tree that hadn't existed for twenty years. Later, I wondered if he had been trying to get my attention. I had the distinct feeling he was trying to warn me about something – and that very evening I became very ill. I was bedridden with some kind of flu for the next three days. But why a ghost would want to warn me about an illness, I have no idea. It seems rather excessive to me."

"Did you say it was just after that tsunami?" asked Carlos.

"Yes, a week, I think, maybe two."

"Well, I do know that stress on fault lines can cause strange things to happen, so maybe that was why it happened."

"It could be, but the Andean fault line is far from Indonesia, plus the family were used to paranormal events happening. Miguel was laughing at me for the rest of the night for thinking it was a real person. You really had to be there to understand it. They told me so many strange things about life there. Moyobamba lies at an altitude of eight hundred metres, on the slope of the Andes as you head into the Amazon, so it certainly lies on a big fault line. Fault lines don't come much bigger than the Andes. And I experienced more things during my stay."

"What other things did you experience there?" asked Juan.

He seemed to have quite an interest in the paranormal. I looked at everyone to see if there were any objections, for this conversation was hardly helping ease the discomfort we were all still feeling. However, they were all looking at me expectantly, so I carried on.

"About a week later, after I had recovered from my illness, I was lying in bed trying to get to sleep. It was hot and sticky and I was very uncomfortable. On the first floor, there were at least six rooms, but none of them had doors. Suddenly, I heard shuffling feet coming towards my room. I thought it was the youngest daughter – she had a slight developmental problem and she used to shuffle along in that way, so when a head peered round the doorway and into the room I thought she was coming to get something from the room, or maybe she was even sleepwalking. I was lying down not two feet away from the door, and I could see this head peering round and looking at me. Then the person came into the room and was standing about twelve inches away from me. Thinking it was the youngest daughter I just closed my eyes, ignored it and went to sleep. The next morning, however, I realised it could not have been her – or any of the family – because of the head height of the person who was there. They must have been about my height, and the whole family, being Peruvian, were about a foot shorter."

"Are you saying it was another ghost?" asked Felipe.

"What other explanation could there be? I was the last one to go to sleep, everyone else was in bed and no one could get inside the building. Being a restaurant and in a dangerous country like Peru, the security is high. The family also had two dogs and they would bark at the slightest unusual sound. There was no other explanation as far as I am concerned. The man in the garden was also about my height, so whether it was the same 'ghost' I don't know."

My story-telling had passed some time, but the incident we'd witnessed still stayed with us. Juan had seemed particularly interested in my story. He had been apparently quite unfazed by our experience at the pyramid and it seemed that, like Miguel in the Peruvian Jungle, this was normal for him. Felipe seemed slightly more concerned but less so than the rest of us, who were all admittedly a little on edge. We returned to finishing off the wine and tried to make an attempt to return to laughter and calm, but before we could relax we all decided it was time to go to bed.

The eeriness about this place had intensified and we were all tremendously unnerved by it. I tried to calm my mind but my thoughts kept returning to the trees. There was definitely someone there, but who, or what? And why was this experience similar to what had happened in Peru? Strange noises of people that could be heard but who left no trace, the reality around us altered as if entering another dimension that wasn't our own? In Peru there was a man standing in the garden and I heard fruit falling from a tree that had only existed twenty years earlier. Was it possible the same thing had just happened to us? Was there a person in the trees who made the sound of cracking wood as he walked, but who had left no physical trace because they did not exist in our time? Or was there an even more sinister reason? Whatever the cause, we didn't really have time to think about it. We had more pressing things to be concerned with, but if we thought it was an isolated incident, we were wrong. Things were about to become a lot worse.

Tuesday 25 May, 2010

What the hell was that? There was definitely someone in the trees, no doubt about it. It wasn't an animal, even I know that, but I'm not too bothered about it. What bothers me is the increasing tension around the site and the ever rising oppression that's surrounding us as we work and sleep... and tomorrow is the day we will go inside that pyramid. I really don't want to go down there. To be honest I just want to leave. I wonder what's down there – an entrance to another dome; the burial tomb of a dead king or queen; a store house of gold; perhaps even a mass-grave of victims, hidden away. If that's the case then why build a pyramid and not just a hole in the ground? No, there's something weird going on here. If it was a dead king or queen then it begs the question – where's the rest of the culture that existed here? There are no other buildings, no other pyramids, no signs of anyone living around here at all. This pyramid sits alone in the middle of nowhere. Something's wrong with this place.

9

SYNCHRONISED SLEEP

I eventually dozed off at about four in the morning. Before then, I hadn't been able to sleep because of the heat and the wine had only succeeded in giving me a slight headache. Certainly I wasn't comatose for long because...

I awoke in the darkness and watched the shadow of a spider spinning its web outside the tent. I decided to quietly creep outside and breathe some air, risking the chance that a few bugs might crawl over me.

Once again the jungle was silent and still and an eerie feeling swept over me. It seemed I was completely alone and fear filled my body to the base of my soul. As I stood up, there was a strange mist rolling towards me on the ground. It surrounded my ankles and quickly swarmed the campsite. Walking towards the source of the mist, I could see it was coming from inside the pyramid, out through the entrance which was completely open from the removal of the slab... even though I was certain we had sealed it the night before. As I stood in front of the pyramid something glimmered in the moonlight above me, and when I looked I could see the dark figure of a man standing on the platform at the top. I anxiously climbed the steps and the silhouette became clearer, until I was standing in front of a Maya priest. His hair was long and matted and a feather headdress adorned his head, reaching up into the sky like a peacock's tail-fan. The priest was old and he seemed very wise with a wrinkled face and black eyes. He stared deep into my soul for what seemed like an eternity, and then he started speaking to me in a language I could not understand while pointing at the sky towards the pole star, Polaris.

My leg jolted and my heart was pounding as I sat up in the tent, sweating and breathing heavy. Thankfully, it was just a dream. Or was it? It is always the second or two after waking where confusion reigns – the dream world and the conscious world collide and the two realities melt into one. The dream had seemed so real, I struggled to be sure I was now actually awake. Many times I had awoken from a vivid dream only to find I was still dreaming. I looked for the spider's web, to make sure I wasn't still in the dream, but there was none. Thankfully I was awake and completely conscious. The dream was so clear and vivid I was tempted to get out of the tent to see if the same scene awaited me, but I was far too scared to move after seeing that Maya priest on the top of the pyramid. Who was he, and what was he trying to tell me?

After managing to sleep a while longer I awoke at dawn to the sound of clattering pots and that unmistakable aroma of coffee. Joining Professor at base camp I tried to wake myself up, the dream still fresh in my memory as if it had been experienced for real. Professor looked equally tired, but he also seemed very stressed and flustered.

"Morning," I said.

"Good morning, Stephen," he said in a downbeat tone. "I am not feeling so good today. Would you like some coffee?"

"Yes please. I feel absolutely shattered myself, and I had a *very* bizarre dream last night."

Professor stared at me as if he was a mannequin in a shop window and his eyes seemed defocused and cloudy. Looking behind me to see if something there had alarmed him, I could see nothing but the impenetrable jungle.

"Are you okay?" I asked.

"I'm fine," he said, although he clearly wasn't. "Tell me your dream, please."

"Basically, I dreamt of a Maya priest on the pyramid."

Professor froze. "That is what I dreamt as well," he said, staring at the floor.

"Really? Oh. *That's* weird," I said, not knowing quite how to respond.

Professor was visibly shaken. Strange events and bizarre coincidences were the norm for me, or at least I was accustomed to them, but for an academic like Professor it was not a field of reality he was comfortable with and it showed in his reactions.

"Tell me your dream in detail, Stephen," he said.

As I described the whole dream, Professor spent the entire time with his head down, stirring his mug of coffee as if it was his last. He didn't look up once as he heard what he obviously didn't want to hear.

"Stephen," he said, finally raising his head, "your dream is identical to mine except for one detail."

"What's that?"

He paused for a moment, not sure if he should even continue the conversation. "The priest did not show me Polaris, he showed me a scroll with strange symbols on it that I did not recognise."

"Really? Can you remember the symbols?"

"Oh yes, every one of them."

"Write them down for me."

"I already have done, here."

He reluctantly showed me a piece of paper and on seeing the symbols I gasped in shock. A shiver ran up my spine and my neck tingled. I couldn't believe it – these were the same symbols that were on the scrolls in Tibet. They were the letters from the Atlantean alphabet.

For a moment, I stared blankly at the piece of paper in my hand. My mind was awash with questions, but suddenly the first clue to my being here was in front of me. There really was a connection between the dome in Tibet and this place, but what? Were the builders of the dome also responsible for this pyramid? Or was this an ancient, worldwide language?

"Professor, you're not going to believe this, but I can translate this for you."

"What? How?"

I cleared my throat, stalling for a moment, not sure how Professor was going to take my explanation.

"This is the alphabet of the Atlanteans. I was shown this in Tibet, and I happen to have the translation in my notebook."

Professor was stunned. He sat there staring at me for a moment as if I required admittance to a mental hospital.

"What did you just say?"

"I said this is the writing of the Atlanteans."

"*Atlanteans...* Atlanteans, as in 'Atlantis'. You are saying this is the writing of the people from Atlantis, a place that supposedly doesn't exist."

"Now you know what I was doing in Tibet."

"You mean you have proof of the existence of Atlantis? Why have you not mentioned this before? With all the weird things going on here you neglected to tell me about this?"

"Yeshe told me that everything would come together in time and in the correct sequence, and that I shouldn't reveal anything until the appropriate moment."

"That is beside the point. You have come from Tibet and you have been sent to me by someone who obviously knows this information. Here I am, telling you everything that is going on here and you decide that I do not need to know something that is probably the most important piece of information in the history of the world. That's wonderful. Thank you."

"I'm sorry, but I can only do what I have been instructed to do."

Professor seemed annoyed but quickly changed his mood as he realised this wasn't the time to be arguing. Things had taken a strange turn and the atmosphere was more than tense, but he ignored it and, instead, turned on his archaeological mind. Suddenly he had grasped that evidence for the existence of Atlantis might well be right here, right in front of him and he wanted to know more.

"Go and get your note book," he insisted, all the while looking at me in a strange way. He must have been wondering who I really was.

Sitting next to Professor, I helped him translate the symbols letter by letter. The letters spelled out the word – *evolution.*

"Evolution. What does that mean?"

"I have no idea," said Professor.

We sat in silence and stared at the word, totally bewildered. We just repeated the word to each other, over and over. We picked up our coffee and sipped as if that might help, but it didn't. Then Carlos appeared from the opposite end of the pyramid. He had been working on the Maya numbers since sunrise, working to find some correlation, any clue that might help us see their meaning. As he sat down he said, smiling "I had the most bizarre dream last night, very weird."

Shifting his bulk and getting comfortable, he suddenly stopped and looked at us, realising he was not receiving any reaction, only to see us frozen on the spot. Professor and I looked at each other and it was obvious we were thinking the same thing; that we should let him tell us the dream, without interrupting him, to see if it was the same as ours.

Carlos proceeded to describe exactly the same dream – except that the ending was, again, different.

"The Maya priest pointed up into the sky. It was strange – it was night time but when I looked up the sun appeared. It was a full sun but I could look at it without my eyes hurting and then, for some reason, it started to brighten even more, like it became bigger, and I could feel it had more energy. Then I woke up."

Once our own dreams had been explained to Carlos, the three of us sat in stunned silence. The atmosphere was very uncomfortable. What was going on? What did all of this mean? Why did a Maya priest appear to us all in the night? Why did he show Professor the Atlantean alphabet? What relevance did it have to the pyramid? And then Felipe appeared from the trees in front of the pyramid.

"Felipe," Carlos called out.

"What?" he asked.

"Did you have any strange dreams last night?"

He walked towards us and sat down. "Yes I did, actually. I was sitting at a bar drinking beer and this woman sat next to me. She was really beautiful, a white woman with blonde hair. I started chatting to her and then I turned back to the bar and drank some more beer. When I turned to look at her again she suddenly changed into a cow with a huge head. I blinked a couple of times and when I looked back at her again she had walked away. When I turned around again she was heading for the door, and I was about to call out when she turned around and waved at me, but this time she had changed again – it was my wife." He paused and looked at our strangely attentive faces. "Why, do you think there is a meaning to that?"

Professor, Carlos and I looked at each other. I held my head in my hands and then laughed out loud.

"What's so funny?" asked Juan, walking into camp.

"Did you have any strange dreams last night, Juan?" Carlos asked as we all continued chuckling.

"No, I rarely remember my dreams. Why?"

"Oh, no reason – but we've decided Felipe needs to see a psychiatrist!"

"Or he needs a new wife!" Professor said.

Felipe was sitting still with an expressionless face, wondering what on earth we were all talking about. Once the giggling had calmed down, we explained our own dreams to Juan and Felipe and then the talk turned serious again as we tried to figure out the meaning of this bizarre turn of events.

"So, we have Polaris, the word 'evolution', and a brightening or intensifying sun. Steve, are you sure it was Polaris?" Carlos asked.

"Well, the sky I was looking at in my dream was the one I'm familiar with back home, so I am very certain it was Polaris. I could see Ursa Major below the pole star with the two right-hand stars directly below, pointing towards it. It was unmistakable."

"You know about astronomy, too?" asked Juan.

"It's one of my interests, yes. Anyway, you cannot study archaeology without studying the stars because you won't be able to get into the mind of the ancients. The stars controlled the lives of our ancestors. No knowledge of astronomy makes you a blind archaeologist."

"Well, we know Polaris is the pole star," Professor said, "so in that sense it ties in with the numbering of the Maya calendar because it is represented in the precession of the equinoxes. In Carlos' dream, we can assume that the Maya priest was showing us the end of the calendar, since the calendar ends during the time period when the pole is directed at Polaris."

"How can you come to that conclusion?" Juan asked.

"It is just an educated guess, to be honest. But really, Juan, we can't ignore the possibility that these strange dreams have something to do with the pyramid. For three people to have the same dream, or as similar as these were, cannot be a coincidence. Therefore, the conclusions must be related to the pyramid. Since we have a calendar stone here which is directly connected with the Maya Sun cycles and which ends in 2012, we can assume that the pole star is related to the time period in which we exist now."

"So," Juan responded, "since we have a Maya calendar which ends in 2012, you think the Maya priest was pointing at Polaris because that is the time period when the calendar ends. But how can you relate that to the precession of the equinoxes?"

"Because the five cycles of the Maya Long Count – five cycles of 5,126 years – amount to 25,630 years, and this has been calculated as the precession of the equinoxes. Even though the exact time of the earth's axial wobble has not been conclusively agreed upon, the calculations are close enough and since the Maya were master astronomers, it is a fair conclusion to make."

Now we were all a little lost. I think we could all see what Professor was saying – that the image of the Maya priest pointing out the pole star could be directly related to the end of the calendar because the calendar ended at a time during the cycle of the precession of the equinoxes when the pole was pointing at Polaris – but it was not an easy concept to grasp.

"Okay," Felipe interjected, "but what about the sun and the word 'evolution'?"

There was silence. Professor buried his head in the notebook, studying the alphabet. The rest of them looked at me.

"And what about the fact that this alphabet translates directly into modern English?" Carlos asked. "Can you explain that?"

"No, I can't," I admitted.

"It doesn't make sense," Carlos said. "This is a language that probably became extinct around ten thousand years ago and yet the letters of the alphabet, all twenty-six of them, can be translated into *modern* English, a language that is only several hundred years old in its current form and is also one of the most modern languages existing today."

"It is a bit older than that, Carlos," Professor interjected.

"Yes, but what I mean is that modern English is different from old English."

"But the alphabet is the same," I pointed out.

"Okay, if we're going to get picky, just two thousand years ago the language in Britain was a concoction of local tribal languages, with a smattering of Roman Latin. So, please explain to me how this alphabet can be translated into the English we use today. I bet it doesn't translate into the Russian alphabet."

"No, it doesn't, not directly," I said, "but this language, besides the African tribal languages, is the mother of every language on the planet."

"How do you know that?" Carlos asked.

"That's what I was told in Tibet."

"So, you are saying this alphabet can be translated into all languages."

"No, I am saying that the *language* can be seen as the mother of all languages, but I don't know the language, or how it sounds. As you say, it is extinct. You have to think of the language and the alphabet as two separate entities."

Carlos shook his head. "None of that explains the fact that this alphabet can be directly translated into modern English. It's totally ridiculous. This has to be a joke."

We all understood what Carlos was saying. There was no explanation as to how these very simple letters – all based on circles – were so easily changed into the English alphabet. The Atlantean alphabet was suddenly looking like a crude and badly created code of the English alphabet. The frustration was clear in everyone but the obvious explanation was being ignored – somehow this alphabet was jumping through time and connecting with the present.

"I think we simply need to look at the facts," Professor cut in. "Quite simply, this is too strange to be real. So, it stands to reason that this must be some kind of elaborate hoax."

"Are you joking?" I asked.

"How else do you explain it, Stephen? I am no expert on languages but the fact that this alphabet can be understood in modern English makes me think this is a hoax. No other ancient language can be read the same way as modern languages – they all used picture references for sounds, rather than individual letters. From that perspective, looking at the evolution of languages, this alphabet fits into the modern age."

Professor was right. But what he didn't know was that these letters were contained in the ancient scrolls in Tibet. I hadn't told the group about the scrolls – and I hadn't even tried to tell them about the dome – and even if I had, this was still an inexplicable situation. I was feeling completely overwhelmed, because there was this nagging thought in my head that somehow Atlantis and this pyramid were connected in a way that was incomprehensible right now. It was almost like the alphabet was created to be read *now*, and maybe that meant it wasn't the Atlantean alphabet at all – maybe it was simply created to be understood today. However strange that sounded, it meant that somewhere along the line the past and the present were interconnected – that the past knew of the present. Was time going around in a loop that was connecting to the present? Was this the real meaning of the Maya calendar? Is this why the calendar is circular? Is the Maya calendar a time piece way beyond our understanding? Whatever the explanation, I was starting to view Yeshe's teachings in a whole different way. One thing that I could not explain, though, was why this pyramid was creating such negative feelings and situations when the dome was positive and full of energy.

"We are going around in circles here," Professor said, "and we're not going to figure it out, so we'd better get on with our job. Stephen, later you will explain to us exactly what was going on in Tibet when you were there. There's no doubt something strange is happening here and you seem to be connecting it with your experiences in Tibet. I need to know why. You owe us an explanation."

I nodded – the only reaction I could give him. He was right. I did owe them all an explanation. My new friends suddenly seemed far more important than the faceless people who were apparently directing our destinies at this time. After all, we were the ones going through these bizarre experiences and the stress of them, while Charles and whoever else was involved were comfortably drinking champagne and eating strawberries without a care in the world. Or so I imagined. Just at that moment, my loyalties were firmly with the group and not at all with Charles, but I felt terribly guilty – I had been holding on to what was, for an archaeologist, the most important piece of information imaginable.

The most devastating aspect for Professor was that now, after a lifetime of archaeology, the world of Atlantis, previously just a fable and a rumour, was now a reality – a place that actually existed and a place that would throw our entire understanding of man's evolution out of the window.

10

INTO THE UNKNOWN

It was already mid-morning and the distractions had put the clock forward on our plans by a couple of hours. Our communal strange dreams had given us a break from thinking about the open pyramid that was waiting for us, but the intensity of the weird events of this morning and the previous night was clearly showing on our faces.

I think we all just wanted to get the job done and get the hell out of there. It was a sharp contrast to my arrival at the site only two days earlier, where high spirits and excitement meant we were all laughing and joking. Now though, it felt as if we were not welcome here and it was apparent that things had taken a turn for the bizarre since the pyramid was opened.

After yet another strong coffee to counteract the tiredness, the sun was almost directly above us and it was now time to go inside the abyss. A plan of action was set out for the day and Professor brought his professional experience to the table.

"One person must remain outside at all times in case of any emergency. We simply do not know how stable the interior structure is and there is a possibility, although remote, that the walls could start to collapse when we are in there."

A volunteer was required but Felipe quickly accepted the task. I was surprised that he volunteered so quickly, thinking that everyone shared my own nervous excitement at the prospect of exploring the interior of the pyramid. But Felipe seemed almost indifferent to what we were about to do – his concern was directed more towards keeping intruders away from the general area. There was something about Felipe that was starting to nag at the edges of my mind. Whenever something interesting was happening, he appeared to be uninterested, such as when Carlos found the numbers on the back of the pyramid and he simply walked away back to base camp. Maybe he simply didn't have the intellectual capacity to understand it all, or maybe he just wasn't interested. Either way, for the most part he wasn't bothered by what was happening and he spent a lot of time by himself whenever he could, often wandering alone in the forest and away from the site. Anyway, his offer to stay outside was accepted and it was agreed that the rest of us would take turns after the initial investigation was completed.

"Carlos and I will go first," Professor announced. "We will be roped when we go in. We will use the bowline-on-a-coil method, using the tree directly opposite the entrance as the 'end man'. That way we will have a strong support in case of any internal collapse."

We all felt this was a little over the top but we all agreed it to be a safe option. Professor always carried caving and mountaineering equipment on his expeditions and he wanted to be sure that if anything bad were to happen, they were both at least connected to the outside and we could locate them easily, even if it was only to recover a body. Felipe, Juan and I would have some hard digging to do if anything like a structural collapse was to occur, for there was no help nearby.

"We simply do not know what is down there," Professor continued, "but we clearly cannot assume we're dealing with an ordinary pyramid and since I get the feeling something is not right I want to make sure we are all safe. We have all seen 'Indiana Jones', but in all seriousness, I take the idea of traps and false doors very seriously. If something does give way and we are all tied to the tree, then we will not fall into a pit of snakes, or something."

For a moment I thought Professor was being serious but a smile crossed his face.

"You really have watched too much Indiana Jones!" laughed Carlos.

"As long as the Professor goes first, we'll be alright!" I said. "In fact, I think Professor should go own on his own and we should sit up here drinking wine!"

"I would agree with that," said Juan, "but if I drink any more of that stuff I'll be sick for a week."

At last the tension was easing, our gentle mocking relieving it just a little, but the task ahead was very serious. I could almost read Professor's mind. I was certain he'd already related the Atlantean alphabet to the pyramid because of his dream, so turning the story of Atlantis from a fable into a real location meant that this place could have built using a level of technology that we might not be familiar with. In fact, it wasn't necessary to make a direct connection between the pyramid and Atlantis – it was obvious we were dealing with something that was outside the realm of normality. From that perspective, was the ghost in the trees and the Maya priest helping us forward, or were they both warning us not to enter the pyramid?

"Carlos and I will go in first and make certain that the interior is structurally sound." Professor turned to me and Juan. "If you two follow us in, then providing you take the same route you will not need ropes. Okay, gentlemen, are we ready?"

"Yes," we all said in unison.

Grabbing a torch each and standing up, for a moment we looked each other in the eye. We all knew instinctively that the next time we faced each other like this the world would be a different place.

"Good luck, men," said Professor.

We all shook hands. This was it. The moment had arrived at last.

My heart started beating faster once Felipe had attached their ropes to the tree and returned to the entrance. The tree was by far the largest one in the visible area and the fact that it was directly opposite the entrance was a coincidence that didn't go unnoticed. All the equipment was high quality caving and climbing gear, so any safety concerns were alleviated once everything was secure. I thought Carlos was correct when he said that Professor had watched too much 'Indiana Jones', but then again we could be eating our words if something bad were to happen. On the outside it looked like a typical pyramid, so one could assume that the interior was also typical, but we all knew there was nothing normal about this place.

The protective sheet over the entrance was removed and Professor took a deep breath before climbing over the wall and onto the first step. He tentatively tested each step by not putting too much weight on them. It seemed he was expecting them to break away under his feet and as this place was five thousand years old, this was a distinct possibility. At the bottom of the steps he shone his torch down the passageway. The rest of us leaned over the wall and shone our torches to add more light. The walls and floors were smooth and seemed reminiscent of the great stonework that adorned the elite Inca buildings in Peru. Carlos, Juan and I climbed the wall and sat on the steps so we could see inside. The passage seemed to come to an abrupt halt about thirty feet along, but then we caught sight of a shadow that hinted of a right hand turn at the end. Professor was halfway down the passageway when he turned to look at us.

"All good so far," he said.

"Well, carry on," said Carlos, "and call me on my mobile if you get into any difficulties!"

The laughter once again broke the tension and this time it echoed deep into the pyramid.

As the three of us shone our torches down the corridor, Professor studied the floor with his, making sure each step on his journey would be safe. The task was laborious and painfully time consuming, but each step was a deeper trek back into unknown history.

By the time Professor was about two-thirds of the way down the passageway, Carlos started to follow, less cautious and far more eager to get to the end. Carlos' actions, lack of fear and impatience made me realise just how much of Professor's behaviour was a little strange. While a sensible and safe approach was necessary under the circumstances, it was apparent that something had unnerved him a great deal. Was it the dream, the mysterious visitor, or just the general atmosphere out here in the middle of nowhere? There was surely more to it than that, something he was not telling us, but this was hardly the moment to ask and, quite frankly, at this moment I didn't want to know the answer.

"There is definitely a right-hand turn at the end," he said, breaking my thoughts, "but the strange thing is there is no wear of any kind. No damp and the walls look like new. I have never seen anything like it. It's as if it's been hermetically sealed."

"Well, I think it's certain we have contaminated it by removing the slab," I said.

There was silence and the sudden realisation that we had committed some kind of sin in the process, as if we had practically destroyed the place already. It was certainly one moment where I wished I'd kept my mouth shut. There was no way we could stop microbes, bugs or mosquitos getting inside, that was for sure, and once those creatures had laid their eggs there would be no stopping the slow but certain deterioration of the inner structure. It was a horrible thought and one that left me feeling extremely guilty, but it actually produced more unanswerable questions – how did the builders manage to construct this place and remove any contaminants? It really was almost as if it had been vacuum sealed. It was, without doubt, a miracle of engineering.

Professor and Carlos continued cautiously towards the end of the corridor while Juan and I sat on the steps waiting patiently at the entrance. As I turned around, Felipe was his normal quiet and serious self, holding the two ropes that were attached to Professor and Carlos and standing about ten feet away from the entrance. To me, he always appeared indifferent. I tried to convince myself that it was simply typical of the hardened, rugged look of living in the jungle environment.

Suddenly everything changed.

"Oh my God!" Professor exclaimed. His tone carried a sense of astonishment and his voice echoed up the passageway towards us.

"What is it?" I called back.

Before the echoed reply returned up the passageway, there was a ritual silence that we had now become accustomed to, but which also meant something exciting had been discovered. In this case, the long silence became tortuous and deafening.

"Earth calling Professor," I cried out.

"You are not going to believe this. You'd better come and see for yourself."

I looked at Juan and simultaneously we got to our feet and headed down the steps and into the corridor. A slight musty smell was noticeable, accompanied by a strange feeling that couldn't be described; a feeling which reminded me of what I'd experienced when visiting the battlefields of the Somme – a sense of deep sadness. As we stepped farther into the past, I looked at the incredible stonework and touched the smoothness of the walls, unable to resist running my hands along them as I walked, like a child scrawling on a wall with a piece of chalk. In the first corridor, the inner wall on the right was a single solid piece of granite. It must have weighed at least two hundred tonnes and it was perfectly smooth and straight, finely cut and polished, levelled out with the accuracy of a spirit level.

When we reached the end, we shone our torches on the walls and my mouth dropped open. I froze on the spot as a wave of shock rippled through my body. The entire second corridor, on both sides, from top to bottom and end to end, was completely covered in writing. The same kind writing that was on the scrolls in Tibet, the same kind of writing that appeared in Professor's dream, the same kind of writing that was copied in my notebook. It was the writing of the Atlanteans.

"A hoax, you say?" I commented to Professor.

Everything Yeshe had said to me in Tibet suddenly fell into place – and raised more questions. Had Yeshe known about this place or had he simply given me information he was instructed to give me? Was it possible that everything I learned in Tibet was linked to this pyramid by pure coincidence? Did the Tibetan scrolls contain information about this pyramid? If so, how could that be? How could texts that were written down at the time of Atlantis talk of a pyramid in the future? And how is it possible that the Atlantean language was still in use only five thousand years ago? Did the builders of the pyramid have any contact with the natives in Central America? There were so many questions but few answers.

There was another long silence as we stood there, our minds awash with questions, confusion and above all, complete awe and wonder. And then, for no reason whatsoever, we started to laugh. It was the kind of spontaneous laughter you would expect at the shock of finding a suitcase of money. This was, however, a million times better than a suitcase full of money.

"Well, Stephen," Professor said, as our laughter died away, "I know what you are here for now!"

I revelled in the idea of the task ahead of me, but the two walls were about twenty-five feet long and ten feet high. This meant there was five hundred square feet of writing to decipher.

"How is this even possible?" asked Carlos.

"What do you mean?" asked Juan.

"We were discussing earlier that this language became extinct ten thousand years ago and now we have to adjust that timescale to five thousand years."

"In fact," Professor interjected, "Stephen is correct. It never actually did become extinct. This could be the mother language of the Olmec."

"What are you talking about?" asked Carlos.

"I mean that we can now assume that not only did Atlantis exist, as Stephen has shown us, but that the story of Atlantis is correct – these people, the survivors, may have spread out around the world and started new colonies."

Professor had jumped ahead to the obvious conclusion. The sudden arrival of human beings in the Americas around ten thousand years ago could now be attributed to the fall of Atlantis and not to a migration from Asia. If this was true then it would be the biggest discovery in human history and the accepted path of human migration would have to be completely rewritten.

It occurred to me at that moment, though I didn't voice my thought, that the Amerindians are oriental looking with slanted eyes – all the original Americans have this feature – so if these people were descendants of Atlantis then it also meant the oriental race was descended from them. Things had come full circle – Yeshe had told me that Tibet was one of the places the Atlanteans migrated to after the fall. Did this mean that the Far East and the Americas were populated at the same time from different directions? Or had there been a migration from the oriental lands to the Americas as was believed in the historical record – a migration during, or at the end of, the last ice age? It was an important question that needed an accurate answer, but Yeshe had not told me *when* the Atlanteans had settled in Tibet, only that they went there after the fall, whenever that was. The scrolls in the dome were ten thousand years old, but they had been copies of the originals which were at least twice that age. That fact gave me a window of at least ten thousand years – from 20,000 BC to 10,000 BC. So, *when* was the fall of Atlantis?

What had become apparent was that there was more going on here than any of us could imagine. This was a vastly important discovery. Professor Sanchez had discovered the ultimate archaeological find in the history of humankind. Nothing could compare to this seemingly unimportant pyramid in the middle of this dreadfully hostile environment.

What we had failed to notice in all the excitement was what awaited us at the end of the second passage. The astonishing walls in the second corridor were so beautifully adorned with writing that none of us had even bothered to look beyond them.

"Look," I said, shining my torch towards the end. In the distance, beyond the corridor, there was a room. From where we stood, we could see the beautifully painted walls – complete with pristine pictures with glorious colours. Strange images that were not discernible from our vantage point required closer inspection.

"You'd better go first," I said to Professor and Carlos.

The darkness of the room ahead felt decidedly ominous. This emotional rollercoaster was taking its toll on my mind and my body and I suddenly felt very tired, but at least the cooler air down here was a break from the belting heat on the outside. Carlos turned to Professor who could only stare back at him. Professor had stopped half way down the second corridor and was suddenly acting very strangely, saying nothing as Carlos walked ahead towards the chamber. Juan followed and I walked a few paces before turning back to look at Professor. He was staring blankly at the walls in front of him.

"Professor," I said. He turned to me, but said nothing and turned back to gaze at the wall, lost in his thoughts. I left him to it, but it wasn't long before he followed the rest of us, still silent and looking a little bewildered.

Standing at the entrance of the room, we shone our torches on the walls. The images were incredible with beautiful colours and a freshness that made them look as if they had been painted the day before.

On the left hand wall as we entered, about one third up from the floor, was an illustration of a pyramid which looked very much like the one we were currently exploring. It had an obvious forty-five degree angle to the sides and the top was cut off to show the platform. Above this a line stretched out from the top and pointed to an unmistakable star system which was painted above – Orion – the most important star system of the ancient Egyptians.

On the wall which faced the entrance, I was once again astonished to find something I had seen before. In the centre of the wall were three big concentric circles – exactly the same as the symbol for Atlantis that had been on the door of the dome in Tibet. Again, lines stretched out from the edge of the image, this time four of them stretching out towards the cardinal points – north, south, east and west. At the top was an unmistakable painting of a stone circle, the typical kind found in Britain and parts of France. In the eastern position was a triangle, a pyramid. On the left hand side was once again what appeared to be the pyramid we were occupying, the same size as the image on the other wall. At the bottom was a step pyramid. The pictures were brightly coloured and only the centre circles were painted black. They stood out from the other images which were grey and brown. Each of the five symbols had a series of dots and dashes near them – Maya numbers – but again it wasn't the later numbering system, it was the same type that Carlos had discovered on the back of the pyramid.

On the wall to our right was a series of very bizarre paintings. Once again I saw the circular image for Atlantis, this time on the left hand side of the wall. Above this was a strange picture of a circle with lines emanating from it – rather like a child's drawing of the sun, complete with rays. Running from left to right, the following images could be seen – a sun-like image next to the first one but with no image underneath and no rays; a circle with a few rays and below this the stone circle design; a circle with more rays and below this a step pyramid; a circle with more than half the rays complete and below it a triangle; a circle with nearly all the rays and what appeared again to be the pyramid we were inside; and finally, the symbol for Atlantis once again but this time the circle above it had a complete set of rays. It was an exact copy of the left hand picture. The only difference between them was that both the symbols for Atlantis had lines emanating from them – the one on the left had a line pointing to the floor, and the one on the right had a line pointing up to the circle. The pictures below the circles were exact copies of the images on the adjacent wall.

"Seven suns," I said without thinking. To me, it looked like a series of images of the sun, starting with a full complete sun, and then ending with another complete sun, with incomplete suns between them. And if they were suns – stars – and assuming they were depicting the Maya Suns, why were there seven of them and not four or five, as the calendar depicts? What did all of this mean? The images were simplistic enough, but at the same time they made no sense.

No one had said a word for quite a while and it seemed everyone's mind was in overdrive trying to comprehend the images.

The Holy Grail of Holy Grails, however, was sitting in the middle of the room. We had all seen it but until now no one had mentioned it as we continued scanning the walls. It seemed like no one wanted to turn round and speak of what was there; like having someone standing next to us and staring at us but not daring to turn round and face them. Finally the silence was broken by Juan.

"What the hell is that?" he asked, as he pointed his torch to the centre of the room.

The room around us became dim as our torches were all directed at the centrepiece, the shadows on the walls behind us like an army of ghosts watching our every move. A large stone, carved from a single block and shaped like a sarcophagus, was sitting there, silent, cold and still. But it wasn't a sarcophagus, it was a solid block of stone – it was the object sitting on the top of this block that we were looking at.

A beautifully carved stone box, about nine feet long and only ten inches wide and eight inches high, lay along the top of the solid block. Approaching the object, we could all see that it was a box, a removable lid clearly discernible. Walking around it, we tried to peer into the line that separated lid from base, but the lid was tightly sealed and rested perfectly on the base – another piece of magnificent and beautifully accurate artwork. Besides the calendar stone, this was the only actual object we had discovered and we realised that a real archaeological find might lie inside the box. One thing was for sure – there were no bodies to be found here. This pyramid was not a tomb. It was something far more mysterious and disturbing.

THE ATLANTEAN ALPHABET

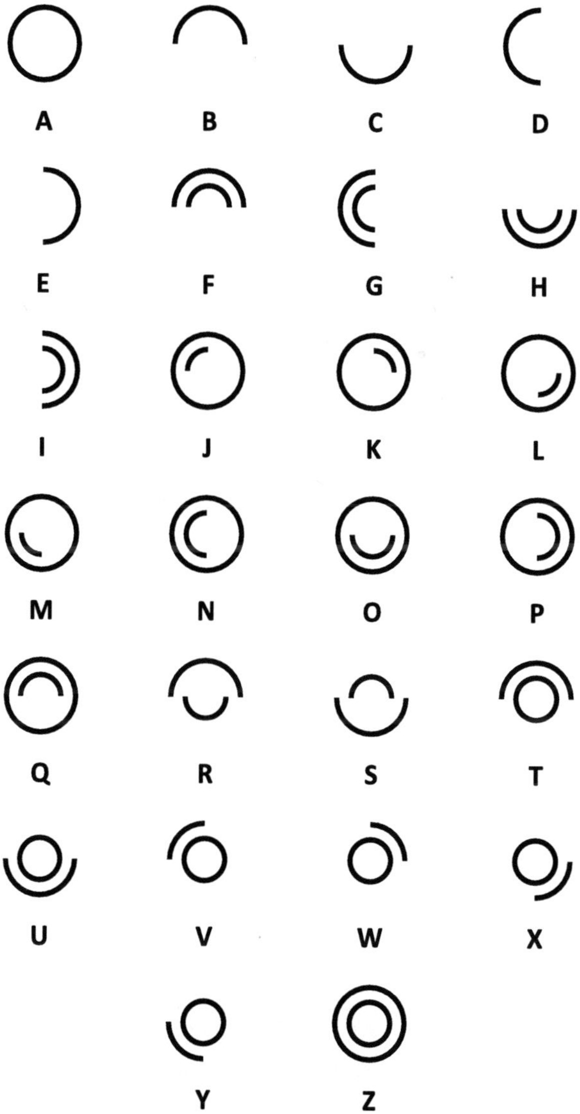

LEFT WALL INSIDE CHAMBER

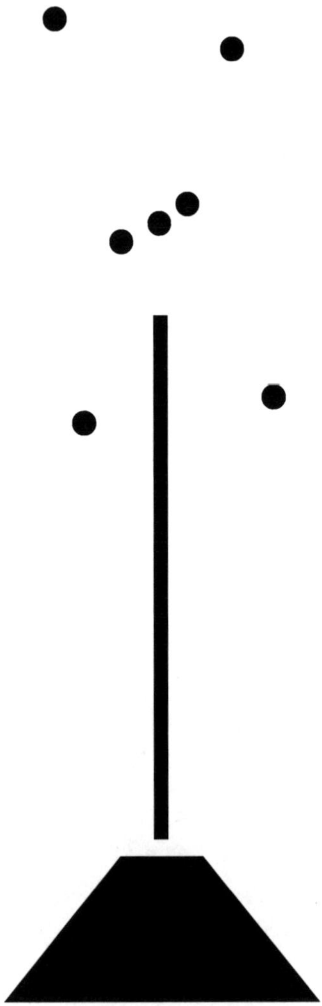

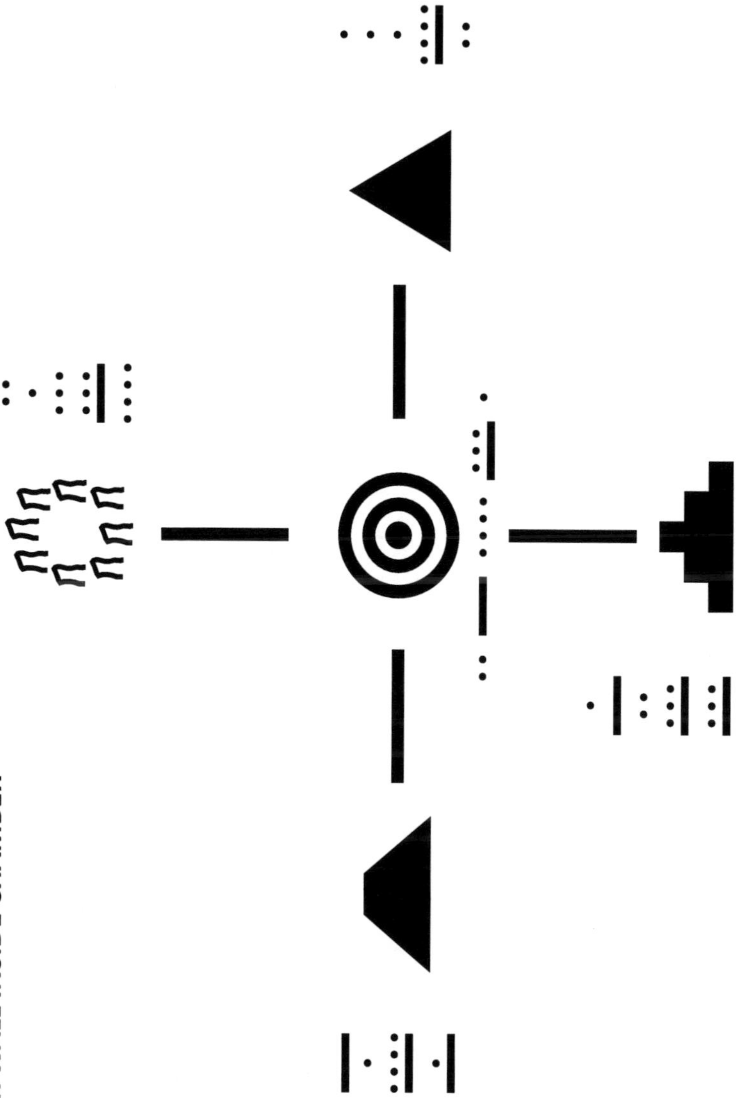

BACK WALL INSIDE CHAMBER

RIGHT WALL INSIDE CHAMBER

11

PROFESSOR UNDER PRESSURE

"Okay," said Professor, "let us take a lunch break and then we can make a plan of action."

"What, now?" asked Carlos, despairingly.

"Yes, now. It's lunchtime."

"Why don't we see what's inside the box?"

"Because it is lunchtime, that's why. Anyway, I am sure Felipe is wondering what is going on." He turned to Juan. "Take my rope back and send in Felipe so he can have a look and then you three get lunch started."

We were all stunned by Professor's decision and looked at each other in dismay. It was akin to finding the Ark of the Covenant after a lifetime of searching and then deciding to turn back, when all that was left was to take a moment to lift the lid and have a look inside. Professor was the team leader, I knew, but since entering the pyramid he had become detached and aloof and his decision seemed out of character. Carlos, Juan and I walked out of the room and back down the corridor, past the incredible writing and out towards the entrance.

Professor was left alone in the room. It seemed he needed a moment or two to comprehend what he had discovered. How must he have been feeling in those moments? His odd behaviour might simply be down to the pressure he suddenly felt – after all, he had discovered a pyramid that completely destroyed the entire history of the Americas. His life's work had been a waste and the theories of the evolution of the Maya, which he had almost singlehandedly formed himself through good scientific study, was now all lost. His reputation as the world's leading Maya archaeologist, built over a forty year career, was now going to be surpassed by a new discovery. How dispiriting it would be to have to come forward and say 'sorry, forget everything I told you before, it's all wrong.' I felt very sad for him – but at the end of the day that is how it all works – new discoveries destroy the old. But the irony was that normally it was a new, fresh scientist – the new graduate on the block – who brought new discoveries to the table, wiping out the old hands as they retired, leaving their life's work to the history books. But Professor Santiago Sanchez was now in a position where his own discovery would wipe out forty years of research of Professor Santiago Sanchez. What a paradox!

The sunlight hurt my eyes as we reached the wall and a bored-looking Felipe stood like a statue in the sweltering heat.

"Felipe," Juan called out, "the professor has fallen down a pit and is impaled on a bed of spikes. He wants you to get the first aid kit and pull him back out!"

The three of us laughed once again, but funnier than the comment was Felipe, who just stood there motionless and expressionless, and this caused us to laugh even more.

"We don't need the ropes anymore," said Carlos, "go on inside, Professor is waiting for you. You won't believe what's in there."

Felipe pulled the ropes back from the entrance and turned back towards the jungle. Carlos shook his head disbelievingly as we watched him slowly detach the ropes from the tree. I admired his professionalism – always finishing a job before starting the next one – but I still wondered about his apparent lack of enthusiasm. He was almost as detached and aloof as Professor. However, a degree in psychology was hardly required to understand was going on here. Everyone was showing signs of inner turmoil and even humour couldn't mask it entirely.

The three of us were standing outside by the time he walked back towards us. "What's wrong, Felipe?" asked Carlos.

Felipe looked at us seriously. He appeared shaken and nervous.

"We are not welcome here," he said, before heading for the entrance of the pyramid.

I looked straight into Carlos' eyes, shrugged my shoulders and raised my eyebrows. Carlos turned his head back towards Felipe.

"Did something happen while we were in there?" he asked him, gently.

Felipe, with one foot on the wall, turned back and stared at Carlos for a moment. Then he scanned the trees as if trying to find some answers in the surrounding jungle canopy before looking back at us.

"Something is watching us," he said.

The euphoria of the morning suddenly disappeared and the fear of the night before returned with a sharp sting. Once again a shiver ran through my body.

"You mean there are people around here?" Carlos asked.

Felipe was about to head into the entrance but stopped again and turned completely around. He walked up to Carlos, took his torch from his hand and looked him in the eyes.

"There is no one here, Carlos, not for kilometres around. I am telling you there is something else here and it is watching us. Maybe if you spend an hour out here alone you will understand what I am saying."

Felipe turned back around and disappeared down the stairs.

None of us said a word, we just looked at each other and then around the site, as if expecting to see something. We all understood exactly what he meant. After the incident last night there had been an eerie feeling and the dreams hadn't helped. All these strange things had started after the lid was removed. Certainly Felipe's perception was believable – spend an hour here alone and this sinister aura would intensify. I suddenly felt very alone and had to fight an internal urgency to get away from this place. While there was an 'otherworldly' feeling here, just like in Tibet, it was much darker. In Tibet, my soul was filled with peace and joy. Here in the jungles of Mexico my soul was filled with fear. It was obvious that Juan and Carlos felt the same. So what was it that we had we stumbled across? Was this place the opposite of the Tibetan dome – a place of evil?

As we walked the few yards to base camp to prepare lunch, I had an overwhelming desire not to spend another night here, and perhaps this was what Felipe had experienced. Feeling isolated and confused, I wanted noise, lights and the busyness of a town. It was as if the energy of this place had crept inside my skin and was attacking my senses, penetrating my inner being and instilling some kind of terror deep in my bones.

"What do you think is wrong with Felipe?" Carlos asked Juan, as he prepared the coffee pot.

"I have known Felipe most of my life. If he says there is something here watching us then that's exactly what's happening. He must have seen something while we were inside. Nothing normally bothers him and he has spent most of his life in the jungle, so it's all familiar to him. You can bet your life something's happened. Anyway, this place shouldn't be here. It comes from another world."

Carlos refrained from commenting as he started to boil water in a saucepan. Juan was right – something wasn't right about this place and there *was* a continuous feeling that some strange force was watching our every move. And certainly it had intensified since we entered the pyramid.

"I keep thinking about the Maya priest in the dream," I said, "but, you know, I have this fear about looking up at the top of the pyramid and just avoid doing it. I know it's there but I don't want to look up."

"I know what you mean," was all Carlos said, before quickly changing the subject. "What do you all want for lunch? We have plenty of rice but our fresh food is dwindling."

"I don't mind, anything," I responded. My stomach was churning with anxiety and this left me with no appetite whatsoever, but I was very thirsty so I set about drinking a litre of water before diving into the coffee.

Professor and Felipe appeared to be taking a long time, but when they eventually emerged from the entrance Felipe looked much calmer.

"What do you think, Felipe?" asked Carlos.

"It's nice and cool down there."

That wasn't quite what Carlos meant, but never mind.

Professor and Felipe sat down and it was more than comforting for us all to be together.

"Right, I think it is obvious things are a little strained around here," said Professor, "so I think we should have a change of plan. Instead of starting work today, we should seal up the entrance, pack up the essentials and head back to Candelaria. I think we are all in need of a decent shower, a proper meal, a good bed, and most of all a cold beer. In the morning we can get fresh supplies and return by lunchtime. I do not want anybody staying here alone, and Felipe thinks it will be safe to leave the site unguarded for a night."

None of us could believe the turnaround in Professor's attitude. Why would he want to leave the site now, when everything was right there in front of us? Surely we should find out what was inside the box and even try to make some sense of the paintings? It was a bizarre decision, but at the same time it was music to my ears – my wishes had been answered. It was also obvious that this decision had come about through whatever discussion Professor and Felipe had inside the pyramid. Something had startled Felipe enough that he wouldn't stay here alone and, knowing the kind of tough person he was, it must have been something quite serious. But it was Professor's change of stance that concerned most of us. It was apparent that scientific professionalism was being overrun by biological reflexes – total fear and the wish to take flight.

"After lunch," he told us, "we will cover the entrance with the plastic sheet and seal it up the best we can. It is not necessary to replace the lid because it will take hours to put back and remove again."

Felipe had calmed down with the news that he was leaving this place, even if it was for only twenty-four hours.

"I don't think anyone will come along while we are away," Felipe said, "but I now think that there are locals who know about this place. Maybe some of the Maya settlements towards the hills know about it, but as the villagers are very superstitious I am sure they stay well clear."

Internally analysing Felipe's comment about the villagers left me a little confused. He said they were superstitious and would stay away, but what did that mean? Were they aware of the paralysing darkness this place emitted?

Carlos started dishing out rice to each of us.

"I think you are right," said Juan, "I think a night in the town will help us put things into perspective. We can all calm down and then tomorrow we will be refreshed and that will help us to start the work. There is strong energy here and I think it has affected all of us."

He was right. We just needed to get away from here for a few hours, look at everything from the outside and then come back refreshed *and* with a new perspective. We tucked into our rice and for the most part we were in silent contemplation. Just the thought of leaving this place was enough to alleviate the stress of this unbearable feeling we were all obviously experiencing.

It took just an hour to get the plastic sheet back into place, seal the gaps, clamp the sides down and place a little earth over the top to camouflage it. The plastic sheet wouldn't easily be seen, even from a short distance. Everything else was left as it was – the tents, the shower, and even base camp was left with unwashed utensils.

Besides the obvious feelings we were encountering there was something wrong with Professor. Whatever misgivings he was having, they were overpowering his professionalism to the point where, even though the most important discovery of his life was right in front of him, he was willing to wait twenty-four hours to find out what it was. I tried to put it out of my mind and hoped the trip back to Candelaria would realign us all and bring back a bit of normality, but it wasn't our emotions that were the problem, it was an angry pyramid – a pyramid that had been awoken from a sleep that had lasted for five thousand years, and it seemed that it didn't like being disturbed. The Curse of Tutankhamun was looking like a child's comedy compared to this nightmare.

12

FOOD FOR THE GODS

The journey back to the town seemed to take forever. The more I thought about the decision to leave the site the more strange it seemed. We had been an afternoon's work away from leaving the site altogether, at least from the archaeological perspective of a preliminary examination. Sure, archaeological study doesn't happen in an afternoon with a site of this magnitude, but there was nothing left to *dig*, and that is the most time-consuming of all archaeological activities. It may have seemed easy to think these things now that we were away from the site and the intense oppression was no longer around us, but aside from that there was no logical explanation for the decision to leave at such short notice. From an archaeological perspective it wasn't the right decision and so Professor's ruling was very peculiar indeed. Getting away from the torment of the atmosphere of that place was a great idea, but we could have been away from it for good had we stayed for the afternoon and finished the work.

"I have arranged for us to stay at a friend's house," Professor said en route. "You should get on well with him, Stephen. He is an English ex-pat and a palaeographer. He moved here in the early nineties. His name is Michael White, and I can tell you he certainly knows his stuff."

"That sounds very interesting, and a bit of a coincidence," I replied.

"What's a palaeogie-thing?" Felipe asked.

"A palaeographer is an expert on ancient writing," Professor replied. "He is a dependable friend and we can talk openly without the worry of anyone overhearing us. I went to see him when I picked you up, Stephen. I told him we would be coming but didn't give him an exact date – not that it matters. None of you need to feel we're intruding – we can all have a hot shower and some great home cooked food from his dear wife, Clara. She is Mexican, by the way."

This was yet another synchronicity. Michael was a palaeographer and no doubt the best person to look at the writing. Professor had arranged for us to stay without even guessing we would have something important to show him.

However, I doubted that even he would have an explanation for what we had discovered. There was no one on earth that could explain how this writing translated into modern English and it seemed almost a cruelty to show it to Michael – he would be another person who would have to throw a lifetime of work out of the window.

"I would have thought that talking at the pyramid would be the best place to stop anyone overhearing us," said Felipe.

"But Michael isn't at the pyramid, idiot!" snapped Professor.

It was another mindless comment from Felipe but he did have a point because Professor hadn't previously made it clear he wanted Michael to look at the writing and, after all, the pyramid *was* the safest place to talk. Since our strange dreams, Professor had changed completely, displaying the traits of someone in psychological trauma. I wasn't sure if he was using Michael as an excuse to get away from that place for a short time – after all, Michael could just as easily have looked at the writing after we'd left permanently – or whether there was something else up his sleeve, something he wasn't telling us.

Michael wasn't quite what I expected. He looked more like a CID officer than an intellectual. He had grey hair, now almost white, which was slightly wiry and dishevelled and he had a considerable moustache of the same colour. He was slim, with a quiet demeanour and a little arrogance sprinkled on the top, although it was more an intelligent aloofness. He was probably good looking in his younger days, with high cheekbones and softness to his features which gave him a sympathetic appearance.

His wife Clara was a small rounded woman. She was a bit older than Michael but with the same weathered brown skin as Juan and Felipe. Despite her small stature she had a strong presence which always dominated the room, her female energy overpowering even the six of us men. At first sight she and Michael seemed an odd couple, but they were clearly very close.

The house was an old colonial style building with large gates on the outer perimeter and an enclosed inner courtyard perfect for sun and conversation. It reminded me very strongly of the house Anjali had described in her story about her NDE – there was a walkway all around the upper floor and it wasn't difficult to imagine her falling over the railing head first onto the concrete below. She had been more than lucky to survive.

Michael and Clara's house must have had at least twenty rooms, far too many for the two of them, which left me wondering how a man who studied ancient writing could afford such a luxurious abode. The fact that they had a child could partly account for it, but that made the size of the place even more bizarre. Without prompting or questioning, the answer soon came as Mike, as he insisted on being called, explained his background.

"I made a lot of money in the eighties selling photocopiers and computers to small companies before all the big boys cornered the market. I got bored with it all and needed another outlet to satisfy my life. Believe me, money doesn't make you happy and for me it just made me restless. In the late eighties my father passed away and when I was clearing out his loft I found some old manuscripts. There was something about them that intrigued me and I wanted to find out what my father had been up to. I sold the business and started researching and reading and eventually I discovered that these very documents had been stolen by the Italians in World War Two. My father acquired them from somewhere when he was in the war, but I never found out where he got them from. It turned out that they were old Spanish chronicles about the conquest of Mexico. So, I came here, learned Spanish and studied palaeography. Then of course I met Clara and my fate was sealed!"

Clara threw him a bemused but affectionate look as she passed the table.

We accepted Mike's offer of showers – fortunately the house had plenty of them – and in what seemed like no time at all, Clara had assembled a huge meal for us on the large wooden table in the sun-strewn courtyard. The table was full with large pots containing different dishes with fajitas, nachos and bread to accompany them and cold drinks and beer to wash down our meals. It was a full Mexican feast, but by late evening there was not a single scrap left.

As we ate, Professor had made it clear to the rest of us just how much he trusted our hosts. He and Mike had become friends after literally bumping into each other at the main university in Mexico City. Mike had been attending a philology conference and at that time Professor was teaching archaeology.

"I flung the door open and it hit him, sending his books flying across the floor," Mike explained, "and as we got chatting we seemed to have an instant bonding. Our friendship started right there as we discussed what was going on in both archaeology and Mayan writing. There was equal respect on both parts."

Sitting at the table, sipping fresh juice, Professor started to tell Mike and Clara the entire story of the pyramid. For the most part they were in stunned silence. Leaning back in the chair and closing my eyes, I tried to imagine being on a beach somewhere, but my mind was full of strange images of triangles, Maya priests and jungle ghosts.

"What do you think it all means?" asked Mike, finally.

"We have no ideas about it yet, not until we have a chance to analyse everything properly."

Professor showed Mike some pictures he had taken on his digital camera while he was alone in the pyramid. "When we decipher the writing," he said, "I am hoping it will give us a complete story of what we are dealing with."

Mike was astonished to hear that I had seen the same writing in Tibet and had the alphabet written in my notebook ready for translation, and now, for the first time, I felt I should reveal most of the details of my Tibetan journey – Chang, Lasya and Yeshe, the Chinese soldiers trying to find us. I related some of the teachings Yeshe had given me and told them the alphabet was the writing of the Atlanteans, but I stopped short of telling them about the dome, only talking of the strange room with the snake crawling along the ceiling. Remembering that Yeshe had said many things would be revealed *at the right time*, I instinctively kept some knowledge to myself, but I did inform them about the scrolls and explained that they were Atlantean.

Poor Mike's face was ashen by the time I had finished and Professor was eyeing me cautiously. It was now obvious that the dome and the pyramid must be linked in some way and also that my being here was no accident. It was also very clear to me that Yeshe knew a lot more than he had ever said. In fact, I hadn't seen the connections myself until I told the whole story.

Given Mike's expertise as a palaeographer, the writing became the central focus of our conversation. The fact that we had a five thousand year-old pyramid and a copy of the Maya calendar seemed to pale into insignificance as everyone recognised that we had evidence that Atlantis really had existed, with even more evidence to back it up – their writing.

"What do you think, Michael?" asked Professor.

"Well, if the story is to be believed – and I have to say I'm leaning that way – the remnants of the Atlantean civilisation migrated around the world after their civilisation was destroyed by a catastrophe. So, it would not be a surprise to find their language and evidence of their legacy scattered over the continents. What is strange, though, is that Steve was sent on some kind of mission to Tibet and then on to here, and in both places there are writings from the Atlantean language. The fact that Steve was sent here with a copy of the alphabet means that someone knows about the pyramid and the most important job is to translate those walls. Maybe all your answers are written in stone."

Feeling six pairs of eyes fix on my face was like being on trial for some crime. Some of them may have guessed that I wasn't telling them the whole truth about Tibet but part of me still felt that it wasn't important for them to know everything. From my perspective, the important thing now was for us to figure out what those pictures meant and decipher the writing – maybe then I would tell them the whole truth. But I wasn't the only one at the table keeping secrets. The more I thought about it, the more it seemed that Professor was acting in a very strange way.

By midnight, the conversation turned to more trivial matters. Juan and Felipe's attempt at staying sober failed miserably, the latter of the two eventually succumbing to the beer and sliding off his chair onto the floor. It was a beautifully warm and clear night and the humidity appeared to be almost eliminated in the courtyard, but every time I looked up at the stars an eerie feeling swept over me as if we were back at the site. I couldn't wait to get back to the pyramid and decipher the writing but at the same time I couldn't dispel a feeling of dread which left me thinking I never wanted to go near the place again. In fact, the feeling of apprehension had intensified since we were away from the site and it was more than likely everyone was feeling the same. This was in sharp contrast to what I had expected. I'm sure we all thought that coming here would remove the feelings and give us renewed enthusiasm, but it seemed that only on completion of the job would we be freed from the torment. It was as if the pyramid itself was calling out to us and it wasn't going to let us be until we had replaced the slab. I felt certain that if we chose to leave things as they were and never go back to the site again, we would be hounded by nightmares for the rest of our lives. This particular pyramid seemed an unforgiving place.

I kept a close eye on Mike, who had spent the evening looking at the writing. From time to time he shook his head and let out a long, deep sigh. It was comforting to be in the presence of another Englishman, even if I didn't know him. Later, when everyone else was finally retiring for the night, I hung back to ask him what he was thinking.

"I have no answers, Steve," he said. "There's no comparison between this writing and any other I've ever seen. Even cuneiform doesn't come close. It's like discovering a six-legged mammal – it just doesn't fit into anything that we know. Not to mention the fact that this writing is supposedly from Atlantis but translates directly into modern English – that's the most bizarre thing I have ever come across. All I can say is that something is wrong."

"What do you mean?"

"It's just wrong. How can an extinct alphabet translate into a modern language? It's totally bizarre. It makes me feel very uncomfortable. I think you guys are dealing with something far beyond the known rules of normality. If I were you, Steve, I would be very careful."

"Why?"

"Can't you see it?" he whispered. "Just step outside and look back at yourself. You've been sent to Tibet and now here. You've been tracked by the Chinese government. You've been sent around the world by God knows who – you don't even know who this person is but he seems to be able to pull whatever strings he or she wishes. And, most importantly, you have in your possession evidence which destroys *all* of our known history. It's dynamite. Don't you think you're being led up the garden path?"

"You mean this might be a hoax? That it's all some kind of joke and someone's just having a laugh?"

"No, I don't think that at all – you're missing the point. If Santiago is convinced that the pyramid hasn't been opened for five thousand years, then I believe that too, and it's indisputable that it contains writing in the same language that you're carrying in your pocket. According to what you've been told, that writing is from Atlantis. This whole thing means that some people know about this already, but they've been keeping it a secret, maybe for thousands of years. If that's the case, then there's a damn good reason for it. If your job is to reveal that information, you'll be the most wanted man on the planet. These people aren't stupid, so they must be on your trail already. If you don't stay one step ahead of the game you're a dead man. If you want my advice, you'll get the hell out of that place as soon as you can."

It wasn't advice I was ready to hear, despite my own misgivings. "That doesn't make sense, Mike. Yeshe told me that he and his people in Tibet are the keepers of this knowledge – yes it is a secret, but they've only been hiding it from those governments that wish to use its power for negative means. They are good people, Mike."

"You still don't get it, do you?"

"I guess not."

"Look Steve, maybe I can see it because I'm not up to my neck in it, like you are. What I am saying is that the thing they have been keeping secret is the *existence* of Atlantis. It's not your friends in Tibet; it's the secret governments you need to worry about. They must know all this exists and they're the ones who have been keeping it out of the history books for a damn good reason. They don't want us to know about it. They want us to think that during that time we were running around the forests chasing hogs with spears. So, you've got to ask yourself – why are they keeping this a secret from us?"

"Maybe they *don't* know about it, Mike."

He leaned back in his chair and let out a long, concerned sigh, and he dropped his arm down behind the back of the chair. His eyes were red from tiredness. He nodded, very slowly, and his lips tightened.

"You can bet they do know, Steve," he finally said. "They will know about it. And they will do whatever they can to keep it secret. Putting the pieces together, from what you've told me I can guarantee that they're not too far behind you. I wouldn't trust anyone, if I were you."

Wednesday 26 May, 2010

What a day! I cannot believe that writing is also in the pyramid. Never in my wildest imagination would I have thought that Tibet and that pyramid could be connected so directly. But what does it mean? What are those strange pictures? What's in that box? And what on earth is going on in general – strange dreams, paranormal events and a continuous feeling of fear? I am even more certain we shouldn't be in that place. Professor has been acting very strange since we went inside the pyramid. I'm sure he's hiding something. And as for what Mike said, it's almost as if it doesn't bother me at all. It scares me a lot, but compared to everything else that's gone on, it's nothing. If we were caught, though, that would be a different story…

13

THE VISITOR

With only a couple of hours sleep after Mike scared the hell out of me, a nearby cockerel woke me at half past six as the early morning sun started to rise in the sky, an orange glow visible on the horizon as if the jungle was on fire. Flocks of birds swept through the air, the cloudless heavens created a blue screen and there was a crisp, albeit warm, freshness to the morning air. As I leaned over the balcony outside my room, a stray dog rummaged through the street to find an early breakfast, his tail wagging and his nose sniffing out every inch of the path. A light wind blew pieces of paper across the road and an old woman was beating a hanging mat with a saucepan, the dust flying out into the air and dispersing into invisibility.

After taking a shower and entering the courtyard, I found that Felipe, Juan, and Carlos had already headed off to the market to collect more supplies. Professor and Mike were whispering to each other at the table.

"Morning," I said as I reached them.

"Good morning," they replied, ceasing their conversation. I had obviously interrupted a private discussion but I wasn't feeling courteous enough to leave them alone again.

"There is breakfast on the table," Clara said, "please help yourself." The table had been cleared of last night's detritus and filled again, this time with fruits, bread and biscuits.

"Excited about your trip?" Mike asked in a typically English fashion.

"Yes, I can't wait to get there and make a start," I said, my words sounding unconvincing even to me.

I glanced at Professor to see if he had an expression of fear, but he kept his eyes on the back wall of the courtyard.

"Make sure you come and stay again when you are finished, seems like we have a lot in common."

"I'd like that," I told him, nodding appreciatively.

"Please do. You'll be welcome to stay as long as you like."

The thought of returning to this wonderful house after more time at the site seemed like heaven. I would happily pay my way here, or should I say Charles would pay my way here – providing he wasn't planning on sending me to the North Pole – and the memory of the great food, hot shower and comfortable bed would stay in my mind until I came back. I was, however, a little surprised that he was extending his hospitality – after what he'd said last night, wasn't he worried that I would be putting him in danger by coming here again?

The others returned from the market and by nine we were ready to leave. All too soon, we were driving away from Mike's comfortable house and heading back towards the creepy jungle.

Everything at base camp was exactly as we had left it. Professor asked that we all sit for a while so that he could explain his plan of action for the coming days, but all of us were surprised by the change of procedure that he put forward.

"Since we left here yesterday," he began, "I have thought deeply about how we should proceed. There is no mistaking the strange events we have all witnessed. I have no doubt that we are dealing with something very unusual here, especially after hearing the full story of Stephen's trip to Tibet. It seems to me that we are not here by chance and that our discovery of this place was timed to perfection."

Professor paused for a moment and took a sip of water, and before anyone could ask why he had the idea that things were predetermined, the answer quickly followed.

"Last night, at Michael's house, I had what I can only describe as a 'night visitor'. This person, or whatever it was, gave me strict instructions on how to proceed. We will remove the plastic sheet and get inside the pyramid. We will set up lighting and take as many photos and details as we need to take. Nothing is to be removed from the pyramid. As an archaeologist, I find that very disappointing because I want to know what is inside the box, but that's not important anymore. We will finish this work by tomorrow evening. The slab is to be replaced before sundown and sealed in its original position. The following morning we will put earth back on top of the slab so that it looks totally undisturbed, and then we will leave the site, making sure there is no trace of our visit. I think there may be other, not-so-pleasant individuals also trying to find this site."

"What are you talking about?" asked Carlos, as if insanity had finally got the better of Professor. For me, the synchronicity between Professor's words and Mike's advice last night was obvious.

"What?" asked Professor, as if nothing was unusual about his statement.

"I asked you what the hell you're talking about," Carlos said.

"Do I have to repeat myself?"

Carlos was speechless for a moment, shaking his head and holding out an open palm as if the gods might offer a better explanation. "What do you mean by a 'night visitor'?"

"Maybe it was just a dream, I don't know."

Carlos was astounded into silence. Dream or not, Professor was taking this very seriously and it was an astonishing revelation, coming from him. He was talking about some kind of paranormal experience – yet another since we opened up the pyramid.

I was mortified at the idea other people were following our scent. "When you say 'not-so-pleasant individuals'," I asked, "what exactly do you mean – the government, or perhaps the military?"

"I don't know. Those that wish to suppress this information, or those who wish to use the knowledge for negative means – who knows who they are. I just know that my... visitor, whatever it was, left me in no doubt that what is written on the walls down there is extremely powerful and someone else is searching for it, and they're not too far behind us. As long as we stick to the plan and the time scale I've just described, we should be okay. It gives us just over twenty-four hours to get in there, get out, and put that lid back in its original position. So let's get started."

"Okay, but let me get this straight," said Juan. "You're saying a ghost visited you in the night, told you some stuff and now you're going to do the things it told you to do. Is that what you're telling us?"

Felipe sniggered and then covered his mouth with his hand.

"I am not saying it was a ghost. It might have been a dream but, if so, it was a very intense dream. I don't mind admitting that it scared me and I have no alternative but to take it as a serious warning."

Juan raised his eyebrows. "I am surprised that you, of all people, would take a dream so seriously."

"Well, I'm more surprised that you want to leave everything in situ," Carlos complained.

"We are *way* out of our depth here, my friend," Professor replied, getting to his feet. "We have evidence that proves the existence of Atlantis or, at the very least, an unknown form of writing. It seems to me that certain organisations or governments must already be aware of this information and that means they have gone to a lot of trouble over the years trying to suppress it. And why? Because it destroys the idea that we are the pinnacle of human evolution, that's why. For the past forty years, Carlos, I have been promoting the idea that the Olmec were the first civilisation in our great country. This bloody pyramid destroys everything I have ever done. You know as well as I do that there are people in this world who will not hesitate to kill to keep their secrets. Now, you can sit there all afternoon if you like, but I am getting far away from this place as quickly as I can."

Sheepish looks were exchanged but Professor had made his point. No secrets would ever be allowed to leave this place. We had to put things back the way they were and leave as soon as we could, before we were caught. How ironic it would be if we were put to death at a Maya pyramid that was *not* used for sacrifice.

Either this was yet another bizarre synchronicity, or Mike and Professor had been discussing the subject as well. Perhaps Professor had overheard our conversation and was making it up – maybe he understood the fear that Mike had presented to me and now he'd decided to get the hell out of this place as soon as possible. But if Professor had overheard the conversation I had with Mike, or had discussed it with him, he was far too clever and intelligent to repeat the same words that Mike had used.

Felipe, understandably in the circumstances, was reluctant to wait outside the pyramid by himself, so Juan agreed to stay with him as the rest of us got to work. We erected a makeshift lighting rig and very soon over a hundred photographs had been taken.

I made sure every inch of the writing had been photographed several times. The difficult thing was making sure when the photographs were put together later they did not overlap or become mixed up, so the first series of photos were of areas just a foot square, from left to right. Then I repeated the process from top to bottom until both the walls had been completed. In between I took more close-up photos showing detail to ensure no mistakes would be made during the translation.

The writing itself was incredible. It had been carved into the walls and then painted – a white background with black symbols. The writing was, without doubt, absolutely beautiful – the artistic effect was breathtaking.

While I was photographing the writing, Carlos and Professor had also spent time in the room taking photos of the wall paintings and the box. They had also carefully measured both the halls and the room, in every direction. Since numbers were appearing wherever we turned, we surmised that there may be mathematical reasoning to the dimensions of the interior, so every possible clue was noted. By late afternoon, our work had been completed way ahead of schedule and the only thing left to do was to see what was inside the box.

Professor decided we should break off for dinner as the sun was setting behind the trees and none of us wished to be inside the pyramid during the night. Inside the pyramid, it was hard to tell whether it was daytime or not but it still had an altogether different and more menacing aura at night time.

Back at base camp, I sat with Professor while dinner was prepared.

"That didn't take as long as I expected," Professor said, "so I think, providing we seal the pyramid up correctly, we can leave tomorrow night."

Those words were like music to our ears. It was an incredible relief that we might only be spending one more night here. The intensity of the stress had increased as the day wore on. It was no longer a feeling that we were being watched by *something*, it was a feeling that we were being watched by *everything*. Even the trees seemed conscious of our presence – it was one of the most bizarre and intensely unnerving feelings I had ever experienced. Normally this kind of feeling lasts for moments, depending on the situation, but this was a continuous feeling that increased my stress levels to breaking point. I found myself thinking someone was behind me, and then to my left, and then on the pyramid. It was the strangest experience and it was almost like the ghosts of the past were everywhere, surrounding our camp and watching our every move.

By the time we finished dinner it was dark and we spent the entire night at base camp, with adequate lighting to dispel the watching aura of the forest. We used one of the battery powered lights that were used inside the pyramid and that was enough to fill base camp with a yellow glow, and with it a sense of security.

And now, finally, we discussed what was going on in this, the strangest, weirdest, and scariest of places.

14

GHOST STORIES

"While I was standing outside holding the ropes, things went a bit weird," said Felipe, as he started our conversation. He seemed relieved to be getting this out in the open, as if he no longer had to hold on to the fear.

"I could hear every word you four were saying," he continued, "the sound is very loud coming from inside the tunnel. Suddenly everything went quiet. I could no longer hear you talking, the trees stopped moving and even the birds stopped singing. It was very strange, almost like time itself had stopped. Then I froze. I couldn't move and I could feel the hairs standing up on my neck and my spine was tingling. It might seem stupid, but I wasn't too bothered about it at the time. It went on for a few seconds, or at least I thought it was a few seconds. Anyway, like I said, I wasn't too bothered about it until I realised someone was standing right behind me. And when I say *right* behind me, I mean *right* behind me. I could feel his breath on my neck and I could hear his breathing. It was definitely a man and I could sense he was tall and largely built. It felt like he was looking inside me, like he was looking into my body, or something. It scared me a lot because I knew there wasn't actually anyone standing behind me. I don't know how long that went on for, it seemed a long time but it was probably only around five or ten seconds. Then he disappeared and everything went back to normal."

It was a hard story to take in, but having several similar experiences during my life, I felt empathy for Felipe. It must have been a truly frightening experience for him, one which must have left him feeling very alone and isolated.

"Wow!" was all Juan said.

"Now I can see why you don't want to be out here alone," added Carlos.

Juan seemed to be the only one who hadn't had a personal experience, except for hearing the cracking wood in the forest a couple of days back, and because of this his curiosity was all the greater. "What about your night visitor?" he asked Professor.

Everyone glanced towards Professor, not knowing if he would react angrily, but he was calmer now than he had been for some time and he clearly felt it was necessary to share Felipe's burden.

"It was not a Maya priest this time," he began, "it was a figure of a woman, but I couldn't give you any real description. I couldn't make out any details or features. The figure just seemed to be floating above the end of my bed. I just sensed it was a woman and the voice inside my head was soft, gentle and feminine. I am not sure if I was asleep or awake, I just know the experience was vivid and real. I've already told you everything else. She just gave me instructions on how to proceed. There's nothing else to tell you."

"Well, that's pretty comforting," I said, "because it sounds to me more like what's known as an angelic visitor."

"What do you mean?" asked Juan.

"Well, it's a rare type of visitation," I began, "but it is reported reasonably frequently. Often when someone is in a 'near-death' situation, or..." I stopped, suddenly remembering a similar experience, when I was seventeen.

"Or, what?" Professor asked, breaking my thoughts.

"It could mean that we're being protected by a higher source."

"What do you mean by that?" asked Carlos.

"Let me tell you about an experience I had years ago," I said. "When I was a teenager living with my parents, my mother and I had some very weird experiences that were pretty scary. Then, one particular night I awoke and there was a girl sitting on the end of my bed. She was right in front of me. She was sitting across my legs, although I couldn't feel her weight. I thought maybe it was just a dream or a mirage, or something, but then I leaned forwards and the image became clearer as I became more conscious – there *was* a girl there, and now I was only about eighteen inches from her face. The scary thing was that her face was blank – there were no features at all. She had long, black wavy hair but still there was no face. But the weirdest thing was, just like Professor said, I could hear her thoughts in my head and her voice was gentle, soft and feminine. She was saying, 'How can he see me? He is not supposed to see me! I can't believe he can see me.' I heard every word of her thoughts. We stared at each other for what seemed like minutes, but in reality it was probably about ten or twelve seconds. When I finally regained control of myself I flew under the covers and didn't come out until morning! I wasn't really scared of her – my body just reacted to the situation.

"The next morning, the end of my bed was ice cold and remained so for two weeks. I knew that meant she was still there, all the time, sitting at the end of my bed. But despite the cold, I knew for sure that she was protecting me against all the bad forces that were in that house – I am certain of it."

My storytelling had created a tense atmosphere and the spirits of the jungle seemed to be wide awake, listening intently to our stories.

"That's an incredible story! I can't believe it," said Juan.

"Yes it is incredible, but every word is as it happened and I don't care what anyone says about it. People have laughed at me, told me I was imagining things, but then that's how people are programmed to think. What I am trying to say is this – she was protecting me. Of that I have no doubt, but in the coming weeks and even years, I used to think 'Where did she come from? Why am I so special that this entity would come to guard and protect me? Did anyone send her? Or did she come of her own free will?' I felt very lucky and blessed that this entity would go out of her way to spend a couple of boring weeks sat on someone's bed! If she was sent by *something*, we have to ask by what? And if she was sent by *someone*, then we have to ask by whom? And where is that place that she came from? It must have been something of a higher nature, don't you think?"

"Are you suggesting that God sent her?" asked Carlos.

I took a deep breath. "No, that's not what I believe. But it all depends on your beliefs, doesn't it? If you believe in God then you would probably say that is where she came from. I just feel that she came from a higher place, something that we don't understand. I don't believe in heaven and hell but I do think that the universe is filled with all sorts of levels of existence. If we remove our preconceived ideas about religion, or more importantly the idea that *this is all there is*, then we stand a better chance of understanding what we're dealing with. The girl on my bed could be described as a kind of angelic visitor, but sometimes these visitors are, like in Felipe's case, something darker and scarier. Are they two different things coming from different places, or are they different elements of the same thing? What I mean is, are they two aspects of the same face? Is 'God' completely neutral, a perfectly balanced combination of good and evil?"

There was silence. I wasn't surprised. "Anyway," I continued, "I don't think we should drag ourselves into a philosophical conversation about this, or we'll be here all week! The point is that Professor's experience, his female visitor, is an indication that we are being protected by something and it's the best protection we could ever wish for. And that also means that whatever secrets we have discovered here are very special and very important."

"Are you saying that we should not be in fear of what is happening to us?" asked Juan.

"Basically, yes, but don't ask me why we're having such contradictory experiences. The Maya priest in our dreams and Professor's night visitor seem to be guiding and helping us, but Felipe's experience and the noises in the forest seem to be trying to scare us. Why is that? Why are we experiencing both positive and negative forces?"

There was silence once again, because there was no answer to those questions. But then Juan, of all people, came up with a possible explanation.

"Maybe the negative experiences are designed to scare people away, almost like they are programmed into the surroundings, like a trigger? Things only really started happening when we opened the lid, so maybe it set off some kind of alarm, like a protection system, that would scare off anyone who was not actually supposed to be here. In that sense these events would occur to anyone. And maybe we're also experiencing guidance because we are the ones who are *supposed* to be here. Anyone who was not supposed to be here would only experience that bad stuff and would be scared away. Maybe that's why the tribes steer clear of this place."

"It is an interesting theory, Juan," Professor interjected, "but how do we explain that the pyramid can somehow activate certain experiences of a paranormal nature? It seems more logical that the things happening must be spontaneous, rather than by design. How would the man that was breathing down Felipe's neck know he would be there at that moment? If it was designed then it seems unlikely, don't you think?"

"I am not so sure," said Carlos. "A lot of stuff has happened since we removed that slab – too many things to be coincidence, if you ask me. We were here for weeks before we opened that lid and the only thing I noticed was a vague feeling that we shouldn't be here. In just the last two days we have had some very weird things happening, and looking at that from a scientific point of view it is statistically improbable that it's all happened by chance."

"Then how do we explain it, Carlos?" asked Professor. "Are you seriously suggesting that opening up the pyramid somehow unleashed a series of paranormal episodes? Whilst I am willing to accept that strange things happen in the world, I have to stop short of accepting that moving a block of stone can create things like this."

"I don't have an explanation," Carlos replied. "I'm just making an observation of something that neither of us can ignore."

“It feels to me like we are being tested by these experiences,” said Juan.

“I agree with that,” said Felipe. “When that man was standing behind me I did feel like he was trying to scare me away. If I wasn’t with you I would never have stopped here. As soon as I arrived I had a feeling I shouldn’t be here, like I should fear this place.”

Juan was a little bemused since he hadn’t experienced anything directly, other than the noise in the trees, but perhaps this had allowed him to come up with his theory more objectively. It must have been hard for him to take all of this in and accept as truth things which were happening outside his personal experiences. He obviously didn’t think that we were all telling lies, but at the back of his mind he must have been thinking that he couldn’t possibly believe it unless he’d seen it for himself. If, however, he had any doubts lingering in the back of his mind they were about to be unequivocally removed.

15

FRAGMENTS OF REALITY

The big lamp hanging from the tree was totally unnecessary as the moon was nearly full but our need for it just showed how nervous we were all feeling. A creepy quietness surrounded us as the conversation mellowed and turned to more trivial matters.

"What do you think of Michael?" asked Professor.

"He's an amazing man," I said, "and living exactly the life I would have lived if I had that kind of money!"

"I am sure Michael has some fascinating documents to show you," Professor continued. "He has spent a lot of time in the field and I think you may be amazed at what documentation he has."

"I am definitely looking forward to it," I replied.

A smile ran across his face. "I think you will be spending a lot of time with him when we are finished here. We will head back there and I think that is where we will be saying our goodbyes."

I was suddenly sad to realise that this adventure would have to come to an end at some point. Even through the fear and the constant thought of wanting to get away from this place, a great bond had grown between us. It seemed to me the kind of bond that soldiers must experience when they have been in battle together – the intense emotions brought on by fear mean that your companions are your only solace, saving you from being alone in the loneliest place imaginable. This place itself wasn't lonely, but it would still be a terrifying situation if you were here alone. Naturally this place could never be compared to the battlefield, but our closeness was a bond that could not be explained in any other way – it was intense fear that had brought us closer together and we relied on each other's support.

"I had a weird experience years ago at Palenque," Professor suddenly said. "In the mid-nineties, I was leading a team excavating an obscure part of the site away from the main pyramids. People don't realise that the majority of Palenque is yet to be excavated and is still covered in jungle. We were excavating a small area that appeared to be a square house, although we never did truly discover its purpose, and the theory that it was some kind of living accommodation was never verified. The working conditions were horrific. It was much hotter than here and the mosquitos attacked us relentlessly. After about two weeks we had little to show for our efforts apart from a small pit about thirty centimetres deep and a metre square. In reality it was just a test pit and we weren't really expecting to find anything.

"We'd stopped for lunch one day when a strange looking gentleman appeared from nowhere. There was something very odd about him – he was dressed in clothes that would have been in fashion in the nineteen forties. He had grey hair, was in his sixties I would say, but his skin was very smooth. That seemed unusual, but he had Mexican-coloured skin with very bright blue eyes and that was even more unusual. His eyes seemed abnormally large, too. He stood there for a few moments looking at our pit and then he looked around at the forest in the distance. I said 'Hello' to him and he turned to look at me and then stared towards the Temple of Inscriptions. My colleagues and I all looked at each other, thinking he was a bit odd. Then he looked straight into my eyes and said, 'That pot you found does not come from here.' He continued staring into my eyes while I told him we had not found any pot. He looked towards the temple again then back at me and said, 'It is a beautiful day for travelling south.' By this time I simply thought he was a bit crazy, an old man losing his marbles, so I just said, 'Yes, it is a lovely day.' With that, he walked back into the forest. That also seemed a bit strange because no pathways went in that direction, so he was going off track. My colleagues and I gave each other a look and dismissed him as an old man approaching senility. So, you can imagine our complete shock when, just a few days later, we did find a pot buried in the earth. And we had only uncovered a couple of inches of it when we all recognised its unmistakable patterns – it was from Nazca!"

"Nazca," I repeated in disbelief.

"Yes, Nazca – it was a small pot with a handle on the top and a spout."

"What the hell was a Nazca pot doing in Mexico?"

"I have absolutely no idea, but I can tell you that information was hushed up. The pot is currently sitting in the vault at the museum. All archaeological miscellanies are kept secret from the public. You have studied in Nazca, have you not, Stephen?"

"Yes, I spent quite a bit of time in Nazca, volunteering on excavations at Cahuachi. Their pottery is certainly the most beautiful of all the South American cultures and, in my opinion, the most beautiful in the world. What was a Nazca pot doing at Palenque? The Nazca disappeared at least a thousand years before."

"The only conclusion we could come to was the pot had been traded and slowly, over time, moved north, place to place, eventually arriving in Palenque. In the end, the really mysterious thing was not the strange location of the pot, but the gentleman who had correctly predicted what we would find. It was very peculiar."

"If the pot was traded slowly over time, why wasn't that information released? There is nothing unusual about it," said Juan, innocently.

"Have you ever heard of strange objects appearing where they should not be? No! It happens occasionally but it is always kept quiet. Occasionally the odd story gets out, but for the most part it is kept under wraps. If the 'experts' cannot explain something, they simply ignore it. In any case, people do not trade in pottery – each culture has its own and any trade is usually within that culture. This is how we can identify the differences between cultures – by their pottery alone. So, our conclusion that this pot had been traded was an explanation that wasn't really good enough. And the thousand years' difference between the cultures made it even more inexplicable."

"Yes, I suppose that's true," Juan nodded.

"I cannot help thinking," Professor continued, "that the gentleman at Palenque is a part of all of this, as if he put something in my mind. On that day, he predicted the future, even though it was only a few days forward. I cannot help feeling that I would not be here today if I had not had that experience, as if somehow everything is linked to a great cycle."

"Yes! I am starting the see the pattern now," said Carlos excitedly. "It is without uncertainty that we are not here by chance and that this group was predetermined."

I smiled at Carlo's peculiar way of speaking. He often used words in strange combinations, but 'without uncertainty' was a good one. "What I am wondering," I asked, "as I am sure we all are, is what does all this mean? Where is all this leading us?"

My question was met with another one of those long silences. It seemed none of us had contemplated the idea that if everything *was* predetermined, then there must be an end result that had far reaching implications. The notion had been mentioned before but no one had really thought about what would actually happen at the end of it all. What was the ultimate goal of all this? All we had were a series of bizarre coincidences, some strange numbers, a few pictures, a Maya calendar much older than it should be and a host of paranormal events that would be enough to scare away God itself, but where was it all going to lead? And then the obvious response came, from Professor.

"I am hoping all the answers are hidden in the writing, Stephen, and that the translation will tell us everything we need to know and what to do with that information at the end. I think we just have to submit to fate and let destiny control things from here on. Since my night visitor, I realise the situation is definitely out of our hands."

Professor was absolutely right, of course, but the idea of having no control over what would happen next left me feeling a little uneasy, to say the least. I agreed with him in that I felt the answers lay in the writing, but after Professor's night visitor the warning was stark and clear – get out as soon as possible. It really seemed that the information we had stumbled across was so important that some unknown individuals wanted to suppress it. But was it really so powerful that it could change the nature of our reality and our belief systems?

Talking of Professor... he had warmed since his strange behaviour yesterday, but he still seemed somewhat detached from the rest of us and it was certain that he had something on his mind. It may have been the stress and the responsibility of the find or perhaps the paranormal events affected him more than anyone had realised, but I had a feeling there was more to it than that. For the next hour he was transfixed by the images on his camera, only popping his head up occasionally to join the conversation.

The rest of us were talking about other things, and Felipe and Juan were asking me questions about England since neither of them had ever left Mexico, let alone travelled to Europe. It was getting late but it seemed none of us felt tired. Base camp seemed unusually quiet, the air was still and only the sound of insects disturbed the peace. As a lull in our conversation took over for a few moments, it was the perfect moment for Professor to make an announcement.

16

SMALL PIECES, A BIG PUZZLE

"I think I have found something," Professor said. "The painting on the centre wall with the Maya numbers next to each of the images..."

"Yes," we all said, expectantly.

Professor raised his head slightly and smirked, amused that we had all spoken at the same time like a class of eager six year-olds waiting to hear a great story.

"Each of the numbers divides into a single number. Two of the numbers are the same ones Carlos found on the back of the pyramid, and on each image the base number is multiplied by two, then three, and so on."

"Really?" Carlos asked as he moved to take a look.

"Yes. 5,096."

None of us had paid much attention to these numbers when we were inside the pyramid. Not only were we still reeling from the glorious carved writing on the inner corridor but the pictures had taken all the attention away from the Maya numbers that were almost inconspicuously written next to each image.

Professor continued. "A different number is encoded into each image – one number for each picture, each one 5,096 more than the last. So, if the centre image represents Atlantis, then we have a set of dates!"

"You're kidding!" I said.

"The number underneath the Atlantis image is 25,480. Now, assuming the calendar stone and all the other evidence points to this pyramid being built 5,096 years before the calendar ends in 2012, then Atlantis dates to 23,468 BC."

"23,000 BC. That's incredible!" said Carlos.

"I know. Most of the people who do believe in the mythology about Atlantis believe it probably disappeared at the end of the ice age, due to the rising of sea levels. But that was around 10,000 BC. This date takes it back more than twice as far."

Carlos was incredulous. "It is hard enough to believe Atlantis existed, but to take it back so far is ridiculous."

"Maybe," Professor agreed, "but another thing – here – the image on the left – it shows a remarkable similarity to our friend sitting behind us."

For a moment I thought Professor was talking about yet another paranormal visitor, but on glancing to my left, thankfully he was talking about the pyramid.

"What is the date next to it?" Carlos asked.

"Below the image it says 5,096."

"That is the number on the back of the pyramid."

"Exactly. And since the image looks the same – a pyramid with a forty-five degree angle – and the numbers are the same we can conclude with good reason that this pyramid was built 5,096 years before the calendar ends, or 5,094 years ago. But I think the most important thing is that we can directly relate the pyramid to the picture. That means that the other pictures are of real structures, and are not just a picture story. We have our first real clue!"

Despite having several pieces of evidence in front of us, we still couldn't take in the information. I was astonished at its simplicity, and yet dumbfounded by its complexity. It was absurd to think that this pyramid, which was supposedly Maya in origin, dated back to 3000 BC. It was a notion that none of us could comprehend, particularly Professor and Carlos, who had always been taught that their Maya ancestry appeared only around 500 BC. However, if we thought that was a shock, it was nothing compared to the indications given in the other pictures.

"Things are going to get even stranger. I have something else too," said Professor.

What is it?" asked Carlos, as he leaned closer to the camera.

"The top picture is unmistakably a stone circle, correct?"

"Definitely, what's the number?"

"20,384."

"What? That's ridiculous. How can stone circles be twenty thousand years old?"

"I am sure it's not just any stone circle. I think these images are specific places and not simply a generalisation of the structures shown. As they point to specific dates I think we can guarantee that each image depicts only one location."

"Do you think it could be Stonehenge?" asked Felipe, his eyes widening as he peered at the camera.

"That is your territory, Stephen, what do you think?" asked Professor.

Felipe passed me the camera.

"If it is, it would blow the lid off British archaeology," I said, "but the picture doesn't show the lintels on the top and this design is more like the earlier stone circles. Anyway, nobody really knows how old Stonehenge is and certainly there were earlier, more basic circle designs on the site before they built the Stonehenge we know today. Twenty thousand years does seem unlikely for Stonehenge. There are hundreds of other stone circles in Britain that are older but the date from this image would take them back another fifteen thousand years! It's just ridiculous."

Juan started to laugh. "I think we have to remove these ideas we have on your beloved archaeology. Already we have evidence that proves archaeology is riddled with errors, so I think we can just forget what we know, or what we think we know, and start again from the beginning. The rewriting of archaeology starts right here, right now, with us."

Felipe started sniggering at Juan's statement because Juan had thumped his hand on the floor three times in unison with the words, "right here, right now, with us." But however silly it may have seemed to Felipe, Juan was right – everything known about archaeology and the history of human civilisation was crumbling to dust in front of our very eyes, like the city of Atlantis itself.

"I think I've also worked out the triangle shape on the right hand side," said Professor. "The number given is 10,192 so I am certain that is the Giza plateau."

"The pyramids of Giza – how?" asked Juan.

"We're all familiar with the work of Robert Bauval, Graham Hancock, John Anthony West and Robert Schoch. You remember their work on the pyramids and the Sphinx? They date the Sphinx at around 10,000 BC, based on the star charts of the time and the water weathering around the sides of the trench. Leo was rising on the horizon during that time period and the Sphinx faces east, directly towards the rising of Leo. So now we have the evidence to back up Bauval's theory – the Sphinx was built in 8180 BC."

"You actually believe that stuff?" asked Carlos, shocked at his mentor's views.

"I think their arguments are irrefutable. Plus the geology around the Sphinx is there for all to see."

"I absolutely agree," I said.

The names Professor had mentioned were an engineer, a journalist, a maverick Egyptologist and a geologist, respectively; heretics in the fields of archaeology and Egyptology. Scientific establishments don't like having their toes stepped on by 'outsiders'. Yet, often the greatest discoveries come from those on the outside. After all, Albert Einstein was a clerk in a patent office. All that, however, was going to change once this discovery was out of the bag. I was also filled with a deep sense of satisfaction because Professor was acknowledging those very sentiments I had voiced in the jeep when we first met. It was, however, more than surprising that someone of his scientific background supported the ideas of Bauval, et al. I wondered how much more of the 'alternative' approach he agreed with but kept quiet about.

"You have studied all this as well, Carlos, so I do not know why you are putting up a defence," said Professor.

"I have, but surely 8180 BC is actually quite far from the date of the rising of Leo through the ecliptic?" he replied in confusion.

"No, it's not," I cut in, "because the time period for each star sign through the ecliptic is simply a division of 360 degrees of a circle divided by twelve, which makes thirty degrees per star sign. It takes seventy-two years for the earth to rotate one degree and if you multiply that by thirty degrees it takes 2,160 years for each star sign to pass through the ecliptic. Multiply that by twelve – the number of star signs – and you get a complete number for the precession of the equinoxes – 25,920 years. However, each star sign is a different size so their relative motion through the sky takes a different amount of time. In other words each star sign does not take 2,160 years to pass through the ecliptic because they vary in length. As far as I remember Leo takes up about thirty-six degrees of the sky and therefore it takes around 2,500 years to pass through the rising sun, not 2,160. The age of Leo ends around 8000 BC. Since no one has ever agreed on the exact date I think it is safe to conclude that this date of 8180 BC is the correct one for the end of the age of Leo."

"You've completely lost me," said Juan.

"Me too," said Felipe.

Even Carlos looked confused, but Professor was grinning like a Cheshire cat.

"Look up into the sky," I started to explain, "and measure the distance between the ends of a star sign. If you take Gemini, for example, and measure the distance between the heads of the twins and the feet, you will notice it covers a certain distance in the sky. Now, if you take another star sign you will notice the distance in the sky covered by that star sign is either greater or lesser than Gemini. So, not all of the star signs cover exactly thirty degrees of the sky, or in this case 2,160 years of the ecliptic. Since the star signs are different sizes then the time it takes for them to cross the ecliptic also varies."

"You've completely lost me," Juan said again, his mouth open in jest.

"Me too," repeated Felipe, still acting the fool.

"Ignore those two. They get like this sometimes," Professor said defensively.

Carlos, on the other hand, was looking thoughtful. "So you're saying that this date of 8180 BC marks the end of the age of Leo. But how can you come to that conclusion based on a picture of a pyramid that has no reference to Egypt whatsoever? And, if you are correct, what does it all mean?"

"It means," Professor said, "that somewhere here, we may find the actual length of the precession of the equinoxes. No one has ever conclusively deduced the exact time the earth takes to wobble on its axis. Since this could well be the date of the end of the age of Leo, there may be other clues as well."

Professor had ignored Carlos' first question and I understood why – there was no real evidence to support what he was saying. However, I did agree that the images on the wall must be pointing to real sites, and the Egyptian pyramids were so important in the grand scheme of things that they had to be represented here. 8180 BC was also the only 'date' that could be linked with Egypt as, although it was a fairly loose assumption, that date fitted in neatly with the arguments regarding the age of the Sphinx. However, all evidence aside, I had another reason for agreeing with Professor, although I couldn't explain it beyond saying that I had a gut feeling he was correct. Before we could move on though, there was another argument to discuss.

"I thought the pyramids had already been dated to the time it is written they were built, that being 2500 BC?" said Carlos.

"Yes," Professor said, "but I have always doubted the methods used for that 'definitive' dating. The mortar used for dating was taken from the top of the pyramid and dated to 3100 BC – but it was later realised that this was older than the mortar on the *bottom* of the pyramid, which was dated at 2850 BC!"

"Uh," Juan said, confused as ever.

"This implies that the top of the pyramid was built before the bottom, which is clearly impossible but I think it is obvious that this mortar work was done later – repair work. Even so, as the oldest mortar is dated to 3100 BC then the pyramid must be older than that date. Anyway, like Stonehenge, I think it is likely there were earlier structures in place prior to the familiar pyramids being built. I think that is a safe conclusion to come to."

Everything was quickly falling into place and the new ideas based on the model were, for a change, easily discernible.

"What about the image at the bottom?" asked Felipe. "That one that looks like a step pyramid – what is the number with it?"

"15,288."

"It's Peru," I said without thinking, as if the answer was given to me from somewhere else.

"Peru?" Carlos questioned. "How did you get that?"

"It's a map, albeit a crude one." It was suddenly obvious to me. "The centre is Atlantis, which is thought to have been somewhere in the Atlantic Ocean. If you look at the whole picture you will see our pyramid on the left, which is west. The top is a stone circle, pointing north, to Britain. East is the location of the Giza pyramids – more evidence for Professor's idea – so the bottom image is south. The only place I know south of the Equator that has those structures is Peru."

"That is strange, but so simple and so obvious," said Juan.

"There are many undiscovered structures in Peru and even completely lost cultures, because they are still covered by sand. Take Caral, for example. That wasn't discovered until very recently and already it has been placed as early as Mesopotamia, probably older. In fact, it could have been the oldest known civilisation in the world in the accepted archaeological record, if it was not for Göbekli Tepe in Turkey. I am sure there are dozens of sites in Peru that are buried deep in the sand but, I have to say, a date of fifteen thousand years ago would surprise me a little."

"Yes, you are absolutely correct," said Professor, looking at the image on the camera.

"How do you know these places are there," Felipe asked, "if they're covered by sand?"

"Good question. Peru, as you know, is a poor country and has little resources available for the luxury of funding archaeology. It also covers a huge land mass – five times the size of Great Britain with half the population – so there are huge expanses of land that are unpopulated. When I was in Nazca, I volunteered on the digs being carried out at Cahuachi. Cahuachi was probably the religious centre and the main city of the Nazca culture. But despite the fact that the Nazca Lines are one of the world's most important archaeological sites, the area of Cahuachi, close to the modern city of Nazca and even intersected by some of the lines, is still mostly covered in sand – there just aren't the resources for the archaeological work required. Sites are being discovered in Peru all the time but unfortunately the *huaqueros* tend to get there first, plundering the sites of most of their important artefacts which end up on the black market."

Professor seemed a little startled at the idea of the black market and he looked into the sky before changing the subject.

"The thing that bothers me," he said, "is that these sites may already be known about, but when archaeologists discover a site, sometimes even with the benefit of hard evidence they are reluctant to take the date back prior to 3000 BC. Since many sites don't have a written date attached to them, the archaeologists proclaim a 'possible' date based only on the known sites on record. That is why I'm certain so many of the world's archaeological sites are dated wrongly and are much older than we think, but I never imagined this was the case in my own garden."

A sadness crossed Professor's face. It was as if he was slowly accepting that throughout his illustrious career he had been living a lie, forced to conform to accepted wisdom in order to succeed – not to mention passing those lies on to others when he was teaching. I was heartened to discover that he was open to the possibility that the accepted archaeological record was full of errors. Being the leading man in his field he was certainly a lone figure in this regard – most archaeologists at the forefront of their specialised area are reluctant to even consider the ideas of others. After all, despite what people may think, their jobs and careers depend on them conforming to preconceived ways of thinking. This is what Professor meant when he said that archaeologists were reluctant to take sites back further than 3000 BC, because it would upset years of documented evidence.

I had mentioned Göbekli Tepe earlier because it was a prime example of this misdating. According to accepted theories, our species was supposed to be running around forests hunting game during the time when this relatively technologically sophisticated culture appeared. Archaeologists are scratching their heads over this site and I could only wonder how many more such sites were yet to be discovered. Since most cultures exist in coastal regions because fish is a staple of their diet, then there is an obvious conclusion that a lot of very old cultures, if they existed, disappeared when sea levels rose at the end of the last ice age, more than ten thousand years ago. And, surely, our pyramid would be the biggest spanner in the works when the information was revealed to the world.

"It is correct," said Carlos reluctantly after studying the pictures for a while. "We would be very stupid to assume anything, but I think we can agree we have certainly stumbled upon some key insights here. Your map idea is unquestionable, Stephen, and as Juan correctly said all this symbolism is simplistic; easy to understand. We even have an alphabet for the translation of the writing. It is almost too easy, which worries me quite a lot."

"I was thinking that a minute ago," Juan said, "why is everything so easy to decipher?"

We all looked at Professor for the answer. He leaned back slightly, took a deep breath and sighed. And then he made a moving, but bold and unusual statement.

"The only thing I can think is that we are *supposed* to be here to discover this. However, I do not think things are that easy. The designs on the other two walls seem a little more complicated but I am sure, as we have said before, all the answers will probably be found in the writing. So yes, maybe it is all too easy, but perhaps this discovery is meant to happen at this moment. We have less than three years to the Maya end date and I am certain that the truth about what that actually means will be found on those walls. Maybe it is a message to mankind, the truth about 2012 and the calendar. So much has been said and predicted, but much of it is wildly inaccurate. Maybe this is why we're feeling such a lot of fear while we're here – because what is really going to occur could be something very special. It's also possible that this is why some people wish to suppress this information – it may have major implications for those who control humanity, as if it describes a new evolution, or something like it."

"Evolution!" I exclaimed.

Everyone looked at me for a moment.

"Oh yes, my dream!" said Professor.

"That is weird," said Felipe.

"Yes, but what did the dream *mean* by 'evolution', exactly?" asked Carlos.

The question left us all confused and quiet. The thought that everything appeared to be easily decipherable was disappearing fast. I looked at Professor.

"When you said the information could reveal a new evolution, what did you mean exactly?"

He took a moment before answering. "I suppose I was talking about an evolution of consciousness, or something like that. It's something that has been talked about often within the New Age movement – they say we are heading into a new consciousness – so I was thinking that maybe this dream is talking about an evolution of that kind."

"That seems very specific to me. I don't think we have enough evidence to suggest that, Professor."

"Yes, I know, but it was just a thought."

Again, the feeling swept over me that Professor knew more than he was telling us. He was making a habit of coming out with explanations and possibilities that would be frowned upon by even the loosest of sceptics. There were only two possible conclusions – either he knew more than he was letting on, or his mind was far ahead of ours. Then it occurred to me that his comment about there being an informer in the group might simply have been a diversionary tactic – because he could be the informer. That kind of diversion could easily come from a mind as clever as his. But my thoughts were broken once again as the conversation returned to the problems.

"What was your dream again, Carlos?" asked Juan.

"He showed me a bright sun, or should I say a sun that became brighter."

Another short silence while we contemplated. My mind was becoming a little hazy with all of this new information. There was too much going on and while there was a lot of confusion, there were glimmers of a breakthrough.

"Okay, right," Professor said, adjusting his position. "Stephen, you said you saw Polaris and we said this could be due to the precession of the equinoxes, correct? My dream was the word 'evolution', and Carlos saw a bright sun... a bright sun...? Stephen – did you say the images on the far wall looked like a brightening sun?"

"Yes, I did and yes, they do. I never made the connection! Let's have a look at those pictures."

Professor clicked through the images on his camera and now it seemed glaringly obvious that we were indeed looking at basic paintings of a sun that was slowly brightening over time. We couldn't be a hundred per cent certain of course, but it did seem the most likely explanation once we added Carlos' dream into the mix, and since the idea of pre-determinism had previously been discussed it seemed to be fulfilling itself. It was almost as if we were completing a jigsaw puzzle that was too easy. However, we had to be cautious because this was not the time to be making bad errors of judgement.

"It does look like a sun that is getting brighter over time," said Felipe.

In some ways Felipe may have been the best person to answer some of the questions, for he seemed to have a 'simple' mind. A simpler mind often sees the most obvious explanations, while intellects like Professor's gravitate to more complicated solutions.

"Agreed," said Professor, "it is a sun, but what is the relation between that and the images underneath? If these are images of a brightening sun, then underneath each sun there are the same pictures as on the other wall, and those have dates attached to them. So, can we assume that something is happening with the sun every 5,096 years?"

Carlos looked at me. "Steve, didn't you ask what it was that was occurring every 5,096 years in the precession cycle that made these dates important?"

"Yes, I did, but I was thinking of the temperature patterns in the earth's record. I don't think there has been a significant increase in temperature every 5,096 years or even a steady increase over time. In fact, I think the temperature has fluctuated. It's only recently that there's been a significant increase due to human activity, or so they say."

"You are correct", said Professor, "so, we ask again, why do we have images of a sun that is brightening over time, and also every 5,096 years? It does not make sense."

"Maybe it is not a sun at all," said Juan.

We all glanced at Juan like he had ruined the mood or destroyed the conversation. Each of us looked at the pictures and suddenly felt that we no longer had any idea what we were looking at. Perhaps Juan was right – maybe it wasn't a sun at all. Finally, Professor broke the ice.

"It must be the sun," he said.

"Why?" asked Carlos.

"Because of the dreams. I don't know why, I just feel this is correct. Polaris links directly to precession due to its location as the current pole star, and it goes without saying that the sun has a direct influence on the planet as the earth changes position on its axis. It is thought the gravitational pull of both the sun and the moon are the reason for precession."

"How does that work?" interrupted Juan.

"The earth is not perfectly round. It bulges at the equator because of the tidal forces caused by the earth's rotation and the gravitational pull of the sun and moon. It is thought the bulge in the planet's form actually causes the earth to wobble on its axis, although it's imperceptible to us. If you could speed up time and make twenty-six thousand years happen in five minutes, you would see the earth turn like a spinning top, or a gyroscope. Anyway, it is still a theory because no one has proved anything. Some people even doubt precession exists at all."

"What doubt is there?"

"Well, there's actually another theory which explains some unusual findings, like the discovery of mammoths that died so suddenly they still had food in their mouths. This was at the end of the ice age, and there were many other large species that suffered extinction at the same time, but it happened so fast that no one has been able to explain it. A very interesting theory is that the earth's entire crust moved over the surface of the planet. It's called crustal displacement."

"You think that's possible?"

"It actually answers a lot of questions, so I wouldn't dismiss it. It certainly explains why all the ice melted so suddenly and so quickly. Also, different areas of the earth are hotter at different times during the supposed wobble of precession – we know that Egypt, for example, was once in a temperate climate. This is certainly the argument about the Great Sphinx – that it has been water weathered and was once in an area that had a lot of rainfall. That is another piece of evidence regarding the age of the Sphinx – maybe the earth's wobble creates different climatic changes on areas of the planet, or is it a crustal displacement that shifts places into other areas? The problem with the Sphinx and the rainfall idea is that crustal displacement would have happened a lot earlier than 8000 BC, so that brings us back to precession as the answer. Or is it even possible that they both occur – crustal displacement *and* precession?"

Suddenly I was struck by a thought which left me momentarily speechless. It felt for a moment as if everything had fallen into place, a kind of 'eureka' moment. I couldn't explain it, but the expressions on the other's faces told me it was a collective feeling.

Only Carlos was unconvinced. "You've just made me realise something," he said, "something that can't be explained. The ice age covered Northern Europe twenty thousand years ago, so how was the stone circle in the images built?"

"It might not be a British circle," I told him. "It could be northern France or even Germany. Other sites have been found in Europe. Circle building wasn't just a British phenomenon, even though 'Britain' never existed back then, and it still places the site of this stone circle in the north, as the image says. But also there's no conclusive evidence about how far south the ice cap was. Some say as far south as London. If the ice was higher in latitude then the area around Stonehenge would have been ice-free."

"I am not sure about this," Carlos argued. "We haven't really asked the obvious questions – why were these sites built every 5,096 years? Why do we have images of what looks like a brightening sun every 5,096 years? And what is the connection between a brightening sun and the building of the sites?"

"That is quite remarkable," said Juan, completely out of context.

Everyone's thoughts were broken and we all looked at Juan and started to laugh. It was almost as if someone else was talking through him. Everyone was laughing – that is, apart from Felipe, who had the same expression on his face as he'd had when we came out of the pyramid the previous day. I was about to ask him what was wrong when he suddenly spoke and broke the atmosphere.

"Okay, you have all worked out your dreams, so can we leave now?"

Before anyone could ask what was wrong the cheerful atmosphere was shattered in an instant as another loud 'crack' came from the trees opposite the pyramid. We all jumped and fell into a fearful silence and yet again my heart was thumping against my ribcage. As the adrenaline started to decrease I looked again at Felipe who was still wearing the same expression. Then he let out a long sigh that indicated he'd now had enough of all this. Turning to grab his rifle he looked at Juan and in silent communication Juan picked up his torch. Felipe flicked off the safety catch and stood up. This time, however, we all got up with him and stood looking towards the trees.

17

MAYA BENEVOLENCE

Once again the jungle fell into an eerie silence and not a single bug or animal could be heard. There was nothing, just a silence that was deafening and penetrating.

"The sound of silence," I thought to myself. Having never heard it before I always assumed it was just an expression but now the sound of silence was loud and disturbing, enough to make a sane man crazy in a very short space of time.

There was nothing to be seen. No movement and no sound. We all edged slowly out of camp towards the trees, scanning the area for any sign of movement. Reluctantly turning towards the pyramid, I scanned the platform and the steps. There was nothing but deathly calm. As we moved towards the trees opposite the entrance, my hair stood on end and my neck and spine tingled. Almost shaking in fear, I sensed a looming presence around us and the air suddenly felt cold and stagnant.

There was absolutely nothing – not even a mosquito could be heard and even the trees were still as if they had frozen in time, just like Felipe had experienced before. We reached the midway point between the pyramid and the trees and stood there, huddled together like scared rats, and a feeling of vulnerability swept over me. Juan shone his torch through the trees and the resulting shadows of the branches seemed like menacing arms trying to reach out and grab us as they moved against the background.

"You knew something was about to happen," whispered Carlos to Felipe.

He didn't answer. He just glanced at us and it seemed he hadn't even heard the words. Then he lowered his rifle and pointed it at the ground, turning on the safety switch. He had realised how useless the rifle would be under the circumstances – there was nothing physical to shoot at.

The silence was excruciating, the wait brutally terrifying and my senses were on heightened alert as we all stood waiting in the timeless moonlight.

Professor was about to speak when Felipe called out.

"There," he said as he pointed towards the big tree opposite the entrance.

Looking towards the dark forest we froze in astonishment. To the left, about ten feet behind the tree, there was a glowing, semi-transparent white ball of light that was about six inches in diameter. It appeared from nowhere and lit up an area about five feet around it, floating slowly and silently through the branches. There was no pattern to its movement, it simply stayed in a small area amongst the branches of the big tree and danced around lightly in its wispy state. None of us could speak. We were frozen to the spot, both terrified and amazed at the same time. What was it – ball lightning? Perhaps it was those earth lights I'd heard about?

Then the ball of light started to make circular movements in an anticlockwise direction, creating a larger circle about three feet in diameter. It then shifted its position to the left and started to move in a clockwise direction, making a smaller circle about one foot in diameter. After a few moments it again moved position, this time slightly higher up the tree, and made an anti-clockwise circular pattern about four feet in diameter. It spun slowly at first and once it returned to its original position it repeated the circular movements of the first two circles, but this time it got faster and faster. The movement became frenetic as it jumped from the first circular movement to the second, then to the third and back again, getting faster and faster.

And then it stopped. It just floated in the branches, motionless. I glanced across at the others who were all standing with gaping mouths, rigid and in a state of bewilderment. After a few moments the ball of light increased to around three times its original size and started to crackle like a burning camp fire. And then it was on the move.

Out from the big tree it headed, moving slowly away from us, parallel to the pyramid but within the tree line. Then it made a ninety-degree turn and headed towards the corner of the pyramid, opposite our camp, its wave-like motion seeming like a boat on water. It stopped near the far corner of the pyramid about ten feet off the ground and for a moment it hung motionless, still crackling. Heat from the object could be felt by all of us.

Suddenly, without warning, the ball exploded and for a moment the whole area was lit up like daylight and the heat was frightening. We all jumped backwards, expecting to be blasted by a force of some kind, but then we watched in awe as a shower of sparks sprinkled towards the ground. As both the heat and light diminished, two apparitions appeared underneath where the ball of light had been. They appeared to be Maya warriors, naked on the upper body but with cloth covering their hips and thighs like skirts. Their chests and arms were covered in black tattoos. One held a spear and the other arm was adorned with a large bracelet. He also wore a large knife attached to a belt. The other warrior held a long staff. They both stared at us and then smiled, as if we were long lost friends returning after many years. And then, as the sparks dissipated, they faded away into the darkness.

The forest quickly returned to normal, the air was humid, the trees were swaying lightly and the bugs fluttered around us.

Normality – if there was such a thing in this place – returned and we were left standing in the darkness once again, out in the open, vulnerable and alone. And yet, for some reason, the feelings of fear had completely disappeared. Every negative emotion we had been experiencing over the days was now gone, as if the ball of light had soaked it all up like a sponge and flung it down a wormhole into another universe. Instead, a feeling of jubilance overpowered me, as if I had just witnessed Man landing on Mars. We were all dumbfounded and in awe at what we had just witnessed. It was undoubtedly the most incredible experience any of us had ever witnessed.

We stumbled the twenty yards back to camp but none of us said a word. We were all shaking and when Felipe tried to drink some water he ended up wearing most of it. We were all happy and exuberant, albeit still in shock. Even Felipe finally had a smile on his face and Juan had, at last, experienced something physical in this powerful place. Excited and hyperactive, it was several moments before we could gather ourselves together enough to talk.

"That was incredible," said Felipe, who was now a different person to the one I had known over the last few days.

"I cannot believe what I just saw. Did that really happen?" asked Juan.

"It certainly did," Carlos replied, "and I don't know about you but I feel like I'm full of energy, as if I have been blasted by something."

"I agree. I feel as if the energy of my teenage years has returned," said the ageing Professor.

They were right. I also felt energised, just like I had at the Tibetan dome, and Carlos was right when he said it felt like we had been blasted by some kind of energy. Surely, there was only one way to find out...

"Last one to the top of the pyramid makes the supper!" suggested Juan, smiling.

We looked at each other with huge grins and without any prompting we stood up and headed for the trees opposite the pyramid.

Standing in a line and giggling like a bunch of kids, we prepared ourselves for the 'pyramid dash'. It was the most ludicrous thing to do under the circumstances, and in one of those strange acts of brain malfunction it became one of my overriding memories of the entire trip. Ask someone what they remember after they witness a horrific scene of some kind and often their most prominent memory is of some obscure and totally irrelevant detail. Standing in the middle with Professor and Carlos to my left and Juan and Felipe to my right was one of the most incredible moments of my life. Almost as if posing for a photograph – *the five men who changed the world of archaeology* – chuckling like children, happy and smiling, for me it was the most powerful moment of all. Here I was, standing alongside two of the best archaeologists who ever lived and who, during the last week, had become very close to me, but we weren't posing for a historic photograph – instead, we were about to behave like juveniles and find out who would reach the top of the pyramid in last place, with the forfeit of making dinner.

"Ready? After three!" said Juan. "One, two, three, go!"

And we were off, running as fast as we could towards the steps. Juan was first to reach them, followed by me and then Felipe, with poor Professor and Carlos already several yards behind. Flying up the side of the pyramid like cheetahs on amphetamines, we reached the platform in the same order, except now poor Professor was bringing up the rear. It was surprising that Carlos, with his very plump frame, had beaten the Professor to the top but he was obviously in better shape than I thought.

On the top of the pyramid we were breathless and excited, and we wandered the platform in joyful exuberance. When we calmed down, we looked outwards at the dark jungle, silent and still in all its beauty, the bright moon showering the tops of the tress with a glowing layer as if the Maya gods had sprinkled icing sugar over this sacred land. Suddenly a feeling swept over me – a feeling I had only experienced once before in my life – a feeling of total calm and inner peace and a sense of freedom which is usually only possible to attain when you are travelling alone. But this was a beautiful, collective moment experienced by us all in silence and it cemented the bonding between us. After some moments we all hugged each other in turn, the emotion of the experience overpowering our male reticence, sharing this precious time – this one special moment before we had to return to reality and finish the task we had been given. And now, at last, we had finally conquered the easiest and yet the most difficult of pyramids. Whatever happened in the last fifteen minutes had removed all the negative feelings that were plaguing our minds and senses, as if a critical point had been reached.

Lasya was correct in everything she had said to me – we were five penguins and we had successfully reached top of the mountain. Fear *had* pushed us forwards after all. It was fear alone that kept us going, kept us pushing on towards the top. And here we were – five men who had overcome their innermost fears to reach the summit.

18

TURNED TABLES

We returned to base camp and Professor was on the receiving end of many jokes since it was apparent that no one had ever seen him cook. This was especially funny for Juan and Felipe, who had known the Professor for many years and had been contracted to carry out all such daily tasks.

"You need to get to the gym," laughed Carlos, basking in the glorious victory over his mentor.

"I am too old for that," he replied, brushing off the idea with a flick of his arm.

"What are you doing, Professor?" asked Felipe, as Professor searched through the fruit box.

"Trying to find some salad and bread!" he said, smiling.

"No, no, no! We want steak, potatoes, caviar, and champagne!"

"Absolutely," I said.

"Hey guys," Juan interjected, "you remember that meal we had at Mike's house?"

"Oh yes," said Carlos, "get a table ready and we will have a feast. Let's all laze around on the hammocks with a few beers, and when we come back there should be a gourmet meal within the hour."

"Yes!" we all shouted together.

Everyone was laughing and poor Professor stood scratching his head wondering how he could create a meal with the limited stock we had.

While Professor was trying to remember what a saucepan was used for, I wandered over to the trees where the ball of light had first appeared. Not once since arriving here had I felt brave enough to go near the trees by myself, even in the daytime, but now the forest seemed like any other. A little bit eerie, sure, but no more than the Amazon jungle at night. Up until the last half hour these trees were so terrifying that I had stayed well clear of them. Now it was almost funny how dreadfully oppressive this place had been. No wonder people stayed away.

Remarkably, Professor did manage to create an excellent dinner within forty minutes. It wasn't the gourmet feast we ordered, but it was close enough; cold chicken, potatoes, rice and salad. We all sat down at base camp and enjoyed a great meal together. There was one big surprise, though.

"Well, you did say champagne," Professor said. "I was going to keep this until we finished, but as we're leaving tomorrow, we may as well celebrate tonight. It's probably a bit warm but I am sure it will do."

With that he pulled out a huge bottle of champagne from his pack. None of us could quite believe it – it was a five litre bottle – and as soon as the cork was removed we were swigging from the bottle like a sports team that had just won promotion. Our spirits were high and the champagne had a rapid effect on our senses. It was certainly a welcome relief from all the stress and tension and the experience we'd just shared gave us a new feeling of optimism and a strange sense of security. A sense that was, perhaps, illusory.

"So, what was that all about?" I asked, once our hyperactivity had lessened.

"I have no idea," said Carlos, "but it felt like we were being welcomed, or something like it."

"I certainly feel welcome," giggled Felipe, who finally seemed to be released from his torture.

"I noticed the ball of light was spinning in the pattern of the Maya calendar wheels," said Professor, suddenly. We all stopped and listened intently, remembering the spinning ball and following his explanation.

"It was mimicking the rotation of the interconnecting wheels – one anti-clockwise, the next clockwise – and when it changed position it was in the place where the wheels would be touching each other, making them turn like the calendar does. So, it was an example of how the wheels turn when they are connected, like cogs in a gear system. Also, they were different sizes, indicating the different lengths of each calendar in relation to the others."

I looked at Carlos in amazement and saw his eyes widen.

"You are right," he said, "that is exactly what happened, very well noticed, my friend."

"The ball also became brighter and larger," Professor continued, looking at Carlos, "just like your dream and in the images on the far wall in the chamber."

"So, are you saying the sun in my dream and the images in the chamber are representing the Maya calendar wheels and not the sun?"

"No because the images and your dream seem to be more in line with the sun. If the dream was meant to be the Maya calendar, then why did the priest not show you the calendar itself?"

"Okay, I am confused," I said. "So which is it – the sun, or the Maya calendar?"

"I think it is both. I think the dream and the pictures in the chamber are representing the sun, but what we have just witnessed is the Maya calendar. But I also think the two are linked together. Precession is represented by the sun and the earth's wobble, but the calendar is representing the time factor."

As usual, Professor's intellect seemed to be working far ahead of ours.

"I have no idea what you are talking about," said Felipe, as he swayed slightly. The champagne had affected him a great deal and it seemed he wasn't accustomed to drinking the bubbly liquid. Then again, he was usually drunk after only a small amount of alcohol so it was obvious that a litre of champagne would do no good to his powers of judgment. Juan laughed at him and then nudged him slightly to see if he could stay upright.

"I can see how the two are interlinked," Carlos said, "and that they are in essence mirrors of the same thing, but how did you come to the conclusion that one is the sun and the other is the Maya calendar, and not the same thing?" The alcohol had affected us all, and now our ability to express ourselves was in question. The bottle of champagne was too big even for five of us.

"Well, in essence, your dream showed the sun. In the chamber, the images look like a brightening sun. The ball of light was obviously showing the rotation of the Maya calendar in visible form. Can I explain it any more clearly for you?"

Felipe giggled again and put his hand on Juan's shoulder. He leant over and spoke quietly in his ear. "You know, my friend, I think they are all a bit crazy."

"Of course they are, amigo, completely and utterly. They have all lost the herd."

Felipe giggled again and then hiccupped. "There's not one cow left if you ask me!"

"Don't worry, amigo, let's just listen. Here, have some more champagne."

He passed the giant bottle to Felipe. There was only a tiny amount left in the bottle and he finished it quickly. If anyone deserved to be drunk this night it was Felipe, who seemed to have suffered more than any of us. Professor, Carlos and I had been watching these two clowns in action and we smiled at each other as we became more amused by their behaviour. They were like a comedy duo when they got going and after the last few days of intense stress, it was great to see.

"So, all three of your dreams have manifested themselves," Juan said.

"We seem to be getting *somewhere,*" said Professor, "and I think we can come to at least one definite conclusion tonight – that the Maya calendar is linked to sun cycles and that the total length of precession has a big part to play in all of this."

Taking a step back, it was pretty incredible to say the least, and how quickly things were making sense and coming together was a dream in itself. An archaeological dream, for sure, but this was swiftly turning away from archaeology and becoming something altogether different – something far more mysterious, if not paranormal. On the other hand, there were many unanswered questions and, like any other archaeological investigation, the more answers we found, the more questions arose. The problem, however, was that all of these ideas were only conjecture and guesswork when compared to scientific thinking. Then again, what was going on around this place was far beyond scientific thinking and applying that kind of rigid methodology was utterly useless, under the circumstances.

"We still do not know what it all means, of course, but I am sure by tomorrow we will have more answers," said Professor.

"I cannot wait to get in there again. I wonder what's in that strange looking box?" asked Carlos.

We all sat there thinking for a moment but nobody dared to make any suggestions. For a start the 'box' was a very strange shape and certainly nothing I could come up with would conform to its odd dimensions.

"A sword?" proposed Juan.

"Possibly, but it would be a very long sword," said Carlos.

Then we were graced with Felipe's wisdom once again. "It's probably empty," he said, "or another staircase, but this time for rats. Or maybe it's a coffin for a dead snake."

"Felipe," said Professor, "I am concerned about the manifestations that are contained in your subconscious mind. If you need help, let me know!"

It was clear that Felipe's ridiculous humour was due to a little too much champagne, but his guess was as good as any. None of us had any real idea what was in there and the speculation soon ceased as we knew we wouldn't find any answers until the next morning.

The conversation ran into the early morning and for the most part we managed to stop talking about our surroundings, entertaining each other with silly stories from our past, both serious and comical. One by one, we fell asleep where we lay and by three o'clock we had all dozed off, the effects of the champagne finally causing unconsciousness. Not surprisingly, Felipe was the first to slip into a deep sleep.

I awoke at six and immediately raised the alarm. There was a storm of mosquitos around us and we immediately ran for cover, diving into the tents and sealing ourselves in. Juan and Felipe abandoned their hammocks and joined us in the tents and we doubled up in our small space. Only Professor was alone. We spent half an hour barbarically killing the mosquitos that had attached themselves to us prior to our escape, and then we sat there for another half hour until the storm passed. I had witnessed this once before in Tarapoto, Peru – millions of mosquitos flying around in a storm of biblical proportions, the sky darkened by the mass. It was, however, an appropriate backdrop to our surroundings – biblical findings now followed by biblical happenings – and it seemed an almost natural part of the adventure we were undertaking, another test of our courage.

We were all groggy, tired and slightly hung over and we were soon drinking as much water as we could. Although the storm had passed, we were doing our best to repel the normal mosquito attacks which were always most ferocious at dawn. A few stragglers from the storm had decided on settling in our area, adding to the numbers.

None of us were hungry, so after a breakfast of water and coffee we were ready to get the job done. Our excitement was coupled with exhaustion and now the sun had filled the area with light, taking even more energy from us as the temperature rose. We knew the time had come to fulfil our destiny, as Professor had so poetically said, but there was a little regret on my part that we had drunk the champagne only a few hours earlier, for now the most important day of my life was about to happen and I had a terrible hangover.

19

THE PYRAMID BUILDERS

The plastic sheeting was removed from the entrance and once again we found ourselves walking down the corridor towards the chamber, this time all five of us together. Now that all our fear had been removed by last night's events, we no longer felt threatened and we concluded it was safe for us all to enter the pyramid without worrying. Bypassing the hall of writing we entered the main chamber and spent a while staring at the images on the walls, recapping our conversation from the previous evening with a clearer view of the images. They seemed different somehow, more alive and vibrant than before, as if they had awakened from slumber – although I rationalised that was probably just because the pictures on Professor's camera could not compare with the real thing.

Our focus was first on the left hand wall, which had not been given much attention before now and we soon found ourselves puzzling over the meaning. It showed our pyramid at the bottom with a straight line emerging from the top of the platform, shooting upwards about midway up the wall. Above this was the unmistakeable star system of Orion – 'Osiris', the main God of the ancient Egyptians – and the straight line was pointing directly towards the central star in the well-known Belt of Orion.

"What is that line coming from the pyramid?" asked Juan.

"I have no idea," said Professor, "but maybe it is coming down from Orion, not going upwards from the pyramid."

"It seems to be connecting with one of the stars in Orion's belt," said Carlos.

"Or it could be the Orion Nebula," I proposed.

"What's that?" asked Juan.

"Just below Orion's Belt is the Orion Nebula, a region where stars are regularly formed – also called a 'stellar nursery'. Whether the line is connecting with that or with one of the stars in the belt we can't tell, but the nebula is also visible to the naked eye, at least on a clear night without city lights."

"Okay," Juan nodded, "so what is the connection between this pyramid and Orion?"

"I have absolutely no idea. As far as I am aware, only the Egyptians revered this star system to such a great extent, although it was recognised by other cultures."

It wasn't until Juan shone his torch over the entire wall that we noticed a small amount of writing in the top right corner. I quickly took out the Atlantean alphabet and translated the few words, which didn't take long because, astonishingly, the words ran from left to right, just as the English language does. This is unusual for ancient texts which normally run right to left, or up and down, like Chinese.

SEEDING – RECONNECTION – RETURN.

"What the hell does that mean?" I asked. I turned to look at the others, who were all just as bewildered.

"No idea," said Carlos.

"I do know one thing," Felipe said, "if the rest of the writing makes as much sense as that you'll be translating it for the *next* five thousand years!"

He was trying to be comical but the thought of the entire text being this obscure certainly wasn't funny at all. The only hope was that the writing in the hall turned out to be complete sentences and not just a string of nonsensical words.

"That line shooting up from the pyramid almost looks like some kind of energy beam, like a laser or something," said Juan.

"It could be," Professor responded.

"If it is, let's hope we don't accidentally turn it on!" Felipe replied.

"Yes, but there's nothing in this pyramid to suggest such a technology," Professor argued. "Maybe it is just a mythological idea of some kind."

"Nothing in this place so far suggests myth," Carlos objected.

"Stephen, take some pictures of that writing and the rest of us will search the other walls for any more hidden writing we may have missed before," Professor ordered.

No other words or numbers were found, so it seemed we had everything we needed from the walls. So now our attention was drawn to the centre of the room where our Holy Grail awaited us, to what was about to become the most important archaeological discovery in history.

We all stood in a line, our overhead lights showering the object with a yellow glow from above and our torches adding extra illumination to the beautiful stone box that lay on top of the huge block. Carlos and I moved to the opposite side of the block and we all checked both the block and the box thoroughly to see if there were any numbers or writing on them, but there was nothing to be found. The box itself was carved with a design reminiscent of modern leaf carvings, but it didn't represent anything we could recognise. The box seemed to be made of sandstone, like the slab, and the block was a solid piece of granite.

"Anything?" Professor asked.

"Nothing at all on this side," said Carlos.

Again we stood there staring at it and then at each other, wondering if we should even attempt to open it at all.

"Okay," Professor finally said, "if Juan and Felipe get at each end we will see if we can lift the lid together. It looks quite heavy. Ready?"

No one said anything this time. There were just a few glances here and there as we all anticipated what might jump out at us.

"Okay, lift from each end and see if it comes up and if it does, I'll help support it in the centre."

Carlos and I stood watching, ready to lend a hand if necessary, but the lid of the box lifted up easily, almost as if it was lubricated and the familiar sound of scraping stone echoed throughout the chamber. The lid was placed on the block and we stepped a little closer and peered inside, and for the first time in five thousand years the most magnificent object glared at us from its resting place.

"Wow!" said Felipe.

"Oh my God," said Carlos.

"What the hell is that?" asked Juan.

Professor was silent. I was speechless. I wanted to speak but I couldn't produce any words.

In the box was a staff about eight feet long. The main shaft was made of an unrecognisable substance. At first it looked like metal, but the next moment it looked plastic, and from another angle it could even have been some kind of wood. It was very hard to tell what it was. Certainly it was not a material we were familiar with or, for that matter, had ever seen before. Elaborately encased at the top of the staff was a large crystal that looked like quartz, although it was very different to any we had witnessed before.

We all leaned forwards and peered into the box to inspect the object more closely. From that perspective, the material making up the shaft of the object appeared even more bizarre – it was almost transparent.

"What the hell is that thing?" repeated Juan.

"I have absolutely no idea," said Professor. "Whatever it is, I have never seen anything like it before."

"What's that inside?" asked Juan, as he got a little closer.

Inside the shaft we could now see a row of crystals stretched along the whole length of the object, and they appeared to be touching end to end. They were different colours but mostly the same size, appearing hexagonal in shape, albeit elongated. As I lifted my head up, the crystals disappeared and I was once again looking at what seemed to be a solid shaft – on leaning forward again, it became transparent and the crystals were visible. It was the most bizarre object I had ever come across.

"Shall we pick it up?" asked Carlos.

"NO!" I shouted, finally managing to find my voice. I imagined the sound of my scream could be heard across the whole of Mexico. Everyone jumped as my cry bounced off the walls like a bullet ricocheting in a war torn street. Professor turned his eyes towards me without moving his head and then cast a bemused glance towards Carlos.

"Stephen...?" Professor said calmly, waiting for my response.

Professor once again glanced at Carlos and then back at the strange object. Standing in silence, a spooky feeling suddenly swept over me because the object seemed almost alive. It felt as if it was somehow communicating, warning us not to touch it, and at the same time I felt a strong presence behind me as if someone was standing there in the darkness, whispering long lost words that were echoing through the walls of time.

"It's a Ptah Wand!" I exclaimed, gasping for breath.

"A what?" asked Carlos.

"A Ptah Wand," I said again. "This was the device that was used to build the Pyramids and the Sphinx and all the other structures like Stonehenge – and even Atlantis itself."

"*That* thing?" asked Felipe, innocently.

"Yes, you see the crystal in the top? It's activated through thought. What I was told in Tibet is that they used this device by pointing it towards a block of stone, or anything else for that matter, and simply by visualising they were able to move huge blocks of stone into place as if they were weightless. That is how the Pyramids of Egypt were built so quickly and why scholars cannot work out how they managed it in such a short time."

"The Egyptians used *this* to build the pyramids?" asked Juan in disbelief.

Professor and Carlos were standing silently with their mouths open. Professor seemed a little angry with me for keeping yet more secrets from him, but there had been no obligation on my part to reveal what I knew. Yeshe had been correct in saying that things would be revealed at certain times, and how on earth could I – or anyone – know this device would be here in Mexico? I turned back to look at Juan.

"Yes. They did. There were apparently very few in existence, maybe just four or five, and I was told there was only one left on the earth and it was buried somewhere in the Gobi desert. I had no idea there was another one. Things are really making sense to me now and I think the five structures on the wall behind us were all built using this device. It seems that after this structure was built they left it here for posterity."

Everyone turned to look back at the wall once again.

"So, if there were five of these things in existence, maybe each one of these places on the wall has one hidden somewhere?"

"It's possible, but I was told one was buried in the Gobi desert."

"That doesn't mean it was," said Carlos, "you were told there was only one left on earth and that wasn't true."

"*All* these places were built with one of these?" asked Juan, still struggling to comprehend.

"Egypt, Britain, Peru, Mexico and even Atlantis itself, this object has been used through twenty-five thousand years, probably more, to build these structures. And countless other places also, no doubt."

"You've got some serious explaining to do," said Carlos.

I looked at Professor who was staring at me, waiting for my explanations.

"I don't have all the answers. I can only tell you what I have been told."

"So, what have you been told? From the beginning, please." Professor clearly wasn't happy.

Taking a deep breath and a letting out a long sigh, I felt a shiver down my spine as if the presence behind me was intensifying, as if the pyramid itself was listening and waiting to hear the truth of our ancients.

"This device, the Ptah Wand, could be operated by just two people. It's far too dangerous for us to handle – the modern mind has become too corrupt and imbalanced – but the mind of the Atlantean was purer. Who knows what damage could be done if we tried to use it. I suppose it would be a bit like giving a computer to a chimpanzee. By the power of thought alone it can be used for many things – lifting stone is just one of them. Using the energy in ley lines and magnetic lines, they were able to levitate the huge blocks along them. It was used all over the world but this knowledge has been completely hushed up by the governments."

"You mean they know about it?" asked Juan.

"You bet they do," I said angrily. "There was another device that was similar – the *Wand of Horus* – which could be used for destruction. While the Ptah Wand can be used for *construction*, the Wand of Horus can be used for *destruction* – two counteracting devices. The Wand of Horus was the device used to cut the stone, like a knife through butter, apparently. The Ptah Wand can be used for destruction too, but less so – it all depends on the mind of the user."

"How does it work?" Professor asked, finally joining the conversation.

"The thoughts of whoever holds it are channelled down the shaft and magnified as they flow along the crystals. Apparently crystals have an energy that flows outwards into higher dimensions, so they can contain higher energies including our own consciousness – our thoughts. By the time the thoughts reach the large crystal at the top, the thought is magnified to a point that it becomes real – it manifests in reality."

"That doesn't make sense," said Felipe.

There was another long pause.

"No, it does make sense," replied Professor, quietly. "This has been taught in all the ancient texts and religions – that our thoughts create our future and we manifest our reality by our own thoughts. That philosophy, since it comes from thousands of years ago, must be the legacy of *this* kind of idea. I am guessing that these people were able to magnify their thoughts using this device because they were more aware of that philosophy. Our modern world has eliminated these traditions and ideas with materialism and technology."

It was obvious that Professor understood clearly what all this meant, but there was one element missing. He looked at me and waited for me to continue.

"The Wand of Horus was the device used to actually cut the stone," I said, "so if you think about the pyramids, for example, there must have been a whole production line of stone cutting, moving and placing the blocks. The sarcophagus in the King's Chamber in the Great Pyramid was also cut out using a Wand of Horus."

"So there must have been many more than five of these devices in existence," said Carlos.

"I can only tell you what I've been told. I guess if the great pyramid took thirty years to build then someone, one day, could try and figure out how many of these things were in use. Apparently, it's been calculated that if it did take thirty years, then one block would have to be put in place every three minutes."

"But some of the blocks of stone used weigh hundreds of tonnes. How is it even possible?"

"I am not sure, Carlos. This is a technology so powerful, so beyond anything we know. There is even a stone in Lebanon, I think, that is more than three thousand tonnes."

"I cannot believe this little thing can lift stones a thousand tonnes in weight."

"But it can. And it did. This is the true power of the human mind, more than anything else. You can even see evidence of this device in use in history."

"Like what?" asked Juan.

"You know the story of Moses, the Ten Commandments, the parting of the seas, turning bread into wine, and all those Biblical stories?"

"Yes."

"They are all fundamentally true – they were all made possible using the Ptah Wand."

"How?"

"When you see a picture of Moses, he is always seen holding a long staff, and if you look closely it is roughly the same length as this – he is holding a Ptah Wand. Some people even think that Moses was an Egyptian Pharaoh or at least royal, which would explain where he got the Wand from. Many early images show Moses holding what looks like an old man's walking stick, probably because the early artists didn't truly understand what they were being asked to represent – or because the real truth was hidden from them. Some images even show a beam of energy coming from the clouds, hitting the staff where the crystal is, and being focused on the earth – the power of God. In the Bible stories, Moses is said to have been in direct contact with God himself but, in reality, the power was from Atlantean technology. The original truths were manipulated in order to create the control that religion still exerts today."

"It is Atlantean technology," Professor cut in, as he turned around and walked to the back wall to stare at the pictures. In that moment, it hit me too. Here we were in possession of an Atlantean device. It must have weighed heavily on Professor – was he going to let this knowledge be announced to the world? Would he be the one responsible for destroying religion, bringing down our belief systems and changing the whole world? Thankfully, Felipe stepped in as my words started to hit home.

"Why is it called a Ptah Wand?" he asked.

"Good question. I have no idea what the original name for this device is, but in Ancient Egypt Ptah was the God of construction, architecture, and design. If you type the word Ptah into an internet search you will see images of the God Ptah, and he is always holding one of these devices. They even show the crystal on the top, or something similar. I am guessing Ptah was the individual who brought this technology to the Egyptians, and therefore was revered as the God of architecture afterwards. Who or *what* he actually was, or where he came from, I have no idea, but it seems he arrived with the purpose of building the Pyramids."

"That is very interesting," said Felipe.

I couldn't help but have a little giggle to myself – he said it in such a serious way, like a child who only pretended to know what I was talking about, but of course he understood fully.

"Let me get this straight," said Juan, "you're saying that these devices were used to build all the ancient structures but the information has been kept secret because the technology came from Atlantis and the governments, or whoever it is, don't want people to know about it because...?"

"Because it destroys *everything,*" said Professor, "and they need us to believe that we are the pinnacle of human evolution. If people knew about this, proof that there was a civilisation in the past that was far more advanced than our own, that would destroy the power they hold over us."

"Tell me – how does it work again?" asked Felipe.

"All the ancient sites were built on very particular places, chosen because they were located on ley lines or meridian points of the earth where the magnetic field is strongest, with the exception of the Giza pyramids which were built in the absolute centre of the earth's land mass. There were other technologies that could easily deduce where the best places were – in fact, even simple dowsing rods still used today can locate these places. They cut the stones and then with this device they were able to transport them along the ley lines to wherever they wished to build their monuments.

"Now, what you have to understand is that *everything* in nature functions because of electromagnetism; the earth is a giant dynamo, and the human brain also functions with electromagnetic waves. If you can tune your mind into the correct frequency, then you can work with the natural background electromagnetism of the earth. This device was basically a way of manipulating nature without causing destruction. That is, provided you don't consider the cutting and removal of the stone as destruction in itself."

"You make it sound so simple," said Juan.

"Are you saying that these people were able to basically levitate stones weighing hundreds of tonnes and float them across the landscape? That sounds far too fanciful to me," said Carlos.

"It's quite straightforward actually, at least theoretically," Professor intervened, "because I do know that some scientists have been able to levitate small objects using a certain frequency of electromagnetic waves, although the technology has been suppressed, but I never imagined that it could be used to such an extent."

"It's true that it has been suppressed," I responded, "but some of these experiments have been filmed and you can find them on the internet and see it for yourself. The knowledge is coming out slowly, but for the most part *this* is the technology they have been keeping from everyone – free energy. They've been keeping this all a secret for two thousand years and more, keeping us in the dark, and it's even said that some scientists have been murdered because they have discovered this energy. The powers that be want to keep the oil flowing because oil equals money, but free energy for all destroys their power.

"In a way, the real secret is that the human mind can have such a huge influence on matter, and they don't want 'rogue states', as they call them, understanding these ideas because then it would be possible to manipulate weapons using the mind. The Wand of Horus is such a device, but even the manipulation of conventional weapons is possible, if the correct technology is applied."

Carlos looked at Professor. It was obvious that they were thinking similar thoughts – were there people in their own country who knew about this? Had they been fed lies during their education which they in turn had fed to their own students? But, more importantly, how much trouble would this discovery bring down on their heads?

The ultimate question was a fairly simple one that had no answer; how many people in the world, which organisations, knew about this information? Were we talking about a handful of individuals, or were we talking about all the mainstream religious groups, governments and secret societies?

"Potentially, this device is extremely dangerous."

The sentence echoed through the chamber. Professor had his back to us, but he spoke in such a serious manner it forced me to pay attention. He turned and looked at me as if something had unnerved him – which wasn't surprising under the circumstances – and in return I stared at him searchingly.

“Yes,” I said, slowly, as I tried to find what was inside his mind, “and very, very powerful, but there’s another element to this technology. It cannot actually function correctly in our world, because it requires the manipulation of a higher dimension, a higher form of energy.”

Professor turned back to the walls and looked at each of the pictures, and then walked back to the object.

“What is it?” Carlos asked Professor, sensing his concern.

“I am not sure, but I get a feeling we need to leave.”

The mood changed in an instant as the realisation of what we were looking at struck home. It hadn’t really sunk in before this moment. Lying in front of us was the device that had been used to build *every* ancient structure on the planet, the device that was used to lift the huge and heavy stones into place – a device so powerful that it was far ahead of any of the technology of our times.

Sleeping peacefully on its bed in front of us was the biggest secret and the most important discovery of the last five thousand years of human history. It was perhaps *the* biggest secret and *the* most important discovery of all time, but there was a sudden realisation that this device must not be revealed to the world. Somehow we had to cover this up, hide the Ptah Wand and get the hell out of Dodge before the cavalry arrived.

20

A MIRACULOUS CLEAN UP

Professor brought us out of trance and down to earth once again.

"Carlos, take as many pictures of this object as you can get. I have a new camera card in my bag. Use this solely for the wand, or whatever it is, and if anything should happen when we leave throw it out of the window or destroy it. Swallow it if you have to, but do not let it get into the wrong hands."

Panic suddenly struck me as the reality of this whole situation hit home. It was truly ridiculous, to be honest – surreal and unreal in equal measure. I wasn't even sure if I was physically there, my mind was floating as if this was all a dream. In this moment, even the dome in Tibet with its moving walls, disappearing scrolls and higher dimensions seemed more realistic than this place.

Professor passed Carlos the camera card and for a moment they both held onto it, staring into each other's eyes. What this must have meant for these two after all their years studying Maya archaeology? This situation made all their hard work completely and utterly futile, for this object, which was at least ten thousand years old, had obviously been constructed using materials not seen before and a technology unknown even today. It was unlike anything that was even supposed to have existed during that time period. It was something more advanced than anything in the modern world and yet, in reality, it was just a feeble looking stick with a few crystals inside.

Professor came back to where we stood and peered again into the box at the Ptah Wand. The sadness in his eyes was clear – it was the pinnacle of his career and the most important archaeological find in history, and yet it had to remain in situ for eternity. Despite his spiritual nature, still he was an archaeologist – and thus a scientist – and I sensed his loss. I really felt for him but the greater goal was more important and he knew it. We had to do what we had been told. We had to respect this site and not forget why we were here, and for the first time it was apparent why Professor had been 'chosen' for this task – any other scientist would have said 'to hell with the warnings, I want my glory', but not him. He was a man of great integrity, and a man intelligent enough to cope with drastic changes in his life. A man capable of understanding what could happen if this ended up in the wrong hands.

"Okay, we're done here," Professor said, as Carlos started taking photos.

"What about the measurements?" Carlos asked.

"Do them when we have cleared the chamber. We need to pack up everything and empty this place of our belongings. Carlos, Felipe, Juan, you put the lid back on the box when the photos are finished. We need to seal the entrance back up, replace the layers of earth and clean this site up as if we have never been here. Stephen, let's get these lights outside. We only have until the end of the day to get all these things done."

"That's going to be a push," Carlos commented, as he programmed the camera.

"I know," Professor responded.

We quickly got to work and within half an hour everything was outside. Carlos was expertly taking the measurements of the room and halls of the pyramid in quick time using an electronic measuring device. Although he had taken preliminary measurements before, this time he took more accurate readings.

And then, one by one, we took turns to spend a few moments alone inside the pyramid. With just a torch for illumination, once alone inside the pyramid I felt a different aura and once again I was convinced I was not alone. This time, however, I sensed the entire chamber was filled with the souls of the dead, watching me from every corner of the room. Wherever I stood, the intensity of eyes staring into me was everywhere, as if the consciousness behind those eyes had no location or reference point. It reminded me of the same bizarre experience I'd had with the light in the entrance room to the dome in Tibet – it either changed location when I focused on it or it was in all places at the same time.

"Thank you," I said aloud, and in a strange way felt that this helped me to make peace with the place, because it still felt as if we had committed some kind of sin by lifting the slab and going inside. The powerful, omnipotent energy this place exuded was strangely sombre, almost as if the ghostly guardians were upset to see us leave. Or maybe it was the structure itself – lost in time and hidden in the jungle, forgotten to history and left to rot alone. Despite its obvious inertness compared to the Tibetan dome, the pyramid felt just as alive and conscious but, while the actual *structure* of the Tibetan dome was alive, the lifeless pyramid seemed to be surrounded by the souls of the dead.

I looked at each of the walls once again, admiring the beautiful images and taking a moment to fix them in my memory. I wanted to make sure I would never forget this place, but even trying to forget it would be impossible, for it had penetrated every one of us in a unique way. Stroking the box containing the Ptah Wand, resting my hand on it for a moment to see if its energy could be felt, I closed my eyes and concentrated. Within moments the centre of my palm became intensely hot and I took my hand away quickly – I certainly didn't want to be waking the wand from its slumber. That was a moment I did not share with the others – it was mine, and mine alone.

As I walked back through the hall of writing, standing for a moment to admire again its beauty and design, I couldn't help wondering how on earth it would be possible to translate all of the letters. It seemed time was not on our side, and now it was time to leave. Time, time, time – that's what all of this was ultimately about. And yet I had already learned in Tibet that time was an illusion to us, here in the third dimension. What a strange paradox this was – everything we do is governed by the clock and the day and the month and the year. And yet time itself does not exist. Time is the devil of our world, the trickster that controls our every waking and sleeping move, but time is also an Ouroboros – a snake eating its own tail – and something about this pyramid was telling us, calling out from the past to the future, that somehow we are all linked as if existing in the same moment.

There was such anguish inside me. It was an emotion like letting go of someone very close and saying goodbye for the last time, never to see that person again. The pyramid had affected us all. It had crept unnoticed into our minds and souls and held onto us like a clinging baby that wanted to be cuddled. Feeling such powerful emotions in those moments, a tear ran down my cheek and as I walked away from the writing hall and back out into the sunlight, as the sun's rays hit my skin, I felt that we, Mankind, would now be entering a new dawn.

Once we had cleared the internal structure, the slab was miraculously replaced within an hour and we set about covering it with the earth that had been piled up next to the pyramid behind base camp. It took another two hours to pack it down and replace the top layer, and then cover it with leaves and small branches. It was a remarkable job and, once finished, we took turns to walk around the pyramid and look at it from farther away, inspecting it for any errors. There really was no sign that there was anything beneath it and since I hadn't seen the original site prior to the earth layers being removed, my objective response was all the more important. It looked like a simple mound of earth once again.

Making one last climb to the top of the pyramid, it was a great struggle to get to the summit. I had to use my hands to help myself scale the last few steps as my body was tired and my limbs ached. I was suddenly very glad that we were leaving soon – now the excitement was nearly all over, my body had started to give up. For a few precious moments, I stood on the top of the pyramid looking at the vast jungle before me, admiring the dense forest and catching a breath of breeze that the height offered. I wasn't alone in needing a few moments of solitude. When I climbed down from the pyramid again, everyone was standing around in their own little daze. Conversation was at a minimum as the site was cleared. We were all too tired and bewildered to talk.

We then set about packing everything else – the tents, all our personal belongings, and base camp, which turned out to be the most difficult of all since the grass and the ground itself had become rather flattened during the several days we had spent there. It was sad to be dismantling our camp, as it had been the scene of many great conversations and stories and our energy was truly marked on that spot, but it was difficult to remould the grass to make it look like no one had been there. We did the best we could and covered it with debris from the jungle floor, comforting ourselves with the certainty that it would take no time at all before the jungle reclaimed the ground that had been flattened by our activities and our backsides.

It was well into the afternoon by the time we were ready to leave and we were all extremely tired. We were all suffering with mosquito bites from this morning, bites that were uncomfortable and itchy. Eventually a few of them would become scars, a permanent reminder of my time here which I wouldn't mind at all.

"The site looks immaculate," Professor finally pronounced. "Say your goodbyes, gentlemen, we need to get back to the jeep before the feeding frenzy starts."

I looked upwards and could see that the sun had started to dip behind the tops of the trees; dusk was heading our way and the mosquitos would soon be back in full force.

This was it. It was time to leave this place and never return, and it would be difficult to walk away – more difficult than we imagined. In a strange way this incredible location belonged to us. It was ours – our special place – the place that for more than five thousand years had been sleeping through a long hibernation, waiting for the time when it would be ready to reveal its secrets to the world.

My emotions overcame me and tears welled up in my eyes. As I stood there staring back at our pyramid, a hand touched my shoulder. I turned and saw that Professor had the same sad expression in his eyes.

"Come on, Stephen, time to go. Let her return to rest," he softly said.

21

FOUR BY SIX

Carlos, Felipe, and Juan were already a hundred yards ahead of us and Professor and I turned to follow them, walking side by side.

"It has been quite an adventure," he said.

"It's been the most awesome week of my life and no words will ever be able to express just how awesome. This was more incredible than Tibet and that's saying something. What about you?"

"It is, without doubt, the pinnacle of my career. It would be nonsense to suggest otherwise. How could anything compare with this?"

I smiled and looked at the trees; their branches were swaying as if waving goodbye. Everything was quiet and subdued and a despondence filled the air. It was time to give the pyramid back to the jungle. Carlos, Felipe, and Juan had disappeared through the forest and Professor and I were alone.

"There are some things I do not quite understand," said Professor. "Why did you not mention the Ptah Wand in your story of Tibet? And did you know what was inside the box based on the shape of it?"

"I certainly had no idea what was in that box," I told him, surprised by the question. "It never crossed my mind once. I suppose there can't be too many things that would fit that box but honestly, I had no idea. Since I had been told that there was only one left in existence and it was in Mongolia, I guess my mind didn't even consider the possibility. As for not mentioning the Ptah Wand, well, I left many things out of that story. I just followed my intuition and told you what I felt was right at the time and kept back what I thought was not. No offence was meant by that, of course, but you know what I'm saying because I know there are things you're keeping quiet as well."

I glanced quickly at Professor. I was taking a risk by being so bold in my words. He seemed quite shocked, as if he thought his secrets had been well hidden, but they were not. I was certain the others knew, as well.

"I don't take offence," he told me. "I think this is all supposed to be, somehow, but I don't really understand it all. Too many strange things have happened for me to make sense of them all. I think we all need a little hindsight."

It didn't surprise me that Professor continued to be tight-lipped, but I seriously started to wonder exactly what he was keeping quiet about. There was something there, something in his eyes that told me he'd been worrying about something since the day we entered the pyramid, but it seemed he couldn't be pushed or forced to talk about it. Whatever it was, he seemed to be dealing with it internally.

"Yes," I said, "hindsight would be good. I hope by tomorrow things will be a little clearer. I am very excited about the translation."

Professor seemed concerned about my words, almost as if he no longer wanted to know what the writing said. His body language suggested he wanted to leave it all behind and go back to his normal life, but we both knew this was no longer possible. We had been committed, whether by chance or design, to be fully responsible for what was revealed in that place. We had all the materials and evidence from the site but now we had to take it with us and start our investigation.

"Is there anything else you can tell me about Tibet?" he asked.

I'd wondered when that question would come along.

"You know, Professor, it's very strange what I feel inside. A part of me wants to reveal everything, but something keeps telling me to hold back. It's not that I'm keeping enormous secrets from you; it's just that I wonder how much of it is relevant to what's going on here. I know it's all connected, but I don't yet know how or why. My intuition just says that I should tell you things as they become necessary. Please don't be too concerned. I honestly believe I'll be telling you more, once we can decipher those walls. I think it all fits together somehow but I don't know why yet."

"Okay, Stephen, I understand, for now at least."

There was a determination in that sentence that told me Professor wasn't going to let this go. He wanted answers and he was sure that more of my experiences in Tibet were relevant to what was happening here in Mexico. But, at that point, even I was still unsure of the connections. I hoped that putting distance between us and the pyramid might help me to put things into perspective.

"What do you think of the Ptah Wand?" I asked.

Professor stopped on the path and turned and faced me, staring into my eyes. "Do you realise what we have found? Do you actually understand what this all means? Do you realise what we are all responsible for?"

"No, Professor, I don't think I do. I haven't had the time to think about it all. Even Tibet hasn't sunk in yet and I am not sure it ever will, but I am very aware of how careful we have to be. And I know everything is down to timing, which is quite ironic considering this is all about a calendar!"

My attempt to change the mood worked, and a smile crossed his face as we continued walking, but it wasn't really a joke – because the particular calendar involved appeared to be ending in a couple of years' time. There was no mistaking the synchronicity that our pyramid had been found at this time, just a little over two years before the *current* Maya calendar supposedly ended. There was little doubt about the timing of these events we were living through, and little doubt that there were great secrets hidden somewhere on those pyramid walls. It was teasing us, beckoning us to try and figure it all out in time. As our conversation came to an end we reached the others, the three of them slouched over the jeep with bags scattered on the ground.

After packing the bags and tents into the back of the jeep we jumped in and Carlos quickly turned on the air conditioning. Within moments we were cooling off in the glorious breeze and the seats felt blissfully comfortable, offering welcome relief to our battered spines.

Just as Carlos put the jeep in to gear and started to turn the jeep around, a bleeping noise came from Professor's bag.

"Oh dear," he said. "This is bad news."

"What do you mean?" I asked.

"That is my pager. It is only to be used in an emergency."

For a moment I thought that Professor was about to receive bad news from home or some work emergency meant he had to go straight back to Mexico City, in which case the timing wasn't so bad since we were just about to leave, but it wasn't either of those things. It was much worse. Professor pulled the pager out from one of the pockets in his bag and turned it to show me. Carlos swung his head around, keeping his foot on the accelerator and the clutch in the biting position.

"I hope you are enjoying your holiday!" the message read.

I was utterly confused. "What does that mean?"

"It means we cannot go to Michael's house. It looks like my night visitor was correct. Carlos, Plan B – get us out of here quick."

Carlos didn't need asking twice and before we could even breathe he floored it and we sped off down the track. The force of the initial acceleration threw us back in our seats and Carlos went as fast as he could without causing any damage to the jeep, but still we were being jolted up and down as the uneven track wasn't exactly ideal for fast driving, even with a 4x4. I must have hit my head on the roof a dozen times. Carlos did finally slow down to a more comfortable speed but thankfully it wasn't long before the track levelled out and he was able to accelerate without too much discomfort for the rest of us. We must have reached speeds of fifty miles per hour on the second leg, and the narrowness of the track made it feel like we were travelling at twice that speed, with branches slashing the sides of the jeep, some of them breaking and falling to the ground. Many times I thought the windows would smash but the sturdy jeep held its own and anyway, the farther we could get away from the pyramid, the better.

"I didn't know there was a Plan B," Felipe finally said, as if he had been thinking about it the whole time, trying to remember when anyone might have mentioned it. He seemed flustered and concerned.

"Don't you remember?" said Juan, taking the thought out my mind, "you must have drunk far too much last night."

He smiled and Felipe looked confused at the thought that he might have missed an entire conversation without realising it but Professor finally put him out of his misery.

"There was no Plan B. We just need to get away from here and find another location to stay because we can't return to Michael's house."

"Why?"

"Because the message I have just received means that there may be others in the area trying to find the location of the pyramid, so we have to get out of the jungle and onto the main road before they get close. And certainly we have to make sure they don't see us or suspect that we have found it ourselves."

Panic rose in me but I was struck by the timing of that message – at exactly the moment we were about to drive away from the jungle – which made me wonder what on earth was going on. That immaculate timing felt like more than pure coincidence or synchronicity. There were far too many of these strange coincidences even for my liking. The more often they happened, the more surreal and ridiculous everything seemed to be, as if we were acting in some farcically cheap Hollywood caper.

"But how would Mike know someone was on the way?" asked Felipe.

"I asked him to watch for *any* suspicious activity in the town. It is the last town before this route so anyone trying to locate the pyramid would pass through there."

"Not if they came from the West," he protested.

That answer seemed to annoy Professor, but it was correct – surely the most likely direction of some approaching government organisation would be from Mexico City, but who or what was it that we were dealing with?

"What about Eloisa?" shouted Carlos as he steered us through the jungle.

"Good idea," said Professor, "but we'd better not make any phone calls, just drive straight there."

It seemed to take forever to get out of the jungle but when we finally reached the main road a huge sense of relief hit me, and for the first time since I arrived at the pyramid it seemed we were finally free. The farther we headed away from the pyramid, and in turn away from the jungle, the more relaxed the atmosphere inside the jeep became.

It was another hour before we reached the main 186 road which stretched for miles east to west, cutting north of Candelaria. We headed west towards Mexico City.

"We should be safe now," said Carlos, and after another two hours of fast driving we turned right off the 186 and onto a dry dirt track.

The road wound through the forest as we made our way up a steep hill and after a short drive we found ourselves at a house that was set deep within the trees, and so far away from the road it was completely camouflaged. It was, in essence, the perfect hiding place. Certainly under the circumstances it was more than we could have wished for and more importantly it was the perfect place to relax and decipher the writing.

The house itself was in a clearing and the trees had obviously been cut down specifically to build this jungle retreat. It was a modest home – a bungalow that had an unusually steep sloping roof, large windows and a thick wooden door that was reminiscent of a log cabin. The house was made of solid stone blocks and a single tree stood in the clearing about twenty yards from the door, and this created a kind of one-way system for vehicles, the tree acting as a roundabout. Even though it was basically a bungalow, it had the charm of a quaint English cottage, and because of this it seemed rather out of place in the stifling Mexican jungle.

Before the jeep had even stopped a woman opened the door, and she stood in the doorway with a huge grin on her face. She was small and slim but with wide hips and her pretty face was framed by long, straight, dark brown hair. Her face was interesting; high cheekbones, deep brown eyes flecked with hazel, full lips covering very white teeth. Her face had that attractive openness which made me instantly curious about her. Her skin was almost as white as mine, which told me she wasn't a native Mexican.

"Professor! Carlos!" she called excitedly, walking over to hug them.

I was introduced to Eloisa Montoya Escobar, and after receiving her soft but firm handshake we were invited inside. Once inside, something of her openness disappeared and she looked at everyone with a cautiousness bordering on suspicion, a natural response since we had arrived uninvited and she must have been wondering why five grubby and dishevelled men were at her door, even if she did know at least two of us.

The house was a huge open-plan design, with two bedrooms on the left, a bathroom, and then the living room and dining room were both in one large open space. The kitchen was slightly higher than the living area, with a single step that gave the impression of a separate room. A huge supporting post near the kitchen, slightly off centre, was the dominating feature of this most beautiful and comfortable home. Birdsong swept through the open window and echoed through the house, and a cat stretched lazily on the windowsill near the front door. With one eye open it gazed at the intruders on its territory, occasionally flicking its tail as if warning us not to make any sudden moves. She was obviously a playful cat with a dark side – one of those felines who would indulge you with play for only a short time before issuing a sharp warning with her claws. She reminded me of Filthy Cat and I wondered if all cats in Mexico were this lazy.

"It's so lovely to see you, Professor," Eloisa said, breaking into a sunny grin as she started to fetch us something to drink, "but I know you have come here for a reason and I can sense something isn't quite right. So, are you going to tell me what's going on? Or do I have to guess?"

Eloisa was obviously a no-nonsense woman but she spoke in a caring way that could get blood out of a stone if required – the kind of woman that would be great with children. Her direct approach could only be admired and it was quite apparent this was a woman who wasn't going to put up with false excuses from anyone. Her house had been invaded in numbers and for this she demanded answers.

"I will tell you everything in a while, once we all settle if you don't mind?"

"Of course not," she said as she handed him a glass of orange juice, her eyes searching his soul for clues.

Eloisa continued pottering around the kitchen as the rest of us sank onto the sofas. Tiredness quickly set in and took hold of our aching bodies, and I suddenly felt as if I was floating; a swift dizziness followed by a sharp pain in the forehead which left my eyesight wandering for a few moments. We were all too tired to talk and when Eloisa noticed this, she suggested we all freshen up before we explained our story to her.

Again we took turns in the shower and Professor suggested I go first as he wanted me to start on the translation as soon as possible. Carlos soon followed as it was his duty to write it all down.

When I'd finished in the shower, Professor and Eloisa were in the garden and Professor was explaining, as best he could, what had happened at the site, although I could hear that he was missing out much of the detail. As expected, he was only telling her what was necessary so she had an overview of the situation. She certainly deserved to be let in on the secret, after all where would we be now without her kind hospitality? If he trusted her with the truth then there must be a good reason.

I didn't interrupt. I settled back on the sofa in front of Professor's laptop, on which I could see that he had already transferred his photographs from his camera. It seemed to me that the screen was glowing, as if the gold of El Dorado was to be found somewhere within, and all I had to do was decipher the clues and the ultimate discovery of archaeology would be ours. But at the same time I wondered – would it really be the ultimate archaeological find? Or would it be nothing but nonsense? Would the writing make sense? Or would it be as obscure as the images in the main chamber? It was worrying to think that the writing might reveal nothing extraordinary and that the only real find might have been the Ptah Wand. I was excited, nervous and eager to get started.

Professor and Eloisa returned from the garden and Eloisa leaned against the kitchen work surface in shock. She looked pale and disorientated and ran her fingers through her hair as if trying somehow to comprehend what she had been told. It seemed that, after being excited to know what was going on, she no longer wanted the burden of involvement in any of this. I didn't really know how much Professor had told her since I had only heard parts of their conversation, but Eloisa seemed amazed and terrified at the same time, the ambiguity leaving her obviously distressed.

"I just can't believe it", she said, over and over again.

Eloisa tried to put things out of her mind by starting to prepare dinner and Professor helped as they continued to talk, their conversation turning to more trivial matters in an attempt to restore some normality.

I started sorting through the photos, making sure they were in the correct order and labelling each one from the sequence in which they were taken. It took time but, once finished, the first task was to check whether the writing was easily decipherable. Carlos appeared and sat next to me, pen in hand, and we started with a straightforward left to right approach since the words on the chamber wall were also written left to right. We checked the first few letters and to our complete dismay, the writing seemed to make no sense whatsoever. It was total gibberish. We then checked the writing backwards, from the top right, but it didn't help. Then we tried up and down, diagonal, the middle in all four directions, the edges and just about everything we could think of, but there was nothing – just a mess of jumbled letters. I put my head in my hands and sighed and then rested my chin on my palm, digging my elbow into the table. How could this be possible? Everything else had fallen into place so quickly, so why did we now find ourselves at a brick wall? Something must be gravely wrong. Had we missed something back at the site?

Carlos was tapping the pen against his chin, his paper still blank except for a strange doodle of a spiral pattern and we could only look at each other in complete dismay.

"I don't believe this," I said, frustrated to the point of anger.

"I know," was all Carlos could say, shaking his head.

"What's wrong?" Professor said, as he approached us from the kitchen.

"We have a big problem," I said.

"I assume it is not going well?" Professor gave me a piercing stare from the edge of the sofa, his eyes sharp and intense. We didn't need to say anything, let alone explain the details.

"So much for things being easy for us – I knew it was too good to be true," said Juan.

He was standing by the window annoying the cat and its tail was wagging furiously with impatience. Juan seemed rather depressed, indifferent, like he just didn't care anymore. His mood was certainly something we didn't need right now. Felipe was on the other sofa, drifting in and out of consciousness with his mouth open and letting out an occasional snort, and Eloisa tried to concentrate on the food preparation although her attention was naturally targeted in our direction. But mostly I was surprised by Professor's reaction; he seemed almost completely unconcerned.

"What have you tried?" asked Professor.

"Everything – up, down, left, right, diagonal – everything. It is not making any sense either way."

"Maybe it is a code and not just writing?" said Carlos.

"It could be," I said, "but then we would need to decode it."

"It probably says nothing. It's just some kind of strange joke, or something," Juan said. I turned in annoyance and in that moment the cat caught him off guard, stretching its long arm and swiping at his wrist.

"Ouch," he said, pulling his arm back.

"Instant Karma," I said as I smiled. That was one thing I had seen coming.

"Juan, do something useful and go and help Eloisa instead of annoying that cat," said Professor.

Juan obeyed the order and sulked his way to the kitchen rubbing his arm. I was impressed by Professor's authority, which clearly continued off-site.

"Try the letters backwards," Carlos suggested.

"What do you mean?" I asked.

"Reverse the alphabet so that 'z' is 'a', and 'a' is 'z'. Maybe that's the code."

It was a reasonable suggestion but after repeating all the possible variations there was still no sign of a breakthrough.

I sat back in the chair and scratched my head in frustration. Professor simply raised his eyebrows and Carlos stared at the screen blankly.

What were we going to do if we couldn't decipher the code? It would be a total disaster, but since the letters were the same as the Atlantean alphabet, there must be a way to decode the text. The question was – how?

As my annoyance reached breaking point, I suddenly laughed as if the cosmic joker had left his mark.

"What?" asked Carlos, who excitedly assumed I had figured it all out.

"Oh, nothing, I suddenly thought we were back at the site. It looks like the adventure is not over after all."

Eloisa called out from the kitchen area – since she had been so quiet I had almost forgotten she was there, which was rude of me, considering we were sitting in her house.

"Let's have dinner," Professor said, "and then we can discuss this to see if we can produce some ideas. Try and get it out of our minds for a few moments and we might work it out."

Carlos and I were more than glad to leave it alone and have a break for a while. My eyes were straining and my head was spinning. Without realising, two hours had passed since we'd sat on the sofa. The pyramid, like the Enigma machine, was not going to give up its secrets so easily.

22

THE SECRET OF SIPÁN

We seated ourselves around a huge and impressive oak table with enough room for a dozen people, let alone the six of us. Eloisa was obviously accustomed to entertaining guests. This huge table had been cut from a single piece of the elegant wood; the tree that was cut down to make this beautiful ornament must have been the mother of all trees, which left me feeling distinctly sad.

"This is solid oak," I said, as I examined the edges, "where did it come from?"

"An oak tree!" Eloisa replied, giggling to herself.

That kind of response was certainly warranted under the circumstances but she never did explain anything about its origins. Why would Eloisa require such a large table when she obviously lived on her own? I was momentarily suspicious of our host and immediately felt guilty for thinking that way. If Professor trusted her with all this information then there could not be anything to worry about. I put my feeling down to the after effects of the events at the pyramid and the paranoia created by the message Professor had received. Any lingering doubts were put to rest when I asked Eloisa what kind of work she did.

"I finished my degree at the university about eighteen months ago. I was studying archaeology in Mexico City. Obviously I was Professor's favourite student!"

Eloisa smiled at Professor and he just raised his left eyebrow which clearly hinted that this wasn't quite the case.

"My husband, Elias, was an undercover police officer working in the city tackling the drug cartels. He was killed about a year ago in a gunfight and then my grandmother, Teresa, died about six months ago. The family said I should live here if I wanted to get away and recover, so I took the opportunity and here I am. My grandfather worked as a forest ranger and it was he who built this house, in the sixties. Professor and my grandfather were good friends, and I have known Professor since I was born. Professor bent some rules to get me into the university, since I married young and never really bothered with school so much."

Eloisa was blunt, honest and matter-of-fact about the whole thing, and nothing else needed to be said.

"I am sorry to hear about your husband and grandmother," I said.

"There is nothing to be sorry about. These things happen in life, but thank you."

"You don't seem to be Mexican – your accent is different."

Eloisa giggled again. "You are correct. I am from Colombia. My mother and father still live there but I was so close to my grandfather I came to Mexico years ago to stay with him here. I wanted to travel a bit and do something different for a while, and I met Elias here and got married. Professor introduced me to him in Mexico City. You should ask Professor how he met my grandfather." She gave a smile like a child causing trouble.

"Huh," was all Professor could say.

"Come on Professor, tell the story. Don't be shy!"

He looked across at Eloisa with an affectionate smile. These two were obviously close but I would never have guessed they went back such a long way. "I am more concerned with when you are going to put your education to good use. You cannot sit here for the rest of your life. There is plenty of work for you to do."

"Don't try to get out of this one," Eloisa smiled.

There was a long pause.

"Professor..." she said slowly, running her fingers across the table in his direction mimicking an insect, rather like a mother would to a child. Professor spoke before the hand reached his plate.

"I was doing a survey with a team near Mexico City," he started. "It was an unimportant Mexica site, containing just one small structure. It actually turned out to be a simple house but we did not know that at the time. We thought it could have been part of a larger site so we considered a wider area for excavation. After a couple of days, a team of loggers turned up and started cutting trees down right next to the site. I am not going to give you a detailed story but we ended up arguing with them and told them not to cut down the trees, but they insisted they had their orders. I tried to reason with them, asking them to wait until we had finished but they continued felling around the site. The tension between our two teams increased so much that, for the most part, we traded insults throughout the whole week. After about three days a tree came crashing down into the excavation area and missed us by a few feet. I was sure they had done this on purpose and I lost my temper. I ran over to Jorge and pushed him to the ground. That was it, really."

"Oh, come on Professor, tell them the truth!" said Eloisa, giggling. "Or do I have to tell them?"

"What do you know, you were not there!"

"Ah, but I have heard this story so many times I probably know it better than you. I wouldn't have slept so soundly if it were not for my grandfather telling me the wonderful 'Tale of Tenochtitlan'!"

Professor smiled at Eloisa, a glint in his eye as if she were his own granddaughter.

"Okay, okay. Well, we had a fight. That's it."

"Professor..." she said again, slow and demanding.

"Okay! I knocked one of his teeth out – which still shames me to this day, but he could have killed us with that tree."

"No, he wouldn't. He knew exactly where that tree would fall."

"What if I had decided to move at the moment the tree came down?"

"But you didn't!"

Eloisa had a big grin on her face, enjoying the comedy and putting Professor in his place. It was great to see and it was a welcome reminder that he had a softer side, even if it was very well hidden most of the time, but what surprised me most was Eloisa's bright smile and immense internal joy. Somehow she had managed to overcome terrible grief in solitude. Either that or she was a master at hiding it all.

"Anyway, to make this story even shorter," Professor continued, "our fight ended all that tension. By the end of the week we were friends and our teams would eat together and have a few drinks every night. After this, Jorge and I were best of friends. I was devastated by his death five years ago, as was Eloisa of course. He is sadly missed. Jorge Montoya was a great man."

It was very sad that Eloisa had lost so much of her family in such a short time. But, to be honest, it was difficult for me to apply the term 'great man' to a person who cut down large numbers of trees for a living. After learning in Tibet about the Buddhist philosophy of non-interference with nature, I was starting to struggle with the massive destruction wrought on our planet. It was such a stark contrast – there was a man like Jorge Montoya chopping down dozens of trees a day, and then there was Lasya, who believed it was wrong to pluck a blade of grass from the ground. What a strange and contradictory world we live in.

As we tucked into much needed nourishment of cold meats, vegetables and salads, the conversation soon returned to the problems with the translation.

"Professor, is there anyone you know who might be able to translate this, like a code breaker, or someone?" I asked.

"I do know someone but, unfortunately, I would not trust him."

Carlos glanced at Professor and I could see he was trying to work out who he meant. With his fork in his mouth he stared at the far wall before seemingly giving up on his quest to work it out. Silence hung over the table and a sense of despair loomed as it seemed all our hard work had come to nothing. The thought that we wouldn't be able to decipher the code was unbearable. It felt as if we had climbed a mountain to reach a pot of gold, only to find the gold disintegrating as we touched it.

Carlos tapped his knife on the side of his plate and as we all looked at him, he said, "Surely there are computer programmes that can break codes?"

We all looked at each other as if the answer had been so obvious but we had failed to notice. But before we could rejoice at the answer to our problem, Professor ruined the excitement.

"I have already thought of that but I'm not going to take that option."

"Why?" asked Juan, daring to question the obvious.

"I am not sure, but I fear that purchasing such a program will alert someone to our quest."

That answer seemed paranoid at worst and downright stupid at best but I wasn't going to question Professor's reasons. Whilst I understood that he was following the strict guidelines laid down by his night visitor, all the time there was something else going on behind the scenes.

"Surely someone else could purchase one from somewhere, maybe abroad, and then post it to us?" suggested Juan.

Suddenly, Professor slammed his fork down on the table with such force everybody jumped.

"I have already gone over this", he shouted, "and anyway it would take far too long!"

Professor was so rarely angered that we all realised something was getting to him. Something had obviously been bothering him for some time, but it surprised me that it was Professor of all people who was starting to show the strain. Everyone was starting to wonder what was going on and even Eloisa seemed concerned by his behaviour.

"Look, I'm sorry," he said. "I have been through this in my mind a dozen times but we cannot involve anyone outside of this group. This is it – we must work it out for ourselves, somehow."

Professor was always one step ahead of us, always outwitting us and always predicting what was to come, but it didn't escape our attention that something beyond this situation was worrying him. And then Felipe, in all his naivety, took the thoughts right out of everyone's mind and dared to ask the question.

"Professor, what is it that bothers you so much? We all know something is wrong and it's been affecting us all."

You could have heard a pin drop as silence struck the table, as if an unwanted visitor had arrived. Professor stared at Felipe without speaking and then Eloisa broke the tension by asking everyone if they would like more to drink. She stood up and wandered round the table filling up our glasses. Eloisa had obviously seen this behaviour in Professor before and seemed to be experienced in how to change the mood quickly. After circling the table she took her seat again and looked at Professor expectantly. He placed his knife and fork gently on to the table. He let out a long sigh as he sat back in his chair and then he told us the story he had been keeping inside for far too long.

"You all know the story of how Sipán, in Peru, was discovered?" he asked.

"Not really," replied Felipe.

I almost laughed again at his idiocy. I knew the story very well, as I am sure Carlos and Eloisa did, but we waited for Professor's version.

"Back in 1987, artefacts started turning up on the black market in Chiclayo – a few gold pieces and similar objects. The police began to investigate and rumours surfaced that a local family, the Bernals, seemed to have come into sudden wealth. They had been coming home with women and new cars and getting drunk regularly. It was not such a difficult thing to work out that they had been involved in looting ancient sites. The police raided their home, one of the family members was shot dead trying to escape, and some artefacts were recovered from the house. Well, that's the official story, the one you would read about if you looked it up in the records. It's a well-known 'historical account' of what happened."

"I am very familiar with the story," I said.

"Me too," followed Carlos.

"Well, there is another version of events that you do not hear about," Professor continued, "because it wasn't just huaqueros, the police and a few archaeologists who were involved. But I must insist, quite categorically, that this story does not go beyond this table. Agreed?"

We all agreed in unison, except for Carlos, who said, "You don't have to even say that, Santi, we are all brothers now, and one sister!"

Carlos glanced at Eloisa and smiled but what struck me was that Carlos had spoken to Professor as his friend and not his mentor, calling him Santi, the familiar version of Santiago. That was quite a strange thing to hear, but Carlos had seen the stress in his friend's face and tried to calm him. What was more surprising was that even Carlos, the man whom Professor trusted with his life, was obviously unaware of the story we were about to hear.

"Are you saying the official story isn't true?" asked Juan.

"No, it is all true, but there were other things going on as well."

Having spent so much time studying Peruvian archaeology and also visiting Sipán, I was intrigued as to what the professor was going to tell us, but no one could have guessed what was to come

"I received a call from one of the archaeologists who had been involved in trying to trace the source of the recovered objects. I was in Mexico City at the time, and it just so happened I was between jobs, following up on some other work. They said they wanted my help and would pay me well if I would take a flight to Peru and help with the investigation. Since I had been involved in other archaeological investigations in Peru it only seemed natural that they would require my expertise. I was not bothered by the financial incentive – I would have done it for free – protecting archaeology before the sites are destroyed is far more important than money. I arrived in Lima the following morning, met the archaeologist, and then took a flight to Chiclayo in the afternoon. He was convinced the artefacts were coming from that area."

"Who was the archaeologist?" asked Carlos, his curiosity piqued.

"I am not going to mention names. You will understand why by the time I finish the story. Anyway, in the evening we had a meeting with the police and a government official and I was given a briefing on the situation. From the start, something did not feel right and I was certain I was not being told the whole story. As the meeting came to an end another man came into the room and was introduced as an undercover agent, working as a black market buyer. His task was to infiltrate the gang responsible for stealing the items. He said he had good information about who was taking the items and where they were coming from. At that point I asked myself why they needed me, if they already knew the source."

Professor broke from the story, took a bite from his plate and had a drink. The rest of us continued to eat, listening in silence.

"Doctor Walter Alva was the official archaeologist appointed to the case. He had no knowledge of what was going on – he is a great man – and it turned out that the archaeologist to whom I had been introduced was collaborating with the government official. In fact, all the men I was introduced to were working for someone in the government, although I don't know who, or in which department. Quite simply, they were just criminals and they were trying to use me for their criminal purposes. The problem was, everyone was backstabbing everyone else and the policeman and the official were in cahoots. One night, the undercover officer told us that he had worked out the exact location the artefacts were coming from and, of course, this was the Sipán temple, about twenty kilometres east of Chiclayo. I will not bother to explain the details, but when we arrived at the site the undercover officer handed over some objects to the official. The official nodded to the policeman who turned around and pulled out his gun. He shot both the archaeologist and the undercover officer at point blank range and then turned the gun on me and pointed it at my head. I was convinced I was about to die."

Professor struggled to swallow his next bite of food. The silence was excruciating and only the cat could be heard as it jumped off the windowsill and headed for its food bowl. Carlos was especially shocked as he had no idea that his friend had been keeping such a burden to himself.

"With the gun pointing at my forehead, the official said, 'the only reason you are not dead is that your country will miss you and will investigate your disappearance. Now, go home, don't come back here and keep your mouth shut.' Suffice to say, I left that place as fast as I could and took the next available flight back to Mexico City."

A stunned silence hung over the room. But something wasn't right about Professor's story. It didn't make sense – why would these people call in an archaeologist from Mexico? What role did he actually play when he was there? From what he had told us, he'd had no influence over what was going on – the location of the artefacts had been found by the undercover agent and it seemed his journey had been wasted. At best, he had been a passive observer over events in which he had no active role, so what was the point of him being there at all? We were all confused but no one wanted to voice our questions. Carlos was looking at Professor very suspiciously; Professor was looking back at him with an expression that clearly said 'don't you dare ask'. We didn't doubt that he was telling us the truth but still, there was a lot more to the story that he wasn't telling us. More to the point, why was he telling us this story in the first place?

I suddenly remembered the message Professor had received on his pager and I found myself suspicious over the timing of that incident, arriving as it did at the very moment we arrived at the jeep. Was it purely coincidence? Or was the Professor himself playing games of which we were unaware?

Then Juan spoke – and perhaps he chose the wrong moment to ask the obvious question. "So, what has this got to do with deciphering the writing?"

His question startled Professor. He looked at Juan as if to say – 'work it out for yourself' – the expression on his face was bizarre and in his eyes I saw a deep, dark stare. For the first time I saw the darker side of Professor. He let out a deep sigh and in the process appeared to release the emotions he had been holding in.

"Look Juan, and all of you." He put his glass down and looked at us one by one. "Perhaps I am the only one who truly knows the deep implications of what we are dealing with. The information we have will change the world. Think about that – it could bring down our society and our religions and if people are prepared to kill over a few pieces of gold then those same people would not hesitate to delete us from history altogether. I admit I am scared. I am scared for you and I do not want any of you to come to harm. You are my responsibility."

"No we are not," Juan interrupted, "I am here by choice and if I die in the process I will be happy to die knowing I have witnessed the most amazing thing imaginable. I am very lucky to be here and whatever happens to me, well, so be it."

"I agree," said Felipe.

"That is not the point," Professor quickly responded. "This information is for the world, not for us. We must ensure this information is released somehow. We are nothing but plastic toy soldiers on a child's play mat and the responsibility weighs heavy on me. I have already decided to retire after this. This is the pinnacle of my career and nothing will match this discovery."

Professor was correct – how could he possibly return to his normal archaeological investigations when this discovery had completely destroyed everything he had ever believed and taught? The pyramid alone took the Maya civilisation back at least another 2,500 years, so how was it possible for him to go back and rewrite all the history he had previously discovered? He had no choice but to call it a day after this. It was a sad moment and it would be another generation or even two before a man of his calibre appeared again in Mexico.

Another long silence hung over the table. Eloisa seemed rather bewildered and she had stayed silent throughout, letting us get on with our discussions. She, if anyone, knew when to keep her mouth shut around Professor. So this time it was Carlos who broke the silence, his annoyance overcoming any loyalty for Professor and his superior knowledge.

"How can you be so sure that this information will bring down our society and our religions?"

"I made the deduction because of the information I was given by my night visitor."

Carlos wasn't convinced and now he had certainly had his fill of his lies and secrets. "Oh, come on Santi, no more games. Enough please."

His annoyance was clear to see. He had had enough. Everyone stopped eating and looked at Professor, waiting for his response. Eloisa glanced at all of us with her head down, wondering what was going to happen next. I had no idea what she was thinking about all of this and I was sure that at times she must have felt like she was invisible, which must have been strange in her own home. Professor stood up, turned around and walked over to the window by the back door. While he stared out into the garden the rest of us looked at each other in bewilderment, except for Carlos who shook his head in annoyance and frustration.

Professor then turned to face us, leaned back against the window ledge and dropped a bombshell.

"I have already deciphered the writing," he said, quietly.

23

CRACKING THE CODES

"WHAT?" Carlos yelled. "What on god's earth is wrong with you?"

I dropped my fork and watched as it bounced off my plate and onto the floor.

"Back at the site I read much of it on the wall," Professor replied, calmly. "I could see the code. I memorised the alphabet from Stephen's notebook and when we were looking at the writing I realised how the code works."

I was amazed and frustrated in equal measure. Whilst I still needed the notebook to translate the letters, Professor had memorised the entire alphabet in the single hour he'd spent looking at it on the day we'd discussed our dreams. It was another testament to his amazing intellect.

"It starts in the centre and works in a circular motion, anti-clockwise," he stated.

I started to laugh. It wasn't funny, though – I was just as annoyed as everyone else but I couldn't help admiring Professor's coolness about the whole thing. He had memorised the entire alphabet and deciphered the code, all in the space of a couple of hours. No wonder he had been 'chosen' for this investigation. The magical weaving of the people involved in this amazing story was even more apparent, and it was nothing less than genius.

Professor must have had his reasons for not telling us this before but as I looked at Carlos, it seemed that cracks were appearing in what had seemed the most unbreakable of friendships. Of course, there was little danger of these two ever falling out for more than a few hours, or days, but Carlos was extremely annoyed.

"Why didn't you mention this before, Santi? It has been stressful enough for us all – you should not be keeping things as important as this hidden from us."

Carlos' point was valid but Professor quickly refuted it.

"I can only go by the instructions I have been given and my intuition. I am sorry you are all upset but this is just far too important to be making any errors of judgement. Please do not forget the strange things that have been happening. I cannot go against the advice I have been given."

Professor walked over to Carlos and put a hand on his shoulder.

"I am sorry, my friend," he said, caringly. Carlos visibly calmed.

"Okay. I understand. I am sorry I got annoyed. I know I should trust you all the time but you should trust us too. We are in this together and if you can't trust us, then who can you trust? I think I am more upset about your Peruvian story – I had no idea you were carrying such a weight on your shoulders."

Remembering what Professor had said in the beginning – that someone in the group might be untrustworthy and may have told someone about the site – I understood that this was enough of a reason for him to have kept quiet about what he knew until he felt in a comfortable position to tell us. But I certainly wasn't going to mention that to anyone else – it wouldn't have been right for me to tell his close companions that Professor had *not* entirely trusted them.

Eloisa was still sitting at the table in silence and Juan and Felipe, amazingly, continued eating as if they might never eat again. Professor walked back to the window and stared out into the garden. Despite that fact that his disagreement with Carlos had been resolved, the atmosphere was still awkward. I walked over to the sofa and flicked through the images on the laptop until I found one clearly showing the centre of the wall. I called Professor over to confirm that this was the right image.

"Yes, that's it," he said. "If you look closely at the 'letter' in the centre, it is not one from the alphabet."

I grabbed the notebook and checked the letters. He was right. The one in the centre was similar to the letter 'z', which contained two complete circles, but with the addition of a tiny dot, or circle, in the centre. It was in fact the same symbol for Atlantis – three circles.

"Wow! Well spotted," I said. I turned to Professor. "Well spotted – get it?"

I started to laugh and Professor rolled his eyes and smiled, my silly joke changing the atmosphere slightly. It was always difficult to use English humour on my new friends.

Juan and Felipe had finally had their fill and sluggishly joined us on the sofa while Carlos helped Eloisa clear the table. They started an uninteresting conversation about the garden as they began to wash the dishes and it seemed Carlos needed a bit of space between himself and Professor, to clear his mind. Talking to Eloisa appeared to be the best way for him to ground himself again.

For a moment I wondered if I should even start to translate the writing. What was it that Professor was so concerned about? I shifted my position to get comfortable, wondering if Professor was going to make me translate the whole text by myself, but as I looked at him he reluctantly asked, "Shall I read it for you?"

"Please," I replied, without hesitation.

"You had better write it down, then."

And so it was to begin. Our lives would never be the same after this evening. We had all been fundamentally changed by our experience at the pyramid but this was the night where all our beliefs would be destroyed. Everything we had been taught in the past, everything we thought we knew, was to be shattered in a matter of hours. It wasn't really the words that caused the foundations of our beliefs to be destroyed – it was the fact that the future was written in stone. Professor read the text out loud.

FOUR SITES MADE AT THE DUSK OF THE DAY
HERE STANDING THE FIFTH AND THE LAST
BEFORE THE FIVE THE GREAT LAND DID LIE
THIS DUSK AND NO MORE WILL PASS
AT THE END OF THE FIVE A RETURN IS DUE
THOSE WHO ARE NOT AT HOME WILL FLY
THE GODDESS MUST BE RETURNED TO HEALTH
AT THE END OF DAY BILLIONS WILL DIE
THE INVADERS AND MANIPULATORS WILL BE REMOVED

"There is a short gap using that three-circled letter and then the text continues," said Professor.

BRING FORTH FEAR AND PERISH IN THY SELF
DREAM HEAVEN OR HELL AND REALITY WILL BE THIS
THE VIRUS WILL COME AND MANY WILL FALL
SCIENCE AND MAGIC WILL COEXIST
THE MOUTH HAS BEEN OPENED AND THE WORDS ARE SEEN
THE EVOLUTION HAS BEGUN

"That's it," Professor said.

"What? There is a lot more writing than that," I protested.

"There is, but they are not words. I will show you the last few words, and then if you can try to read backwards, you will see."

He pointed to a letter in the photo and I started to read it from the translation although, unlike Professor, I still needed the book to check each letter. After the words *the evolution has begun* I started to read the next part, but there was no sense in the words. Professor was correct; it was just the alphabet, repeated time and time again.

"What about the other wall?" I asked.

"I didn't find anything on there. It was all nonsense as far as I could tell. It was not very difficult to find and decipher the code."

"It would have been if you hadn't been here!"

For a moment I stopped as something ran through my body, a strange feeling about everything which was hard to decipher. The idea that everything was predetermined and that Professor was supposed to be the one to find the site at the exact moment suddenly seemed to make sense. It was right at the back of my consciousness and I could see it in images – an explanation of it all that made sense – but my conscious mind wasn't capable of forming words to explain it and my stupid animal brain wasn't clever enough to comprehend it. It was there, tantalising and yet fleeting in my mind, but before I could grasp it properly, all the images disappeared from view.

"I don't believe it. Is that all there is?" asked Juan, as disappointed as the rest of us.

"Do you not think that is enough? Did you actually hear the words? Already this information is dynamite!"

Professor was right yet again. He leaned towards the screen.

"Do you see the last letter from the last word, *begun*? If you look closely there is a very thin line, like a razor cut, separating that from the next letter. It's deliberate, marking the end of the text."

And what a text it was. For the first time ever, words from the past that told of the future were written in stone. We weren't dealing with copied stories, like the biblical texts which had been obscured by the writing hand of Man; these were words that apparently told us precisely when and what was going to happen. But what exactly was it telling us?

I sat back in the chair in wonder.

"So what's it all about?" I asked.

"It's the worst poem I've ever heard!" said Felipe.

"It's not a poem," said Professor. "Using this, we can confirm the pictures that are in the main chamber. Each picture has a number corresponding to when the sites were built, at intervals of 5,096 years each. So, this text confirms that these sites were built in the years that are stated on the walls, which means Atlantis did exist twenty-five thousand years ago, or thereabouts, and each site was built at the end of each 5,096-year period."

"Well, you've had enough time to think about it all," Carlos griped.

Professor gave Carlos a tired glance.

"How did you work that out?" asked Juan.

"Well, the second line says that the pyramid is the fifth site – *here standing the fifth and the last* – and the first line says the others were *made at the dusk of the day*, so I concluded that these referred to the drawings in the chamber, the previous four sites, built at the end of each 5,096-year period. *The dusk of the day* is referring to the end of a cycle of 5,096 years. The third line – *before the five the great land did lie* – seems to be talking about Atlantis. The fourth line – *this dusk and no more will pass* – seems to be stating that no more sites will be built, but I am not sure about the rest of it."

"Maybe they aren't saying that," said Carlos. "The fourth line could be talking about the end of the calendar. It says *this dusk and no more will pass*, which means the end of a 5,096-year period, and there is no more after."

"The problem with that," I interrupted, "is that the Sun cycles of the Maya calendar are 5,126 years long, and not 5,096 years. There's a discrepancy of thirty years. The Sun cycles of the calendar are 5,126 years long, and these sites were built every 5,096 years. There's got to be something wrong somewhere."

"Maybe there isn't anything wrong," replied Professor. "We have to look at the evidence. At the site we have undoubted proof that the pyramid and the other sites were built at intervals of 5,096 years. Yet the entrance was sealed with the calendar stone, a calendar which has cycles of 5,126 years. There has got to be a reason for that. Maybe they are trying to tell us something."

Professor was right. There seemed to be nothing left to chance. Everything was too perfectly written, literally in stone, in front of us. The numbers were marked clearly at the site, but what could be the reason for a thirty year difference between them? Over a complete set of five Maya Sun cycles, that added up to a difference of 150 years. That was far too much to be a mistake – the Maya were far too advanced and far too clever to be making mistakes in their calculations. The site could be seen as an amalgamation of both Atlantean and Maya but since the Maya culture did not actually exist for another 2,500 years then this site had to be connected with Atlantis. Professor must be correct in stating that, at the very least, this was a 'mother culture' and this meant the Maya calendar was not Maya at all – it was Atlantean. The symbol for Atlantis was three circles, the letters were all made from circles and the Maya calendar was also circular. Surely that could not be a coincidence.

"So what's going to be returning, at the end of the five dusks?" Juan asked, referring to the fifth line. "And what does it mean by '*those who are not at home will fly*'?"

There was another long silence.

"I don't know," said Professor. "But I think the bit about the *goddess* could be referring to the planet – Mother Earth – which must be returned to health."

"That makes sense. But who are these invaders that must be removed?" I asked.

Everyone looked at everyone else. No one said a thing.

"At the end of the day billions will die," Felipe said out loud.

These were terrifying words if they were to be taken literally and they couldn't have appeared more literal. There was no riddle in that line. It said what it said and since the human population had reached billions only in the last hundred years or so, it was more than scary.

"And about this virus, what is that?" asked Juan. "Is that what will cause billions to die?"

"Maybe," responded Professor, "and it says that billions will die '*at the end of the day*'. So does that mean at the end of the calendar?"

A shiver went through my body, a shiver of pure terror at the possibility that billions of people could die at the end of the Maya calendar, possibly because of a virus, and there were only two-and-a-half years before we reached that point.

We spent a few hours driving ourselves crazy with various explanations for the words in the text but nothing came forward that had any substance. The only thing that seemed clear to us all was that a virus might kill billions of people. Or was it just a riddle? Were they just words, pointing to something else that wasn't literal? Was there a hidden meaning to them, like the rest of the text?

By late evening we had all had enough of guesswork and despite our best efforts we concluded that there was nothing else we could reliably deduce. We had gone around in circles and back to the beginning several times.

"Whatever we have done by opening this pyramid, whatever it is that will happen, there is no more for us to do," said Professor. "I am tired. I have had enough and I want to go home to my wife."

"I agree, but first I need to sort out the measurements." Carlos went over to the kitchen table to work with his measurements and see if there was any meaningful correlation in them. He spent half an hour examining them before reporting that he could see nothing significant.

It was time to call it a night. We thanked Eloisa for her hospitality and retired to our beds, although Felipe and Juan had to sleep on the sofa and the floor respectively, as there were not enough beds for us all.

Professor, Carlos and I shared a large room that looked out onto the driveway at the front of the house. The room contained a bunk bed and a single bed and I guessed it must have been Eloisa's room when she had visited her grandfather as a child, with her parents. Carlos and Professor were asleep within moments. The evening was warm and humid and very still, and only the chorus of cicadas could be heard outside.

Friday 28 May, 2010

What does that writing mean? The only thing that keeps ringing around my head is the statement that billions of people will die. Is that literal? Will billions of people really die or is this some kind of cryptic code like the end of the Maya Calendar itself and its 'end of the world' prediction? Everyone knows the world won't really 'end', it's just some kind of astronomical cycle, but is this different? I can see now why Professor was acting so strange – he knew all along what that writing said. He's a truly amazing person. I can't imagine what he and Carlos are going through. For me, this is one amazing adventure, but for them their entire life's work has been completely destroyed. So, what happens next? Where do we go from here? What are we supposed to do with this information? Nothing's really come from this and there's not much else we can do.

Lying in bed I started drifting into sleep, that strange state when one is neither unconscious nor awake. It was a blissful feeling as I floated in the netherworld but then suddenly an image appeared in my mind like a photograph, breaking the peaceful feeling and filling my soul with an urgency that told me to take notice. It was a picture representing the solar year, a circle with 365 squares marked around its edge, reminiscent of the Maya calendar itself. The little squares were numbered from 1 to 360, but the last five days were black and I instantly recognised them as the five unnamed days of the Maya Haab calendar.

Immediately sitting bolt upright, I realised this was a sign, the feeling of a presence palpable in the humid night, as if the ghosts of the pyramid were still with us. Knowing instantly how significant this was, I got out of bed as quietly as I could and took out a pen and a notebook from my backpack. By a stroke of luck there was a calculator in a drawer in the desk next to the bed. It really didn't feel as if I had been dreaming; it felt more like an intuitive spiritual experience, as if the image was sent to me by some divine force. Straight away I understood that there was a connection between those five unnamed days of the year and the five Sun cycles of the Maya calendar. I just needed to find out what it was. Making sure Professor and Carlos didn't wake I climbed back into bed and set to work.

I realised now that the five unnamed days of the Haab calendar had been ignored by everyone. The Maya solar calendar, the Haab, was 360 days long. To compensate for the discrepancy they added on the five days to make up the solar year. Those days were considered unlucky, and anyone born on those days was doomed to a bad life. Was it really possible that there was a link between those five days and the five cycles? What if...?

Then a flash went through my mind; a memory of a lecture I had attended many years before. The lecture was about, among other things, the number 666 and its relation to the Christian faith. Many centuries ago the number 666 was regarded with deep suspicion because of its relation to the devil. However, the lecture revealed that this number was sacred to geometric design, nature, the fraction two-thirds, and that the 'powers that be' had enforced the notion of the devil so that people wouldn't dare look at this number and thus, certain secrets could be kept from the public. It wasn't necessarily a theory I agreed with, but it was interesting enough for me to have remembered it. Were those five extra days that gave one a life of doom in the Maya kingdom the same as someone going to hell if they dabbled with the number 666 in the Christian world?

So, I wondered – what if the five unnamed Maya days were acting in the same way – keeping the secret hidden. What if there was a great significance to the five days that had been kept from the Maya population, thus leading to today's researchers not crediting them with any importance? Were today's researchers blind to the truth because they thought the Maya were a little stupid and the five days were just an addition to the calendar to make sure it didn't wander through the years? Was it a diversion? It was just an intuition but I had to find out if there was a connection between the five days and the five cycles. After all, there were five in each and knowing the Maya that probably wasn't a coincidence. For the entire night I worked on the calculations.

What I was to discover completely took my breath away. I didn't sleep at all and by sunrise my mind was cracking up with the lack of sleep and playing around with numbers all night, but it wasn't just my mind that was cracking – I had cracked the secret code of the Maya calendar.

24

A SPANNER IN THE COGS OF THE MAYA CALENDAR

The next morning I waited impatiently for everyone to wake, drinking coffee and pacing up and down the kitchen like a lost lamb. Eloisa appeared first, the unusual disturbance in her own home causing her to wake prematurely. She looked at me, obviously wondering what was wrong, but she only said, "Good morning," as she yawned her way to the back door to let in some fresh air.

Professor appeared next and he was back to his old self. At least that was his outward appearance but inside it was likely he entertained a deep concern about everything that was going on around him.

"You're quiet, Stephen, are you okay?" he asked, meandering towards the kettle.

"We all need to sit at the table. I need to speak with you all."

Professor glanced at me inquisitively and he could see how serious I was, not to mention that I probably looked like hell. He didn't ask why, he just called everyone to sit at the table. No arguing, it was done, simply and quietly. Professor knew there was something of major importance that needed to be discussed.

"Are you okay? You're shaking!" said Carlos.

He was right, I was shaking. I was tired but I couldn't get my discovery out of my mind and I needed to share it quickly before the information became confusing and obscure. Messing with numbers always left me feeling a bit weird and the lack of sleep wasn't helping at all.

"You'll be shaking too when I've finished!" I replied.

First, I told them about the strange image that had come into my mind and the feeling that had accompanied it, and then I set about explaining what I'd subsequently discovered.

"I wanted to find out if there was more to this number five. I started with a simple question and came up with a revelation. There are fifty-two years in the Calendar Round, and the Maya and the Aztecs celebrated at the end of this long cycle, but what was the significance of those fifty-two years in relation to the number five? So, I looked at a simple equation – there are fifty-two years in the Calendar Round and five unnamed days in the Haab calendar, so I simply multiplied them together – 52 times 5, equals 260!"

There was a little confusion in the room. It was so simple that no one had noticed the obvious. If either Professor or Carlos had said, 'I know that', then I could have believed that I was wrong in thinking that this was a discovery of something entirely new, but their reaction told me that even they hadn't noticed this simple multiplication. It was the most ridiculous thing I had ever encountered because one hardly needed to be a great mathematician to work it out. The connection was clear for all to see – 260 is the number of days in the Tzolk'in calendar.

"I couldn't believe it either," I continued, "and here is the next obvious part – you can reverse this – there are five unnamed days in each year and when you multiply that by the number of years in the Calendar Round you get 260 unnamed days every fifty-two years. It is the same number of days in the Tzolk'in calendar – 260. From this starting point I knew I was on to something, so I continued to look more closely at these numbers."

In the meantime I had written the information on a piece of paper that I'd pinned to the supporting beam, facing the table – thankfully Eloisa didn't mind this desecration of her kitchen pillar. Felipe was scratching his head already but it was Juan who started the debate.

"Are you saying the Tzolk'in is the basic component of the Calendar Round?"

"Of course it is. The Calendar Round stems from the Tzolk'in and the Haab, so they are components of it," Professor replied. "Please continue."

"An extension, if you like, of the Calendar Round is the Sun cycle and we all know this is 5,126 years long. So I took the number fifty-two and tried to see if it could be calculated into 5,126. Unfortunately nothing fitted with the larger number and I was about to give up when I found something that totally shocked me. If you multiply 52 by 98 you get 5,096."

"What does that mean?" asked Felipe, struggling to keep up.

Carlos' eyes suddenly sprung open and his expression changed in an instant – he looked as if his wife had just told him she was pregnant. He stood up so fast that his chair was sent scooting backwards, scraping on the wooden slats of the kitchen floor.

"Puta Madre!" he shouted. Knowing what this profanity meant left me laughing inside but Professor was never impressed by bad language and looked at Carlos scornfully across the table.

"Carlos! Please. Not in front of a lady!"

"Sorry," he said.

Professor leaned forward on the table, his eyes lighting up as he rested his chin on his fists and his elbows on the table. He gave me a strange look and smiled. His eyes penetrated my soul like never before.

"I took both the numbers – the accepted 5,126 and the new number 5,096 and did another calculation. If you divide 5,126 by fifty-two you get the calculation 98.5769. It's fractional, and we all know the Maya did not use fractions, right? So, let's divide the new number 5,096 by fifty-two. You get exactly ninety-eight. So, it is obvious there is more to the number 5,096."

"Okay," said Professor, "I can see what is happening here, keep going."

"Let me give you something else. Take the number 5,126 and add the individual numbers together – five plus one plus two plus six – it equals fourteen. No significance. Now add the numbers five, zero, nine and six."

I waited for a moment.

"Twenty!" shouted Felipe, excitedly. He was so happy to have actually given a correct answer during one of our discussions!

"Yes, twenty," I continued, "the base number of the Tzolk'in and the Maya counting system. It is their first main number after the unit of one, like our ten. These numbers come up again. If you take the solar year as 365 days and deduct the Tzolk'in, you get 105. If you take the 360-day Haab, however, and deduct the Tzolk'in you get 100, and from that 100 you have twenty times five, that magic number five again and the base twenty."

I looked at Professor. He knew what was happening here and I was almost certain that his mind had already jumped ahead and calculated some of the things I was about to disclose. During the night I had wondered why someone of his intellect had not seen this before, but he was an archaeologist, not a mathematician, and the Maya calendar was not his area of expertise. He was an expert on the Maya, not their calendar.

Suddenly I remembered what Charles had said to me back at home on the first day – *"And in many ways the most important ability you have is a strange talent for memorising numbers."* Stopping for a moment and thinking about those words, I wondered if Charles had known exactly what was going to happen here. Was all this foreseen long ago?

Professor was looking at me in a way I had never seen before. He had a smile on his face and he was staring at me as if I was the latest prodigy. He seemed in awe of what was coming from these calculations, but a prodigy I was not. It was just a dream, another part of those strange events that had occurred at the pyramid. Somehow the pyramid had changed all of us – the way we thought, the way we perceived reality. I tried not to think about it all too much and continued to concentrate on the here and now.

"There is something else there too – the number ninety-eight is also additions of the base eighteen and base twenty systems – four times twenty, plus one times eighteen, equalling ninety-eight. There are also five of those units that make up the number ninety-eight."

"What do you mean?" asked Felipe.

"Well, there are four twenties and one eighteen, so four plus one, equals five. The numbers keep coming forward – five and twenty. Five unnamed days and five Sun cycles; twenty is the base number of the Tzolk'in. The base twenty of the Tzolk'in makes up the Haab, as well as the Tzolk'in itself, and when you take the 360 days of the Haab you have five days left over in the solar year. So, the Haab *was* significant to the Maya, but not because they were using the calendar to calculate the solar year – *it was pointing to something else."*

"So, what was it pointing to?" asked Juan.

"I am not sure, but let me continue. If you take 5,096 and multiply that by five, you get 25,480. This is now the complete number for the five Maya Sun cycles. The other number is 5,126 and if you multiply that by five you get 25,630. This number is thought to be the number of years of the *precession of the equinoxes*, the wobble in the earth's axial spin. Not even today's scientists can agree on the length of time of precession, but it is thought to be around 26,000 years. I am thinking now that the correct and exact number for precession is 25,480 years. This is what it points to."

"How can you come to that conclusion? Maybe it's just *numbers* and the precession has nothing to do with it," said Carlos.

"It's possible, but do you remember my dream? The Maya priest was pointing to Polaris – the Pole star. Professor's dream had a word, which led him to work out the writing on the walls. Carlos – your dream had a brightening sun and you worked out the Sun cycles. My dream was about this – precession. I feel those dreams were actually implanting us with information, which means they were not dreams at all."

"So what have cows got to do with it?" asked Felipe.

A sudden silence was then broken with roars of laughter. It was always Felipe who managed to break any tension that was around. It was almost like his whole purpose here was to combat stress and anxiety and to keep us all with our feet on the ground.

Eloisa took the opportunity to offer us more coffee and lay breakfast on the table. All the while, she had been pottering around behind us in the kitchen. She must surely have been wondering what on earth was going on and why her quiet life had been invaded by a group of people who were about to change the world.

"There is another calculation," I carried on. "If you take the accepted number of the five Maya Sun cycles – 25,630 – and divide that by twenty, you get 1281.5. This is, again, a fractional number, but if you divide the new number 25,480 by twenty, you get 1274 – a round number. And there is more."

I started to scribble more numbers onto the piece of paper.

"25,630 divided by fifty-two = 492.8846. Yet again, another fractional number, disliked by the Maya, but if you take the new number with the same calculation – 25,480 divided by fifty-two – you get 490 exactly. And nine minus four equals five. Our five unnamed days again. Wherever I look the numbers keep coming up – 5; 20; 98; 5,096. The number 5,126 no longer applies and this number is calculated by adding the five unnamed days at the end of the calendar. It's the removal of those five days that unlocks the secret. The five days were unnamed for a reason. That is the clue. It has nothing to do with their calendar in that sense. They did not add those days to compensate for the solar year. There was a much deeper reason for it."

I stopped and allowed everyone to take a breather, including myself. I wanted to sleep so much but I realised I had gone beyond tiredness and out the other side again.

"I think my brain is about to explode!" said Juan.

"You're not the only one," said Professor. "This is astonishing, Stephen, and you say this came from a dream?"

"Yes. Well, kind of. I was half asleep and half awake. You know that state of being, I'm sure."

Professor nodded and kept his eyes on the pillar.

"But I need to take this further," I said, "it goes beyond this and into other realms. If you take the solar year – 365 days – and multiply that by the fifty-two years in the Calendar Round, you get 18,980. We all know this is the calculation that gives us the Calendar Round – the simplest even division of the Haab and the Tzolk'in. If you then divide that number by the Tzolk'in itself – 260 – you get the number seventy-three. However, if you remove the five unnamed days from the Haab and multiply that by fifty-two you get 18,720. Now divide that number by 260, and you get seventy-two."

I stood and waited but I was met with confused faces.

"I think you will have to fill us in on that one," said Carlos whose expertise, like Professor, was not the Maya calendar.

"Seventy-two times two equals 144," I said.

Another long silence before Professor spoke.

"The number 144 occurs often in ancient scriptures," he said. "In the Bible, the number 144,000 comes up a few times and this is also the number of days in the Maya Baktun, equal to 400 years in the original 360-day Haab. And let us not forget a circle has 360 degrees, not 365."

"It also means," I continued, "that the Calendar Round, thought to be fifty-two solar years, was not originally in solar years, or 18,920 days. It was 18,720 days, based on the calculation of 360 by fifty-two, not 365 by fifty-two. In other words the Calendar Round is not simply fifty-two *years* – it is fifty-two cycles of 360 days. You also get the number 18,980 by multiplying 260 by seventy-three, but if you use the number seventy-two then you get 18,720."

A sudden dizzy spell stopped me for a brief moment. All these numbers and the lack of sleep meant that I was now struggling to comprehend everything. Even though these calculations had come to me during the night, talking about them now was a very stressful undertaking. Thinking I was about to faint, I reached for a glass of water.

"Is there anything else you need to tell us from these numbers?" Professor asked.

"Yes," I said, "there is another calculation here as well, in reverse again – seventy-two multiplied by five, gives us 360 once again, the Haab calendar with the five unnamed days missing. It also works with the seventy-three calculation which equals 365 – the solar year. And yet another one – 144 multiplied by five equals 720. So, these calculations are telling us the significant number is five because it is the removal of the five unnamed days which is important. It is this calculation that tells us the number 5,096 is correct and not 5,126 or even 5,125, which is also another version of the Maya calendar. It brings us back to the beginning in many ways. The Maya really were pointing out something with their Haab calendar. It wasn't a rough calculation of the solar year. They were hiding these secret numbers and calculations inside it and, just like the number 666, the number five – the five unnamed days – was a number to fear. It contained their secrets and maybe the general population were kept in the dark. Excuse the pun."

"Why did you mention 5,125?" asked Juan.

"Some texts state the number of years as 5,125 or even 5,125.36 for one Sun cycle. There has never been any real definitive number."

"I can make sense of this," said Professor, referring to the previous point. "Only in the first century do we see the five days added to the Haab so that it conforms to the solar year. It makes you wonder if somewhere along the line knowledge was lost and the priests did the best they could to figure it out, but based it on the solar year thinking the 365-day Haab was the significant factor, and added those days in after they came to that conclusion. Maybe it is just a convenience that they added them to the Haab. The Haab calendar would still be out by one quarter day and they already knew the exact length of the solar year. They are not actually doing *anything* to make it accurate – the Haab calendar will still wander through the years even if it takes slightly longer than the older one. It is also possible they knew about this already but then hid the truth by covering it with the solar year calendar. The original Haab had nothing to do with the solar year at all. It has no relation to the solar year from that perspective. Like you say, it is a deception."

"And the pyramid of Kukulkan blatantly incorporates the numbers of the solar year, hiding the original Haab and forcing everyone to concentrate on the solar year. It's almost as if they are laughing at us," Carlos added.

"Not anymore," said Juan, who was reclined in his chair and had slid down to the point that only his head could be seen over the table.

Eloisa sat chewing on a piece of toast, silent and bemused, staring into space as if a ghost had appeared across the room.

"Do you have anything else, Stephen, before we discuss the implications of this?" asked Professor.

"Yes, there is more. In the general Maya calendar one Baktun is equal to 394.5205 years. We get this calculation by using 144,000 days and dividing them by 365. But once again we all know the Maya did not use fractions, so why is the Baktun a fractional number? However, if we use the other calculation – 144,000 – and divide that by 360 we get exactly 400 'years'. Also, if you use the accepted number of years in a Maya Sun cycle and divide it by thirteen it equals 394.3076 years – yet another fractional number. However, taking the new number 5,096, and dividing that by thirteen you get a round number which is 392 years. The number thirteen is also a base number in the Tzolk'in calendar, since it comprises of 260 days – twenty by thirteen – the thirteen weeks of twenty days that make up the calendar. Again it points to the accepted calendar as being a deception of some kind."

"Why is it a deception? I don't understand that," asked Juan.

"Because the Maya never used fractions in their numbering system," said Professor, understanding everything. "The fact that calculations using those commonly accepted numbers bring up fractions all over the place should have told us that something was wrong, but no one has ever questioned it before. All the other Maya calculations, like the Katun and the Baktun, are always calculations of the base twenty numbering system, giving round numbers all the way through. If you use the number 5,126, based on the solar year number 365, they come out as fractional numbers, but with our new number of 5,096, based on the original 360-day Haab, all the fractions are removed. We have to take into consideration the fact that our pyramid was built 2,500 years before the Maya civilisation supposedly came into existence. At some point in time the number was either changed, or miscalculated in some way."

"I don't understand that, can you show me?" asked Juan.

"Stephen, will you do the honours?" proposed Professor.

"Certainly," I said, but before I started writing the numbers onto paper there was one more thing I wanted to reveal.

"There is one other incredible calculation I found, and it is in fact the only fraction. If you take the number 5,096 and divide it by the Tzolk'in – 260 – you get 19.6."

"What's the relevance of that?" asked Juan.

Professor appeared totally gobsmacked, understanding the importance of this at once. I smiled and continued writing, leaving him to answer.

"The interesting thing about that number is the Pyramid of the Sun at Teotihuacan sits at exactly 19.6 degrees north of the equator."

"So are you saying these numbers are Aztec?" asked Felipe.

"No, Felipe, you're heading in the wrong direction," Professor replied. "Although The Aztecs were contemporaries of the Maya, their culture started much later, up to two thousand years later, but we do know that their huge city of Teotihuacan was not built by them – it was already there long before they arrived. In fact, the city of Teotihuacan was already around fifteen hundred years old when the Aztec arrived. That is, of course, if you believe the dates that have been applied to the site. Who actually built the city of Teotihuacan is a total mystery. No one knows who these mysterious, but obviously highly advanced people were.

I almost dropped the pen as Professor's words echoed around the kitchen. I turned around to see that Professor, Carlos and I had the same expression on our faces, like we had suddenly realised who assassinated John F. Kennedy.

We were speechless and alarmed and staring into empty space but Felipe was as confused as ever.

"Well?" he asked.

"It looks like our pyramid builders may have also constructed Teotihuacan," Professor replied.

I said nothing but turned back to my calculations. By the time I had written down all the calculations, there were several pieces of paper on the pillar and an impressive set of simple mathematical equations for all to see:

52 x 5 = 260 = the number of days in the Tzolk'in calendar.
52 x 5 = 260 = the number of unnamed days in a 52-year Calendar Round.

1 Sun cycle is considered to be 5,125 or 5,126 years in the 'accepted' calendar.

1 Sun cycle is actually 5,096 years, based on the figure given at the pyramid.

52 x 100 = 5200
52 x 99 = 5148
52 x 98 = 5096

The Maya did not use fractions in their calculating system.
5126 ÷ 52 = 98.57692307
5096 ÷ 52 = 98

The new number gives us our base 20 when added together.
5126 = 5 + 1 + 2 + 6 = 14
5096 = 5 + 0 + 9 + 6 = 20

The days of the solar year versus the Haab.
365 – 260 = 105
360 – 260 = 100 = (20 x 5)

Our new Maya Sun cycle number gives units of the base numbers.
98 = (4 x 20) + (1 x 18)
4 + 1 = 5

The calculation of the new Maya Sun cycle gives a corrected figure for the precession of the equinoxes.

5126 x 5 = 25630 years

5096 x 5 = 25480 years

The new figure for the precession of the equinoxes brings up no fractions.

25630 ÷ 20 = 1281.5

25480 ÷ 20 = 1274

25630 ÷ 52 = 492.8846153

25480 ÷ 52 = 490

(9 – 4 = 5)

The number for the precession of the equinoxes brings out a calculation of the base numbers.

25630 x 52 = 1332760

1 + 3 + 3 + 2 + 7 + 6 + 0 = 22

25480 x 52 = 1324960

1 + 3 + 2 + 4 + 9 + 6 + 0 = 25 (20 + 5 or 1 x 20 + 1 x 5)

The original Haab calendar, not the solar year with the 5 unnamed days, gives us one degree of the precession of the equinoxes.

365 x 52 = 18980

18980 ÷ 260 = 73

360 x 52 = 18720

18720 ÷ 260 = 72 = one degree

Doubling the single degree of the precession of the equinoxes gives us the figure which appears in many ancient cultures, including the Christian Bible.

73 x 2 = 146

73 x 5 = 365

72 x 2 = 144

72 x 5 = 360

146 x 5 = 730

144 x 5 = 720

The number 144,000, which appears in many ancient cultures, divides correctly without fractions.

144000 ÷ 365 = 394.5205 years

144000 ÷ 360 = 400

The new corrected figure given by the pyramid gives us no fractions, and thus the number of years in a Baktun.

5126 ÷ 13 = 394.30769

5096 ÷ 13 = 392

The fraction given by the division of the new number with the Tzolk'in calendar gives us the location of Teotihuacan.

5126 ÷ 260 = 19.7153

5096 ÷ 260 = 19.6 (degrees north of the equator)

"We must also understand that the Maya knew the exact length of the solar year," I said, "because they did not calculate it as 365 days exactly, or 365.2425 days, as we do. They calculated it more accurately – 365.242036 days. If you use either 365 or 365.242 you get fractional numbers. But if you use exactly 360 days, you always get round numbers. It is one thing I have never understood – why the Maya supposedly used a 365-day solar year but didn't add the leap year like we do. I am proposing that if they were actually using a solar calendar they were clever enough to make this adjustment."

"I agree," replied Carlos, "something doesn't add up. They knew precisely the length of the solar year but it had no importance to them whatsoever."

"I would agree," said Professor, "but when you live in the tropics there is no concern for seasons – you do not need to worry about planting crops at a certain time of year, or worry about a cold winter. They could plant maize, their staple crop, at any time of the year and they knew exactly how long it would take to grow – 260 days, or nine months. That's also the gestation cycle of the human female – they are both 260 days long. It goes without saying that if the Maya were concerned with implementing the solar year, we would see evidence of it being used. Their calculations are so accurate that they knew the exact length of the solar year but they never felt the need to use it."

"I don't understand," said Juan.

"What I mean is they understood the exact length of the solar year, calculating it to the point of stupidity, incorporated the numbers into the pyramid of Kukulkan, measured it, understood it and everything else, but they were not concerned about it. Their other calendars were far more important to them."

"What does it all mean then, exactly?" asked Carlos.

"It means that the number five," I answered, "previously 'hidden' between the Haab calendar and the solar year and stated as unnamed days that were considered unlucky, actually encodes secret information. It is telling us the original calendar is the real one, based on the figure of 5,096, and not 5,126. The later calendar consisting of 5,126 years was either a miscalculation of the later Maya, or it was used as a clever deception to hide the real numbers."

"But why would they hide it? What would be the point?" questioned Juan.

"There could be many reasons," Professor responded, "and as Stephen said, the number 666, considered to be the 'number of the beast' and feared by those in the past, actually encodes numbers of the secret geometry of nature. It is also believed that a lot of architecture and various designs encode secret information, like the US Dollar Bill and its all-seeing eye on top of the pyramid – many believe that to be a secret code relevant to the Freemasons or the Knights Templar. There are lots of other examples, too."

"So, let me get this straight," said Carlos, looking at me, "the original calendar, which is what our pyramid has encoded, is the definitive version and the later calendar based on the solar year is incorrect. So does this mean the year 2012 is not the correct ending of the Maya calendar?"

"Well, the original calendar is based on Maya Sun cycles of 5,126 years each, starting in 3114 BC and ending in 2012, but if we take the new number of 5,096 years then the calendar would have ended in 1982 – thirty years difference. However, that is assuming that the calendar started in 3114 BC."

"And if we take five Maya Sun cycles we have a miscalculation of 150 years," said Juan.

"Yes, and that would mean the calendar ended in 1862!" I replied.

"But we cannot be certain when the entire cycle started," said Carlos. "We cannot go back 25,480 years and know exactly when the five Suns started. Something is wrong here."

"No, it's not wrong," said Professor.

We all looked at him and waited. He stood up and wandered away from the table and looked out of the window. He turned around and leaned against the windowpane, his face white as a sheet.

"It never started in the past at any time. It has started now. The writing on the wall in the pyramid – *The mouth has been opened and the words are seen. The evolution has begun.* The calendar has only just started – *WE have started it!"*

"Okay, you have completely lost me," said Juan.

Professor turned around to face the table.

"The calendar ended the other day when we took the lid off and opened the pyramid – 5,096 years after the pyramid was closed. We know the pyramid was built 5,096 years ago. It does not give a date as to the actual year it was built, but it was designed so that it would be opened 5,096 years later – *exactly* 5,096 years after it was closed. The calendar never started, and it never ended."

25

EUREKA

A silence deeper than I had ever heard before hung over the room, as if we were all facing the judgment of a supreme God. Professor's words sounded like total lunacy and yet there was truth in what he was saying. The number given on the pyramid, and the calculations, undoubtedly pointed to the number 5,096. Since a Maya Sun cycle was the same number of years and we arrived 5,096 years later, it meant that the cycle was ended by us when we removed the slab. As for the number 5, 0, 9 and 6 on the outside of the pyramid, they could not be giving us a starting *year*, because there was no reference point. The only thing it could be saying was that it was built 5,096 years *after* a certain point in time. Although I was struggling to comprehend everything, it was clear what Professor was saying – whether we had opened the pyramid in 1982, or in 2012, or now in 2010 didn't matter. What mattered was that only when the pyramid was opened did the date of its completion become a reality – it would always have been built 5,096 years before it was opened, regardless of what year it was!

Suddenly I had another 'eureka' moment. I remembered what Yeshe was telling me about time not being linear, that everything was linked by cycles, and that time had no ending and no beginning. Everything in the Maya calendar was also circular – the calendars themselves and even the cogs of each calendar wheel turn when they are put together visually.

"I think I understand what you are talking about," I said. "In a strange twist of fate, we were the ones who actually ended the Maya calendar! It doesn't matter when the pyramid was built. What does the word 'Maya' actually mean? It means 'illusion'. In this sense time is an illusion. If we had arrived in the year 2000, or 2020, the pyramid would still have been placed there 5,096 years previously! Regardless of when the pyramid was built, the calendar only ended when the pyramid was opened and the words were read."

"That is way too much for me to comprehend," said Juan.

With that he stood up and went over to the sofa, quickly followed by Felipe.

"You're right," said Professor, "the clue is in the word – Maya. Why were the Maya so called? It is a Sanskrit word – an ancient Indian word – meaning 'illusion'. It is based on the fact that we do not experience reality itself, but only a projection of it, which is created by us – our own illusion. Therefore the calendar has no beginning and no ending in itself. It only ends when we project ourselves upon it – in this case, when we opened the pyramid."

It was so simple and yet almost impossible to understand, but there was a real truth in there – a truth that science itself sets as our fundamental reality, whether we like it or not. The foundation of quantum physics bases itself around the *Uncertainty Principle,* a notion proposed in 1926 by one of the geniuses of that time, Werner Heisenberg who, in many ways, surpassed Einstein himself. The Uncertainty Principle's basic premise is that if one knows the location of a particle, then its direction is less known, and vice versa. It was understood that only when a person observes the particle does it actually conform to any particular state. In layman's terms it means that only our observation of the particle determines its actual location *and* direction.

This dilemma was aptly shown in Erwin Schrödinger's thought experiment, known as *Schrödinger's Cat*. In the experiment, a cat is sitting in a closed box. Inside the box with the cat there is a hammer and a vial of poison. The observer does not know if the cat is alive or dead until he opens the box and takes a look – has the hammer smashed open the vial of poison and killed the cat, or is the vial of poison still intact and the cat still alive? But the problem is that the cat is both alive and dead at the same time. Only the observer, once the box is opened, can determine either scenario to be real.

The same principle exists with Heisenberg's Uncertainty Principle, and the basic facts are that our reality is constructed by ourselves – nothing is real or determined until our observation, or interaction, brings it into being. Strangely, this has also been the fundamental teaching of many ancient scriptures dating back thousands of years – including the Sanskrit word 'Maya' – that our reality is created by ourselves.

When Mahatma Gandhi said, *"A man is but the product of his thoughts. What he thinks, he becomes,"* he meant that our reality is created by our thoughts and actions. We attract things to us by those thoughts, good or bad. Our expectations of the world manifest around us in reality. In India this is also known as *karma*. Reality truly is an illusion. But was this the correct interpretation or was there an alternative?

"So, the calendar had neither begun, nor had ended, until we opened the pyramid," I said out loud.

"That is what I'm thinking," Professor responded, "but I could be wrong."

There was a long, drawn out silence that seemed last an age before Carlos spoke.

"I don't know. It all seems a bit weird to me."

"Yeah, like everything was *normal* at the pyramid!" shouted a sarcastic Felipe from the sofa.

"It feels right to me," I said. "I can't quite put my finger on it but somehow this makes sense. The pyramid doesn't actually give a year of construction. It just gives us the length of one Sun cycle. Everything points to one Sun cycle and the writing does state clearly what Professor said – that the words have been read and the evolution has begun – as if it is telling us evolution only begins when the pyramid is opened."

I stopped in my tracks once again.

"What does it mean by 'evolution', anyway?" I asked.

"I don't know," said Professor. "I have been thinking about that since I read it. I guess we will just have to find out."

"Well, I don't hear or feel any earthquakes, do you?" laughed Juan.

"What was it the Maya said about the end of this cycle?" I asked.

"According to the interpretation, the world would be destroyed by earthquakes, as Juan just mentioned," Professor responded, "but since everything about the Maya is illusory surely it has a non-literal meaning? Maybe the interpretation of 'earthquake' refers to something more illusory, rather than a literal earth-shaking – an earthquake of emotions, perhaps."

Something fell into place in my mind.

"Yes, I understand that. We are at a point in our evolution where everything is coming to a head – population growth, industry, the raping of the planet, the emptying of the seas, the cutting of the rainforests, mass extinction of species – all these things are unsustainable. It can't continue. And it does say the word 'evolution' in the text, so maybe we are about to evolve, rather than be destroyed. Maybe, just maybe, the evolution will occur in our own consciousness – an evolution where we change our way of thinking so that we can stop the destruction of the planet. In that sense, it could be earthquakes in our own minds."

"Sounds too perfect for me," said Juan.

"It is too perfect," responded Professor, "but then it really is the only way forward because if we do continue this way then the future for our species is rather grim. But whether that's the true message of the pyramid is another matter. At the end of the day, whatever happens will happen and there is nothing we can do about it. We have to accept we have stumbled across something by opening this pyramid and there is no point in us speculating or we will be here for another 5,096 years. We just need to move forward from here. We have done our job and now it is time to move on. Let fate take over and do its thing. There is nothing more for us to do."

Professor's words were a kind of closure on everything. It suddenly felt as if everything had come to an end and it really was time for us to move on from here. We had completed our task. We had been through hell and back. The strange events at the pyramid had taken their toll on us all. The stress had been immense and it seemed like ten years had passed in those few remarkable, unforgettable and certainly unbelievable days.

And yet, somehow I felt as if my body had been invigorated by the pyramid, as if it had breathed new life into me. It felt like I had been rewarded for completing our task – rewarded with a newly vitalised body. The more I thought about the little, seemingly unimportant things the more similar the pyramid and the dome in Tibet seemed.

I was suddenly reminded of the Holy Grail story, the one where Sir Galahad eventually lands on the island where the Grail is located. He enters a room that contains hundreds of Chalices and he must choose the correct one – the Holy Grail itself. Many knights have previously entered the room and pointed to the brightest and most beautiful chalice and in doing so they suffer death for their wrong choice, but Sir Galahad picks out a dirty, broken, dull chalice and his judgment is correct. For me, our pyramid was that dirty, broken chalice – a godforsaken pyramid in the middle of the most hostile environment where only the strong would survive, where the unworthy would be frightened away by the immense power and energy the pyramid gave off and where the paranormal events would turn any normal man to stone. But somehow, we had managed to get through it as a team, conquering our fears and carrying out the task we had been given. And we had succeeded. What we had unleashed would only reveal itself in the future – any attempt we might make to say what we had actually achieved was conjecture at best.

Whatever pride or fulfilment we may have felt now, I realised that we were all just pawns in a game created by the gods themselves. And to be a pawn on the chessboard of the gods was the greatest feeling I had ever had. It was a great honour to have been chosen for this game and I felt I had achieved whatever had been expected of me. Now, it seemed that Chang's death really had been part of a greater picture. Chang was a white pawn that had fallen whilst fighting the black demons of our own souls and consciousness, and those of the elite who keep great secrets from us in order to control us all – a fallen soldier on the battlefield of the gods – his was the death of a true hero. I owed everything to him for he had paved the way for *my own* evolution to begin.

But was it an evolution of my subconscious mind, or an evolution of my physical being? Was it an evolution of the planet itself, or a physical manifestation of reality that we would see around us? What was *really* going to happen to us – the human species – as we enter the darkest days since our physical evolution on planet Earth? I thought about our poisoned seas, a rapidly deteriorating atmosphere, the depletion of fossil fuels, broken nuclear reactors spilling dangerous radiation into the atmosphere, the reduction of our rainforests, our manipulation of nature causing imbalance on a vast scale, an uncontrollable population explosion and a million other things – all steps on a sure route to disaster of unimaginable magnitude. I thought about the fact that all this was being ignored, all for the sake of greed and profit, born of a badly designed economic system whose driving force was the greed for money. We are the most *intelligent* creatures on the planet, and yet without doubt we are the most stupid and ignorant.

While contemplating these ideas I started to wonder – where are we going? What kind of a future are we creating for our children and our grandchildren? There was one thing that was certain in all of this, one thing that stuck out amongst the chaos and confusion – the pyramid seemed to be telling us that something was going to happen, that billions of people would die because of some kind of virus. Was that the literal meaning? Or was it some kind of obscure anecdote? And if it was meant to be taken literally, then would the virus be a natural occurrence or would it be of our own making? Were we about to receive collective global catastrophic karma, or were the gods angry with the human race? Or was it all a complete and total *Maya*?

26

THE LAST STEP

Everyone was in silent contemplation. Eloisa cleared the table and Professor helped her clean the dishes. Felipe and Juan went out into the garden and Carlos was on the sofa, pretending to read a book but in reality half asleep. Joining him there, I felt a sudden and irresistible urge to go to sleep myself. My brain and body were battered and my mind was breaking down; strange visions and numbers were flying around in my consciousness, dancing around in circles and waves.

I awoke several hours later. A late lunch was being prepared and despite only having a few hours' sleep I felt renewed and full of energy. I walked to the bathroom to grab a shower, washing away the numbers that still plagued my mind like a nest of ants crawling all over me; I watched as the numbers fell off my skin and spun away down the plughole – fives, twenties... It was as if they jumped out of my mind and became solid objects, my brain needing a complete clear-out before insanity crept up on me unawares.

Lunch was a joyous affair, without a single mention of the pyramid or Maya numbers. For that brief time, it was as if none of it had even happened. We laughed and joked and talked about all manner of normal things. It was wonderful to feel that the shackles of stress and responsibility had been removed, but something was nagging me in the back of my mind. Something was missing and I couldn't figure out what it was – and then, suddenly an image of Carlos standing on the top of the pyramid came to me.

"Carlos, did you really find nothing interesting in all those measurements you took?"

"There was nothing useful, although I didn't spend that much time with them. All the measurements seemed quite usual. The chamber, for example, is measured out accurately, the shorter walls being two thirds the length of the longer walls, but they really seem typical of any rectangular shape."

"Can I take a look?"

"Feel free."

Sitting back on the sofa I took Carlos' complete measurements for the entire inner structure and the outer dimensions of the pyramid, and after an hour I was scratching my head. He was correct, there was a certain mathematical constant to it all – the rectangular halls and the chamber were accurately measured out – but there was nothing to denote a system that we were familiar with. I was about to put the paper down when a voice inside my head told me to keep going.

After another fifteen minutes my mind was going around in circles and despite the inner voice, I was too tired to continue. Placing the paper on the table and leaning my head against the back of the sofa I stretched my arms as high as I could, letting out a long, tired sigh of frustration. In a flash, suddenly something appeared in my mind's eye – the numbers of the Haab and the Tzolk'in calendars – 260 and 360. Obviously those numbers hadn't completely been washed away by my shower. I was about to dismiss them when I felt a perceptible nudge on my shoulder and a vision accompanying it – a vision with those two numbers again. On the top of the page I wrote the numbers 260 and 360 side by side. Although there was no logic to it, I knew exactly what to do next.

Looking more closely at Carlos' measurements I did a simple equation and suddenly a number jumped out at me. Grabbing a calculator I did another one, and another, and another and every time the same round numbers were coming out. Suddenly everything fell into place.

"You're not going to believe this," I called out.

Everyone stopped what they were doing and looked at me.

"Have you found something?" Carlos asked.

"Have I found something? You bet I have, but I don't know how to explain it. I think it's 'table time' again!"

Once we were all seated, Eloisa removed the pieces of paper from the pillar and replaced them with Carlos' calculations.

"Carlos' measurements are accurate to several decimal points. That's a nice bit of kit you've got there, Carlos, because if the measurements were taken back a decimal point or two I might not have noticed it."

"*What*?" asked Felipe, impatiently.

"As Carlos said, the measurements for the main chamber are accurate in that the shorter walls are two thirds the length of the longer walls, giving an accurate rectangular shape. The measurements are 6.096 metres for the shorter walls and 9.144 metres for the longer walls."

"So?" Felipe said.

I couldn't suppress the smile on my face. "You're not familiar with feet and inches, are you?"

"No, why?" asked Professor.

"Because that pyramid, inside and out, was designed and built using feet and inches!"

"That's ridiculous! It can't be," proclaimed Carlos.

"Ridiculous and unbelievable, but true I'm afraid. 6.096 metres is twenty feet, and 9.144 metres is thirty feet. And every other one of your measurements also converts into feet and inches accurately. In fact you can forget inches – it's measured out in feet alone – too many times to be a coincidence. Even the stone block with the Ptah Wand, the box containing the wand itself, the hall of writing and the first passageway, are all measured in feet. And let's not forget the pyramid itself which is seventy-six feet long corner to corner, and fifty-five feet along each edge."

"You have got to be joking!" said Professor.

"No! Even the corridors are exactly six feet wide, the platform on the top of the pyramid ten feet square and the calendar stone six feet square. The only measurement I can see slightly out of sync is the steps. Carlos measured the steps to be approximately fifteen centimetres high for each of the fifty-two, but since the pyramid is exactly 7.766 meters high, having fifty-two steps at fifteen centimetres would make the pyramid exactly 7.8 metres high, a slight discrepancy of 0.04 metres. Now, if we convert that into feet and inches each step comes out as 0.49 feet – almost half a foot, or almost six inches high – a discrepancy of 0.08 inches if my mathematics is correct. Either way, both of those measurements is slightly off a round figure."

"A little bit of subsidence could easily explain that since the steps would have been walked on. I would assume it would have been the most difficult part to make accurate, and the steps appear to have been added to the structure rather than built into it," Carlos replied.

"I have saved the best until last," I said, "but rest assured this one will floor you. Excuse my pun," I smiled.

"What is it?" asked Professor.

"The pyramid is 7.766 metres high, which is 25.48 feet."

I waited to see if anyone would notice but I was met with a silence.

"Enlighten us please, the suspense is killing us," said Carlos.

"Multiply that by two and you get...?"

"50.96" said Carlos.

"Yes. 5,096! Once again the magic number appears. I bet we'll find it elsewhere too if we keep looking."

"This is ridiculous," said Professor. "Not only do we have a written language that translates directly into modern English, but the builders used British feet and inches to build the pyramid. I give up!"

"Yes, and if my memory serves me correctly, that measurement system wasn't introduced until somewhere around the sixteenth century. I could be wrong, but I think it may have been Queen Elizabeth I who altered the system slightly, giving us the modern format."

"I do know that the 'foot' was originally from Ancient Egypt," Professor replied, "which would indicate origins from Atlantis with our new data – but then, that can't be applied here, because you're saying this measurement is from the British foot."

There was a lot of confusion during the next half hour as we tried to figure out the origins of feet and inches. We couldn't come to any conclusions; without access to data our conversation was running blind. While I hadn't really studied the history of feet and inches I was aware that the British system was introduced by the Romans two thousand years ago, but theirs was an earlier version. There was another system brought in by the 1066 invasion of the Normans, but the system in place here at the pyramid was the modern version used in Britain today. It was much later that I discovered there was another system introduced in the Indus Valley of India and also in Mesopotamia around the same time as the Egyptians, so in our accepted version of history there was no real origin of the foot measurement. It appeared to have sprung up in several places at once. However, it was the Indus Valley which produced the earliest and most accurate system. Was this once again the legacy of the Atlanteans after the fall? Had the migrating Atlanteans taken their measuring systems with them? Was the cycle coming around in a loop once again, completing another 'Sun' of the calendar? After all, it was five thousand years since the Indians, Egyptians and Mesopotamians came up with these measurements.

Either the builders of the pyramid had incorporated a modern way of measuring, which was just as impossibly confusing as the fact that their writing translated into modern English, or somehow this was an original unit of measurement that had been rediscovered or reinvented later. Either time was coming around in cycles, or there was some knowledge of the future. I could just about accept that the measurement system could have been rediscovered, but I couldn't accept that about the written language –

languages do not become rediscovered in that way; they evolve. So, there seemed to be two very weird, but very real, things happening. One was that time was somehow going around in a loop, and the other was that the future was being foreseen to a great accuracy. The question was – were they in essence the same thing? Is the future linked to the past in ways we cannot understand? And is 'cause and effect' just an aspect of our reality that is also illusory?

Bewildered faces showed that everyone's powers of reasoning were stretched beyond belief. Even the cat seemed confused. It must have been sensing the strange aura that was being created by the five strangers invading its territory. This was too much for us, too much for our mere human brains to comprehend. The next step would be insanity for us all, and Professor had seemingly had enough of it.

He had given an order that we should all stop trying to think this out, and he was right. There was nothing more we could do, nothing more for us to understand. Whenever we found more answers, they only raised more questions which only increased our confusion. Our heads would have exploded if we'd continued. For me, the only logical way to get to grips with any of this was to walk away and come back to the data sometime in the future when the dust had settled. We had more than enough information to take away with us, but what was it, exactly, that we had discovered? At the end of the day, there was too much information for us to make any sense of it all. We had carried out our tasks with great care and attention to detail, the site was left intact, and there was no indication of how we should proceed from now on. We had no hard evidence except for the photos and no way of telling the world what had happened. We certainly couldn't take the risk of revealing the Ptah Wand, so I wondered – what was the point of it all? Why was I sent here in the first place if we weren't going to tell the world about it?

"Right, that's it. I have had enough," Professor said.

"What do you mean?" asked Juan.

"I've had enough. That's it. I am going home. Pack your things everyone, we are leaving."

"What, now? Are you sure?" asked Carlos.

"Carlos, not only do we have a five thousand year-old alphabet that translates into modern English but now we have discovered that the pyramid was measured out using feet and inches. I cannot cope with this anymore. I am leaving. You can stay if you want but I am going home and I never want to hear about that bloody pyramid again as long as I live."

Professor's sudden turn caught us all off guard and shocked us, but his statement said it all – this was too much for him, and he was right. It was totally ridiculous. It was incomprehensible to the point that it really did seem like a joke. Maybe it was a set-up after all. Maybe some people had recently built the pyramid and planted all the evidence, fooling Professor and Carlos completely. Maybe the walls had actually been recently painted, as they had appeared to be. Maybe the Ptah Wand was a fake, made by a clever artist. Maybe I had been sent to Mexico to take part in one of the greatest hoaxes of all time. But then one would have to ask why? Whatever the reasons, Professor had reached breaking point and the rest of us had no real problem accepting his pronouncement. It was time to leave.

Soon we were all hugging Eloisa with great thanks and allowing her to return to her normal life. Whether her life would ever be normal again was open to debate and whatever she thought about it all was even more of a mystery, but one thing was clear – Eloisa could be trusted completely.

Leaving Eloisa's house and heading down the track to the main road there was an odd sense of loss, as if we had just been to a funeral. I was empty inside and yet I also had a feeling that somehow everything was going to be fine. The fear that for so many days had clung to my body like a spider on its web was now replaced with an optimism that was refreshing and clear and it felt as if the future, whilst it might be traumatic, was also going to be fruitful. I felt that the growing pains that are the teenage years in the evolution of the human race were over and now it was time to enter into adulthood. It was time for us, as a species, to grow up and accept the consequences of everything that had come to pass, of everything we were doing, and how we would treat the planet in the future. Maybe that is what this was all about – maybe the five thousand-year cycle of the Maya calendar was about to go back to the beginning again.

My world had changed within an evening but now it was clear the entire world would also change. What was to come, however, was both terrifying and amazing in equal measure. I didn't realise it in those moments, but the story was far from over.

We were the lucky few who had access to knowledge that was given prior to events that were to come. Why we five had been fortunate enough to witness these events in the Mexican jungle was a question that would never be answered, but I had my suspicions as to what was really going on. It is something I will keep in my heart for eternity. Only time will tell the truth of the events that are contained in this, the most ridiculous of true stories.

27

THE PHONE CALL

As we turned onto the main road and drove back towards the city the sun shone through the rear window, illuminating the jeep and filling the air with a new vibration. Everything was out of our hands and there was no more we could do to influence the events around us. Our job was complete. Our mission had been accomplished. And now, sadly, it was almost time to part company with my new friends. What we had been through, although not life-threatening, had created a bond that would be everlasting even if we never saw each other again. It was impossible to witness such events and not be affected by them in some way, and we had been changed in a manner that was unusual, to say the least. Even today, when I think of those amazing men, I feel as if we are communicating on some level or another, as if our consciousness is reaching out across the great oceans and connecting.

As we headed back towards Candelaria, it was late afternoon and the sun started to drop, creating long shadows across the open fields as the rays penetrated the tall forest trees. Where forest met road we were in shadow but as we drove out across the vast pastures sunlight struck the inside of the jeep, like a torch shining into a dark cave.

"So, what was really going on with the Maya?" asked Juan.

"We are not dealing with the Maya any more, Juan," Professor replied, lethargically.

"What do you mean?"

"This has nothing to do with the Maya. We are dealing with an unknown people who left no trace of their civilisation except for that pyramid, as far as we know. Whoever built that pyramid were the direct descendants of Atlantis – an ancient people who had technology that was way ahead of ours. The Maya somehow inherited all this stuff from them but, if my perception is correct, they may have been a little confused by it all."

"How did they get hold of all this information?"

"I have no idea. I really don't know anything anymore. Everything is wrong. I have always been confused by certain things and now some of those things make sense, but I still don't have the answers."

"What things?"

"The Olmec Heads, for a start. Despite strong opposition from mainstream science they do seem to show various races of people. I now suspect they may be related to the Atlanteans as well. Then there's the confusion of how the Maya calendar ever came into existence. Its complexities are so profound that if it was originally Atlantean, those complexities would make sense. In other words, that calendar is so advanced that I've always wondered how the Maya made such accurate measurements with the technology they supposedly had."

"So, you think the Olmec were the Atlanteans?"

"That's possible, yes. The Maya supposedly descended from the Olmec and the Olmec pretty much appeared from nowhere about four or five thousand years ago. Maybe the Maya gods are in fact the Atlanteans. I have no idea who the Maya are anymore."

Carlos looked in the rear-view mirror and, like the cycles of the Maya calendar turning back to the beginning again, it was as if I was back in the jeep with Professor and Carlos on the first day we'd met.

"Turn left down the next track," said Professor.

The rest of us had been silent since we left Eloisa's and suddenly the sound of Professor's command echoed in the jeep, returning my mind for a moment back to the pyramid. Carlos didn't ask why. We were all beyond questioning anything. He just looked in the rear-view mirror again for a moment and then turned down the track.

"Stop here," requested Professor, as we reached a spot far enough away from the main road not to be seen.

"What's wrong?" asked Carlos.

"I don't know. Something is bothering me. I just need to get out and breathe."

With that, Professor climbed out of the jeep and started to wander towards a fence that overlooked fields, the sun slowly sinking in the background.

For some reason, Professor's reaction made me remember to call Charles. Surely he must be waiting for news. I got out of the jeep and took the phone from my pack, careful not to let the others see what I was searching for. I walked in the opposite direction to Professor, towards some trees at the edge of a deep forest.

Once I was out of earshot, I took a deep breath and was about to dial the number when I realised what it was.

"Five, zero, nine, six," I said out loud. "Son of a bitch!"

My words seemed to echo through the forest. That phone number had simply not occurred to me before now. I hadn't felt it necessary to call Charles until now – in fact I had practically forgotten him altogether in all the excitement. Although it was clear to see, my mind almost couldn't make the connection – Charles obviously knew about the number 5,096. But surely it hadn't been discovered until this last week? That pyramid had lain hidden for a long time, so did this mean there were written documents somewhere that told of this place? Since Charles had sent me here in the first place he must have known about it but how much did he know? I was determined to find out.

The connection was made in a second and there, once again, was that distinctive voice that was compassionate and yet always left me feeling nervous.

"Mister Maybury. How good to hear from you. I assume you have finished at the site?"

"Yes, we have."

"That is great news! Now do you understand everything? Do you understand why you have been involved in this expedition?"

"Are you kidding? I'm even more confused now than ever before. But then I haven't really had time to digest it all."

"I thought you might say that, but it doesn't matter. In time you will understand more. In years to come, everything will make sense to you."

I took a deep breath. It was frustrating to realise that I would learn nothing from him. He was never going to tell me anything. I really was just a pawn in a game, being moved around the board by the giant hand that was Charles. Where was the point in all of this? Sure, I had been lucky to witness these events and to be in possession of knowledge that was still kept secret from the rest of the world, but why? Why, why, why? I wanted to scream out loud in frustration. And then, suddenly, everything changed.

"I assume my task is over?" I asked.

"Oh no, your task has not even begun. This journey of yours is far from over. I am assuming you have kept your diary as requested?"

Now what the hell was he talking about? I waited for a moment before answering.

"Yes. There may be a day or two missing, but all the vital information is there."

"Good. When you return to the town you will stay with Michael for a short time but soon you will be on the move again. From there, you will figure out the next phase of this great mystery. It is part of the larger picture."

"Mike is involved in this too? You know him as well?"

"No. I do not know him, he does not know me and we have never engaged in any contact. What you must understand is that people like Michael are monitored very closely. People like Michael are closer to the truth than anyone and that makes them very dangerous individuals to certain other individuals."

"How can a palaeographer be a threat?"

"He knows more than he will ever divulge, I can assure you, although it has little to do with what has happened to you recently. What you must realise is that the origin of writing can pinpoint the origin of humanity and, as you have just discovered, the origin of humanity is not as you were taught at school. Now Michael has seen that writing, he knows even more than you do."

"But if he is such a threat, then why do you want me to stay with him?"

"Mexico is considered to be significantly open to certain subjects of interest – along with Brazil it is a kind of maverick country. Michael's location keeps him out of the way of those threats. He didn't settle in Mexico because he liked the scenery, I can assure you. He is a very clever man. You will be protected if anything gets out of hand, I'll make sure of that."

I suddenly wondered what kind of danger I might be in – especially as some unscrupulous organisations might be trying to find out about the pyramid and its contents.

"You're sure you can protect me?"

"One must know one's enemy or there is no one to fight. Games of this nature are conducted in ways that people don't realise. Both sides agree with one another not to touch certain members of their army so that the games can be played out. Officers are rarely killed, they are usually spared. It's the lower ranks that are expendable. It's all a game, you see."

"Sounds like a sick game to me."

"And now you have become a player in that game."

"But I never asked to be a part of this, for Christ's sake."

Anger fuelled my words as I realised that I was in much deeper than I had ever wanted to be. I had thought this would just be an adventure. A dangerous one, for sure, but the dangers I had foreseen were more along the lines of deadly jungle diseases or fatal snake bites. I had never wanted to become a 'player', as he put it.

"What you must realise is how close you are to the truth – the truth about *everything*. Those that get close to the truth are usually killed. You know, *'bizarre accident kills renowned scientist'* – you've seen the headlines. To get to the truth, one must be protected. You are protected by me and because of this you will get to the truth. After all, this is your ultimate dream, is it not?"

I had to think about that. He was correct. All my life, all I'd ever wanted to know was the truth about reality – the truth about our world – where we come from, who we are.

"Many who know the truth are protected by secret societies or government agencies, the Church and similar organisations."

"You mean like the Freemasons."

"Yes, but one needs to attain the status of a very high degree of order to know the truth. Most Freemasons don't know anything, as is the case in most societies or organisations. They think they are just a part of a group that protects them from getting a parking ticket. What you have become is a player of the highest order. You have joined the elite, my friend."

"What about the others?"

"Oh, don't worry about them, they'll be fine, you have my word on that. Now, you need to get back into town and make a start. You need to get there soon."

"How do you know I am not in the town already?"

"I know exactly where you are to the nearest five metres. I can track your movements from the phone, even when it is turned off."

I should have been annoyed but nothing fazed me anymore. I was tired of his games, tired of travelling and certainly tired from the heat of Mexico. I had definitely had enough. My stress levels had been raised to breaking point in the last week. I certainly didn't want to continue with this, but he knew as well as I did that I wouldn't give up now. He knew I would do exactly what he asked of me. I was putty in his hands.

I said nothing and waited for his next move. When it came, it was check-mate.

"So, your task is about to start, Mr Maybury. Are you ready for it?"

"You mean I haven't actually carried out my task yet?"

"No, you haven't."

"So, you have sent me half-way around the world for what?"

"You could call it an observational exercise, if you want."

"An observational exercise," I laughed.

"To obtain a degree, one must learn the subject in detail. There must be background knowledge and experience obtained in the field before one can call himself a Bachelor of Science."

"So, what now – are you sending me a certificate?"

For the first time I actually heard him laugh.

"Your task is that you will write a book about everything you have seen. This knowledge must be released to the wider public. However, it cannot be revealed by those of a scientific background and that is why you have been ultimately chosen for this task."

"You want me to write a book?" I laughed again. "You are joking, right?"

"What do you think the diary was for?"

"I thought you wanted to read it when I got home," I replied sarcastically.

"I have little interest in what has happened on this journey of yours. There is nothing I don't already know."

"Somehow your words don't shock me, but how do you expect me to write about this? I don't have any real writing experience."

"It will come to you, don't worry. You don't need to have a flair for writing or use fancy words like those ostentatious, ego-filled, highly educated snobs. You just need to get this story out into the public domain. It will work out just fine. And don't worry about how it will be published; that also has already been arranged. You will receive further instructions when the book is completed."

"Oh yes, the man that can do anything, I forgot. Why don't you write it yourself?"

"How can I write this book myself? I have not seen the places that you have visited. You are the first people to see inside that pyramid for more than five thousand years."

"Then how the hell do you know about it?"

"Are we in England again, Mister Maybury? You know not to ask questions that cannot be answered but if you really want the truth – I have no idea what is inside that pyramid and neither do I need to know."

"You're a really weird person, do you know that?"

Once again I heard him laugh down the phone. Suddenly I must be appealing to his sense of humour.

"Maybe I am, but it does not change the situation. Go back to Michael's house and start writing that book while it is reasonably fresh in your mind. You do not have long so don't waste time. That book must be released at a certain point in time. Now go, and call me at the end of the year. You won't be in Mexico, Tibet or even England, by that time."

"What about this calendar ending in 2012?"

"Which calendar is that?"

"The Maya calendar, obviously".

"Oh, *that* calendar. That's just a sheet covering a box."

"What do you mean?"

"It's like a pretty picture on the front of an annual Gregorian calendar that you might buy each year. You don't know what's inside until you turn the pages. People have no idea what that calendar means."

"What about the calendar stone at the site?"

"It's the same thing, just quite a bit older."

"I don't understand."

"You probably have half the answers already. You'll more than likely discover the other half soon enough."

There was nothing more I could ask him regarding the calendar. He was clearly going to remain aloof and distant about it, so I changed the subject.

"Why do I have to stay with Michael?"

"You could stay in your own accommodation if you wish. You have the funds to do so, but you wouldn't receive such great home-cooked meals now, would you. Anyway, you won't be there for long but take some rest for a few weeks and start writing. Good luck."

"But how am I going to write this? How do I know what to write and what not to write? Surely I cannot reveal *everything* I have seen?"

"No, you'll probably write about fifty per cent of it. Most of the things you discovered in Tibet must remain a secret. Remember – we don't want a *revolution* to start, but the *evolution* has already begun..."

28

A SAD FAREWELL

"Son of a bitch," I yelled into the forest, disturbing a bird in the tree above my head. I looked up and saw the bird with its head turned to one side looking down at me, wondering whether I was a threat or not.

"What are you looking at?" I asked. "It's alright for you. You're free from all this crap."

My frustration was intense but it certainly wasn't the bird's fault. I suddenly felt bad about channelling negative energy towards that innocent creature.

"Sorry," I said quietly and then I strolled back towards the jeep in a sulk.

"Are you okay?" asked Felipe when I arrived. "Everyone thought you had run off, but I told them not to worry."

I nodded, trying to hide the phone up my sleeve while cupping it in my hand. It was small enough not to be noticed.

"Where's Professor?" I asked.

"Everyone is ready to leave," Felipe said, looking at me in a strange way.

It was disturbing to think he may have overheard the conversation but searching his eyes I concluded this wasn't the case. In any case, I had really gone beyond worrying – if he had overheard the conversation then so what? We would be parting company soon enough anyway.

Staring up into the sky through the trees, I felt nothing. It seemed that somehow my life had become a meaningless and transparent journey. The irony was that it wasn't even my journey, it was someone else's. The wonderful feeling within me just a short time ago had been removed by Charles's latest task for me and my new status as one of the 'elite' left me feeling even more vulnerable than before.

Watching a flock of parrots fly overhead, the bright green colours illuminating the sky, something stirred within me. It wasn't something I could explain. I just sighed, as if even a beautiful sight such as those parrots meant nothing. How did I ever get myself into this mess? But there was no going back now. I was already in far too deep. I climbed into the jeep, dejected and demoralised, and yet there was also a new feeling underneath that demoralisation, telling me that somehow, there would be a new future – a new future of hope.

Nothing was said as we returned to the main road. Everyone seemed exhausted from what had happened and it was catching up on all of us. I stared out the window for a moment and watched as the trees whizzed past, blurry from the speed which we were travelling.

We reached the plaza near Mike's house and Carlos pulled up about a hundred yards away from the entrance. We all got out of the jeep and I retrieved my back pack.

"Well, this is it," said Professor, "we will not be meeting again. Maybe in the distant future, but it is unlikely. We all have to protect ourselves now."

"What about you? What are you going to do?"

"I shall hand in my resignation."

Everyone turned towards Professor in a bewildered hush.

"Don't look so shocked. I have already mentioned this. There are others who are deserving of my position. I think this is the correct time to pass this responsibility of mine on to someone else. I have done more than enough during my years. I will head off to the coast somewhere with my wife and enjoy my twilight years. She deserves it as much as I do."

"But your knowledge is irreplaceable. How will they cope without you?"

"I will always be a phone call away if they need my help but that is as far as I wish to continue. I will no longer do any field work. And anyway, what is the point in continuing with all these lies? Everything I have worked for in the past, every piece of knowledge about the history of the Maya is wrong, or at least out of synchronisation. I do not have the energy to correct things now. "

Professor still seemed a little confused and disorientated.

"You're not going to write this up and report it?" asked Juan.

"Are you joking? I don't think revealing the existence of that pyramid is a good idea, especially with that strange device sitting inside it. Somehow I feel things will right themselves in time. I think we all know we have unleashed an unstoppable force that will do the work for us. None of us can talk about this to anyone. I cannot even tell my wife about this, so be warned."

"I don't understand," said Juan, "if you're not going to report this then what was the point of it all?"

"Come on, Juan, you are more intelligent than this. If we report this, show all the evidence and bring it out into the public domain we'll be hounded for the rest of our lives. All of human history will be destroyed. Religion will be brought to its knees. I cannot even comprehend it, Juan. We have evidence that Atlantis existed and we have evidence of a technology that surpasses our own and is so powerful we cannot even handle it. If this gets out, some bastards will go and find that place and they'll dig up the whole of Mexico if they have to. This is bigger than any of us can handle. Anyway, whoever sent Stephen here is the one who will know what to do. Let them deal with it. This is their war, not ours. It is better for us if we go about our lives and forget we were ever involved in this. It is the only way for us."

Tears filled his eyes. I could tell this was not an easy decision for him to make, but as he said – how could anything give him the will to continue after what had happened in the last week? No discovery could spark that fire within. He had already made the ultimate archaeological discovery – the biggest and most important discovery in human history. The saddest thing for me, and possibly for him, was that he couldn't take any credit for this discovery. No one could. There could be no name attached to these findings – this was a finding for all humanity. Looking at him with great sadness, I knew that secrecy was the only way to stop an avalanche of media interest.

"I doubt anyone would believe this story, anyway," I replied.

Professor smiled. "Yes, it does seem rather ridiculous when you think about it. Anyway, I cannot think to trust anyone with it."

"I trust *you,* Professor, and you three."

I looked at Carlos, Juan, and Felipe in turn. They smiled at me one by one, and with a glint in their eyes that told of a remarkable story – a story of friendship, of bonding, of fear and wonder.

This last week had been the most special of my life. Nothing would ever compare to this. We had witnessed the most incredible and unbelievable things imaginable and after sharing them with these remarkable men, this was one of the saddest moments of my life. I never actually said 'goodbye'. None of us did, for this was a story that would continue far into the future and beyond.

We hugged each other and looked deep into each other's eyes.

"What about you, Carlos?" I asked.

"I don't know. I'll just go home and take a break, I think. Then we'll see what happens."

"What about you two?" I asked Juan and Felipe.

Juan shrugged his shoulders and lifted an eyebrow, turning his mouth up on one side.

"I am thinking of getting a dusty cat," said Felipe.

With a frown and a sigh, everyone turned to look at Felipe. Professor shook his head and looked skywards. It was the most ridiculous of answers but what did we expect from a man whose mind was never where it should be? I smiled at Felipe and I think the message was that he was going to forget that he was ever involved in this and go back to his normal life. I think that was true for Juan too. It wasn't in their nature to be concerned with this episode. They'd simply had an experience that they wouldn't forget and maybe in later years they would sit around the camp fire in their Maya village and tell their grandchildren of a remarkable story – a mythical adventure that happened to some people many years before. A story, maybe, that would be passed down for generations.

"Good luck with Michael," Professor said. "I am sure you will enjoy your stay here."

"Thank you – I am sure I will too."

Juan, Carlos and Felipe climbed back into the jeep. Professor hesitated, obviously sensing that I hadn't quite finished with him. We took a few steps away from the jeep.

"I wanted to ask you something. I have a feeling your night visitor was a lie and that no one was coming to find the site. Is that correct?"

He smiled and seemed almost pleased that I had figured it out.

"No, there was no night visitor. I needed time. I did not want to go back to Michael's house and discuss this because I am still convinced we have a traitor in our midst, albeit maybe a 'friendly' one. But I did have a very strong feeling that whatever we found in that pyramid must remain there. Somehow I knew that if we took anything away, it would put everyone's life in danger. I had to give a very good reason for leaving that thing in its box, especially for Carlos. Archaeologists do not find priceless objects and then put them back."

"You're *very* lucky everyone believed you."

"Then I guess we will call it fate."

"Don't you mean luck?"

"I have used the term 'luck' for my entire career, but after this experience I realise that luck had little to do with it – many things in my life were simply destined to happen. There is never any luck in a man's life, only destiny. I knew very early on at the site that things were not as they appeared. I took off my scientific hat and replaced it with my intuition."

I smiled and nodded my head.

"Good *destiny*," he said.

With that he got back in the jeep. Carlos started the engine and drove off down the road. The dust lifted in the air, obscuring the back of the jeep as they sped away westwards towards Mexico City. As the dust dispersed, I took a moment to think but my mind was as empty as my heart. Taking a deep breath, with tears streaming down my face I turned back towards the plaza.

I couldn't agree with Professor's viewpoint and I didn't believe there was an informer in the group. I didn't want to believe it...

And then I stopped. I suddenly remembered what Felipe had said.

"I am thinking of getting a dusty cat," I repeated.

I turned back towards the road. The dust had settled and the jeep had disappeared into eternity.

29

NOT ANOTHER ONE!

"There is never any luck in a man's life, only destiny."

Professor's words were ringing around my head and coupled with Felipe's potentially meaningful comment about a dusty cat, instead of entering Mike's house I walked as fast as I could towards the plaza and the hotel. I needed to gather my things and vacate the room anyway.

Was Felipe aware of Filthy Cat? *Dusty cat* wasn't a name you would randomly say for no reason, surely? But then Felipe was capable of saying all kinds of random and stupid things. Was it just another of those ridiculous coincidences that had been present throughout my journey in Mexico? Was it a message that was given to me but which Felipe was unaware of, saying it without thinking, some higher source making him say those words without him really knowing why? By now I'd simply had a gutful of that, but something kept nagging at me. Nothing, anymore, was as it seemed.

On reaching the hotel the man on reception welcomed me back with a smile and an uncertain look of dismay. Climbing the stairs and reaching the top floor Filthy Cat was sleeping on his chair.

"Hello Filthy Cat," I said, "you won't believe what's happened while I've been away."

He seemed pleased to see me and enjoyed being stroked as the dust was removed from his coat once again. He started to purr and I stroked him a few more times.

"You really are a dusty cat, aren't you," I said.

It was yet another moment where I froze. Only by stroking Filthy Cat and saying those words did it hit home. I stood up and rapidly headed for the room.

Opening the door I jumped in amazement for sitting on one of the beds was a very strange looking man. My mind was going around in circles and a liquid blackness seemed to wash over me as I stared blankly into his face. The intuition was correct. Felipe's comment about getting a dusty cat was a code for me to return to the hotel and this could only mean one thing – Professor was correct – there *was* someone in the group that wasn't to be trusted. He truly was the most intelligent person I had ever met.

After all this, it was actually dopey Felipe who had been involved in this 'conspiracy'. Felipe, the stupid idiot who seemed to have no idea about anything, was the one who actually knew *everything*. No wonder he was so docile and laid back.

A million thoughts and images went through my mind and I couldn't believe it. Felipe, the little bastard, knew everything that was going on. I was furious. I could have killed him if he'd been sitting in the room instead of this strange man. All that fear and terror that had horrified and frightened the life out of us, and all this time Felipe had known about it.

The strange man sat on the bed and watched me in silence. He could see my mind was going in circles and he waited patiently for me to acknowledge him. I locked eyes with him as my anger started to calm. He was tall and thin, rather like Dzengin, with wiry hair and penetrating icy blue eyes that told a thousand tales. I knew this man was special in some way, almost as if he was a chosen angel sent down to earth to fulfil a prophecy. He certainly wasn't Mexican. In fact I had no idea where he came from. He seemed mixed race, with his European eyes and brown skin. He appeared wise beyond anyone I had encountered before and his fifty-or-so years belied his ageless soul. If Professor was the most intelligent man I had ever met, it seemed this stranger was the wisest.

"Who are you?" I asked.

"Who I am is not important," he responded.

"OH GOD," I shouted, "NOT ANOTHER ONE!"

I buried my face in my hands and flopped defeated onto the bed.

"How did you get in here anyway?" I asked.

"The same way any other unwanted visitor would – through the back door."

"I have had enough of all this shit, okay? Whatever you have to say, I am not interested. I have had enough. Understand?"

"If I leave, you won't get all the answers you are looking for."

"Oh right, so you are going to tell me *everything* I want to know?" I said sarcastically, raising my hands in the air like a priest giving a sermon.

"Yes."

"Sure you will!" Once again my sarcasm seemed to reach new heights.

"I will tell you why you have been on this journey and what that pyramid is all about. So yes, I will tell you *everything.*"

He returned my sarcasm in equal measure.

I sat bolt upright on the bed.

"Do you really mean *everything*?"

"Well, maybe not everything, perhaps ninety-nine per cent, but not here. Let's go."

"So, what's your name?" I asked as we passed Filthy Cat curled up in his chair. Filthy Cat seemed displeased that he was being disturbed yet again and his head turned in our direction with his usual look of *'what the hell do you think you're doing, interrupting my peace?',* but his demeanour changed when he saw me and received another stroke. Maybe it was this unusual man he disliked.

"See you later," I said.

The strange man looked at me as if I wasn't normal.

"You can call me whatever you like."

"What about 'Elena'," I said sarcastically, as we reached the stairs.

"I would prefer a gender-accurate name, to be honest. Some people call me Kalden."

"Kalden – isn't that a Tibetan name?"

"Yes. It means 'of the Golden Age'."

I wasn't surprised by this name. The aura of wisdom that emanated from Kalden suited this name perfectly.

"But you're not from Tibet," I said, hoping he might give me a clue as to his origins.

"No I am not, but where I was born or who my parents are have no relevance. And by the way, don't ask me any questions about the person who has funded your voyage, because you will be disappointed."

I was disappointed. That was going to be my first question.

"So, we're down to ninety-nine per cent already. Looks like you'll be answering all my other questions."

"Then maybe my prediction of ninety-nine per cent was far too optimistic," he responded.

Kalden never changed his expression. He never smiled and never gave any indication as to his emotion or mood. He was a professional at this and I imagined he would be an interrogator's nightmare.

The man on reception seemed perplexed that one man had entered but two were leaving. When we reached the door I turned and watched as he scratched his head while running his finger down the pages of the guest book. On the other side of the plaza, Kalden's car was parked outside the restaurant where I'd spent my first evening in Candelaria. There was nothing to note about this car. It was as inconspicuous as every other car – dusty, old and needing a bit of attention. I concluded it had been borrowed from somewhere.

As we climbed inside, Kalden did something strange. He pulled out a peculiar-looking device from his pocket, placed it on the dashboard and pressed a button.

"What is that?" I asked.

"It detects any kind of spying devices which might have been placed in the car during my absence."

"You mean, like a voice recorder, or something?"

"Yes. Or even a bomb. It will detect magnetic pulses, among other things. This is one of the most advanced pieces of equipment you'll ever see. It will even tell us if a satellite is directed at the car, listening to our conversation from the skies. Yes, they have that technology now."

I laughed. "That's a bit paranoid, don't you think? And surely a satellite doesn't focus on a specific place – it covers a large area."

"Don't underestimate what you are dealing with here. It's true what they say, you know, that the military is technologically years ahead of the rest of us. Thousands of people have been killed keeping these things secret. We are talking about the absolute secrets of everything, not satellites or military technology. I'm talking about what you've just discovered recently. These are the things that the 'powers that be' don't want the population to know about. It's time your joking came to an end, my friend. What you have seen in the last week is enough to get you killed already. That professor you were working with is well aware of this. I assume you noticed his fear during your expedition?"

"He was a little strange at times, yes."

"Then take note. Even though he is *the* world's authority on Maya archaeology and totally irreplaceable, they would not hesitate to dispose of him if they knew what he knows. This is why he will go into hiding now."

"You mean, retiring?"

"Call it whatever you like. He became well aware of the dangers involved and after his experience in Peru all those years ago he understands fully how people can be killed for the smallest amounts of gold. From the moment he dropped you off back in Candelaria, you are the only one who will take this forward. You are the one responsible for this venture now. Everything is down to you. So start taking it a little more seriously or you will be buried in the jungle somewhere. You need to get this book written and released before anyone figures it out."

"I don't know exactly how to do it, to be honest," I replied.

"You have to write it as a fictional novel."

"What do you mean?"

"No one is going to believe a story like this is true. A five thousand year-old Maya pyramid containing writing from a civilisation that most people don't believe existed and which translates directly into modern-day English! It is totally absurd. No one will believe it. That is why it must be a work of fiction. That way when word gets around about the content it will be too late to do anything about. If you write it as non-fiction, no one will take it seriously and you'll be ridiculed and laughed at. It is too controversial and you are forbidden to provide any evidence for it, but a fictional version is viable."

"Yes, but surely no one will believe it if it's written as fiction?"

"Don't underestimate the ability of people to see the truth in things. People will *feel* the content is real and they'll put the pieces together on their own."

I tried to catch him out by challenging him.

"Surely if there was a bomb in the car it would have exploded before we got inside, when the door opened. So waiting until we got in before you put that device on seems a little silly, don't you think?"

"You see, I am not so paranoid after all. Anyway, most car bombs detonate when you turn the key. A bomb that detonates when you open the door takes too long to install. In the middle of a busy plaza strange behaviour would have been noticed. Besides, I was watching out the window of your hotel room before your arrival. I am not bothered about bombs. I am more concerned with surveillance. It matters very little if I am dead but it matters if people know things. You're in this up to your neck, my friend. From now on keep your head down and your wits about you. We don't have much time, so you'd better start asking important questions and let me worry about the rest of it."

We drove out of the town and headed south towards the border, but after a few miles we turned right down a track and ended up at the end of a clearing near some farmland. There was no one in sight. We were completely alone, on top of a small hill with a panoramic view giving us more than advance notice of approaching ears.

"It's time for you to ask your questions, my friend," Kalden said, "but prepare yourself – the world you are familiar with will be no more."

PART III

THE FUTURE

1

THE PYRAMID AND THE CALENDAR

As the wind picked up and howled through a gap in the window, creating an eerie sound like a wolf calling out in the forest, I sat back in the seat and took a deep breath.

"What was Felipe's role in all of this? It's obvious he's involved."

"Next question," was the reply.

It was apparent Kalden would offer no information about anyone who was involved with Charles, or anyone connected to the greater picture, although that shouldn't have been a surprise. By now I had become accustomed to the wall of silence from these strange, enigmatic people.

"What about Juan?" I asked, trying to get at least one tantalising clue from him.

"Juan is an excellent tracker and along with Felipe works with that professor Sanchez when required. Besides this he has no involvement. Felipe and Juan have been friends since childhood. Let's just say that professor of yours has been unknowingly groomed by Felipe for this expedition for a very long time."

From this it was obvious that Juan had no idea about Felipe's secret life, but I was suspicious as to what extent Felipe was involved. I doubted he knew as much as Charles or Kalden, for example, so I assumed he was more of an on-site worker rather than one of those who sat behind the scenes. Felipe was not the kind of person I would have trusted with great secrets. Then again he played the fool to a masterful degree. I had never suspected him. Even Professor, who had been correct in his suspicion that someone in the group was leaking information, probably had no idea it was Felipe. It would have been logical for Professor to have suspected Carlos, if anyone. Felipe was a master of disguise of the highest order – even Professor, the most intelligent person I had ever met, had been outwitted by him and this was evidence which proved Felipe *was* very clever indeed.

"I assume the bowl that was found by Felipe was faked to get Professor on board?"

"That is correct. The bowl was found in North West Mexico about a decade ago. It is from an as yet unidentified culture that existed there about five thousand years ago. It is a unique piece. No other items have been found. It was likely to have been from a remote farming community."

"So, why choose Professor Sanchez?"

"I would think that answer was obvious. He was the only one capable of handling the site and deciphering the contents. He is one of the most intellectual people on the planet. His IQ is about a hundred and sixty. He is the Einstein of archaeology but he also has another aspect of his personality that is unique – he is open to experiences of a non-scientific nature and clever enough not to dismiss them. He will always accommodate them into the scientific findings around him and try to make connections between them, although he generally keeps this to himself. More often than not, strange paranormal events happen around the discovery of pyramids and ancient sites but they are not reported, and digs can create unusual phenomena."

"What about the spear head that was found near the site?"

"I am unaware of this information, so I would assume it to be genuine. There are some villages in that area. They may have known about the site but had an instinctive fear of it. They would have felt the energy that emanated from it and stayed away. Some of the local tribes, although living in the modern world in many ways, still maintain old traditions and superstitions. However, I would go carefully with the term 'superstitious' – these people are just more in tune with their surroundings than we might be."

Kalden's words were a kind of disclosure – a hint that the site emitted an energy which could be felt by anyone who came close to it. I hadn't realised how strong this energy was on my arrival at the pyramid because there was far too much excitement, but I do remember the slight reluctance and hesitation on the part of Carlos and Professor to walk the last few metres and that was *before* we opened the lid and all hell was let loose.

Certainly any superstitious villagers would stay well away from a place in which they felt an odd energy and, as Kalden said, 'village' people would be more in tune with the environment than those from modern towns and cities.

"So the pyramid gives off an energy that keeps people away," I repeated, "but how come the area surrounding the pyramid was cleared? And why was the pyramid still almost completely intact after five thousand years?"

"The energy that surrounds that pyramid is similar to that which you discovered in Tibet. Its higher rate of vibration maintains the area in a state of stasis. However, now the pyramid has been activated it will be swallowed up by the jungle. It will never be found again. The rate of growth will be accelerated almost as if a switch is turned and everything catches up with time."

"So, five thousand years of growth will happen in... how long?"

"It won't be five thousand years of growth. It doesn't catch up with time in that sense but the trees and bushes will have accelerated growth, about three to four times normal, until a state of equilibrium occurs. Although the subterranean chambers of the pyramid will remain intact, it has been designed in such a way that the top collapses downwards and inwards and once the trees cover it over it will be unrecognisable as a pyramid. That is the sole reason a forty-five degree angle was used in its construction. Anything steeper and it would be noticeable even after collapse. This is also why it has a flat platform on the top and between ground level and the platform there is an empty space inside except for a few supporting pillars. In a short space of time, just a few weeks, it will blend with its surroundings and never be revealed again."

"All that will happen in just a few weeks? How is that even possible?"

"You have no idea what you are dealing with here. This is way beyond anything you've experienced before. We're talking about higher dimensional frequencies and even that place in Tibet is nothing compared to that pyramid. Just take my word for it."

That was a strange statement for me to accept. The dome seemed totally surreal with its higher technology, and the pyramid was just a stone structure and not much different to many other pyramids. There was obviously more to this than I was aware of, or was ever going to be told.

"So, how did the pyramid *know* we were going to be there to open it at that time?"

"You already know the answer to that question – you learned about time in Tibet. Time is not linear, as we think it is, but the reality is too much for the human mind to comprehend at the moment. Let's just say universes have always existed, there is more than one universe and there are 'Big Bangs' happening all the time. There is no beginning and there is no end. The universe does not end, ever. Time loops back on itself, so in a bizarre way your arrival at the pyramid had already happened even before it was built! But what you don't want is for your mind to go crazy when you have an important task to complete. Just accept it. Time is not the way we think it to be. It is not linear and often cause and effect are not so straightforward. Let me tell you that some things you do in your future will have an effect on your past! Accept that as fact and then leave the subject of time alone. It is like thinking about what happened before the Big Bang. You keep going back and back thinking *something* must have been there before it and *something* must have created that *something* for there to have been a Big Bang in the first place. It has no end and no beginning and it never makes any sense. You *will* go crazy if you think about it too much. Past and future are very similar things so please, for your own sanity, leave it alone."

Pausing for a moment and thinking about it, I agreed that it had driven me crazy in the past when I had considered what was *before* the Big Bang. I mean, how could there be nothing? Something must have created the tiny speck that exploded into the universe. So what was it? And what was it that created the thing that created the tiny speck that created the universe? Whatever question you ask, you always end up at some point with *nothing.* Nothing existed. But that is a concept the human mind cannot grasp. How can *something* come from *nothing*? It's simply not possible. We are always taught that energy cannot be destroyed and instead it is always transformed into something else – $E=Mc^2$, right? So if, as Kalden said, there is no beginning and there is no end then Einstein's equation is correct when it is applied to the question of 'before' the Big Bang because there is no such thing as 'before' the Big Bang. The element of time is a good example of how we humans know very little in reality and do not have the brain capacity to understand many things. However, science often gives the impression it understands our reality and I am always suspicious of the arrogance of some scientists who believe they almost have it wrapped up – that all they have to do is dot the i's and cross the t's and everything about the universe would be understood. Science itself often stands on its own arrogant pedestal – but in one sentence Kalden had proved that all our science is wrong. Time, he said, was *not* linear – future and past exist at the same time. The world truly is a *Maya* and therefore no human, scientist or otherwise, will ever understand its secrets. I was amazed that Professor had pretty much understood this as the only explanation of what had been happening at the pyramid.

"Why is the pyramid almost camouflaged when you look at it from certain angles?" I asked.

"Its design is extremely advanced. Our current way of life is thousands of years behind this kind of technology. And remember, this building is partly fourth-dimensional, like your structure in Tibet."

"Who built the pyramid?"

"You are asking the wrong questions, my friend."

Kalden looked straight forward and waited.

"When was the pyramid built?"

"It was built around five thousand years ago. But you already know that."

"Why was it built?"

"Now, *that* is a question – *why* was it built? It was the last of the five sacred sites. The other four were what you may term 'marker' sites, pinpointing certain dates in the great cycles but this one was intended to be kept hidden, to house the device and to be opened at this time and closed again. Remember, certain sites exist on a different frequency. This is why you experienced so much paranormal activity at the pyramid. You could say it is in a different time. Now it has been activated and the countdown has begun. It was activated the moment you opened that lid."

"What do you mean by 'activated'?"

"It is like a clock and like any other clock when you wind it up it starts ticking down to a certain point in time. The opening of that lid started the timer and it was supposed to be opened on exactly the day it was opened. It was about three hours out but that is not a problem. That was solely down to your professor's hesitation when he started to realise certain things were going on. Anyway, in the grand scheme of things, three hours isn't going to make any difference. Everything has gone as planned."

Sitting back and letting out a long, deep sigh I scratched my head and wondered if this was all a dream. It all sounded so ridiculous and I was struggling with the reality of it all. It only made sense when I thought about the dome in Tibet being on a slightly different frequency – the fourth dimension.

"So, the timer caused the pyramid to start changing its frequency and after a time it becomes fourth-dimensional?"

"The pyramid is already fourth-dimensional. Like that dome in Tibet it exists in both frequencies at the same time but that pyramid has a darker element to it, hence the weird things that happen. The timer has more to do with events happening in the world. That pyramid has more power than you can imagine."

But, on the contrary, I could imagine. We had witnessed the terrifying paranormal events that surrounded those days and which were still haunting me to this day – dreams that were real, spinning balls of light in the trees, noises of people that were there but weren't and visits from the ancient Maya. No, nothing in my wildest imagination could envisage those things, but they happened. They happened right in front of us.

"So, what are the other four sites you mentioned that were 'marker sites'?"

"Those are the four you saw on the back wall inside the pyramid."

"Yes, but what are they and where are they?"

"You already know the answer to this – Egypt, Britain, Peru and Mexico. And then there's Tibet."

"I didn't see the Tibetan site there."

"No, but there must be six sites not five, once you include Atlantis and Tibet. In a way the Tibetan dome was the first site and the last. If the fall of Atlantis was twenty-five thousand years ago then you have five cycles of five thousand years or so until you reach today. The reason the Tibetan dome is not on there is because it still exists."

"But so do the pyramids and Stonehenge."

"Yes, but the Dome is Atlantean and it contains the scrolls, or did, and it must never be found by those wishing to use its powers."

"Why are these places called marker sites?"

"Because each one was built in an interval between the cycles – the five cycles of 5,096 years. They were built as an attempt to reconnect with the higher levels because each 5,000-year Sun cycle brings about a shift in the frequency of the planet. You could say it is like a long-term weather pattern. They were built in the places where the connection was strongest and, like the wandering magnetic pole, it appears in different places over time."

"So, with the building of these sites, did they make contact, so to speak?"

"Oh yes, they did, but not contact in the way you may think. In essence they were made to connect with the higher dimension but although they increased the vibrations of the people who were involved they could never quite raise the frequency enough so that they would return to that level. The dome in Tibet came closest because it was actually built using the technology that existed on Atlantis. That is why it exists in both levels at the same time."

"I thought it was lowered from a higher frequency?"

"It was built during the fall hence it exists in both levels at the same time. Don't assume that the fall happened overnight. It was a long process. For a time people were manifesting in both frequencies."

"I thought the fall of Atlantis happened overnight? I thought it was some kind of cataclysm like an earthquake or a meteor strike, or melting ice."

"No, it was not. That is something else."

Although Yeshe had explained the fall of Atlantis to me before, I wanted to check if Kalden would give me the same answer, for I felt it important to filter out any discrepancies.

"So, none of these cultures ever raised the frequency high enough to reach the higher dimension."

"None of those from the five sites managed it, but others did."

"Like who?"

"Like The Maya! They managed it about a thousand years ago, hence you hear rumours that they disappeared. Although at least three million Maya still exist today, earlier a large number of them raised their frequency and entered the higher dimension. Archaeologists say there was a 'collapse' of their civilisation but they simply disappeared. So did the Clovis people who existed a long time back around the place that today is called *Sedona.* It is also the reason why so many spiritual people are attracted to that place, because the energy still exists there, although like most places it is diluted to around one per cent of its original power."

Now I understood why certain cultures suddenly disappeared. In many archaeological sites evidence of habitation, from things like pottery and fires, suddenly stops at a certain point in time and there is no suggestion that the people moved to other places and there is no legacy or genetic lineage appearing in another area. Scientifically, these cultures literally vanished into thin air, but I had no idea *how* literal that statement was!

"What about the fall of Atlantis in respect of the flood myths?" I asked. "Surely the timing of the fall fits in with the melting of the ice during the ending of the ice age?"

"No, those two things have been confused. While there were places and even large towns that were destroyed during the meltdown the actual 'fall' refers to the lowering of the frequency. Many cities, what we would probably call a large village or a small town these days, were destroyed at the end of the last ice age in the great floods. These incidents have been mixed up with the fall. In a strange way it has helped to cover up the real 'fall' and keep that knowledge hidden. After all, civilisations destroyed by water are far more believable than civilisations dropping from one dimension to another, right?"

"Indeed."

"The real truth about the fall is that it was the lowering of the frequency. *The fall* – this expression relates to the emotional state of the people – the waves in the mind, not in the sea. The *waves* that destroyed Atlantis were not literal. Like many of the religious texts the story is an allegory. Atlantis was not destroyed by a cataclysm and swallowed by the sea. Atlantis itself did not disappear beneath the waves, the people did. In a way it was confused with the catastrophes that were going on later during the end of the ice age. It's a bit like a fifteen thousand-year game of 'Chinese Whispers'. Twenty-five thousand years ago the people of Atlantis lowered their frequency and by about ten thousand years ago most places that existed were destroyed by the great floods. The connection is that the end of the fall, the last stages, coincided with the great ice melt. The fall had taken fifteen thousand years from start to finish. So in that sense there were two different 'falls' but Atlantis was not destroyed, it was the lowering of the frequency – the *fall from grace*."

"So, the story of Adam and Eve is the same thing?"

"Yes but there is another aspect of that story which we will come to later."

I could see very clearly how these Biblical-sized events could easily be mixed up during ten thousand years of storytelling since the end of the ice age and how this metaphor ended up as the story of Adam and Eve. It was quite clear the story of Adam and Eve was more related to the fall of Atlantis than to a literal translation. Adam and Eve's *fall from grace* was not an act of God ejecting them from the Garden of Eden. The *Garden of Eden* was in fact Atlantis and it wasn't God who cast them out – it was they, the Atlanteans, who were to blame. In essence, it is there in the story of Adam and Eve – they were tempted to eat the apple from the tree of knowledge, and this was another metaphor.

"What caused the ice age to end, anyway?" I asked.

"There were several factors and most of them are a part of a cycle. The first aspect is the *Milankovitch Cycle*, the orbit of the Earth around the sun which periodically moves the earth farther away. That cycle is about a hundred thousand years long and ice ages occur at this frequency, usually lasting for sixty-five thousand years, followed by a thirty-five thousand year warm period before the cycle starts again. The second factor is the precession of the equinoxes, the wobble of the earth. There are also the ocean currents, mainly the Atlantic Conveyor, which can shut down, allowing colder fresh water to fill the oceans. Then there is the release of carbon dioxide and methane, which can alter over time. You see, there is never just one factor involved."

"What about extinction of species? Because I know that certain species became extinct at different times."

"Ah, I see where you are going. Some of these animals, like the cave bear, became extinct during the ice age as temperature changes killed off their food supplies. The mastodon became extinct around twelve thousand years ago as a rapid ice melt meant the Atlanteans were able to push farther north into the Americas, forcing the mastodon to retreat, and again there was no food for them since the ice age had destroyed their habitat. They also came into contact with the Clovis People who hunted them. The woolly mammoth, the cave lion and the giant deer all became extinct about ten thousand years ago and this was caused by an asteroid that struck the planet in the ice cap in north America, hence why there is no physical evidence of it.

"But this impact had a contradictory effect – the ice which had been melting and which created a corridor that allowed humans to populate the Americas from Asia now froze over again, and this has been called the 'mini ice age'. It was caused by the atmosphere blocking out the sun for a considerable time. At the same time it turned parts of Russia into a frozen wasteland. It basically altered all the weather patterns in the northern hemisphere, causing most of them to flip from one extreme to another. But the impact zone created another freeze. Some of the animals did survive and those that were left were hunted into extinction by the spread of humans who were searching for food. These animals would have died out even without human hunters, so don't feel bad about it. There weren't that many of them left."

"It sounds like the extinction of the dinosaurs."

"Yes, it is very similar. The asteroid that finished off the dinosaurs was just the end of a whole line of climatic changes, just like the ice age extinctions. One does have to question the synchronicity, don't you think?"

Kalden smiled at me. I knew what he was trying to say – there was nothing natural about these cycles – there was some kind of planned evolution that was way beyond my comprehension. The synchronicities that had been occurring during my journey were a kind of initiation into how the universe works, both on a universal level and a personal one. Synchronicity was proving to be an element of our reality that was as real as solid objects, but it was too much for me. I found it scary that cycles of life brought about mass extinctions by design, for it meant that we were not immune to this action and no matter what technology we brought forth we could not escape the wrath of the 'gods'. It was time to move on to something that didn't rattle my bones.

"So, these marker sites – is Stonehenge really twenty thousand years old?"

"Yes. It was modified various times over thousands of years but the original is very old. The problem with the dating of these sites is due to archaeologists wanting to fit things into preconceived models of human evolution. Just because archaeologists find a few bones that can be dated to a certain time period doesn't mean they can be directly related to the site in which they are found. It's like finding a camper's stove discarded in a thousand year-old Maya temple and then saying the temple must be of the same age. The other important thing here is that these vibrational frequencies have a connection with acoustics."

"You mean sound? How do they have a connection with sound?"

"Some scientists have noticed strange acoustic effects at certain ancient sites. Echo effects coming from inside stone circles and other sites, and amazing acoustics that even opera houses cannot match. These effects are the result of the building techniques used to try and connect with the higher dimensions. Archaeologists have been somewhat blind in their search for the truth for they are only looking for physical evidence at these sites. What these people did was use sound vibration to raise the frequency of their immediate surroundings in what you might call a 'trance state' and in that state they could connect, albeit briefly, with the higher frequency."

"That sounds a bit like shamanism."

"Shamanism is one aspect of this activity that is a branch of the original. Over time the connection to the higher frequency became diluted and weak and some people realised that certain substances could be used as a tool to reconnect with the higher dimensions. Shamanism became a world-wide religion for thousands of years as people all over the planet tried to connect with the higher frequency but, all too often, these substances take the individual to other realms, not the dimension they are hoping to reach."

"What do you mean?"

"We won't go into this too much but there are many different levels of existence, many dimensions and many places. These substances that have been taken by different cultures – for example, ayahuasca in South America and the psilocybin mushroom in the northern hemisphere – don't help the partaker connect with the dimension that we are referring to. However, they were as close as they could get and at least they were connecting with some kind of spiritual aspect of reality. And, for the record, these substances have been made illegal in most countries because those that control things don't want people to connect with the higher realms. They want to keep people firmly dumbed down. But that's another discussion and we are going way off track."

The conversation didn't require explanation as I understood what Kalden meant. Shamanic practices had been going on for thousands of years and every culture was using some form of 'hallucinogenic' substance (although the term 'hallucinogen' implies a false reality created by the brain, which is wrong) and they connected with the 'spirit world' by taking these plants. This aspect of our reality, which was in fact the *main function* of reality for even my own ancient culture of Britain, has been completely ignored and forgotten. But there is no doubt that taking substances was a central part of religious practices at places like Stonehenge – an aspect of our ancient traditions that has been completely ignored and removed from history by archaeologists and scientists. And it was true what Kalden said – archaeologists look at sites purely from the scientific perspective and they try to find evidence that backs up loose, if not ludicrous, theories of what places like Stonehenge were actually built for. There is no doubt that the truth will be found when we take into account their religious practices and, in the case of the ancient British, this undoubtedly involved the use of the tiny mushroom which contains the substance known as psilocybin. Many ancient sites were built with these religious practices in mind. While science tries to find practical reasons for a place like Stonehenge, suggesting that it was an astronomical observatory or a 'place of the dead', there is no reference to the fact that these people were building these sites for a different purpose entirely – they were trying to connect with higher dimensions and they were using drugs and acoustics as some of their tools to achieve this. It is that scientific tunnel vision, the idea that everything must be measured accurately, which brings about a one-sided, one-dimensional view of our history and our origins. Science by its methodical nature removes the spiritual element of our reality, crushes alternative theories and in the process *destroys* knowledge. And that, ironically, is going against what the scientific method is supposed to be about, but it is not science as a discipline that shoots itself in the foot, it is the scientists themselves – the arrogant human minds who consider these ideas to be ludicrous and who keep the rest of us from understanding our past because of the monopoly they hold on knowledge.

"Where were we?" I asked. "I'm lost."

"We were talking about the timing of the pyramid being opened."

"Oh yes. That seems like an ice age ago! Okay, so let me get this straight. We were meant to be there when we were and the pyramid was supposed to be opened at the exact moment it was opened and it started a countdown of some kind."

"Correct."

"What exactly is it counting down to?"

"It is counting down the final days of the calendar, of course – five dark days – five unnamed days of darkness until the *beginning* of the cycle. That is the secret of the number five that was hidden in the solar year calendar."

"Five dark days," I repeated, thoughtfully. "So, there was significance in all the calculations I had discovered. But only five days until the calendar ends? I thought it ended in 2012?"

"Oh yes, I heard a rumour that you had figured out all the calculations. But you also know the date of 2012 is based around the other calendar, which is calculated using the solar year."

"So, the Maya Calendar is wrong?"

"Well no, it's not wrong, it's just that it was a later copy of the original but unfortunately it was flawed. When it was discovered by Maya priests they noticed it incorporated the 365-day solar year and not the 360-day Haab even though that is there too, so they calculated it using a 365-day year. In summary, they assumed the calendar had been made using the solar year and not the 360-day Haab, so when they applied it they had to create the five dark days because they were using the base twenty. They made adjustments through astronomical observations which ended in them calculating everything correctly from the solar year perspective, but the big thing here is these are two different calendars predicting two different things."

"What do you mean?"

"The well-known Maya calendar predicts when our solar system lines up with the galactic centre, and the precession of the equinoxes. It has nothing to do with the version you worked out. The calculations were not wrong in that sense. That calendar was unwittingly designed to hide the *real* calendar – the one you worked out. The later Maya who discovered the original calendar had no idea what it meant. By making their own calculations they discovered the solar system would line up with the galactic centre at this time so they thought that is what the calendar meant, but it was a very clever and ingenious deception on the part of the makers of the original calendar. In essence, this is a calendar hidden behind another calendar. And, for the record, modern scholars have calculated the Maya calendar based on inscriptions that were used by the Maya and these interpret the later calendar."

"So, what you are saying is the Maya calendar is not Maya at all?"

"Of course it isn't. How do you think they made such incredibly accurate astronomical observations with the technology they had? This technology came from Atlantis. The counting system of base twenty came from Atlantis too. It's all to do with circular mathematics and as you know Atlantis was circular."

"So, what is the calendar hidden behind another calendar?"

"The 365-day calendar ending in 2012 is based on scientific or astronomical observations. You could say it is a 'material' calendar, but the 360-day calendar is a 'spiritual' calendar, rather like the Tzolk'in, predicting less obvious things. The 360-day calendar is far more complicated because it has many variations in comparison to the well-known version."

"Listen, I am getting confused here. Tell me – what exactly did I work out? What are these five dark days? And it is only five days from when we opened the pyramid? I don't understand this."

"What you have to understand is that these are two different calendars. When the Maya acquired the original calendar they thought it contained miscalculations. They assumed that it was a rough calculation of the precession of the equinoxes, but it isn't."

"So, the calendar at the pyramid has nothing to do with the precession of the equinoxes?"

"No. It has to do with something else which we will come to in a moment. The Maya realised the solar system lines up with the galactic centre at the end of the five cycles, and they also made a slight adjustment with the precession of the equinoxes which is why in your calendar there is a difference of thirty years per cycle. The Maya had no idea what the cycles meant but by making astronomical calculations they could see the cycle of precession and concluded that the earlier calendar must have contained a miscalculation. Excluding the Atlanteans, the Maya were the best astronomers the world has ever seen."

Struggling to grasp what Kalden was saying, I tried to use basic images in my mind to comprehend why there were two different calendars, but this difficulty was compounded by the fact that both versions existed within the same calendar! It seemed the earlier calendar, rather than being a more accurate version of the later Maya time piece, was actually predicting something different. While the later calendar used by the Maya accurately predicted the precession of the equinoxes and the time when our solar system lines up with the galactic centre, the original, definitive, Atlantean version was predicting something entirely different. But what was it?

2

THE RIDDLE OF THE ATLANTEANS

Getting out of the car and going for a walk, the world outside seemed a different place, another planet that was unfamiliar and with new rules of nature which had to be grasped before I could move forwards.

"What about the writing inside the pyramid? What does it all mean?"

"The opening of the pyramid triggers a change in the planet's vibration. With this higher vibration changes occur all over the planet, affecting every living being that exists on it. Anyone who is not in balance with the new frequency will not survive when it increases."

"Is that what it means about a virus and billions of people dying?"

"Yes, but it is not a virus as we understand it. Do you remember what you learned in Tibet about the vibrational rate of people's souls? The increased vibration, not a virus, will cause death. If a person is only vibrating at ten thousand pulses per nanosecond then they will not be in tune with the new vibration of around sixteen thousand pulses per nanosecond. The earth has already been increasing its vibration – it's called the *Schumann Frequency* – and it is around thirteen hertz at the moment. It will continue to rise. This increased energy comes from the sun."

"Hang on a minute," I said.

Something clicked in my mind and I could physically see what Kalden was telling me in pictures. The images on the right hand wall of the chamber showed a brightening sun at intervals of 5,096 years so this must be a description of the sun's energy increasing over time until it reaches full capacity. The Schumann Frequency – the background vibration of the planet itself, predicted by German physicist Winfried Otto Schumann years ago and monitored for decades – has been increasing in frequency year by year from seven hertz to its current rate of around thirteen hertz. Its sudden increase in recent years has baffled scientists but now Kalden had given an explanation as to why it was occurring.

"That is correct," he said. "Those images of the sun inside the pyramid are referencing a periodic increase in the sun's energy, rather like a long-term weather pattern. It occurs every five thousand years but increases in intensity each time, until it reaches five cycles lasting a total of twenty-five thousand years, or thereabouts, and this is what your dating system is ultimately about. However, there are many complexities about this cycle and some questions that cannot be answered."

"So, this increased energy causes the death of those who are not in tune with the new vibration?" I asked.

"This is where things get complicated," Kalden stated, "because there are two outcomes, two possibilities, and two things that happen at the same time. And then there are two further outcomes from both of those things. Just remember, as you know, the electron exists in two places at once and this is how you'll grasp these concepts. Things split off into two different directions giving a fourfold future of possibilities, but you must understand that they *all* happen. Are you ready?"

"I guess."

"Then hold on to your underwear!"

I would have been ready, if I could have comprehended what he was saying. Understanding the nature of the electron was the only way for me to grasp what was coming for this, it turns out, is scientific proof of our reality.

"First of all we need to look at the line that mentions a virus. There are two possibilities with this. The first possibility is a man-made virus. One thing that is agreed amongst those elitists who control everything is that there are too many people on the planet and since population growth is practically exponential it can be agreed by almost everyone. One thing these elitists wish to do, one thing they have been discussing for a long time is how to reduce the world's population. They have made several attempts at creating viruses to see how they spread. That Swine Flu is one example"

"That was man-made?"

"Yes. It was created in a laboratory. When they create a virus they also create the vaccine, the cure for it. I won't mention which company created that particular virus but they released it in Mexico and waited to see how quickly it would spread, and then announced that they'd found a cure for it, but they had the vaccine all along. Not only does this routine allow them to see how their viruses work but it also makes them billions of dollars in profit from the sale of the vaccine. That particular virus was much weaker than they had anticipated and it died out very quickly although it killed about two hundred thousand people. Their plan backfired because they were left with a warehouse full of very expensive vaccine. To cut their losses, they now mix it in with the annual flu jab that many countries offer to the elderly and even the young. The problem with these jabs is they are extremely dangerous, cause a lot of damage to DNA and contain lethal chemicals like formaldehyde."

"Who is doing this? Who are these people?"

"They are the people who control the world. I won't mention names, but we're talking about the owners of the banks, oil companies and pharmaceuticals. It is literally a handful of individuals. They have been called by many names – the 'illuminati' is one of them, but that's a rather commercial conspiracy theory tag. There is no real name given to them – they are just the people who run the world, and they are in that position because of the wealth they have gained through the three most profitable systems of our times, which I mentioned just now."

"This spreading of viruses is really shocking. I can't believe they would do such things."

"That's nothing, I can assure you. The worst thing is that some of the chemicals in the vaccines offered to the public actually damage the pineal gland and this stops people from interacting with the spiritual aspect of reality."

"What do you mean by that?"

"It keeps people 'dumbed down'. The closing of the pineal gland causes a shutdown of our spiritual senses, thus ensuring people only believe in a material world. You'll understand more about that later. Also, many companies experiment on the poor in places like Africa and India, giving out drugs in trials that kill thousands of innocent people, who line up for it with the offer of a few dollars from the company and with the 'guarantee' that they are safe."

"That's really sick."

"It gets worse. They have been making plans to create super viruses, ones that will wipe out huge swathes of the human population. They are even trying to create viruses that will kill off certain races, like the Chinese, for example."

"How is that even possible?"

"Well, this is the real reason for their human genome projects which have sprung up all over the world. They are trying to figure out how genetics are passed down from one generation to another. Like the Nazis with their skull measuring in Tibet during the 1930s, these genome projects are a cover for what they are really doing – designing viruses that will attack only certain races, or types, of people. If you could, for example, wipe out the Black race and the Oriental race there would be a far more sustainable level of human beings left on the planet. Or, if you targeted just the Indians and the Chinese then the world's population would be cut by a third."

"I don't believe it," I said.

This was by far one of the sickest things I had ever heard. I thought that Nazism was over but this was exactly the same concept. The Nazis tried to wipe out certain 'types' of people, like homosexuals and people with disabilities, in the hope these 'genetic' traits would be eliminated from society. It appears the work of the Nazis continues to this very day. Yeshe had never mentioned any of this when I was in Tibet.

"This sounds like the Nazi regime."

"Where do you think they got the ideas from in the first place?" Kalden responded. "They have even taken this one step further – trying to find ways of wiping out those they consider 'useless eaters' – the general working class population and especially those that don't like to work or don't conform to the system. They want to know if there is a difference in the genetic code between those that are successful and those that are, well, useless in their eyes. That's the reason for the genome projects."

"Do you think there is actually a gene that dictates future success?"

"There could be, but it's far more complicated than you can imagine and anyway they won't have enough time to find this out because in an act of pure irony it will be they who succumb to the virus. And that brings me on to the second point."

I ran my hands through my hair and let out a long, deep sigh of shock and horror. It was unbelievable to think that those we consider to be looking after us, those who are running things, could be so evil and sick minded.

"The second interpretation of the 'virus' mentioned in the pyramid is that it is natural. A virus made by the earth itself – the Mother Earth, Gaia, or whatever you want to call it. But it is not a virus in the common meaning of the term. This one is all to do with the changes in the vibrational rate of the individual. It is a natural process, and this one is all to do with the way people think. *'Bring forth fear and perish in thy self'* it says in that pyramid of yours. It has to do with that age-old saying that what we put out as thought comes back to us as real events. Karma, if you like. But when the shift happens, when the vibrations rise up to a certain level, this will take on a whole new meaning. And it is very simple – those who think bad thoughts, put out negative emotions, anger, hatred, lies, and things like this will be the ones who will succumb to the 'virus'."

"What do you mean? I don't understand this."

"Everything I am telling you is written in those two paragraphs in the pyramid. It says – *'At the end of the five a return is due. Those who are not at home will fly. The goddess must be returned to health. At the end of the day billions will die. The invaders and manipulators will be removed'.* The first line of that part is referring to the return of the same rate of vibration that existed at the time of Atlantis – the fourth dimensional state of being. The second line is telling us that those people who are not in tune with that frequency will perish. The Earth must be returned to health because she is being eaten by the cancer that is the human race and this requires the death of billions of people. But what you must understand is this – the last line is actually talking about those very same people who are making those other viruses to kill everyone! It's a race between nature and nurture, if you like. Which one will come first – the man-made virus or the natural one?"

"So, we are returning to a state of being that is a higher frequency, the same state that existed at the time of Atlantis, and because it is a higher frequency anyone who is not vibrating at that higher rate will die because their vibration will not be in tune with the new frequency."

"I could not have put it better myself. Well done!"

"But billions of people? That seems so cruel."

"When was nature ever kind? Nature is cruel. Look over there," he said, pointing at the trees, "you see how those vines swallow up everything, curling around every available piece of space? That is nature and even the very trees have to fight for survival. Every tree's seeds are spread as widely as possible in the hope that new trees will be created, whilst the trees already standing try to fight off other trees that may grow and uproot them. But you know it's not cruel when you look at the bigger picture. Let me give you an example. Which is more important – the survival of our species or the survival of the planet?"

"The survival of the planet, because without the planet there are none of us left."

"That is exactly what this is all about – the survival of the Earth itself. If we continue on this path then there is only one outcome – both the planet and the human species will become extinct. Of course, the planet may right itself, but with all this damage it could take millions of years to get back to a state of equilibrium. So, there must be a way that nature can reduce the world's population and it is intelligent enough to know how to do it. This is your *evolution*, my friend – the planet will only allow those who vibrate at a high frequency to survive, because those who vibrate at a low frequency are the ones destroying the planet. And they are the individuals who are the *manipulators* and the *invaders*. They are the ones who must go. They are the ones who have put the human race into slavery. They are the ones who keep the wealth to themselves while others starve to death. They are the ones that make people pay more and more taxes and raise the price of food while dining on lavish dinners that cost thousands. These people will be the first to die off. So, rejoice in that knowledge! And for the record, these are the people your friend Charles and others are fighting against."

"But how is that even possible? I mean, how does the Earth 'know' how to react to things? And surely not everyone who has money is a bad person? I have met some lovely, kind people who are wealthy. Surely that's a negative stereotype."

"No, not everyone who has large amounts of monetary wealth is a bad person, you are correct, but let's just generalise for the sake of comprehension. And let me also tell you poor people will also die in the virus. What is going to happen has nothing to do with wealth in that sense, it's all to do with how people think. What people don't realise is that Planet Earth is a living being. It has a consciousness. Not a consciousness like our own, but rather like a plant, or even like that place in Tibet. A plant will react to certain stimuli, like sunlight or water. Let me give you a good example. Giraffes like to eat the acacia tree. They like to eat the leaves of the acacia tree but a giraffe would, in normal circumstances, stay at the same tree and eat all the leaves until there is nothing left. That means the tree will die, and in time there will be no food for the giraffes to eat. In one of those wonderful balances of nature the acacia tree, when the leaves start to be eaten by the giraffe, releases a substance into the air called 'ethylene'. This chemical travels downwind and alerts other trees to the arrival of the herbivores. Once this signal is given the acacia trees start producing leaf tannin in quantities that are poisonous to a giraffe. The giraffe knows this so it will only eat a few of the lower leaves and then it will move on to the next group of trees. The giraffe is even clever enough not to eat the leaves from the trees that are downwind. This natural balance ensures the survival of both the giraffe and the acacia tree. Now, not only is this a good example of how nature is in a perfect balance, but the acacia tree is also an example of how the earth reacts to a threat over longer periods of time. You can also see from this example how human activity can completely destroy natural balances by just the simplest of interventions."

It was a disturbing situation. If the acacia tree reacts in such a way from just a few leaves being eaten then imagine how the entire earth could react to the massive destruction we are causing – all that oil being removed and spilt, all those trees being cut down, all that pollution in the seas, all that radiation leaking from various places, and all the life being destroyed. We have, without question, more than disturbed the natural balance on the planet. So maybe we deserve some kind of retribution?

"However," Kalden continued, "you must also understand that although the consciousness of the earth is like a plant and since everything living on the earth is, in a way, alive *because* of the earth, then the earth has the collective consciousness of all the creatures living on it. The earth is a part of us and vice versa. When we 'hurt' the earth, we hurt ourselves."

Looking on the ground I noticed an ant walking over a bit of bark that had crumbled away from a fallen tree. I picked it up and watched as the ant wandered across its surface, and when it reached the edge I turned it over as the ant continued walking along. I could have done this all day and the ant might be none the wiser but it made me think about this ant living in its world. It is a world we are unaware of and care little about. We walk across the land, crushing ants beneath our feet without realising and then huge machinery comes along and destroys the entire habitat of not just the ants but thousands of small creatures that we care nothing for, and yet they also have a part in the balance of nature. And what is all this for? So we can have a nice wooden table in our room or so that soya bean farms, which we don't really need, can be planted in the cleared forest.

Suddenly the irony of Lasya's pandas became apparent and it was almost comical. Her pandas, it turned out, are the earth itself and we human beings are the ones who must be sacrificed to save it.

3

THE SHIFT

Breaking off once again to gather my thoughts, another thing clicked inside my head; something Yeshe had told me. He said that certain souls would not be allowed to enter the dome, and that ninety-five per cent of the planet was filled with souls called 'Yhevics' – people who were incarnated after the fall of Atlantis. It is these souls who have been responsible for the carnage wreaked on the planet – the oil extraction, the industrial age, the cutting down of the forests and the era of waste.

"So does this mean that all the Yhevic souls will die off and the original Atlantean souls will survive the changes?" I asked.

"No, it doesn't. If this shift had happened many years ago then that would have been the case but all souls have been given a chance to prove themselves through repeated lives. The question is; how many of them have learned the lessons?"

"It still seems extremely sad that people I may know, including myself for that matter, may die. It seems too simplistic and surely it's not the fault of a person which soul group they may belong to?"

"It's the cruelty of nature again, isn't it, and no one has really listened to those great teachers, have they? I mean, what was the message of the messengers – the Buddha, and various others? It's all about helping others and having a lack of selfishness. How many people are really like that? Now don't get confused with religion here because religion is the curse of humanity. It has nothing to do with religion. Most religious people are hypocrites of the highest order. Religious people often don't do good deeds because they are genuinely like that, they do good deeds because they think they are getting Brownie points from their god, or that their good deeds will guarantee their entry into whatever passes for a positive afterlife. Either way their reasons are selfish or born out of fear. And then you have those people who hide behind religion – on the outside they are the pillar of the local community but behind closed doors they abuse children, for example. Just remember that what you put out comes back to you. I have no sympathy if either you or anyone else you know succumbs to the 'virus' when it comes.

Anyone can change their rate of vibration and survive this thing. It's up to them."

"That seems a bit harsh, Kalden."

"I am not here to be kind. I am only here to tell you the truth. There has already been an example of this virus in our history. Back in the fourteenth century, Europe was decimated by a disease known as the *'Black Death',* later identified as the Bubonic Plague. Half of Europe was wiped out by this disease and millions of people died. But have you ever noticed anything strange about this disease? Have you ever wondered why so many people were afflicted with this disease and yet others were able to wander among the dead, the dying and the infected without catching the disease at all?"

"No, I have never questioned that. I just assumed they had a natural immunity."

"Amazing what people never think about, isn't it. The fact is whatever it was that was killing all those people was not Bubonic Plague at all – it was something else. It was something that was affecting some people but not others. Bubonic plague is highly infectious and will attack anyone who comes into close contact with it. It is one of the most lethal diseases known to man. Thankfully it has now been virtually eradicated but outbreaks do still occur and it can be cured with a course of antibiotics. However, it wasn't the poor rat that was causing the disease of the fourteenth century – it was something else – it was the earth itself putting out a frequency to reduce the population. In physical terms an illness or disease manifests in our bodies – a physical illness – but the actual cause of the Black Death was a different vibration of the earth's frequency. It did not originate in fleas or rats. The poor rat was given a bad name but the Black Death did also occur around that time. Like the hidden Maya calendar, the virus that was caused by the earth's change in frequency was hidden behind the mask of Bubonic Plague. If that disease had never happened, then the world would have a much larger population than it has now. And this is about to happen again – but on a different level entirely."

"So, the Black Death was a natural virus caused by a frequency change in the planet."

"Yes. But this new virus will be worse because it won't be an increase in the Schumann Frequency – it will be caused by the sun itself, which is far more powerful. Things will become very complicated for you now, because I will tell you the other aspect of this situation, the other outcome."

"What does that mean?"

"Just keep in mind, as I mentioned, there are always two outcomes. Because of the nature of the electron, and thus our reality, there is another scenario that plays out. It's an alternative version that happens at the same time. While things have been stable for some time at this level, the new increased vibration will cause a split in reality. So, in one reality those of a lower vibration will die off and those of a higher vibration will witness these events, that which will be termed a 'virus'. But the alternative version will also be played out. In that reality the increased vibration causes a split in humanity – while the people vibrating at a higher rate will return to the state of the fourth dimension, the lower vibrational people will be stuck in this reality. The earth will literally split into two versions of itself, both existing but they will be invisible to each other. What people will physically see is exactly what happened during the fall of Atlantis but while Atlantis was disappearing in front of people, this time it will reappear. Remember the electron is both a wave and a particle – spirit and matter – both existing at the same time."

"So, you are saying that two versions of reality will exist at the same time? How is that possible?"

"Keep in mind the nature of the electron in that it exists in two places at once – both realities exist at the same time but are invisible to each other. The other aspect is that you won't know which reality you will enter into until you decide for yourself."

"You mean, like Schrödinger's Cat – we don't know if the cat is dead or alive until we look in the box."

"That is it, exactly. You can choose the spiritual path or the material path – the wave or the particle. The idea that we create our own reality will take on a whole new meaning. That which we call karma will be almost instantaneous in some ways. Because the way we think determines our future and our vibration, each individual soul must make a decision as to which reality they will enter into. Although it is purely subconscious, the way we think will determine our future – we will create our future for ourselves. All those things that were happening in the past – moving huge blocks of stone and feats of magic – will be available again because the higher vibration will increase the energy available. When the actual split is occurring, people will be able to manifest matter from the aether by thought alone, turn bread into wine, levitate, and all these things that are considered science fiction today but were a normal part of our reality in the past. That is the line in the writing that says *science and magic will coexist.*"

"So, when the frequency of vibration starts to increase these things that were considered magic in the past will be happening as a normal part of our reality?"

"Yes. And also in that reality, while the split is occurring, those that are on the lower frequency will witness those people moving into the higher frequency. They literally disappear in front of them. Since the reality splits into two, people starting on the higher vibration will be able to materialise and dematerialise at will – shifting between the two realities until the end of the changes. These people are what we call the 'vanguard', as they will be trying to get others to raise their vibration high enough to join them in the higher frequency. But so many people will fear this, so many will be terrified of seeing these things happen, it is actually this feature that causes the split between people in many ways."

"How does that work?"

"Those that embrace the new reality will naturally rise up. Those that go into fear mode will not. You could see it as a weird version of Darwin's natural selection but in a different way. It's that line again in the pyramid which says *'bring forth fear and perish in thy self'*."

"So, they cause their own downfall by their internal fear?"

"That is exactly true, yes, but this is slightly different than the line which says *dream heaven or hell and reality will be this.* The former of those two lines is referring to the actual shift and the latter is referring to those that will die in the virus. It's the same thing happening at the same time but in two realities."

"I don't understand the difference."

"In one reality people will literally die in what could be termed a 'virus' epidemic, whilst in the other reality the people will be left to perish on the vibration that is existing now. The planet must raise its vibrations to survive and evolve as a planetary being. The one that exists now – the third dimensional version – will be a ghost image of the planet when the other version raises its vibration. The best way to understand this is to think that that earth is a chrysalis that will burst forth into a higher reality, leaving the shell behind – the earth will turn into a beautiful butterfly. Those who are left on the shell will perish in that reality. In both versions the entire planet is being transformed. Those that are living on the planet have a choice – either now in this life, or maybe the choice has been made through many lifetimes."

"I thought that the original Atlantean souls were able to make this transformation?"

"Most of them will, yes. Those that have been destroying the planet for so long will perish and whether you see that as cruel or not I care little about."

I couldn't really see anything at this point. My mind's eye was blind from being overloaded with all of this information. It was so ridiculous it was hard to believe and yet there was something in Kalden's story which made total sense – everything was already known about. All it took was to put the pieces of our reality together and it made sense but it took a concentrated effort to understand it because what I had to do was bring science, philosophy and spirituality together into one. Only then was it understandable. Only when one saw the whole did the image of reality manifest. For example, cementing the ideas that our thoughts create our world and that the electron exists in two places at once – two philosophies independent from one another from completely different sources – only when I brought these ideas together did they make sense. And that is how the future will be. The writing was correct – science and magic must coexist. At the moment science is too far from spirituality and spirituality is too far from science. I could see that by marrying these two subjects Schrödinger's cat would no longer be dead *and* alive – it would be one or the other and bringing the two subjects together allows for one of those realities to exist. That is what the writing is trying to tell us – once we, as a species, decide which reality we wish to live in then we would create that reality for ourselves. We would no longer be living in a reality of possibilities – the fourth dimension offers a more distinct and determined future. Therefore Schrödinger's Cat would either be dead *or* alive, not dead *and* alive – our decisions will become final.

"And this is what is meant by *the evolution has begun,*" continued Kalden, "it's the next phase of the evolution of our species, but it's not a physical evolution, it's a spiritual evolution. We evolve beyond the physical realm and back into the etheric realm. It's a natural process that exists throughout the universe but you must understand this is a planetary evolution *and* a human evolution – it's not just the human species evolving, it's also the universe itself."

We were still walking at a steady pace but long before the car had disappeared from view. Along a track that headed down towards a farmhouse I took a few moments to try and comprehend how our future would evolve. It was almost impossible to understand that two completely different things would happen to people at once and then a thought struck me – what about God? Was science correct in its continued measurements which stated that

God cannot possibly exist, or were the religious groups correct that there was indeed a God responsible for the entire universe and our very being?

Which one was correct – science or religion, the particle or the wave?

4

THE SOURCE

"The problem with God is the interpretation of what it is," Kalden said. "We seem to have this inbuilt idea that God is in some way similar to us, especially in regard to its consciousness. We assume that God thinks like we humans. What we know about God is this – there is what is called a 'source' – that thing which is conscious and exists throughout the entire universe. It is the creator of the universe, certainly, but also it is so far beyond our comprehension that we fail to understand the basics of what it is."

"So how does God come into the equation of these changes that are going to occur?"

"It doesn't. God is completely neutral on these matters. Everything is down to our species, both collectively and individually. The reason these events are coming to fruition is simply a state of the evolutionary path of both human beings and planet Earth. What happens to individual people is down to them as individuals and again I stress that this is to do with the way people think. We have had enough lives to sort ourselves out in some form or another. What you must understand is that a being, a soul if you like, leaves that state of consciousness that is God and eventually returns to it. That is the sum total of God's involvement."

"He just leaves us to it?"

"*It* leaves us to it – there is no sexual ambiguity – God is neither male nor female. You have to understand that although we separate from the source during our own personal creation, we return to it at the end of a great cycle – the *end* of the universe. Although, in reality there is no end, so don't get confused. What people fail to recognise is that since the entire universe is God, then everything that exists in it is also God – and that includes inert objects. Every single atom in the universe – be it inside a table, a car, a person, or a planet – is God. It's all one thing."

"Then how do we become separate from God?"

"We are never separated from God because we are all God! But the process is a simple one when you are referring to the soul. The soul of an individual person is like a stone that you drop from a height. When it hits the floor it smashes into hundreds or even thousands of pieces. Each one of those pieces is a conscious life that the soul must live through. When the cycle is complete all those lives coalesce into that stone and it becomes whole once again, and then it returns to the source itself, rather like a baby reuniting with its mother after a long journey. The experience of each individual soul is to learn everything imaginable in the universe and in our reality that is love, hate, violence, fear and all the other animalistic emotions, as well as soul emotions. The human state is a very basic one compared to the millions of possibilities, and I can assure you no one can comprehend the magnitude involved. For the record, crystalline structures are the most intelligent beings in the universe. They exist in many of the dimensions, from the third dimension all the way up to the ninth dimension, and can communicate between the dimensions. Some planets have only crystalline life on them. Trust me when I say that the universe abounds with wonders you cannot imagine."

"How many dimensions are there?"

"There are eleven in total. The Source is the eleventh dimension. In religion there seems to be a perception that between us and God is nothing, so that there can be a direct connection between the two, but in fact there are many levels of existence, many ways to experience the universe. Life is not so simple."

"So the religions on earth have misinterpreted the idea of God?"

"Well, you would have to ask every individual person's view of what God is to answer that question because I guess everyone has their own personal viewpoint, but the religions that enforce ideas have it wrong, mostly. Many do not propose or enforce religious tolerance and instead create division amongst people but the basic messages written in religion are decent and fair."

"But they aren't the ideas of God."

"No, God has never been here. I mean it's here all the time, it's everywhere and in everyone and in everything, but the source has never popped its head in and said *'hello'*. All the religious teachings are written by the hand of Man. All the religious personalities were perhaps decent people who tried to give the ideas of how we should treat each other and what rules we should abide by. After all, *thou shalt not kill* isn't a bad idea because you only end up harming yourself and, more importantly, the source itself."

"So, what is the source? I mean, what does it look like?"

"Nobody knows. It could be a giant lobster for all we know but you are missing the point – you are God, I am God, we are all God, and everything in the universe is God."

"What do you mean by that?"

"Reality is an illusion. It is actually like a mirror reality. Since the universe is consciousness it tries to manifest itself wherever possible in the physical realm in the form of living entities. When you are asleep, you return to that universal consciousness realm to 'download', if you like. Everything that has happened in your waking day is recorded and then downloaded into your spiritual memory. You could say life is like a football match – when you are asleep you are in the changing room, receiving instructions on how to perform in the match, and what duties to carry out. When you wake up you are a player in the field – the stadium of life. The sports stadium is somewhat an illusion, is it not? Tens of thousands of people watch you perform on the field and you try not to make mistakes. It is an illusory world – a game. When you reach half time or the end of the match you return to the changing room to recharge and take rest, and to take further instruction for the second half, or the next match. Life is like that – the stadium – the illusion of performers. But the real world is back in the changing room – in spirit. Consciousness is the real reality and where you are truly judged – your own mind."

I had never heard life being compared to a football match! But it made sense, and it could be compared to any other sport. It was a funny analogy but one that struck a chord with me, especially the part about the changing room – our sleep or death – being the real reality.

"So, the judgement that is spoken of in the Bible is not a judgement by a God, but a judgement of our own self?" I asked.

"Of course it is. Since there are no 'gods' in that respect how can they judge you? And surely the only one who knows you is you? How can someone else judge you, God or otherwise, when so many things are dependent on what has happened to you? How can there be a set of rules that apply to all living beings when everyone sees the world differently? The only fair way is to judge yourself. When people have a 'near death experience' and talk of their life being flashed before them, they are being shown their own faults and allowed to decide for themselves what they did wrong and what they did well. There are basic rules of course, such as the Ten Commandments – although only three of those are spiritual rules, the rest are designed by Man – obvious basic rules that everyone should adhere to. But most other elements are the different ideas that exist between people, which are often caused by different upbringings and different views on life. What you have to understand is that since everything is consciousness, including yourself, then how can you be judged by something else? It is all the same thing – *everything is consciousness*. People really don't understand that – *we are all gods, we are all God, we are all consciousness and we are the universe as the universe is us. We are a physical manifestation of the universe itself and the universe is a reflection of us*."

It was so simple and obvious. It was a statement of the fundamental laws of the universe. So many people look outside of themselves for explanations and reasons, without ever once looking within. People want to find a reason that exists outside them, so that they don't have to take any responsibility for their actions. Some people blame others for things that are in fact their own fault. For example, a mother might blame a child for knocking a cup of coffee off the table and onto the floor, shouting at the child for being unobservant when, in fact, the blame is attached to the mother for placing the cup too close to the edge of the table. The funny thing, though, is that people worship a God and even fear that God. From what Kalden was saying, in essence they fear themselves.

"In reference to the changes that are coming, what about religious leaders?"

"They'll be going down with the others in the first wave."

I was totally confused by this. "Surely religious leaders are decent and kind?"

"Are you kidding?" Kalden replied. "They are warped individuals who are just as power hungry as world leaders – but please understand I am talking about the few at the top, not all of them. Most of them, you're right, have good intentions. But those at the top have controlled the masses for more than two thousand years with fear and punishment and pure lies. Many organised religions are rife with paedophilia and to make matters worse they know the *real* secrets. They keep those secrets from everyone to maintain their power."

"You mean like Jesus having children, that kind of thing?"

"Jesus? Jesus of Nazareth? He was nobody! Whether he had children or not is of no relevance and the Church knows this. I can tell you the truth about Jesus and it is relevant to our discussion. The one that is known as Jesus of Nazareth, or Jesus Christ, was not the poor *'son of a carpenter'*. The words were manipulated and changed to conform to the aims of the early Christians. Jesus' title was actually *'son of a master of the crafts'*, which is completely different. The first one implies poverty but the second title, the real one, was given to someone of high standing in society. This is because his father, the real influence on his life and the man responsible for his position was a magician – Joseph of Arimathea."

"Joseph of Arimathea was Jesus' father? I thought he was his uncle."

"Yes. Mary was the wife of Joseph and was his mother, and Joseph was his father. Don't you think it's a bit strange that both his parents *and* his uncle and aunt were called Mary and Joseph? Joseph of Arimathea was one of the richest men in the world at that time. He made the equivalent of billions from importing tin from Britain and he had a base in Glastonbury, hence all the myths of his visits there. Tin was the gold of the day back then. He also had an entire fishing fleet, hence the connection between Jesus and fishing, and Jesus spent much of his life in Tibet learning the spiritual crafts, paid for by his father, hence the so-called 'missing years' in his life. But what you must understand is the real secrets that have always been hidden by the Church. The word 'Christ' comes from the word 'Christos' – the energy of the sun."

"Christos. What is that?"

"It is literally the *spiritual* energy of the sun – the unseen energy that allows life to thrive. In fact it is this energy that is responsible for raising the vibration of the planet. It is this energy that is responsible for everything, even the virus. It is also what is being shown on the wall inside that pyramid – the increased amount of the sun's rays in each image is referencing the increased spiritual energy from the sun, which we discussed earlier. Five thousand years ago the sun increased in intensity, as it did five thousand years before, and as it is doing now. It was during these times that the marker sites were built, trying to capture the energy that is given off by the sun. This energy has been called 'Christos' energy. It is the Christ Monad, the spiritual energy of the sun. It is also the energy that allows the Ptah Wand to function. It's all about aligning oneself with that energy. Prior to the time of Christ this energy could be collected and stored and used to create feats of magic. It was also the energy that was stored in the Ark of the Covenant, hence the great power it had."

"The Ark of the Covenant contained Christos energy?"

"Yes, and it becomes extremely powerful and dangerous if it's in the wrong hands. It was the ancient Egyptians who created the Ark of the Covenant. Their pyramids were created to focus Christos energy into the chambers and then it was stored in the Ark. Pyramids by their shape focus energy onto a certain point. Pyramids sprang up all over the world but only the Egyptians mastered the technique of storing Christos energy."

"So, it was the Egyptians who created the Ark of the Covenant and it was also the Egyptians who passed on the story of Atlantis to Solon."

"Yes. Now you're making the connections. It was the Atlanteans who originally accessed the Christos energy and that knowledge was learned by the ancient Egyptians a long time ago. I'm not talking about the Egyptians from the Old Kingdom – I'm referring to the original Egyptians who created the sphinx ten thousand years ago. Although the Christos energy was more freely available in those days, by the time of Jesus only the wealthy were able to gain access to it. This is why Jesus was known as 'Christ' – because he had access to Christos energy and this was why Jesus' powers were supposedly that of God – the facts were manipulated by the early Christians. Of course, the masses were unaware of the Christos. Now, as then, the secret is kept within a few closed circles."

I laughed out loud.

"So, Jesus was just a magician – a son of a master of the crafts! But what about all the teachings he created – all the things that make him the *Son of God* in the Bible?"

"Having access to the energy of the Christos allows you to do things that could also be done during the time of Atlantis – levitate, move blocks of stone, and so on. In the days of Jesus Christ there was a prophet on every street corner but since Jesus had the Christos energy he was able to perform what people considered feats of magic – miracles – and thus they believed he was special. The Christian movement spread the belief that he was the Son of God but all he was doing was using magic."

"So, he basically bought the title?"

"In a way, yes he did. There was a huge movement going on back then and people were fed up with Roman rule so they created a new religion using the secret energy of the Christos and pulled the wool over the people's eyes with the tricks they created. Those twelve apostles sitting around the table with Jesus were in fact a bunch of rich kids who created the entire movement. Funny, isn't it?"

I wanted to laugh, but found it difficult to be amused by the idea. It showed exactly how religions or ideas can be manipulated by a few people who are determined to control the masses.

"So this is the secret that the Church knows about? How do you know about it?"

"Yes, this is their real secret but they like to keep their power. One has to laugh when people rally around leaders of Churches as if they have some authority over them. Take the Catholic Church, for example. Who is the Pope? He's just an elected person, like a government leader. He is no one special. They don't even allow women to become Pope. Do you think Jesus or God discriminates between man and woman? Funny, isn't it! Mary was supposedly the vessel for the Immaculate Conception and the most revered woman in the Catholic tradition. The Virgin Mary is worshipped by the Catholics and yet they don't allow women to become Pope! Such hypocrisy – and the masses lap it up without even thinking about it. The thing that makes me laugh the most is that people are so weak that they need a Church in the first place to connect with God! God is in everyone and yet the Christian religion, for example, says that the only way to God is through Jesus Christ. That alone should alert you to the fact that this is a group of people, an organisation, who want to control you or obtain wealth from you. 'Come to us and we'll show you the correct way to God'. It's utter stupidity! Connections for the weak minded, candy for the child."

Kalden was right. Why did people turn to organised religion to find God? Is it the fear of loneliness? Being in a group with similar minded people is certainly what I would consider 'flock behaviour'. Is this how people think? Are we humans so weak that we need others to guide us? Can we not find the God which exists within? Some people even identify themselves with others of the same religion by wearing the same clothing. It was obvious from what Kalden was saying the mistake that people make is they think that God is *external* to them when it is *internal*. I also remembered what Anjali had said about the way she was brought up by her parents – that we are all individual souls who walk the path alone. Was she trying to tell me the same thing? Was she trying to say that God exists in all of us and we don't need other people or religion to fall back on? And did she understand that our souls are on a journey that would determine our survival, independent of relying on others for support?

"And look what these religious groups have done in the past, like the Spanish," Kalden continued, "all over Central and South America people were slaughtered in their thousands if they didn't conform to Christianity. This outright murder is in complete contrast with what the Bible says. And please don't get me wrong – there is nothing bad in religion – it's the people who control the religion that are the problem. Man himself is the criminal here, not the religious texts or the idea of God."

"How do you know these secrets?" I asked, fully expecting the subject to be swiftly changed.

"We have the original written texts from Simon Magus, the founder of the Gnostics. In fact, they are the only original texts from that time that speak the truth. Simon was a part of the group along with Jesus and the other twelve, but he was ousted by them as a 'heretic' and has even been labelled as the Devil himself. However, the truth is a little different. Peter the Fisherman was jealous of Simon Magus' powers. Simon had understood how to use the Christos energy to its full potential but wanted to use it for good purposes. Sure, people like Jesus could heal the sick and perform other remarkable feats but Simon Magus wanted to allow the power to be available to a wider audience. The group didn't agree and one day, when Simon was levitating in front of a group of people, Peter used his own magic to bring him crashing down to the floor. He broke his hip and this eventually led to his death. In the meantime, though, Simon Magus came up with a different philosophy – Gnosticism – that was not so concerned with controlling people. If history had been different and the group of thirteen not so power hungry and selfish then it's possible that Christianity may not have got off the floor in the first place and Gnosticism could have become the dominant religion. Basically what Simon Magus wanted to do was share the knowledge of Christos energy so that everyone could have access to it but the Christian, or Christos, group wanted to keep it secret. After all, if the secret got out then their plan to enforce the idea that Jesus was the Son of God would have been in ruins."

"It was a plan to enforce that idea?"

"Well, more a conspiracy. It was an idea that came from normal people that the group used and magnified greatly. They saw how they could use this idea to create an uprising against the Romans and rid themselves of Paganism. They wanted the idea of monotheism to take hold which, incidentally, originated in Egypt with the Pharaoh Akhenaton."

"What about Jesus' crucifixion, was that a part of the plan?"

"Yes, and this is the greatest genius of their plan. The group planned and executed a military-style manoeuvre that was highly risky at the very least. The Romans knew they had the Christos energy and wanted to gain access to it – to find the Ark of the Covenant. They had been trying to find the group for that reason. Judas agreed to inform the Romans where Jesus was. When they arrested Jesus, they crucified him because he would not reveal where the Christos was being stored. The ingenious part of this was the group knew Jesus would be crucified, so while he was on the cross they gave him a drink they had pre-prepared. In this drink was a drug similar to what is used in the Voodoo religion to create 'zombies'. After a few hours of drinking this substance the person appears to be dead. Once the Romans agreed that Jesus was dead, after piercing him in the abdomen, they allowed his body to be taken down from the cross. He was taken to the tomb where Joseph of Arimathea, Jesus' father, used the Christos energy to awaken him again. The group then used that to their advantage by saying Jesus had risen from the dead and this proved that he was the Son of God."

"That's one hell of a risky plan."

"It was, but since they had the Christos they knew they could revive Jesus easily enough. He suffered horrendously in a physical way but it was all worth it from his point of view. And it was yet another slap in the face for the Romans."

"It all seems like a strange thing to do. I mean, it's so dangerous."

"Yes, but think of all those secret spies who risked their lives during World War Two. They knew what would happen if they were ever caught and many of them were, women included. What Jesus suffered physically was nothing compared to what some of those people went through, or at best the same kind of physical torture. This idea that what Jesus went through was for 'all of humanity' is nonsense. Many other people have experienced much worse forms of torture and they have taken risks knowing this would be the outcome. Jesus' life is nothing special from that perspective; there are Jesus Christs all over the world, even today. The only difference between the tortured victims of World War Two and Jesus Christ is the Christos energy which gave Jesus certain powers. Besides that, they have all taken great risks for the greater good. From that perspective, in the time of Jesus Christ the Romans could be seen as the Nazis. Can you imagine what torture the Nazis would have meted out to their victims if they knew their captives had a secret power they could get their hands on?"

"So, Jesus was using his powers to selfish ends – to enforce the idea he was someone special when he was not."

"There is actually nothing wrong with what Jesus did. He did heal the sick using the Christos energy – balancing the soul and thus any physical ailment. He did create 'miracles' and many other things. He wasn't a bad person. But the real issue is that Jesus' powers did not come from God, they came from the Christos energy. While Simon Magus wanted everyone to know about it, the others wanted to keep it a secret. Then everything started to turn in such a way that the group could see something unfolding in front of their eyes –

they could overthrow the Romans and create a new movement. It was basically a revolution."

"So, Jesus wasn't a bad person?"

"Of course he wasn't. Bad people don't heal the sick when they have power like that, they abuse it. The group didn't abuse it in that way, they just allowed things to unfold and when people started to follow them and the movement gained in popularity they realised how they could use it to their advantage. They were very intelligent people who managed to manipulate things in such a way that a worldwide religion was formed from it all. And eventually the movement got so big that the Romans couldn't deal with it and had to absorb it into their own religion, thus creating the Roman Catholic Church. This is why the centre of that religion is based in Rome. And they – the Christian Church and the Roman Catholic Church – both know the truth about it all. It's not really what Jesus and the group did back then that is, or ever was, wrong. The problem is that those people who hold the power of these religions have kept these secrets from the people. They have used this power to manipulate the minds of the masses and control them with fear for far too long. The early Catholics were concerned that the truth about Jesus could come out so they used his mother, Mary, as their focus in a kind of *two-fingers up* to the Christians. They manipulated their own history by saying Mary was the Immaculate Conception. From this you had two religions – Catholicism and Christianity. Since the Christians were in conflict with the Romans, the Romans wanted their own version when the powerful new religion brought down their own Pagan gods along with the Roman Empire. The movement became so powerful that the Romans had no choice but to absorb the new faith into their culture. That's why there has been a division between the two for so long, even though in essence they are the same thing – because of the Christos. The Romans never gained access to it."

"So, who has the Christos energy and where is the Ark of the Covenant?"

Kalden frowned and shook his head. "You really think I'm going to tell you that?"

We took another break and continued walking along the track, which wound down into the valley below before snaking back up parallel to us. Along the bottom was a small stream that soothed the ears as it trickled through rocks and pebbles. As the night reached its peak the animals stirred in the bushes and cold air hit my face as the tree-covered path hugged the flow of water. Now I felt ready to know more about how the sun's energy can be used.

5

THE FIFTH ELEMENT

"It's basically the manipulation of the aether – the etheric band of reality," Kalden said.

"How does that work?"

"There are five fundamental elements in the universe – four material elements that exist in the third dimension – earth, fire, water and air, and then there is the fifth element – the aether – and this is the spiritual element of the universe that exists in all dimensions. In its third dimensional state it is what is called 'dark energy' by scientists. They have no idea what it really is but it is the fabric of the universe itself – the thing that holds the universe together – it *is* the universe. It is this energy that is the consciousness of the universe – it is God itself – the fabric of reality manipulated by the consciousness of every living entity that exists within it. It is a mirror of itself. What happens is the fabric of reality breaks through into this world and shows itself to us. It is already happening. It has been happening for quite some time. That Maya calendar does not end at a single date in that respect – it is a window of time."

"But what are its practical functions?"

"It is the manipulation of the aether that creates things like free energy. Etheric energy runs through all the dimensions and it is this which is responsible for creating all the mystical elements of reality – time, gravity, paranormal events, and so on. They all come from that aspect of reality. It is created by stars – this is the energy they give off, pumping it out into the universe around them and keeping the universe in a stable state. It binds the dimensions together too. In essence it is the universe itself and thus 'God'. This is why all the ancients worshipped the sun as their main God. Our ancestors understood these concepts. It is ironic that modern scientists consider our ancestors to be primitive in their thinking, don't you think? Anyway, the aether is also the energy that is contained within pyramids and they focus that energy by their shape – they naturally conform with the aether because the basic shape of an etheric atom is pyramidal."

"That's confusing. So, are you saying that stars are God?"

"*Everything* is God! I have already explained that. You can think of stars as pumping the aether from higher dimensions into this one, creating the third-dimensional universe. Stars create this dimension of existence by allowing the aether to flow through them."

"So, how is it stored and then used?"

"Certain devices that were Atlantean were used to store the energy and it could be absorbed into the body, or should I say soul. Once a person has this energy inside them they can manipulate their surroundings since the energy contained within them is in harmony with what is around them. It's that simple. It's all to do with aligning oneself with electromagnetic frequencies, just as the builders of the pyramids did. And this is how they moved their huge blocks of stone with the Ptah Wand. When you use that device, Christos energy runs through the body like electricity."

"So, when the ancients built the pyramids the etheric element – Christos – was stored and then they were able to manipulate it, like we might manipulate the element of fire?"

"That is correct. During the time of Atlantis the Christos energy was available to everyone since it was everywhere. You must remember that it is a spiritual element and therefore a higher spiritual people will be able to automatically connect with it. In other words, it is a natural element in the fourth dimension. In our world it is not such a dominant element. The other four elements are dominant and the etheric element is more subtle, like gravity, which is another manifestation of the aether. What will happen now is we are about to return to a state that existed in the past and therefore the etheric element will be more apparent in our reality, and this is why the way we think is important. It is also the reason why the Atlantean world devolved into the third dimension – the thoughts of the people caused this and not reality itself."

"So, our entire reality will be created by our thoughts."

"It already is, but after the shift it will be more obvious. The first thing people will notice is what you might call 'instant karma'. For example, someone might bump into you in the street by accident and you might shout at them rudely and unforgivingly. When you turn the next corner the exact same thing will happen to you and then you'll notice it. You'll think 'oh, that was strange'. People will actually start seeing their negative, and even positive, actions returning to them within moments. Strange synchronicities will increase also, connections that will become too obvious to dismiss."

"So, when the earth splits into two realities the aether will be more abundant in the higher reality."

"In essence, yes, but the other realities are ghost realities. It all has to do with the collective consciousness of the people on the planet. If you think of a creeper plant that is growing up a wall it will stop at a barrier and try to grow around it. Or, if one part of a plant dies because it is broken at some point then another part of it will start to grow. However, in some ways the part of the plant that was broken still exists, like certain ghosts. It is the same principle that applies to some real ghosts – they are branches from one reality or time line that never quite made it and started to fade out and sometimes we can witness these realities and interact with them. However, most ghosts are in fact branches of time that are not faded out but interact with the one we exist in now. It's all to do with time being non-linear."

"I don't understand that. So, what are ghosts?"

"Since time is not linear, events that happen here are, in a sense, happening at all times. Time lines split from one another and cause branches that fan out in all directions and sometimes these lines can intersect during different time periods, either past, present or future. In our dimension it mostly happens with the past and this is why people often see what would be termed 'ghosts' – we see an intersection from our time into the past as the time lines cross through one another. Since negative energy can disrupt the flow of natural time it causes rifts in the time line that become distorted and this is often why ghost sightings can occur in places like battlefields. This is also the reason why people can feel strange things in places like old castles and murder sites. Anyone who has been to the World War One killing grounds will tell you this. But there are many different types of ghosts and not all of them can be explained in this way."

"So, different branches of reality break off from the main line and they fade out as if they never existed, but how does that reality appear to those on the other reality?"

"Just think about it. Often when people lose an arm in an accident they can still feel they have an arm but over time that sensation disappears. Their arm doesn't really exist but at the same time it does."

To be honest, I couldn't quite grasp what Kalden was telling me. It was too complicated and nonsensical. How can something exist and not exist at the same time? I understood the cat in the box scenario – that reality only comes into existence when we look at it – but this was an extension that seemed beyond comprehension.

"When you apply this to our reality, to what is going to happen, it is our thoughts that will determine the reality and if we survive or not," Kalden continued, "so that we can create heaven or hell, both collectively and individually. All of these complications are written in those few words inside the pyramid. Each sentence is like an encyclopaedia of knowledge."

"It's all a little confusing, really."

"It's actually very simple, when you're able to visualise it. If we return to physics, this discipline has had a problem for nearly a century because two scientists, a father and son ironically, both received the Nobel Prize – J. J. Thomson for proving the electron was a particle and his son, George Thomson, for proving the electron was a wave. Ever since, scientists have been trying to decide – is the electron a particle or a wave? The electron was proved to be both a particle and a wave in those experiments, but how can it be both at the same time? In fact, the entire nature of our reality was at stake. Physics underwent a revolution during that time because between those two Nobel Prizes, Albert Einstein developed his Theory of General Relativity. Anyway, the real point is that the electron is a wave and a particle at the same time, but how this actually functions in reality is something that people can't understand.

"In our everyday life, we see the electron as a particle. Everything we see is solid, so in this space in which we exist, everything is made up of particles, but these particles spread out like a wave. This wave aspect exists not only in the other reality, but in other dimensions too. This is why time is not linear and why past, present and future are all the same. Now, imagine standing in the middle of a circle; in the middle everything is solid, but spreading out from the circle everything becomes a wave. This wave spreads out from the middle of the circle, into the future in front of you and the past behind you. You can imagine it like throwing a stone into a puddle – the stone in the centre is a solid, particle-filled object and the wave that spreads out from it is the reaction caused by you throwing the stone. These waves spread out into the future as a result of the impact of the stone. They spread into the past too, since the waves go in all directions at the same time, but let's concentrate on the future."

"Hang on, I think I understand this. So, our thoughts and actions in this reality behave like the waves in the puddle and exist in the future and this is why we create our own future – our karma."

"That is exactly true, yes. The waves that stretch into the past have already been caused by previous actions. In a sense, what we are doing now is walking into the future, which has already happened based on our actions of the past or present. The future has already been created. Naturally, these waves can be changed in the present at any time but certain fatalistic events are created in this way. It is also how the dimensions are created. The fourth dimension – where Atlantis existed – would appear like a wave to us but to them it is a solid reality, and to them we are existing in a wave-like dream reality. Ghosts appear like ghosts and not solid people because they are echoes of the past or even the future. It is also why the writing on the walls of the pyramid can be directly translated in English – they are echoes of the past and the future. So, now you should be able to understand why past, present and future is the same and also why time is not linear. Time does not behave like the solid particle we perceive it to be in this reality. Time behaves like the wave and it can be bent in different directions."

"So, people think that time is linear only because we exist in the particle reality, where the electron is stable."

"Yes, but remember the universe is consciousness, and therefore our thoughts are the things that actually create our reality and manipulate it. Solid objects are made from particles but thoughts are made from waves. It is our consciousness that creates a solid reality."

"So, how is it that some people see and *interact* with ghosts or some scene from the past or future?"

"Yes, these things have happened and have been documented. Various cases are on record of very strange events occurring that seemingly cannot be understood or explained, so they are dismissed by scientists. But if you apply this understanding of reality then it all makes sense. Interactions occur when two timelines cross over one another or when the rippling effect can be observed from the standpoint of the 'particle' location. You can even go into the future by bending time – and it has been done already. It is one of the biggest secrets that the controllers keep from the people."

"How is it possible to bend time?"

"We know that large bodies bend time, and this is called 'gravity'. But it is not strictly true that gravity causes the bending of time because *gravity is time,* and *time is gravity*. They are not different things. Large bodies, like a planet, effect time and this has been proven in experiments with clocks that have been placed on the space shuttle, for example. The clock travelling away from the earth slows down. This experiment alone proves that time is not linear but scientists still choose to ignore the fact. They still prefer to believe that time is linear and cannot be manipulated and that time travel is not possible. Now, if you bend time enough, it creates a distortion in the wave fabric of reality – a vortex – and since it is a wave and not solid, objects can be passed along the wave and appear in the future."

"So time travel is possible?"

"Of course it is, but scientists are always reluctant to sway from Einstein's theories. Einstein's work is not wrong; it's a bit like Newtonian physics – it only applies to the particle aspect of reality. It is the latest physics, like that stuff going on at CERN, that will prove the other elements of reality. They are already finding things they cannot explain and when they get their heads out of their textbooks they will discover that dark energy is the fifth element."

"So, in summary, dark energy – the aether – is the universal consciousness. It is God. It is the universe itself. And every action we make has an effect on it. We distort it by our actions but also by our thoughts. This is how we create our own futures – our actions and thoughts distort the dark energy around us and this has a rippling effect through space and time. This rippling comes back to us – our thoughts manifest as reality and our actions return as karma. These things are not conducive to religious or spiritual belief systems – they are the basic functions of the universe itself, but the problem is that we live in a reality that is dominated by solid, particle elements and therefore we perceive things as being solid and time as being linear. But the spiritual element, the aether, is more malleable and is affected by consciousness. And this is how the universe works."

"Correct. And karma often returns as a physical illness. There are two types of physical illness – the normal virus-type of illness brought on by the depletion of the soul, which might be caused by stress or something like that. This has to do with our thoughts. There are viruses everywhere but not everyone gets ill. If your soul is in balance then your natural body will combat the virus but if it isn't then you are vulnerable to a cold or flu, or even something worse. There are those with natural immunity to certain viruses, of course, but that's another issue. The other type of illness is much worse and this is caused by karma – either from a previous life or the thoughts and actions in this life. Many awful diseases are the result of past life karma. It's actually a bad system, because the person has no memory of what they may or may not have done in a previous life, but that's just the way it is."

"So, things like cancer, AIDS, and diseases like this are often caused by previous life karma."

"Correct. Cancers were rare a hundred years ago – about one in thirty people compared to one in three today – and AIDS did not exist. The huge increase in energy has created a bottleneck of physical manifestations – they manifest in great numbers as we reach the end times. You must remember there are no such things as 'luck' or 'bad luck' in this world – we create it all ourselves. It's like a complicated program that is incomprehensible to us."

"And this is what the ancient teachings have been saying all along."

"Yes, and isn't it ironic that modern science has been ignoring these sentiments for so long. The ancients were well aware of these universal laws. This is why Buddhism is the highest religion. In Buddhism it is even forbidden to pluck a flower from the ground as this affects the universal consciousness and interferes with the natural cycle of things. Yhevic human beings are a destructive creature by nature and their every action has a huge effect on not only the reality in the space around them but also in their own internal reality."

I could now see clearly why I was sent to Tibet – to understand these laws. I had seen at first hand the way Tibetans live their lives – not interfering with nature and maintaining a balance within themselves and the environment around them. At the end of the day though, Buddhism was just another religion. Perhaps more in line with the true nature of the universe, but nonetheless still a religion. I understood that the dome itself was only relevant in terms of understanding the past but it was not by chance that the dome was in Tibet. These people were the direct descendants of the Atlanteans. It was the Atlantean way of thinking and conducting oneself. Whether these practices were still in place since the time of Atlantis or whether the historical character of the Buddha himself revived them is something that will never be discovered, but it was clear to me that Atlantis was a great culture and it existed on a higher frequency because of the way people thought. It was their thinking that created their higher nature and enabled them to exist on a higher frequency.

Kalden suggested we take another short break in our discussion and as we walked up the track we took a left turn and headed to the top of a hill. When we reached a gate the car could just be made out in the background, glinting in the moonlight. In the distance a dark mass of clouds obscured the stars and was heading our way, like an ominous omen of negativity.

6

ATOP THE PYRAMID

"How many people actually know about what is going to happen? Obviously you know, and certain other people know, otherwise I wouldn't have been sent on this journey."

"The people that know are generally those at the top of, what you might term, the pyramid. The general public are at the bottom of that pyramid and then you have the government at the next level and the military brass at the next level, and so on. If you go all the way to the top of the pyramid, you find the people who are really running the world - religious groups, bankers and giant corporations, as we mentioned earlier. The religious groups know because they have the original documents and the rest know because their wealth controls the world. They can move mountains if they wish. The problem is they keep this secret from the rest of the world because they want to keep power and keep people in servitude."

"I thought the governments were in control of the population?"

"No, they are not. They are simply puppets for the giant corporations and because of this the corporations literally get away with murder. If a corporation wants a certain law to be passed which will enable them to them to carry out some kind of activity which was hitherto illegal, then it will be done. They pollute rivers with chemicals and many other things to which governments turn a blind eye, and yet in some countries the average person is bound by stupid laws that forbid them to drop litter, for example. It's hypocrisy of the highest order. Even scientists are ordered to produce favourable results so that corporations can continue with certain activities. Take the mobile phone industry. Mobile phones are injurious to health and can cause brain tumours but since scientists are paid by the corporations to carry out their research then the results of their experiments will have a favourable outcome for the corporation, so all evidence pertaining to these findings is kept secret and different results produced for the public. Tobacco is another example of where the damage to health became all too obvious. It could no longer be ignored by the tobacco companies. You might think the government ordered the tobacco companies to put health warnings on their cigarette packets because it was 'the right thing to do'. But it wasn't for that reason at all. They did it because people started suing the tobacco companies for not warning them of the dangers. If the tobacco companies lost class actions against them they would have all gone bankrupt and governments would have lost billions in tax revenue.

"This is why the news we receive is nothing but lies and sleight of hand. It's to keep people's attention focused on something other than what they are sneakily doing behind everyone's back. Law and the news are both nothing but hypocrisy because the government preaches to everyone how to behave and yet they conduct such indiscriminate illegal activities themselves, including wars. What people don't realise is that the population has the power and not the government. I find it strange that people don't realise this because governments pass laws that the people don't want which is in fact illegal in itself. They create situations and then offer the solutions."

"What do you mean by that?"

"They create a false situation, telling the public they are in danger and then they say 'don't worry, we will keep you all safe' and then offer a solution to the problem, but most of the time the situation is created by them so that corporations, or some other organisation, can pass a law to benefit themselves and in the process slowly tighten the noose around the public's neck with tighter laws. One example is that so-called 'terrorist threat' that occurred where they supposedly infiltrated a gang that was going to blow up airplanes by taking chemicals on board. Then they actually blew up a disused plane by putting explosives on it and they showed this on TV to allow the public to see how dangerous this was. By doing this they put fear into the general public. Then they offered the solution – from now on no one can take liquids on board an airplane in quantities greater than a hundred millilitres and it needs to go through scanners at the airports inside clear plastic bags. But there was no terrorist cell attempting to do this."

"I had wondered about that. So, what was the purpose of it?"

"It's really all about putting fear into the public, making them think there are terrorists everywhere trying to kill everyone. The stupid thing is you cannot take a three hundred millilitre bottle of water, which is inert, on board a plane but you can take a one hundred millilitre bottle of perfume which is in fact a flammable liquid! It's totally insane. The point is there really is no terrorist threat to the UK or the USA, certainly not in the way they make out.

If there was then there would be bombs going off all the time, but there aren't."

"How do you explain the bombings in London, then?"

"Easy. Brainwash a few kids, which is easily done by the way, and them give them instructions on what to do."

"It doesn't make sense. I mean, why would they do this, what is the point?"

"What you must understand is they want the public kept in fear at all times. During the Cold War everyone feared that the Russians would come and start a nuclear war. It never happened and it never was going to happen. There was so much propaganda in films and TV that it made people scared. When the Soviet Union collapsed in 1989 there was no longer anyone to fear. And that's when this whole thing started. A new plan, a new bogeyman was required to scare the public. And that bogeyman was to become Muslims – 'terrorists'. Have you ever thought of the name 'terrorist'? It's nonsense, because I can assure you that people in certain places in the world consider the US military are the terrorists. War is terror, is it not? How can you fight a war against terrorists when war creates terror? What they do is make you fear the terrorists so they can justify killing innocent civilians just so they can control the flow of oil, among other things. If the public hate Muslims, which is what they have managed to achieve in the US, then killing Muslims becomes a perfectly acceptable activity, since it was Muslims who brought down the Twin Towers. But it has nothing to do with religion, or Muslims. When there is some event, what usually happens is that some vigilante group will go and set fire to a mosque or two, and then they say on TV that they shouldn't be doing this, but it's that kind of hatred they are trying to create in the first place. It's all predetermined."

"But I mean what is the point? Why are they doing this? Why would they kill their own people with bombs and keep them in fear? It doesn't make sense."

"What is it that you can't understand? Think about it – if people are living in fear then what is happening to them on a spiritual level?"

When Kalden said those words, it hit me immediately.

"It keeps their vibration at a low level."

Kalden smiled at me.

"That's it, my friend. And that is what *all* of this is about. If the population lived in harmony and was happy, these people would have no control over everyone, but if they keep them at a low vibration then they won't be able to raise themselves up during the changes. Those in control want to bring them all down with them. They know what's coming. They know about the changes. They are instigating a kind of 'Nineteen eighty-four' situation – tightening laws by the day, monitoring nearly everyone with street cameras, monitoring their internet use, among other things – all to bring about totalitarian control over the public. It's a long-term plan and it's all designed in the same way – TV, films – everything is propaganda filling the minds of people with fear. Films contain violence and horror and the news is about putting out fear. It's only when you stop watching TV for a long time and then go back to it that you realise the impact these things actually have on you."

"But there are some good programs on TV that are educational." Even as I said that, it sounded trite.

"Do you think so? Do you really believe that? Historical documentaries are often wrong because, for example, you now know the truth about Atlantis. Children's educational programs are even worse. The problem is that television puts your brain into an alpha wave state – a trance. It is addictive and when you take a child away from the TV they can become irritable and angry. Since the flicker rate of a TV is determined by the rate of frames per second that the human eye and brain can perceive, subliminal messages inserted into programmes go directly into your subconscious, without you noticing, because you are in a state of trance."

"Like what?"

"A political party can suggest you vote for them, or a company can make you buy a specific product. A certain popular fizzy drink corporation does this all the time."

"And it actually works?"

"It works very well indeed. This is why they want everyone plugged in with new digital television because digital signals are much clearer. Have you ever woken up after watching TV with something in your mind that you cannot get rid of, like a thought of a certain food? And then you go and buy it because it's in your mind all day?"

I laughed.

"Yes, that has happened to me once or twice in the past, but you'll be glad to know I haven't watched TV for years."

"I know. That's one of the reasons you're here – you have a clear mind. They also want children plugged in from a very young age so they can be easily manipulated as adults. By the time today's children reach adulthood, their minds have been so manipulated that they are putty in the hands of the elite.

Have you ever sat in a public place and listened to people's conversations? It's amazing how many of them talk about television programmes or films or computer games. It's amazing how much rubbish their minds are filled with. The idea of spirituality has been removed from people by an organised programme that has been designed to unplug people from reality. The reality they live in now is so far removed from 'truth' it is ridiculous."

"This is totally crazy."

"There are other things too. They now have a program where they take blood from new born babies to record their DNA. At a hospital the nurses will always take the new born baby away from the mother at some point after the birth and say they are 'doing tests'. All your doctor's records are now being computerised along with your police record, if you have one. Although your doctor's records are your property and you have the rights by law to gain access to them at any time, if you go to your doctor and ask to see them you'll be shocked at how they react. They really don't like it and they'll do whatever they can to put you off. Just try it and you'll see. I could talk about these things all night. Everything about you and everyone else is being stored in a centralised computer. They want to have every detail about every person. Of course, this is only happening at the moment in certain countries, like the USA and the UK, Europe and China, but eventually it will be a worldwide program as a part of their agenda, what some people are calling a New World Order."

"That is really scary. Why are they doing this?"

"As I said, it's for totalitarian control but don't worry because it will never happen. It will never get that far because the changes that are coming, including the virus, will put an end to it all."

This was all mind-blowing information. On the one hand it came across as total fantasy – but on the other, everything he said was making sense and I was starting to build a picture of it all that really flowed quite well. However, as soon as I thought I was beginning to understand our reality and where we came from, Kalden revealed the biggest challenge to our accepted beliefs. It was this that would destroy everything we know, both outside and in. It was this that the religious groups, the people running the world and the secret societies were keeping from us. And it was keeping this secret hidden from us that was enabling 'them' to keep control of us.

It was ironic because, like the cycle of time itself, we ended with this secret by going back to the beginning of the story.

7

THE SECRET OF SECRETS

"So, the Ptah wand was the device used to build all these sites and that is Atlantean technology, so..."

"No, it isn't," Kalden replied.

"Then where did it come from?"

"That technology is extraterrestrial."

"Extraterrestrial? You mean aliens?" I laughed.

"No, I don't mean that at all. You seem to be missing a chapter here. What I mean is that the technology does not originate on Earth. The crystals used in that device do not originate on this planet. Don't be fooled into thinking that 'extraterrestrial' means 'alien species'. It just means that it is not terrestrial. That's a mistake many people make."

"But then you are suggesting that the Atlanteans are extraterrestrial."

"You are totally missing the point here – *we all are*."

"Now you are confusing me."

"Look, human beings have existed on this planet for millions of years but in a higher frequency. When you are in the fourth dimension you are in the etheric band of reality, part material and part etheric, like the electron. From that reality not only is it possible to travel across space, it is also possible to manifest material from the aether. It can be obtained and then lowered down into the material frequency, or even from higher dimensions down to the fourth dimension."

"I don't understand that."

"Have you been listening to anything I have said? I told you already that the universe is consciousness, and therefore everything is created by consciousness, by our minds."

"I understand that, but I don't get how it applies to the Atlanteans and the Ptah Wand."

"Look, very recently in Ahmedabad, India, an eighty-two year old yogi called Prahlad Jani spent fifteen days being monitored in hospital. During that time he had no food or water and doctors were absolutely baffled as to why his health did not deteriorate in any way. They thought he might be getting his sustenance from the sun, as a plant might, but scientifically he should have been dead after a week without water. What this gentleman was doing was connecting with the aether – the fourth dimension – and bringing down 'manna from heaven'. You see, the aether is an element, just like the other four in our dimension, through which we receive our sustenance. In the future, in the fourth dimension, this is how we will all live. It is also how they lived during the time of Atlantis – the fourth dimension is a spiritual realm and since it is made up of consciousness, and the universe is also consciousness, then it is also possible to travel across the universe since we are connected to the whole."

What Kalden was saying was that Prahlad Jani was literally connecting with the aether – the fourth dimension. Somehow he was able to tap into the etheric band of reality and get all his sustenance from the aether, the spiritual element. While the four fundamental elements of the third dimension are required to live in this reality, the aether is the element required to survive in the fourth dimension. Now that the sun is already increasing its frequency as we come to the end of the five cycles, that energy is breaking through and becoming available in this reality. Already we are seeing the veils to the aether breaking down. The changes have already begun.

"It will make sense when you go away and think about it," Kalden said. "I admit that right now your mind is filled with too much information and you are probably confused, but some day, maybe a week or even a month, you'll wake up one the morning and it will all fall into place. Trust me on that. Let's just say I am programming your mind with all the information and your subconscious requires time to decode it all. The most important thing you must remember is that this is all to do with the sun – *all of it*. The sun is responsible for everything – generating the aether, the universal consciousness, planetary changes and also weather patterns and global warming. All the talk about global warming being down to human intervention is nonsense. It's another one of their fear programs, and since they drop depleted uranium all over the planet and let off nuclear bombs don't you think they are being hypocritical when they ask you to use a low wattage light bulb? The sun is changing its frequency so fast it is the energy from the sun that is causing all these events, including earthquakes and even global human events – they are interlinked. They blame global warming on human activity so they can make everyone believe we need more nuclear power stations. That is yet another fear programme put out so that the population thinks it needs a cleaner energy to power our world. It is total nonsense and they know it. Sure, human activity is adding to it, but it is minimal."

"Okay. If you are just programming my mind can you give me the short version?"

"I can only give you the information you need, short or otherwise. Now, what you must understand is that the human body is the universal standard for intellectual consciousness to manifest in physical form. That is why the religious texts say that 'man was made in the image of God'. Although that is not strictly true since no one knows what God is – and it certainly isn't a man – the fact remains that the human form is the vehicle used for this consciousness experience. Humans exist all over the universe. Most of the extraterrestrials, about ninety per cent, are human in appearance. Some are even so much like us you would not tell the difference. That is why we are all extraterrestrial – we travel across the universe in a higher dimension and then bring the physical manifestation down into lower dimensions. The universe abounds with life. That is the point of the universe's existence – to create life. Earth is not the only planet where humans exist. We are a universal form, although naturally planetary differences create slight variations in our physical appearance."

"Humans are a universal form? How is that possible? How do they travel between planets and stars?"

"Just imagine that every liveable planet is seeded and on each planet there is a programme – an evolutionary programme that is universal. Many planets that can harbour life will eventually have human beings living on them because it is part of the evolution of the planet."

"So, you are saying that our planet is just a program, like a computer virus, or something?"

"The whole point of the universe is to create life and for each individual creation to experience that life. Everything is alive – even the stars themselves. The source that creates everything is responsible for each individual life. Thus you are a part of the source and eventually you return to it. In essence, the universe and everything in it is consciousness. This is why your thoughts create your reality – your thoughts are also a part of the universe – they are a reflection of you, and this is why they come back to you. Since the universe itself is consciousness, that consciousness will always try to manifest itself into a living being to experience a life. This life can exist on different levels – levels that exist on different frequencies, like dimensions.

The universal consciousness, if you like, naturally manifests an existence on a physical dimension. It is a way of self-propagation, a way of self-learning and self-manifestation. I think the writer and thinker Michael Cremo has called it *'Devolution'*. There is no such thing as evolution as described by Darwin, it is a genetic programme that is brought down from the source into a third, fourth, or fifth dimensional reality, and from that perspective your DNA is your soul."

"So, the physical body evolves naturally and the soul is the extension of 'God' that manifests in all living things."

"That is correct. But we have a problem here on planet Earth. The Human form naturally exists in the fourth dimension of existence and it has done so on this planet for millions of years. But it is possible, like the electron, to flip between realities based on thought, both individually and collectively. Individually you can lower yourself down and wander around the lower dimension for a while before raising yourself up again but the collective consciousness of a population must be stable to enable it to stay in one dimension or another."

"And this is why human footprints have been found that are millions of years old?"

"Correct. All the old cave art, skeletons of human beings, and even footprints, as you say, are much older than the time when human beings actually existed here as a population. What these people did was lower themselves down, some of them even became stuck here, and what they were doing with their cave art was giving descriptions of the higher dimensions in many of them. This is why the images seem obscure to us. Some of them are scenes of hunting, which came later when they became trapped here, but the older ones are like fingerprints."

I was starting to understand these ideas. I could slowly see the bigger picture coming into view but it required a leap of understanding and a change of my own consciousness to see it all.

"What you are saying is that human beings have existed here for millions of years, mostly in a higher frequency, and occasionally they lowered themselves down and left traces of themselves in various places. But at some point in history this entire civilisation – what we would call 'Atlantis' – lowered down to this frequency and became trapped here."

"Correct."

"So, when did that happen?"

"The fall started around twenty-five thousand years ago and the cycle was complete ten thousand years ago."

"And that's the meaning of the Atlantean calendar."

"Correct. It is cyclical."

"I cannot make sense of this."

"Look at all the other animals and creatures, all living in harmony and with the balance of nature. It's been like this for millions of years and then suddenly the Homo sapiens comes along and 'bang', it all goes wrong. Why is that, do you think?"

"I actually have no idea. Darwinian Evolution appears to be problematic but I am not sure about any alternatives. Certainly the story of Adam and Eve is incorrect."

"Both those theories are wrong. I repeat – the story of Adam and Eve is in fact a metaphor for the fall of Atlantis. In the story of Adam and Eve it says that Eve was tempted to eat from the tree of knowledge and then she gave the apple to Adam. After they ate the apple, they were expelled from the Garden of Eden. It is an allegory of the real story. The people were tempted to have dominion over their affairs – to individually control their lives in a material sense, rather than collectively in a spiritual manner – their thoughts became impure and this created an imbalance in the society, and over time the frequency lowered. Once it hit a tipping point the whole system collapsed and the people found they could no longer access Atlantis – they were now in the third dimensional frequency we see around us. They had no choice but to move away from the area. Many perished but thousands managed to get to the existing continents by boat. This is how the legacy of Atlantis can be found all over the world – different civilisations that apparently had no contact with one another building similar structures and containing similar stories in their ancient texts and worshipping systems."

"So the story of Adam and Eve, like Plato's fall of Atlantis, describes the lowering of the frequency into this reality."

"Yes. Adam means 'Adamic', or 'Atlantean', or even 'Aryan'."

"So, when you say 'Atlantis', where was it on this frequency, and where did they all go after the fall?"

"It was located in the Atlantic Ocean. It still is. The survivors went to South America and India, initially. From India they spread to Tibet and Egypt. In the Americas they spread northwards."

"So, we are talking about the Oriental race?"

"No, we are not. The Atlanteans were white, like Europeans."

"I don't understand. How come all the South Americans look oriental? And you're also saying the ancient Egyptians were white? That's ridiculous!"

"In Egypt the Atlenteans built the Sphinx and then they disappeared. The South Americans look oriental because the oriental race populated the Americas at the end of the ice age, but the Atlanteans were already there."

"So, where is the evidence of them? How did they end up in Europe?"

"The Atlantean physical form has disappeared through dilution. The Europeans are not the Atlanteans."

"I really don't understand this. It doesn't make sense. Where are they all? And where did the rest of the people come from – the oriental, black and white races?"

"Ah, now you are asking *the* question. Like the story of Adam and Eve, in the Vedic scriptures of India Man is also created from a single male – Yama Vaivasyata who, with his twin sister Yami, produced the entire human race. In the Hopi myth from North America Man was also created from two deities. The Dogon tribe of Africa talk directly about the human race being genetically engineered. As Eve was made from Adam's rib, and Yami was Yama's twin, the same story is being told – that of a genetically engineered race. These kinds of stories come up all over the world but they all have a common origin. You only have to look at the myths of all ancient cultures and tribes and you'll find a similar story, even if it seems obscure. The point being, they all have a common origin and that origin is the truth."

"What then, is the serpent in the story of Adam and Eve, because it was Eve who was first persuaded by the snake to eat the apple? And why does the snake appear in so many ancient cultures?"

"Ah, this is complicated, and you must remember that the snake does not appear in all of the tales of Adam and Eve. The name 'Adam' being interpreted as the first man is referring to the first wave of humans to arrive on the lower third dimension – the Adamic. The snake is the reason the Adamics were tempted to lower their frequency in the first place and that is what the story was about. They were tempted to lower their frequency and thus have dominion over their own affairs, for in the higher fourth dimension there is less manoeuvrability and it requires higher thought processes to exist there. One must not be selfish or cruel or materialistic, as we have discussed regarding the changes that are coming."

"So who tempted the Atlanteans with dominion over their affairs? Did they do it themselves?"

"The Sumerian texts give us the story, although much of it is missing and obscure. Our entire system of organisation and civilisation is based on the Sumerian texts but it is always missing the 'origins' section because it is considered a myth. When the Atlanteans arrived on the third dimension after the fall they found there already existed another human being – the *black headed people.* This, of course, is the African race."

"I don't understand that. Are you saying there are different types of human being on this planet?"

"The Black race is descended from the other lineages already existing on planet Earth. They are a native species, the natural species of the planet."

"Are you saying the other races are genetically engineered?"

"The Black race is what you might call a 'native' of planet earth. They have been here a long time. The white race is the created species. The white race is the destructive version of the human on planet earth."

As a white person I suddenly felt terribly guilty. All this destruction of the planet which has occurred very recently has been caused by the white man and his thirst for progress.

"The truth of the matter is this," Kalden continued, "the Black race has one biological mother, the Oriental race also has one biological mother, but the European race has seven biological mothers. This has been termed the 'Seven Daughters of Eve'. Eve was a template for the creation of other females but they were not literally her daughters."

"They were created? Manufactured? It doesn't make sense. You are saying that the Black race evolved on the planet, the Oriental race – well, who knows where they fit in to all this, and the White race is a destructive version of the Homo sapiens that was genetically engineered! It's total lunacy."

"It is."

"Great! Anyway, I thought you said that what exists are Atlantean souls but not physical Atlanteans? And I thought you said we devolve and consciousness tries to manifest in living things?"

"I also said that God is neutral to what goes on in the universe. Every culture on the planet says the same thing – gods came down from the skies, taught them the laws of nature and architecture, gave them all this knowledge and then left again. But we were created by them – we are manufactured, genetically engineered, made."

"But by whom? Who are they?"

"You will never know that answer. I will tell you what you need to know but not the details."

"How is that even possible?"

"Just look at nature again. Lions eat gazelles, spiders eat flies, sharks eat fish, bees pollinate flowers – everything is in balance. Then we come along and the balance of nature is messed up completely, and worst of all we start taking oil from the ground and eventually work out how to split the atom, and all this in a very short space of time."

"What about all the other ape families?"

"That is where the genetic material came from to create our species. The Neanderthal was the first attempt. That is the only other species that was created by outside influences but the problem was it wasn't aggressive enough, so they made another version. That's why there is no missing link – it doesn't exist. And all these alleged lines of monkeys and apes that lead to humans is just the imaginings of scientists who want to fit everything into Darwin's theory."

"I thought you just said the Black race was native to the planet, so how can they be manufactured along with the other races, and why create an aggressive species when the results can clearly be seen all over the world?"

Kalden was silent. Cracks were appearing in his story. I decided to go along with him but it was clear something wasn't right. I changed the subject to make sure he didn't know I understood his deception.

"What do you mean the Neanderthal wasn't aggressive enough?"

"This is all in the ancient texts – you only have to read them. The Sumerian texts tell us we were created to mine. That is what we are – miners – and since our creation we've been digging holes in the ground. The male was created to mine and the female created to make more miners. Simple! Plus the human female was designed to be receptive all year round making sure a population explosion was inevitable."

"To mine for what?"

"You'll have to research that yourself."

I took a deep breath and stopped. My mind was awash with information that I could not digest. Despite the discrepancies something struck a chord with me. Something about this all made sense. I mean, here we are, the human species. We literally came out of nowhere and spread around the planet and started eating up everything, and for me the application of Darwin's Evolution was never adequate to explain it all. But here we had again a testament to Darwin's genius – even he believed there was some kind of divine intervention that was the original spark. Was that divine intervention from the gods that the ancient cultures had written down in their stories? But who were these gods? If Kalden said God, the source, doesn't interfere with the universe then was he referring to an extraterrestrial species? And how was it possible that human beings were created by some outside influence and yet the Atlanteans, who are also human, arrived by lowering their frequency? I had to find out more.

"So, where did we start? Where were we first created?"

"And now we are back to Adam and Eve, aren't we, but you must look at the other races. Do you think there has been enough time in the fifty thousand years since humans supposedly left Africa for there to be the kind of evolution that would create white skin, blonde hair, blue eyes, and then the Oriental race with their slanted eyes and short height? If you think that slanted eyes are the product of a cold climate, then why don't the Northern Europeans have this feature?"

"I have never thought about it."

"They are different races because they are different species – all human, yes, but different. Look at the Black race. They tend to have larger bones, the femur is longer, their bone structure generally more robust like the Neanderthal, and they can run faster, but the white man has a different bone structure. And you just look at the Olympic Games for this evidence – the Black race wins the sprinting, but you'll never see a Black person in the swimming pool. You don't even need to be a specialist to tell the difference between the races – even the skulls are very different."

"What about the similarity between us and the ape skeletons?"

"The reason we look almost identical to monkey and ape skeletons, even though they are a different size, is because they were the genetic template for our species. I mean, we couldn't look too different from what was already here and we needed to be adapted to the environment. The skeletons do look similar, but their differences show we are a different species. No monkey ever walked on two legs but with slight genetic manipulation these alterations could be achieved. And here we are, walking on two legs and digging up the entire planet."

"So, let me get this straight – we are a genetically manufactured species based on the ape family, you're not going to tell me where we came from but all the ancient texts say that gods came down and taught us everything and they were the ones who created us."

"That's about it, yes. And your friend, Mister Ptah, was one of these gods. All of the ancient gods are these people. This is why they are more often than not portrayed as half-human, half-creature in ancient texts. You just have to look at ancient Egypt for this evidence."

"And these things came from Orion. This is why the Egyptians worshipped Osiris – the God of Orion, and this is why Orion is painted inside the pyramid."

"Correct."

"And the words above that painting say – *seeding, reconnection, return*. So, are we returning to the gods?"

"No. What has happened is that everything has become too corrupt and there have been outside influences that have taken control of things."

"What do you mean outside influences?"

"I cannot tell you. I can say, however, that things have got out of hand, you could say, and they need sorting out. Even though a species can be created and can cause havoc on a planet, nature always has a way of correcting itself. And that's where we are at now. This is where the virus comes in to it. Whether we like it or not we are a nothing, an abomination of nature, a species that should not exist."

"But I thought you said we have a soul?"

"Of course we do. Everything has a soul. Whether you are a manufactured species – created by outside influences – or a natural one you still have a soul because the entire universe and everything in it is consciousness, so it is all connected together."

"It's all very confusing, Kalden."

"But when you get your head around it, it's very simple. The problem is that we have this programming, whether we are religious or not, that God is an entity that created us. But it wasn't God that created us, it was something else. However, God is the entire universe and everything in it."

"So even though the collective universal consciousness is God and everything in it is God we weren't created by that consciousness. We were created by something else but since everything in the universe is God, then we were still created by the universal consciousness!"

"Something like that. You must remember that the universal consciousness that is responsible for the creation of the universe is not responsible for what goes on in the universe. You could say it made the universe and then let it unfold by itself."

"Okay, I am going to go crazy if this carries on. So, the gods that created us are not the true God, the universal consciousness."

"That is correct. The two have been somewhat confused. The gods that created us were what you could term 'living entities' but the true God of the universe is something so complex it is impossible for us to understand. All religions come from the fact that we were physically created by something other than the true universal consciousness. So, the God or gods of religion are in fact the things that created our species. The Egyptian Gods were real –

they were real entities that created us. All the gods of Ancient Egypt are depicted as half-animal, because no human ever understood what they really were. They could literally materialise in any form they wished. I suppose what we might call shape-shifters. They had to look something like us otherwise we would die of a heart attack simply by seeing them. What they actually are is something so weird you'll never understand it. They don't even come from this dimension. It is too much for us to comprehend, hence why they keep it all secret. The Western religions have controlled things for two thousand years by keeping it hidden. Now the new religion, science, is doing the same thing – hiding it. In religion we were created by a wonderful being that loves us – God. Now science says we evolved from the natural forms on the planet. It's funny really – both those ideas are correct. It's a combination of the two – science and nature."

"You are really confusing me. On the one hand we are created and yet you say, for example, the Black race is native to this planet. It doesn't make sense."

"The Black race was just the first creation after the Neanderthal. There are many times when these events occur in history. Remember that time is not linear and then you'll understand."

It was a long time before I spoke again. We started wandering back towards the car as the black clouds rolled in from the east. Suddenly I realised I hadn't seen a drop of rain since my arrival in Mexico and that was strange for a tropical jungle.

"So, what is the point in writing this all down?"

"We are heading back to the frequency of Atlantis – the fourth dimension. Nature has a way of giving living entities the chance to live. Everyone is given the opportunity to live. We are souls that have been reincarnating here for a long time. The fourth dimension that was Atlantis became a holding area for souls – a kind of holiday in between lives – a heaven-like area for recuperation. But it was a trap. The souls of human beings could not go beyond that place unless they ascended. That is, those that did such great deeds for humanity were allowed to break free from the cycle of reincarnation and move on to the fifth dimension and beyond. People like the Buddha. But for the rest of us it has always been a case of reincarnation. We are here because we have not become such great people."

"What about the people that do evil things?"

"There is another place that could be termed Hell, I suppose, but it is nothing like the Christian version of it. In fact it is cold, not hot – a place where souls become dormant. That is the worst fate for a soul – to live in a non-existing state – but those souls are always eventually reincarnated. They get another chance but their karma will be harsh. People suffer so much because of their own karma. It has nothing to do with the universal consciousness for it is neutral – we have created our own reality – our own hell. The problem now is that things have become so imbalanced, so destructive, that the earth itself will step in and return things to balance. The Earth is in direct contact, you could say, with the universal consciousness, and it sort of 'requests permission' to return to a state of balance. This is what the virus is all about. This information, written down, gives people an opportunity to prepare themselves for what is coming. Karma becomes instant. The fourth dimension, where the souls of the dead recuperate, will be destroyed. This is why there are so many people on the planet right now – the fourth dimensional recuperation area is being cleaned out and all souls that ever existed are being returned to earth to face the ultimate judgement. That's written in the texts, too – the judgment."

"It's cruel. Since we are not a natural species, but created, how can we be responsible for the destruction we have caused? After all, we were created to mine, you said. So, that is exactly what we were programmed to do."

"It's all a bit of a trick, really. You see, these entities that passed on the word of the universal consciousness – people like the Buddha – told us how to live, how to conduct ourselves as people, how to be good to one another. Even the entities that created us gave us these teachings – they are all written down. But it is our own hand – our own conscious doing – that has manifested the greed, the cruelty and the selfishness that exists in many people. You know, these entities that created us are not all bad."

"It still seems a bit cruel. I mean, it's not our fault what we are."

"But we go back to before, don't we. Nature is cruel. Creatures eat other creatures. There's nothing worse than being eaten alive, I can assure you. But that is nature. The difference is that lions eat gazelles because they have to eat, and that's an act of nature itself, but the human species created cruelties that are not in nature, that are out of balance. It is this sickness that exists in us that must be purged. In the beginning we were so pure it is unimaginable to us now. We have created our world, no one else. This world exists in the way it does because we created it by our thoughts. It could still be a Garden of Eden if we had not become so selfish and cruel."

"So, I have to write this down so that people can get a chance the raise their vibrations and be ready, but even I know that not everyone on the planet is going to read this."

"You don't have to worry about that. This book is just a part of a growing movement, if you like. The awareness that exists now is growing all over the planet. Those that keep these secrets will be the first to go. Then we will know where we come from. The gods will return just as was written down in the very beginning, so everyone gets a chance. This process will not happen overnight. It will be long and drawn out. It is already happening – you just have to look at what's going on in the world. But when the virus kicks in, you'll know about it. That will be the beginning of the end. All the collective karma will come at the same time. It will be hell on earth. The planet will be cleansed. Our species removed. So, prepare yourself."

"But I thought you said before that there were different versions of reality that happen at the same time? That there are different realities – some where we stay on earth, some where we survive? This is all a contradiction."

Kalden smiled and for a while he said nothing.

"You need to sit down and think about it. You will make sense of it eventually. All this will happen, and then it won't happen."

"What do you mean 'all this will happen, and then it won't'? Now you're just messing with my head."

And then suddenly Kalden started to shout, his booming voice startling me and it felt as if I was right back at the beginning in the café with Charles.

"DON'T YOU UNDERSTAND? DON'T YOU GET IT? IT'S ALL AN ILLUSION. REALITY IS AN ILLUSION. THE UNIVERSE IS AN ILLUSION. ALL CREATED BY OUR MINDS! It's evolution, my friend. It all goes on inside of us. Nothing is external to our minds. Who do you think created us? Really, tell me – what is it that created us?"

"You said it was the gods – these entities that came from somewhere which created a species of miners."

"Oh yes, I did, didn't I. That's funny, isn't it?"

"So what, you're now saying we created ourselves? How is that possible?"

"You're not getting it at all."

"I'm not getting it because you are purposely confusing me."

"I'm not confusing anything. I have already given you the answers. And you haven't learned anything from your pyramid, have you? That calendar only started when you opened the pyramid. That is the clue for you. That is there for you to understand how this all works. *The universe only reacts when we project our consciousness onto it. Reality only exists when we look at it.* That pyramid was your initiation into this field. It is telling you how it all works. It is a Maya – an illusion. *Everything that exists in this reality is an illusion and only because we create it ourselves. That* is your answer. *That* is the truth."

To say I was struggling with Kalden's explanation of our reality and where we come from was an understatement. After all this information, what he had really given me was confusion, contradiction, truth and possibly even lies. Nothing was real. Nothing made sense. Either things happened or they didn't. Either the future was written or it wasn't. I wasn't sure if Kalden was telling me the truth about everything or whether he was simply leading me somewhere – maybe these stories were just anecdotes. On the one hand our future was already written. Like the pyramid, our future was already known about. And yet our future was not known until we projected ourselves onto it. How was it possible that these things can be happening at the same time?

I understood the principles. I understood that Schrödinger's Cat, at least at the quantum level, tells us that reality is not real until we look at it, but then in our everyday world it seems that everything is already there - the way the world appears to us suggests reality is *external* to our minds. But Kalden was saying that it isn't. He was saying we create it ourselves.

"It's all happening at once," Kalden explained, "all these possibilities are created at the same time. It's that version of reality that says these things are all happening at once. All the possibilities are there at the same time. Each decision we make is like a fork in the road – do we go left, or do we go right? It's that decision that determines our reality. In the everyday world we see around us we only perceive one of those possibilities but the others are happening as well."

"This is all too confusing, Kalden. My mind is overloaded, I think. I cannot make sense of any of this."

"Well, you have to figure this out for yourself. And now it is time to leave. My job is done. I have told you all you need to know. Let's go."

"That's it? You're not going to tell me anything else?"

"I have told you everything that you need to know, everything that you need to write down, anyway."

"But it's not enough. I cannot possibly figure this out."

"But you will. Life is an illusion, my friend, a Maya. That is the key for you to understand all of this. Never let that truth slip from your consciousness or you will lose the path. Why do you think that pyramid was found in Mexico? Why is it a *Maya* pyramid? It's an illusion, that's why."

Kalden walked away and headed for the car leaving me more confused than I had ever been before. There was nothing left in the way of coherent thoughts, only fragments of reality that didn't blend together, like a cheese and chocolate sandwich coated with seaweed sauce.

Wandering in a daze a few metres behind Kalden, I tried to think but I couldn't. At the very least I needed to sleep. It seemed I had gained more information in the last two weeks than I had in the last ten years and all I needed right now was rest. There was no way I could even attempt to figure this out now. Kalden was right, it was time to leave, and maybe there was nothing else he could tell me. Maybe he had told me everything I needed to know. Only time would tell.

Time, again. I was sick of that word already. Time – that fundamental element of our reality is just an illusion – the biggest illusion of them all. Time is the cosmic trickster, the joker that laughs at us when our backs are turned. Belief is another falsity we put so much effort into, since everything is illusory. The more effort we put into an idea, the more we are fooling ourselves and the more the cosmic trickster laughs at us, because in reality we are only creating that thing by our belief, but it doesn't really exist.

The biggest illusion is the certainty we place in our reality, our world. It is not solid at all and it never was. It's a world made of elastic that can be manipulated, stretched and bent, and not a solid reality that has any defined edges. But strangely that bending of reality affects everything around it and if we put any negative or positive thoughts into that manipulation then the world somehow returns to its original state through *us,* and in the process those actions have an effect on our souls, bodies, and the world around us, changing the way we perceive it. It's that perception which is always subjective and never objective, and because of this the universe is a bubble of infinite and individual *untruth*. The universe never reveals itself to us – we only see a tiny portion of it, like the visual range of the electromagnetic spectrum, and to assume that tiny portion of reality is truth is a mistake too many of us make. We are the biggest fools in this universe of illusion. The certainties we place on everything around us is only for the comfort of our being, the way our fearful minds find a way to survive, for we instinctively know there is some mysterious element of our reality that makes us all uncomfortable. It is there, hidden and yet perceivable.

We all know deep in our souls that there is something else going on. We can all feel it inside but we mask it with whatever material we can get our hands on, whatever distraction we can find to keep it under the carpet. Is it a survival instinct or is it fear? Are we too scared to switch off our devices, go to the mountains alone and let the real world surface from within? Is it really that scary for us to feel the world as it really is? What is it we are really scared of? The truth is we are all scared of ourselves and nothing else. Since we create the reality around us, which is not real, then what we fear is our own consciousness.

8

THE FINAL LAP

The car wasn't too far away and I soon joined Kalden in a tired silence. I had no idea what to make of it all. Literally hours before, I had just returned from Eloisa's house and Kalden was waiting for me in the hotel. With all that had happened in the last few days, with all the information and lack of sleep, it was hardly surprising I couldn't make head or tail of what he was telling me. But Kalden had planted a seed in my mind... and surely that seed would grow.

The journey back to Candelaria was quiet. Kalden, whoever he was, was an incredible person. My original perception of him as being a wise soul was never in doubt. He was an extremely gentle person considering he carried a huge weight on his shoulders. He was, like Charles, involved in something that very few people know about. He was one of those keepers that Yeshe had told me about. He was burdened with knowledge that would have driven others insane - my overriding emotion was one of admiration.

Despite the uncertainty and doubt in my mind it was obvious that focusing on one element was the key to understanding everything – our reality is an illusion. Somewhere in that phrase were all the answers. But maybe there was no answer. Maybe the fact that there was no answer *was* the answer.

We reached the main road again and headed back to Candelaria. As I looked out of the window the wind blew across the plain and the distant trees seemed to be waving at me, as if guiding me towards the truth, the tops bending towards the east. They looked old and wise and I wondered how long they had been there. How old were they? How many storms had they survived? And how many generations of human life had they outlived?

"You'd better get started on this book as soon as you get back to Michael's," said Kalden, "and don't forget you will have to change names and locations where you can."

"I doubt anyone is going to believe this story, anyway, especially if it is released as a work of fiction," I replied.

"Don't underestimate the power of those involved in this. And anyone reading this book will make their own decisions about whether it is true or not. I guess people will feel inside that this information is correct. And by the time people are reading it, maybe some of the things that have been written will have already happened. Trust in yourself, and trust in those that have given you this task."

"How can anyone make their own decisions on whether it is true or not when there are nothing but contradictions in this story?"

Kalden glanced at me as if I hadn't listened to anything he had said.

"There may be contradictions, but for some people one element will be correct and others may connect with another aspect. It's all ambiguous anyway, but either way, everything is true. And sooner or later this virus will happen. People will start dying mysteriously as the vibrations increase. Suicides will increase dramatically although those statistics won't be released to the public. As the energy increases strange things will happen, either to us directly or to those around us. People will read this information and something will stir within them and when something strange happens they'll think 'Oh, I read about this somewhere', and then they'll start making their own connections, and thus their own future, one way or the other. You won't realise the power of this thing until you write it all down."

"I guess I'll have to take your word on all of that."

I wasn't playing devil's advocate. I knew what Kalden was saying and I understood the principles of his teachings. In fact I understood it all. I wasn't a novice at this and this was ultimately the reason why I sitting next to him. Only now did I understand why the mixture of knowledge I had was so important. While the contradictions made my mind spin, it all made sense in a strangely lucid way.

We reached the city about an hour later. The chaos of Candelaria was a great example of the truth that the life to which we are all accustomed is an illusion and this created an uncomfortable feeling. The unnatural buildings, people travelling in metal boxes with wheels, the lack of greenery and the constant bombardment of noise left me feeling out of place and alone. The loneliness was within, a feeling of emptiness, and now everything around me seemed even more false. I realised it was down to me alone to reveal this story to the world. I never asked for such an obligation and the commitment required seemed far too much to bear, certainly at this point in time. The only hope was that with time things would naturally unfold and somehow the book would write itself.

Kalden parked outside the restaurant again and turned towards me. For a moment his eyes were averted and he stared at the floor, seemingly trying to put together his final words before he would disappear forever, along with everyone else I had so far encountered.

"Don't have any fear, you will be okay. Many people will throw abuse at you for this information, but don't worry. It's just their internal fear. People's feathers become ruffled when they come across something that scares them but everyone will see it for themselves eventually. Let them deal with it in their own way. You will come across outright aggressive objection. Don't let those people unnerve you in any way. Everyone is on their own path and everyone has their own karmic judgment coming, one way or another."

"I am not concerned about that, Kalden. Nothing can scare me more than what I have been through in the last month. I have faced death and many other things. I have seen it all for myself. The biggest fear I have is only about my own ability to carry this out."

"That's exactly what I have been saying. The fear is within, not without. People think they are scared of something that exists outside of them, but that fear is always within and I can only reiterate that nothing is external to our minds or souls. Now, go and write this book. It will cause a storm eventually."

I smiled and looked out across the plaza. I felt a deep sadness inside of me and sighed. Kalden started the engine.

"In a few weeks you'll be heading somewhere else," he said.

"What do you mean?"

"You'll see. It'll come to you at the correct moment. Just call it destiny."

Kalden held out his arm and we shook hands. I could feel the remnant of his strong grip on my hand for a short time afterwards, just like the ghost image of another reality that still existed. I smiled about that. In fact, I still smile to this day for I see the things he told me wherever I turn, manifesting in everyday life around me.

Kalden drove away from the plaza, and once we said goodbye I never saw him again, like everyone else in this story. All, that is, except for one person...

I returned to the hotel, ashen-faced and tired. Filthy Cat was sleeping in his chair. I cleaned the dust off my hands before returning to my room. I also gave up on the diary. There was nothing more that I needed to write. And I also realised it wasn't necessary. It was just an exercise Charles had given me – to practise writing. Instead, I fell on the bed and slept for twelve hours.

The following afternoon I checked out of the hotel and headed for Michael's house. For some reason saying goodbye to my new feline friend was more difficult than many of my other partings. There's something about animals that leaves me feeling sad and despondent. Maybe it's the destruction we have caused on this planet, destroying the balance of nature and disturbing the natural cycles of life, although in many ways cats and dogs are arguably the only two animals that have actually benefitted from human interaction.

I shook the hand of the man on reception and thanked him for my stay. The dust from Filthy Cat now covered his palm and there was something about that moment that made me smile.

Crossing the plaza everything seemed false and surreal. I walked the side streets, reached Michael's house, took a deep breath and knocked on the door.

9

A NEW DAWN

Michael was more than pleased to see me but not once did we discuss the pyramid or the writing. Somehow that surprised me but I concluded that he brushed it all under the carpet, like any true scientist – the idea that writing from an extinct language could be directly translated into English was surely too much for a palaeographer. It was no different from Professor Sanchez's reaction when he discovered that all Mexican civilisations had a common origin from a world that existed in a higher dimension. I wondered which one of those was more devastating. However, as Kalden had said, Michael knew more than he was letting on and I wasn't going to push him to talk about it.

Michael and Clara left me in peace for several weeks while I got stuck into writing. We spent meal times together but for the most part I locked myself away while the important aspects of the book were written down.

There were so many confusing things that had happened in the last few weeks it was hard to make sense of anything but, just as Kalden had said, connections were slowly being made in my mind that enabled me to build a picture of reality and the scenario of our future. Despite the confusion of everything Kalden told me – the ludicrous stories of our origins and the contradictions – the three teachings from the scrolls and the writing in the pyramid were at the forefront of my mind at all times. These were the pieces of evidence that ended up becoming the central focus. The scrolls had stated we were created by the divine source, that time was the illusion of our world, and that our thoughts create our reality. The pyramid warned of a global virus that would wipe out billions, that karma would become instantaneous based on our thoughts, that we would return to a higher state of vibration and that the cycles of the sun were the cause of life itself, both physically and spiritually, and all future changes that were to occur. Despite all the strange happenings, the coincidences, the synchronicities and the beautiful people I had met, these simple pieces of writing were all that was left to take with me.

One morning, when my writing came to a halt, something dawned on me. It was more a revelation really, a realisation that things were not as I expected them to be. Everything had changed. Suddenly a glimmer of light stretched out across the universe and landed into my heart like a gamma ray burst from a distant dying star. It was a sign. It was the thing that Kalden said I would realise in a few weeks. I looked in my backpack to check if the piece of paper was still there. It was.

I made all the necessary arrangements and packed everything ready to leave. But I wasn't leaving for home. There was nothing left for me there anymore. I was not the same person. The Steve that existed in England just six weeks before was a different life, in a different time. All my worldly possessions meant nothing to me. I even imagined Charles had already anticipated this, emptied my flat and put my things into storage, paid all the bills and the rent, and terminated the contract. The broken relationship which I had run away from by going on this trip in the first place seemed like a drop in the ocean compared to the events that had happened in the few weeks before I stopped at Michael's house. In just this short time it was as if my entire being had been turned inside out and rearranged. All the emotions I felt about it, the internal pulling at my soul which had hurt immensely, seemed like just a heated discussion compared to my life now. All the jealousy and possessiveness that filled her soul and caused so many issues were a pathetic and total waste of life. I could only pity her. Even my friends and my family were now just people on their own personal soul journey. I love them all very much but this adventure was part of a greater picture, part of a drastically more important situation. I hoped that someday they would understand why I would never return home. No, I could never go back there, not now.

And so I realised that this journey was a never ending adventure. I could not go back. My life had become like the pyramid – an Ouroboros. I had to keep following the clues, keep moving forwards and hope that by my life's end I would reach my own tail. So I decided to keep going, keep moving, and there was only one place for me to go if I was to continue on this spiritual journey.

I said goodbye to Michael and Clara and once again caught the bus back to Cancún. I left a present for them both on the table in my room – a substantial amount of money I took from the bank account left for me by Charles. I had to pay for their amazing hospitality somehow. Or at least Charles did. Financial rewards are never a replacement for what is in your heart but I hoped the gesture would be understood.

The following day I was flying back to the United States for the connecting flight and once on the second plane I settled in to a long journey. I flew first class, of course, but this time I was with other passengers in the normal first class section. Although this journey was my own choice, it was still Charles' doing. This was my destiny, after all. He knew all along I would never go back home and, looking back, he had chosen the perfect moment to catch me off guard and force me to make a quick decision. I had always been an impulsive person by nature and he knew this very well.

It's funny that previously I had asked so many times 'why me?', but now, with everything I had learned, I understood that there was no other person capable of doing this. The particular blend of knowledge and perception I had was unique and perfectly toned for this adventure. Everyone has a reason to live. Every soul that exists is perfectly tuned to this reality by the magical weaving of the 'source'. Everyone has an ability that fits in somewhere. Whether we are a cleaner or the leader of a country we are all as important as everyone else. Albert Einstein once said *'try not to become a man of success, but rather try to become a man of value'*. The false ladders that people feel they have to climb are an illusion, for life is not about climbing ladders. And yet our civilisation is a testament to the organisation that we human beings are capable of. The only problem is the hierarchical system we have in place which creates these false ladders in the first place. Queen or homeless, we are all the same. Looking down on someone solely because of their standing in society should only bring shame on the person looking down. Likewise those that look up at people who they perceive to be above them equally need their heads examined.

We can have a civilisation, but we must work towards one where everyone is equal. Stop trying to climb ladders. Climbing ladders often involves stepping on the hands of others and this is bad for the soul. Be yourself. Believe in yourself. Be free. Be happy. We are all teeth in the cogs of the wheels of the Maya calendar. The cogs are our reality. The Maya calendar is the 'source' itself. We are the teeth that bind it all together. If one tooth in the gear breaks, another must replace it or the system collapses – this is why we are just as important as anyone else, above us or below.

As the plane started its crossing of the Atlantic Ocean I pulled out the piece of paper again from my small bag and stared at the email address. My instinct told me Anjali would be waiting for my arrival.

After everything I had learned, after everything I had seen, there was only one place for this journey to continue – India – the home of Mohandas 'Mahatma' Gandhi, and the Buddha. I had realised in a flash of inspiration that it was India that held the secrets I needed for the next phase of this adventure. It is India that contains the oldest knowledge. It is Indian thought that holds the clues, for nothing is black and white in India like in our own culture – there is always a middle road. It also dawned on me that India was one of the places where the first Atlanteans had settled after the fall.

I took the phone and locked myself in the small toilet.

"An unexpected call. What can I do for you?" Charles said, sounding almost annoyed.

"I just thought you better know I'm leaving Mexico."

"And heading for India, yes."

"How did you know?"

"You figured it all out, that's why. This is all a part of your destiny. It's all a part of the grand plan, but you don't have to call me and tell me things like this. You're on your own now. You've created the path for yourself. I am sure you and Anjali will get along very well. She's a very insightful and beautiful woman, but let me tell you – time is of the essence."

"Why?"

"You'll find out soon enough but I will say that those unscrupulous people that Professor Sanchez made up will be hunting you like a dog, in India. You'll need to go carefully but Anjali will lead the way."

"What do you mean? Are you trying to tell me that Professor actually created those people from his mind and made them real?"

"Yes and no. There is someone in India who is a major threat to these people – those playing the game for the other team – you need to get all the information out of him before they catch up with you. Anjali will be your guide. She is protecting him but you'll need to be on the move once you get there."

"You mean I have to go through all this again?"

"Oh no, this is on a much deeper level."

"What do you mean?"

"You're flying to Cochin, I see," he said, ignoring my question.

"How do you know?"

"I am sure Anjali will be more than pleased to see you."

He let out a laugh and put the phone down. I understood that laugh. It was a laugh that said the attraction I had for Anjali was mutual, but I didn't care for that right now. I practically ignored the conversation like it didn't exist. Instead I settled into my seat, leaned back, closed my eyes and I thought of everything that had recently happened.

Somehow, despite the serious mess that the human race now found itself, we must regain the way of thinking that brings everything back into balance. We have to stop the greed, remove the monetary aspect of our civilisation and live in a world of peace and balance, but despite my optimism from gaining this knowledge we seem so far away from this that it's not surprising that many people would have to die in order to regain this way of being. And at the end of the day we only have ourselves to blame. If we can get to the stage where we can teach the next generation to think in these positive terms then perhaps we can bring about a return of the Atlantean world. It seemed, whether we liked it or not, that this was being forced on the human race through the warnings contained in the pyramid. We have had our warnings. We have had our chances. Now it is time for the universal consciousness – for the bending of time and space – to realign itself and bring about mass karma on the human population. Now I understood that this was not the cruelty of nature. It is not God's wrath or an Armageddon like those which are written in religious texts. It is only the fruits of our own labour, our own karma returning to give us what we deserve. And can any of us say that we are perfect? Can any of us say we have conducted our lives like saints? Can any of us say we have lived our lives in a completely unselfish manner? No, we are selfish creatures by our nature. And we cannot blame this on our animal bodies – our flesh and blood, or our natural biological behaviours – for inside each one of us is a soul. And whenever we have committed a sin of some kind there is always that part inside of us that tells us what we are doing is wrong. And despite those internal warnings we continue to commit these sins and ignore our own souls.

It seemed ironic to me, and even funny, that these warnings and teachings have been there all along. In all the religious texts and other writings and teachings the way to conduct our lives has been there from the beginning. But we have sold our souls for the comforts of selfishness and greed. We have manipulated nature along the way through the advent of medicine and mass-farming, allowing our population to grow to unnatural and unsustainable numbers. We have created such an imbalance in the earth's natural cycles that thousands of species have become and are becoming extinct. We have polluted the seas and fished them to breaking point. We have cut down the lungs of the earth and polluted the atmosphere. We have created new and dangerous diseases by playing God. Our economic systems are already breaking down. The earth's natural systems are also breaking down. Our civilisation, like all those before it, is on the verge of collapse.

And now all these events are going to come back to us on a grand scale. Our collective consciousness – the behaviour of all of humanity – is going to return to us, both individually and collectively, in a form of mass karma that will leave no soul untouched. It has already started.

The year 2012 marks the end of the Maya calendar in astronomical terms, and the end of the fifth Sun in spiritual terms, but the year 2013 marks the beginning of the karmic cycle of humanity which will last for decades. It is the beginning of the sixth Sun, the new spiritual dawn. It is *The Evolution* of the human race. Everyone will start to see strange things happening around them. Little synchronicities at first, but then more bizarre events will start happening. We all need to keep our ears to the ground and our eyes focused and act accordingly when we notice them. We all need to think positively and treat others the way we wish to be treated.

Listen.

Look.

Hold on to your saddle as tight as you can.

Here comes one hell of a ride.

Are you ready for it?

Acknowledgements

First and foremost I am eternally grateful to Melanie Warren of Gazelle Books, who has been there from the very beginning of this journey and has never lost faith in my writing ability or the story I had to tell. Melanie has read the manuscript many times and acted as editor and proof-reader. Melanie Warren can be contacted via (www.lancashirefolk.com)

I would like to thank my website developer and designer, Dan Trayner, for long hours spent patiently refining the website and creating the illustrations in the book. (www.dantrayner.co.uk)

Artist Valerie Helmers for producing a magnificent cover illustration that encapsulates every aspect of the focal point of the book.

A special thank you to Elena Morozova for providing emotional support during the last couple of years.

Lobsang Dawa, whose Buddhist wisdom and experience as a monk in Tibet was hugely inspirational.

A special thank you to Ian Aiken for the many days I've been given to complete this project.

Deepest gratitude to Luke Selman for proof reading.

Thank you to the true life characters who appear in this book - Eloisa Montoya Escobar, Michael White and Peter Froude (RIP).

Gary Samdaliri for his continuous spiritual support and friendship – without you this book would never have been conceived – and also Mark Johnson, Soto, Bill, Florence, Rudolph S, Simon M, Squanto, Arthur Briggs, Brother Simon.

Erin Furner and Nicole Leggett, who have given me spiritual guidance and friendship when I have needed it most.

Thanks to all the café staff, who are now my friends and who put up with me sitting in the corner, day after day, for years on end whilst I wrote this book; Karl Hendy, Stephen Kay, Kate Gruzinskaya, Agnese Zvaigzne, Tsujimura Tamami, Galina Pavlova, Kiera Jose, Dominika Pakulska and any others I forgot to mention. Thank you all for keeping it going when the chips were down...

Thank you to all the subscribers on my website (www.stephenmaybury.co.uk) who have waited extremely patiently for this book to be published, and to those who responded with words of advice when the sample chapter was sent out.

Gratitude is also due to all those other friends and family who have been there from the beginning and have supported me throughout; Maria Zhuravleva, Dave Sayers, Ali Marron, Matt Todd, Kjell Van Zoen, Kim Van Zoen, Regan Smith and many more. If I've forgotten you, complain and I'll make sure you go in the next book!

Last, but not least, a personal thank you to author Graham Hancock for his inspiration and words of encouragement.